I0654901

Naked in the Winter Wind

The Fairies Saga

(Includes: Amnesia,
Abandoned, and
Adoptions)

Dani Haviland

Previously released as three separate books:
Amnesia: Naked in the Winter Wind, I,
**Abandoned: Naked in the Winter Wind, II,* and
***Adoptions: Naked in the Winter Wind, III*

Naked in the Winter Wind and *The Fairies Saga* are works of fiction.
Names, places, characters, and incidents are the product of the author's
imagination or used fictitiously for the reader's entertainment. Any
resemblance to persons living, dead, or fictional, events, business
establishments, or locales, is entirely coincidental.

Copyright 2011 by Dani Haviland
Published by Chill Out!
ISBN 978-09840308-3-5
All rights reserved

SOMETHING SPECIAL:

Just so you won't get confused about who's who, I put a cast of
characters on the last page of this book. I figured it was the easiest place
to find. And if while reading, you find that someone is narrating the
story—that it's in the first person—that's just Evie taking over.
Sometimes that old lady in a young person's body just won't shush!

Contents

*1 Not in my plans

October 30, 2012
Greensboro, North Carolina

It wasn't a bad place to be—it was actually quite beautiful and inspiring—but being in North Carolina had not been in my plans. I loved Alaska and didn't like leaving home when we still had over eight hours of daylight. Every Alaskan knew the time to take a trip 'Outside' was between late November and mid-February, when the short, dim days, ice-sealed windows, and cars and trucks all slush-painted the same color of road-grime gray were sure to affect even a sourdough Alaskan with the winter blues.

But this was the week my daughter had scheduled her vacation. I hadn't seen Leah in years—and we didn't talk much—but we had business to take care of. She and I needed to review her late father's estate before the end of the year. It wasn't complicated or contested, but I didn't want to do it over the telephone.

Leroy and I married when I found out I was pregnant. We stayed married for nearly twenty years for Leah's sake. It was the wrong thing to do, and he and I both realized it too late. Soon afterwards, I moved to Alaska for a fresh start. Leah stayed in Arizona to finish her nursing degree.

Leroy and I had been divorced for only two years when he found out he had cancer and, well, he and Leah got closer, and she and I became emotionally distant. If I had done something wrong, I never found out what it was.

I had arrived late last night, full of hope that her attitude toward me had changed in the last year or two. Her smile at the gate was promising, the ride from the airport was cordial, but the unusually brisk, chilly weather outside followed us into Leah's stark, white-walled, one bedroom apartment. I wasn't sure if her icy attitude was intentional, so decided not to respond to it. It wasn't anything I had done lately anyway: she was still angry about the divorce. That was her problem, not mine. I got over it—so did her father—but her sour lemon sorbet attitude toward me still hadn't thawed nor sweetened.

I was an incurable optimist, though. Life would change for her in due time. At some point, she'd realize grudges and hard feelings were

1

stumbling stones, not building blocks. Good attitudes and forgiveness could overcome all of life's obstacles, even death and taxes.

Leah had grown up in the desert—sweltering Scottsdale, Arizona—but moved to North Carolina after her father's death. I had hoped she would join me in Alaska—and there we could repair our mother/daughter bond—but she had her own dreams. Alaska was too new for her, not enough history. She wanted to live where the land had a tale to tell.

She had her nursing degree and could have worked anywhere. It wasn't as if she had relatives near Greensboro—we were pretty much our only family. She hadn't any friends there either, but that wasn't a problem. Leah's persona didn't threaten other women, and men didn't feel as if they had to suck in their guts when she was around. Give her a week and she'd have enough friends to play both sides of a softball game.

In her opinion, North Carolina, the first of the thirteen colonies to join the United States, was ideal. She went on and on about how great the state was, telling me about the major battles fought there during the Revolutionary War, how pivotal it was to America gaining her freedom from Britain, and then later, the great achievements it made in civil rights. Her history narratives were endless.

She could preach her patriotism all she wanted, but I knew the real reason she chose North Carolina: it was the home of Jody and Sarah Pomeroy, the fictional heroes of the *Lost* saga, the historical romance novels she was so passionate about.

Last year Leah gave me a paperback copy of 'Lost' for Christmas. She put a little note on the handmade gift tag that said the book was about the most perfect man in the world. Of course, that got my attention, but it took a stubborn case of drug-resistant pneumonia, and the sick days that came with it, for me to investigate her claim. Two days, 800 pages, and a box and a half of tissues later, I discovered the epic was just the first in a long series.

The bacterial pneumonia army refused to relinquish its hold on my lungs, so off to the doctor—again—for a new salvo of antibiotics. I picked up the prescription for the latest super drug, the next three books in the saga, and eight cans of chicken soup, all at the same time. Those big box stores were so convenient at times.

Well, the new wonder drug didn't work—evidently, this strain just had to run its course—but I didn't care. My recliner and electric blanket created the ideal winter retreat for devouring the complete series of time travel novels.

2

Lisa Sinclaire's words took me away to the Uprising in Scotland and then later, to the American Revolution in North Carolina. I shared the passions and challenges Jody and Sarah Pomeroy, and their friends and family, faced through the years, culminating with their fight for self-rule in a new America.

Leah was right about the main character. Jody Pomeroy was the ideal male. Smart, strong, and compassionate, but unfortunately, only a fictional character of the 18th century.

So, here I am in gray and boring 2012. Leah has the next seven days off, and I don't have to return to frigid Fairbanks for another five. Her enthusiasm about exploring the actual battlegrounds of the Revolutionary War, treading over the same stones once covered in patriot blood and sweat, and bringing me into the 'real' world of the Pomeroys, was contagious. Now I was looking forward to melding with history, too.

Ж

Before I came out here, I was hopeful but insecure about how we'd get along. I wasn't sure if Leah really wanted to spend her vacation time with me or not, but now it was a moot point. She gave me the news when I came to pick her up after work: no road trip. She had to fill in for another nurse at the hospital. I couldn't tell if she was happy about the opportunity to escape from my presence or not. Her explanation was simple and civil, no smirks or sighs to let me know how she really felt.

Earlier today, Leah's counterpart on shift rotation fell and twisted her ankle while chasing her little Pomeranian. Apparently, the big Labrador retriever next door had smelled Foo Foo's *eau de heat* and jumped the fence to romance her. Nurse Donna didn't want the two of them mixing it up—that was understandable—but she tripped in her rescue effort and sprained her ankle. It was a good thing her husband was home to rescue her and the Pom. There won't be any *Laboranians*—or would that be *Pomerievers?*—this season.

Donna's twisted ankle would keep her busy in her Lazy Boy recliner, rotating ice and heat packs for a few days. Nurse Gata, the ornery floor supervisor, agreed to take one of the days, but dumped the rest of the schedule on Leah.

We used her one day off to go to the bank and do some 'initial at the Xs and sign and date on the last pages.' Leroy never bothered to take my name off his retirement and life insurance policies after our divorce. Legally the money was mine, but morally, I felt it was hers.

With the help of the chubby, curly-haired bank clerk wearing the

3

'Disco Rocks' tie clip, I changed all the accounts over from 'Leroy or Dani' to 'Leah.' I think the bank officer wrote down her phone number, too. Another man falls to Leah's unintentional charms.

I brought my financial information with me so I could change over my meager portfolio contents and bank accounts to 'Dani or Leah with right of survivorship.' I also made sure she had the latest version of my 'just in case file': 'just in case' something happens to me, here are the emergency contacts, bank account numbers, life insurance policies, blah, blah, blah. I've never subscribed to the 'if I don't have it written down, nothing can happen to me' theory. Probate courts were swamped because of that common delusion. Hey, I know I'm not immortal, and when I die, I'd like my friends and family to miss me, not curse me for being so disorganized.

All this estate planning was making me feel vulnerable. My mortality was something I didn't think about, much less dwell on. Its eventuality was depressing. Except for the pneumonia a while back, I was in good health for an old broad of sixty. True, I was about fifty pounds overweight and my blood pressure was a tad high, but I probably had twenty good years left. Of course, a logging truck might run a red light and rob me of my last few years. It happened to my grandmother and, even though I always double-checked intersections before entering, it could happen to me, too. There's no telling what tomorrow will bring, no matter how healthy or prepared a person is.

Ж

There were five uncommitted and potentially fabulous days to go before my return flight to Fairbanks. I had psyched myself up for this road trip and still wanted to go explore the local history, maybe catch a second autumn parade of leaves, before returning to Alaska, subzero weather, and those short, dismal, and lonesome days of winter.

Leah had planned this trip for us months ago. She plotted our itinerary, downloaded narratives on the battles, procured local information flyers, and compiled the works in a binder. This morning she handed me the blue plastic notebook containing her amateur thesis and the keys to her little purple Prius.

"I can take the bus for a couple of days. Go ahead and take the trip for both of us." She handed me a purple felt-tipped pen. "Make notes in the margins for me at each stop. I'll take the trip later and look at your remarks. It's not the same as going together, but it's the best I can do."

I gave her a big hug, this time not feeling like I was invading her

4

space.

"Thanks, that's a great idea. You add your notes to mine, we can both take a bunch of pictures, and then I'll put together two memory books. It's easy enough to do on the computer and will keep me busy this winter. I hope you can take your trip soon. You've been working lots of hours."

I saw 'the look,' the 'don't tell me how to run my life' look, when I mentioned her work. I let it slide and changed the subject. "If I'm not up when you leave, would you wake me? I'm still on Alaska Time, but I want to head out early. I might stay at one of those Revolutionary War era bed and breakfasts tomorrow night to get the full experience, but I might be home, too. I'll have my cell phone with me, so I'll let you know if I decide to stay over."

Ж

I wasn't the least bit sleepy. It was ten o'clock at night but felt like six to me. I grabbed my backpack and started loading it with the bounty from my afternoon shopping trip at the sportsman's paradise store. I had zero desire to sleep in the open but bought one of those itty-bitty solar blankets to use as a tarp or poncho just in case the remnants of Hurricane Sandy decided to precipitate instead of blow. A hand-powered lantern, a small pot, and an eight-pack of those freeze-dried emergency meals rounded out my purchased goods. I still had the rest of the big bag of Leah's favorite homemade trail mix I had made, so in it went, too. A change of clothes, a couple bottles of water, a first aid kit, and my reading glasses filled out my daypack. This feisty old lady was now ready to walk and roll.

Ж

Leah cracked open the door and poked her head into my...er, her room. She had insisted on giving me her bedroom and had taken the couch.

"It's 5:30. Are you sure you want to get up this early? I left the car keys on the kitchen table. There's half a pot of coffee if you want some. Have fun!" she said.

"Okay, I can do this. Body, you are in North Carolina and have to obey its time law," I said, babbling to myself. I looked up and saw Leah's head pulling away from the open doorway. "Oh, thanks, Leah; don't wait up for me."

I was tempted to roll over and go back to sleep. "Nope, sleep on the plane ride home. Up, up you sloth-y body, you." I almost used the phrase 'You can sleep when you're dead,' but was afraid that I'd be hexing,

5

cursing, or jinxing myself if I did. "Okay, you strong, beautiful, and vigorous body, let's go check out our great American history!"

I bounced out of bed and groaned as my feet hit the floor. My body hadn't listened to my command. My size nines were always tender from the ankles down after I'd been off them for an hour or more. It seemed that my foot bones fell out of place when air hit the bottoms of them. It invariably took me ten to fifteen tender-footed realignment steps to get my achy knees, hips, and ankles unlocked first thing every morning. Those were always the most painful steps of the day, but I was tough. At least I could still walk, even if I had to do warm-up exercises first.

After a bowl of oatmeal and all my vitamins, minerals, and achy-joint medications, I was ready for a quick shower, then my road trip.

The more I thought about it, the more I realized I shouldn't be in such a hurry to complete the tour. One day, two days, or four: what difference did it make? None to Leah; she'd be working the whole time. She was used to eating dinner at home or going out with friends. I'm sure she wouldn't miss me if I stayed out late, or even overnight. If I came back too soon, I'd be bored or frustrated because I didn't have anything to do or anybody not to do it with.

I stretched my arms up high over my head, and out to either side. "There," I announced as I broke the imaginary time chains that bound my wrists. "Gone!"

I grabbed my backpack, the folder, and the keys, then skipped around the apartment. "Yee-hah!" I had just removed my self-imposed time restraints and it felt so good. "As long as I'm back in time for Leah to take me to the airport on Sunday, I'm good. Road trip for one, coming up!"

I opened the blue binder and there it was. The first leg of my tour was only a few miles away. New Garden Road led right to Guilford Courthouse National Military Park, the site of the battle that turned the tide of the Revolutionary War. In a few minutes, I'd be walking the same grounds as those heroes did over 230 years ago.

The mechanical noise of the modern heavy equipment in the background, altering the earth—probably constructing another shopping mall—was sacrilegious, but what could be done? Certainly we couldn't restrict progress, insist that every aspect of the historical grounds conform to the Revolutionary War spirit.

Not even the park rangers were in period dress. Unlike nearby Old Salem or Bethabara where volunteers clothed in era reproductions greeted visitors and showed off tools, furniture, and structures from the 18th century, here one had to look at the sterile displays or watch the video presentations to get into the spirit.

I don't think I could sit through those movies again, though—too emotional—but I was tempted to buy the DVDs for Leah. Nah; it wouldn't have the same effect. She wouldn't have the soldiers' ghosts sitting next to her while she watched.

After checking out the gifts, books, and videos in the museum, I was ready for the tour of the grounds. There weren't any historical structures here—the original courthouse was long gone—but the monuments listed on the flyer looked impressive.

As I drove down the narrow, one-way park road, bulging sporadically with parking lots for the numbered points of interest pullouts, an expansive graveyard loomed on the right. The huge granite monoliths—well, maybe not huge, but big and easily identified as personal memorials through the private property owner's chain link fence—brought unexpected tears.

So many men fell here—unnamed, but not unappreciated—without even a simple stone to mark their individual spots. It wasn't hard to imagine those greenhorn soldiers in what was referred to as the battle's First Line—the rag-tag full time farmers/part time militiamen who were the first line of defense against the incoming seasoned British troops. I, too, probably would have bolted at the sight and sound of those smartly uniformed and experienced Red Coats, marching in formation towards me with rifles, grim faced and self-assured, while I only had a pitchfork or maybe a single-shot blunderbuss.

These woods, densely woven with all sizes and shapes of trees, had to be alluring, calling to the terrified. Even with sparse leaves—I doubt they were fully foliaged in mid-March—they offered quick concealment, the lush forest floor of fallen vegetation and mast hiding any traces of unauthorized or illicit escape routes taken by the frightened.

The video that I had watched earlier said that there had been three lines of defense, their positions orchestrated by Nathaneal Greene, the slippery American commander who led General Cornwallis across rivers and valleys for weeks, intentionally wearing out the British Lord and his experienced soldiers. General Greene had stayed at least half-a-day ahead of the British until he had them where he wanted them: Guilford Courthouse, the little wide spot in the woods that is now part of Greensboro, North Carolina. His clever tactics forced Cornwallis to come to him and his well-rested American patriots on this chosen turf. Greene was fully aware that the long, early morning march would wear out the British. The miserable rain and chill of the morning was an added irritant to the already weary state of Cornwallis's troops.

War is always unpredictable, and usually horrid for at least one side, but on March 15, 1781, the day of the battle, cannons, poor communication, lack of weapons, untrained soldiers, and the deliberate misdirection by Lt. Colonel Henry 'Lighthorse' Lee – Robert E. Lee's father—exacerbated the chaos. At one point, the British fired on their own men in order to break up a skirmish. Yes, the British won the battle, but their troops were so disseminated, they never recovered – Cornwallis wound up surrendering a few months later. America won the Revolutionary War because of the battle at Guilford Courthouse.

I glanced at the flyer and saw that this was the location of the Third Line, the site of the last siege. Off in the distance, I saw a tall monolith, a monument of some sort, shining white in the sunshine. My legs didn't hurt—yet—and I still had wind left, so I left the car in the pullout and took the earthen path to investigate.

Along the way, I snapped a few pictures with my digital camera. One of them was of my smartphone at the bottom of an oak tree, showing the relative size of the palm-sized unit to the mammoth sentinel. Odd, this same tree was probably here 231 years ago.

That thought invoked the first minor trembler. As I walked across the broad, open field, making sure I stayed on the crushed gravel path—the spirits of the past began to manifest themselves, tickling me with their presence. The sensation was like an air wrinkle, the movement of space created when someone reaches across you for a saltshaker—you're aware of the person's proximity, but not touched.

These *feelings* were compounding, multiplying, as I strode across the field. There still wasn't any physical contact, but I was eerily aware of their 'presence,' goose bumps rising on my arms, the little hairs poking straight out as if someone had just blown across them.

I stopped short of my destination and read the details about this site in the flyer. The monument in the distance was in the wrong place. The field where I was standing now was the actual site of the battle, not where the monolith ahead, tall, impressive, and intimidating, had been erected years ago.

I felt intrusive, as if I were sleeping in someone else's bed and the sheets had not been changed. It wasn't that the ghosts cared—they just wanted me to know that this ground was theirs. They had fought for it, bled to death for it, and they'd appreciate my respect.

Shoot, I not only respected them and their sacrifices, I was thankful for them. I had voted absentee just before I left Alaska. Because of these souls' heroic—or desperate—acts, I was not only able to select regional representatives, but judges, and the president, too. I also had a very vocal say in what I was willing to pay for taxes. Thanks so much, men—we're all grateful.

Ж

It's a good thing Leah kept a box of tissues in her car. I had already used all the ones in my pockets during the movies and now, outside at the monuments, I had almost resorted to using my sleeves. At first, I was a bit self-conscious about the tears, but I couldn't stop, so didn't even try. Those early Americans had so little but fought for independence with a passion now called radicalism. They weren't crazy, though. They knew what they wanted: the freedoms so eloquently spelled out in our Bill of Rights.

We Americans have had our Constitutional rights for so many generations that many U.S.-born citizens seemed to forget—or maybe they never learned—life wasn't always free. Now that I'm walking these grounds, seeing the exhibits with the actual artifacts that were a part of our predecessors' lives, I wonder how these men and women found the time and the physical and emotional strength to fight.

Their quality of life, low by today's standards, entailed hard work and long hours just to survive. Sometimes that wasn't enough. Disease, poor hygiene, and lack of proper medical treatment caused many early deaths. Transportation was slow, and goods for sale or trade were limited. If they wanted it, they pretty much had to grow it, trap it, or make it themselves. Most of the colonials wore homespun clothes, lived in homes they built, and worked literally from dawn to dusk to grow the crops and raise or hunt the animals that were their sustenance.

I wonder if I would have been able to handle their lifestyle. Now if I'm hungry, I usually take one of three options: nuke something in the microwave, jump in the car and go to a restaurant, or make a sandwich with store bought bread and peanut butter and bananas. Just about anything a person could want or need now is available at your front door in twenty-four hours with internet orders and next day shipping. I'm ashamed to say I'm spoiled, having everything so accessible. I get upset when I can't find the right style of shoes or my favorite sprouted grain bread. How would I feel if I had to plant, harvest, mill, mix, knead, and bake my bread in an oven that I had to chop wood to heat? Yes, I can sew a pair of pants, but I don't have to weave the cloth, and I have a wide choice of patterns, sharp shears, and an electric sewing machine, all of which reduce production time considerably. Well, I wouldn't want to give up any of this now, but after being so vividly reminded of the labor intensive lives these early Americans had, I think I'll be a little more grateful for the electricity to nuke that potato and the vast choices I have for a comfortable pair of shoes for my old lady tender feet. I don't know how our forefathers managed to win, but I'm glad they did.

After I reloaded my stash of tissues, I returned to my tour of the park where I learned that the confrontation here at Guilford Courthouse was one of the bloodiest battles fought in the war, but was also pivotal in winning it. I walked and I cried, amazed then grateful, and then overwhelmed again. It almost felt like my old menopausal mood swings, but without the anxiety. I guess what I had was a case of passionate patriotism. I suppose if I was going to be infected with something that made my nose run and eyes tear, it might as well be this.

Maybe I was just being overly sensitive. Either that or the souls of those who gave their lives for freedom were reaching out to anyone who was susceptible. Yup, that's me—a soft touch for a ghost.

I walked back to the parking lot, head bowed down to hide my red, bleary eyes, and saw garbage on the ground. Why were we trashing this country? Was it too much trouble to stuff that powerbar wrapper in your pocket, dude? I mean really, do you know how long it takes plastic, even a thin candy wrapper, to decompose? Well, I don't know either, but I'm sure it's a long time. Take it home and put it in the trash so it can rot in a landfill with all its cousins.

I looked around and saw others were staring at me. Maybe I'd been speaking out loud. "Trash," I said boldly as I crumpled the wrapper and placed it in the garbage receptacle. "Trash can." I lifted my head and walked proudly back to Leah's little car. I shouldn't be embarrassed about being patriotic and environmentally responsible, so I wasn't.

I knew I was emotionally distressed, but I was probably suffering from low blood sugar, too. The oatmeal and coffee had long ago metabolized, and I was running on empty, both nutritionally and emotionally. I don't know if I have the personal fortitude to continue this Revolutionary War trek through central North Carolina or not. I hadn't expected to be this patriotic. Before I make a decision to cut short my expedition though, I should eat. The first restaurant offering real food—not boxed or bagged fare—would get me as a customer. I didn't know what I wanted to eat, but did know I wanted to finish the meal with cherry pie.

"And that has nothing to do with you, George," I said as I looked up to the sky.

*2 Master Simon

I was able to stop my leaky face and pull myself together once I was out of the park, away from all those spirits in the woods. I was about two miles out when I saw a man lying flat on his back near the side of the road, one hand on his forehead. I could tell something wasn't right. Okay, I was feeling brave. I looked behind me, didn't see any cars or trucks coming, so made a quick U-turn, pulling to a stop about five yards away from him.

After what seemed like forever, I located the car's flashers and turned them on. Then, just to be on the safe side, I stuffed Leah's keys deep into the left pocket of my sweatpants. I doubted that this was a setup with someone faking an injury in order to steal the car, but I was still leery. I took my itty-bitty cell phone out of the cup holder and put it into my other pocket. I could call 911 if something did go sour; the phone's security system and GPS could locate me wherever I was. I paused and grabbed my water bottle—I guess I didn't want to approach the stranger empty handed—and got out of the car.

"Are you okay?" I asked.

The man pulled his hand away from his forehead. "Pardon me?" he replied in a European accent. I couldn't place it as French or English, but it certainly wasn't American.

I inched nearer and squatted down next to him. He looked at me in awe, as if I had two heads and was sprouting a third. "I said, are you okay?"

I could see he wasn't, though. By the looks of his disheveled clothes, bruised cheek, the cut above his left eyebrow, and his blank stare, he was the victim of an assault. He pulled his hand away from his face, turned it over, and examined it—it was bleeding, too.

"Here, let me see," I said and checked out the cut and bruised palm. Apparently, he had tried to deflect the blows, but by the look of his face, he wasn't too effective. There weren't any calluses on his hands either—he wasn't a laborer. The lace on the edge of his cuff looked handmade and his cloak and shoes made him look as if he were in the wrong century. If he wasn't an actor or guide at one of the nearby museums, he was a nut.

"Can you walk?" The man looked a little loopy but managed to nod his head. "Okay, on three." I reached for his good right hand. "One, two, three," I said, but he didn't budge.

"You're supposed to try to stand up when I say three," I explained, trying to hide my exasperation.

"Oh, I'm sorry, I didn't understand," he replied, and leaned forward in anticipation.

"One, two, three, go." This time he cooperated and got to his feet.

He was quite short and sturdily built, but not fat. He was still a bit unsteady but standing by himself. The phrase 'dazed and confused' came to my mind when I looked at him. He probably shouldn't be left alone, especially near traffic. "Hey, let's go to a restaurant and get something to eat. They'll have a restroom there where I can clean your wounds. I have a first aid kit and Band-Aids in the car. Are you game?"

"Game?" he asked, obviously confused. "Oh, yes, I am game," he answered with a weak facial tic. "And thank you for your assistance."

"Sure; my name's Dani Madigan. What's yours?"

"My name is Master, er," he stuttered, then quickly recovered and finished with, "Please, just call me Simon."

"Okay, Simon." I fished the keys out of my pocket and clicked the button to unlock the doors. Simon was standing on the left side of the car, waiting for me. "If you don't mind, I'd like to drive. Come over to this side."

"Oh, I'm sorry. European automobiles, they're different, you know," he explained as I opened the passenger door for him.

Hmm, so he isn't from around here.

He climbed in gingerly, obviously in pain. I noticed he was staring forward, his right hand cradling his left—he was probably in shock, too.

"Here, let me help you." I reached across his chest for the seatbelt and he flinched. "State law, you know. Click it or ticket and all that." I acted as if nothing had happened and fastened the seatbelt. The last thing I wanted was for some strange man—or any man for that matter—to think that I'd made a pass at him.

It was a very short trip. Four blocks away, I found The Duck Inn, a quaint little café that looked like a decent place for real food and fast first aid. The parking lot was nearly empty, too—only an old Dodge pickup in the back—so an odd couple like us, the male member in period costume and hairstyle, probably wouldn't attract too many stares.

I grabbed my backpack from the backseat, got out, and went around and opened the door for Simon.

"Thank you, madam. I'm sorry to be such an inconvenience," he said, his bottom lip twitching in an attempt at a smile.

13

"No worries; I don't like to eat alone anyway. After you, sir," I said brightly, and opened the glass door with the hand-scribbled 'Open' sign taped to it.

The first thing I saw as we walked in was a little dessert carousel containing two cherry pies, a chocolate cake, and a couple of white-topped pastries. The little devil on my left shoulder suggested we have lemon meringue pie for dinner and cherry pie for dessert, but I didn't listen to him. I resisted the urge to tell my demon to shush. I didn't want Simon to think I was a nut within the first ten minutes of meeting me—that should take at least an hour or two.

We walked past the counter and, sure enough, there was only one other patron, seated by the far window. The waitress—Frankie according to her nametag—walked over with two menus in hand. "Sit anywhere you like," she said in her light southern accent, pointing to the six tables. I chose the one in back, conveniently located near the restrooms. She handed me two ragged edged laminated menus and smiled. "The special of the day is pot roast and homemade rolls. Would you like to start with something to drink?"

"A glass of water and a glass of milk, too, please. Oh, and go ahead and get me the stew. That sounds yummy." I looked around and saw Simon was already heading toward the restrooms. "Make that two stews and add a cup of hot tea," and gave her back the menus.

The waitress attended to her other customer, a dark-haired, good-looking, and well-dressed man in his mid to late twenties. "Would you like some more, sir?" she asked with a flirtatious grin.

"Oh, no, no, thank you. Two bowls are enough for me. I want to save room for some of that cherry pie, but don't bring it to me just yet. I'd like to sit here and study this map for a bit longer, if you don't mind."

"No problem, sir, just let me know when you're ready for dessert," Frankie said in a sultry tone with a shoulder twitch that suggested that pie wasn't the only sweet dish she had in mind. It wasn't any of my business, and he didn't seem too receptive either way. His nose was already stuck back in the parchment-colored map.

Okay, Dani, pay attention to your own situation; head back to the restrooms and check on your new acquaintance.

Simon was leaving the men's room just as I got there. "Wait, come in here with me," I said as I pulled him by his elbow toward the ladies room. "I want to clean up those owies."

Simon was shocked, either at my touch or by my words, or maybe

14

both, and took a step back. "The cuts, I want to wash the cuts with soap and water before an infection gets started. I have antibiotic cream and Band-Aids in here," I said and lifted up my backpack. "Come on, I'll prop the door open if it makes you feel better."

I nudged the tall, stainless steel, swinging-door-topped garbage can toward the doorjamb. "Come over here by the mirror, the light's better here."

I turned on the hot water, grabbed the washcloth out of my bag, and worked up a good lather with the restroom's liquid soap. I wiped and washed and scrubbed his hands and face, then rinsed and rinsed again. I urged him over to the hand dryer and pushed the big button.

"Oh, my stars!" he exclaimed when it roared into action.

I giggled, but managed to say with a straight face, "Yeah, I hate them, too, but I think in this case, it's better than a hand towel. Here, let me put this goop on you." I opened the little foil packet of triple antibiotic and squeezed it onto the abrasions on his hand and the cut above his eyebrow. "Here, hold still. I'm going to put a couple of Band-Aids over these to keep the acky-pucky in and the dirt and fuzz out."

I managed to put the yellow happy-face bandages on his hand and forehead without laughing. He brought his hand up to inspect the smiley faces that decorated his dressing. "That's it!" I exclaimed just a little too loudly.

What I had been thinking when I said, 'That's it,' was that Simon looked like E.T. the Extraterrestrial from the Steven Spielberg movie. Well, not exactly like him, but from a distance and with clothes on, E.T. could be the brother of my new man friend, Simon.

I kicked the trashcan out of the way and held the door back for him, nodding to the table I had chosen. "That's it, I mean..." I stammered, lowering both my voice and emotional level. Just then, Frankie arrived with our dinner and drinks, saving me from further explanations.

"Here you go," Frankie said as she set down two big bowls of stew and a basket of yeast rolls. Simon, quite the gentleman, used his good right hand to pull out the chair for me. "Let me know if you want more," she said. "We have plenty in back. I got carried away. I thought I was making enough for the weekend crowd. It's only Wednesday so, *manga!*"

"*Grazie,*" I replied and saluted her with a dinner roll. Simon quickly grabbed one and copied my salute. The good-looking man at the other table glanced up from his studying. I smiled broadly at him, shrugged my shoulder, and went to work on my bowl of meat and vegetables. I guess

15

not everyone understood my silly sense of humor.

We finished our meal in silence. I covertly kept an eye on the intriguing young man at the other table, foreign yet familiar, as I ate the wonderfully spicy stew and two of the yeast rolls. The food tasted great and I wanted more, but decided I'd rather save room for that cherry pie I'd been craving.

Simon had only eaten a small amount of his food—evidently he still wasn't feeling well—and was now in his own private world, staring at his bandaged hand. Frankie came by to bus the table and Simon's eyes suddenly lit up as if he had just had an epiphany. He backed away and said, "If you don't mind, I'd like to excuse myself for a moment."

He was in such a hurry that he didn't wait for my reply, but instead rushed out the front door. He stood in the parking lot, the sunshine reflecting through the sparse hair on his balding head, and looked from the Band-Aid on his hand to the sun and back again.

I got up and walked over to the other patron in the café, the man who seemed to be drawing me to him without trying. "Would you care to join us for some cherry pie?" I asked.

He quickly scooted his chair back and stood to address me. "Thank you, I'd be delighted."

He was certainly a gentleman, but not as tall as I thought he'd be with such broad shoulders. "Oh, here, allow me," he said, and offered me a chair.

Instead, I remained standing, trying to get a better look at the latte-colored paper. "What's this?" I asked, genuinely curious. The markings on the antique-looking chart weren't the black, red, and blue lines of a modern street map, just a bunch of squiggly lines and curiously drawn symbols on thick parchment-like paper. For all I knew, it was a map to all the bars and strip joints in the area. I couldn't help but smile at my perverse thought.

He returned my smile. "I'm not sure what this is. I bought it this morning from a young man who said it was older than America. That isn't verifiable without testing—replicas are getting very good these days. I've never seen a map quite like it, though. It doesn't have a title, key, legend, or place names—at least that are in a script that I can read. I'm sorry; I didn't introduce myself. I am James Melbourne. I am here in your country to perform genealogical research. It seems my great-uncle many times over, Lord Julian Hart, was an early settler in this area. He was here for your Revolutionary War. There is, however, much debate as to where his loyalties lay."

Just then, Simon walked in and saw the two of us. His eyes were wide, his jaw slack in surprise. "My map! Where did you get my map?" He scurried over to stand in front of it, then reached out and tentatively touched it, verifying its existence, as if it were a puppy that had just returned from the dead.

James and I stared, first at Simon, and then at each other. "Hopefully, sir, I have not just paid top dollar for a stolen artifact. Are you saying this is yours?"

Simon looked up, confused and mute now, his head shaking almost imperceptibly. James continued in his rich baritone voice in a genteel but slightly condescending manner. "Sir, I hate to inform you, but I just paid five hundred American dollars for this map. Can you prove to me that it is yours? Sir? Sir?"

Simon had just transitioned from extreme bewilderment to shock and was now hyperventilating. I jumped into the middle of the uncertainty and assumed the role of mediator. "Okay, guys, my turn. Let's all sit down."

I led Simon back to our table, handed him his cup of tea, and waited to speak until he had calmed down enough to take a sip.

"Now, how about some introductions: James Melbourne, this is Master Simon, Simon this is James Melbourne—from England, I presume?" James nodded and I continued. "If nobody's in a hurry, let's sit here and get this figured out. James, would you like a cup of coffee or tea? I know I said we were getting ready for pie, but I'd like to wait just a bit if you don't mind."

The ever-vigilant Frankie was at the younger man's elbow in a flash, ready with the coffee pot and a cup. "Coffee, my lord," she said, eyelashes fluttering. I think she dipped into a curtsey, too.

"No, thank you; nothing for me right now," he replied, barely glancing at her, his eyes focused on the strange little man who was almost in a trance. Simon was still breathing, but rapidly—practically panting— and still mute.

"May I see the map, please?" I asked.

Rather than hand it to me, though, James stood up and brought a chair over from the next table, offering to share his space.

"Thank you," I said. I got up to join him, but first pulled over still another chair for Simon, placing it on the opposite side of the table before I settled down beside James.

"Simon, here, you can look over the map while we sort this out."

Simon took a long, slow deep breath as he got up from his chair. He waddled over to us, eased himself into the seat, then stroked the edge of the table in front of his precious map, not wanting to disturb the actual document. He was also holding his breath, a good cure for his hyperventilating.

"It's okay, you can breathe now. I don't think it's going to blow away," I said. "So, are there any identifying marks on this map—or whatever it is—that will verify your ownership?"

I knew Simon had heard me, but he was still 'involved' with the parchment, fawning over it without actually touching it, as if it were his newborn son. After a pregnant pause, he disengaged his fascination with it and stood up to address me, formal in both his manner and tone.

"Madame, when you found me, I was recovering from an assault that had occurred just moments after sunrise this morning. The bast..., fiend who attacked me also took my purse and this map. The map was in a black velvet sheathe and the purse was tan doeskin leather. There were a substantial number of gold coins in the purse, but they are of no concern. I have an important appointment tomorrow morning and I need this," he indicated the map with a loving sweep, his good hand floating just above its surface, "in order to get to where I am going."

I had been watching James's face while Simon gave his explanation. He was probably a good poker player—stone-faced for most of the dissertation—but with the mention of the black velvet sheathe, he had paled. To his credit, he quickly recovered, but I had seen his tell.

"Simon, are there any marks on the map indicating it belongs to you?" I asked.

He shook his head, dejectedly looking at the floor.

"How about the sheath; did it have distinctive stitching, or anything else that would identify it as being yours?" I was addressing Simon but looking at James as I asked the question.

"It did have a coin on the yellow cording that secured it. It was an ancient coin with two holes drilled in it. It was quite valuable, so the thief may have cut it off."

I looked at James with a raised eyebrow. "Does this sound familiar?" I asked.

James got up and walked to the coat rack by the door. He took down a duster-length beige raincoat and brought it with him to the table. He sat down, laid it across his knees, and reached into a side pocket. "Whose face is on the coin?" he asked.

18

"Pegasus was on one side and Athena on the other. It came to me with the two small holes near the edge of the coin, but I doubt it had been struck that way. It was a silver coin, not gold." Simon looked from James to me and then back again. "You've seen it, haven't you?" he asked accusingly.

"It looks like I have been robbed, too," James said as he pulled out a folded square of black velvet. He placed it on the table and carefully opened it out. There, strung on a bright yellow twisted cord, was a silver coin, embossed with a flying horse.

*3 Map taker and a ride

"Wow!" was all I could say, and it sure sounded stupid when it came out. It was a real Greek coin—real and ancient.

"I mean," I said, trying to recover from the momentary shock, "let's think about this for a minute. How did you meet the man who sold you this map? Did you find it on eBay or something?"

"On eBay?" asked Simon. "What's an eBay?"

"It's a buyers and sellers venue," answered James, "and no, I did not buy it on eBay nor did I solicit its purchase. An oddly dressed man approached me earlier this afternoon. He had heard I was doing genealogical research and said he had a document I needed."

"So, had you told him or anyone else what your research involved?" I asked, then took a sip of water.

"No, I assumed he had overheard me ask the park ranger if there were registers of soldiers from either side of the Guilford Courthouse battle on file at the museum or possibly anywhere else. But I made no mention of my family."

"Where did you first meet him—had you ever seen him before?" I asked, my eyes narrowing with my subconscious cross-examination.

"He first approached me approximately two hours ago at the museum and no, I had never seen him before." James pulled back his shoulders and stuck out his chin, offended with the apparent interrogation. "I thought perhaps he worked there when I saw his unusual shoes, apparently handmade, but poorly crafted. He was in colonial period dress and all looked appropriate except for his shoddy shoes. Ms. Madigan, I am beginning to feel as if you believe I did something wrong."

"No, not at all. I was looking for a lead on who sold you this so you could get a refund, and Simon could have his map back. I don't have any personal interest in this at all. I'm not even from around here. I'm on vacation from Alaska."

This seemed to put James at ease. He took a deep breath as if to say, 'What now?'

"Let's see if I have this straight," I said. "Simon was beat up early this morning and robbed of some valuable personal property. Several hours later, a man offered to sell you something he said you needed. Did you know it was a map?"

"When the man said he had a document, I was hoping it was a list of names or a journal. I hadn't asked about anything else. When I arrived here for lunch and finally got it completely opened out, I was a bit confused and rather agitated," James said, his face reddening with the memory.

"Yes, I know what you mean," I said, giving James a moment to recover. "You didn't know the man wasn't honest. What exactly does a thief look like, anyhow? You don't look like an easy target to me, but, then again, I'm not a thief. Maybe you just looked like you had money. He had this parchment and thought it might be valuable, even if it was just a laundry list," I said and rolled my eyes, grinning.

My attempt at levity failed—they were a dour pair—so I changed tactics. "So, it might be the thief saw Simon as a weak man with an 'old document' and you as a rich foreigner looking for answers in an 'old document.' He didn't happen to have any gold coins he wanted to sell, did he?"

"No, coins were never mentioned. I doubt he saw the coin on the cord or he would have taken that, too. It was tucked into the fabric of the casing and wasn't visible at first." James paused and started to say more, hesitated again, then continued. "The man just seemed so insistent I have this. That's why I've been examining it so intently. It's as if it's a cryptogram and I just need a few key characters to decode it. Or I suppose it could be he was just one hell of a salesman. Please, excuse my vulgarity."

"You're excused. So, can I have a crack at it? I'm pretty good with codes and puzzles," I said with a smirk and double eyebrow pop a la Groucho Marx.

As James said, "Please, be my guest," Simon blurted out, "Oh, no, don't be concerned. It's just mish mosh."

James and I looked wide-eyed at each other in disbelief, then back at Simon.

"Mish mosh? You treat this…this…piece of dried up old sheepskin as if it were made of gold leaf, and then say its mish mosh? I don't think so," I said and cracked my knuckles. "Don't tell me what I can be concerned about! I'm on this like a dung beetle on a pile of shit, if you'll excuse the vulgarity."

"Vulgarity excused, madam," James replied, grinning as he pulled back the curtains. "May I offer you better light?"

James turned his attention to the short man, scowling as he spoke. "Mister Simon, shall we leave the lady to her research while we go

21

outside? I think we have some business to transact." His left hand hovered above Simon's shoulder, ready to guide him and their frail relationship outside, to the privacy of the parking lot.

"That's Master Simon to you, sir," Simon said, bristling at the nearness of James's touch. He shrugged away from the hand, and pushed through the café's glass door, positioning himself so that now he was leading the way.

Well, I'll be. I didn't slip when I called him Master Simon. I wondered who'd come out on top if the two of them ever went at it. And, if they spent much time together, it would be a definite when, not if, they went at it.

Ten minutes later, the men returned to their respective diner tables. Neither one had an 'I won!' look on his face, so apparently nothing had been accomplished in their powwow.

I didn't want them to know I hadn't answered the riddle of the map, so I grinned broadly, hoping to make them think I had made progress. The sheepskin sheet before me, its field of black squiggly lines randomly intersecting at spiral flourishes, was as logical as ants on a sugar cookie and had me stumped. The only writing—sparse notes near the spirals— were scribbled in runes, not letters. That didn't help me either; I didn't have any elfin translation skills.

James spoke first, "Well?"

"I'm getting there," I lied, "how about you two?"

"Since there wasn't any useful information for me in this 'document,' and I did get an unforeseen bonus in the ancient Greek coin, we agreed that he could have the map and I would keep the coin. With the right agent, I should at least be able to get my money back."

James retrieved his coat and turned to face me. "Ms. Madigan, it has been a pleasure meeting you. You have quite the talent for managing diplomacy without incurring bruised egos. You have been most instrumental in obtaining a resolution to this dilemma. If there is anything you need, please don't hesitate to call."

James handed me his business card. It was embossed, of course, and had his family's coat of arms on it. It was definitely the classiest card I had ever seen. Ooh, and he was a member of the House of Lords. He was 'Lord' James Melbourne!

"I'll put it in here where it won't get lost," I said, sucking down my smirk at negotiating with British almost-royalty. I picked up my backpack, unzipped the top, and saw that there was already something in the skinny inside pocket. "Hey, I found one of my cards! I didn't think I had brought any with me, but here."

I handed him my colorful little desktop published business card with a huge bouquet of homegrown roses set as the background.

"Goodness! This is beautiful. I didn't know roses came in such a wide range of colors and forms."

"Thanks, I guess this is like the Little Red Hen of cards. I grew the roses, I arranged the roses, I photographed the roses, and then I designed and printed the roses-themed cards all by myself." I realized too late that I was babbling. If I apologized, it would call even more attention to my nervous blithering, so I just stopped talking.

James saw my blush of embarrassment and smiled. "The Little Red Hen was one of my favorite stories when I was a child. I actually had my grandfather show me how to raise wheat and grind it so I could bake my own loaf of bread. The result wasn't very pretty—more like a big fat cracker—and tasted horrid, but we had fun."

James's face was aglow with his childhood memory. He paused, and his demeanor turned from light to somber. He looked me in the eyes and spoke softly so that only I could hear. "Please, let me know if you find out anything about this map. My gut instinct tells me there really is something in it for me. I've learned it's always best to heed those feelings. And something's not quite right with this Simon character. I believe he knows more than he's telling us." He nodded and smiled. "You have my numbers."

"And you have mine. If you're ever in Alaska, look me up. I'll give you the three-hour tour. Well, at least three hours; it's a pretty big state, you know."

"I just might do that." He turned to face Simon, who was now on the other side of the table, absorbed in his search for the hidden secrets of the map. James raised his voice in order to break the man's focused trance. "Good day to you, Master Simon. I hope you find what you are looking for."

Simon backed away from the table and stood as tall as his short frame would stretch. "Thank you, sir, for your integrity and justice in returning my property. I hope you find what you are looking for also." He then saluted James, without a roll in his hand this time, and said, "*Grazie!*"

"*Grazie* and *ciao*," James replied, returning the salute.

And then James was gone, walking away, dignified but engaging, holding the little silver coin in the air, looking at it as if it also held a secret.

Ж

"Circles: circles within circles, but not concentric," I babbled, hoping to make sense out of something, anything, by verbalizing my clues. "Two off-center circles, like the ones punched in that coin and like the little eyes on the happy faces on your Band-Aids…that's it!" The possible key to the mysterious map presented itself like sap on a pine tree, hard to see until found, and then hard to ignore.

Simon's eyes grew perfectly round as he looked at me, hopeful that I had found the answer for him.

"Yes, look here." I was so excited, like a little girl with a new dolly. I tore off little pieces of paper napkin to use as my markers. "Now, if you join these locations," I used my finger to draw a line over the markers, "they're like the smile on a face, and here's the eye."

The map now looked like a child's self-portrait, little toilet tissue teeth arranged in a semicircular broad grin, and one white eye. "Now, I think there should be another marker here." I pointed to a blank area, glaringly devoid of any of the ancient character markings, where I thought the other eye 'marker' should be. "If this were a treasure map, this is where the X would be. See, those mountains are the smile, here's one eye and here; here's what you're looking for," I said with confidence. Then my insecurity kicked in. "You were looking for something, weren't you?"

Simon's anticipation segued from hope to shock to glee, an asymmetrical smile growing ever so slowly, but definitely making an appearance. I don't think he had ever smiled by the way his face pulled taut at the sides of his mouth.

"Do you know where this is?" he asked.

"Well, I can probably figure it out." I turned around to look for Frankie. She was sitting at the cash register, sipping a cup of coffee and looking forlorn. Her pretty English lord had left. Oh, well. She had the weekend to look forward to. Maybe another foreigner or three would stray in. Someone was bound to strike her fancy.

"Frankie," I called out, breaking her reverie, "do you have a map of North Carolina around here?"

Without saying a word, she reached under the podium and produced two brand new maps, adorned with full color advertisements framing the edges. "We got lots of 'em. Let me know if you want more. Are you two ready for your pie yet?"

"Oh, snap—Simon, would you like more tea with your cherry pie?"

24

"Snap?" He looked down and around to see what he was missing. He saw I was looking at him, waiting for an answer. "Yes, more tea, if you would, please."

Frankie asked, "Do you want your pie a la mode?"

"A la mode? What's that?" Simon asked.

Before Frankie could explain, I said, "Yes, make that two cherry pies a la mode and two hot teas, please." I turned to Simon and asked, "You're not from around here, are you?"

"Well, yes and no. I haven't been here in a *very* long time. Many things have changed since then. I know I've only been back for a short while, but I want to go back home. Could you help me a bit more? I hate to be such a burden, but..."

I interrupted him before he could beg. "I'd be glad to help. Remember, I'm here on vacation and can pretty much do whatever I please. My daughter and I were supposed to go on this Revolutionary War battleground expedition together, but she was called back to work. I had just returned from the first site when I found you. I was very impressed with the Guilford Courthouse Museum and Park but, quite frankly, I was over-stimulated, overwhelmed by all I saw. I wasn't sure if I wanted to continue to the other locations, so coming across you and James was a welcome distraction. Now, where are we going and when do you want to leave?"

"I'm not sure." Simon put the colorful advertising map next to his archaic black-inked parchment and looked for further parallels. He tore more pieces of napkin, transferring his reference points to those on the advertising map. "I'm supposed to meet a friend. He said he would leave a note for me. Actually, he said 'notes' for me. I have no idea where to look for them and...I'm...well, I guess I'm getting a bit overwhelmed myself. You, my dear young lady, are a Godsend. With your help, I have at least found the general location of my, shall we say, rendezvous. I'm supposed to meet him this evening, or at the latest, at the break of dawn tomorrow."

"Thank you," I said softly, the blush rushing from my neck to my cheeks.

"You're thanking me? It is I who am thanking you. What are you thanking me for?"

I giggled like a schoolgirl in embarrassment. "For calling me a young lady and being sincere when you said it. It's been a long time since I've been called *that* with a straight face. Now, changing the subject, who is your friend? Can we call him?"

"No, Leonard doesn't have a telephone. He just pops in—is that the right phrase?—when he feels like it. He is a terribly brilliant man and sometimes forgets that we aren't as quick as he is. There's no telling what form his notes will take either. Do you think you could take me to this place?" he asked as he pointed to a spot on the colored, commercial map.

Frankie arrived with the two bowls of cherry pie a la mode, a small pitcher of hot water, and a basket of assorted tea bags. "I don't mean to rush you, and I'm not, but I wanted to remind you that it's Halloween and some strange characters will be prowling the area as soon as it gets dark… and that's not too long from now. I hope you remembered to lock your car."

I reached into my pocket for the keys and pushed the button. The electronic notes indicated that if it hadn't been locked before, it was now. Simon jumped at the 'peep peep' noise. "Thanks for reminding me. Go ahead and bring me the check. We'll be leaving as soon as we're done with dessert."

Simon picked up his fork and took a bite of ice cream. "Frozen custard? Is that what you meant when you ordered pie a la mode?"

"Well, this is probably ice cream. I haven't heard of frozen custard in ages. Sometimes they use frozen yogurt instead, but either way, it sure kicks up the taste experience a notch or two."

Simon plunged his fork into the ice cream and took three big bites in rapid succession. "Watch out for brain freeze," I cautioned just as he dropped the fork and slapped his hand to his forehead, his eyes squeezed tight in pain. "Don't try to talk; just take a sip of tea. Oops, no tea yet. Here," I poured plain hot water into the remains of his tea from our late lunch, "sip this so it'll thaw out your brain cells."

Simon obeyed and breathed slowly and deeply to try to contain his pain. I wanted to tell him that he looked like a woman doing the Lamaze breathing technique for labor, but I decided it was better to let him suffer in silence. He didn't need to groan at my bad jokes, too. Of course, I doubt my little foreign friend had ever heard of the Lamaze method. He didn't look like a family man. "Better?" I asked softly.

"Yes, thank you. I doubt I will ever do *that* again," he said emphatically. He turned his bowl around and eased a piece of the cherry pie onto his fork. He savored it, then pointed to the map and asked, "So, would it be possible for you to take me here in that little car of yours?"

"It's my daughter's car, but there shouldn't be a problem." I looked at where he had placed the torn napkin marker on the advertising map. "Hey, that's Hanging Rock Park! I've heard about that place. It has an awesome rock formation there. I can't remember what it's called, but it looks like someone pressed a big thumb under a hill and pushed a chunk of it straight up."

Frankie came up, the ever-present carafe of hot water in hand. "It's called a monadnock. That's an Indian name meaning isolated mountain. I heard the land on the top is supposed to be sacred ground. The park service must not think it's too sacred, though. This one," she pointed to the area we had marked on the map, "is still accessible on foot by a hiking trail. We have some park flyers on the wall by the bathrooms. If you're going up there, it might be handier to have one of those detailed maps rather than this," she said, pointing to the advertising map we were using.

I pushed away from the table and groaned as I stood up, putting my more-than-ample weight on my arthritic feet. I took a few more steps toward the bathroom and said, "I'll be right back; it might be a while before I get to use indoor plumbing again."

I studied the reflection in the mirror as I washed ice cream off my hands. You're not too decrepit-looking for being close to—oh, how can that be?—sixty years old. Remember when you were a kid? You thought you'd be parked in a rocking chair at sixty, crocheting doilies, just waiting to die. Here you are today, thousands of miles from home, traipsing around North Carolina with what appears to be a treasure map, and a couple—no, you're down to only one—mysterious foreigner looking for who knows what, using the flimsiest of clues: an old piece of parchment with odd scribbling on it. Cripes, you're even volunteering to drive wherever to find whatever!

I know men go through mid-life crises, but for me to do this is ridiculous. I don't have anything to prove! I have half a mind to cancel this crazy mission.

I walked out of the bathroom and there was Simon, looking as happy as a four-year-old about to open Christmas presents. He strutted up to me with his arm held out for mine. "Shall we?" he asked.

"We shall," I replied, "why not?"

Ж

I estimated the drive to the park should take us just over an hour, but after ten minutes, the heavy silence made it feel as if I'd already traveled a full day. Neither of us was in the mood for conversation, and I didn't want to play disc jockey on the radio, searching for a decent station.

Although he wasn't doing anything wrong, it felt odd riding next to

Simon. I guess it was because I was sitting so close to someone I wasn't related to and barely knew. At least he didn't stink. Actually, he had a distinctive herbal aroma about him that was quite pleasant. It reminded me of playing on my backyard swing as a child. He smelled of mulberry leaves in summer, dusty bark, and sisal rope, with some kiddy sweat thrown in to round out the perfume. And, now that I was aware of it, the odd, complex scent was having a calming effect on me.

Simon kept looking out the window—for clues, I suppose. I had to keep my eye on the road and watch for highway signs. A late afternoon shower had made this gold and copper-leafed landscape appear severely clear, eerily bright in contrast to the gray sky above us and the intrusive dark road—slick, shiny, and sinuous—in front of us. I laughed: at least I didn't have to worry about a moose jumping out in front of us like in Alaska.

What I did see were rows of headstones on either side of the narrow road, and not just in one town, but in several. The two-lane highway actually bisected graveyards! I thought it was extremely disrespectful at first, but then realized that the communities were actually encompassing those who had died, keeping them in their daily lives. An interesting concept I never would have considered. This part of the country was definitely different from anywhere I had lived.

Ж

The entrance to Hanging Rock Park was well marked and easy to find with the GPS navigator built into my smartphone. As soon as we stopped, Simon bolted out of the car. He tried the front door of the visitor center, but it was locked. No one was on duty—it had closed at five. Simon peered through the glass, craning his neck, searching for clues.

I left him there and proceeded to the elaborate bulletin board on the sidewalk—an unattended booth adorned with colorful posters about wildflowers, the trails, and the region's history. It looked to me like a good place to start. A handmade poster was pinned to the upper left corner of the kiosk. The unusual pins securing it, brass I think, had strange little marks all around the heads.

"Hey, look here, Simon," I called out, "It's Mona Lisa. At least there's someone here to greet us."

Simon scurried over and nudged me aside so he was standing directly in front of the handbill-sized poster of the classic smiling maiden. If he hadn't been so intent on what he was doing, I would have called him positively rude. "Well?" I asked.

"Leonard did it, I'm sure he did. Now I know I'm on the right path! Hmm, I believe I need to go that way," he said. He carefully pulled out the pins and looked at the etchings on the heads.

"Why don't you look on the undersides, too," I suggested.

Simon turned them over and beamed with approval, but not at me. "Thank you very much for your assistance," he said curtly. "I take it you can find your way back." He turned away from me and strutted across the parking lot to the first paved foot trail, head held high, oblivious of anything other than his quest.

I was stunned, speechless for a whole thirty seconds, and then unexpected anger flooded in.

"Whoa, dude. Would you at least tell me what this is all about?" I started to run after him, then stopped, disgusted with myself.

I hated the idea of chasing after a man, any man, but there was such a feeling of incompleteness in all of this, it literally squeezed my gut. I guessed what I needed was closure or finality or something like that. For some reason, there was a tenuous attachment to either this strange little man or to the whole oddball mission. I remembered James said he felt the map had something to do with him. I was starting to feel the same way, that it—or maybe it was Simon—was part of me, too.

"Simon," I called out using my mad mama voice. "Simon, you stop right where you are, mister." I wasn't going to run after him, and I wasn't hysterical, even if I sounded like it. I was thoroughly pissed, though.

The hostility in my voice worked. Simon stopped, turned around, and looked at me as if I were a squawking parrot. "That's *Master* Simon," he said.

"No, it's not. If you were a *master*," I said snidely, "you would have figured this out all by yourself, without the help of a *mere* woman. What in the hell is going on?"

"Madame," he began, now using a condescending tone, which I found even ruder than just blowing me off, "I am here to find my destiny. At first light, I will depart this world to join my family. Please, leave me in peace."

"Okay," I said, and turned around to head back to the car. He was being melodramatic and, in my estimation, was looking for me to plead with him to come back, or at least ask him for details. Not gonna happen.

I continued walking towards the little purple Prius, surreptitiously watching Simon's reflection in the car door window. I wouldn't give him the satisfaction of seeing me turn around to watch him, but I was getting a perverse pleasure seeing his image fidget. I could tell he wanted to come back and say something else to me, but his pride was a lot bigger than he was.

Rats! Now it was my turn to be antsy. I had reached the car and I would have to get in—which would mean losing sight of his reflected image—or remain standing alongside it like an idiot—which would make it look as if I were waiting for him to come back. Two breaths later though, it didn't make a difference. Simon was walking slowly; slowly walking away from me.

Okay, if Simon was determined to meet his family in the great beyond that was his choice. But, dang it, I couldn't let someone commit suicide, no matter how justified he thought it was. And, no matter how crazy he was, he shouldn't believe that jumping off a mountain or whatever would be the solution to his problems.

"Who is crazier, the crazy person or the crazy person who follows him?" I grumbled as I put on my coat. I started a little mental checklist of what I should take with me. "I'll need my coat, water... Heck, I'll just take the whole backpack; that should do it.

"Okay, I don't want to take the keys with me. Leah said she always leaves them under the right rear bumper, so I'll put them there." I stashed the keys on top of the muddy body part that connected to the plastic bumper. "Okay, a quick call to Leah first. Rats, I'm still talking to myself."

I dialed Leah's cell phone number and got her voice mail. "Hi, I'm not here so leave a message or call back. Bye." Great, she wasn't available so I wouldn't have to explain myself to her, at least not now.

"Hi Leah; it's Mom. I won't be coming home tonight. I'll be back sometime tomorrow, depending on how the day goes. Don't work too hard." I winced at saying the wrong words on the recording. 'Don't work too hard' were flash words for her, at least when I said them. I quickly added, "I love you. I'll call you later, Honey."

And I would call her later and tell her what was going on—unless I saw her in person first. Right now, I didn't want to tell her about my emotional morning at the museum and picking up a hitchhiker in 18th-century garb. If I told her that I'd involved myself in another spontaneous escapade, she'd add another hash mark to the 'irresponsible' side of my already lopsided good/not-so-good judgment scorecard. That would mean I'd be on the unbalanced side again, at least in her opinion.

Whatever—I had other, more important concerns, and they didn't involve what someone thought of me. I was probably the only one around who cared for that goofy-looking little man who called himself Master

Simon. I pulled on my backpack and adjusted the straps to distribute the weight across my shoulders. "Okay, suicide prevention team 'A,' ready, willing, and hopefully able, to stop one lonely little man from jumping off a cliff into the great beyond."

*4 Leonardo the First

The wind was picking up, whispering harsh, unintelligible secrets through the trees. The brisk breeze caused the leaves and branches to bump against each other as they noisily tried to find a resting place. This unsolicited but welcomed racket benefitted my situation: I didn't have to worry about Simon hearing me as I shuffled down the path, stalking him for his own good.

After the first ten minutes, I could no longer hear the highway noises. The only sounds were natural: the wind in the trees, a creek rushing down a ravine somewhere, and the crunchy-cereal sound of my boots on the granite rubble path.

Darkness and the unknown were quickly replacing dusk and the last remnants of my daytime adventure. Still, the Park Service's enhanced deer path was easy to follow and, at times, I could see Simon ahead of me. Our route was like a roller coaster track: when our aspects were just right, I could see him on the twisting and undulating trail ahead of me. He wasn't turning around, looking for me—or anyone else for that matter. Either he was sure he wouldn't be followed, or he didn't care. Absorbed in his quest for his friend, he was oblivious to his surroundings.

I struggled forward, concentrating on taking deep, steady breaths, trying to keep my heart rate down on the aggressive hike. It was definitely not moderate as described on the poster, at least for me. I thought I was in good shape for an old broad, but evidently, I was not. The old man ahead of me didn't seem challenged by the steep intervals, though.

I was silently cursing my obese, weak body, not paying attention to how close I was to my psych patient, when I almost blew it. All of a sudden, there he was. Simon had come to a complete stop in the middle of the trail, a stone's throw ahead of me. He was bent over, picking up some sort of artifact.

I tiptoed over to a stand of tall, scrubby bushes off the path, and sidled closer to sneak a peek at his discovery. He had what looked like a toy airplane in his hands, but even from this far away, I could tell that what he had was not a child's toy, but a fine, miniature scale reproduction of a glider. It appeared new to him by the way he was examining it, running his fingers over the framework, holding it up to the fading light, looking for gaps or clues or whatever.

It looked like a Leonardo da Vinci replica to me. I had received a book of paper airplanes based on some of his designs for my birthday, twelfth I think, and I was positive that this was one of them. However, this one wasn't made of pre-printed craft paper and plastic rods. It appeared to be made of parchment stretched over a wooden frame, held together with catgut or some other coarse, straw-colored binding. If it was a clue, it was a classy one.

I saw Simon look up and smile. I followed his gaze. Someone was approaching. Was it a man in a dress? Yes, it was an older, longhaired man in a cream-colored, flowing robe, strutting down from the upper trail, a big smile of welcome on his face. Well, either he was a nut or he really was Leonardo da Vinci, back from the 16th—or was that 15th?—century. Ah, this must be his friend, Leonard. So this must be the special rendezvous Simon was so eager to make.

Okay...now I got it: Halloween! His friend dressed up like Leonardo and hung a print of the Mona Lisa in the parking lot with some sort of clue on the underside of the pins. That led Simon to this custom-built glider model. Leonard da Vinci-themed clues for Simon from his friend named Leonard. Cute and clever, even if it was a little over the top.

So why did Simon say all that crap about suicide earlier? Maybe I just read more into it than there was.

I backed away from my leafless lookout, plopped my weary butt down on the hard ground, and rested my forehead on my knees. I wanted to melt down, to evaporate into the atmosphere; better yet, to be teleported back to my recliner in Fairbanks. Here I was, four time zones off my body's natural biorhythm, six thousand land miles from home, severed from my comfortably boring daily routine, and involved with a cryptic and crotchety old man.

I looked up at the two men—smiling and chatting away, happy to be in each other's presence. Simon had met up with his friend—all was well in their little world. It was time for me to leave. My outlandish adventure was over.

I still didn't want Simon to know I had followed him, so I decided I'd hang back here and recuperate from the long hike—in silent mode, of course—until they were gone.

The two men's arms and hands were flying up and out, visually amplifying their vibrant conversation, their words lost in the air between us.

Oh shoot, I couldn't help myself. Even though I knew it was wrong, I wanted to eavesdrop. I crawled forward, trying to catch the excited pair's tête-à-tête. The wind shifted, and I both heard and smelled them, the appetizing aroma of manicotti and olive oil causing my stomach to rumble in response. I clutched my belly, trying to muffle the growl, but they were oblivious to me or anything other than each other.

I could hear their words now, but it didn't help much—they were speaking Italian. Yes, Mister D., you are so into character that you're speaking the language. I had never learned Italian, but I was pretty good at Spanish, so was able to follow the gist of their conversation. Apparently, the two of them were going to hang out until the sun came up. Then they'd go home together, hand in hand, "*Il grande salto dalla montagna,*" the big jump down the mountain.

"What?" I gasped out loud, then crouched low to the ground, wishing I could crawl into it and hide. Crap, they *were* going to commit suicide—together!

They hadn't heard me and were still chatting away, not a care in the world, fully animated, their heads, hands, and arms in constant motion. It was like watching an old Jerry Lewis and Dean Martin routine. They were acting like schoolboys, excited about playing hooky during test week, actually *happy* about dying!

Leonardo reached down, grabbed a fistful of dead leaves, and tossed them straight up in the air—maybe he was checking for wind speed or direction. He shook his head, "*Non qui,*" picked up the plane, and motioned for Simon to follow him.

The two scuttled off the established trail, up a side path, with me doggedly trailing behind them. They stopped talking, and instead focused their energy on the increasingly steep climb. The going was rough for me, too, but the odd mix of curiosity and compassion that drove me was more powerful than the fatigue that was urging me to quit. This worn out, but indomitable old lady was going to keep up with those two oddly dressed—and one of them certifiably ornery—old men, determined to intervene so a life or two wouldn't be tossed into the wind.

Leonardo, leading the way, stopped without warning. He put on the brakes so suddenly that Simon bumped into him. Of course, that meant I had to stop quickly, too, but my reflexes weren't fast enough. I took one too many steps, and the last one was noisy.

I froze and squeezed my eyes tight, hoping it would help me become invisible. Even if it didn't, with eyes shut, I wouldn't see the look in their eyes when they realized that some weirdo woman had followed them up the long, arduous trail, then off the beaten path.

Nothing was happening though—my existence not acknowledged—at least verbally. Maybe they hadn't seen me. I still didn't want to open my eyes to find out, so continued in stealth mode, just in case. My shallow breathing was beginning to catch up with me. I had the overwhelming urge to take in a big, healthy lungful of air, but stifled it, and instead concentrated on blending in with the living woodwork.

"*Sento l'odore delle rosa,*" Leonardo said.

I think he said he smelled roses.

"*No, percepisco le rosa,*" he corrected.

Did he say he perceived—or was that he sensed—roses? Oh, crap: I think he meant me.

A single set of footfalls approached, stopping directly in front of me; another pair shuffled up and stopped behind those. Neither man spoke, adding to my apprehension. I doubt either of them were happy to see me, the woman who had been trailing them for over an hour.

The whisper-soft flap of wings overhead broke the awkward silence. I tilted my head back, opened my eyes, and saw a big, bulky, mottled-brown bird suspended in the thermals above. I glanced over and saw the two men watch as the bird floated in the lake of air above us. In tandem, they nodded to one another in complete understanding, like an old married couple. They didn't say a word, but looked at me, then each other, and then back at me again. Maybe they thought the owl was an omen or something. I let it ride, glad that they weren't upset with their stalker.

"Okay, okay, I followed you. But I only came to make sure you were okay." Both men smiled at my apprehension, or maybe it was at my naivety. I paused, then clarified my statement, "It's just I was afraid you were going to kill yourself by jumping off a cliff, and I didn't want that to happen. You seemed…"

I stopped right there. Both men's good-natured grins fell, and their mouths dropped open in amazement. For some reason, their pale, shocked faces empowered me. I didn't say a word, though. I just watched them with half a smile, waiting for one of them to finish my sentence for me.

Simon spoke first, clearing his throat to begin. "Ahem. Madame, I thank you for your concern, but you need not worry. We have everything under control."

I looked at him, my head cocked and eyebrows raised, but still I said nothing. The 'look' worked. He was obviously hiding something because he suddenly had a very guilty look on his face. I glanced over at his friend

35

and nodded, then looked back, asking Simon wordlessly, "Who's he?"

Simon pulled himself together, literally, before answering. The little man shifted his shoulders within his coat, cleared his throat again, and pulled his elbows into his waist, as if to pull up his pants. "Madame Madigan, may I present Leonardo da Vinci, my friend and traveling partner. Leonardo, this is Dani—is that Danielle?—Madigan."

Leonardo bent over and kissed my hand, which seemed to have risen by itself to his mouth. "*Siete la signora di rosa?*"

"Yes, they sometimes call me the rose lady. How did you know? Do I smell like roses?" I lifted my forearm to my face, sniffed, and then realized I was more relaxed now that my presence was acknowledged.

"No, you do not smell of roses. I sensed you. You are not like the others. You are kind and not selfish. That is why you followed. You did not believe the treasure was gold or jewels, did you?" Leonardo was speaking English, but with the most intriguing Italian accent.

"Nah, gold and jewels don't trip my trigger, uh, they're not important. They're just rocks dug out of the ground—traded, purchased, stolen, or given away freely. Now human life, that's very complicated and precious. Created in God's image and recreated every generation out of nothing but a little egg and a sperm too small to see with the naked eye. Once a person has left this earthly plane, he's gone forever. True, you once could buy and sell people as slaves, but thank You, Lord, it's illegal to do that anymore. Humans are high maintenance. You have to feed them, protect them from the elements, and then still, they can just up and die when you least expect it. Precious metals and jewels can sit in crypts for millennia without fading or deteriorating. Just don't try that with a person. Oh, excuse me, I'm babbling again."

"Some would say that is why gold and jewels are more valuable," Leonardo countered. "They retain their worth through the years and are easy to transport, don't require special handling, and are quite durable."

"Yeah, well, a rock is a rock, and only man has decided that gold and diamonds are more valuable than," I bent over and picked up a walnut-sized stone, "this." I tossed it up in the air, caught it, and then threw it into the ravine the owl had hovered over earlier. "Whoa!"

The rock wasn't falling, but instead was drifting down, as if on a cushion of air. I squatted down and picked up a bigger rock, this one tennis-ball sized. I threw it underhanded into the same area and watched as it arched in the air. It, too, sank slowly, until it was out of sight. I couldn't see the bottom of the ravine and listened in vain for nearly a minute, waiting for the rock's report.

I looked back to Simon and Leonardo, wondering if they had seen my little pitching exhibition. They had but didn't seem surprised. Their identical reaction—both still very much in tune with each other—was pinch-faced, eyebrow-crowding concern.

Simon gulped, his mouth empty of words. He was very aware of the gravitational anomaly but didn't know how he should react to it. Instead, he glossed over the phenomenal results of the rock tossing. "My, my; how fascinating. Madame Madigan, it is getting late, but the moon is rising now, and you should have enough light to find your way back to your car."

I glared at him but said nothing. He fidgeted a little and then looked at Leonardo, who replied nonverbally with shrugged shoulders.

Simon tried again. "I feel a bit of a chill coming on. Shall we build a fire to warm our hands?"

"That sounds like a splendid idea," Leonardo agreed loudly and with too much enthusiasm. He kicked aside rubbish and leaf matter to expose a site for a fire pit and began gathering fallen twigs and branches. "I'd love to hear about your roses. I hear they are quite different from the once-blooming Rosa albas I'm familiar with."

I mumbled something like, "sure," and shuffled about, picking up loose twigs, adding them to the pile. At least for now, I didn't have to worry about old men jumping off cliffs.

I brushed small granite pieces off a boulder I planned to use as a seat, then looked up and saw that both men were staring at me. "Yesss?" I drawled. When they didn't reply, I added sarcastically, "Is there something you need?"

Leonardo, who seemed to be the alpha male of the two, said, "You are just so beautiful."

I tucked my double chin down and frowned at him like, 'Are you nuts?' but replied with the polite words, insincerely spoken, "Thank you."

Simon was fidgeting again. I think I was intruding on his quality time with his friend and he wanted me gone. I smiled at him and looked away. "Almost a full moon tonight," I said to the sky, speaking just to change the uncomfortable topic. "I'm glad I'm not in town with all the Halloweeners."

Leonardo stared at Simon, a puzzled frown on his face. "*Samhain,*" Simon said as a one-word explanation.

I started at the sound of the strange word and, turning back, saw Leonardo nodding his tacit acknowledgment. He poured something on the poor excuse of a fire. It flared up and stayed big; it had to be more than lighter fluid he was using.

"Would you care for an aperitif?" he asked as he held up a small, long-necked green bottle.

"No, thanks, I'm fine." After his little display of alchemy, I didn't want any of his potions passing my lips.

I saw a look pass between the two of them that seemed to say, 'Rats, foiled again.'

Leonardo started making small talk about roses. I was wary but polite, certain that he was just trying to gain my trust. Whatever. I was just killing time with the empty conversation, recuperating from the long hike, and waiting until the moon was higher, bright enough to see the path back to the parking lot. I had been wrong about Simon's suicide risk. I knew that now. These two just wanted to be alone. I was more than ready to go back to Greensboro proper and Leah's bed, but I didn't want to do it in the dark. I wasn't going to tell them that, though.

"How about a jumble?" Simon asked. "I forgot I had brought along some of these wonderful sweet cakes for my journey." He pulled out a small beige cloth packet and opened it. Inside were four intact cookies and several big broken pieces. "It seems they are a little worse for the travel. I'm sure my encounter this morning had something to do with it." He picked up and inspected one of the more substantial chunks before eating it.

Well, the cookies looked good, and he did eat one first, and it had been a long walk; I guessed it was safe enough if I just took a small piece. I doubted Simon, or his baker, would be lacing cookies with LSD or angel dust.

I looked into the cloth container, took out a small bit of broken shortbread, and put it in my mouth. It wasn't very sweet—more like a spiced butter cookie than oatmeal or chocolate chip—and had a rich, smooth texture. I closed my eyes, withdrawing from visual distraction in order to focus on the intriguing spice. I looked up, ready to ask what it was, when I saw both men staring, watching for my reaction. It was then that my tongue started to tingle.

"I hope this doesn't have almonds in it; I'm allergic to them. My tongue is itching, and why are you two staring at me?"

I was becoming—oh dear, all I could think of was—befuddled.

I heard a woman's voice singing a nonsense song, but couldn't see her when I looked around. The two men in front of me were laughing as their bodies segued from normal human beings into the Looney Tune characters of Elmer Fudd and Yosemite Sam. Yosemite was asking me if I wanted to dance and, well, I couldn't help but accept. Elmer was cheerily clapping and stomping his feet in time to the music that was coming from everywhere. I danced and twirled with my cartoon partner until I begged to sit down on the giant mushroom near the fire.

Now Elmer and Sam were nose to nose, speaking so rapidly I couldn't understand them and, dag nab it, there weren't any balloons over their heads with words in them like in the comics. The two men didn't seem very happy. I guess that wascally wabbit got away again...

Out of nowhere, I heard a woman's high-pitched voice call out, "My, my, this toadstool is too hard and lumpy. I think I'd rather sit down over there, on that small sofa."

The plump and perplexed old woman who had just ingested hallucinogenic carbohydrates adjusted her backpack and walked toward the stony outcropping, intent on more comfortable accommodations.

"Ooooh, nice," she said as she walked across what she thought was a crisp graham cracker path to a mammoth marshmallow settee.

"Stop," shouted the two men as she swan-dived into the great, white cumulus cloud of a couch.

But they were too late to stop her. Instead, they followed her over the cliff, each grabbing one of her feet.

The crisp autumn air in my face quickly brought me out of the spell. Oh, crap! I was falling! Actually, drifting, but still moving downwards. I was sure to hit bottom eventually. I felt a pair of hands on each ankle, grasping and then clutching their way, hand over hand, up my body until each man had a death grip on a wrist. I looked back and forth between them, all of a sudden stone cold sober and scared. What I saw looking back at me was not fear, but anger.

"She's ruined it, Simon! You should never have let her follow you," screamed Leonardo.

"I didn't mean for her to come, but what could I do?" Simon yelled back. "She saved my life, and if you had just left a note rather than your idiotic clues, I wouldn't have needed her!"

"I'm right here, guys. I can hear you, you know." I pulled my hands away from them and turned over to look up at the sky. "When are we going to... Oh, shit!" I exclaimed, seeing the trees at my side. The ground had jumped up beside me, right here, right now, and then it was all over.

Ж

Simon and Leonardo had made many leaps before. They knew how to land, but they had drugged the concerned old lady. She was both ignorant and incapacitated. She didn't know what she doing when she walked out onto that cloud. She would have had a good chance of survival if she had just received some training, or at least a few quick words telling her to bring her legs down and land feet first, as if jumping off a fence. Instead, the two men had been bickering, and she had landed on her back. If she were alive, it would be a miracle. The rate of descent hadn't been too fast, but she hadn't been prepared.

Ж

Leonardo picked up her hand and let it drop. "She's dead; let's go," he said coldly, and looked around to locate the moon. He didn't have a compass, and the cloudy night obscured the stars. He needed to get his bearings so they could leave in the right direction immediately.

Simon knelt down by Dani's side and put his ear to her chest. Thump thump, thump thump. She was alive, but not breathing. He pushed up and in on her belly, trying to get her diaphragm to move, but still no breath.

"You need to blow in her mouth if you want her to live. I say just leave her. She wouldn't survive in this time anyway. She's not prepared."

Simon looked into the face of the sweet, middle-aged lady who had come to his aid when no one would even look at him. She cleaned and bandaged his wounds, fed him, took him where he asked to go, and didn't ask for anything in return.

He took a deep breath, pinched her nose, and blew into her mouth. "Ugh." He shuddered. Close physical contact repulsed him.

He sat up and waited to see if he needed to repeat the resuscitation procedure. Probably—she still wasn't breathing. He took in another deep breath, resigned himself to the unsavory task, and bent over her once again.

Dani gasped in a deep breath and immediately cried, "Ow," wincing as she exhaled. She squeezed her eyes closed, attempting to shut out the pain, and tried to sit up. She didn't make it. She had landed on her backpack and couldn't move.

"Here, let me get rid of this," Simon said as he rolled his would-be patron over, took her arms out of the straps, and shoved the bag aside. He settled her carefully onto her back again. "How many fingers do you see?"

"Huh?" she replied.

Simon turned her head from side to side and saw blood coming from her ears. He took her hand and squeezed her fingers together: no response

40

of discomfort or pain. He tightened his grip, but her features remained blank. He reached over, grabbed a bit of skin just above her ankle, and pinched it: still no sign of any feeling in her extremities.

Master Simon made his very first heartfelt decision. He reached into his pocket, pulled out a little blue facet-cut bottle, and uncorked it. "Here, take a sip of this," he said as he put the jewel-like container to her lips.

"No!" screamed Leonardo. "That's mine!"

The sudden shout caused Simon's patient to gasp in surprise, causing sixty-year-old Dani Madigan to gulp a very large dose of the rare and valuable medicine. She would never be the same again.

Simon held the bottle up to the dim moonlight. "I think there's still some left. If not, we can go back to Florida and get more. The fountain is still there; let's take more bottles this time. I think Leonardo Junior wanted some, too, did he not?"

Leonardo was furious. "I did not come all this way for more elixir. That is what *you* were supposed to do. And no, my son said he wants to live his life without staying young. He is actually embracing his aging, the fool."

"He is not a fool! You taught him many basic concepts, but he has progressed far beyond your lessons to develop his own great projects and art works. He will make his mark in history his own way. Leave him be."

Leonardo da Vinci the Elder looked over at the still-unconscious female on the ground. She didn't look as big as she did when he first saw her. It must be the moonlight playing tricks on his eyes. He picked up the old woman's backpack and threw it into the bushes. "Let's go. Either she'll make it or she won't. You had better hope she doesn't remember any of this. If anyone does find her, they'll think she's mad."

Simon bent over the unconscious woman's body and pinched her wrist. It jerked away from his fingers. He reached into his coat one more time and pulled out a small envelope. He opened it and took out a twist of pollen stem. He pried open his friend's mouth and stuck it under her tongue. "Remember nothing, my dear, remember nothing."

*5 So, here I was...

October 31, 1781

Someone was sweeping an ostrich feather under my nose, or maybe it was just my hair blowing across my face. Either way, the tickle was enough to wake me out of a sound sleep. I tried to brush whatever away, but couldn't. My body was unresponsive, rigid, and felt heavy, as if made of solid oak. Something was wrong here. Everything was out of focus, moving in slow motion, or not at all. Suddenly, I sneezed the mother of all sneezes. Wham! Now that felt good, and I think it jumpstarted my heart, too.

Oh, crap; where am I? Lying on my back—somewhere. The high cirrus clouds above me seem to be racing ahead of a winter storm. The smell of moist, moldy leaves nearby is pleasant, but doesn't help me know where I am. I shut my eyes and inhale deeply, filling my lungs to the top of my shoulders with the cool, heavily oxygenated air. I let it out slowly, and panic...

"Who am I?"

I know I'm me, but I can't remember my name. Shoot, I don't know what day, or even what month it is—or year! I lift my head and look down at my body. My clothes seem familiar: gray polar fleece sweatpants and a green buffalo-checked flannel shirt with a white cotton undershirt. I'm wearing my favorite jacket, too. Hey, that's something! I know it's my favorite and, now that I think about it, I remember I made this myself.

"Great," I mumble sarcastically, "all I know about me is that I can sew, and I only know that because of the coat I'm wearing. There has to be more to me than that!"

Hmph, maybe I fell and hit my head. Right, that would explain waking up flat on my back and without a memory. Evidently, I'm not the type to freak out. My momentary panic has now become rabid curiosity. Who am I?

I check my pockets for clues. I have a Leatherman multi-tool, a wad of tissues, a couple of brightly colored handkerchiefs, a ballpoint pen without any advertising blurb, and three safety pins. There's nothing special about any of this. I'm still anonymous. Something doesn't feel right though. I know something is missing.

What I'm not missing is a case of cottonmouth. First order of

42

business: find water. Before I can do that, though, I have to figure out how to stand up. I don't hurt anywhere, but for some reason I have pudding for muscles. After three frustrating attempts at standing, I'm able to get my feet under me. I feel like I just won a wrestling match with myself. Hey, look at that. I'm wearing tan hiking boots. They blend right into the ground, and cool—they're on the right feet, too!

Now, where's my water bottle? That's what's missing—my backpack! I had a backpack with at least one water bottle in it. I don't know what else was in it, or even what it looks like, but I know I had water and a backpack at some point. Yeah, well, wishing for the backpack and water bottle doesn't make them magically appear. Maybe there's a creek or stream nearby. If I were an animal looking for water, how would I find it? I'd sniff it out, that's how. Okay. I can do that.

Sniff, sniff. Turn ninety degrees. Sniff, sniff. Hey, that's it! Maybe I'm from the desert and that's why I can smell water so easily. There, that big oak-looking tree has deep green vegetation underneath it. I'll bet there's a spring feeding it.

I pull away the thick, spongy mass covering the top of the wet spot with my hands. It's moist all right, but there isn't enough water to drink. I paw at it furiously, trying to enlarge the pit, hoping to speed up the water flow. Ergh! Okay, I guess I'll just have to wait for it to fill. I start laughing hysterically. Yeah, right. What was it that poster said—or was it a tee shirt? 'God give me patience and I want it NOW!' Well, Lord, I want a tall glass of water, but I'll settle for a muddy puddle…and the sooner the better.

The damp spot appears to be getting wetter. Groundwater they call it. I remember digging a hole for a mailbox post in Fairbanks. I couldn't dig down even one foot without hitting the water table there. Fairbanks, that's Alaska! That must be where I'm from. No time to think about that now; I need to figure out how to get a drink.

I look around and see a few fallen trees, lots of branches and twigs, then finally locate a broken sapling, just the right length to use as a pry bar. After a few jabs and pushes, I'm able to lever several of the bigger rocks out of my little oasis. Then it's down to my knees for the dirty work. I dredge out as much sand and muck as I can with my hands and create a fair-sized bowl. The water can move in faster now; less restriction or something like that. I guess I should have paid more attention in science class.

My face won't fit into my slow-filling excavation, but I have two handkerchiefs I can use as sponges. I can slake my thirst with one while the other gets nice and sopping wet. I shake off the pocket fuzz and set them into my sandy, earthen sink. Umm... Sucking on a wet hankie is such a primitive joy: a wonderful, albeit small, blessing.

I don't want to leave and to try to find civilization because there's water here. I'm sure there are other sources, but I'm too scared and insecure to leave this place—wherever 'this place' is.

Then again, I should probably stay put and improvise some sort of shelter. Yeah, right. I have plenty of trees to build with, but no way of getting them down. There are lots of twigs and branches for a fire, but I don't have matches. Well, at least my legs still work. I can jog in place until someone finds me, or I can think of another way to stay warm, whichever comes first. Where's a nosy neighbor when you need one?

*6 Woof

"Woof, woof."

Now there's a familiar sound. At least a dog barking is better than a wolf snarling or a bear growling. Maybe this means there's a cabin nearby. A folksy, backwoods log cabin, or even a shack would do, with a friendly sort in residence. Actually, any place where I could warm my frozen fingers and find out how to get to civilization would be fine by me. Maybe I'll get lucky and score a cup of hot cocoa, too.

Of course, most of the vacation cabins are abandoned for the winter this late in the fall. I'll be lucky to find a doghouse to climb into. Well, right now a doghouse sounds pretty good. It looks like it's going to snow, and all I have is the coat on my back. Yeah, well, the Pollyanna part of me realizes that at least the coat is warm, has a hood, and I'm wearing boots.

"Woof, woof." Okay, back to reality, woman. That's not a warning bark I hear—it's an animal in distress.

"Here boy, here boy," I call out. I have no idea where the dog is, but I can tell he's in trouble.

"Woof, woof, whheee?"

Woof, woof, whine? What the heck? I carefully step over the uneven ground, thick clumps of leaves, and fallen trees as I search for the source of the sound, but still wind up tripping on the bottoms of my pants. For some reason, they keep falling down. Dang, how come they're so big all of a sudden?

"Woof?"

Oh, my God!" There's a huge dog in that tree, and he's hanging upside down! At least, I think it's a dog. Whatever it is, that big four-legged, mud covered, hog-tied critter has a foot-long chunk of wood wedged in his mouth.

Poor, pathetic animal, he has to be a dog; he's stopped woofing now that he's seen me. Those sad, puppy-dog eyes are begging me to help him. I'm not too sure about that, though. He's surprisingly quiet now, but I know better than to get close to a strange dog, even one who looks gentle. Dogs are still animals, even if they have been domesticated for thousands of years.

Oh, well, I'll take a chance. At least with that stick in his mouth, he can't bite me. I suck down my anxiety and, keeping my eyes low, approach him cautiously, my knuckles extended for him to sniff. Out of the corner of my eye, I can see that his lip is back, teeth bared, but he's not snarling at me. It's that wooden gag screwing up his mouth, distorting his face. But his eyes, the true character indicators, aren't hostile.

"Poor baby, poor baby," I repeat softly. My soothing voice must be working, at least for one of us. Now I'm more at ease.

"Okay, baby, here we go." I reach up and cut the suspension rope with my Leatherman tool, letting him drop into the pile of leaves below. It's a short fall, but I think he's been through worse. No, I know he has. I rush to his side. My maternal, or whatever it is with a dog—pet-ernal maybe?—instincts have kicked in. I have no fear of this dark-furred beast.

The poor battered canine has been repeatedly thwacked and probably booted, too. There's a bloody gash across his snout, and his chops are raw where the rough bark scraped. He lifts his weary head and seems to whimper, "Set me loose, please."

"Not, yet, baby; just wait a minute," I reply to his non-verbal request. Logic tells me I need to get the wood out of his mouth now, while he's still securely bound, or I may never have another chance, or at least a safe one. Okay, time to put on my orthodontist hat.

I try to be gentle, but that's both futile and exasperating. I need to be aggressive. "I have to get this out first, then I'll untie you. Please be patient with me; I'm new at this."

The stick still won't budge, even when I get my back and butt into it, pulling on it with all my weight. It's crammed all the way back between his molars, wedged in so he can't push it out with his tongue. Even though he's not threatening me, I'm cautious around his canines; they're huge! Whoever did this dirty deed probably drew back a bloody stump, or at least I hope he did. I'm certain the person—or persons—who did this got hurt in the process. It had to be 'persons' though; I can't image even two big men overcoming this huge beast. I sure hope the dog drew first blood, and lots of it!

"Poor baby, poor baby," I repeat soothingly as I try to figure out a new tactic. I can almost swear he winces when I say 'baby.' I look down at his belly. Okay, now I see: he's a male. He's also a trusting one by the way he's patiently waiting for me to figure out how to get this done.

"Sorry, fella. Let's try this. I know it's going to be painful, but please, pretty please, don't bite me. I have to open your mouth extra wide, and it's gonna hurt."

I come at the short chunk of tree trunk from the back of his head, stick my thumbs in his mouth, and hyper-extend his tight jaw. "There we go," I grunt as I push the wood out with my fingers.

It's gone now, but his mouth still won't close. It's going to be a while before his jaw muscles return to normal. I don't think he could bite me now, even if he wanted to.

Finally, time to free him from his crude bindings. "Okay, big boy, let's get you out of this convoluted torture chamber."

I could swear he glared at me when I called him big boy. "Okay, bear with me; I'll let you tell me your name when your mouth gets back to working order. Now, you see this: it's my Leatherman." I flip the tool open like the guys do and open up the pliers. "The inside of this is for cutting wire. It works great on rope, too."

I approach him cautiously, and with just a couple of snips, cut through the crudely twisted sisal. He collapses into a heap at my feet with an audible groan. I check him for broken bones or other wounds but can't find anything obvious. He's dirty but seems to be intact; at least he has all his pieces, and I can't feel any breaks. I know he's grateful to be free, but he's still stunned and can't—or won't—move yet.

He looks like a chocolate-brown Malamute under the mud and filth, and appears to have a tan, raccoon-like mask. I brush away some of the debris from his coat. He definitely likes the attention I'm giving him and snuggles into me. I'm starting to like this big guy and feel comfortable with him. I hum a random nonsense tune and massage his ears, taking care to avoid the raw spots. He rubs his face against my legs, showing his appreciation, and then struggles to stand up. He makes it but is still wobbly.

I'm sure he's thirsty, so I try to lead him to my water hole. He walks off in the other direction instead, pauses, takes another step, looks back at me with those big coffee-colored eyes, and moves forward again. He only has to do this twice before I realize he wants me to follow him. I've heard 'you can't teach an old dog new tricks,' but evidently this feral dog can teach a lost woman how to obey and follow.

About thirty yards from where I found him is a free running stream. We both drink our fill. I'm content and feel as if I've found a new friend. "Well, dear," I tell him, avoiding the nicknames 'boy' and 'baby,' "I sure hope you can help me find my way back to...?"

I'm shocked back into my new reality. I don't know where I am, much less where I was going or what I was doing before I woke up at the bottom of that cliff. I face him and smile at his loyalty. "Hi, glad to make your acquaintance. My name is…."

I waver in shock, my head suddenly too heavy for my neck. *I still don't know who I am!*

My knees unlock one at a time and I collapse awkwardly onto my bottom. My arms reach out to grasp the ground behind me, instinct kicking in to avoid a complete head-cracking faint. My mind shuts down momentarily to avoid overload, and then reboots. I'm awake, mostly alert, and have no choice but to park my body and emotions here—in the middle of I don't know where.

What happened? And why?

I gradually drift back into reality. Poor dog, I must be scaring him. He bumps into my shoulder as if to say, "It's going to be okay."

My eyes start tearing up, either from fear or from the affection that this hound is showing me…or both. He puts his snout under my chin.

"Okay, I got it. Chin up. Stop feeling sorry for yourself. Sorry, Rocky, I didn't mean to upset you. After all, you're the one that was trussed up like a birthday piñata with a tree trunk crammed in your mouth."

"Woof, woof, howl!"

Rocky; I just called him Rocky. "Rocky?" I repeat, this time as a question.

"Hoooowwlll"

"Is that your name: Rocky?"

"Howl, howl, woof, woof."

"I guess that means yes. Now, can you tell me my name?"

"Mmmfff," was his embarrassed, almost human reply.

"I guess not."

*7 Ian Found

Rocky's ears perked up and then lay back flat against his skull. His eyes squinted and he snarled, momentarily scaring me. Don't panic, self—whoever self is—he's not mad at you.

"What is it, Rocky? Is someone else in trouble? Did Timmy fall down the well? Are there zombies coming? Good grief! I must have a concussion or I'm hallucinating. I'm talking to a massive wolf/dog creature and expecting an answer!"

Well, I do get an answer. Rocky makes eye contact with me, gives another snarl that I don't take personally, and then heads out to answer the call in the woods. He's after something or someone, that's for sure.

Concussed, confused, or just plain crazy, it seems like going with the dog is the logical thing to do. He's good at finding water and probably a good hunter, too. He likes me and, well, I'm kind of fond of him, too. That and I don't know what else to do. If he's heading into trouble, I can always hang back and hide in these dense woods. Since lead, follow, or get out of the way are my options, I think I'll follow.

So, off I go into the bleak unknown, blindly following my canine leader into the night. I'm either fearless or foolish, but definitely fast. I've made good time covering a lot of unknown terrain, but now I'm getting a hitch in my side. Okay, time to take a break, catch my breath, and hike up my sweatpants that seem to be three sizes too big. There's cording in the elastic waistband so, after working at the knot a bit, I get it untied and cinch it up tight so—hopefully—they won't fall down again.

I'm getting hot with all this running, but I'm not going to take off my coat; it's starting to snow now. That's good. I don't know where the creek is, but I'm getting thirsty again. As soon as there's enough snow accumulation, I'll make myself a fresh snowcone, even if it has to be unflavored.

The thought of a wet, frosty treat makes me even thirstier. If I just had my water bottle... I *know* I had one in my backpack. I wish I could go back and look for it now. Oh, well, no time to reflect on the loss—I have to find Rocky. With his apparent affinity towards trouble, he's probably headed for that noisy fiery glow ahead.

I doubt I'm a Marine, Green Beret, or an Indian scout, but there's such a ruckus coming from the bonfire crowd ahead, I could be coming in with a flock of sheep and still wouldn't be heard. I'll do my best, though, to be quiet, and won't call out for Rocky. I'm sure I'll find him when he wants to be found.

More than a campfire, the blaze is huge, maybe ten feet across and at least twice as high. Eight singing men, all shabbily dressed and sloppy drunk, surround it. Two of them share a fallen log; the rest are standing, although several are leaning against each other in order to remain upright. Several rifles and what appear to be baseball bats are propped up against a boulder, the amber-hued armory and sports locker an ominous and precarious six feet from the blaze. I definitely want to keep away from that crowd!

There's still no sign of Rocky. I stop, look, sniff, and listen, but can't detect anything with the primary senses. The sixth sense is kicking in, though. I'm sure something is going on. The tension in the air is tangible, I feel as if I can pluck it like a banjo, but I don't have the *huevos* to go any further. Even if I weren't such a chicken, I have that flash bulb blindness thing going on from looking at the campfire. There's nothing to do now but wait and watch to see what happens. Hmph, I think I can handle those two tasks.

I turn away from the fire, eyes squeezed tight, subtracting the visual distraction of the massive blaze, and listen for the dog. A few moments later, I hear it—movement beyond the edge of the firelight, away from the gang of eight. Now that my eyes have adjusted to the low light, I can see Rocky nudging a big bag. The object of his attention—a muddy, lumpy, over-sized gunnysack—appears to be moving. I think there's a person in there! No good could come from eight drunken men holding a person hostage in a bag.

Rocky's ministrations go unnoticed. These men are more interested in their liquor, and barking out their bawdy bar song, than noticing what's going on, practically under their noses. They're drinking from one of those ceramic moonshine jugs like the ones in the old western and hillbilly movies. For my sake, I hope their supply doesn't run out too soon. They won't be paying much attention to anything but their brew until it's gone. And by then, they'll be even drunker still, and less able to see, fight, or give pursuit.

Rocky is still intent on getting that bag opened. Watching his efforts, I have visions of a kidnapped young woman, trussed up like he was, and then stuffed into that bag, on hold for later—the carousers' dessert.

Okay, snap decision made. I'll sneak around the perimeter and help

Rocky drag the bag into the woods. It would be safer to open it away from the gathering, but I'd better hurry. Some of these guys are starting to act antsy. Drunk, rowdy, and excitable men—what am I thinking! Well, I know what I'm thinking. If I were in that bag, I'd want someone to come rescue me.

The snapping of twigs and crackling of leaves smashed by my running footsteps are lost in the loud flats and sharps of the challenged choir's lame but dogged attempt at song. The tune almost sounds like our national anthem, but their words are so slurred, that they could be singing the ABCs and I wouldn't recognize them.

I stop to hike up my perpetually drooping drawers at just the right time; one of the gang has just stepped into the woods to take a leak. If I hadn't paused to pull up my pants, our paths would have crossed. Too close for comfort, but I keep thinking of that poor creature in the bag. Then again, it might be Rocky's mate. Well, she would be worth rescuing, too.

Rocky's ears flatten and his lip curls up—he senses someone approaching—but he doesn't make a sound. He lifts his nose, sniffs the air, recognizes my scent, and then goes back to work, biting the ropes securing the bag, pulling at them with his long canines, pawing at them in frustration and urgency.

I gingerly pat the bag; it's definitely a human inside, not a dog. It's a bony person, too—I think I hit an elbow. The response is a small movement. Great, the person is still alive.

I use whispers and hand gestures to let Rocky know that I want to drag the bag away from here and *then* open it. If he doesn't understand what I'm saying, at least he's letting me take charge.

I grab and tug, first at one end, then the other, and then in the middle, trying to find a good place to hold on to the awkward package. I settle for grabbing the foot end because I can grasp ankles easier than a neck or shoulders.

The load is heavy, but the damp, fallen leaves in the woods are like grease on a griddle, and we slip right along. The trail is rough for the bag person—bumpy with tree roots, stones, and fallen branches indiscriminately jabbing and poking into the coarse fabric. Still, banging along an uneven path is better than staying put and being at the mercy of those yahoos who bagged him or her.

Former hostage in tow, I manage to travel at least half an hour before needing a break. I had been feeling pretty powerful—adrenaline will do that—but now I need to get a second wind.

A rocky outcrop with a stand of bushes in front becomes our temporary refuge. The gang's fire is no longer visible, but the bag has cut a definite path. It's still snowing, which should help conceal our route, but it won't completely cover it. "Stay still and be quiet. I'm going to try to erase our tracks," I whisper to the person in the sack.

There isn't a response from the bag, neither noise nor movement. Well, 'in for a penny, in for a pound' they say. I just hope I'm not dragging around a dead body. I'm sure it was moving earlier. And, if I don't want to join the non-living, I'll get those tracks erased soon—even a one-eyed drunk could follow our trail.

I backtrack and use a fallen limb to blend the snowy ridges into the ruts. I return to the bag and whisper to the hostage to hold still. I use my Leatherman tool to snip, snip, snip with the wire cutter jaws. Done. I pull the ropes away, locate the opening of the rough gunnysack, and use the knife to enlarge the exit for the hostage's broad, bony, but inert shoulders.

It isn't a woman, but a man, who Rocky and I have rescued, and he's still alive. I quickly cut off his gag, but he's oblivious to my ministrations. He's dazed, stunned, or whatever, and doesn't—or can't—move. I prop him up against the rock face and ask if he can walk. No response: he just sits there, slumped over, forehead to belly. I decide to leave him there— still bagged for warmth—until I can figure out what to do next.

Well, first off, I'd better find a decent hiding place with better protection from the weather than these prickly bushes provide. No, I'd better make that my second priority. Before I do anything else, I want to, or need to—I'm not sure which—perform a well-being check of my rescued hostage.

As I lean in to see his face, I feel a slight breeze. It smells different from the air around us. I remember something from somewhere—of course, I don't know where—that caves breathe. Oh, yeah, and there are always lots of bushes and trees by a cave's entrance, too. I search for the source of the musty scent, probing the bushes with a long branch for a hidden sanctuary, while my Señor Zombie keeps guard.

Voila! Just like in the movies: a well-hidden cave, this one with a low ceiling. I just wish I had a flashlight! All I have is the moonlight, which, I'm happy to notice, is brighter than normal due to its reflection off the falling snow. I poke the broken branch deep inside the apparent entrance and never hit a back wall. It's more than six feet—the length of my extended arm with the branch—to the rear of the cave. I sweep the branch across the floor, checking for snakes or other critter inhabitants, pull out the stick, and sniff it. No stink, fur, or snakeskin remnants, so I think we'll be safe.

I lift the man's face with both hands and look him in the eyes, ready to tell him we have to move. Good God, he's a mess! Evidently they put him in the sack to contain him while they beat him with bats or sticks or whatever. All I can see of him is his head and shoulders. He's all red and blue and purple—not a trace of pinkish flesh tone anywhere. His face is puffy and lumpy, and his eyes are swelled shut. He looks like Paul Newman as Rocky Marciano in 'Someone Up There Likes Me.' Well, I know someone up there likes me, too, because He led me away from those vile characters to a safe place, a cave we can hide in. And He likes this man, too. He has just helped him escape further punishment—or maybe even death—from those mangy creeps.

Now for the tough part: settling in. Moving the man into the cave is like handling an enormous water balloon: heavy, awkward, and with unpredictable reactions to my pushing and pulling. Poor Rocky tries to help by nudging while I pull, but it is my adrenaline-fueled stubbornness peppered with fear that finally gives me enough strength to get him into our dry little refuge.

Once inside the cave, relaxing slightly and recovering from relocating my rescuee, I get a brainstorm. I pull, tug, and then manage to wrangle Man the rest of the way out of the gunnysack. I quickly put my coat around his bruised shoulders, grab the empty bag, and call softly to Rocky, motioning for him to follow me.

I take the gunnysack back to the point where we left the trail and fill it with rocks. "Rocky, take this back over there so they think we left that way," I tell him softly, using broad gestures, pointing to the virgin snow area.

Well, I'll be! The dog understands English with my improvised sign language accent and is heading out to perform the diversion.

I start to sweep snow back over the tracks we just made, and then realize it's snowing so fast and heavily, they're already covered. I sprint back to the cave and crawl inside, just in time.

The drunken horde's noisy singing hits a raucous finale, and then it's quiet. Only one man is speaking, as if they're having a meeting. The speaker is shouting, slurring his words, "Fun time's over men; it's time to finish off this vermin once and fer all. By now that damned wolf creature is deid and canna help this thievin' polecat. Bring out yer dirks, men, and we'll carve up our cooked white Injun..."

Evidently, they were looking at the bag—or where the bag had been. Their drunken singing had been loud, but it was nothing compared to the deafening rage of men deprived of their booty. Actually, it sounds funny. I'm too far away to see anything, but I can hear men cursing and yelling, stumbling over pots and each other, with absolutely no sense of order.

I grin broadly, overcome with complete satisfaction—we are safe. Man and I are secure in our little cave, the snow continuing to cover all traces of where we are. And I know Rocky can take care of himself. Man is in bad shape, still flat on his back, unable to move by himself, but still, we are safe.

I suddenly realize how cold I am. Dang, I'm not just chilly, I'm 'teeth rattling in my mouth, hurting my jawbones up to my ears' shivering cold. Now that I've slowed down, no longer running or hauling a heavy, male-loaded gunnysack, I'm not generating any body heat. Man has my coat, and I don't want to take it away from him—he needs it, too. But, crap: now I'm shaking so badly, my spine feels like it's curling up the wrong direction.

Ah, to heck with being proper. I grab the coat sleeve with his arm still in it and snuggle beneath it, my back to his chest and belly. I drop his coated arm over my side so he's unwittingly holding me. Rocky sneaks in, so I guess he can warm Man's feet and lower legs while I take care of the upper torso. I'm wearing insulated boots and polar fleece pants, so I'm set.

I feel Man make a definitive movement for the first time. He readjusts his left arm across me and grabs my boob. Well, Man may be asleep and half-dead, but his maleness is still alive.

*8 Cave life

I slept warmly, but uneasily in our hollow hideout, listening to the calls and curses of our sobriety challenged search party who were, gratefully, heading in the wrong direction. Their angry voices eventually evaporated into the serene silence of the early winter storm. The ragged mob never discovered our ruse. The rock-laden gunnysack Rocky dragged away from our site hadn't been very heavy, but still made a discoverable trail, a clever misdirection if I do say so myself. Of course, as drunk as they were, and with as much snow as we had, I probably could have left it at only one rock in the bag and fooled them.

Even though it's dark and still snowing, I can see the eastern sky brightening, so I guess tomorrow is almost here. And, because it looks like my rescuee and I are going to be here for a while, I should investigate our new accommodations more thoroughly. The ceilings aren't vaulted—shoot, they're not even shoulder height,—so I have to assume the rugrat position to check out the back.

Six feet in, I'm panting, totally out of breath, terrified, and sweating profusely despite the chill. I'm having a full-blown panic attack! I didn't know I had claustrophobia, but apparently, I do—and I have it big time.

It's really not that cramped in here, but that fact doesn't stop my debilitating perception of being smothered and choked. I twist around quickly and race on my hands and kneecaps to the front of the cave. I won't—can't—go further back into this cave than my hands or feet will reach. Claustrophobia and fear of the dark don't go well with camping out in an unexplored cave. Where's a Holiday Inn when you need one?

I take a few calming breaths to try and slow my heart rate and rid myself of that choking feeling, but it's not enough—I need to be outside. I tap Man on the shoulder and point to the opening. Duh! He can't see me because it's still dark. "Excuse me," I say softly. No reaction. I say it again, much louder, but still nothing. Either he's in a deep sleep or he doesn't hear me.

I realize I have to go outside for another reason, too. I really, really have to pee. I crawl over him and accidentally bump his shoulder in the process. He gasps deeply, holds his breath for a moment, and then settles back, back into his deep sleep. I don't know why he's sleeping so much. I'll check the extent of his damages as soon as there's enough daylight.

Right now, there's nothing I can do for him but keep him warm.

I, on the other hand, am healthy enough to go outside and go potty all by myself. After that's taken care of, I'll put together my long-awaited snowcone. I'll get the makings from a source far away from my latrine, of course. It's always nice to have a plan and something to look forward to. Weird: I'm actually getting excited about making arrangements to take a leak and eat snow. I'm either really bored or still asleep.

I duck behind a bush for privacy for my little toilet. Why do I feel like I need to be discreet? There isn't anyone around as far as I can see. I dig in my pants pocket and find some wadded-up tissues to use as toilet paper, kick aside the snow and leaves, and then squat to do my business. I pee for about five minutes—or so it seems—wipe and throw the tissue into the makeshift toilet bowl. Whoa! There's fresh blood on that tissue—I'm bleeding! I haven't had a period in years. I know stress can cause a body to react strangely, but I'm an old lady and menopausal, for goodness sakes. Oh well, I have more tissues and a couple of handkerchiefs, so I guess I'll have to get creative with my sanitary arrangements. I'd better get something to eat, too. I feel cramps coming on and an empty stomach makes them worse.

Rocky's nowhere around. Hopefully he's scoping out the area, making sure we're safe. Then again, maybe he's finding us breakfast. I'm sure it won't be vegetarian fare. I doubt there's any late-season fruit around, and the squirrels have probably stashed away all the nuts. I've never skinned or gutted freshly killed prey, but I'm so hungry, I'm sure I could figure it out in a hurry. It's a good thing I can handle rare meat. Medium rare would be better, but I haven't seen any self-igniting hibachis around either.

The next thing I need to do is reposition my rescued hostage so I can make use of the increasing daylight to check his wounds. I never really thought about it until just now—was the man I rescued last night a horrible criminal? Maybe I should have been more cautious about who I picked up off the forest floor—it might have been wiser to leave the bagged-up bandit where he was. But my gut argues that those creeps who tortured and detained him looked more like a lynch mob—nothing at all like a duly elected sheriff and his deputies. I doubt they held a trial with a real judge or magistrate, either. There was also the secreted location of their execution site to consider, and the fact that the backwoods group had to get drunk to do their dirty deeds. Ugh! Those maggots of the male persuasion who hurt him were too vile to be called men. Besides, if my banged-up guy is evil, I can handle him. He can't even lift his head.

*9 First Aid

Smack! A lanky portion of my botanical front door—a sharp-leafed holly branch—springs back and assaults me, snagging my left earlobe as I try to sidle unscathed into my new home. I stomp down a low-lying branch, separating it from the parent plant, and install its forked end as a wedge between the shrub and the rock face. No more scratches when I pass through now. My hands already look like I've been playing with a catnipped kitten.

I look up, back into the chilly blackness of the cave. Ergh! All I can see is frustration. There's nothing I can do for Man until 'real' daylight appears. Even then, all I'll be able to see is the extent of his injuries—I can't treat them. My jaws clench, both from aggravation and to keep my teeth from rattling. I'm shivering uncontrollably—not even two warm muscles to rub together to create heat. He's still wearing my coat, so in order to keep from freezing, I have to find some way to keep moving or cuddle up to the stranger.

Okay, enough with the cuddling—I need to do something a little more useful than that. Hmm, maybe I can clear the floor. At least I can do that by feel.

The sharp, loose stones on the ground make a lousy carpet and cut into my palms and knees as I work. Grrrr. It seems that the more of them I brush away, the more that miraculously appear. Doggedly continuing my task toward the rear of the cave, concentrating on clearing away the rubble, I look up and panic smacks me breathless. How'd I get back here again?

The walls are closing in on me—I swear they are. The four-foot high ceiling is pulsing down, threatening to crush me into the rocky dust. I can't move. I start gasping for air, unable to get enough oxygen. It feels as if a Clydesdale is sitting on my chest. Oh, crap: I'm hyperventilating. I have to get out of here fast. Double crap: I can't remember how to move!

I get a flash image, a picture of me turning in a half circle toward the open air. Suddenly, I'm outside again. I must have acted out the visual, because here I am, unaware of scooting, crawling, or moving a muscle. I'm safe, in the open, and am suffering nothing more than a panic hangover.

I clutch my erstwhile security blanket—the rock face of the entrance behind me—and indulge myself with a couple of minutes of doing nothing. I know I need to take care of the man, but I won't do him any good until I stop shaking. I close my eyes and concentrate on breathing, trying to relax all my muscles one at a time, hoping to remember, find, or create a peaceful safe zone.

I'm reclining, safe in an urban backyard fortress, watching the tall palm trees wash the wind above the adobe wall. The green scent of freshly cut grass mixes with the spicy undertones of the vibrant red Chrysler Imperial rose bush, carpeted beneath with snowy alyssum. The orchestra of eclectic wind chimes, clinking and tinkling under the eaves, accompanies the mourning dove calls. The plastic straps of the chaise lounge are sticky under my bare legs. My whole body relaxes with the warmth of the sun, gentle on my face in the early hours of a desert day. Mmmm...

Moments pass while I bathe myself in my blissful daydream. My eyes open reluctantly to reality and the chill of the dim, damp morning. Light snow is falling on my face, not warm sunrays. That backyard fantasy was so real, it has to be a genuine memory. That won't help me now, so I blink back my delightful scenario to savor at a later time.

My mini mind-vacation has done the trick. I believe I can handle just about anything now. I can handle 'any' thing, but I don't want to handle 'every' thing, and that is what I'm up against. No food, no water, totally lost, winter snow falling, no source of heat nor way to start a fire, and in custody of a man who may not survive the day. "Take one step at a time— baby steps, lady, baby steps. First, attend to the injured."

I flick away a few more rocks, then use a relatively straight-edged stone to smooth the floor at the cave entrance, creating a temporary examination area. I'm not aware of having any medical training, but I know how to clean a wound and...what am I going to use? All I have is the snow outside. I don't know if there's a stream around here. How would I transport water, even if I found it? I don't have any bottles, cups, or pans.

I whisper under my breath, "I don't even have a pot to piss in." I start to giggle at my little joke, then start into stage-two laughter: snorting. I have a hard time stopping, but finally achieve some semblance of calm. Well, I guess that's a good thing. If I start into stage-three—laughing out loud uncontrollably—I'll know I've lost it. But by then, I doubt I'll care.

I try to reposition Man by pulling his shoulders towards the entrance and the soon-to-be-bright-enough daylight. His body bends sideways at the waist, following the direction of my tug. Now he's formed a perfect right angle. That can't be good.

I climb over him and shove his middle into alignment with his neck and shoulders, then crawl toward the back of the cave. I quickly push his legs in the right direction and scurry back to my safe zone. Phew! That was so quick, claustrophobia-induced panic never got a chance to snag me.

I grab him under his armpits and tug. Nothing. I readjust my grip and pull, but even after changing the angle of my approach a dozen more times, I still can't budge him. I'm plenty determined, but that doesn't make me strong enough.

It's time to try a new tactic. I sit down, open out my legs, and scoot as close as I can to him, gently lifting his head into my lap. My thighs under his shoulders, I wiggle further down, lifting him upright as I go, until his upper body slumps forward. I give him a bear hug and grasp my forearms, shadowing him, as I pull him towards me. His battered face flops sideways and rests against my resolute jaw as I dig my heels into the floor and inch backwards, dragging him with me. A couple more butt scoots and he's into the daylight. I sigh in victory, glad to see he's still breathing.

I pull out from under his body and get my first good look him. The first thing I see is the strip of filthy rag wrapped around his head, covering both ears. It's still in place, even after he was banged around in the bag, dragged through the woods, and shoved and repositioned in the cave. I untie the knot and try to take it off. It's stuck on—his impromptu dressing glued to his scalp with his own dried blood. If I pull it away now, I'll probably reopen his wounds, and that's sure to hurt. I'll attend to it later.

Next: his face. It's puffy and marked all over, as if his attackers took a fiery stick or poker and branded him, repeatedly burning his cheeks. He's also been hit in the face so many times, I can't tell where one swelling stops and another one starts. I don't know what he was hit with, but Man survived one long, continuous bashing. I can't see any part of his face that isn't injured or covered in welts, bruises, burns, or blood blisters.

He has a nasty two-inch-wide rug burn all the way around his neck, as if he had been strung up and used as a human piñata. It's also swollen, but since he's still breathing, it doesn't seem to be life-threatening. If I had lotion or a balm of some sort to put on it, he'd be more comfortable, but I don't have anything but snow.

I sit on my heels, trying to figure out what to do next in my primitive triage. I recall a TV series—or was that a movie?—about doctors and nurses in a war zone. All the casualties were laid out on cots or gurneys. A trained doctor would make the rounds, an attendant beside him taking notes as he performed quick assessments. The most severely wounded were taken into a field hospital. The tented facility was staffed with trained surgeons in fairly sterile conditions, with adequate surgical supplies and medications on hand. Right now, I would trade my left kidney for a fire, some warm water and soap, and a couple of blankets. Well, wish in one hand and poop in the other, and see which one fills up first. At least I haven't found any gashes that need to be stitched or discovered any broken bones. Maybe I can fill one of my handkerchiefs with snow to use as a compress to relieve some of the swelling.

When Rocky gets back, I'm sure I can get him to understand that I need water. Of course, then I'll need to figure a way to transport it. The only thing I have to bring back water in is my mouth. I doubt Man would want me to give him a drink by spitting second-hand water through his lips. Eww, gross! I guess I can try giving him bits of snow. At least that wouldn't choke him.

"Eeek!" Rocky is poking his nose into my ear, giving me a cold wet willie, to get my attention. If it is possible for a dog to smile—and I know it is—he is positively radiant with excitement. "Okay, Rocky, I'm glad to see you, too. Did you bring us breakfast?"

I look around, half expecting to see a dead squirrel or some other critter, and almost miss his gift. Then I see it.

"Oh, Rocky, I love you!" I'm so happy that tears well up, making my nose run. He's found my lost backpack! Evidently it smelled enough like me that when he caught a whiff of it, he hunted it down. "Thank you, Rocky, and thank You, Lord; thank You for this wonderful helper." I give Rocky a big hug and wipe my face and my tears of joy in his fur.

I open the pack and grab one of the two slushy water bottles, take a quick nip, and exhale in satisfaction. A fine wine couldn't be more appreciated.

First order of business: get some water through Man's bloody and bruised lips. "Here you go, you need to get hydrated."

I can't get him to open his mouth, so dribble a few drops on his lips. Feeling the wetness, they part, and out pokes a bit of pink tongue.

"You can get a bit more into you now, can't you, Man?"

As soon as I say 'Man,' Rocky starts yipping. Maybe I've missed something, so I look around to make sure the bad guys haven't returned. But Rocky is looking at the man. "What? Did I say his name? Is his name Man?"

Rocky cants his head to the side as if to ask, "Huh?"

"Okay, let's see if you can tell me his name. How about Ann?"

61

Rocky dips his snout as if to say, "Keep going…"

"Ban, Can, Dan…that's a good one. No? Okay, E-Ann…"

Rocky goes ballistic, woofing and howling, dancing around in tight circles.

The excited outcries of my canine *compadre* cause the man I now presume is E-Ann, or Ian, to turn his head toward the ruckus. "Rocky?" he whispers hoarsely.

Rocky puts his nose in Ian's face and starts licking. Well, at least I'm getting help with the cleaning. Rocky finishes the quick tongue-washing and lies next to Ian's head. Ian—sensing his nearness—nuzzles into Rocky's ruff and goes back to sleep.

I think he's going to make it. At least now he knows he's not alone and has a friend nearby.

Okay, back to business. Ian's shirt is made of some sort of leather, buckskin I think, and reeks more than a litter box two weeks past dumping. It's stained with I don't want to imagine what, but there isn't any blood soaking through, at least in front, so that's good. Apparently, he's been bruised and bashed, but not stabbed. Stinky or not, I'll leave the shirt on so he doesn't get chilled. If he had major injuries, I'm sure there would be more blood.

His pants are unusual. I expected Carhartts, camo, or denim jeans of some sort. Isn't that what all backwoodsmen wear? These are totally different—they're buckskin leather.

I glide my hand over the outside seam. Shoot! That's *his* skin at his hip—he's wearing a diaper! Well, I guess it's called a breechclout, but it sure looks like a leather diaper to me. At least it's covering his privates; with this limited light, his skin, the breechclout, and his leggings all looked the same color—sure had me fooled!

I wouldn't think it proper to check between the buttons—or under the breechclout in this case—of an unconscious man, even if it looked like there was a need. I can, and do, check his non-personal lower parts, though, patting his legs down the rough-sewn outside seams, past his knees to his ankles. That's when I notice his feet. Now I know what needs to be taken care of first.

It was dark when I got him out of the bag and into the cave. I hadn't noticed at the time whether or not he was wearing shoes—not that it made a difference—after all, he wasn't walking. But now I see he is, and had been, barefoot.

The tops of his feet are lacerated—bad enough to need tending to right away—but the bottoms are hideous! They're slashed, charred, and blistered. It looks as if Ian walked through fire, but unlike the holy men who pass over fiery coals unscathed, his feet are both cooked and cut.

The sight of burned skin and singed hair makes me gag, but something has to be done, and I'm the only one around who can help him. He's still in a deep sleep—or a coma—so he certainly can't do it himself, and Rocky lacks opposable thumbs.

I pull up his leggings to check further—all clear above the ankles. It's a good thing the leather wasn't flammable, or his legs would be burnt as well.

"Hang in there," I tell him, trying to strengthen my own resolve, "it'll be all right." I doubt he hears me, but Rocky does. He glances up, then puts his head back on his paws, his nose back into Ian's ribs.

Rocky! He just brought me my backpack! There has to be more than those two water bottles in there! I snatch it up out of the corner and tear at the Velcro closure. It feels like Christmas with the excitement of unknown presents and gifts. I *must* have amnesia because I have no idea what's inside this nylon package.

Cool!—or rather warm—there's a brand new solar blanket in here. I pull and tug at the wrapper, then finally wind up using my teeth to get it out of its package. As I spit out plastic bits, I remember the one thing I *do* have is a knife. Oh, well. I spread the silvery shroud over Ian and tuck the edges under his body, leaving his tender tootsies exposed for my ministrations. "Hmph," I chuckle to myself. My impromptu bedding arrangement make him look like a huge, foil-wrapped burrito with a head and feet.

I dig further into my nylon treasure and find two plastic baggies—one with crackers and the other with cheese—and inspiration strikes! I make a quick little cheese sandwich and dump the rest of the contents into the pack. I stuff the baggies into my coat pocket and push the backpack towards Rocky, my in-house heater. I don't want the goodies to freeze any more than they already have.

I make my way past my barbed evergreen entryway to the chilly outside air. I take a deep, bracing breath—not a trace of smog here. Shaking out the baggies as I walk along, I look for a drift of clean snow. Actually, all the snow is clean, but there are lots of twigs, pine needles, and windblown tree trash embedded in most of the accumulations. I don't want to apply a lumpy cold compress to my patient's battered and burned feet. I open out the makeshift ice bags and put in a double fist-sized clump of virgin snow. I quickly press it against my coat to get the air out and it's zipping time. *Voila!*

Back at the cave, I stop to look into the backpack again. Great! I have both a pack of baby wipes and a small bottle of hand sanitizer. I grab them and take a quick swig of water, bracing myself for the challenge.

"Ian, I have to wash your feet and see if I can get out the grit and glass in them."

There's no reply, although I can tell by his breathing he's not in a deep sleep. "Ian," I say louder, as if to someone who is hard of hearing, "can you hear me?"

Ian's long black eyelashes jiggle—he's unable to open his eyes because of the swelling. He turns his head to the side as if to offer his 'good' ear for hearing.

Okay, I get it; he can't hear very well. "Ian," I say as loud as I can without shouting, "I am going to clean your feet and put ice bags on them. It's probably going to hurt, but it'll be easier for both of us if you don't kick me."

I'm not sure, but I think I heard him make a noise. I'll take that as an assent.

I get halfway back to where I'm going to do my doctoring when I realize I can't see. A big grin comes across my face. I don't have enough light to see, but I have the power to change that now. One of the goodies I saw in my backpack was a flashlight.

I climb over Ian once again to retrieve my little treasure—a fistful of light. I take out the cute little camping gadget and turn it over for closer inspection. It can be configured as a handheld light, set down on the ground or a stump as a lamp, or hung from a tree for use as a camp lantern. It also has a little AM/FM radio and is powered by a hand crank. Cool, I don't have to worry about batteries.

I wind up the dynamo and give it a shot. The little lantern gives a comforting glow to the confines of the cave, and the pale-colored limestone walls reflect the artificial light, enhancing its effect.

Most of the pieces of debris in Ian's soles are big enough to grab with my fingernails although my multi-tool's little knife blade does a good job of flicking out the tiny slivers. I do my best not to pierce the blisters dotting his soles. What I thought was charred skin was evidently ash and washes away. The baby wipes smell good, are pre-loaded with cleanser, and are very soft, much softer than a terrycloth washrag. I notice, too, that the synthetic fabric will snag on any little bits of glass that I can't see.

I'm doing my best to be gentle, but occasionally I feel Ian's muscles twitch while I'm extracting a particularly difficult shard. He doesn't say a word, though. He's either stubborn or stoic—or both.

Now, time to apply the hand sanitizer. If it kills germs on unwashed hands, it should work as an antiseptic on wounds, too. Or I hope so—it's the only thing I have.

Ian gulps in air, begins panting in pain, but otherwise doesn't move.

Dang! Now I remember—bottled germ killer is mostly alcohol. Alcohol on an open wound would get a three-minute scream and a bucketful of four-letter words from me. Ian must have thought when I said don't move, I also meant don't yell.

I quickly grab the bandanas and use them to secure the snow-filled baggies to the soles of his feet. The soft snow conforms to fit his arches. I make a mental note not to leave them on too long. He doesn't need frostbite on top of all of his other miseries.

I climb back towards the sunlight and Ian's face. I follow up Rocky's face cleaning with a more thorough job, using the baby wipes. He looks like he hasn't shaved in about a week, and that makes it hard to clean his face. Another thing I don't have is a razor, but I think his skin is clean enough without a shave. And, thank You, Lord, it turns out that what I thought were hot poker wounds on his face, are a series of star-shaped tattoos. I think his nose is broken, too, but I don't know anything about fixing it, so I'll leave it alone. At least he can still breathe through it.

It looks like he's asleep again. I don't know if that's good for his health, but it's easier for me. I don't feel so invasive if he's unaware of me.

I had checked the front of his shirt earlier and it wasn't bloody, but I never checked his sides. If Ian had been protecting his chest and stomach, his ribs and back quite possibly received most of the blows.

I move his hand to check his side, but when the light hits it, I stop, sick to my stomach—again.

I hadn't looked at his hands earlier; I never even thought about them. It was too dark to see much beyond my nose when I cut his bindings. I just found the rope and freed him. I hadn't checked them when I did my triage because, well, I didn't think about it. When I saw his feet, I knew they needed taken care of stat. Maybe I should have continued with my examination, but I can't change history; I can only go forward. Maybe it's not too late.

His hands and fingers are horrendous. They're going to need more than baby wipes and shard removal. They're swollen and battered and look more like purple baseball mitts than hands. I doubt that even a piece of dental floss could be wedged between any of his three middle fingers. Gratefully, there aren't any obvious breaks or gashes, and all digits are pointing in the right direction. Maybe it's good that I practiced my procedure on his feet first. This isn't going to be easy or pleasant for either of us.

Feet: I suddenly remember the ice bags on his feet. It's time to take them off. I crawl to the back of the cave and remove them. I don't have a problem with claustrophobia this time. I'm on a mission. I don't even realize that I've just emerged from a cramped space until I hear the birds singing outside and remember the mourning doves I was meditating on earlier.

I dart into the sunshine, reload the bags with snow, and then get back to work. A quick washing of the cuts on his hands with the baby wipes and it's time for the hand sanitizer. This time I'm ready. As soon as I apply the germ killer, I pack the snow-stuffed baggies around his hands, pre-empting the fiery effect.

Now where was I? Right, I wanted to check his sides. I gently tug at his buckskin shirt, but the way he's laying, I can't pull it up. There is, however, just enough wiggle room for me to put one hand up inside it. Wiggle is the right word, too. I wedge my hand up the right side of the shirt, skimming my hand over his skin to feel for broken bones, cuts, or whatever on his lean torso. As I near his armpit, he starts squirming. Evidently, Ian is ticklish.

Moving my hand across his chest doesn't seem to disturb him, but when I get near his left armpit, he starts squirming again. I don't find any injuries, so move my hand down, toward his stomach. Instead of moving away from me, though, Ian seems to be pushing his belly up towards my hand. I hear an "mmm"—it sounds as if he's enjoying my inspection. I stop, hold still a moment, and then reach up towards his liver. No swelling, although I don't know what I'd do if he did have internal injuries. I almost pull my hand out all the way, but then give in to the temptation to tickle those swirly hairs near his navel again.

"Mmmmm," he murmurs louder still, his grin heard, but not seen.

I had better stop this. Both of us are enjoying it too much. He's asleep, and doesn't even know who I am. I scold myself silently and hope he doesn't remember any of this when he comes to.

I look out at the sky and guess it to be about noon. I'm not a woodsman by any stretch of the imagination, but when the sun is directly overhead, it's probably noon in every land and in every season. I figure I've been playing doctor for nearly four hours now. I'm due for a break.

I grab the backpack and clutch it to me. I know it's mine, I'm positive it belongs to me, but at the same time, I don't know what else is in it. Strange familiar items: how contrary. I upend the contents onto my freshly swept foyer, then hold the empty bag up to the daylight, looking for a nametag. Bummer. There's a space for a name, but it's shiny and blank: nothing has ever been written on it.

Well, Miss Ann Nonymous, here's what else you have to make your rustic life more comfortable: reading glasses in a hard-sided needlepoint case, a large zippered plastic bag of what looks like homemade granola, a long reach butane lighter, a waterproof container of matches, Thinsulate-lined gloves, neon green plastic Crocs, a folding pocket saw, a tube of hand cream, some spare clothing, a mess kit with a metal plate, cup, and utensils, eight packages of freeze-dried meals, a hand towel and two washcloths, a short stack of paper napkins, a travel size pack of cotton swabs, a hank of blue and white braided nylon rope, and a quart-sized pot with lid

Cool! Now I have a pot to cook in and two ways to create fire. My means are frugal, but definitely better than they were a few hours ago and, joy of all small joys: I have something to use as toilet paper. Woo Hoo! That reminds me, it's time for my personal hygiene check. Hopefully, this is just a spotting episode and not a full blown, cramping, bloating, farting menstrual period.

After attending to my renewed fertility issue, I want to see if I can build a fire. "Fertility issue! Who can I impress with my puns now? Ah, just hush up and get some firewood.

"Uh-oh, I'm talking to myself. Did I just say that out loud? Uh, yes, I did. Oh, well, I guess I don't have to worry about embarrassing myself—it's not like someone will come along and hear me!"

Come along? Crap! I had forgotten about those creepy men from last night. I've been so busy attending to Ian, and then thrilled at the return of my backpack full of goodies that I forgot there was an enemy out there. 'An enemy of my friend is my enemy?' or was it 'A friend of my enemy is my enemy'? Either way, I need to shut up. I don't want to attract any unsavory characters with my babbling.

It's a cloudless sky today and the air is still, which I'm pretty sure means it's going to be colder tonight than last night. At least we can have a fire. I have wood nearby and both butane lighter and matches, but I'm not sure where to set up the fire ring. If I put it at the front of the cave entrance, I'll have to make sure it's far enough away from the holly bushes, or whatever they are, that they don't catch fire. Or maybe that would be so they don't catch smolder since the wood is green. That's all I need to do—send smoke signals to alert the bad guys of our location. I hope they've gone on to bigger and better tasks, like falling off cliffs! Either way, I'd better gather some wood now, while I still have daylight.

I search my little area for firewood, but all I find is either wet or damp from the fresh snow. It's not ideal, but hopefully usable—and at least it's not frozen to the ground.

Hmph! With all that seems to be going wrong, I realize I can still find things to be grateful for: a sunny day, wood and a lighter for a fire, a dry place to lie, and gloves. Ian's hands remind me of how vulnerable man's most valuable and versatile tools can be. I know the wood I'm gathering is rough and difficult to carry, but I have protection from slivers, thorns, and the cold. I'm healthy, and the task is nothing I can't do.

Yeah, well, what I *need* to do is remove the bandage on Ian's head and see why there was blood coming out of his ears last night. That's something I *can* do, but not something I *want* to do. I'll see to other stuff first.

Ж

Okay, I should probably stash the wood in the back of the cave so it isn't ignited by a stray spark. That would really ruin my day, a wall of fire at my threshold, blocking my exit, trapping me and my comatose patient in an oversized pizza oven.

I crank up the lantern, put the wire bail of the lamp in my mouth, grab two armloads of wood, squat down and duck-walk back to the newly-designated fuel depot. It's not so scary back here now that I can see. Maybe I don't have claustrophobia after all.

I can't find a level spot for the lantern, so I smooth out a sandy mound and set it there. Even with the lamp's limited glow, this place is nice and cozy, not terrifying at all. I carefully arrange the firewood in my little indoor woodshed: the larger pieces stacked on the right, the kindling and smaller branches on the left.

I reach for the lantern and notice a fresh dusting of sand on top of it. I look up and see the lantern's light illuminating little flecks of dirt as they sift down from a high crevice at the back of the cave's otherwise low ceiling. I'm not sure, but I think there's a hole up there. Cool! If it's big enough, I can place the fire back here, then the crack in the ceiling can be the chimney.

It's actually fun building my little fire starter house, using twigs for walls and the paper and plastic packaging from the solar blanket as flooring. Now for the best part: torching it with the butane lighter. Yup, the smoke is going straight up, drawing through the cleft in the rocks. The back wall will reflect the heat toward the front, and I won't have to Jack-Be-Nimble to go outside.

Back to my front yard, once again, to gather more fuel for the fire before it gets dark. I spot a jumble of wood down the rise that looks like it would make an easily accessed, ready-made woodpile. I skip down to it and see it's bigger than I thought, maybe eight feet across. I wiggle the end of a decent-sized piece from the giant Jenga timber puzzle, carefully extracting it to add to my indoor wood box. Hmm, the ends are chiseled. I do believe that what I have here is a beaver dam that has somehow washed ashore. I know I'm not standing on ice now, but the presence of this dam means there should be a river or lake nearby. I'll check it out later. Right now, I have a pan, snow, and a fire, so I can put off my search for fresh water. Just one more armload of logs, and then this Paula Bunyan will do her best to emulate Florence Nightingale.

Ж

Ian is still unconscious. I dump the melted snow from the hand baggies into my precious aluminum pot. For now, it can stay parked on the flat rock at the fire's edge, keeping the water warm and handy for the task I dread the most: Ian's cranial rag bandage removal.

I guess I've put this off long enough. It's time to assess the damage to his ears. I squeak out a quick prayer, "Please help me, Lord," and then return to the fire and my urgent care center.

Plop. I watch the washcloth float atop the warm water of my improvised sink. It soaks until saturated, then drops to the bottom, waiting to be employed as my all-in-one emergency room repair appliance. I squeeze it out minimally, gently turn Ian's head to the right, and place it over the filthy rag stuck to his ear.

While the water is softening the bandage, I recheck the swelling of his face, cranking up the dynamo on the lantern for a closer look. Ian starts at the noise, but doesn't wake. Looking closer, I see the swelling has gone down around his mouth, but his eyes are still swollen shut—he doesn't react to the light.

"Here goes," I say softly, more to myself than him since he's hard of

69

hearing. I need all the encouragement I can get, even if it's only from me. I gently pull at the now pliable rag bandage, but it's not coming loose—it's still stuck to his face. I rewet the washcloth, gently urging the rag away, trickling extra drops of water on the leading edge as I tug. He grimaces and I pause, but he's still out.

I bite my bottom lip in concentration as I continue working it loose until it finally releases with a pop, just in front of his ear. I bring the lantern closer and see there's a rock wedged in his ear canal. I pry it out with my fingernail. It's sticky, but not with blood. If I didn't know better, I'd believe it was honey.

I rinse and rewet the washcloth, setting it under the left side of his head to soften the bandage while I check his right ear. I still can't see worth a darn, in spite of the artificial and natural lights.

"Aha!" I exclaim loudly then add, "Oops, sorry." Oh well, he didn't hear me anyway. I just remembered seeing a pair of reading glasses in the backpack. I reach in and locate the needlepoint case by feel, take the glasses out, give them a quick blow to knock off the lint and dust from the lenses, and set them on my nose. I guess I'm as ready as I'll ever be.

Changing the focus on the lantern from the broad, floodlight mode to a focused, directional beam also helps. The ear canal is goopy with honey and blood but doesn't stink with rot. Thank You, Lord, for that.

I carefully insert one of the cotton swabs and twirl it around. Those swab packages always have the same warning: do not insert into ear canal. Well, what are they for, then—fastidious nose pickers? Thanks for the warning, Mr. Swab Manufacturer, but I think I'll continue to use these as ear swabs, despite your warning.

The crud on the swab has bits of wood bark in it, but otherwise is just dirt, blood, and honey. I dip the other end of the swab into the warm water and clean out his ear canal as carefully as I can. There are small scrapes, but no obvious infection. This was easier than I thought.

I'm sure glad those inbred creeps used honey and not mud to plug his ears. I get cold chills just thinking about it. Honey is a natural antibiotic, so the minor internal cuts and abrasions have already been protected. Right now, cleanliness and fresh air are the next steps in healing. If he has a burst eardrum or inner ear infection, I'll be able to tell because any new drainage will be visible against the cleaned skin.

Removing the bandage on the other side is easier. The wet washcloth soaked all the way through to his skin so I didn't even have to tug. Just like before, a rock was wedged in his ear canal. It's almost as if they didn't want him to hear, so they sealed his ears with a small stone and filled the gaps with honey. I used the same clean-up procedure, grateful once again for the swabs.

Yeah, that one side was easier, but now my back is hurting from all the hunching over and reaching across. There's not much room to maneuver in here, so I'll have to rearrange a body or two.

I roll Ian's shoulders to the left, manage to get my legs under his shoulders again and, after a few more body tilts for him and a fanny repositioning for me, place his head in my lap. This is much easier on my back and shoulders, and the view is better, too. It's also starting to get cold, so his body heat is welcome. Even if it does get well below freezing tonight, we should be cozy with a fire, a blanket, a big furry dog, and our shared heat. We have food and water—I think we'll be fine. I just hope Ian pulls out of it. Except for his brief acknowledgement of Rocky, he's been unconscious for way too long.

*10 Ass over teakettle

I've done all I can for Ian and I'm spent, both physically and emotionally. I need a break from the intensity and frustration, the challenge of repairing a broken man in a primitive existence. I don't know whether to scream or cry.

I brush his dark, stringy, wayward hair off his face—again—carefully lift his head from my lap, scoot out from underneath, and let Rocky take over the comforting.

My rumbling tummy reminds me that it's been ages since I had a real meal. I giggle despite my circumstances. I really can't remember how long it's been, or even what I used to eat.

The crackers and cheese earlier were great for a snack, but now I'm ravenous. I doubt Ian will be able to consume anything other than sips of water, Rocky can take care of his own nutritional needs, so it's only me I need to feed. I have those freeze-dried meals in my backpack, and all I need for a glorious spaghetti meal—or maybe I'll try the beef stroganoff—is water. Ah, back to a positive attitude!

I take the pan I've been using as a washbasin, squeeze the washcloth into it, and offer it to Rocky. He hasn't wanted to leave Ian all morning, and I'm sure he's thirsty. "It's not as good as toilet water, but if you don't want it, I'll get some fresh snow and melt it for you." No need to bother, I guess—he's already slurped it up.

I place the moist, wrung-out washcloth on Ian's face. The evaporation of water from the cloth should be cool enough to help reduce the swelling. Hopefully he'll be able to open his eyes again soon. I remove the bandanas from his hands and stuff the baggies in my pocket to take outside and refill with snow.

"Sure glad I have these," I say to myself, realizing how valuable the bags are as a compact and lightweight means of bringing snow inside to melt for water. With the warmth of my small fire and the body heat of two people and a big, furry dog, the snow would probably melt overnight inside my new home. Still, I'll store the water in the pot with the lid on it, so dust from the chimney cleft doesn't sift down into it. Keeping it covered will also keep Rocky from drinking it all.

I double-check my pocket to make sure I have the empty baggies, turn off the lantern, and stuff it in the foyer of the cave entrance. If I put it there, it's easily accessed when I come in or leave. I learned long ago that it's best to have a place for everything and everything in its place. At least that's why I always put my keys in my left coat pocket and my cell phone in my right.

My cell phone! I have a cell phone! I recheck my pocket and find it—tucked down deep and easy to miss between the coat's thick seams. I bulldoze my way through the front-door brambles, running away from the cave and its earthen interference, out into the open clearing. Maybe I can get a strong signal here and call for help. I have no idea where I am, but all cell phones have a GPS built into them now. If I can get a signal and make a call, we can be rescued in short order, then Ian can get proper medical attention.

So far, I've only been *reacting* to situations, taking care of what was immediately needed. I have spent the last 24 hours extracting a wolf/dog from an exotic snare, rescuing a man from a drunken mob, making a home out of a hole in a hill, and playing emergency room nurse to my rescued human piñata. Now I have a mission: take assertive action to get two people rescued from a remote and primitive situation, and get them to food, warmth, and one of them to a hospital.

My pro-active plan starts right now. First, find a spot with good reception. I know I need to be higher. Cell phone signals and radio waves travel in a straight path—line of sight or something like that. That means I have to get to a place that's in the clear. This hill, this mini-mountain that houses our cave, is one of the tallest in the area, and certainly the closest. I'll try it first.

Upward progress proves to be my first challenge. I start the ascent up the crumbly slope with a big step, and promptly lose my footing. Scaling the fractured rock here is as slippery as crossing a swift-moving creek in high heels. Baby steps, woman, baby steps.

I hold back my enthusiasm to race to the peak. I'm so amped at the thought of being rescued that I can hardly contain my joy. I want to sing out loud, let the world know how happy I am, but remember to be quiet just before the first syllable leaves my lips. I might be found by the wrong people—I keep forgetting about that.

I don't have a piton hammer, ice cleats, or anything other than my gloved hands to help me scale this stony monster. I'm certain rock climbing never appealed to me, because it sure doesn't now. As far as I'm concerned, rocks should be pushed out of the way or driven around, not climbed up or over. Isn't that what bulldozers and four-wheel-drive pickup trucks are for?

Since I don't have a clearly defined path, I'll just stop complaining about my challenge and take care of it the old-fashioned way. I step back and take a minute to study the mountain's terrain, hoping an easy route will reveal itself. Okay, so going up the west side of the opening looks like the easiest way. I double-check the phone to make sure it's still turned on, lock the keypad, and stuff it into my coat pocket. The right hand side pocket, the same pocket I always use. Habit is a comfort to me, an inherently important and essential part of me. I'm sure of that—amnesia or not.

I get about half way up the hill and check the phone for a signal. Still no bars, but the battery has full power. That's a good thing. "Onward and upward! Trudge, trudge, here come da judge. Step one, step two, top of hill, I'm comin' to you." Softly singing silly songs is a nice distraction and really does make the climb easier.

I notice small puffs of smoke coming out of the top of the hill. That must be my chimney! I scamper over a few more rocks and come to my exhaust vent. It's a small rock fissure with a short but ancient juniper shrub growing into it. Well, my chimney will draw better, and I'll be able to build a larger fire, if I enlarge the opening. All I need to do is pull it out, roots and all.

"Wait a minute now, girl, don't get distracted. You came up here to check for a cell phone signal. Oops, I'm talking to myself again. Well, at least I'm talking softly and not giggling, snorting, or laughing hysterically."

I check for a signal. Still no bars, not even a flicker. I almost drop the phone putting it back into my pocket. "That's not the way to drop a call," I say under my breath, then snort at my own pun. Okay, better safe than slipping out of my pocket and losing it down the hill. I unzip my coat and put the slim smartphone inside a zippered pocket over my left breast. "Now that's better," I say to myself. "Ergh, I just can't seem to hush!"

"Okay, it's time to play chimney sweep and get rid of those vegetative clogs. Ah, what the heck, I can see for miles, and there's no one around. I'm going to sing as loud as I want. Chim Chiminey, Chim Chiminey, Chim Chim Cheroooo. A chimney sweep's life is as…. Dang, those are some tough roots."

I pull, grunt, fart, grab the shrub again with both hands, bend my knees, and really put my legs into it. I groan the next refrain, "A chimney sweep's life is as sweet as…

"Oh, no!" My foot slips, I lose my grip, and now I'm stumbling backwards. I catch myself, take two steps forward, and grasp the leaves and branches in front of me, managing to regain my balance by clutching onto that stubborn bush. "Whew, that was close. I'm not going to do that again!

"Oh, crap."

The roots lose their hold, and so do I. The scraggly shrub flies into the air as I plummet backwards, flailing and panicking, falling and bumping, crashing, and then falling again. My right hand smacks a boulder on the way down and is hyper-extended. I hug it close to my chest as I roll to a stop. I take a quick breath and struggle to get up. I'm unsteady on my feet, like I'm standing in a small boat on rough seas, but still upright—for a split second. Suddenly, I'm skidding down the same path I just came up. I have totally lost control again and, by reflex, roll up like an armadillo, protecting my insides.

The tumbling and careening goes on and on, like a bagful of bowling balls down a flight of stairs. I realize your life—or something like it— really does flash before your eyes in situations like this. It isn't my whole life, though, only the last few hours, replayed in fast-forward mode. It still doesn't make any sense—they're just disjointed images with flickers of emotion.

I open up from my balled-up position—the pitching and rolling is over—and put my legs out to slow my descent, skidding to a stop on my side, feet first, as if coming in to home plate. I roll over onto my back, look up at the cloudy sky, and then there's nothing.

*11 Bashed and battered

I must have passed out there at the end. My skull feels like it's split down the back. If it's not cracked open like a pistachio, it's at least crunched like a peanut shell. I reach around to check, scared of what I might find. The skull is intact, but the scalp is definitely split: my fingers are tacky. I bring my hand in front of my face and force my eyes open. Oh, I wish I hadn't looked. I can handle someone else's blood, but the sight of my own makes me sick.

And sick I am. I roll over onto my side, heave a couple of times, but only bring up a little water. Well, that's one good thing about having an empty stomach. That is, if retching can be good in any way, form, or location.

I roll onto my belly to get up and am made painfully aware of the multiple bruises and contusions I just received. I try to ignore them since there isn't anything I can do about them right now. I push up with my right hand—or try to—and my wrist gives way. I curl into the fetal position, cursing in pain and frustration, trying to resist the urge to give in and cry. I try again, this time pushing with my elbows on my knees. As soon as I'm near vertical, I break into a cold sweat and get so dizzy that I have to drop back to the security of the ground.

Well, it looks like I'll have to crawl home. I can probably do that. At least my knees seem to be okay. I check my arms—the elbows are okay, too. I guess the heavy padding of my coat and my instinctive tuck and roll maneuver cut down on the number—or at least the severity—of my injuries.

As I do my 'begging for mercy' belly-scoot across the rocky ground, I realize I'm not getting out of this part of the ordeal unscathed. The joints are okay, but the uneven ground is driving rocks and tree parts of all sizes into my bony knees. It looks to be only a hundred yards to the cave, but it may as well be 100 miles. I don't think I can make it.

Rocky finds me and gives a quick "yip" in greeting. He puts his head down and sniffs my chin as if to ask, "Are you okay?"

"No, I'm not okay. Would you stay with me until I get home? I don't feel so good."

I crawl in the direction of the cave and start to get nauseous again. I faintly remember something about concussions and vomiting. That, and don't let a person with a head injury fall asleep. Now that's not fair. All I want to do is lie down and sleep! "Ah, to hell with it," I mumble, and curl up for a nap before I finish my journey.

Ж

As my consciousness slowly returns, I feel movement—up and up higher, up and up higher. What am I? A cloud? A butterfly? I feel as if I'm floating, but I'm tethered to one spot and can't move away. There's another movement up, then another one even higher. My face—I have a face, and something is passing over it, touching it. And it's cool when the movement stops.

Oh, gross! It's a tongue licking my cheek and nose!

"Ouch!" My head—that I was unaware I even had a second ago— feels as if it's going to explode. I open my eyes and see a long pink tongue and lots of teeth. It's Rocky. I try to speak, but all that comes out is a low groan. That's all I have. And then I am no more.

*12 Fall recovery

Rocky rushed into the cave, barking and yowling, trying to wake Ian. He was still in a comatose state, but Rocky didn't know that. For all he knew, Ian was just napping. When the noise didn't work, he went back to face licking. Ian did respond to that. At least he turned his head away.

Rocky wouldn't stop his persistent request for help, though. He licked again and again, and then bit Ian on the ear lobe. Ian started at the pain and brought up his hand to knock away the nibbler. But his canine companion was insistent—he employed more licking, and when that didn't work, he howled, right next to his friend's ear.

That got Ian's attention. He managed to open his swollen eyes, but still couldn't see. He reached up and pulled the thick, soft cloth off of his face. Where was he?

The place was unfamiliar, but his dog was with him. Rocky was upset about something and wouldn't stop making loud and obnoxious noises. The dog moved toward the opening of the cave, then turned around and came back. Ian got up onto his elbows to investigate. He might be confused about where he was and why, but he knew Rocky wanted him to follow him outside. The dog had never steered him wrong before. Experience had shown him it was best to do what the animal wanted.

Ian rolled over, felt the pain of bruised bones and muscles from his shoulders to his hips, and recalled being tortured and beaten by the gang of eight. No time to reflect on that travesty of justice now—he needed to find out why Rocky was so excited.

He crawled through the holly bushes and saw where the commotion was. He rose, but quickly dropped back to his knees in agony. His bare feet were cut and raw. His knees were still intact though, so he 'walked' twenty feet on his kneecaps over rocks, twigs, and snow to Rocky.

The dog was poking his nose in the face of someone lying on the ground. The sun was low and his vision limited further by his swollen eyes, but the prone person didn't appear to be moving. He came closer, pulled back the long hair of the teenage boy—not even old enough to have a beard—and saw that he was still breathing. A fresh, reddish bruise covered the left side of his face, but his limbs all pointed in the right direction. The thick coat and his youth probably helped him survive the obvious fall. He turned the lad's head carefully and saw the bloody gash on the back of his scalp. He and Rocky were going to have to get the boy moved inside quickly. By the smell of the moist wind in his face, a heavy snowstorm was on the way.

Ian's attempts at rousing the youth were futile. He tried again to stand up, but the pain of his feet wouldn't tolerate his own body weight, much less the additional burden of another person's. It would take too long to find materials to make a travois, so that wasn't an option.

The jacket! The boy's jacket was big enough that he could have Rocky drag him by the hood. He carefully positioned the hood for use as a tow bridle. "Rocky, come help me drag this boy into the cave."

Rocky cocked his head to one side in confusion, then padded to his side.

"Pull here, man—that's it."

Rocky took one bite of the hood and released it, backed up two steps, and sat down, refusing to participate in the task. He didn't like the taste of that fake fur trim.

"Rocky, ye have to help me, I canna do it by myself."

The dog came back, grabbed a mouthful of hood, and started walking backwards. As soon as the slack was out, and he felt the weight of the makeshift sled, he stopped. This was too heavy.

"Come on, I really need ye to pull."

Rocky gave a big tug, and the hood popped off, causing him to take a few awkward steps backwards to regain his balance, and leaving him with part of the coat in his mouth. He quickly performed the doggy version of spitting, and then wiped his tongue on his own coat, trying to get the remnants of fake fur out of his mouth. Ugh, that phony animal pelt was disgusting, and it nearly made him fall on his butt!

Ian picked up the hood, turned it over, and saw that there were brads of some sort pressed into the cloth. He wadded it up, made sure the dog saw him, and tossed it into the brush. "Come on, Rocky, I threw that nasty thing away. It's gone. Here, grab the collar."

Well, Rocky bit into the nape of the jacket and tugged, but it just wasn't feasible. "Thanks fer tryin', but we'll be pullin' the head off the lad if we keep yankin' on the coat that way."

Snowflakes joined Ian's mobilization challenge, the odd-shaped blobs sticking to his eyelashes and blurring his already marginal vision, chilling and wetting his swollen hands, making clutching and grasping even more difficult. He tried a new tactic: crawling under the boy. Maybe he could carry him on his back and shoulders. That would have worked fine, but when he bent forward to assume the position, he discovered his hands were nearly as tender as his feet.

"Weel, mon, what isna beat on ye? Seems that only yer arse and yer belly arena screamin' wi' pain. Ye can crawl on yer belly or crawl on yer arse. Crawl on my arse?"

That actually seemed to be the only valid option. Ian scooted under the boy's head, laid it in his lap, then 'walked' on his butt to the cave entrance. "Left cheek, right cheek, left cheek, ow! Right cheek, left cheek, cursed rocks and stones. Stop smilin', ye damned dog. If ye hadda done yer job, I wouldna be here, shreddin' my backside."

Ian scooted backwards into the cave, the unconscious body warm, but inert, in his lap. Access through the tangled botanical portal was easier than it should have been because the branches of the guardian shrub were propped away from the cave's entrance with a forked stick. That meant fewer scratches when coming and going, but unfortunately, it was also a sign that there were occupants inside. He reached up and knocked away the greenwood prop rod. The prickly branches sprung back into place, quickly re-concealing the hideout's location. He didn't know where he was, but he didn't want anyone else to know either.

After a few more feet of walking on his fanny across the smaller interior pebbles, they were both safely inside. He carefully set the boy's head down and, after several lifts, tugs, and twists, had him situated so that they both had their feet toward the rear of the cave where the small fire was burning. It was an odd placement for a fire ring, but seemed to be working. The smoke was drifting up and away, not out the entrance, nor was it polluting the air in the small cavern.

He picked up a piece of wood between his wrists and tossed it on the fire, encouraging a more generous blaze. He hadn't noticed the smoke plume when he was outside—it evidently dissipated quickly—and the snowflakes coming down now were the size of babies' fists. If someone was dumb enough to be searching for him in this mess, it was doubtful any little puffs of smoke would be seen.

Ж

"What kind of wool or skin is this?" Ian asked aloud as he ran the back of his hand over the unconscious evacuee's pants.

Well, his young charge didn't answer, and Rocky evidently didn't know or care. At least he didn't seem to have the disdain for the wool that he did for the hood's faux fur.

The hood—it was still by the entrance. Ian snaked his long arm under the base of the sentinel bush, swept his tender fingers across the ground, and located the soft, fuzzy remnant. He managed to grasp it between his thumb and fingers, working his digits like a flesh mitten. He brought it in, tucked the fur portion inside—creating a small pillow—and placed it under the boy's head to relieve the pressure on his wound. He arranged the shiny covering he had found himself wrapped in, over the boy's legs. How anyone could make silver so soft and warm was beyond him. Maybe it was from Italy. Those Italians were always using precious metals to make everyday goods.

Rocky moved over to the entrance of the cave, circled three times, and then lay down, his furry back a mammalian shield against the winter storm trying to blow inside.

"I'm glad ye like the cold. Ye make a good barn door." Ian said. He found the pot with the melted snow, put the pan to his mouth, and took a long drink. "Supper can wait a bit. I canna remember when I last ate, but I'm sure an hour more willna make a difference."

He dipped the soft cloth he had found on his head into the rest of the water and wiped the young boy's face. He turned the head to the side. It was dark in the cave, but he could feel the gravelly sand and leaf matter in the wound. "Ye have mighty thick hair there. Hold still while I clean out the bits and pieces lodged in yer scalp."

He carefully urged the skin apart and washed out the wound with the soft cloth and warm water. He couldn't stitch it closed, so he just pushed the skin back together, securing his work with a bandana bandage.

"Weel, Rocky, do ye think he'll make it? Hmph! Do ye think *we'll* make it? Now we're three bucks without a bit of food or any way to get it—no dirk, no rifle, no arrows. I dinna suppose you feel like headin' oot into that mess to bring us supper, do ye?"

Rocky came over to the prone patient and pushed his nose into the crotch area.

"Get away, that's rude, Rocky," Ian said absently, concentrating on finding a way to get food; he was suddenly hungry.

Rocky did it again, and this time woofed, trying to get Ian's attention.

"What, did the lad hurt his private parts or somethin'?"

"Woof, woof."

"Okay, I'll check it out, but it doesna feel right. It's rather personal with humans, ye ken."

Ian lifted the young man's jacket, looking for the buttons so he could get the pants down. There weren't any, but he did find a thin rope holding

81

them up. He huffed in frustration; he couldn't untie the rope because his hands were too swollen to work the knot. The pants did look like they were too big, though.

"Worth a try," he said, and pulled on the pants with the outside of his palms held together like fire tongs. After a long minute of tugging first one side, and then the other, he had the pants down. All he could see in the dim firelight was that the boy was wearing strange undergarments. Ian grabbed a stick of wood and set it on the fire to flame up. While his back was turned, Rocky came over and started nosing the boy in the crotch again.

"Stop that—it's bad manners." Ian picked up the now flaming piece of wood and held it over the area Rocky was so excited about. He could smell the blood, too. But it didn't smell like blood from a wound. It smelled like a woman.

It was blood, and *he* was a woman! Apparently, she was on her courses. She was messy down there, but it would only be a minor clean up. He really didn't want to intrude, but if he didn't, her pants would be soiled. "Lord, dinna let her wake up. This isna lust or desire, I'm simply tryin' to be my brother's, er, sister's keeper. And please, Lord, let her heal. She helped me, now let me be a tool in Yer hands to help her. Amen."

It had been quite a while since Ian had prayed. He had thought God didn't care about him and that was why the men had come to kill him. It just wasn't in him to let them take his life, though. He was born a fighter, would most likely die one, too—but it looked like today was not the day for it. Hopefully, it wouldn't be hers either.

He had done all he could for her—which wasn't much beyond washing her with snow water and giving her a pillow. Sleep was just possibly the best medicine. And it was definitely the only one available.

*13 Caving

Now what should he do? He looked down at himself in the dim light. His clothes were disgusting. He pulled off his filthy buckskin shirt with an angry vengeance, threw it down beside the fire, and then scooped handfuls of dirt onto the smears of blood, vomit, and piss that covered it. He rubbed the powdery soil into the leather with a circular motion, using the still somewhat undamaged outside edge of his hand. He flipped it over and furiously repeated the process. He performed his 'dry cleaning' method several times until the shirt was soft again and 'cleaner,' then shook it out, and tossed it into the farthest recess of the cave.

Next, he untied his leather belt, dropping his breechclout and attached leggings at the same time. They were in worse shape than his shirt. The bastards who bound and beat him had made him walk through hot embers and broken glass. He remembered one man shouting and laughing, "Hey, his feet are on fire," and started to piss on him. Then they all joined in. He sniffed, then groaned with the unwelcome recollection. Apparently, at some point in one of his beatings, he had shat himself. He scooped dirt onto the pile of buckskin. It was doubtful his clothes would ever be clean enough, but these were the only ones he had.

Even though he was now naked, Ian wasn't cold despite the snow falling outside. His body had grown warm with his newly awakened rage. He grabbed the gray rag that had bound his head, dipped it into the water, and began cleaning his lower body as best he could. When he was done, he threw the cloth into the fire. Not only did he not want to be reminded of shitting himself and being pissed on, he didn't want there to be any chance the rag could be used for any other purpose. He rubbed the leggings and breechclout into the ground, performing the cleaning chore a second time by using the rough flooring as his washboard. When he was done, he took a flat rock and pushed the disgusting soil he had used for laundering into the fire, purging it of the remaining stink and filth, then threw the pants into the pile with the shirt.

Burning the remnants of his shame helped, but he still felt emotionally dirty. He grabbed the pan and squatted in front of the fire, pouring the warmed snow water over his loins, scrubbing vigorously with just his hands. His rage was building. How dare someone—or some *ones*—make him hate his own body, humiliate him, and make him lose control of his bowels. His anger was making him hot all over. He started slapping himself, cursing in all the languages he knew …

"Ow."

The cry of pain brought him back to reality. The voice wasn't very loud—he wasn't even sure if it was real. He more felt than heard the noise. He looked over at the lass. Her mouth was moving, but no noise was coming out. Her eyes were still closed—she must be moaning in her sleep.

Ian's angry tirade had worn him out. He was still physically weak, and the lass's rescue had used up what little strength he had. If only this had happened last year, last month, or even last week, when he was his normal self—healthy and clear-headed—then moving a mysterious, unconscious young female over snowy and rough terrain would not only have been a fairly simple task, it would have been intriguing, and hopefully, pleasurable.

Right now, his mind and body were spent. He hadn't eaten in days, had been beaten to a pulp by a group of degenerate heathens, and had been awakened from a deep, comatose sleep by his dog biting him on the ear. He didn't know where he was or how long he had been unconscious. All he wanted to do was go back to sleep. Before he could do that, though, he needed to put another log on the fire, offer Rocky the leftover water, and scoop up more snow for melting.

Too much had just happened. For self-preservation, he closed off all thoughts, consciously numbing his brain, as if packed in ice. By using this old trick, he could force his raw hands to work just a little longer.

Ж

It seemed as if it took hours to get those small tasks done, but he knew he would be glad he had done them in the morning. "Rocky, watch fer bad men and dinna let the fire go out. I canna stay awake another minute. I'll deal with everythin' else in the morn. Dinna wake me unless men or beasts attack. And no more ear bitin', ye mangy cur," he said, bumping shoulders with Rocky.

Ian readied himself emotionally for his new sleeping arrangements. He had to lie next to the lass. Healthy, tired, or half-dead, that situation appealed to him. He had to lie parallel to her; there wasn't much room in the cave. He positioned himself carefully, making sure he didn't touch the unknown young woman—she might be someone's wife. He shuddered at the thought that she might belong to one of the men who had kidnapped him. "Nae, not her," he whispered softly.

The cold wind and snow were blowing into the cave now, skirting around Rocky's massive bulk that only partially blocked the entrance. His feet were warmed by the fire, and the proximity of the dog was keeping his head warm, but his bare torso was shaking from the frigid air and cold ground. Lying near the lass was pleasant enough, but she didn't radiate much heat from a foot away.

His mind ached for sleep, but his naked body was shuddering, too cold to relax enough for slumber. The fire would die down during the night, and their stony shelter would be even icier in the morning. The only coat and blanket were being used by her. He was sure she wouldn't mind sharing with him.

"Weel, I hope she'd share," he whispered. He gingerly took the coat off her, put his arm in the right sleeve, then lay down next to her, cradling her back against his chest. He turned the blanket sideways so it covered the lower half of both of their bodies. A few minor adjustments and their legs and hips were covered. He pulled her body close to his, then stuck his arm into one sleeve, leaving the side of the jacket draped over her.

"Lord, I dinna ken what I did to deserve this comfort, but I thank Ye. Please, jest keep us safe, and let me know what Ye want me to do. Amen, and good night." And with that, Ian fell into a deep, restful sleep.

Ж

"Mmm," Ian crooned as he awoke, immersed in a comfortable, warm feeling, as if he had just eaten a hearty dinner and was sitting around the hearth with friends and family, trading stories and drinking whisky. He was enjoying that twilight zone between dreaming and reality where thought and substance merge, holding a warm, beautiful woman and...

His eyes popped open, but the rest of him froze. This wasn't a dream. His left hand was holding a very soft, very real breast. He realized that one part of his anatomy was definitely aware of her authenticity. He pulled away from her, adjusted his early morning stiffness so he wasn't poking her, and then snuggled back, almost to the same position. This time, though, he placed his hand lower so he wasn't cupping her breast but could still enjoy its nearness and warmth.

Ian tried to return to that peaceful, sleepy place again, but bits and pieces of his recent torture exploded like lightning flashes in a summer storm, revealing a dying animal. He squeezed his eyes tight, clenching his jaws with the effort, trying to keep out images of his own personal horror, but all it did was make his face hurt.

He was wide-awake now, and fully aware that he was uncomfortable in another way. It felt as if he hadn't taken a piss in days. He gingerly pulled his arm out of the coat, leaving the sleeve under her head as a pillow, draping the rest of it around her upper body.

He started to stand, but quickly dropped back to the ground, reminded of two of his infirmities: his wounded feet. Still on his knees, he made his way to the opening of the cave. He reached upwards, arched his spine, and took in deep recharging breaths: the crisp autumn air refreshing, invigorating.

It was as good a time as any to mark his territory. "Ahh…" The relief of his bladder also helped clear his mind of the wooly fluff of his long and deep slumber. He couldn't remember the last time he had slept so hard, but did know he hadn't been able to sleep peacefully in years. He hurt all over, but felt alive and human again.

Suddenly, mental images of his abduction and torture burst forward into his conscious mind again. He quickly pushed them back. There were better things to think of than seeking revenge. Right now, right here—just a few feet away—there was a warm human female in need of someone to take care of her. Whether she was the one who rescued him and tended to his injuries, he didn't know. But if she was, she was one hell of a woman; one he wanted in good health. He wanted to thank her properly.

He reentered the cave and found a colorful bandana by the makeshift bed. He sniffed it—it smelled clean—so he dipped it into the pan of warm water. He dabbed it on her lips to see if she would lick the drops. No luck. He tried again, this time with success. She wasn't awake, but her instinct to suck was there. Her full lips pulled at the cloth, getting all the moisture out of it. He took it away, rewet it, and tried again. Not this time— evidently, she had had enough. She sighed softly, and then sank back into her deep sleep.

Ian couldn't decide what needed done first. He felt worthless. He was limited because of his feet. He couldn't walk at all, nor go very far by butt-scooting or kneeling, and couldn't even hold a dirk—not that he had one anymore. "Rocky, go find us some breakfast," he said in frustration.

Rocky jumped up and headed out through the hedged entrance, not looking back, knocking the bushes further away from the access, eager to hunt for his family's food.

"Weel, there's somethin' I can do." Ian took a piece of the stacked firewood between his palms and used it to pull the branches back over the opening. He'd figure a way to make a more permanent closure later.

He walked on his knees to the improvised bed to check on his charge. She was beautiful—even if she was drooling a bit. "Are ye awake? Can I

86

do somethin' fer ye?" He saw her mouth move again, but still no sound. He bent over, close to her face, and asked again louder, "Can I help ye?"

Her eyelashes fluttered, but her eyes stayed closed. No reply—she was still unconscious. "Weel, get yer rest," he mumbled, then turned away to get the pan of water.

Ж

I was suddenly awake, although I didn't remember falling asleep or anyone trying to rouse me. I saw Ian at the fire. He must have awakened while I was sleeping. He was naked, so I averted my eyes. I couldn't help myself, though, and glanced up again to look at his long, knobby back that ended with a dark, fuzzy crack.

"Hello, Ian. Are you feeling better?" I said, making sure my eyes were low and my voice loud.

Ian swung his torso halfway around and nearly tossed the water on me. I couldn't help but grin. "Ouch!" The grinning hurt my face. I shut my eyes and gulped in embarrassment, afraid that I was staring at his nakedness or that he'd think I was. "What happened to your clothes? I'm sure I left them on you."

Ian grabbed the blanket from my legs and held it over his middle.

"Aye, they were on me when I awoke, but they were so filthy, I couldna bear to be in them. I cleaned them and me up a bit. They're in the back, airin' out. I was jest about to see if they were wearable when ye started moanin'."

"Go ahead and get dressed," I said, my eyes still closed. "I won't look."

"I dinna mind if ye look. I've never been bashful. It's jest ye gave me a start. I was afraid ye'd never wake up. Are ye thirsty?"

"Yes, I'd love a drink. Is there anything to eat?"

"I sent Rocky out to bring us some breakfast. I hope it's somethin' easy to fix. I was, um, relieved of my dirk."

Ian held the pan up to my mouth. I looked down into the bottom of it as I drank. I pulled my head back and with my eyes, offered him the last of it. He accepted it and said, "Thank ye."

His eyes widened in realization. "Ye called me Ian. How did ye ken my name?"

I told him the truth: "Rocky told me."

"Are ye telling me ye understand that beast?"

"No, it's more like we played a game of twenty questions and I won. Actually, it only took a few guesses to figure out your name. He acted all excited when I called you "Man." From there I deduced that you weren't an Ann, Ban, Can, or Dan. When I asked about 'E-Ann' he went nuts. He's a smart dog—or is he a wolf?"

"I dinna ken, he was a weaned pup when I found him. He and I have been together a long time. I think he's more like a brother to me than my own brothers. At least he's here—they're both back in Scotland."

"So that's where you're from. Do you live around here now?"

"Right now, I have no home," he said glumly. "Um, I think I'll get my clothes on now if ye dinna mind."

I turned over, onto my belly, and tried to get up. "Ouch!" It was that darned right wrist. I dropped to my elbows and managed to roll back onto my fanny.

Ian stopped at my yelp and saw I was holding my hand. "Is there somethin' I can do for ye?"

"Yes," I replied a little too curtly. "Can you tell if I broke a bone?"

"Aye, if it's severe, I can."

Ian gently took my hand from my chest, stretched it out, and then turned it over. It wasn't as painful that way. Then he pushed on it. "Ouch! That's where it hurts," I complained, bringing my hand back to my chest.

"I think ye've naught but a sprain. Dinna use it for a few days, and it should be fine. Do ye want me to bind it for ye? I found a bright colored kerchief that would look right bonnie."

I giggled, "Yes, please do, doctor. But I doubt your bandaging could look as magnificent as what I had on you yesterday. Your hands were purple and swollen, so I packed them with bags of snow and bound them with psychedelic bandanas."

"Weel, first, I am nae a doctor. And second, thank ye fer tendin' to my hands. The last I recall, I was wonderin' if they were gonna fall off at the wrists, the way the ropes were bindin' them so tightly. And third, what is cycle deltic?"

"Psychedelic, you know, flower power—I survived the '60s and all that?"

"Weel, I guess I can say I survived the '60s, and I ken that flour is powdered wheat, but I dinna ken about cycle deltic."

"Psychedelic is bright colors in wild patterns, like that bandana."

"Aye, I'll take yer word fer it. Now, let me have yer hand, and I'll bind the kerchief 'round it. How's yer heid?"

"I have a splitting headache, but I think I'll survive. At least I can sit up straight. But this is weird—I can't remember my name. It's funny that I know your name, but not my own."

I was a bit hesitant to say anything more about my memory loss, but I had to ask. "Did you know me before today or yesterday?"

"Nae, I canna say I did. Do ye remember where yer from or yer parents' names?"

"No, but I do recall a little bit about taking care of you and Rocky. I don't remember my birthday or address, but do know how to talk, obviously."

My memory loss had bothered me at first, but now I was intrigued. "Tell me what you know about me; maybe that'll spark a memory," I suggested happily.

"I recall Rocky bitin' my ear to wake me and get me to come outside. Once I was out there, I saw a body on the ground. I thought ye were a lad because of the clothes. Ye were alive but ailin'." Ian shrugged his shoulder. "Then it started snowin'. Rocky and I had the devil of a time gettin' ye inside. I cleaned ye up a bit, found out ye were a lass," Ian mumbled something incomprehensible, "and then, weel, I just bundled us up, fell asleep, and here we are."

"Okay, do you have any idea where we are?"

"I'm most sure we're still in North Carolina, somewhere away from the coast. I canna smell the ocean, and the mountains arena so tall here, so we're somewhere in the interior. Do ye ken where ye were goin' when ye found me, or where ye were comin' from?"

"Not a clue on either. I do know North Carolina is one of the fifty United States, but don't know what day it is, or even what year. God, I don't even know my own name." I was getting frustrated now. "I don't know how old I am, whether I have family or not—even what I look like."

I looked deep into Ian's eyes, "Ian, this is getting scary. Lie to me, tell me who I am, give me a history. Pretend you've known me all your life. If I have amnesia, I'll know the truth when I hear it, or at least I hope I do. Right now, I feel like I'm standing naked in the winter wind. I just want to be warm and safe, with someone who cares about me." I was starting to shake all over, and it wasn't from any injuries. I was scared witless.

"Oh aye, Evie, the game of pretend is over." Ian gathered me close to him in an amicable way. "Ye bumped yer heid when ye were out lookin' for Rocky. We came up here last week on our way to visit my great-uncle Angus and his family. We got separated, and then some mean men kidnapped me. Ye hid out, came and rescued me, and brought me here. Yer, uh, seventeen years old and we've been together fer, uh, six months.

We're newlyweds, ye ken," he added, with a grin that nearly split his swollen bottom lip.

"Thanks, I needed that." I was serious. Now I had a name and a little bit of recent history, even if it was a fairy tale.

*14 Amnesia and Love

Ian hadn't dressed yet, but still had the blanket in his lap. His stomach started growling and mine followed suit. "It sounds like our stomachs are performing a duet."

"Aye, our stomachs must think our throats have been slit. Oh, sorry; that really wasna proper."

"No, that's okay. My mom used to say the same thing. That and, 'I'm so hungry, the big ones are eating on the little ones.'"

"What?" Ian asked, his eyebrows lifting in shock. His eyes tried to follow suit, but only managed to part enough that I could see they were brown. "People eatin' bairns?"

"Nooo. She said that in the old days, when people had tapeworms, they'd say the big ones—that is, the big tapeworms—would start eating on the little ones—the little tapeworms—when a person got real hungry. She had all sorts of old sayings."

"Aye, maybe the wee fiends in my gut are feudin' and that's why the noise. We've naught but water to quiet the wame. I wish I could do more fer ye."

"Well, I feel better already. I just recalled having a mother, even if I don't remember anything about her except what I just said. Hmm, I seem to be able to remember stuff if I don't try."

We endured an awkward pause, neither of us knowing what to say or do next. I was uneasy: totally clothed, sitting in a small, dim cave with a naked man who just claimed to be my newlywed husband. At least he was a gentleman and not getting fresh, allowing me to recover from the amnesia. I didn't know what he had done with his clothes, but if his nakedness didn't bother him, I'd just pretend that he was wearing a fuzzy, flesh-toned bodysuit and do my best not to stare.

"Whoa!" I exclaimed as a burst of memory hit. "Here, lie back down. I have a surprise for you."

I helped Ian lie back on the little patch of cleared dirt floor that had been our bed. He was taking care to keep the solar blanket over his unmentionables. He was still a man, after all, and a well-built one, too. Oops, keep thinking flesh-toned body suit...

I took a deep breath and grabbed my backpack. Yes, I knew it was mine, and that in itself made me happy. It had been sitting undisturbed by

91

the cave entrance since I don't know when. "Here we go: my magic bag." I scooted next to him and peeked inside, not letting him see what was in it.

"Yer bag is magic?" he asked, rising to his elbow to look over my shoulder.

"No, not really. It's just I know that this is *my* bag, but I don't remember what I put in it. It will be a bit of a magic—a surprise for both of us—to see what's in here. I'm pretty sure I have some food, though."

"Ooh... Hmmm... Nope... Ah...Yes!" I glanced up at Ian's face every time I made a noise of discovery. At "yes," he sat up all the way, his back straightened in anticipation.

"We have us a five-course meal in here, Ian," I said with a Southern twang. I reverted to my normal tone, "They're small courses, but, hey, we can pretend we're feasting. Open up for the oats."

Ian closed his eyes and opened his mouth obediently. I put a small oat cluster from the granola mix onto the end of his tongue.

"This feels like oats in the mouth, but doesna taste like porritch or feed fer horses. It tastes like I'm eatin' bits o' fancy cake."

"That's because it's sweetened with honey and cinnamon. It's part of a snack mix to keep your energy up. Are you ready for the next course?"

His mouth popped open like a baby bird. I placed a cashew in it. "Make sure to chew that well. You haven't eaten in a while, and we don't want your belly cramping up."

Ian sighed deeply, then almost purred in contentment, a spoiled tabby, enjoying the attention. He carefully chewed the nut, a blissful smile appearing, incongruent to his battered and swollen face. "This is delicious! What is it?"

"It's a jumbo-sized cashew. Most people use peanuts or almonds in their mixes, but I like cashews better. They're my favorite nut," I said, and popped one in my mouth.

"I think they're my favorite now, too. What do ye have next, if I'm not bein' too greedy?"

"Here is the bread of our little repast—a pretzel." These were miniature-sized pretzels in the mix, but I could tell that they, too, were new to Ian. He chewed thoroughly, either from my warning about belly cramps or because he wanted to savor the taste.

"Now, for our fruit salad..." I grabbed a piece of dried pineapple and a few shreds of the coconut, and put them on his outstretched pink tongue. I put some in my mouth, too. I was enjoying this as much as he was.

"Now what was that? It tastes familiar, but I canna recall what it is."

"That's piña colada, also known as dried pineapple and coconut. Now, for our last course: dessert. We can have more in an hour or so when we're sure our stomachs can tolerate food. My head still hurts, and I think I'd better take it easy. Open wide," I prompted, then placed a dark chocolate chip in his mouth.

"Now that's chocolate," he said, "but better than any I've ever had—nothin' like they had in Edinburgh. There they prepared it as a hot drink, and it was bitter tastin'. My cousin did tell me there were other ways to eat it. Can I have another? I promise not to get sick and waste it."

"Sure, but be careful..." I said as I gave him one more. I wanted to say, 'Be careful; don't become a chocoholic.' Sharing the old wives' tale, 'Chocolate is considered a substitute for love,' also crossed my mind about the time my eyes drifted down to his naked shoulders and slightly hairy chest.

Was this man really my husband? I know that if I were able to order one from a catalog, I'd choose him. Well, except for the beat up part. Kind, helpful, sweet disposition, well equipped, ahem...

I got up, sniffed back my unsettling thoughts, and headed for the exit and the non-naked air outside. "I'll be right back; don't go anywhere."

"I'll stay right here where ye put me," he said, then snuggled down into the coat, wearing nothing but a satiated grin under that thin, shiny, solar blanket.

I fought my way through those nasty holly bushes to my little latrine, solitude—and hopefully—composure. My head still ached, but I was no longer nauseous. I was, however, becoming highly aroused.

I came back in and sat down beside Ian, who was now lying on the floor. He was provocative without trying, exuding a tantalizing male musk, unmitigated by the stink of men's cologne or deodorant. Right here at my feet was a beautiful, hard and lean—and very naked—male body. The man was well mannered, a bit worse for the thrashing...but otherwise Ian was practically perfect husband material, and quite possibly mine. And we were very alone.

Ah! What the hell...

I took my two shirts off over my head, rolled them up, and set them down next to each other. Thumbs stuck in my waistband, I shimmied out of my sweatpants, shook them out, and folded them neatly. I was using the extra time and attention I was paying to my clothing either to compose myself or to try and talk me out of what I was going to do next, I'm not sure which.

Ian was watching me through slits of puffy eyes, not saying a word. He'd make a great poker player with the way he could hide his feelings. And he wasn't grinning or leering at me either. That meant I was correct in my gut feeling about him.

"Pick up your head. I need the coat."

He obeyed wordlessly. I gave him the rolled-up shirts and motioned for him to put them down for use as a pillow. "Now scoot over a bit and let me spread these over you."

"Ye'll freeze in jest yer undergarments!" he exclaimed, his tone letting me know he was both shocked and being a gentleman at the same time.

"Just hold still and don't argue, okay?"

"Yes, ma'am," he said meekly, stifling a grin.

"Okay, turn on your side; yes, that's it." I was positioning him so we could spoon together with the blanket, coat, and fleece pants spread over us. I was also trying to figure out why I felt so comfortable with him. I thought his custom-made, functional fairy tale—that I was his newlywed wife—was to plug the hole of my memory loss, to make me feel at ease with him and our situation. However, it felt right; it was a perfect fit. Whether or not I really was his wife—and that was actually a possibility, I guess—I certainly felt like I was.

Ian moved onto his right side again. Rather than spoon next to him, though, I slid under the blanket and clothing comforter ensemble, and snuggled into his chest, nuzzling him just below his collarbones. He gently settled his chin on top of my head. I couldn't see his face, but I knew he was enjoying this as much as I was.

There were no words between us, but it wasn't awkward. I rubbed my nose into the hair at the top of his chest. I couldn't stop myself. His body was giving off those hard to describe pheromones. He had a distinctive smell: a blend of male musk and a forest wet after an autumn rain. I couldn't get enough of it. I was rubbing my cheeks, nose, and lips into him, deeply inhaling his scent. I wanted to paint his fuzzy chest, using my face as the brush. I kept my hands above waist level so I didn't grab or clutch places that might not be mine to seize. I was also using considerable restraint, not yanking off my sports bra and rubbing my breasts all over him.

I felt his hand come up my back. He was gently stroking me, saying words I didn't comprehend, but somehow knew. Spoken in a foreign language, but related through our bodies, his words didn't need translation.

94

I reached around him as best I could in our awkward arrangement on the hard, stony ground, and held him tight, nearly squeezing the breath out of both of us.

I loosened my hold and pulled my face back a few inches from his chest. "Ian, I know this is strange for you. I don't know who I am or why I'm here, but I do feel that you're mine, and we were meant to be together. I'm not crazy; I can't be, because this is so real."

Ian pulled away from me enough that I could see his face. His eyes were still puffy, but red now—and it wasn't from the beatings. He had been crying. I could see the wetness under his eyes and nose. "And I say to ye, it doesna matter who ye are, because yer mine. Please, dinna ever leave me. I couldna bear it."

And with that, I received the full mouth and soul of the man I knew as Ian and gave him mine in return. The force of the emotion pulsed from his lips and tongue to mine, coursing down my chest and belly, warming that juncture of legs and torso that leads to procreation.

My toes were curled and making their own love to Ian's feet. I suddenly remembered that his were still damaged, tender, and certainly sore. I pulled away and rolled onto my back, panting, taking in deep calming breaths that almost made me lose consciousness.

"Oh, boy," escaped my lips as I stared at the ceiling of our little residence. I sure hadn't expected this to happen!

*15 A primitive marriage

The kissing was great, but both of us were holding back. It wasn't that either of us didn't want to go further. His nether regions made it evident that he was ready—there was still enough blood in his body to head south when excited. I was still dizzy from my fall, and he was being respectful. Yes, we were both highly aroused, but also very weak.

We lay together, holding each other for quite a while. Time by a clock didn't exist; not that either one of us had a timepiece. We took turns emitting big sighs of contentment, followed by extra squeezes of reassurance. There really wasn't much for us to do but talk, hold each other, or sleep. Neither one of us was strong enough to do the chores that needed to be done: to search for a source of water other than snow, gather wood, and to find civilization.

I spoke first. "If it's all the same to you, can we just lie here for a bit? I don't have much energy, and I really do have a headache."

"Aye, that's verra sensible. If we are to be together forever, there's no rush fer the joinin'. I would like to have a bit more vigor to serve ye properly, too. I'd hate to faint halfway through makin' love to my wife fer the first time."

"First time? So…I'm not already your wife, but you want me to be? Aren't we supposed to have some sort of rite or ceremony? I don't think it would be appropriate to sleep with a man unless I was married to him. At least to have sex with him; we've already slept together the other way."

"Weel, the Indians around here simply let the women choose their mate. That's about all there is to it fer them, just selectin' their man. If he no longer pleases her, she kicks him out and gets another. It seems to work fine fer them, but always did seem a bit unfair to me and the other menfolk."

I didn't say anything, but Ian could tell from my face that I was thinking hard about something. I was trying to rationalize a marriage to an unknown, injured man who I had just recently rescued from a death squad. I very much wanted to be his wife. Okay, what I really wanted was to jump his bones and ride him until he couldn't draw another breath. But I was serious—I wanted to be married first.

My face went through a few more grins, grimaces, and frowns as I thought of the many forms of marriage I had heard of. Polygamy, arranged

96

marriages, shotgun weddings, standing before a justice of the peace, those huge elaborate affairs with doves, roses, and limousines. Right now, I didn't even have a scrap of paper to write a marriage contract on. How was I going to be married to him?

And then inspiration hit.

"I am Christian, and I believe God is in charge of this situation and everything else. I have free will and also know right from wrong. I want to do this properly so we're not just two lonely people having comfort sex. So, Ian, will you be my husband before God and man? Will you keep me to love and cherish, through sickness and health, for better and for worse, forever and ever?"

"Aye, I will. And will ye have me, too; to love and honor, through good times and bad, feast and famine, hale or infirm, fer better or worse, even if I am jest a mangy man not worthy to wipe the dirt from yer feet, forever and ever?"

"I will. Lord, please bless us, and recognize us as married, even if we didn't have a preacher and witnesses. Thank You for bringing us together. Amen." I took a deep breath, put my hands on either side of his face, and looked deeply into his eyes. "Do you feel married now?"

"Aye, even more than I did ten minutes ago. And I also believe it was God who brought us together. I havena told ye, but I lost contact with Him fer a while. Ye see, I was livin' with the Tuscarora, and they believe differently than the white man. I lived as a heathen, my life rough and unsettled. Then there were problems. It wasna goin' very weel fer me with them, and they asked me to leave. I had lived with the Indians fer so long, I dinna feel right livin' alongside the white man and, weel, then the Indians dinna want me either.

"So, I lived mostly by myself fer a long time, with jest Rocky fer company. I felt verra empty and alone. I thought the Lord was punishin' me fer not havin' Him in my life. I dinna ken how to get back with Him to make things right. I dinna want to go to a priest, and dinna ken where to find one anyhow. I had heard the Protestants say ye could talk to the Lord Christ directly. A man dinna need a priest or minister but could do it all by himself. So I decided to give it a try. It took a long time, but I started talkin' to Him again. I prayed fer forgiveness of my sins. It took me two years to ask God fer anything except fer the forgiveness. Then I asked Him fer a wife.

"If He dinna listen to me, weel, I guessed I'd ken that I would need to search out a priest to hear my confessions and requests. Of course, the priest couldna give me a wife," he said, and leaned down, grinning at me with his last words.

"The Lord did hear me, though, because yer here with me now. But He did give me my punishment fer my bad deeds before I found ye. Or I suppose it was before ye found *me*."

I looked up at the ceiling, then over at him. "I've been very blessed in my life. Of course, my memory is only about 24 hours long, but I know in my soul that I'm on the right track. Our housing accommodations may be rough, but we're dry, have wood for our fire, and a bit of food. We'll do fine, as long as we're together, I know it."

*16 Consummation

The ground that was our bed was definitely getting lumpier—not that it had ever been soft or supportive. It was probably because our bodies had been shifting the caked dirt away from the stones, making it feel like we were lying on one of those mattresses of nails that Hindu holy men were so fond of.

"I hate to ask you to move again, but could you sit up?"

Ian rocked and scooted back and forth, looking like the steely in play on a pinball machine, until he was finally upright. He raised one eyebrow as if to ask, "Now what?" I didn't say a word, but laid out the coat that had covered us, setting it out like a feather mattress on our 'bed frame,' the cave floor.

"Are you sure you want to be married to me?" I asked, hoping for words of encouragement. "I mean, we've only known each other for a short time, and I'll understand if you want to change your mind…"

I really was quite fond of him—and our kissing and words of betrothal had been very encouraging—but I was still insecure. On the other hand, now I wished I hadn't said anything. Lying next to him was giving me wifely urges that only he could satisfy.

"Aye, I'm sure I want ye fer my bride, but our weddin' really isna bindin' without the, um, joinin'." Ian's eyes lit up as he glanced at my bosom, and then darkened into a frown as he looked further up, at my forehead, remembering that I had told him I had a headache.

I gulped down a breath of fortitude and declared as nonchalantly as I could, "Sure glad my headache's gone. Are you feeling better, too?"

"Aye, I'm feelin' *verra* hale," he declared, his sinewy chest puffed out in pride. "Must be that marriage agrees with me."

He laid the back of his hand across mine, gliding it over my wrist, up the curve of my arm, to my shoulder, the hairs on my goose pimples rising not from the cold, but from anticipation. I followed his lead, and stroked my hand up the back of his, mimicking his route, but proceeding further, up to his neck and slightly bearded jaw line, culminating the introductory gesture with a caress and a gentle kiss next to his swollen lip.

Our soft and timid touches, warily exploring each other's bodies, soon became more insistent, eager for more intimacy, our primal cravings overcoming our puritanical hesitancy. It was awkward for the first few moments, but lust won out, desire overcoming the physical limits of his injuries and his general weakness from lack of nutrition.

An hour after our primitive wedding ceremony, we were man and wife, having 'known' each other in the Biblical way to make our marriage 'legal.'

He spent all of his physical reserves pleasuring me. Well, almost all— he did save a couple of calories of energy for himself there at the end.

When he finished, his whole body crumpled into a controlled collapse on top of me. He was panting heavily, the musky, aromatic beads of his efforts dribbling down his chest and forehead onto me. "Oh, sorry," he puffed as he wiped them away with the back of his wrist, and then carefully rolled off of me.

All the tension and insecurities were gone from my body and mind. With great effort, I forced an eye open, pushing through the grin that encompassed my whole face, looking at him one more time before I melted into the coat mattress and oblivion. "Not cold now, are we?" I crooned.

"Aye, 'tis true enough, though if we dinna get covered soon, we'll both die of the ague."

His words, breathlessly spoken, didn't hide the smile in his voice. He pulled the silver shroud over both of us and settled in next to me. I was totally relaxed and at peace, and glad that one of us could move. I wasn't ready to die, and now, neither was he.

*17 Living on Love

Who says you can't live on love? That's what we did for the first five days. Well, sort of. We did have a wee bit of granola and those barely palatable dehydrated meals to nosh on, but I didn't consider those real foods. They were, however, enough to maintain our basic metabolic functions. If we starved to death, at least we would die happy.

We thoroughly explored each other's bodies, discovering our rhythms and pushing our physical limits. I had been thoroughly embarrassed at first. I hadn't known—must have been memory loss from the head bashing—that I was on my period when we made love for the first time. I was a bit disgusted at the mess, but it didn't bother Ian. He shrugged, kissed me on the forehead, and proceeded to clean up the both of us. If it didn't bother him, I wasn't going to let it hold me back either.

That first time was so intense; I still shudder when I remember all we did and how good I felt. Now, the second time, I'd rather forget about that episode. It hurt so badly, I had tears rolling down both cheeks. I screamed out as he entered me, and when he stopped and asked if he had hurt me, I lied and told him to go ahead, I was just excited. I knew it would get better, and it did. It was only that one time, though. If I didn't know better, I'd swear I had just lost my virginity.

In between the wild and passionate rides, he entertained me with his fascinating tales of growing up in Scotland, his journey to America, getting shanghaied to the Caribbean, and his life with the Indians. I didn't have anything to contribute to our chats, but I was enthralled. His tales were stranger than fiction to me, and he enjoyed sharing his personal history.

Then days six, seven, and eight came and went. We were without food, and Ian was getting morose. He would hardly speak. The stories had stopped, and my questions were answered with a shrug or maybe a mumble. I thought I knew what it was: he was the man of the family—the head of our little two-person clan—and he couldn't provide food or even fetch water for us.

His wounded body was healing, but his ego wasn't doing so well. The good news that he was on the mend was lost in his frustration that it wasn't happening as fast as he wanted. He never developed any infections—the germ killer worked—but his soles looked like crazy quilts, with odd-

101

shaped red and pink patches in different stages of healing. He was able to take a few more steps each day, but he was still a tenderfoot.

His ears were clear, there was no more swelling around his eyes, and as far as we could tell, his vision and hearing hadn't been permanently affected. His fingers were still a mess, though. They were either fractured or he had those confounded soft tissue injuries that took longer to mend than broken bones. They pointed in the right direction, but the middle three digits on both hands were still swollen and tender.

Whatever the problem was, he couldn't grasp anything and had to use the outside edges of his palms to gather up whatever he needed to hold. I insisted on feeding him. Not only did I enjoy the intimacy of the act, but when he tried to do it, food went flipping all over the place. I didn't want to waste what little food we did have. But I didn't tell him that.

Rocky was still gone. Ian didn't seem too concerned: he said it happened every year about this time. The she-wolves went into heat in the winter and, well, Rocky would come back when he was ready. He usually had a few bite marks around his ears, but also sported a cocky grin and triumphant gait. It would have been nice to have him here to fetch squirrels or rabbits for supper—we were down to rationing the last few cashews.

I couldn't hunt, but was happy to get out of the cave every day to fetch water. It was a necessary task, but also allowed me to escape the gloom of the cave and Ian's obvious depression. I recognized the signs; all he wanted to do was sleep. He didn't even respond to my snuggling and pawing anymore.

I wanted to believe it was only cabin fever. Although technically it wasn't a cabin, he couldn't—or wouldn't—go far from our residence. He'd leave a few times a day for his toilet, and then return to his morose attitude and slumber. We couldn't go anywhere together because we had to take turns wearing the coat. So, he'd sleep all day and I'd fetch water, wood, or make tinder—debarking twigs and shaving wooden curls just to pass the time.

I tried to talk him into wearing my spare sweatpants, but he preferred his old breechclout and leggings. He did agree to wear my spare shirt, though, a short-sleeved tee shirt. I was still puzzled about how come the clothes in my backpack were at least two sizes too big for me. I didn't think oversize-clothes were the style, but the ones Ian had found me in were baggy, too. Well, whatever the reason, it was good because the shirt fit him better than it did me.

I brought my Leatherman with me every time I went to sit and wait for the water pan to fill, the all-purpose pot's lip set at the declivity of the slow-seeping spring. It was a sluggish process—it seemed to take half a day—but it was all we had available. The worst part was that I felt so vulnerable, just sitting there. I didn't want to admit to Ian, or even to myself, that I was worried about bandits. It wasn't that I was paranoid, but I was definitely on high alert.

Each day I ventured a little further away from home to scout out a faster flowing spring. With the increasingly cold, dry weather, we hadn't had snow on the ground for an easy water source in ages. It was clear again today, which meant cold again tonight, and slim to no chance of fresh snowfall. "It has to warm up to snow," I said aloud.

I decided to do something about the water situation: I stopped, knelt, and said an earnest, heartfelt prayer for food and a better way to get water. Praying worked immediately. I didn't find a cafeteria or a babbling brook right away, but I did get a wonderful sense of calm. I knew everything was going to be okay.

I stood up and made sure I knew where I was. I could still see the dense, dark green, overgrown holly bush that marked the opening of our cave. I climbed on top of a boulder to look for some wet or mossy rocks—spring markers—or better yet, a stream or a creek.

Then I heard it.

It sounded like a strangled duck. I looked toward the noise and saw movement near an overgrown, shrubby area. I hopped down from the rock, grabbed my pot, and headed toward the sound. Duck soup sounded good to me.

As I got closer, the noise didn't sound duck-like at all. I knew that noise: it was an elk! I had no idea why I knew it was an elk, but I was positive it was.

I licked my finger and stuck it up in the air to determine the wind direction. I wanted to be downwind as I approached any wildlife, especially one three times bigger than me!

I got closer and saw why the animal was making so much noise: it was stuck. It had walked out on thin ice, fallen through and thrashed wildly, trying to get out, and was now totally trapped.

Ice! Elk meat! That sounded better than duck soup to me. If there was ice, that meant there was water. If there was water, there might be fish, too. But, an elk! If I could manage to kill it and haul it back to camp, we'd have a winter's worth of meat, plus a hide for warmth, and maybe moccasins for Ian.

I backed up against a tree to gather my wits and review what I had available to accomplish this enormous feat.

First, there was me. Ian couldn't help, and I didn't want to make him feel worse than he already did about being worthless for heavy tasks. I felt it best not to let him know what was going on. My excuse to him was going to be that I had to work fast, that I didn't have time to go back to ask him for help. That really was the truth, so I rationalized that knowing ahead of time what I was going to say wasn't lying.

Second, I had my pan, the clothes and jacket on my back, and my Leatherman. But I needed a plan. I had to kill the beasty and then haul it uphill, all the way back to the cave where Ian could help me butcher it. It was time to ask for help again…back to my knees.

"Lord, I thank You for the food and water You've delivered. Now, if You would, could You please give me Your knowledge of what to do next? In Jesus's name, Amen."

I was halfway to my feet when I realized what I needed to do. I needed to harness the elk and pull him—no, no antlers, so this must be a her—out of the partially frozen pond. Once out, I could use elk power, the animal's own energy, to move the soon-to-be-foodstuffs to the cave.

I didn't have a harness, but I did have some rope with me. I had reclaimed Ian's bindings and used the coarse rope for a belt, folding up the length twice—quadrupling it—and tying it together every six inches with bits of fray in order to keep it together in one continuous, but usable, length. I took off my gloves and belt, and pulled apart the series of square knots, flipping whiskers of sisal all over the place. I opened out the length, tied a slipknot in one end, and then put my gloves back on.

I tiptoed to her. The elk, unnervingly quiet, didn't fear me. Or maybe she was just too worn out to care. I threw the noose over her nodding head.

"It's okay, honey, it'll all be over in a few minutes. Come on," I said, urging the animal to step onto a pile of fallen branches I had set out to use as a ramp. I felt like a fool, calling encouragements to an animal I planned to be eating for the next two or three months.

I got cooperation when I rubbed behind her soft, mousey-brown ears. She took what looked like a running start—it was actually a lunge—and then gave a horrendous wail as her front hooves hit solid ground. I tugged as hard as I could, pulling on the rope as if I, too, were trying to escape the watery trap, hoping she'd keep up her momentum, that her back legs would follow the front ones out of the icy bath.

104

We made it. She was weak, wobbly, and just about to fall over sideways. I ran to her side and shoved her back into balance. Glancing down, I saw her problem. She had a broken front leg—no veterinarian degree needed for that diagnosis. I would have had to put her down to put her out of her misery, even if I hadn't planned on making her our food source. There was no way I could drag a carcass that big up to the cave, though. I was going to have to coax her uphill—get her closer to home and the pantry.

Rather than climb the rise, I wound up leading her on a route parallel from where we were. I'd still have to drag or haul sections of meat uphill, but I wouldn't have to worry about wolves at our front door, sniffing out the remains. There was lots of wood left in my beaver-dam woodpile, too. I could probably fabricate a cache box with some of it, to contain and elevate the meat so scavengers, large or small, couldn't get to it.

The elk finally fell down and refused to move. I took off my coat, offered an improvised prayer of thanks, and then performed the *coup de grace*. I stabbed the blade of my Leatherman tool into her neck, hitting the carotid artery on the first try, and then yanked down to open the wound and increase the blood flow, moving away quickly so I didn't get a blood shower.

She looked at me—not with fear or anger—but with thanksgiving. Her struggle was over, and she was ceding her spent body to me. "Thank you," I said to my unnamed elk. "And thank You, Lord, for all You have given us."

The heat of excitement was over, and now the cold and dampness were penetrating—and constraining—my hands and chest. I was panting from my efforts and had to keep reminding myself to breathe through my nose. Unfortunately, I had already sucked in too much cold air through my mouth and now my lungs burned. I wiped my chill-stiffened palms and fingers on wisps of dried grass and clumsily stuck my marginally responsive arms into my coat.

I caught a second wind and ran uphill to the cave, jaws clenched against the frigid air, full of adrenaline fire, and eager to tell Ian what had happened. I stumbled through the bushy entrance, almost falling down as I blurted out, "I got an elk! It was just there, and I had to act fast. I managed to kill it, but do you think you can help me with the rest, butcher it, I mean?"

I babbled on, saying I needed to know how to field dress an elk because I knew nothing about it, that I doubted it was a skill I had ever had.

Ian was a blur of movement. I guessed what he had needed was to be an asset—he needed to be needed. He slipped his feet into the front of my neon green Crocs and shuffled down the hill, sniffing the air, quickly beelining to the sacrificial site, my directions unneeded.

He had brought the folding saw with him, and I still had the Leatherman, the only two cutting tools available to us. I handed mine to him and stepped out of his way—I didn't know what to do. He made a few stabs and slashes, yanked down and over in a couple of spots, and then stopped. I didn't watch the butchering process because, even though I knew this was a necessary part of our survival, I was still squeamish. That, and I had begun to like her. I'm glad I never called her anything beyond 'honey'— that would have really personalized her.

"I said, did ye ken this was a female?" Ian asked, apparently not for the first time. I nodded, still stunned. "Weel, she was pregnant with twins. That means we'll have some mighty tender meat and verra soft pelts. Can ye help me here?"

I was an air-breathing robot, only performing the simple tasks he asked of me. Ian, if he even noticed, didn't comment. He was busy and obviously happy about it. He appeared to be working at double speed. Each stroke of his arm, every cut or shifting of the carcass, had a purpose. There was no conversation, only a quick request for assistance once in a while.

We didn't have much time before it got dark. The air was still and that was good. I knew that before long, wolves, and maybe coyotes or panthers, would catch the smell of the fresh kill and come in for their share.

"I need to get water," I said. I hadn't spoken for what seemed like hours, and my voice started out as a squeak. "I forgot to tell you, we have a lake or creek or something, just over there," I pointed. "I'll be right back."

I grabbed the pot and hiked to where I had found the she-elk. The site where she had fallen in, and I had dragged her out, was still open. I eased the edge of the pot into the water and let it fill. I was suddenly aware of how cold the pot was. I must have left my gloves back at the field-dressing site. I pulled my coat sleeve down over my hand to insulate it from the cold handle.

For some reason, I turned the wrong way when I stood up and had to turn all the way around to head in the right direction. That's when I saw him. He was as big as Rocky, his upper lip lifted in a silent snarl, all his teeth showing. I must have smelled like a meat market. I froze.

I sent up a quick prayer, "Help!" and then stood up straight. I curled my upper lip and snarled right back. "Don't even think about it, dude. You go get your own dinner," I said menacingly. Then I flipped my head up, chin pointed at him as if to say, "Scoot, go away."

The wolf stuck his nose up, sniffed, growled quickly, and then turned away, running back into the woods in the opposite direction from where Ian was. I chuckled, nervous yet relieved. Apparently, he had caught a she-wolf scent. The stronger drive won out. The need to breed beat out the need to feed in the instincts of many, if not all, animals, two-legged or four. At least, that seemed to be the case here.

Ж

Ian had devised a sort of tall meat locker. Well, it wasn't a locker per se, but he had suspended the skinned carcass from a sturdy tree branch with the blue and white braided rope I had in my backpack. He had skinned her and folded up the hide. He had also gutted and skinned the two premature calves and had what I supposed were the edible innards and veal split between the two calf-hide bundles. "Do you need some help?" I asked.

"Aye, I'd appreciate it. It looks like a big dinner tonight. If ye could handle this parcel of meat, I'll carry the rest and the big hide. It still needs a lot of scrapin'. I was hopin' ye could help with that."

Ian turned out his hands. They were worse for the wear and tear, that is, cut and saw, of the ordeal. They hadn't completely healed, but the adrenaline of the butchering had overcome any pain in his broken fingers and still tender hands. He was hurting—I was sure of that—but he was also happy. He had found his worth. He was a man again.

The climb uphill to our cave was triumphant. Earlier in the day, I had gone for water, alone because Ian couldn't/wouldn't walk. My stomach and pantry were both empty. Now, we had both food and hope. Ian was back from depression, and *that* was better than having the meat.

I was stowing the bundle of veal in the deepest, chilliest crevices at the rear of the cave, when I realized how much of his maleness had returned. He was rubbing my bottom in a frisky way as I knelt, pushing the packages back as far as possible. It had been days since he had initiated any intimacy. How did that song go, 'It feels like the first time?' Welcome back, husband!

Ж

The next day was a lazy day. We had gathered firewood and water earlier, and were snuggled down for the rest of the afternoon, just waiting for nightfall. Elk steak was the fare for supper. All was calm on the surface, but something had been bugging me recently, so I decided to bring it up and give it a shot. "Why did those men attack you, and how could you possibly believe God would punish you by using scum like that to do His work?"

Ian grimaced. I could tell he was uncomfortable, but I wasn't sure why. I knew he was embarrassed about all aspects of his capture, hazing, and torture. We had never talked about it before because of that. And maybe I had just put him on the spot with questioning his intelligence.

"I'm sorry. I didn't mean that you were stupid to think God worked with creeps. It's just that, well—I'm sorry. I don't want to make you think about what happened. It's in the past. Let's forget about it and just think about the here and now, okay?"

Ian closed his eyes, took a deep breath, and held it for what seemed like forever. He let it out in a burst and finally opened his eyes. He looked wrong—as if there were someone else behind those orbs. It scared me. He looked directly at me without any sign of tenderness.

"I will forget and remember what I choose," he said flatly. He blinked a couple of times, and then started again, this time with the Ian I knew behind the eyes and voice, "Let's not talk about it, aye?"

My jaw dropped open when he—or his evil twin—spoke to me. I closed my mouth, swallowed, and said, "Sure."

And that was that.

*18 The Cougar that came to supper

Ian had reclaimed his position in life and now took an interest in the day-to-day chores. It wasn't as if he could do much himself—both the blisters he had received from the butchering, and the fingers that were still mending, limited him. The blisters never seemed to bother him, nothing more than an occasional gasp or flinch, but I doubt he would have said anything if they had.

Today he showed me how to scrape hides. It wasn't very complicated, a simple task—one he could have done himself—so I figured he had an ulterior motive.

"Show me what ye learned," he said, and handed me my Leatherman.

"Okay, Huck," I said sarcastically.

"What?" he asked, totally confused. "My name's Ian. I've never been called Huck in my life."

"You know, whitewashing picket fences, Tom Sawyer..." But Ian was clueless. "Oh, shoot," I said in quick recovery. "You went to school in Scotland, right?"

He nodded hesitantly, unsure of where this was going.

"Huck is a fictional character in a couple of American folklore books, stories about life in Missouri before slavery ended. Real cute books; next time I'm near a library, I'll check them out for you."

"Hmph," Ian snorted, with an attitude I didn't recognize; nor did I want to. I ignored it and went on with my task, showing off my hide-scraping skills, a talent I was evidently born with.

I wasted no time in finding an appropriately shaped sharp rock to use for scraping so I could save my knife's keen edge for other purposes. One of those uses was to whittle a needle out of a rib bone and carve an eye into it. I wanted to make something and insisted that Ian tell me rather than show me how. The moccasins I eventually fashioned for him were obviously my first attempt. They weren't identical in design but were functional and almost the same size. He didn't complain, but then again, he never did complain about anything.

Ж

"What color are my eyes?" I asked.

"What?" Ian answered in surprise.

"What is not a color," I chided. "I don't have a mirror, and I don't

109

know what color my eyes are." I leaned in close to him, almost nose to nose, so he would have to look at me.

"Weel, they're kinda like a summer bog. There's a bit of brown in them and lots of green, like the moss on the north side of a tree durin' the wet season. Why do ye wanna ken?"

"I suppose it must be a female thing. I don't know. I just wanted to know what I looked like. I can see I have straight brown hair, and I was hoping I had blue eyes or long eyelashes or something else that was pretty. I don't have any big moles or scars on my face, do I?" My hands flew up to my cheeks—skimming my flesh, searching for irregularities—as I suddenly became more insecure.

"No, no moles or scars, and yer jest about as pretty as any lass could be or any lad could want. I guess I'm not verra romantic. I shoulda told ye how pretty ye are." Ian bent down and brought my hand to his lips. He kissed it in a very proper, gentlemanly way, and continued his kissing all the way up my forearm to my shoulders. He then became very *improper* as he nibbled my neck while surreptitiously copping a feel a little lower. He worked his way back down with more kisses, and then stopped abruptly, teasing me by not following through after getting me all hot and bothered.

"Ye do have a wee mole," he flattered, "very wee and pale, more like a freckle, aye, right there." He nudged a spot on the right side of my face just above my lip with the knuckle of his index finger. He stroked it lightly and—when he was just under my nose—flipped up his finger, pushing my nose up in the air, and laughed out loud.

"You got me! Just you wait, mister, you won't see it coming when I get you back."

Ж

We had been together for about seven weeks now. We kept time by the moon phases and were up to our second new moon together. We were doing well with our store of preserved elk meat and a reliable water source nearby. We were able to get fish on a regular basis now, pretty much whenever we wanted a change from the elk meat. A little bread or rice, fruit, or vegetables would have been nice, but at least we had the protein group and wouldn't starve to death.

I had constructed a fishing rod out of a straight stick, a safety pin, and some of my dental floss. Ian hadn't ever seen nylon thread or a safety pin, and was amazed at how strong my little set-up was.

It wasn't the first time Ian was surprised at what I thought was a common item. I still didn't know 'when' I was. I was afraid to ask, and he wasn't keen on volunteering any dates. He spoke of his past, but never with any sort of political or historical marker mentioned. He had sailed to the Caribbean as a youth—was shanghaied, he said—but I knew pirates had been around since men sailed to sea. Current events were avoided with an immediate, "I dinna care fer politics," comment and a quick change of subject.

I guess what year it was didn't make a difference. If by some fluke of man-made science or nature I had transported to another time, there was nothing I could do about it. I was here, today, with a man I loved so much that I had married him—and I didn't want to leave. I didn't know or care where I was from. I was happy where I was now.

And that was that, for me.

Ж

We hadn't seen anyone but each other since Ian's 'incident,' and that was good. Rocky was usually around but had taken off two days earlier on another one of his Romeo escapades. This time, I wasn't concerned; I knew he'd be back when he was ready for human companionship.

Today I stayed back at the cave—again—while Ian took the pan and went to the lake to get water. He said he would do the fetching since I didn't feel well. Actually, I didn't have any symptoms of illness—no chills, aches, fever, or nausea. I just didn't have any energy. We had been eating well and getting plenty of horizontal exercise, but I was always tired. From the time I woke up, well after dawn, until I fell asleep shortly after sundown, I was beat. I tried to take at least one nap a day, but even that didn't seem to help. I figured I was either going to get better or worse, but so far, I was wrong. This had been going on for a lunar month, and I still felt the same way every day—just tired.

Ж

"Now I want ye to get yer rest. And make sure ye remember to eat. I'm gonna check the area. I got this itchy, crawlin' feelin' that somethin' isna right. Ye stay here, and I'll be back in a day or two, maybe three or four. Is there anythin' ye need before I leave?"

Ian had made sure the pot was full of water, that there was plenty of wood stacked in the back, and that the fire was burning well. It was cold today, so he was taking the coat we shared, leaving me with the stiff but warm elk-hide robe.

He came over and rubbed my back and shoulders, gradually making his way up to my neck with his now healed hands. He gently stroked the underside of my chin, making me purr like a kitten with a belly full of

111

salmon. I knew he didn't want to go beyond first base. He was content just to pleasure me with the caressing and attention he knew I loved. If he had wanted to go all the way, he wouldn't still have the coat and moccasins on. I reached out to him, "Take care out there. I love you."

"As I do ye. I'll be verra careful—I wouldna want to damage our, er, yer coat," he said, bending to give me a peck on the lips. "I'll be back before ye get a chance to miss me." He turned and quietly pulled back the branches, set them right again, and then was gone.

I dozed on and off for I didn't know how long, then had to get up—again—for a potty break. I'd swear I was peeing more than I was drinking. I did my business but didn't want to go back inside right away. It was sunny and there wasn't any wind, rain, or snow intruding on the perfect day. It seemed like a good time to bask in the bright winter sun's rays. After spending so much time in the cave, I was probably lacking vitamin D, which might explain my lack of energy. I leaned back against the rock face and addressed the sun, ready to charge my solar batteries and get those much-needed sunshine vitamins.

After twenty minutes or so of achieving irradiated contentment, I forced myself to move. Now I knew why the cat always chose to lie in the sunny spot—I was just about purring myself. Unfortunately, my bones and muscles had settled into the rock's concave contour.

I groaned, leaned forward, and rose to re-evaluate our site. My little world—or rather, our little world—what were we going to do when spring came? Would Ian take me to meet his family, would we go live with the Indians, or would we just be nomads, always trying to stay one step ahead of those heathens who had tried to kill him?

I shook off the uneasiness. Solar regeneration and reflection period was over; time to be productive. I decided to check out the landscape from a different perspective. If I had just arrived here, what would I do? I'd find a reference point, that's what I'd do. And I'd do it from a high place so I could see in all directions, too. I looked around and spotted a trail I had never seen—or at least never paid attention to—before. That trickle of a deer path up there was probably where I had been climbing when I fell and cracked my head several weeks ago. Worth taking another look, I thought. But this time, I'd be more careful. I wanted to make sure I returned to square one on my feet—not on my back—and with both my skull and memory intact.

I didn't have climbing gear but was confident that I could manage. The way was clear and there weren't any obvious obstacles. The wind was calm, and that was a good thing. All I had to keep me warm as I climbed the tall hill—or was it a short mountain?—were my two shirts and the sun. Either way, this tall earthen lump was still the highest rise in the area and had the best vantage point.

I took baby steps up the path. Haste makes waste—and I wasn't going to risk getting wasted again. I tested every step before putting my weight down. I wanted to make sure I didn't slip or start a rockslide. I was also using the three-point system. I always had three points—two feet and a hand or two hands and one foot—touching a solid object before I ventured another move. It was slow progress, but gave me peace of mind: slow, steady, and safe.

That worked for thirty minutes or so. Then, almost halfway up, I got scared. There was nothing to be afraid of, but I was starting to freak out. Panic attack? Nah, well, maybe. Whatever it was, I wanted to go back home to my stony shell, puny fire, and stinky elk-hide robe. The view from the hilltop could remain a mystery for another day.

I picked my way back down the hill just as carefully as I had edged my way up. I was intent on what I was doing and almost missed hearing it. Someone, or something, was rifling through my cave! I didn't have a weapon and didn't know if I had the courage to fire a gun even if I had one. I hung back, hoping that whoever or whatever was intruding would just get what they wanted and leave.

Ian! Oh my God, if he came back and didn't notice that someone—or something—was in there, he might be attacked. I decided to bypass the cave's entrance and head straight to the route we used for fetching water. If Ian was already on his way back, I could intercept him.

As I got closer to our front yard, I heard a noise like someone in pain. The yowl was coming from our front porch. If someone was injured, I couldn't just leave him in pain, even if he was a bad guy. Well, I'd take a peek and see if that someone looked harmless or not. But, no matter what, if it was one of those creeps who attacked Ian, I was outta here! He could take care of any injuries himself!

I was wrong, and wrong again. First, he wasn't outside the cave, he was inside it. Second, he wasn't a man. *She* was a wildcat: a cougar, a big old mountain lion! I'd seen pictures of them in books; I must have if I recognized her so quickly. I just didn't know they were so huge! Her body was as long as Ian's, and that wasn't counting her yard-long tail. She looked like she was only half-alive though. She was panting and her head was flopped sideways on the ground, her tongue not quite fitting back into her jaws. The good news was that I didn't see any frothing at her mouth. She was in trouble, but not rabid.

Apparently, she was heading toward the food cache at the back of the cave when she collapsed. She must have smelled the meat but didn't have the strength to walk those last few feet to get to it.

I managed to inch close enough to her for a quick inspection. Both her front paws were injured. Coarse twine was wrapped around them, and it had cut off the circulation. It looked like she would lose her paws, or die, if I didn't get them unbound. I gasped as I flashed back to Ian's poor hands when I found him. Could it be that those heathens got to her, too?

I talked softly to the languishing feline. "Hey, Lady, I'll be quick." I looked up to see her reaction to me touching her. If she knew I was there, it didn't bother her. She was panting slowly, near death I think, and didn't even flinch involuntarily as I cut the sisal cording that had evidently been part of a noose-style trap.

"Here, let me give you a drink." I poured water into the shallow mess kit plate and offered it to her. She wasn't able to do anything but roll her eyes. She wasn't much of a threat now but could be if she was in good health.

I did my best to dribble water into her mouth, managing to get in a few drops. At least now she could pull her tongue back into her face. I pulled out the elk shinbone I had planned to use for broth and lay it within reach of her. If she wanted to chew on something, she could chew on the bone rather than my hand. That is, if she found enough strength to lift her head.

"Pussy cat, pussy cat, you're delicious, duh dum, de dum dum," I hummed some song. I wished I knew all the words, but it didn't make a difference to her. Music soothes the savage beast, all right. She was too weak to move, but still seemed quite mellow for a wild animal. I figured it was because she knew I was here to help her. That or she realized 'what's the use in fighting?' Nah; animals would fight to the last breath, or at least so I'd heard, somewhere, I thought.

I shook off the insecurity of not knowing how I knew what I knew. She evidently realized I wouldn't hurt her. "Okay, Lady, I want you to rest and get your strength back so you can get better and go back home."

I adjusted my bed to accommodate my new roommate, and lay down for my afternoon nap, positioning myself in front of the entrance. If I didn't hear Ian approach, he'd still have to step on me before getting in all the way and finding a cougar in the larder. Better a squished Evie than a spooked, injured wildcat were my final thoughts as I drifted to sleep.

Sometime later, I awoke. Time wasn't measured in minutes or hours for me, just morning, noon, and night. There was nothing to do, no one to talk to, and nothing to read. Read: I just remembered reading the back of cereal boxes at breakfast when I was a kid. Hey, a childhood memory! Now if I could only have about a kazillion more, that'd be nice—I think.

Evening came and Ian was still gone. Oh well, I didn't feel like anything was wrong. He was in good physical health now and had been taking care of himself for years. Worry wouldn't help, anyway. "Lord, please keep him safe. In Jesus's name, Amen." Now, all was good.

I checked in on my feline patient. She had been gnawing on the shinbone and was now licking her paws. "Hey there, Lady, are you doing better now?"

She looked up from her cleaning, purred, and then gave me a quick, "Rawol."

"That's good. I think it's just you and me tonight, Lady. I'll try not to snore too loudly. Care for a bedtime story?"

Just as the words left my lips, I realized I didn't know any bedtime stories. "Okay, then I'll just sing and hum. Pussy cat, pussy cat, I love you, yes, I do...."

I didn't know if she liked my singing or not, but she did get closer to me. It was dark and getting colder. I was on the chilly side of the cave. I always slept on top of the elk robe to keep as much of the ground chill away as I could. I was depending on the fire to stay warm tonight, especially since I didn't have Ian's warmth, but I had let the fire die down to just a few hardwood embers because cats didn't like fire, or so I thought.

I covered all my exposed areas as best I could with the little solar blanket and curled into the fetal position. It didn't help. I was shivering uncontrollably. Lady saw my situation, raised up, and pussyfooted over to me, stepping gingerly on her still tender feet. She lay down behind me and placed one big paw on top of my head.

"Oh, Lord, help me now," I prayed quickly. Lady started licking the back of my head. My long hair immediately got tangled in her mouth. "Just a minute," I said, and turned over. "Maybe bangs would be easier for you to clean."

Lick, lick; it was just fine by her. For me it was a bit rough though, literally. Her tongue was coarse, stinky, and very muscular. "Thanks, that's enough for tonight," I said and scooted away a couple of inches, close enough for warmth, but not touching her.

She took the hint and paid attention to her own grooming instead, licking her paw, swiping it across her face, cleaning off leftover dinner. I turned over and slept warm and comfortably that night, totally at peace with God, my surroundings, and myself.

*19 Kidnapped

The next morning, I visited my little beachfront property to fetch water. Ian still hadn't returned from his trip to search for intruders. Before he left, he said he hadn't heard or seen anyone, but that his 'wame was in a knot,' and he wouldn't be able to eat or sleep until he made sure the two of us were safe. He needed to confirm or dismiss his suspicions, and I could understand that. It was better for him to be out securing our domain than to stay back here with me, worrying, and imagining the worst.

I had left Lady in the cave, contentedly cleaning her fur. I figured she'd leave when her feet were healed or she felt like it. I knew she was a wildcat and unpredictable. I also knew I couldn't just kick her out! I mean, I was only one woman, and she was twice my size, and one notch above me on the food chain.

I didn't mind sharing the cave space with her; I actually enjoyed her company. I did make sure she knew my voice, though. I sang when I left, and I'd sing when I came back. It was an easy way to announce my departures and arrivals...and I certainly didn't want to spook an injured mountain lion.

I was quick about getting the water. Ian had the jacket, and it was too cold for me to be outside for very long with just two shirts for warmth. The winter weather wasn't too intense, but it wasn't cozy either.

He came out of nowhere. I didn't even have a chance to get half a scream out when his grimy hand clamped over my mouth and nose, nearly smothering me. I wanted to bite him, but the force of his hand pushing my face back towards my ears made it impossible to open my mouth. I couldn't see who it was, but he couldn't be much taller than I was by the way he was holding me against his cheek. I could smell him—although I wished I couldn't. Foul wouldn't even begin to describe his odor.

His stink was the last thing I remembered.

I woke up with a start, shuddering with cold. I was propped up against a broad, rough tree trunk, my hands and feet securely bound with torn rags, my fingers icy cold from the loss of circulation. Indistinct voices were in the area, but no one was close to me. I was foggy-headed, disoriented, and trying to figure out where I was, when the miasma hit me. The stench made me want to throw up immediately.

And then I remembered: abducted.

I didn't know stink could have layers. Without even trying, I could smell everything from bacon to feces, horse sweat to straw, with the lingering aroma of alcohol and body odor topping the others. I managed to tuck my chin to my chest and breathed my own body odor, the familiar musty scent calming my queasy stomach.

I couldn't see, not because it was night, but because I was blindfolded. The greasy rag obscured most, but not all, of my vision. My captors were sloppy in addition to being stinky. They had left a gap in my masking, and I could see the ground. If I tipped my head back, I could probably see my assailant. Or at least I was pretty sure I would be able to.

Footfalls stopped in front of me. "Chee lookth good enough to et, dun't chee, Abe," uttered one hick. The man sounded as if he were missing quite a few teeth. He smacked his lips, and then slurped back the slobbery saliva into his mouth. I felt his breath close to me and then—Gross!—he licked my face! "Tasteth good, too. Now why'd ye have to wear a man's thirt; those bubbies are too purdy to hide away."

I felt his hands pawing at my breasts, trying to get through the flannel shirt to my crawling, goose-pimply skin beneath. I froze. Pop, pop, pop. He ripped my shirt open and started grabbing at the t-shirt underneath. I didn't want to give him the pleasure—perverted or otherwise—of watching me squirm. I grimaced, sniffed repeatedly, and squeezed my eyes tight under the blindfold, blinking back my tears of fear and frustration.

Then I heard them: out of sync footsteps marching towards us. One determined person had a lame foot or leg—I could hear it dragging. "Watch out fer her and dinna git too close," a voice boomed, apparently from Gimpy. "Dinna ever trust a bitch." He snorted in a wad of mucous then spat, hurling a loogie very close to my left side.

I couldn't help but flinch, and that gave them all a big laugh.

"Oooh, thirsty are ye? I got more where that come from," cooed Gimpy. The spittle spewer followed through with another big snort, stopping for dramatic effect before he lobbed another spit bomb, almost on top of the other one. His cohorts laughed again, hooting and cheering their hideous hero.

I didn't move, barely breathed, and did my best to keep a stoic face. I didn't want them to get more wound up. Hopefully, they would get bored with my lack of reaction to their taunts and would let me go. Yeah, right, like that would ever happen. Well, I could hope.

Hope. That's what I needed! I needed to pray, pray right now. And I needed to do it loudly and with self-assurance.

"Dear Lord," I called out, the initial squeak becoming a forceful and commanding voice, "Thank You for this beautiful day. Thank You, too, for my good health. I ask You now for Your help in this hour of need. My host today seems to have a cold and needs his lungs healed. These kind gentlemen also need help finding their home because they're apparently lost. They need help, too, with their eyesight because I believe they think they've found and trussed up a deer. Please guide them home and provide them with good vision and a stocked larder. In Jesus's name, Amen."

"Ha, ha, ha, ha. Ye think that God is gonna help ye? Think agin, ye slut. Why I…"

Whack! A loud bang exploded right next to me. It sounded as if someone got hit upside the head with a two by four. I ventured a peak through the blindfold and found out I was close to being right. A very short but wide, tough-looking old woman wearing an oversized coat was holding a hefty chunk of firewood in her hand, and it looked like she was getting ready to swing it again.

"Dinna I tell ye to get a whore! This is a good, God-fearin' girl. And lookie here," she prodded my belly with the piece of wood, "she's with child. Ye dinna wanna chance hurtin' an unborn bairn, do ye? Let 'er go and tell 'er yer sorry. Go aheid, do it—now!" barked the old woman.

No one moved. "But, Ma," groaned the man called Abe as he shuffled toward her.

"Now, I said! Do ye need another thump upside the heid?"

I felt hands fumbling with the ropes. Abe was obeying Ma. The nauseating stink was back, but I felt like my prayer was being answered. I was almost free.

The woman referred to as Ma made shooing noises to the person removing my bindings. She gently pushed aside my hair and untied the blindfold. "Sorry 'bout that, darlin'. Those boys get a little wound up sometimes, and, weel, a good woman wouldna have anythin' to do wi' 'em. There's some whores down the way that will take their minds off their…er…weel, I think ye ken what I mean. I told 'em ye were with child to scare 'em off. Now, let's clean ye up a bit, and then we'll get ye back to yer home."

I rolled over onto my knees, lifted my head, said, "Thank You, Lord," and then looked over to Ma and said, "Thank you, ma'am."

The oddly attired woman with the big heart offered me her hand and helped me to my feet. "Men," she said with disdain as she dusted off her skirts, "the little head rules the big 'un, evra time!"

119

I looked at her gapped-tooth smile and grinned back at her. I didn't want to get too chummy with her, but she did have a good sense of humor. "I don't know where I am, ma'am. If you could show me the way back to where the men, um, found me, I'd appreciate it."

Ma turned away from me and called out in a booming voice, "Abe, git yer sorry butt over here, and bring Glory." She turned back to me and explained, "Glory's the mule. Yer light enou' that she'll let ye ride 'er. Ye couldna been too far away from here. The boys was only gone but half a day er so."

Abe walked up to us, leading Glory by her reins of knotted and twisted fabric scraps. Her tattered and ancient saddle had been patched with various colors and grades of both tanned leather and rawhide. It had been mended many times, but looked safe enough to carry me.

"Sorry 'bout the cunfusion, ma'am. Can I hep ye up inta the saddle?"

Abe looked a little too eager to boost me onto the mule. He had been deprived of his jollies and probably wanted very much to have his hands on my backside.

"No thanks, I can manage," I replied courteously. I grabbed the front of the saddle where the horn should have been, and put my foot into the stirrup, glad that I was wearing pants. "I'm ready to go if you'll just lead the way, please."

I wore a faint, polite smile on my face, but my insides were like a convenience store slushy drink—cold and unstable. The physical side of me was desperately holding back vomit. I took quick, frantic gulps of air to try and keep my stomach calm. I glanced at the pathetic male next to me. Part of me wanted to grab the reins and bolt away from him without regard to whose mule I was riding. Another part wanted to find a safe spot to sit down and weep until the tears ran dry. I didn't want him near me, but knew I needed Abe to guide me back to where he had found me. I was desperate to get back to that little hole in the mountain that I called home.

I thought I was in control of my emotions, and then realized that tears were rolling down my cheeks. I sniffed my runny nose and wiped my face with my sleeve, trying to clear away the tears while I pushed my fear down deep into my gut—I could be afraid later.

Ma had been right about the distance. Only a couple hours later, Abe stopped and offered to help me get down. I shook my head and slid off the short-legged animal by myself.

"Sorry 'bout the misunderstandin' there, ma'am. No hard feelin's, I hope," he said, then hung his head down. He looked at his feet, shod with worn-out, poorly made boots, and pushed together a small pile of twigs and mud. He obviously didn't want to leave me. He really was pathetic, and a whore who was offered money might be the only one who would have sex with him. Maybe if he cleaned up a bit, he would have a better chance of attracting a woman, but I wasn't the one to suggest it. I didn't want to become his friend—I wanted to be clear of him as soon as possible.

"No harm, no foul," I said. He looked at me as if I were speaking Greek. "Oh, I'll be fine. Thanks for returning me to where you…found me. Uh, good-bye, and have a safe trip back."

"Thanks," he said as he pushed his hair away from his eyes. He looked down at his dirty hand and wiped it on his trousers. Maybe he would learn to clean up his appearance all by himself. I hoped so, for his sake.

I didn't move until Abe was out of view. I didn't want him to see which direction I took to get home. He was finally out of eyesight and earshot; I no longer heard the plodding of him or the mule down the hill. I felt myself relax for the first time in probably six hours.

Suddenly, I had to pee so badly, my belly ached and my eyes watered—my stress had been so great, my bladder had stopped working. That was a minor blessing in itself; I didn't have to drop my drawers in front of strangers during my capture. "Thanks again, Lord," I said to the Man above.

Fluid output taken care of, I walked to the edge of the lake. "My lake, my water, my fish," I pronounced. I guzzled down two cupfuls of water, and then refilled the pan I had dropped during my capture. "Fresh water for Lady, if she's still there."

I started up the rise. I felt a smile begin to cover my face. It was time to sing for my houseguest. "What's new pussycat, wo, oh, wo, wo, wo…."

I made it home quickly, walking with so much of a lilt that I was almost skipping.

Suddenly, it hit me: Ian! I hoped he hadn't come home to find a cougar in the living room.

"Hey, honey, I'm home," I hollered before I pulled back the front door bush. Suddenly, I felt a chill. After my recent experience of abduction by strangers, I was afraid there might be someone inside who I wasn't expecting.

"Hello, hello; anyone in there?" Oh, this fear was ridiculous. And paranoia was not healthy for me or anyone else.

"Rowal."

Lady was still home. I pulled open the branches and chuckled, then remembered to continue singing my refrain.

How funny was that? I was afraid to go into a cave until I heard a mountain lion roar. Only then would it be safe to go in. Welcome to my strange and unusual world.

Ж

Lady was mending nicely. It looked as if there wouldn't be any permanent damage to her feet. I knew she was a wild cat and would leave when she felt like it. That was cool. I didn't think it was a good idea for Rocky to have competition for favorite feral friend of the family.

I tried not to talk to myself as a rule, but made sure I at least hummed as I went about munching my little elk jerky dinner and making up a bed. I was and wasn't lonely. I really liked being by myself at times, but it was nice to know someone was coming home to me. It looked like Lady and I would be the only two sleeping at home tonight, though.

The fire was banked for the night. I was snuggled down with my backpack as a pillow and the 'metal' blanket—Ian said it must be from Italy—over my body. I was still cold—I wished Lady would join me again like that first night. I couldn't keep still. I was fidgeting, turning from side to side, my legs jerking—unwillingly trying to generate heat by movement.

Lady had been content, settled down near the low-burning fire, munching the last shinbone I had extracted from our elevated cache, before I lay down and started my tossing and twitching. I guess I was disturbing her because she came over to me, lowered her head, turned in a circle twice, and set one big paw in the middle of my chest. It was if she were saying, "Sit still!"

"Okay, I'll try, but I'm cold. Why don't you sleep here again?" I asked and patted the space between me and the entrance.

Lady kneaded her paws into my chest with her claws retracted. I guessed this was the feline version of a goodnight story. She stopped after about a dozen hearty pokes and lay on her side next to me. I looked over at her to say good night and then saw it—her belly was moving. My Lady was pregnant.

Pregnant! Old Ma had said I was pregnant to scare her boys away from me. I couldn't be pregnant, could I? Well, I guess I knew *how* I could be. I hadn't even thought of the possible consequences—or was that effects?—of our intimacy. Well, if I were, there was nothing to do about it now.

*20 Re-encounter

Ian refused to give up on his reconnaissance mission—quitting wasn't in him. He didn't want anyone coming into his territory or anywhere near it, discovering him or his wife. Even though he hadn't seen the enemy or any signs of him, the feeling that something wasn't right hadn't left. He could actually feel the proximity of evil—the uneasiness like centipedes crawling up his legs, crossing over his belly, seeking the tender spots on his face—and that made him nervous.

Evie was secure at their cave site with food, water, and wood for the fire. She'd be fine for a few more days. He wouldn't stop his search until the uneasiness was gone or he found the cause of it. His instincts for self-preservation were working again. It felt good to have a family to protect.

He smelled the horses before he heard or saw them. The crudely saddled, sorrowful equines were hobbled near a massive oak tree at the edge of an impromptu encampment. Eight shabbily dressed men were shuffling about, kicking and scooting their boots in the fallen leaves and muddy snow, apparently searching for a lost object.

Ian slipped through the trees toward their camp, staying quiet and hidden just in case the men weren't friendlies. Comrade, stranger, or foe: his manner had always been to stay invisible until he wanted to be seen.

Ian recognized their voices as soon as he was close enough to hear them. His hand automatically went to his side where his dirk should have been. He didn't have so much as a sharpened stick for a weapon. His jaws clenched tight, so tight, he felt a molar move. He inhaled and exhaled once slowly to compose himself, and then went back into stealth mode, holding back the urge to vomit.

It was them.

He thought the heathens had moved out of the area after they had tortured and nearly killed him last fall. Was it only eight or nine weeks ago? They were still here, though, or were back again.

When he first encountered the gang last summer, he was sure they weren't locals. They had the gear and social structure of a traveling band of misfits, like colonial gypsies. What could possibly interest them here? These Carolina backwoods held only riches for hunters and trappers. They'd have better pickings working the larger towns or ports where they'd have a bigger pool of potential suckers. Then again, these men didn't seem to have either brains or ambition.

Ian stayed out of sight and downwind. The gang was preoccupied and

124

wouldn't be aware of his presence, but the horses were smarter than they were—they would smell a stranger and get excited and possibly alert the idiots.

The men had given up on their ground search and were now clustered together in the center of the clearing, like gnats on a molasses drop, arguing amongst themselves about which direction they should take.

"Dammit, Joel, now ye went and lost the coin. Now we'll never know if it wuz heids er tails, and wuz we suppost to go east or west. And that wuz my last coin, dag nab it!"

The grumblings continued, now on a different topic—they were low on food. "Not even a weevily bannock crumb...."

One loud, deep voice boomed out over the others. "Weel, you can all jest figure it out fer yerselfs. I gotta go take a shit. And don't go tryin' to take off without me agin, ye hear? Goddam good fer nuthin' idjits..."

The fireman grumbled and hobbled away from the group. Ian recognized him by both his voice and his gait. Ian's feet began burning with the memory. He was the one who had led the mob in his capture and torture those few weeks ago.

The fireman laughed when his captive's feet caught fire as he walked the gauntlet over burning coals. He made a joke of it, pissing on them, urging the others to join in the water sport. It was Ian's most humiliating memory, and it was back in his head now, dancing in circles, taunting his spirit.

Ian wanted to isolate the fireman from the others for more than one reason. Besides wanting his revenge for the indignity, the bearded bastard was wearing his boots. Evie's moccasins were special to him, but they were no match for his old boot's tough leather soles. He wanted them back.

It looked as if the fireman was a bit bashful. He walked for several minutes before dropping his pants and squatting to do his business. Ian sneaked up to within eight feet of him and waited for his opportunity.

The man took a deep breath, as if to grunt, then suddenly turned toward Ian. Ian dropped to his belly just as the man let out a big belch. "Ah, that feels better," the fireman commented aloud, and turned forward again, contentedly scratching his hairy buttocks.

Ian remained face down on the mess of crusty snow, twigs, and leaves. He thought his position was obvious, but the fireman wasn't looking for him, so hadn't seen him.

The man with the bellyache stayed in his squat for hours—or so it seemed to Ian—exuding an eye-watering, stomach-churning stench. Ian wanted to wait until he was done so he wouldn't have to step in his crap, but the man was really and truly full of shit.

Ian brought up his hand to cover his nose, then heard it. The man heard it, too, and quickly jumped up, tugging on his pants, trying to get them up and fastened in mid-squirt.

"Hello there, would you tell Dani you found her phone…"

Ian didn't pay attention to the words. He was too busy running toward his intended victim, knocking him forward, quickly grabbing and twisting his neck; swiftly, coolly, and effectively breaking it with the pop, snap that indicated the deed was done.

Ian dragged the body away from the site of retribution, into the twiggy underbrush, and waited, his heart racing. The voice had stopped. It sounded as if it had come from his chest! How could that be? He shook his head to clear out the echo of the voice; he had to take care of this situation first.

He grabbed the dead man's right foot and twisted off the boot. The left one was easier to remove and came off at the first tug. At least there wasn't any crap on them. Just the same, he rubbed the boots with crusty snow and dead leaves. He wanted to get the man's stench off of them. He'd give them a good scouring when he got back to the cave and its supply of dry, leafless soil.

He frisked the corpse and recovered a poor excuse for a knife, its blade nicked, the handle wrapped in a soiled rag. It, too, was probably stolen. There were a couple of pewter buttons and a ribbon in the fireman's pockets. He left them there; he had no use for them. He *would* take the shabby knife, though; consider it payment for the trouble he had to go through to retrieve his own property. The dirk they stole from him when he had been captured—a keen edged blade with a bone handle, carved by his first wife—was gone, probably sold for cheap whisky or loose women. His face flared in renewed anger at its loss. If it were possible to kill the fireman again, he'd do it. The dirk was all he had left of Robin.

Ian waited to see if the others would return to check on their cohort. An hour went by. The dead body was stinking more now that the wind had calmed. No one came. Evidently, they didn't care, and neither did he.

He left the fetid hulk where it was and headed away from the vermin's campsite, carrying his boots. If he wore them now, someone might pick up the scent and follow him back. Those men might be stupid, but that didn't mean one of them didn't have a good hunting dog that could track him. Then again, they were probably so dim-witted, they wouldn't even think to try.

So, one mystery solved and another discovered. The 'feelings' he had been having were because the heathens were back in his home territory. He didn't like knowing that they were nearby but felt better now that he had a knife for protection. He also felt worse, though, because those idiots might come back and, finding their slain companion, hunt for the killer. It was time to leave, to take Evie away from here.

And what was that spirit voice? Where did it come from? And why did it sound like Evie?

Ian backtracked to the lake where he and Evie fetched their water. He located his private little grotto, settled in, and built a small fire. Once inside, he recreated the same movements he had made in the grove when he had heard the woman's voice. He dropped to his belly, just as he had done before, then moved his hand up to cover his nose.

Nothing.

He squatted near the fire and cursed in exasperation. What happened? He was sure he had heard it. He stood up, too mad to stay still, and then saw it—the jacket. That's what was different—he was wearing Evie's coat at the time.

He settled his arms into the sleeves, leaving the ragged metallic seam closure in front open like always, and then dropped to his belly.

It was back.

"Hello there, would you tell Dani you found her phone? I guess I've lost it again. You can call…"

And then there was silence. He wasn't hallucinating, was he?

Ian repeated the movement a third time and was saved his sanity: the voice was real. He quickly patted the jacket, searching for the source of the sound. His hand passed over his heart, muffling the words.

The voice without a body was coming from a small, hard piece of the coat, situated close to the heart area, but near the oxter, too. He took it off and found one of those wee seams Evie called zippers inside, just above the hardness. He pulled the metal tab and found a little black packet inside the pocket.

There wasn't any noise coming from it now. It was shiny on one side and appeared to be made of a dark, smoky-colored glass. The other side was smooth, its texture like leather, but hard and tough like metal. It had markings, etchings maybe, and a wee hole with a glass button embedded into it. On one side were small slits with pieces of metal pushed into the

127

leather. It was a sturdy parcel, but looked like it was delicate, too. He didn't think it was dangerous, or meant to be, but it was definitely quiet and harmless now.

That voice; he knew that voice. It was Evie. What did it say? "Hello" and "tell Danny you found her fone?"

He had already decided not to go back to the cave tonight. He had just taken a life and, even though the man deserved to die, he felt he shouldn't be close to Evie until he was cleansed. She was in no danger where she was, and he was close enough that he would know if anyone approached their home. He also needed to be away from her to think about this new development.

He pulled out the wee box again. He remembered a few things Cousin Ramona had told him about some of the goods in her time—little boxes with pictures and voices, and music that came out of them. Could this be one of those? Maybe, but he hadn't thought they'd be this small.

Evie had said a few things in the past two months that made him wonder about not *where* she was from, but *when* she was from. She couldn't remember anything in particular about her life before her fall, but had told him she knew North Carolina was one of the fifty united states. The *fifty* states she had said. He didn't tell her he had only heard of thirteen, and that they were called colonies or commonwealths.

He thought at the time she was just babbling from the head bashing. But then there was the time she called him Huck and said something about 'before slavery ended' and Missouri—wherever that was. There was also her backpack and all the things in it: the fancy knife, the lantern, the food bags, water bottles made of soft glass, and the thin metal blanket. He knew they couldn't possibly be from Italy—but he wouldn't tell her that.

She couldn't even recall her own name, although she did like the name Evie he had given her. Could she be that Danny? The voice sounded like her, but Danny was a boy's name.

He didn't want to believe she was like Auntie Sarah, Cousin Ramona, and her husband Gregg—fairies, travelers through time—but there was no other explanation.

Ian's mind was going in circles. He couldn't complete a thought because there were no beginnings or endings to the person he knew as Evie. She just 'was,' was who she was—beautiful, compassionate, intelligent, resourceful—but ignorant of life as he knew it. He had already decided to keep joking about how clever those Italians were when using her tools, trying to make her believe that that's where they were from. He never commented when she mentioned events or knowledge he knew were not of this time. He kept hoping she would forget about those, too, and would believe they were all a dream. He wanted to make her understand that this land, this time, was her reality—and where she belonged.

But this was her coat he was wearing, the one he had found her in. He held onto the wee box and pushed the flat, shiny piece on the top. It was flush with the rest of the box. It didn't stick up, but did push in slightly at his touch. He heard a small musical tone and the glass lit up with pretty blue colors dancing across its surface. Suddenly, a fine painting of a multi-colored cat appeared, then quickly faded, went back to smoky black, and then there she was...

Evie.

Only it wasn't the Evie he knew. This woman *looked* like Evie but was 30 or 40 years older and fat. Not obese fat, but fat like an older woman tends to get if she's lived an easy life. The picture of the plump, mature woman with a sly smile covered the whole glass side of the box.

"Hello there, would you tell Dani you found her phone? I guess I've lost it again. You can call..." The voice and picture disappeared even faster than it had appeared.

Maybe this was Evie's mother and she just sounded like her. "Yeah, and maybe wee magic boxes jest fall out of the sky with pretty young lasses attached to them; pretty lasses who make ye fall in love with them, and then go back to their own time like Auntie Sarah and Cousin Ramona did, rippin' out yer heart, and leaving ye as an empty shell."

Ian's head dropped forward into his hands. He rubbed his forehead so hard and for so long, he was inadvertently inflicting pain on himself. He pulled his hands back and saw that they were still filthy from the trip. He gently picked up the dark box and put it back into the hidden pocket of the jacket. If Evie hadn't found it by now, she probably wouldn't—if he put it back where he found it.

He couldn't believe she was deceitful. If she did know who she was or where she was from, she would have told him by now. He would talk to her about it, but he would talk about it when he was ready. Right now, he wanted to cleanse himself of the day's events. Talking was the last thing he wanted to do.

*21 Journey to New Bern

Ian was fully aware that I didn't like his idea of leaving our home—I wouldn't budge, and he had had to do all the packing. It really wasn't much of a sit in; there wasn't much to get together, just my backpack and the elk-hide bundle containing our preserved meat.

I sat on a moss-covered log, elbows on my knees, hands cupping my jaws. "Pbbtt." I pursed my lips again and blew a complete raspberry serenade. "Pbbtt, pbbtt, pbbbbbbb…."

"Now, what kinda song is that?" he asked as he kicked the remains of the fire into the snowy rubble around us, hiding all evidence of our first night's campsite.

"It's a protest song. Only I don't know any words I can sing that won't make you angry, so I'll just make rude noises. Pbbt, pbbt, pbbbbbbt."

"Ye ken, I wouldna do this if it wasna necessary. I ken you liked it at the cave, but we're not safe there anymore. We canna go back again. Now, I'll find my auntie and she'll ken how to help ye. As I said before, she's a great healer. I think she can aid ye with the fatigue, and yer memories, too. I trust her, and I want ye to tell her everythin' ye ken. If ye can be mended, she's the one to do it. Now, ye may not like this, but I'll have to leave ye with her fer jest a short while. But then I'll be back before ye have a chance to miss me."

"But you know I don't care if I can remember my past or not. I just want to be with you. I miss you now, and you haven't even left."

"Now, I'm yer husband and ye must do as I say. And I say to come with me."

Ian's voice was stern and compassionate at the same time. I could feel the love and pain in his voice and, no matter how much I didn't want to go, I knew I'd do as he asked.

"I'll follow you to the ends of the earth. It's just that when you say you have to go and leave me behind, I kind of freak out. Can't we just pretend we're only visiting your family and not talk about me needing help or you taking off?"

"Aye, darlin', that will suit me fine. Now, would ye please put on yer coat so we can get started?"

"Yes, dear," I replied dutifully, nearly choking as I swallowed the sarcasm. I stood up and reluctantly slipped into my jacket.

"I have a question, though." I took a deep breath, paused, then blurted out, "Where are we now, where are we going, and how long will it take?"

"Weel, that's more than one question, but we're somewhere in the middle of North Carolina. We're headed to New Bern to see my Great-uncle Angus and his family. He'll ken where my Uncle Jody and Auntie Sarah are. Uncle Jody can help me to, weel, we willna talk of that now, but any time I need help, he's there fer me, and me fer him, too. As fer how many days it will take, I'd say that depends on the weather and how yer feelin'."

"Hmph," I grunted. I almost had the hang of that Scottish all-purpose response. I really wanted to stay in the wild with him forever. I knew it wasn't possible, though, at least not now.

A couple of days ago, one of those vile thugs who had almost beaten him to death two months back, found our home. Ian told me that if it hadn't been for Rocky intercepting the man before he got to the cave, we would have been captured, maybe even murdered. As it turned out, he said, the man escaped, managed to limp back to his horse, and got away.

It was good for us that the creep left his boots and knife behind. When Ian told me how it happened, I thought it was odd. I guess the man had literally been scared out of the boots. Either that or he took them off to sneak up on us and didn't get a chance to retrieve them after being discovered. Yeah, one look at Rocky and the man probably dropped his knife and ran.

Even though it was a sorry excuse for a knife, it did have a hard cutting edge. It was nice to have as a spare, but the boots were a definite blessing. They were big enough to fit Ian, too. My first attempt at moccasins were nearly worn through, and he needed something.

When he came back from the confrontation, Ian told me we had to move out quickly. "We were found," he said bluntly, "and now we have to leave." He mentioned something about 'taking care of the man,' and then stammered onto another subject. I didn't want to ask how he had taken care of him since he had just said the man had escaped. He didn't seem too keen on volunteering the information and, in this case, I preferred the story be left as a mystery.

So, I supposed, there was no way out of it—we had to make an exodus. Those creeps were sure to come looking for their missing comrade. And if they knew Ian was around, they might try to recapture him, too. It was also possible that I had been seen, and that was real scary.

131

If the heathens didn't want to keep me just to anger Ian further—or for their own personal, carnal pleasures—Ian said they were sure to know that a healthy young white woman would fetch a good price on the slave market. I realized he was right; we had to leave now and get us—me—to a safer spot.

Ж

The first few days of travel were easy enough. The sun was shining and the air was still, so the trek itself was quite pleasant. We were back to the original triad. Lady had left just hours before Ian came home, then Rocky returned from another of his personal forays soon thereafter. I doubt Lady would have wanted to join the road trip anyway; she had her own agenda with impending motherhood.

Rocky seemed to be enjoying his human family's journey. Every day, the oversized canine got up early and patrolled the perimeter of our campsite. After circling the area a couple of times, he'd give a "wuff," then head back into the brush to catch a bird or a squirrel, or maybe snag a fish from a creek. He must be part retriever—sometimes he even brought back some of his fare for me to cook. We still had plenty of elk, but I appreciated the change from the smoked or jerked lean meat. I really did believe Rocky liked to help Ian take care of me; it seemed I had become his pet.

Because Ian didn't have to stop to hunt for breakfast or dinner, we made good time. Setting up camp had become a quick and easy routine. Ian chose the site, grabbed wood for the fire, and got it started. I unpacked the pot and plate, prepared dinner, and set up our bedding. If we hadn't done it already, Ian would refill the water bottles. Rocky sat contentedly at the edge of the activity, watching us labor, eating his dinner raw. He seemed to enjoy our routine, too.

After we finished our evening meal, and I had cleaned and put away both our dishes, Ian and I would sit, always his left arm wrapped around my shoulders, cuddled together in front of the fire—every night, in the same position, facing the same direction, west. We watched the sun dip below the horizon, streaks of weak winter clouds sometimes joining the glowing orb's nighttime disappearing act, treating us to a brilliant—or 'psycho deltic' as Ian would say—sunset. We didn't talk much. I still had amnesia, he had already shared the highlights of his youth—and I definitely didn't want to bring up any recent events—so we just chilled, Rocky's furry back next to ours. The fire was too hot for him, but he liked being close to us.

When it came time for bed, Rocky would saunter away, leaving us alone until we had settled down. He would lay a considerate ten feet away, his muzzle on top of his front paws, eyes shifting back and forth, up and down, following our movements. He waited until all activity was over, and then lay at our feet.

I loved my daily grind. The days always started and ended the same. The weather and locations of our evening campsites were different, but the familiarity of doing the same chores, in the same order, was comforting to me. I didn't think about the future or wonder about my past—it was just the here and now that mattered. Any fright or anxiety I may have had at the onset of our trek was sedated by the rhythm of the days and nights. Yup, Prozac and Zoloft couldn't even come close to the soothing effects of a consistent routine and love.

Around one week into our exodus, I sensed a change in Ian. He had an edge about him, as if he knew something was going to happen soon—he was anticipating it.

"Okay, what's going on?" I asked as I nudged him shoulder-to-shoulder, trying to be light without directly questioning his wariness.

"Oh, I'm sorry, it's jest that we're verra close to New Bern and I want to make sure we get there soon. I guess I'm excited about seeing Angus and his family again. He was like a grandfather to me. My mother's father died when she was a wee lass. Angus was her uncle, her father's brother. He had been married to his first wife—that would be Margaret—fer more than twenty years. She had been barren, so it was jest the two of them. Then she died and it was jest him. A year or so later, he took a young—verra young—bride. He and his new wife—that would be *Mary* Margaret—soon had six wee 'uns. She dinna seem to mind that he was older, and he loved havin' a big family."

His words were sincere enough, but didn't feel right. He was holding back, hiding something. I was sure he knew more than he was telling me. Two days later, when I finally got the nerve to ask him what was wrong, he shrugged, snorted, and then grumbled, "Nothin'."

Well, his *nothin'* was sure preoccupying him. He was uncharacteristically quiet, almost like a sound vacuum. All of my attempts at conversation were dispassionately ignored. He focused on trivial issues, obsessively double-checking every rock, ridge, and gully we passed.

That night, I didn't want to go to sleep. I felt like I was losing him a little bit at a time, and if I didn't grab onto him right now, he'd be lost to me forever. I wanted to memorize everything about him, the way his

133

eyebrows moved when he dreamed, the crooked bend of his nose, those star-shaped tattoos across his cheekbones, his musky, wet woodland scent, the curves of his shoulders, and the deep dips beneath his collarbones. I stayed awake as long as I could, just breathing in the smell of him, feeling the tickle of his chest hairs on my nose, the rise and fall of his ribcage as he breathed, and the little snorts he gave when in a deep sleep.

Rocky was ill at ease, too. Either he was sensing something from Ian, or he was concerned that I wasn't sleeping. I rubbed my foot into his fur, trying to let him know I was glad he was with us, and that I was okay. He picked up his head and did something he had never done before—he licked me.

I finally dozed off just before dawn. Or at least I think that's when it was. I had spent a long night impressing the essence of my husband into my mind and soul, and reflecting on the world around me, my life as I knew it now.

My life now—that was all I knew. What was it like before my fall? Did I live in a big house, or in a hovel? Did I have a husband and children? If I had a family, did they miss me, and were they trying to find me? Why did Ian, whom I loved so much, still seem so different from me? Was the rest of his family like him, clever in the backwoods ways, but ignorant of modern life? Where were the paved roads, planes, and power lines in this part of the country? Where was I that plastic bottles, zippers, and battery-powered lights were unheard of? And why was Ian always trying to get me to believe my gear was from Italy? I didn't know anything about the local geography, but New Bern sounded like the name of a city to me, not just a collection of cabins. Come to think of it, though, I've never even seen a cabin here. I was beginning to feel like I was in the Twilight Zone. Now I just wished I knew what the Twilight Zone was.

The next morning, Ian was louder than needed as we headed out. If I didn't know better—and I didn't—I'd believe he was signaling someone. He was carrying the elk harvest bundle on his back. The only load I had was my backpack and the ominous feeling that something was about to happen.

"Are ye comfortable with the pack?" he hollered, when a soft comment would have sufficed.

It was unsettling. Well, at least I was pretty sure something was going on. He had never put on airs for me before, so I didn't know what to expect.

If he was louder than usual, I was quieter. I was concentrating on the landscape as we trudged along, searching for anything that didn't belong. Actually, I was trudging and he was marching. I'd peek at Ian when I didn't think he was watching. He was looking straight ahead with an expression between sadness and apprehension. I thought he would be happy to see his great-uncle, but if he was, he sure wasn't showing it.

"Are you sure you're happy about seeing Uncle Angus again?" I asked, making certain I had a good view of his face and expression.

"Oh, aye, it's been a while since I've seen him. Like I told ye, he has quite the family. I'll be glad to see 'em. That, and I'm hopin' they'll have a bit of bread to eat. And maybe a little sweet jam to go with it, aye? I'm sure Mary Margaret will have a bit of soap and some hot water fer ye to clean with. I think ye'll like that. Women seem to like smellin' good."

Ian sounded happy, but there was a shadow of sadness in his face as he spoke. "We'll have maybe one more night in the woods, and then we'll be in New Bern, stayin' in a house with four walls and a roof. Do ye think ye'll miss sleepin' out under the stars?" he asked absently.

"Well, if I do, I'll just grab a couple of blankets and head outside. That's easier than trying to build a house here in the wilderness, out of nothing but wishes and wants!" I smiled at what I thought was a clever remark, but his face remained stoic, his mind elsewhere.

We traveled the rest of the day in relative silence. I tried to talk to him a couple of times, but he was so involved in what was going on in his head that he didn't hear me. Rather than call his attention to not listening to me, I just ignored it and went on with the trudging. I'd find out sooner or later what was coming our way. I was curious, but not afraid, and sure that he wouldn't lead us—or at least me—into harm's way.

That night we set up what was supposed to be our last campsite under the open sky. We had a light dinner of jerky and broth, and went to bed early. Ian was more loving and tender than…well, ever. He paid attention to every part of my body, beginning at the top of my head. He gently parted my bangs, kissed my forehead, my cheeks, and then showed me how highly erogenous my ears could be. He slowly and effectively worked his lovemaking south, paying homage to my breasts and belly, stroking and massaging both the insides and outsides of my thighs, pausing to taste and tickle the innermost spots, then continued all the way down to my feet and ankles, actually making me blush with what he did to my toes.

It was as if he were making love to me for the last time. That thought had crossed my mind about the time he was suckling my shoulders, but I

135

ignored it, not wanting to convert any of my passionate emotions into worry. I was totally involved in the here and now, feeling more loved and fulfilled than I had ever thought possible.

The last thought I had before I fell asleep was, 'I wonder if this grin will ever leave my face.' I felt him pull the elk robe over my shoulders, and then I slept so hard, I didn't even dream.

Ж

I awoke flat on my back to the smell of bacon frying. I hadn't smelled bacon since—duh! I couldn't remember when—but I did recognize that smoky, comforting aroma. I rolled my head to the side and saw I was alone under the elk-hide robe. Ian was squatted next to the fire, turning the bacon so it wouldn't burn. His fingers darted into the frying pan, flipped the meat quickly, and then pulled back, as if a piece had bit him. He raised his hand to his mouth and sucked the greasy digits, soothing the burns while taking a quick taste of our unexpected breakfast fare.

He wasn't by himself. A tall man dressed in Native American garb was standing next to him. I didn't think he was native though: his brown hair was greased back and tied with a thong, and was wavy, with blond streaks in it.

I stayed quiet in order to hear them, resisting the overwhelming urge to turn over. I was fully awake now, and uncomfortably aware of how stiff and sore my back was. I couldn't understand what they were saying anyhow because it wasn't English. Hmm, I wondered if I spoke languages other than English? Time would tell on that one.

Ian must have sensed I was awake because he stood up and turned around. "Evie, we have company this morning. He's brought good news along with a bit of bacon. Ye do like bacon, aye?"

"Oh, the bacon smells great. Who's your friend?" I asked as I brushed the hair out of my face. I stayed under the elk-hide robe, touching myself discretely to make sure I had my clothes on. I still had on both my shirts, but my panties were around one ankle. I tugged them up, pulled my fleecy pillow out from under my head and turned it back into my pants, and managed to wiggle into them without knocking off the elk robe. Modesty ensured, I arose awkwardly and stepped into my boots to greet our breakfast provider.

"Pleased to make your acquaintance, ma'am," the tall, good-looking stranger said, then bent into a deep bow. His dress was native, but his accent was genuine English, as in English from England. It wasn't Cockney or coarse, but proper, highfalutin diction, and formal enough to

136

be used in the King's court. He was about the same height as Ian, but was filled out, more meat than bones in the chest and shoulders.

"Oh, and this is Little Bear," Ian added quickly. "He says he kens where Uncle Jody is and that we can be there in jest two days. I ken ye were expectin' to be with my Uncle Angus this afternoon, but Uncle Jody and Auntie Sarah are in the other direction. Are ye up to travelin' jest a couple more days?"

I hated to be reminded of my chronic fatigue. I knew if I had a normal energy level, we could travel faster and longer. The two-day trip would probably be just one long day if it weren't for me. "Oh, I'm sure I'll be fine. Little Bear, you didn't happen to bring coffee and a pot to cook it in, did you? Maybe I could move faster and longer if I had caffeine."

"It just so happens that I do have coffee. I don't believe I have ever heard of caffeine though. Now, if you will excuse me, I'll go down to the creek and fill the pot with water. It shouldn't be too much longer until we have fresh coffee for you."

Little Bear gave a short bow to excuse himself, then walked over to his mule and the leather saddlebag on her back. The flap was decorated with an etching of a small bear attacking a big man who looked as if he had a crown on his head. The bag had cut fringe on the bottom edge and an unusual knotted closure. Little Bear's hands worked swiftly as he retrieved a small enameled coffee pot, dark blue flecked with white. I watched him quickly and quietly shuffle down the ravine toward the creek. It was if his feet never touched the ground. I realized I had been staring but justified it to myself as looking at the mule and artwork, not the man.

I turned back to Ian and looked him right in the eyes. I didn't say anything but waited for him to speak first. He squatted down again, avoiding my glare, and began rolling up our bedding, trying to look busy. That was hard to do since, beyond the elk robe, there wasn't much to pack.

I guessed it was up to me to say something. "Will Little Bear be coming with us?" I asked cheerily, a mock smile plastered on my face.

Ian's mouth hung open in disbelief—he hadn't expected that. He probably thought I was going to whine and complain about not going to New Bern or having to travel two days more than originally planned. He closed his mouth and composed himself as the fake smile on my face became real; I liked being unpredictable.

"Oh, aye, I suppose he'll be joinin' us," he said as he stood up. "He was already travelin' in that direction when he found our site. We, um, have been friends fer a couple of years or more. He's a great scout and a

137

good man to have on yer side in a fight. I suppose ye already figured out he isna from around here originally?"

"Yes, it's quite obvious by his manners. Oh, and I think I did detect a bit of an English accent," I drolled, winking at the understatement.

Little Bear was next to the fire, putting the coffee grounds in the pot. He had sneaked in—or rather, had come back so quietly I hadn't noticed his return. Being able to move swiftly and silently like that was certainly an enviable skill. His stealth was a little unnerving to be sure. It was a good thing he was a friend, not a foe. Cool, a friend—someone else to talk to.

But that wasn't how it played out. It was a quick and, for me, uncomfortably quiet breakfast of coffee and bacon. I supposed they had already done all their talking before I woke up, and there was nothing important enough to be said to me.

I came back from my potty break and saw we were ready to go. My measly clean up chores had already been done. The breakfast pots and dishes were already packed away, and Ian was lashing our bundles onto Little Bear's mule. There was still a little bit of room left on her back for our portage, so neither of us had any load to carry.

Little Bear had been trapping all winter and had acquired an impressively large cache of beaver and mink pelts. They stank, but I had smelled worse. I didn't, however, want to think about that all-too-recent episode.

I had never told Ian about the kidnapping. He didn't need anyone else on his retaliation/extermination list, and we were now far away from Abe and his family. Anyhow, the stink was tolerable, and I would just have to remember it was only dead animal skins—not degenerate males—that were the source of the foul odor.

Little Bear led the way, and Ian and I were close behind. We traveled slowly because of me. The pokey pace made it easier for me to maneuver away from the prevailing scent of the uncured pelts and was also convenient for making quick getaways for my frustratingly frequent potty stops.

At midday, Little Bear signaled a halt to our journey with a raised hand. He didn't unpack the mule, but did remove his daypack. He opened it up and took out a package of what looked like parchment wrapped with a leather thong.

Ian came over to join him and announced, "Ye'll be stayin' here fer a long dinner break. I'll go on ahead to check out somethin' suspect. It's probably nothin', though. Ye'll be fine here with Little Bear. He's brought out a special treat fer ye."

Ian leaned over and gave me a quick kiss on the cheek, almost blushing as he glanced over at Little Bear. Evidently, he was uncomfortable with public displays of affection.

He then stood tall and said something that sounded almost like a military command to Little Bear. They were speaking that foreign language again—I couldn't make out even one of the words.

Ian disappeared into the brush. He, too, was as silent as daylight as he traveled through the tangle of evergreen trees and shrubs, bare branches, and those tan weedy plants that still had dead leaves and seedpods clinging to them. He had lost any trace of a limp from his foot injuries weeks ago, and his hands were completely healed, too. His ears and eyes were sharp, sharper than mine were. If they had been better before the incident, he must have had super powers.

I wished I could say the same about his mental health. Of course, I didn't know him before his trial by torture, but I didn't think anyone who went through life so sullen and quiet would be considered normal. I kept telling myself that he could *still* be normal, but that he just hadn't finished recovering. I only had myself to compare his temperament to. Maybe I was the odd one—overly perky and outgoing—and he was the normal one.

Yes, I was perky and handling life 'jest fine.' Well, the last two weeks were fine, but today was just wrong! Instance by instance, nothing was amiss, but the overall, anxious effect it had on me was more than just uncomfortable.

I knew what it was, though: my lifestyle had been turned inside out and crinkled. There was a new person in my life. That alone was extraordinary, but now he was a traveling companion, too. Okay, I'd adjust to that. But, the only other person I knew in the whole world had just left, too, supposedly for only a few hours.

To frazzle my nerves even more, the little chores I performed daily had been taken away from me, as well. I not only missed, but also *needed* my routine to keep sane: clean the fish, fry the fish, wash the pan.

Ergh! I was going to have to accept these changes, whether I wanted to or not. I promised myself I would make a concerted effort to be calm and coherent with my new companion. Hmph!

Little Bear was now setting up a campsite for us. He had dragged a fallen log next to the cleared area—apparently our new dining room. He had also amassed a small store of firewood in record time, as well as constructed a little teepee of kindling and dried seedpods in the center of the fire ring. He struck his flint, smacking the implement in rapid-fire succession, and the sparks flew, the mini-tent catching fire quickly. I watched, fascinated by the crackling pumpkin-colored flames, as he added larger pieces of wood, settling the odd shaped chunks together to form a perfect pyramid of timber, the slits of golden light trying to escape from within the self-consuming structure he had just constructed.

"Would you like a cup of coffee with your lunch, madam?" he asked, his dimples enhancing his smile.

"Oh, yes, that would be great. Can I help you get anything?"

"I believe I have everything we need right here. Would you like to read a bit while the coffee is brewing?"

"You have books?"

"Yes and no. I have only one book. Last year I traded for *Gulliver's Travels,* but I have gathered a few of the political flyers that blew into the trees along the way. They might be a bit too radical for you, though. I wouldn't want to offend you with their inflammatory contents."

"Oh, no, thank you anyway. I think I'll just wait for lunch. I didn't know I was so hungry until we stopped moving. I'm ravenous."

It wasn't very cold, but I was rubbing my hands together briskly, wanting to do *something* with them. I looked down and was disgusted at what I saw. It seemed that no matter how hard I tried, my hands got dirty simply from walking through the woods. It was as if the dirt and grime leapt from the ground and bushes onto my hands, even managing to snuggle their filthy way under my fingernails. I was sure my face was just as soiled as my hands. I looked down and saw the little grunge worms I had made by rubbing my palms together. I hated being dirty and grimaced as I wiped them off on my pants.

My pants—I owned two pair of pants and three shirts. I usually wore two shirts at the same time to keep warm. I kept on the spandex and cotton sports bra to help retain body heat. When it got too cold or was windy, I put on both pairs of sweat pants. Ian had returned to wearing his breechclout and leggings again; he had rubbed enough dirt into them that they were clean of the filth from his capture. We still didn't talk about that subject.

"Ma'am?" Little Bear asked, as if it was not the first time he had called me.

"Oh, I'm sorry; I guess I was off in la-la land again. What did you say?"

"The coffee is ready, and I have your lunch for you." He pointed to the log that was to be our dinner bench. He had opened up the parcel of parchment and laid it open like a fragile platter. I sat down and placed it on my knees.

"Is this pemmican?" I asked. It looked like powdered meat mixed with dried fruit and fat. I took a pinch of it and didn't hesitate to pop it in my mouth because, well, it would have been rude not to eat it. Ian told me before he left that it was special, and I was sure Little Bear wouldn't have offered it to me if it was poison! There was that, and I was also very hungry.

"Yes, it is, but it's a special blend. I came upon a big stand of huckleberries last fall and picked the dried fruits before the bears got them. Normally, pemmican doesn't have the berries in it. They're good for keeping your teeth. Oh, I'm sorry; you didn't need to hear that. You have beautiful teeth."

Little Bear was apparently embarrassed that he was being so familiar and talking so much. I doubted he was used to speaking to anyone but his mule. "Would you like your coffee now?" he asked sheepishly, handing me his tin cup.

"Yes, please." I took a cautious sip. The coffee was bland and slightly bitter. I hadn't seen him throw away the coffee grounds from this morning's batch, so I was fairly certain he had reused them. Still, it was palatable and, hopefully, had some caffeine left in it.

I knew my stomach filled up slower than my mouth, so I ate slowly to make sure I didn't eat too much. The hot coffee would probably swell the dried food in the mix, and I didn't want to get bloated. I paced myself and took small bites, chewing thoroughly, although the minced blend was fine enough even for the toothless, willing to wait a half hour for the full belly feeling to hit.

We ate in an awkward, slightly uneasy silence. I was curious about Little Bear, but not afraid of him. Was it simply native lore that made him aware of the need for the vitamins in berries to prevent scurvy and tooth loss? I decided to play mental poker with the man to see what he had in his hand, er, head.

"Little Bear," I began. He jumped a couple of inches when I spoke. He must have been deep into his own little world—I had startled him. "Before you came to live and trap out here, were you perchance a doctor or something?"

As soon as I said 'or something,' I could have smacked myself. How

141

rude was it to ask someone 'were you something?'

"Yes, I was something," he answered with a smile.

I smiled back weakly.

"I was a student of chemistry and medicine in Glasgow. I learned much from my professor, William Cullen. However, before I could finish my studies and become fully accredited as a medical doctor, I became—how should I put it?—*involved* in some controversial political discussions that made it necessary for me to change venues. It seemed the Colonies were a good place to come to pursue freedom of thought."

"You don't sound like you're from Scotland," I said aloud before I could think. *Ergh: think first, speak second!*

"Um, would you do me a favor?" I asked haltingly. *That's right, ask for a generic favor first, get the okay, and then go for it.*

"Yes, I'd be glad to, if I can," he replied politely.

Phew! He ignored that little bit about not sounding like he was from Scotland.

I refolded the parchment packet, set it down beside me on the log, and stood up. I moved in front of him—he was still seated—and asked, "Since you've been trained as a physician, would you tell me what you can about me, just from looking at me? You can touch me, too, like a doctor, if you need to."

I put my arms out to the side and pivoted slowly in place, like a clumsy ballerina at extra slow speed.

"All right," he said softly.

I stopped my personal carousel and waited to see what was next. He got up and stood very close to me. *Oh, God! He was in my personal space! I shut my eyes to hide any fear that might be spilling out. 'He's a doctor, he's a doctor,' I kept reminding myself.*

I felt his hands on both sides of my face, holding my head, moving it up and down, and side to side, prodding behind my ears. He gently pushed my arms back down to my sides. I felt two of his fingers on the front of my chin. "Open, please," he said.

I obeyed and even took the initiative of sticking out my tongue. "Aahh," I intoned without being asked. He paused, then pushed my mouth closed. Next, he pulled down my bottom eyelids. I did the look up, look down, look all around routine, and then closed my eyes again. He moved to my side, tilted my head, pulled back my hair, and looked in my ear, moving around me to perform the same inspection on the other side. He took my hands, turned both of them over, and then dropped the left hand.

He was rubbing the fingers on my right hand lightly when I ventured a peek. He was examining my middle finger. He looked up, saw that I was watching him, smiled, and then put my hand down.

"Don't be afraid," he said, "I'm not going to hurt you, but I need to touch you a bit more."

I nodded quickly before I changed my mind. I felt his hands start at my jaw. His fingers felt my glands, working their way down to my throat and out to my shoulders. I squirmed and giggled a bit when he felt under my armpits. I was ticklish and couldn't hold still for that part. He patted around my breasts but kept clear of the nipple areas. I squirmed and giggled again when he felt my ribs and waist. He walked his hands around my abdomen and, almost as an afterthought, slid his hands down the outside of my legs.

I couldn't feel any more touching, so opened my eyes. He was sitting on the log, sipping a bit of his weak coffee.

"Okay," I said with mock self-confidence, "first, tell me what Ian told you about me, and then tell me what you deduced from your physical examination."

Little Bear gestured with his hand for me to sit down on the log. I was starting to shake—from nerves more than cold—so wrapped my arms around my breasts, and tucked my hands under my armpits. I slowly walked toward him and sat down, but further away on the makeshift bench than he had indicated. I was still a bit apprehensive about a man who had just 'felt me up,' even if I had asked him to do it, and he had been discreet and performed it in a completely professional capacity.

"Well, first, Ian told me nothing about you other than that you were his wife. Men are like that, you know—not too much on conversation unless it's about hunting, fishing, or politics. But he did want me to know you were his." I raised my eyebrows at this, but stayed mute, waiting for him to continue.

He scooted sideways so he could face me while speaking. His body language, with knees spread open and hands moving while talking, indicated he was opening up to me.

"Now, for the rest of it," he continued, "I'd say you were born into a good family with at least a bit of money, ate well, possibly went to school, but either way, you learned to read and write, and are still in good health."

"How did you come to that conclusion?"

"You have all of your teeth and your bones are straight—no scurvy or rickets—so you ate well as a youth. You asked about books, so I deduced that you could read, but that might have been a ruse. You do, however, have a small callus on the first knuckle of the middle finger of your right hand, the type often received from holding a pen for writing. You have a gold chain with gold nuggets attached to it around your neck, so you had at least a small dowry. Your skin is smooth—no swollen glands or sores— your hair thick and shiny, and your eyes are clear, so you're in good health now. All in all, I'd say you're a very healthy young woman of about 18 years and are approximately four months pregnant."

"Huh?" I gasped.

"Excuse me, which part is wrong?" he asked sincerely, his head canted to the side.

"I'm pregnant? FOUR months pregnant?" I screeched. "How can that be?" Now I was panting, trying not to hyperventilate.

"Well, I suppose the same way all other females got pregnant, save the Virgin Mother. I'm sure you won't have any problems with the delivery, though. You're a young, healthy woman with nicely spaced hips. By the way, that fatigue you have is very common in the early stages of pregnancy. It should be ending soon. The middle trimester, that is the middle three months of a normal nine-month pregnancy, is the most comfortable part, I hear. Many women say they feel better and stronger then than at any other time in their lives. Are you all right?"

I was in shock, sitting on the ground now, having slid forward off the log. The rough bark had scratched my back on the way down—through both my shirts. Suddenly I was cold back there, the winter air chilling the dribbling blood.

I knew my eyes were wide-open and staring. I was completely incapable of movement, though. It was as if I had been knocked out cold, except there was a small portion of me—like a wandering eye peering out of a cutout on a painted portrait on the wall—that wasn't paralyzed. 'It' was aware of what was going on with my body. As much as I wanted to move, my carcass had no power of its own. 'It' was in control of everything, and movement wasn't allowed. Blink, blink. That was all I could do, and even that was not a conscious movement.

My mouth was hanging open. I could feel my tongue starting to dry out, but I couldn't move. Now it was shutting, but not with my effort. Little Bear had gently placed the side of his forefinger under my chin and closed it. He put my palms in my lap and pulled my shoulders forward. He twisted and maneuvered my unresponsive body gently so I was lying flat on the ground. 'It' watched as he brought over his daypack and positioned it under my feet. I was aware of him leaving again, and then he was back. He had retrieved his own blanket and was covering me with it.

"It's okay, little one. I thought you knew. Don't worry; you'll be fine. You rest now, and I'm sure you'll feel better when you wake. You've been on this journey for a long time. It's probably just now catching up with you."

Little Bear brushed the hair out of my eyes and murmured something I didn't understand. It felt like he was saying a prayer or a blessing over me. It was in that same foreign language he and Ian had been speaking earlier. Foreign language—it wasn't foreign at all. It was the native language of where we were now. With that last thought, I achieved total unconsciousness.

I was flying high in the sky, observing the canopy of shimmering treetops beneath me, the wind ruffling the odd-shaped leaves, changing the values of the summer-hued living canvas like bits of yellow and green glass in a kaleidoscope. I scanned the landscape, searching for the hidden paths of the narrow, silvery creeks that slipped through gullies and glades to join their mother, the bloated river, as it sashayed to meet the sequined sea, the pater oceanus. The air smelled clean and brisk. There was no stress in this land, only peace—complete serenity.

I dropped altitude for a closer look, but then couldn't rise again. I was falling slowly, like a hot air balloon that had lost its fire. I was trying not to become tangled in the high overhead power lines that were quickly cropping up where the trees had been. I turned my head and realized I was trapped by those same electrical wires that were all around me, writhing like snakes in a fire. I couldn't move without being electrocuted. Now the power lines were smoking, emitting the smell of apple pie and corn bread. I was trapped in a sweet-smelling hell, falling, frustrated, and scared.

A fly landed on my nose and I swatted it away, bringing me out of my nightmarish nap. I realized I wasn't paralyzed at all, but was safe on the ground without any wires threatening me. That tantalizing aroma was still here, though. At least the good part of the dream had remained. I rolled over and saw the back of Little Bear, busily cooking something over the fire.

"Eh, what's up, Doc?" I asked brightly.

"Eek!" Little Bear squealed like a little girl, nearly tumbling forward into the fire. I hadn't meant to startle him, but I had. These frontiersmen were all so tough and proud of their keen sense of hearing, so my ability to surprise my host was extra sweet.

"Doc?" he asked.

At first, he was unsure of my use of the title, but then he realized I was making some sort of joke, and regained his composure. "Oh, I'm just putting together a bit of dinner. I hope you weren't expecting much. I had some dried apples and decided to add them to the cornmeal. We'll have sweet cakes for supper. How are you feeling after your little nap?"

"I feel fine, thank you. Dinner smells great." Reality started to come back, with uneasiness and frustration on its heels. "Oh, dear, I just remembered; you said I'm pregnant." I put my chin on my fist. "Are you sure about that?" I asked, giving him the 'sad, puppy-dog eyes' look in hopes he'd change his diagnosis.

"My dear, only you can know for sure. But whether you are or are not, you'll need to eat to keep up your strength. Now, it looks like Ian won't be back tonight. We'll be fine here, though—water at hand, plenty of firewood, and clear skies. We should stay dry, even without a roof o'er our heads. Come, let's eat."

The two of us ate a quiet, spartan dinner together. I was glad I didn't feel awkward around him since he had been 'touching me' earlier. That subject never came up again.

"How far are we from New Bern?" I asked, just trying to make conversation. It was a moot point really, since we were now heading away from it and toward Uncle Jody's home.

"New Bern? Oh, at least a hundred miles, I'd say. Why do you ask?"

I swallowed hard. *So, that's why Ian has been so antsy—we've been going away from New Bern the whole time. He's wanted to go to his aunt and uncle's home since we left but didn't have the nerve to tell me.*

"Oh, it's just a town where Ian has some relatives. Please, don't tell him I asked. He's a bit sensitive about that part of his family."

I didn't want Ian to find out I was onto his switch—last minute or otherwise. It was bad enough that I knew he was intentionally deceiving me. I was sure he was only doing it so I could see his aunt, the healer, sooner—but why did he feel like he had to lie to me?

Rather than get moody, I decided I'd get distracted. Since I didn't have much of a history to share—and didn't want to tell Little Bear about what I did recall—reading would be a great diversion for both of us. "Would you like me to read?"

He gladly accepted my proposal. He brought his saddlebag over to the bench and took out a carefully wrapped, leather bound book, placing the tome in my hands genteelly, sharing his gift with aplomb.

I sat next to the fire, using its warm brightness to supplement the fading daylight. I soon became wrapped up in the story, forgetting my plight and becoming immersed in the fictional hero's. I had forgotten how interesting 'Gulliver's Travels' was.

I saw Little Bear's eyes close, and a smile settled on his slightly bearded face. Actually, I think he was enjoying the sound of a woman's voice more than the story. He had admitted earlier that he hadn't seen a female human in nearly six months.

Hours passed; eventually my eyes started tearing and my legs started twitching. I was getting tired and needed my sleep. "That's it for the reading tonight. Is there anything we need to do before we turn in?"

Little Bear was still sitting on the ground, his long legs stretched out luxuriously. He gave a full body stretch, yawned, and, almost as an afterthought, covered his mouth. "No, and there's not much to take care of in the morning. I'll see if I can catch a few fish for our breakfast, and then we'll wait for Ian to return. You can catch up on your reading, if you'd like."

"Maybe I'll try some fishing, too," I mumbled as I rearranged my bedding. "See you in the morning. If I forgot to say it earlier, thanks for dinner and, well, everything."

I quickly pulled the elk robe over my head. I didn't want to talk. I never realized how miserable it was not having something, anything, to look forward to. I didn't have to fuss for breakfast, wood for the fire was taken care of, and, gee, I was useless!

My life as I knew it had been taking care of Ian, and then journeying with him to be with his family. I had always been busy and been needed. My chores had been defined by necessity. Now I was getting depressed because I wasn't needed. Weird; this seemed like a problem I'd had before. Maybe it was from my former life. That was something else I didn't want to think about. Go to sleep, woman. I began counting backwards: one hundred, ninety-nine, ninety-eight...

Ж

Something was wrong: I didn't hear any birds chirping. Then I heard something else: the garbled tones of Ian and Little Bear. They were standing together on the far side of the fire. I couldn't hear what they were saying, but I doubt the volume of their voices made a difference. The singsong rhythm meant they weren't speaking English. I lay still, waiting to see how long it took them to notice I was awake.

It didn't take long. They both stopped talking and turned toward me, looking to see if my eyes were open. "What, did I just stop snoring or something?" I asked defensively.

"No, darlin', ye have a beautiful musical tone when ye sleep. The melody stopped and we both noticed. Are ye well?"

"Oh, I'll do," I answered morosely. I huffed, suddenly angry, recalling my suspicions about why he'd left. "Did you get your 'business' taken care of?" I snapped.

I wanted to be cool, indifferent, but my voice betrayed my true feelings. I didn't like being the second banana for my head ape; I wanted the top banana position. What business did he have that was more important than me, his wife?

"Now, dinna worry about my business, mind ye. We can be at my uncle's house before sunset. We'll have to leave soon, though. That is, if yer up to it."

The genuine concern in his voice made me feel guilty about my original snotty attitude. "I'm sorry for being so short. How was your trip?"

I got up slowly and awkwardly, accepting his helping hand. I remembered how uncomfortable he was when he gave me a kiss good-bye the day before, so leaned into him, my face to his shoulder, and gave him a big hug, saving my 'welcome home' kiss for later. I did sneak a quick little pat on his bottom as I finished the hug, though; making sure Little Bear was on the blind side of my personal gesture. Still in our embrace, I looked up and saw Ian give me a big grin. Whatever had happened in the last twenty hours or so, he seemed to feel better about himself now than he had before he left.

Ж

It only took a few grabs and stashes to get all our gear packed, and then we were on our way. We were all in good spirits. The men were walking at their normal rate, but their legs were longer than mine, and I had to kick it up a notch to keep up. I was fine with the brisk pace because I had excess energy to burn. I was hyper—wound up like a ten-inch rubber band—about meeting Ian's family.

We walked for hours without taking a real break. I scooted off for my personal comfort moments, i.e. potty breaks, but I was quick, and we never had to come to a complete halt. Ian had offered to stop for lunch so I could get off my feet, but I declined. I was excited and wanted to keep going. It was almost as if I could smell new people, new experiences, on the horizon. But the aroma of civilization was just an illusion, fabricated out of my own hopes. Still, it was enticing, pulling me along into the fantasy. I

148

was like a kitten tracking down the scent of a catnip-filled toy that had been dragged through the yard, intrigued and determined to get to the treasure, even though it wasn't visible. I wanted to see other people, people who wore clothes that didn't reek of dead animal skins, and hopefully, at least one other female person. Oh, to be in the presence of estrogen and hairbrushes!

Now, only one obstacle lay in our path: the river. It was angry, swift, and swollen, and seemed to be in a hurry to reach the ocean—or wherever its destination might be. There was no shoreline. Bushes and trees from the forest, once free standing, disappeared into its flow, the newly immersed botanicals struggling to keep their earthen hold. There wasn't any scouring on the banks either—the water had reached a new high point and was twisting and torquing tree limbs and branches, creating a series of giant sparrow's nests along its route.

Nope, I didn't want to cross it, but I knew it was the shortest—and possibly the only—route. The men wouldn't lead us—lead me—across a river that wasn't conquerable, would they? My first thought was, no, they would keep me out of harm's way because I was a female—frail, delicate, and all that nonsense. Then again, there was twice the amount of testosterone at work here. I hoped they weren't underestimating the severity of the situation because they didn't want to appear apprehensive in front of me—or each other.

"I shall lead the way," Ian announced formally.

Little Bear's eyes opened wide at the proclamation, but his mouth stayed closed.

Ian turned to look at me with doe eyes. "If there's a problem, I'll be the one in peril. Once across, ye can follow safely since I'll have found the shallow spots and will be able to lend ye a hand. Little Bear and the mule can bring up the rear."

Ian looked so proud of his decision that I hated to make a comment. However, our lives and safety were at stake. "Can I make a suggestion?" I asked cautiously.

"Aye, of course." Ian appeared shocked and chagrined that I would even think to add to or amend his command, but he was wearing his courtesy coat, allowing me to offer an opinion.

I saw a giggle in Little Bear's eyes, but he was doing a good job of hiding the smirk that had crossed his face when I spoke up, quickly getting it under control, making sure Ian never saw it.

Very cautiously, and with spousal respect, I offered my proposal. "I have that fancy blue Italian rope in my backpack. We can tie it around your waist. If you slip or get carried away, we can pull you back. Once you get to the other side, you can tie it off to a tree. I'll have something to hang onto the whole way across; I can grab it if I start to fall. I don't think it'll work for the mule, but at least Little Bear and I will be safer when we cross."

I could tell I had put Ian on the spot with my idea. It was a wise plan and he knew it.

"Of course, we would be using the rope. I thought ye understood that," he countered…or…rather, covered up.

My big smile was half smirk, "Oh, yes dear, I guess you did mean that. I must be getting a bit fuddle-headed with fatigue."

I glanced over at Little Bear. He had his forefinger curved over to his upper lip, obviously using his hand to hide a grin, and possibly stifling a chuckle to boot.

It was never wise to insult or belittle a spouse or friend, especially in front of others. I wasn't going to do it now or ever. I just wished that Ian hadn't tried to make me look small by claiming my idea as his own. Insecurity was possibly impairing his judgment. If it was because he was jealous of another man—that bright, intelligent, good-looking man with material goods in the way of furs who had joined our little company— well, I hope it left when Little Bear did, and never came back again.

The trip across the river was anxious, but successful. Unfortunately, I started developing a headache as soon we made it to the other side. Its onslaught was sudden and excruciating. I didn't say anything because— besides the fact that the men couldn't do anything about it—I didn't want to delay our arrival.

We stopped for a short break as soon as we reached solid ground so Little Bear could readjust the mule's load. I rested with my feet up while they did the work. I also ate a little of the pemmican and drank lots of water. The headache was probably the result of dehydration from the extra effort of the long, arduous trek. Hopefully, the food and water would take care of it. I didn't want to meet new family with a migraine!

We had only traveled about twenty minutes more when Little Bear signaled us to a stop. "My friends, this is where we part company. I have enjoyed your companionship and camaraderie. I will always treasure the memory of our time together."

Ian walked up to him and said something in that native language. The two of them unlashed our meager portion of the mule's load: my backpack and his bundle with our foodstuffs and robe. They exchanged a few more hand gestures that reminded me of a salute, and then they were done.

Little Bear turned to me and bowed deeply. "Madam, it has definitely been a pleasure. I wish you well in all of your endeavors and with your new family." He winked at the word 'family,' then brought my hand to his lips and gave the lightest of kisses.

I hated to admit it, but his gesture gave me shivers up my spine—and not of disgust either. He was well mannered, good looking, kind, and generous. I smiled at him, said, "Thank you," then looked up at Ian.

Oops. If looks could hit, Little Bear would have just been roundhouse punched. Thankfully, Little Bear was oblivious to the glare and was already heading off to his destination in the opposite direction.

I walked over to Ian, took his hands in mine, brought him close, and stood on my tiptoes, face to face with his stony countenance. "Remember who I'll be sleeping with tonight," I admonished. "Jealousy is only for the insecure. I have given you no reason to be jealous, and Little Bear has shown us nothing but kindness. There's no harm in a little kiss on the paw. You'd probably enjoy one, too, if you hadn't seen a woman in six months. If you did the same to another female, I wouldn't be jealous. You'd still come home to me, wouldn't you?"

Ian's face relaxed. "Aye, I would. I guess I'm anxious to be gettin'— oh, I wish I could say 'home.' Come on, we'd best be goin'. We still have a couple of hours of daylight. Hopefully we'll get there before it's completely dark." Ian bent down, stared deep into my eyes, and then gave me a long, wet, full-mouthed kiss that took my breath away, literally.

"Wow," I exclaimed, grinning broadly, "I feel better. We'd better go before I decide to set up camp right now and put off our arrival until tomorrow, so we can spend some quality time together."

"I'm not quite sure what ye mean by 'quality,' but yer givin' me quite the appetite, and it's nae fer food. Aye, but I do think its best we leave right now. I dinna trust the weather to keep fine fer another day. I dinna want to make the last few miles in a late winter storm."

We shared a tight hug and a gentle, less passionate kiss, then were back on our way, the jealousy episode forgotten—I hoped. Ian was such a guarded person, I didn't know if it still bothered him or not. For all I knew, he was planning his revenge.

Revenge: that was probably why Ian had disappeared for two days. He never got over the attack I had rescued him from. I was pretty sure that in his mind, the only recompense for his pain and humiliation was the elimination of his tormentors. He wouldn't talk about it, and I knew now not to bring it up. I had once mentioned that I believed God would punish those men for what they did. Ian puckered up all over when I said that. "Let's not speak of God and those heathens in the same breath," he had said. And so I never spoke of it again.

The rest of the trip was easy going for our feet and legs. Most of the snow was gone, so we could see where the stumble-sized rocks, holes, and fallen branches were. The lack of leaves on the bushes and trees made the straighter, shorter routes easier to see. If it had been any other season, the foliage would have hidden the ground and everything else except the sky, and maybe even that.

Yes, my feet and legs were fine, but my headache was increasing by the furlong. The sun was getting low, and we were losing our light. Ian had told me an hour earlier that we were only about two miles away. I knew a usual walking pace was about three miles per hour, but we were traveling slower because of the uneven terrain, and even more so because of me.

I didn't say anything, but Ian, of course, saw something was wrong. My head hurt so much I could hardly walk. I was lagging behind, even at our slow pace.

He took the few steps back to where I was, and placed one hand on my shoulder, lifting my chin with the other. "Is there something wrong, darlin'? Is it that yer afraid of meetin' my family?"

I winced as I looked up at him. I started to shake my head 'no,' then thought better of it. "It's my head; it feels like my skull has shrunk and my brains are being squeezed out my eye sockets. I, I..."

I quickly turned away from Ian and threw up, managing to miss my boots. Ian offered me his—rather my—handkerchief and patiently, quietly waited while I cleaned up.

I turned into him, laid my cheek against his chest, and gave a long, slow sigh. "I feel better now," I said. "I *do* want to meet your family, I want it very much. I don't feel very well, and would love a nap, but, then again, I don't want to stop while we're so close. So, if I get so sick that I can't walk, you have my permission to sling me over your shoulder and haul my whiney butt there."

Ian looked down at my upturned face, leaned forward, and kissed me on the forehead, discretely avoiding my mouth. "It will be jest fine when we get there, I promise." He put his hands on my shoulders, held me at arm's length, and asked, "Now, are ye ready fer this, or shall I toss ye over my shoulder like a lamb right now?"

I brought up my arm and sniggered a laugh into the back of my hand. "Oh, I think I have a few good steps left in me. But if I start to fall, please, catch me before I hit the ground."

We took off with Ian at point and me trying to keep up. I did fine for the first ten minutes or so. Then the sun got so low that the shadows cast on the ground were confusing me. I couldn't differentiate between depths and heights of holes, roots, and stones—the ground configuration in general. I felt stupid stepping over fallen branches that weren't there, and tripping over what I thought was a dip in the ground.

Ian looked behind and saw my confusion. "Here, jest hold my arm; I'll escort ye. I'll tell ye if there's a hole, or somethin' ye need to step over."

I glanced up and saw that Ian was putting on a show for me. I caught the end of his broad gesture of bowing before me, showing me the way. I managed a slight smile. At least, I hoped he saw it as a smile. It felt like a sneer coming from my lips—the right side of my face wasn't turning up where it should.

I didn't think it was possible, but the headache got worse. I was seeing bright explosions of light—popping like white fireworks—inside my eyeballs. My field of vision was closing in on itself, swirling tighter and tighter. What had started out as narrowed vision was now reduced to a dangerously limited field, like looking through a long length of garden hose. Even the little bit of light and shadow I was able to see hurt my eyes, my face, my whole head.

It took all of my concentration to maintain the minimal requirements of composure. Walking, breathing, not barfing, all at the same time—it was a complex, difficult juggle for me. There was no way I could add talking to my performance, so we walked in silence.

Ian seemed to have a lot on his mind, too, but I doubted it was trying to keep intense pain in check. I didn't even try to think about him or meeting his family. Step, breathe, step, step, gasp, hold breath, step, step, try not to fall down, step, push fingertips of right hand over spot in middle of forehead and press, hoping for relief, wince, then continue plodding along.

Something happened; I must have fallen down, or at least tripped. Ian reached out and grabbed me, containing my collapse, and then the pain and awareness were gone.

*22 Jody's encounters

Little Bear continued on his trek, enjoying his grin of contentment. It was all he had left from his brief visit with young Evie, but that day-and-a-half encounter with her gave him more warmth than he had felt in years—probably since he had lived in his grandmother's comfortable manse. It wasn't lust he felt, but pure happiness to be able to spend time with such a wonderful and intelligent young woman. He frowned briefly. She wasn't his—that would have been nice—but surely Ian wouldn't let her or the baby come to any harm, no matter what he had planned.

He stopped when he heard the rustle but shrugged it off as squirrels or some other small animal life, and used the break to adjust the load on the back of his mule.

One of these days, maybe he'd find a wife…

Ж

Jody was on his way home from a scouting mission when he spotted the golden-haired man wearing Indian buckskin. The two of them had seen each other previously at the trader's in Gibsonville but didn't know each other except by sight. It seemed like a good time to stop for a break and an introduction.

"Hallo!"

The loud voice boomed out and startled Little Bear. He turned around and couldn't see anyone. Suddenly the traveler, a big white man with red hair, appeared fifteen feet in front of him. By his size, he should have made more noise in his approach, but the gregarious man apparently knew his way around these woods and had been able to sneak up on him.

The two exchanged names and greetings, and then transitioned into brief hunting and weather reports, avoiding any controversial issues. Little Bear no longer cared about what was going on with the war, as long as the Colonists and the Loyalists didn't get in the way of his trapping.

After a few moments, Little Bear realized that he was actually enjoying their light repartee. He had never cared much for social calls before—he relished his solitude and had always been his own best company—but now felt lonely since Ian and Evie were gone.

"Would you care to have supper with me?" Little Bear offered, hoping the congenial man would stay a bit longer.

Jody grinned, "I'd be delighted, sir," and gave a grandiose deep bow to his host. It had been a long time since breakfast, and he only had a chunk of hard cheese left for a meal.

The two shared what little food they had. "Do you know of anyone nearby with cornmeal to barter?" Little Bear asked. "I had two guests just recently, and my supplies are nearly depleted. I enjoyed their company, and didn't mind sharing, but my stores were already low when they arrived. If there's a settler or trader nearby where I could get cornmeal, flour, and several other items for a few furs, I'd feel better about the long trip I have ahead of me."

That remark provided the opening Jody was looking for. "The Kelleys up the river would probably be happy to do some tradin'. Their home will be the first ye come to after the fork. Look fer about a dozen wee'uns runnin' around."

Jody paused to chew another bite of jerky before saying more, beginning cautiously, "Ye said ye had some travelers sharin' yer company recently. It wouldna have been a verra tall young man and an older—but not elderly—fair-haired man, rather slightly built, would it? They may or may not be wearin', um, uniforms."

"No," grinned Little Bear, "This couple was a young man and his wife. He dressed like an Indian and could speak Tuscaroran fluently, but usually spoke English. He had the same Scots accent as you, but his wife didn't sound like she was from the same area. I couldn't place her accent, but she was a bright young lass. Pretty too; she had that glow about her that all women get when they're with child."

Little Bear squirmed a bit and adjusted himself on the rock seat, happy to have someone to talk to. "Her husband was tall, gawky, with jet black hair that wouldn't stay out of his face, and that nose!" he said with a grin. "That lad must have had more than just fists to his face to get a nose like that."

"Ian," mumbled Jody.

"Yes, sir, that's his white name—or at least what she called him. I've always known him as Star Walker."

"Ye said a young couple..." Jody led on, hoping Little Bear would finish the thought.

"Oh, yes, sweet little Evie, his wife," his voice drifted a bit. He realized he was musing and continued. "Beautiful young lady, but oddly dressed. It was a bit of a shock to her when she found out that she was with child. She hadn't known and passed out when I told her."

"What?" Jody exclaimed. He wanted to get up and strangle the man,

155

but contained himself. "How did ye ken she was with child when she dinna?"

"Oh, I nearly completed my studies as a doctor several years ago. I was just a few days shy of getting my degree back in Scotland when...well, that's another story, for another time. Politics, you know. Yes, yes, the lass was confused about herself. She asked me to tell her what I could by looking at her and examining her in my capacity as a doctor. It was as if she didn't know who she was and wanted me to tell her what I could determine. I didn't get too familiar with her; believe me when I say that."

Little Bear was eager to share the story but had seen the fire in Jody's eyes and heard it in his voice. "I just checked her about the neck, looked into her eyes, had her move around a bit, and patted her little belly—with all of her clothes on, of course. Do you know this couple?"

"Aye and no; the lad is me blitherin' clotheid of a nephew, Ian Kincaid. I dinna ken anythin' of the lass or of him even bein' marrit. When did ye see them, and did they say where they were heided?"

"Ian said they were going to see family. We parted company at noontime today. I did hear him say something about an Aunt Clara; I think that was her name. Do you have a sister named Clara who is a healer per chance?"

"Nae, but I have a wife named Sarah who is." Jody remained seated on the rock, his shoulders now slumped forward as he turned his head slowly side to side in disbelief. *What was that idiot up to now? And draggin' around a pregnant wife—what could he be thinkin'?*

Jody suddenly sat up straight, took a deep breath, put his hands on his knees, and stood up. "Thank ye, sir, fer sharin' yer meal with me. And thank ye for lettin' me ken about my family. It really doesna matter, but is the lass an Indian?"

"Oh no, she's a white woman, for sure. I figure she's about eighteen years old, brown hair, a bit tall, from a good family—she can read and write you see—and just a joy to be around. She does dress a bit oddly, though. She wears pants, but that might be because that's all she has. They didn't seem to have much."

"Ian never was one to care much fer worldly possessions. If she stays with him, I'm sure they'll both be fine. At least he's not as likely to go off on some hare-brained crusade with a wife and a wee bairn on the way. Now, if ye do happen to meet a verra tall young man—a bit taller than me, still—and a slight, fair-haired man about my age, travelin' together, please let them ken where the Pomeroy homestead is. That's two miles north of the old mill, mind ye. They're not familiar with this area, ye see. And I would feel verra bad if they fell into harm's way."

"I'll watch and listen for news of them. I will be most discreet, I assure you." Little Bear heard both the concern—and the warning—for the safety of Jody's friends in his voice. He had just met the man, but already liked him. He reached out to shake his hand.

Jody grasped it firmly and shook it heartily. "Weel, they say the Lord works in mysterious ways. It seems that since He couldna send me a letter, He sent me a courier with news of my kin. May the Lord be with ye on your travels and keep ye safe."

"And the same to you, my brother in God. I hope I didn't cause you any distress."

Little Bear was genuinely concerned. He didn't think he had betrayed a trust when he shared Evie's pregnancy. Yes, if this man, Jody Pomeroy, was her kin, he seemed the type who would help family, and with Evie a lady in waiting and living on the road, she would need it. Especially with what Ian had in mind.

Ж

Ian arrived at the cabin just after sundown. The windows were covered, but slivers of light were peeking through the gaps. Smoke was wafting out the chimney, the smell of burnt pine blending with the aroma of freshly baked bread. He could tell by the carving on the lintel that if Uncle Jody wasn't living here now, he had been at one time. The wooden beam—carved with an interlaced apple blossom motif—was the same design as the engraved wedding ring he had given Aunt Sarah.

He started to shrug at how romantic his uncle was. Oof! That didn't work. He was still carrying Evie, his elk-hide bundle, and her backpack. "Stop delayin', man," he grumbled to himself. "Get on wi' it."

He couldn't knock on the door because his hands were full of passed-out female. He thought of bumping it with his shoulder or head, but couldn't because Evie was sprawled out, various parts of her body hanging between him and the entrance. He decided he'd kick the door. He followed his first feeble thump with a hardy boot, briefly losing his balance, performing a fancy two-step pirouette and shuffle in recovery.

Sarah called from the other side of the door, "Who's there?"

She must be alone, he thought. She sounds as if she's trying to be in command, but the quiver in her voice is unmistakable.

"It's me, Auntie Sarah. Can I come in, please?" Ian's voice squeaked at the end of his supplication. He cringed at his emotional regression. He felt like a child who had been out after dark and was going to get in trouble for coming home late.

Yes, he had to let her go, to leave Evie so she could go back to her own time, to the friends and family she left behind. And he had to be free— single and unencumbered—to take care of his own business, or he would never feel like a man again.

Sarah opened the door, drying her hands on the linen cloth tucked into her apron. Her mouth dropped open at the sight of him and his load.

"Um, can we come in, please?" he asked again, bringing Sarah out of her momentary shock.

"Oh, sorry, of course—here, let me help you."

Sarah tried to take first one, and then the other bag that Ian was carrying, but the straps were tangled with Evie's dangling limbs. The most she could do was clear a path to the chaise lounge so he could set down the apparently sleeping young lady.

Ian bent over the couch and managed to get Evie laid out without dropping her. *He picked up her fallen hand and placed it on her belly, swallowing his grimace. They hadn't spoken of it, but he knew he was leaving behind more than just Evie. Whether he still loved her or not didn't make a difference—he had loved his first wife, too. Robin had sent him away after both of their children died before they even had the chance to breathe air. That was the other reason he had to send Evie away—he couldn't stand the loss of another bairn.*

Ian let out an involuntary groan as he straightened up. He was spent but didn't want to sit down. He knew he wouldn't want to get up again if he did. And he had to leave—before he changed his mind.

He grabbed his bag and set Evie's backpack at the foot of the couch while Sarah arranged a quilt over her. "Where's Uncle Jody?" he asked without preamble.

"No hi, hello, or go to hell? You just barge in here with an unconscious female slung over your shoulder and ask where your uncle is? Well, to put your mind at ease," she said sarcastically, "he heard you were looking for him. He had planned on heading east this morning, but, depending on what he finds or doesn't find—including you—he might be back as early as tomorrow night."

Sarah turned back to the center of her attention, "What's going on here?" she asked as she nodded at the frowning, comatose female dressed in baggy pants, plaid shirt, and an odd, dark green coat.

Ian slung his improvised pack over his shoulder, grabbed the knife on the table, and sliced off a generous chunk of bread from the freshly baked loaf. "Thanks," he said as he raised the bread in both salute and farewell. "This is Evie. She's my new wife. She has a sair heid and is tired all the time. Would ye see to her, please?"

That was all he could think to say, and it was hard getting out even that much. He saw Sarah had turned around and was already busy, starting a hands-on examination of her new patient. He made use of the opportunity and slipped out the door.

"Ian? Ian? Ian?" Sarah's call started with a soft voice, but ended up as a hoarse whisper, bellowing for her nephew. Seeing he had obviously sneaked out, she rose from her patient's side and ran to the door, flinging it wide open. "Ian? Ian, what's going on? Come back here right now, mister!" she called, her voice escalating to an angry and bossy reproach.

But it was too late. He heard her but knew she couldn't see him. He also knew she wouldn't leave her new patient alone to search for him. And, there was no way he was going back.

Ian walked away from the house with long, confident strides, his burden relieved, his destination his own choice. He didn't have any intention of finding Jody and never had. It was just the opposite—he wanted to be as far away from him as possible. He knew if his uncle were aware of his plans, he would try to talk him into forgiving the bastards.

He wanted, needed, to be alone, to immerse and surround himself with hate and anger, to seal off and forget everything about forgiveness and mercy he had been taught all his life. He wanted to call up every bit of Indian warrior vengeance he had left in him and exercise it, cultivate it, until it was stronger and more powerful and potent than any white man's justice.

Leaving was what was best for Evie. He was sure of it. He hadn't said much when he left her at the house. He couldn't tell his aunt how they had met—or the stories she had told him about the fifty United States of America, and 'President' George Washington. Aunt Sarah would find out about her soon enough—even sooner if she saw the strange items Evie had in her backpack. In no time, she would discover that Evie was from the future, even if Evie herself wasn't aware of it. And by then, he'd be gone. Sarah could help Evie get back to her own people, her own family, and to her own time.

He was both relieved and sad about losing her. He wished he could erase the last two and a half months from his memory—pretend it never happened. He loved Evie more than he thought he could ever love anyone. But that adoration also meant he was vulnerable. She could hurt him more than knives, fists, and fire ever could—or had. True, she wouldn't intentionally cause him pain or trouble, but she was better off with her own kind, in her own time.

Yes, it was best for her—and for him.

He couldn't get that voice out of his head. Whether that old woman in the wee black box was Evie or not, one thing was certain: Evie was a time traveler like Sarah and Ramona. Nothing but heartbreak could come from her being in his life.

Sending her back was all he could think about since he had heard that voice: 'Tell Danny you found her fone.' The only time he didn't think about it was when she was gazing into his eyes. Evie loved him; he knew that by the way she looked at him, touched him, and smiled at him when she first saw him in the mornings.

He had thought about it one last time as he walked up to his aunt's front door. But he always came back to the same conclusion: he had to leave Evie with Sarah and never return. His aunt was the best person—possibly the only person—to take care of her. Of that, he was certain.

Having Evie out of his life was the first step in achieving what he hoped was peace. The second step was getting his revenge, and the third step, well—he'd figure that one out later. Right now, he wanted to find out where the heathens' camp was. With the elimination of the whiner yesterday, he was only two vermin down. He still had six more of those foul 'judges' to get rid of. It would be difficult to do with a wife and child in his life—that is, if the bairn even lived. He had already lost two wee'uns and couldn't bear the loss of a third. Hopefully, midwives had better skills and herbs in Evie's future time.

Ж

The trail away from Uncle Jody's home was well marked, and it didn't take much talent to get away quickly and quietly. He felt like he had wings. His mind and body were now free from the responsibility of caring for—or even considering the needs of—another person. He felt as if he was already changing from white man husband back to Indian warrior. All conscious thought could now be focused on composing and perfecting his revenge.

His deep thinking was probably the reason he was out of tune with his environment. He didn't hear or see anything out of place—the night

160

sounds were low and soft, and not a leaf or branch had been crunched. He was absorbed in his plans of devising new methods of torture and payback when a large, strong hand came from behind and grabbed him by the mouth, cutting off his breath. At the same time, another hand grabbed his wrist and flipped it up behind him, twisting it so hard, he thought his arm was going to break.

"Gettin' pretty sloppy in yer old age there, arena ye, nephew?"

It was Uncle Jody.

Ian didn't know whether he was more mad or embarrassed at being caught off guard. Either way, he was blushing red as a fevered bairn from forehead to toe and twice as hot as a midsummer's day.

Jody quickly released his nephew.

"Aye, I guess I am. Glad to see ye," Ian lied. Jody wasn't the last person he wanted to see, but he wasn't very high up on his list either.

"So what brings ye here?" Jody asked, offering Ian a jug of the hard cider he had picked up from his secret cache at the edge of his property.

Ian took a long sip, savoring both the brew and the opportunity to compose himself and a story. The cider was ice cold and chilled his throat as it went down. His body was hot from the fast pace he'd been keeping, and hotter still from the flush of embarrassment he had just suffered at being surprised by his uncle. He took another sip, taking care not to drink too fast and get what Evie called 'brain freeze.'

"Well, where have ye been and how have ye been keepin' busy?" Jody asked. "We havena heard from ye in ages. We dinna even ken if ye were still alive." He wasn't going to make it easy for Ian to be evasive. He also wanted to get right to the heart of the subject, so he could get back to the house and see what was going on with Sarah and the lass.

Ian felt like he had just been made the Christmas goose and put on the dinner table for Uncle Jody to carve. He had the feeling his kin knew something, but what? He took another small sip of cider but acted as if he were savoring a big mouthful. He knew his uncle could see right through any lie he told, so he decided to tell the truth, omitting some—most—of the major points.

"Weel," he drawled, "I've been here and there, and neither place had writin' paper, so I suppose that's why ye havena heard from me. But, as ye can see, I'm jest as great as ever!" Ian kicked back and put his hands behind his head, leaned against a tree, and looked up for the first star in the sky. That was clever, he thought. He grinned widely, very satisfied with himself.

161

"Oh, so that's the way it is, is it? Nothin' excitin' in yer life? Tell me, how'd ye lose yer dirk, *boy*?"

Ian blushed red again, this time with anger. There was no way he was going to tell his uncle that his favorite dirk had been taken from him, and that only yesterday he had broken off the only knife he owned in the ribs of a mongrel of a man who had shamed, beaten, and planned to kill him last fall. He would rather suffer the indignation of not having a dirk than to let his uncle know he had broken it while wreaking vengeance. And *boy!* He was a man—how dare Jody call him a boy!

"It's none of yer business!" he shouted as he jumped up, face to face with his uncle.

Jody's two eyebrows crowded into one as his whole face came together in a snarl on hearing his nephew's boorish tone. He pulled back his shoulders, using the movement to calm down and try to rein in his anger and disgust.

"Oh, so droppin' off yer wife—and her bein' in a family way—at my house is none of my business? Maybe lettin' ye run around the woods, yer head so high in the clouds I coulda come up behind ye and taken it off had I wanted, is nae my business either. But it *would* be my business to let yer mam ken that her son was runnin' all over the country, gettin' lasses in a family way, and droppin' 'em at my doorstep, while the *boy* goes about, tryin' to kill men without so much as a dirk in his belt!"

The men were face-to-face and ready for battle, a battle of strong emotions, and maybe fists.

Ian was both angry and hurt when he heard the facts presented from a viewpoint that wasn't his. Shoulders back, chin up, he shouted, "Ye dinna understand, I had to do it!" He closed his eyes and his voice softened, "It was what was best for her."

Jody wasn't ready to calm down, though. He hollered back, his enraged words blasting forth a mere twelve inches from Ian's face, "What do ye mean, best fer her? How could ye leave yer wife and unborn bairn with someone else, even family, while ye went out and tried to get yerself killed?"

Ian's wrath flared up again. "I'm not tryin' to get myself killed! I have to, to, take care of some business." He wanted to say more but realized there was no explaining vengeance to a man who had learned to live and cope with the horrors of his past by using forgiveness. Ian turned away and headed into the woods, picking up his pack as he walked past it.

"Oh, so that's how it is, eh? Ye jest walk away from yer family so ye can take care of yer *business*? Dinna ye ken that takin' care of yer family is the most important business there is? Or are ye too much of a coward to take on any responsibility?"

Ian dropped the pack, turned around, and glared at Jody. He was too far away to throw a punch, but close enough to go for a tackle.

Jody saw the rush and stepped aside at the last moment, avoiding the hit and sending Ian headfirst into the scrub. "Oooh, the wee lad doesna like bein' called a coward now, does he? Well, a coward is what ye are if ye go and desert yer family. Coward or nae, tell me, why did ye leave her? If ye dinna want her, then why did ye marry her?"

Ian picked himself up from his tumble in the bushes. Jody was right; he deserved some sort of explanation. He walked over to his uncle and motioned to the ground. "Let's sit."

Jody sat on a fallen log, his face and stare, hard as granite. It would take one hell of a story for him to forgive his nephew for abandoning his pregnant wife.

"Evie's a traveler, like Sarah, from another time, but I dinna think she kens it. She shouldna be here. As soon as she gets to feelin' better, Auntie Sarah can send her back." Ian shrugged his shoulders, like this simple explanation was all that was needed.

Jody's eyes turned from stone to fire. "Ye dinna even let Evie make the decision? She's yer wife—whether by priest, handfast, or the Indian way—and it's yer job to take care of her."

Jody shook his head in amazement and disgust. "Ye kent she was with child, and yet ye jest left her? What kind of man are ye?" The rage was too much for Jody; he couldn't sit still. He stood up and paced, at first ignoring Ian, then glancing back at him, snorting and shaking his head again in disapproval.

"Aye, but it wasna my bairn!" Ian protested. "She was already with child when I met her: her belly grew real fast. I had only been with her two and a half moons and she was like Robin at four moons when I, I, left her with Sarah."

Ian pulled his knees up to his chin. He was motionless, as if he were a part of the ground beneath him, small as the ant crawling over the end of his boot. He hugged his knees and rocked back and forth, wishing he could be anywhere but here.

"Yer child or nae, she is still yer wife, and it's yer responsibility to take care of her and the bairn. And that means from right now until yer *deid*," Jody said, as if there were no exceptions or arguments acceptable.

163

But Ian had managed to compose himself. He stood up to his uncle, this time calm and determined. He was wearing his shield of futility. No matter what was said to him, his decision was made, and it was futile, useless, to argue with him.

"Ye were never a whole man without Auntie Sarah, my mam used to say. Then she came back, and ye were whole once more. Then ye got sick, she left again, and we thought ye were gonna die. Ye wanted to die without her, dinna ye? Well, Uncle, I dinna want to go through that. I may not be a man to ye, but whatever I am, I want it to be whole. Send Evie back; it's best for everyone."

**23 I Woke Myself Screaming

January 11, 1781
Pomeroy Point, North Carolina

Somewhere nearby, there was hysterical screaming. A woman was shrieking without pause, her pitch rising and falling with her gasps for breath, her protests never diminishing.

I reach up to push the hair out of my face and realize that I am the one who is producing those hideous wails. Panic-stricken and overwhelmed, I can't stop myself. Screaming is me: there is no thought or emotion—just horrid noises emanating from my core, surging up, and blasting out a fissure—my mouth, I think.

The chaos slowly subsides, or at least the volume is decreasing, but now my essence is being invaded, attacked. It feels as if a giant jellyfish is enveloping me—tentacles grabbing and pulling my newly discovered body into its mass, eager to consume me. A thundering growl erupts from a point deep within me, "Get your hands off of me!"

"Okay, okay, everyone, leave her alone."

A woman with a soft English accent is speaking, but I don't recognize her voice. I hear the authority in her tone, though, and so do the others. The pawing ceases, my panic subsiding enough that I can breathe.

A woman's voice I don't recognize: "Hmph," escapes directly from my chest, completely bypassing my clenched jaws. I have only encountered a fistful of people since I've had a memory, and this woman is definitely not Ma.

A couple more parts of my physical being are now making themselves uncomfortably known: my tongue is swollen, and my throat raw and raspy from my hullabaloo. My body needs fluids. I take two slow, deep breaths, attempting to pull myself together. I become conscious of the fact that 'I' will have to snap back into reality; no one else can do it for me. And the sooner I get it done, the better.

"Water, please?" I implored squeakily, my eyes squeezed shut to avoid stimulation.

Hearing the swish of fabric nearby, I forced one eye open and saw the backside of a woman as she ushered everyone out of the room, her curly golden brown locks, kissed with the silver highlights of maturity, escaping the ribbon-tied queue, to cascade down her back. Her full-length colonial-style dress was a non-descript neutral color, but the shawl around her shoulders was a bright sunny yellow. She turned and smiled at me. "Are you sure you don't want something stronger, whisky maybe?"

"That sounds like a good idea," I whispered hoarsely, then swallowed hard, trying to get my mouth moist enough to speak louder. "Can you put a little honey and milk in it, though? I'm not used to whisky, and I'm not even sure I should be drinking alcohol."

My apparent hostess opened the door, said something to someone outside, and returned to the kitchen area. She took two containers from the cupboard: a honey pot and a bottle of whisky. A moment later, she answered the knock at the door and returned with a small pitcher of milk. She poured a shot of whisky into a stoneware cup, added a dollop of honey, then a healthy splash of milk. "Do you want it warmed?" she asked as she reached for the hot poker set in the ashes.

"Uh, no thanks; cold is fine."

I sipped the concoction. Just as I had hoped, it tasted like crème liqueur. I brought the brim of the cup to my bottom lip and inhaled the musty scent of the milk, concentrating on the sweet yet sharp taste of the drink, trying to exclude all distractions, meditating on the creamy texture, letting my thoughts settle and synchronize gracefully.

"Have you ever tried it like this?" I asked hesitantly. I really didn't want to engage in conversation, but didn't want to be rude either.

"No, we usually drink it straight. It either fixes what ails you or allows you to not care about it anymore." She paused a moment, then asked, "What do you mean you aren't sure you should be drinking alcohol?"

The tranquility of floating inside my cup of bliss is shattered by her words, reminding me that I need to come back and face my new reality: pregnant and alone, my husband gallivanting off to parts unknown, probably to 'get even' with those men who had terrorized him last year. Ouch, this new reality is uncomfortable—and anxious—but not as scary as my transition from unconsciousness earlier. Waking up in the presence of strangers, with a real roof over my head, and with a noggin stretched to bursting with vibrant, disjointed, and unbidden information is more than one shock too many for me.

At least I feel safe with my new guardian, even if I don't have a clue about what's going on. But whether she's the one in charge, or it's some ornery ogre just outside who's calling the shots, I know she can't help me—I am the only one who can really take care of me.

I delayed my response, "Before I answer any questions, who are you, and where is Ian?"

"Well, Ian brought you in a bit ago, said that you were his wife, that you had a headache, and that you were tired all the time. He, um, left to search for his Uncle Jody. They should be catching up with each other soon. By the way, I'm Ian's aunt, Sarah Pomeroy, Jody's wife. You can call me Sarah."

"Oh, boy," I murmured, dipping my nose back into my drink, glad that I was sitting down.

I continued sipping to stall for time, but I couldn't lose myself in the cup again. It was as if the warm swim I had been enjoying had suddenly become an icy shower.

What should I say— I think I know you?

I have never met either of them, but for some reason, I know who she and Uncle Jody are, sort of. My memory is coming back in huge surges now, like tidal waves, overwhelming me, threatening to knock me off my nut again. And what I am 'knowing' has nothing to do with what Ian told me.

"I think I'd better lie down again if it's okay. I...I...oh, boy."

Sarah rushed towards me, arms out to catch me in case I fell. "Here you go; don't try to do too much now."

Faint averted, she led me to the chaise lounge and helped me lie back. "Would you care for a cool cloth?"

"Thanks, that would be wonderful, Sarah. And a tall glass of water, too, please. I think I'm dehydrated, and the whisky and milk won't help that."

Sarah made another trip to the door, whispered to someone outside, and came back to my side. She laid her cool hand on my forehead—a mother's touch, not a healer's. "Now, is that better?"

I nodded, but I could tell she was still confused.

"I've never heard anyone around here say the word 'dehydrated,' much less know what it meant. Are you a healer?" she asked, her eyes narrowed with suspicion.

I snorted, biting off the rest of my laugh before it sneaked out. "No, it's just basic knowledge where I'm from. Ian says *you're* quite the healer, though. Are you a doctor or a nurse?"

My question took her off guard. She blinked a couple of times, then paused before replying, wringing her hands, choosing her words carefully. "You know, when I first got here, I told someone I was a nurse. He

167

thought I meant 'wet nurse.' Women aren't doctors here in America, or even England, and a nurse isn't considered a person with medical training." She raised a single eyebrow. "Where did you say you were from?"

"I didn't say, and you know that," I replied, sporting a smug grin. Her face dropped, and I felt bad about my attitude. "Sorry, I'm not trying to be rude; it's just that I have a problem with my memory. A big problem, as in I don't have one. I fell and cracked my head pretty good the day after I found Ian. At least, I think it was the day after I found him. Anyhow, until an hour ago, I only remembered bits and pieces of things that happened before I woke up one morning with a concussion and Ian taking care of me. That was just over two months ago. Now, all of a sudden, I'm overloaded with memories. I think that's why I was screaming when I woke up. But it's weird. The things I'm remembering aren't personal memories. I *know*, but don't *remember*, if that makes any sense. I know about people, technologies, events that…well, stuff that might make people around here think I'm a witch."

I finished my short biographical dissertation with a sigh and an opening big enough for her to climb right into. And, by the look on her face, she knew exactly what I was talking about.

"Oh, crap," I said before she could respond to my observation. I sat upright and groaned, but not in pain. Volumes of information were once again surging into my gray matter, but this time without the headaches and hysterics.

I still don't know who I am, but now I recognize Sarah, both by her name and from the detailed descriptions of her given by Lisa Sinclaire, author of the romance novel series, 'Lost.' I don't remember reading the stories, but I know all about Sarah, and her husband, too—Jody Pomeroy, the most perfect man in the world, 18th century hero of the Second Rising in Scotland, now an American patriot. The 'Lost' saga was supposed to be historical fiction, lusty science fiction fantasy, but Sarah Pomeroy is standing right in front of me. She really is a 20th century time traveler!

Neither of us said anything. We both looked around the room, avoiding each other's eyes, not even glancing in each other's direction. She took a few hesitant steps away from me and sat at the kitchen table, gathering the fabric of her skirt as if pleating it. She could just as well have been biting her fingernails—she wasn't very good at hiding her nervousness. The silence was oppressive; neither of us knew what to do or say next.

168

"I also know that you know what I'm talking about," I ventured, reaching out to touch her arm, pleading with both my eyes and my voice.

Her mouth twitched side to side, as if chewing her words before letting them out. She took a deep breath and said in a chilly, clinical tone, "May I see your left arm, please?"

"You could if it wasn't so darned inconvenient to take off these shirts." I paused then added, "How about if I just tell you that, yes, I have a smallpox vaccination scar and a few fillings, too?" I pulled my mouth open wide with my index finger, rolled my eyes comically, and showed off my lower right silvery molars.

Sarah's mouth dropped open in surprise, then shut quickly as she gulped hard, swallowing her shock. She stood up, took a deep, soul-cleansing breath, and smiled, at peace with her decision to trust.

The real-life fictional character reached out and squeezed me close and hard. She finally loosened her grip and allowed air space between us, but didn't let go. She was crying and trying to talk at the same time, not making any sense at all, babbling with joy between more embraces and sniffling. I returned the hugs and patted her on the back as I rocked her to and fro like a young child.

A firm, insistent knocking at the door interrupted our emotional revelation. Sarah broke away, straightened her dress, and wiped her face with her apron. A brief sniff and a swipe of her hands through her hair for composure, and she was ready to greet the visitor.

"Ma'am, here's the cloth and pitcher of water ye wanted. Ye have a couple of other visitors here, too. They're waitin' fer ye over by the barn. I told them ye were busy with a sick woman, but they said they'd wait fer ye."

"Thank you, Dottie," Sarah said and accepted the folded cloth and ewer of water. She closed the door and looked around, obviously searching for another cup.

"Sarah, why don't you finish this whisky and we can reuse the cup for water? You look like you could use it more than me right now anyhow."

Sarah set down the pitcher, took the proffered cup with both hands, and gulped it down. "This is good; I'll have to remember this. It's easy on the stomach, too." She poured a splash of water into the cup, swished it around to capture the last, sweet drops of *crème*, drank it, refilled it with water, and handed the non-brew to me.

A couple of deep, joyful sighs and Sarah had regained her wits. "Would you mind waiting here for me? I need to see who our visitors are and what they need." She paused at the door. "I really want to talk to you," she added, looking like a child who had just received a new bike and had to wait to ride it.

"It doesn't look like I can go anywhere for a while. Ian's gone, and I'm all alone, stranger in a strange land."

"Robert Heinlein, right?"

"You got it, sister. Hurry back."

"Don't worry," she said as she pushed open the door, "I will."

**24 New Accommodations

I walked the perimeter of the room. It was an elegant room—if you were a priest taking a vow of poverty. Not even a simple curtain adorned the tiny window. There were no pictures or decorations on the walls, and no rugs on the earthen floor. I could tell it was as clean as it could be under the circumstances. There were still sweep marks on the hard packed dirt floor, and the crude broom that had made them was in the corner. The kitchen table was roughly made of native pine, but clean and sturdy. The neatly patched chaise lounge—coarse homespun beige fabric over the worn, shiny pale green brocade—had once been an elegant piece of furniture. "At least it's still comfortable," I sighed as I kicked back for a little nap.

Ж Ж

Thumps and jostling noises just outside the door woke me out of a sound sleep. Someone was excited, but I couldn't understand enough of the frantic conversation to figure out what the problem was. The female voices faded as they walked away, but I didn't hear Sarah's distinctive accent among them.

I waited a few moments—fear of the unknown, I guess—then nudged open the door and looked out. I couldn't see anything, but heard rumblings coming from the other side of the yard. I sucked in a lungful of bravery, grabbed my coat, and slipped outside.

I tiptoed toward the outbuilding, trying to be as quiet as Ian or Little Bear would be. Several horses and a couple of mules were in front of the barn-like structure, voices and light seeping from the partially opened doors. I kept my eyes to the ground, literally watching where I put every step, negotiating the uneven path, rutted by wagon wheels or heavy sleds that had slogged through the once snowy mud. The frozen crisscrossed ground created a veritable icy, earthen obstacle course. With the ruckus going on in the barn, I didn't have to worry about anyone hearing me, but I did have to worry about spraining an ankle.

I approached from the blind side of the building; sidling close to the newly-split wood walls so as not to be seen through the foot-wide gap between the doors, but not so close that I'd get splinters. A lantern was hanging from a nail on the center support pole, its amber glow strong enough that I could see the objects of the men's attention. Two huge burlap bags were lying on the straw-strewn earthen floor—muffled curses coming from one of them—and three grungy men were prodding them with their shoddy boots.

Oh, God—*déjà' vu* all over again.

I didn't know who or what were in the bags, but it didn't matter. I was pissed!

I strutted in boldly and demanded, "What the hell is going on here?"

"Who's she?" a slack-jawed, snaggle-toothed teenager asked, "and who let her in?"

I pushed by him, ignoring his comment, and planted myself solidly in front of the burlap sacks. I whipped out my Leatherman and pulled out the knife blade. "Hold still," I said loudly to the writhing person in the first sack. I sliced through the top of the bag, just under the knotted rope that secured it, and then pulled the coarse and dirty fabric away from the shoulders of a small, well-built, and finely clothed—but now disheveled—gentleman.

The man's diaphanous blond hair was flying all over from static electricity, his blue eyes brilliant with hostility. I didn't know who he was, but I'd be ticked, too, under the circumstances. The grimy brown rag crammed in his mouth, tied in the back with a haphazard knot, muffled his curse words, but not their emotional color. I pulled the bag down further, past his shoulders, and saw that—just as I had thought—his whole upper body was bound.

"'Git her away from him; she's gonna to let him loose," a greasy-looking man squeaked in fear as he cowered against the brass and leather horse accoutrements hanging on the wall.

I whipped around and growled, "Watch it!" at the two skinny, rag-clothed men approaching.

They froze; everyone could see how angry I was, even in this dim light. "Don't even think about it!" I snarled and waved the knife in front of me threateningly. All three backed away, stunned by the knife, my voice, or by the fact that it was a woman holding them at bay.

I turned my attention back to my half-exposed hostage. He, too, had stopped with my command. I dug my fingers into his gag and wrestled it down over his chin. "Are you hurt?" I asked, looking into his angry and very blue, long-lashed eyes. I didn't take my gaze from his. If he was a creep, I'd be able to see it in his reaction to me, his champion.

"I'm well enough, I think. Thank you, madam. Now, if you would be so kind as to…"

172

He didn't get a chance to finish. As soon as he said, "Thank you" with sincerity, I flipped the Leatherman around and revealed the wire cutters.

My fancy wrist action and the flash of metal caught everyone's attention. Clip, clip; two quick snips, and Blondie was untied, albeit still in the bag.

The prisoner wavered, but kept his eyes fixed on me—he was stunned by my appearance or actions, or both. He looked almost comical, like an awe-struck character in an old slapstick comedy: his blond hair splayed out around his head like a lion's mane, his eyes stern, but mouth hanging open in confusion. His light brown eyebrows crowded together and seemed to ask, 'What did you do with that knife to turn it into scissors?'

Time stood still as everyone gawked at me; only the sputtering of the candle flame as bits of straw chaff drifted into it disturbed the silence of the winter night. The hostage realized his stare, closed his mouth, and cleared his throat. The bag next to him was suddenly alive, wiggling, and writhing. He tipped his head, wordlessly asking me, "Would you help him, too?"

"Can I trust you to stay here until I find out what's going on?" I asked.

"You have my word, madam," he replied formally and courteously, his head dipping into a bow, the rest of his body limited by his situation.

"How about the other bag—is it okay to let him out, too?"

"I'll vouch for him also." Blondie squared his shoulders and picked off the cut ropes clinging to him with disdain, dropping them to the ground like lint from a jacket, and then began extricating himself as gracefully as possible from the rough sack. I noticed he was wearing a Colonial-period uniform, slightly dirty, but otherwise respectable.

I grabbed the ropes on the second gunnysack, and tried to remember the order of colors on Revolutionary War uniforms. I remembered that the young American army had used colors opposite of the British uniforms, but I couldn't recall if we were red on blue or blue on red. The man had a British accent, but that didn't mean anything. I shook my head to clear it and resumed my immediate task.

"Hold still or you might get cut," I warned the occupant of the bulging bag. "I'm trying to get you out of there."

It was harder to open this sack because the man was so big—not fat, but power-forward basketball-player huge. He must have been shoehorned in. I was surprised he fit at all. His struggles to escape had also tightened the knots.

"Freeze," I said. He stopped squirming immediately. I patted along the front of the bag, searching for a spot that wasn't taut with body parts. I flipped the Leatherman around and used the long blade to slice through the coarse fabric, pulling the cloth away bit by bit, sawing through it in segments. Even at that, it took less than half a minute to free him.

He was younger than the other man was—maybe in his early twenties, probably younger. His long golden-brown wavy hair had come out of its queue, the dark ribbon dangling unceremoniously on the shoulder of his dusty uniform. The jacket was the same design as Blondie's, but with less braid trim. "Hold still again," I told him, and cut through his gag.

I touched the young man's shoulder to steady myself as I walked around him. He was muscular, not wiry strong like Ian. I gulped, pushing the memory of my errant husband back into the pit of my gut. Now wasn't the time to deal with Ian and my abandonment issues.

I pulled the remnants of the sack from the young man's back, cut the coarse ropes binding his hands, and noticed a big blue lump on the side of his head. "Thank you," he said as he sat up straight, twisting the kinks out of his back, neck, and shoulders before arising.

I had only glanced at the others in the room when I came in, but now that the hostages were free, I paid closer attention to the young ruffians. They were terrified. They had edged away from me as far as possible, practically becoming the caulking in the split-timber walls. It didn't look like they wanted to leave, but I doubted they were going to challenge me or try to re-subdue their prisoners. Now that their hostages were unbound, they might have reason to fear them, but I didn't. I had asked for and received the word of a gentleman.

"Sirs, can you tell me why you were detained in such an uncouth manner?" I asked the disheveled duo, my words formal, but my mouth lopsided with a smile of sarcasm.

"I am Lord Julian Hart, of His Majesty's Royal Army, and this is my stepson, Lieutenant Wallace Urquhart, Viscount Cavendish. I assure you, I have no idea why we have been abducted in this rude and senseless manner."

I take two steps back and bump into the support pole, nearly knocking down the lantern. I feel as if I'm going to pass out. I suddenly recognize these two, or at least realize who they are, just as I had Sarah. I have never met any of these people, but I know all about them. There's no time to reflect on this now, though; I have to maintain control of the situation in

174

front of me first.

To cover my awkwardness, I said, "Oops," as if I had just lost my balance. I sucked in a calming breath and coolly asked, "Now, what's your side of the story, boys?"

Snaggle Tooth spoke up, "Ma'am, sirs, we canna tell ye yet why we did it. We dinna mean to harm the men, it's jest that the big 'un here, he was kinda hard to handle. We had to knock him upside the heid so he'd cooperate into the bag. Sorry, sir, fer the knot thair. It's jest that, weel, we was tryin' to save ye."

"Save us?" Lord Julian blared. "Who in God's name would think that rendering us unconscious and dragging us to God only knows where would save us?"

"Sorry, sir, I canna tell ye. But it really was fer yer own good." The look on Snaggle Tooth's face was sincere. The others mumbled and nodded in agreement, but no one would say more.

"Okay then, Lord Julian and Lord Wallace, would you accompany me into the house? Since we still haven't figured out what's going on, I guess you'll be spending at least tonight here." I turned to the ragtag trio and addressed them, "Men, if you'd like to make your camp here, I'm sure the lady of the house wouldn't mind."

"But ma'am, I…er… don't ye think ye ought to have one of us with ye for protection?" Snaggle Tooth asked.

"Lord Wallace, your stepfather gave his word to stay here with me until this was all resolved. Will you do the same? Oh, and neither of you will hurt me or tie me up, right?" All I had to secure these men with was old-fashioned integrity, but from what I remembered from history, it was stronger than the ropes that had bound them.

"Yes, ma'am; we are at your service," he replied, ending his acknowledgment with a courteous bow.

"Okay, then let's get out of here."

The three of us left the greasy kidnappers where they were and headed toward the house. We were mute, unsure of a safe topic of conversation, the oppressive silence clinging to us like wood-smoke to clothes.

The sound of another possible intrusion—at least one more horse and rider coming in—hurried our footsteps. It was nighttime, we were already skittish, and few people traveled in the dark.

Lord Julian quickly ushered us into the house. He was taking charge now, and I was glad to cede the responsibility. My adrenaline had subsided and, although I no longer had a headache, I was exhausted and wanted to lie down.

I stumbled in the darkness to the chaise lounge. The fire had burned down to an ashy orange glow and there weren't any candles lit. I quickly thought of using my flashlight but shook my head wordlessly. I didn't even know if Ian had left my backpack here. If he had, I certainly wasn't going to pull out a 21st century bag covered in zippers and Velcro or use an electric light in front of 18th century soldiers!

Julian was watching the action outside from the small kitchen window. I didn't need to see what was going on; I could tell by the noises that the rider or riders were coming directly to the house, not stopping at the barn to take care of their horses as friends or family would. These must be strangers.

Strangers. That reminded me, where were Sarah and the women who were helping her when I arrived? Everyone seemed to have disappeared.

Footfalls on the steps sent me bolting to join the men against the wall beside the door, hiding from first view of whoever was coming in from outside.

The door opened wide and in walked Sarah. "Halloo, are you awake?" she called toward the chaise, her voice low so as not to wake me if I were asleep.

I stepped out from behind her and announced, "I'm right here," startling her so much that she faltered. I allowed her a moment to gather her wits, then said, "It's dark in here, and I don't know where the candles are."

"Oh, I'll take care of that. How about you; how are you feeling? Are you okay?" she asked, the back of her hand to my forehead, checking for fever.

"Yes and no. The headache is gone, but I'm lightheaded. Is there anything quick to eat? I have low blood sugar and I feel like I'm going to faint."

"I've got some bread, and there's cheese here in the cupboard. Oh, and the candles are… Jesus! Where did you come from?"

Julian moved away from his shadowy spot near the door. "Hello, Mrs. Pomeroy. As to where I came from, I recently emerged from a filthy gunnysack, which I was introduced to—very much against my will—for transport to your barn from…let's just say from an undisclosed military location. Evidently some ill-informed renegades decided that abduction and bondage were the appropriate methods of making sure my stepson and

I were transported to your barn. You do remember Wallace, don't you?"

At his introduction, Wallace stepped forward. "Good evening to you, Mrs. Pomeroy. I hope you are well."

I grabbed the cloth given to me earlier, poured water over it and slapped it on my forehead, then plopped back down onto the chaise.

These people are storybook characters who have come to life and suddenly manifested themselves—body, scent, sound, and personality— right in front of me. This is a lot—maybe too much—for me to deal with!

I put down the cloth, grabbed the pitcher, and drank directly from the rim. I didn't know where the cup I had used earlier was, and at this point, I really didn't care about good manners. I did wish I had more of that *crème liqueur*, though.

Sarah lit a taper, tossed the punk into the fire, and asked Julian, "Are you saying you were kidnapped?"

"It appears so, although I haven't heard any mention of a ransom. We would still be in those sacks were it not for this brave young lady," Julian said and nodded to me, obviously waiting for an introduction.

"Oh, I'm sorry," I responded, rising to my elbows. "I'm Sarah's sister who she didn't know she had. I kind of dropped in by surprise this afternoon, and well…just call me Evie."

The sounds of more activity came from outside—voices calling, feet shuffling, animals whinnying—interrupting our conversation. Julian rushed to the window and I followed, Sarah close behind.

Apparently the young kidnappers had packed up and were leaving, the shreds of their gunnysacks rolled into two chaotic bundles, lashed to the back of a short-legged donkey.

"I hope they're not bringing back any more captives," I said dryly as I looked over Julian's shoulder. "It's getting kind of crowded around here."

I got a snort, a chuckle, and an eye roll out of my impromptu audience. I looked at Wallace and noticed he was starting to waver. "Sir, I think you need the couch more than I do. Sit here and I'll get you a drink of water."

I led the young man by the elbow to the chaise, found the cup, and poured water for him. I rewet the cloth and handed it to him. "Leave this on the bump. The coolness should make the swelling go down and maybe ease the pain a bit, too. It does hurt, doesn't it?"

"Yes, ma'am, it does smart a bit. Thank you for your help." Wallace eased back into the chaise, his long legs dangling over the end, arms resting at his sides, elbows tucked in close, so they didn't dangle, too.

177

I readjusted the rag, which had slipped off as he settled in. I placed it across his cheeks and brow, covering his eyes, making sure I left him room to breathe. "Try to relax. It's okay to fall asleep, but I'm going to wake you every half hour or so, just to make sure you don't have a concussion. We don't want you to slip into a coma now, do we?"

He nodded in reply, but didn't speak, instead relaxing into a slow, steady breathing rhythm, preparing himself for sleep.

I looked up at the hollow silence—something felt wrong. Sarah and Julian were both staring at me.

"Are you a healer, too?" Julian asked. "You seem to have the touch, although your bedside manner is much gentler than your kind sister's." Julian turned and looked at Sarah with the last part of his remark, giving her a sly smirk of sarcasm.

"It's just that she's not used to dealing with you ornery men. She'll learn," she replied with an even bigger grin.

"Well, Wallace doesn't seem ornery to me. I think it's just a bruise though." My voice and attitude quickly changed to one gently imploring. "Sarah, do you know anything about this situation, why anyone would kidnap these two and drop them practically at your doorstep?" I wanted to be the one to start the inquiry so I could set a friendly tone.

Sarah nodded towards the broom and she, Julian, and I retreated to that corner for our discussion. She answered in a hoarse, frustrated whisper, "I know nothing about this. I didn't even know you were in the area, Julian. And why would I want to kidnap you?"

"Sarah, I didn't think you were responsible for abducting Wallace or myself, but we are on opposite sides of this confounded revolution. Maybe there is something political behind this. I didn't recognize the men who took us, but I wager by their accents, they're colonials."

"Julian, I'm sorry for what happened to you. Please, allow me to offer you and your son hospitality, at least. I'm hoping Jody will be back soon. He went on a short errand. He didn't tell me exactly where he was going, but said it was to fetch Ian. Just after he left, Ian showed up here and asked me to take care of his new wife, Evie. Then he went to find Jody. I'm sure they'll locate each other and return shortly. After all," Sarah laughed nervously, trying to make a joke to put us all at ease, "Ian will have to come back for Evie, and I'm sure Jody will want to meet his new niece."

"Oh, so you are both a niece *and* a sister-in-law to Jody? He'll be glad to have more kin here. I know he misses his daughter and her family. Quite the thrifty Scot: two relatives in one," he said, giving me a sincere smile of appreciation, the dimples in his cheeks and tone of his voice letting me know that he was jesting, not being rude.

I blushed in embarrassment and tried to hide my glow, even though it was probably too dark to be seen. I babbled on about family, remarking on Jody and Sarah's daughter. "I never met Mona, her husband, or their children. I'm sure they were wonderful people."

I wince, realizing that I have started an awkward topic, at least as far as Sarah and I are concerned. Julian's comment seemed to support that her daughter and family had left, but how would I know her name?

I quickly changed the subject. "Wallace seems to have fallen asleep. I'm sure he'll be fine for a while. Bread and cheese, anyone?" I suggested, and held up the loaf of bread, smiling at the prospect of feasting on non-game food.

The uneasiness remained, but we all ignored it. Sarah brought out the cheese, along with a knife and plates, and set the spartan fare on the table. I didn't know how 18th century people ate bread and cheese, but I was doing it my way. I quickly sliced away and made little sandwiches, happy to be busy. "Anyone ever hear of mayonnaise?" I quipped, and took a big bite of dry sandwich.

**25 Fathers Revealed

Sarah retrieved the bottle of whisky and two short glasses from the cupboard while I rescued the cup from Wallace's sleeping hand before it spilled on him. I paused to gaze at him as he settled himself into a comfortable position. He was so beautiful. I doubted that I'd ever seen a man so perfect. He was tall, easy on the eyes, well educated, and very polite. I wasn't lusting after him—I was just appreciating God's handiwork. I sighed with loneliness; I was very much in love with Ian and the tightness in my chest reminded me of how much I missed him, even if it had only been a few hours.

Very little was said beyond 'please' and 'thank you' at our little soirée. Just about any topic—food, weather, or health—would end up pertaining to the war or the men's kidnapping.

My mind is busy—frustrated, but not panicked—quietly trying to put it all together. My innate knowledge about these people isn't from personal memories. I don't remember doing it, but I swear I learned all about Sarah and her family from romantic time travel novels. The title 'Lost' keeps popping into my head. I 'know' Sarah was born in 20th century England and that she had lived for a long time in modern-day America. She has to be aware of the outcome of the Revolutionary War. Certainly, she would have told her husband about it. Jody knows she is from his future, and if she's told him the American Colonists will win this war, I'm sure he believes her.

I 'know' they had tried to change history before by trying to stop Bonnie Prince Charlie from his ill-fated quest to return to the throne of England. That didn't work. I shook my head: why do I know this? I'll try and solve that mystery later. Right now, I have to see if I can keep these two rescued former-hostages here, out of harm's way, and away from fighting for the losing side.

Julian and Wallace are on the wrong team in this war, but I don't know whether it's because of birthright, patriotism, or military professionalism. Julian is a British subject and a current or former officer by his dress. Wallace also appears to be an officer in His Majesty's army—or whatever they call themselves. I just remember referring to them as Redcoats.

Redcoats—that's it! The British wore red coats and the Americans—

180

when they had uniforms—wore blue coats, their design the same as the British but the colors reversed.

Images and memories are pouring in again. I recall visiting Washington, D.C. and standing at the Twilight Tattoo ceremony, watching soldiers parade by in uniforms representative of all the different wars the United States had been in. I also remember crying when I realized that America has been fighting in wars and 'conflicts' and losing men for well over 200 years.

I don't want to lose these two, no matter which side they're on. I just 'rescued' them, and I feel kind of protective towards them. I need to find a way to keep them from going back to the war and their units. Besides, if they become active military again, they might shoot some of the good guys, the American patriots.

Sarah cleared her throat as if to make a statement. Julian and I looked at her, waiting for the words that wouldn't come. Her face suddenly emptied of emotion. It was obvious she had changed her mind about what she was going to say. She swallowed, and then tried again. "Uh, I hope you and Wallace have been in good health." She grimaced as soon as the words were out of her mouth. She realized her *faux pas*, but it was too late; she had already spoken.

"Well, up until this morning, we were quite well, Mrs. Pomeroy." Julian's voice had a cold, formal—almost sinister—tone. "I expect we will be back to our normal healthy selves in short order. The bump on the head Wallace received doesn't appear to be serious. We shall be on our way in the morning."

"Uh, excuse me, Julian," I said. "You gave me your word that you would stay here until we found out who kidnapped you, remember?"

"As I recall, I said I would stay here until we found out what was going on. It appears that it was just, well, just..."

"Then you *do* agree with me that we still don't know what's going on. So you'll stay here until we find out, right, like you said?" His word was the only tool I had to keep him and Wallace here, and I was going to make sure I used it as long as I could.

"Well, I suppose Wallace could use a bit more time to recuperate. I see he is resting well now. This uprising has bothered him quite a bit. He has had trouble with the concept of taking advantage of, and even killing, people in their own towns for the benefit of the Crown. He likes living here and has made this country his home."

Now I've got to try and keep them here—no matter how! These are

181

good guys. They're just playing for the wrong team.

I leaned forward, placed my elbows on my knees, and with a determined and sincere scowl on my face, peered deeply into Julian's eyes. "Julian, I need to tell you something about Sarah and me. It's very hard to believe, but it's important for you to know so you'll change your allegiance in this war. It's a matter of life or death."

I turned to face Sarah. Her face had paled at my words. I whispered, "I think it's the only way, Sarah. We have to save him and Wallace."

"What is she talking about, Mrs. Pomeroy?" asked Julian, his voice still chilly and now indignant.

Sarah gulped, cast her eyes down, took a deep breath to compose herself, then brought her chin up, making sure she looked him in the eyes. "Evie and I are different, Julian. Mona and Gregg were, too. I think you could see that, at least with Mona and me."

"Well, I did see that there was something *different* about the two of you. I reasoned your daughter was like you in her bluntness because of the way you reared her. I find that Evie is also very bold and direct in her speech and actions. It is quite plain that you are sisters. I dare say, I would hate to meet with your mother."

"Both our mothers are dead," I said.

I don't know if I just lied. I 'know' Sarah's mother is dead, and it feels as if my mother is, too. At least, she is dead as far as having a memory of her. No, wait, she isn't even born yet!

I sucked in a deep breath and did my best to get back on track. "We don't have the same mother, but we're family of a different sort. Not related by blood, but, Sarah…" I paused, searching for words, "can I tell him more?"

"In for a penny, in for a pound," she said in defeat and sat down hard on the chair. "Might as well."

"Julian, would you go out that door if I told you you'd be killed as soon as you went through it, even if you couldn't see or hear any evidence of danger?"

"I would think you were either rude or mad to say so, woman. I would exit, although I would be on high alert."

"If I told you that Wallace would die if he went through that door, would you risk his life, too?"

"In that case, I would probably go first and make sure the way was clear. I would not risk his life, although I wouldn't want him to be a coward, imprisoned by fear, rumor, or superstition. No, I wouldn't want to hold him back, but I would take extreme precautions for his safety before letting him leave."

"Julian, Sarah and I know things because what is happening here and now is the past for us, even though we're living in it as we speak. We are not witches or oracles; we don't see into the future. We know the outcomes of major events of today because, well, they're history for us. America is going to win this war, and there's nothing you or anyone else can do about it."

"Hmph!" Julian snorted, crossed his arms in front of his chest, and turned away from me, shutting me out with his body language and attitude.

"Really, you can't change the outcome. You see, Sarah also knew Bonnie Prince Charlie and the Scots would lose their Uprising. She and Jody intervened and tried to change history, but couldn't, didn't, make a difference. By the way, did he tell you that he meant to die at Culloden?"

"Yes, he did," admitted Julian.

"Did you think that he would ever leave Sarah, pregnant and alone, to go into a battle that he knew he'd lose?"

"Well, men who are soldiers do what they have to..."

I didn't let him finish. The newfound memories in my head were organizing and sorting themselves without me consciously thinking about what I was going to say next. It was my heart speaking out of desperation. I wanted, needed, to keep these two British soldiers from fighting against this new, semi-established America.

"He sent her home to be safe, and I don't mean to Italy. She went back to her time, a future time two hundred years hence, and he knew he would never see her again. There she bore his child, Mona, safely because of the benefit of modern medical science. This same future is where Mona grew up and learned all about the American Revolution and Presidents George Washington, John Adams, and Thomas Jefferson in her history classes. Julian, I understand that this is a lot to handle, but Sarah and I know what is going to happen because for us, it already *has* happened. And, hey, you might as well be with us on the winning side."

Julian wasn't even trying to hide his shock. His jaw slackened when I spoke of our presidents, but when I finished, he sat up straight. He shook his head, physically trying to erase what he had just heard. "No, your story is absolutely incredulous. It is impossible to appear and disappear into different centuries just like that," he said as he snapped his fingers. "Do not deem me a simpleton, madam, one who would even consider your 'time traveling' explanation as an excuse for Sarah's and your brazenness.

183

You were simply raised in an uncouth and semi-civilized culture, God only knows where."

"I was born in New Haven, Connecticut, in a hospital located less than a mile from Yale University. I believe the university is there now, but I think it's called a college. Many famous people have graduated from Yale including Nathan Hale and several signers of the Declaration of Independence. But you see, the hospital I was born in, St. Raphael's, hasn't even been built yet."

Julian puffed out his chest and lifted his chin. He didn't have a weapon, so I knew I was safe, but he was still intimidating.

"I am not a fool, so do not speak foolish words to me, madam. There is nothing you can say that will convince me that you speak the truth."

"Well, if the truth is too fantastic for you, I'll have to try a different approach. How about I tell you hidden things, things that even Sarah doesn't know, about you and your cousin?"

"I think that you are playing at cards right now, madam, and are bluffing."

I reached across the table and grabbed Julian's right hand. I lowered it beneath the table and tickled the inside of his palm, causing his fingers to curl, and then slid my index finger between his thumb and first finger in the imitation of carnal intimacy. "Are you sure I'm bluffing? Do you want me to reveal more of what I know?" I asked as I released my grip.

He pulled back his hand, casually wiped it on his trousers, and returned it to the tabletop. "I don't think that will be necessary. What is so important that you would think of blackmailing me and my family?"

"Normally I wouldn't even think about extortion, but I'm desperate. I'll do just about anything to save your life and Wallace's. Now, you may not believe me, but Sarah knew the outcome of Charles' attempt to regain the crown in the Second Uprising, even before he whispered his plan to his closest advisor. She had learned all about it in history books.

"When the time came close, she told Jody, 'Don't go to Culloden; it will be a bloodbath.' He said not to worry; he wouldn't. He had a plan.

"Jody convinced his captain that he and his men all had small pox and needed to be quarantined, hospitalized. Stinging nettles and beet juice did the trick. He led his spotted men to the abbey of Ste. Anne where the abbess accepted him and the 'infirm'…and the cask of wine he donated.

"Sarah was with them. She had disguised herself as a young man in order to stay with Jody. But the game plan had changed. She was pregnant again. She and Jody had already lost one child to her inadequate womb;

she didn't want to lose another one, too. She knew that the only way their child had a chance of surviving was with modern medicine. Besides, she knew what lay ahead. They might be able to survive the upcoming battle at Culloden, but times would be rough afterwards, as bad as the slaughter itself, or worse. There would be horrible reprisals, purges, and starvation: never enough food to eat for those left alive, much less for a time traveler—a 'fairy'—and her newborn.

"Jody agreed that she should return to her own time, but if there were any way she could come back, he'd wait for her. She wouldn't let him wait, though. She told him to get on with his life and that she and the babe would do the same. He was hurt, didn't believe that she could love him as much as he loved her, or she wouldn't have said such a thing. But he had to let her go, and sent her on her way, back to her time, to your future.

"His men were able to return home over the course of the next two weeks, leaving the good sisters and the ramshackle hospital two at a time. But that wasn't for Jody.

"As soon as Sarah was gone, he was on his way to Culloden...where he meant to die.

"He was captured, grievously wounded, but instead of dying, he was saved by you. You remembered him, right? He was the man who had reached in and pulled you out of that whirlpool when your boat overturned in the campaigns, remember?"

Julian's stiff back loosened. He had been tense, absorbed with my story, but now that I had brought him into it, he relaxed and nodded. He remembered.

"So, rather than put a bullet in his eye, you sent him on his way."

Julian sighed as he recalled that day. "I sent him back to his family at Barden Hall. I really didn't think he'd make it, but I gave him a gentleman's chance. I gambled and he won."

"You both won, Julian." I said. "He became your friend after he was recaptured, right?"

Julian nodded again.

"It wasn't until events occurred in Sarah's life—in her time, your future—that she even looked to see if Jody's plan had succeeded, to see if he and his men had escaped the slaughter and survived the aftermath. She looked through piles and piles of historical documents, with the help of Ramona and Gregg, before she found him in the prison journals at Fort William. Oh, and by the way, thank you for keeping such good records.

"It seemed that time was progressing in the past—your present—and

185

her 20th century at the same rate, so, well, that's when Sarah entertained the idea of coming back to him. She looked but couldn't find any trace of him remarrying or having other children. Their daughter, Ramona, was all grown up, had a great education, and a wonderful fiancé, Gregg. The outlook for their future was rosy. So, if time was progressing at a constant rate, Sarah wanted to come back to Jody.

"She was irate that he had gone back to Culloden, but what good would holding on to her anger do? He was two hundred years in her past…and certainly dead by now. The only way to make it right, to apologize for leaving him with a heart full of hurt—and to smack him for going to Culloden—was to go back. You see, she had been wrong: she hadn't been able to go forward with her life without him."

"Then what about Ramona and Gregg?' Julian asked.

I know Julian doesn't believe me, but he still wants to follow my logic. I can respect that—at least he is listening and trying to understand.

"Apparently Ramona wanted to meet her father. She wanted to dash back in time, get acquainted with Dad, see Mom once more, and then return to her fiancé and the 20th century after taking her little 'time vacation.' Of course, she didn't tell Gregg about the plan. She figured, rightfully so, that he'd try to talk her out of it. Well, Gregg was—is—a pretty smart character and figured out where she had disappeared to. He didn't know why she left, but he loved her and didn't want to lose her, so he decided to follow her. Lots of confusion ensued after he got here, much of which you already know. They wound up having a family and stayed here in this time for several years. It wasn't until baby Rebecca was born with a heart defect that they decided their family had to return back to their time—your future. Modern surgery was able to save Rebecca's life. Now they're all living happily ever after at Barden Hall."

"They made it? They're okay?" Sarah asked, tears streaming and hands wrenching. "Oh, thank You, Lord, I knew You'd see to them. Thank You, thank You…" she praised, and then started sobbing uncontrollably.

I looked over and smiled at her tears and sniffles enhanced radiance. She was ecstatic, and relieved, with the unfounded, inspired—but I was certain that it was true—news I had shared. I turned back to Julian and said, "So, unbelievable as it is, Gregg MacKay and family, two of whom were born in this 18th century, are alive and well in the 21st century."

"Assume for a moment that I believe you. Why are you telling me this?"

"Because…because…I don't want you and Wallace to fight on the side of the British army," I blurted out in exasperation. "Don't you see? America wins this war. It is still a country more than 200 years later in the 21st century. Slavery is abolished less than a hundred years from now, and women and blacks get to vote. In the 20th century, men will fly to the moon and people begin regular travel through the air all around the world. You can fly across this country—which will have fifty states by then and range from the Atlantic to the Pacific Oceans and almost to the North Pole—and do it in hours, not months."

"I do believe you are crazy, madam." Julian snorted. "People flying through the air, indeed. Ridiculous."

"Well, they'll be in airplanes, kind of like long carriages, but I guess it's easier for me to realize that I've gone back in time than it is for you to believe that I'm from the future. After all, I have the knowledge of what's going to happen and you…well…I guess I haven't been able to show you solid, tangible proof."

All was still. Sarah was wiping her face, composing herself after finding out her daughter and her family had returned safely to live at Jody's family estate in Scotland. Julian, face red in anger, was staring at the floor, squishing a small dirt clod with the toe of his boot.

Sarah tried to speak, but only managed a pleading squeak, "Oh, Julian."

"Wait! I've got it! Tangible proof! Sarah, did Ian leave my bag when he brought me here?"

Sarah opened the wooden chest, took out my backpack, and handed it to me as if she were awarding me an Academy Award. She cleared her throat and threw back her shoulders. "Here you are," she said with a confident smile.

"*Voila!*" I said and pulled out an empty plastic Ziploc baggie. "Have you ever seen one of these?"

"It looks like a bladder of some sort." Julian leaned forward to look at it, but didn't want to touch it.

"Here, look at this." I opened up the zippered top and set the bag on the table. Holding it open with one hand, I poured water from the ewer into it. I zipped it closed and held it upside down, just like in the commercials. "Ever seen anything like that?"

Sarah came over and looked closer. "They put zippers on plastic bags now? We only had the fold top kind when I came back. What else do you have in there?" she asked as she peered into the bag. "How about this?" she asked me, and pulled out the folded sheet of aluminum foil, crinkled

187

from being folded so many times, but still intact.

"Oh, I'm sorry, you'll want to see this, too, won't you, Julian?" Sarah began unfolding the thin metal sheet. Julian took it in, but didn't seem too impressed.

"Or this," I said. I held up, squeezed, and flexed my souvenir plastic water bottle shaped like a locomotive. "Practically indestructible and totally waterproof; just don't get it too hot or it'll melt."

Julian didn't say anything with his mouth, but his eyes were open so wide, his eyelashes were touching his eyebrows. It looked like his breathing was a bit rapid, too.

"You're not going to faint on us are you, Julian?" I asked, grinning like the cat that just ate the caviar. I was making progress.

His answer was to sit down with a thud. "Most amazing, madam," he admitted, "flexible glass?"

"Not quite," I answered, but didn't expound on my wonder bottle. "Did you see this when I was cutting you loose?" I asked and pulled the Leatherman out of my pocket.

"No, I think I was a bit preoccupied at the time, trying to extricate myself from that filthy sack," Julian growled, recalling his recent imprisonment.

"Here, check this out then." I held the Leatherman flat in my palm, then turned it back on itself to reveal the pliers. "See," I said as I picked up a pebble from the floor with the tool. "Now, this is where I grabbed the rope and cut through it." I showed him the sharpened inner jaws of the tool. Next, I opened out the little mini scissors, screwdrivers, corkscrew, files, and knives one at a time, and then returned it to its original, blocky configuration. Just to add a flourish, I whipped the tool around, exposing the pliers in one quick flick of the wrist.

Julian's head snapped back, his face once again trying to stay composed, but failing. I gave him a genuine smile; I knew I had him with the technology.

He sighed in resignation. "All right, you now have my full attention as well as my awe and respect. But why are Wallace and I so important to you; why us and not someone else?"

"I'll do whatever I can to save you. You are more than just a good friend to Sarah and Jody. You are the father of his son. Saving the lives of you two, well, it can be so easy or so hard. It all depends on whether or not you believe me."

A hard look suddenly took over Julian's face. It was obvious to Sarah and me that he was both angry and disgusted, but why?

He shouted at me in a hoarse whisper, "What do you mean 'I am the father of his son'?"

"Yes, madam, do you mean to say that Mr. Pomeroy is my father?" It was a softly spoken, but urgent question from the now upright Wallace Urquhart, Viscount Cavendish.

I looked at Sarah, then Wallace and Julian, and then back again to a stunned and pained Sarah. I glanced up and saw that Jody had slipped in, and was now standing quietly behind her, his face totally devoid of any emotion, but his hand was white-knuckled. He had a firm grip on Sarah's arm and was unintentionally hurting her. 'Oh, boy,' flashed through my mind. 'Think fast.'

The three of them knew Jody was Wallace's biological father. For that same unknown reason, I 'knew,' too. Jody had sired a child under duress when he and Sarah were separated by a couple of centuries. That part was fuzzy for me, but I did know it was a huge secret, and one that Wallace obviously had been protected from his entire life.

I slowly walked the few steps over to the chaise, hoping for—and then getting—inspiration. "Wallace, I need your assistance to explain this." He looked puzzled, but nodded in agreement: he'd help me. I continued, "Unbutton the top few buttons of your coat and shirt, please."

He lifted his chin up and worked the buttons without question. After he had the top four of both undone, he sat up straight and looked at me, not saying a word, but the blank stare of his blue eyes and crowded eyebrows inquiring, "Now what?"

"Let me see," I said. I fumbled inside his shirt with my chilly, shaking hands. He was either very good at hiding his feelings or he didn't have any to share. He wasn't shying away from me or acting embarrassed, but dutifully submitted to my nervous, probing fingers. I had just challenged his parentage, but he remained still and quiet. He was sitting in front of the two men I had just said were his fathers, keeping his eyes vacant, not looking at either of them, nor saying a word. Yet even in his silence, I could tell he trusted me. Not many men of this time would submit to an unknown woman fumbling inside their shirt, touching their bare skin, without being drunk or in a bawdy house. I had essentially called him a bastard, but he was stoic. Evidently, this wasn't the first time his parentage had been questioned…although I wouldn't doubt that it was the first time in the presence of his stepfather, Julian. And, I knew by the set of his jaw that he wanted to know the truth, no matter how unsettling it was.

"Here," I said as I wrapped my fingers around the worn, wood bead necklace I found tucked inside his shirt. I looked at Julian, "Did you know about this, Julian?"

"That appears to be a Catholic rosary. No, Wallace has never shown it to me," he replied icily. He started to say more, but literally bit his lip.

I was certain he was biting off the question about what this had to do with Wallace's parentage. I nodded to him, one corner of my mouth raised in a slight smile of appreciation, to thank him for his restraint and courtesy in this odd and curious exposé.

"I didn't think so," I said. "Would you care to tell us about its history, Wallace?"

The wary young man looked abashed as he started to explain, a slight flush rising from his exposed neck, his words spoken just above a whisper. "I got my first and only spanking from the man who gave this to me. I was only about five years old and spoiled rotten. I had just built a fire in one of the horse stalls. I was trying to roast an ear of corn. I wanted to make the kernels pop up like they had at the faire. The blaze got out of control, but our groom, Mac, doused it before it spread and did any real damage. He paddled my bottom as punishment. I threatened to have him dismissed for doing it. He said it didn't matter because he was already going to leave. Those words hurt me much more than any spanking ever could.

"I didn't have any friends when I was young. There was just my grandfather and a household full of doting women and servants letting me run wild, doing whatever I wanted. Every chance I found, I slipped outside to spend time with the groom and the horses."

Wallace was beginning to speak louder now. We were all still on edge, though, eager to hear the rest of the story.

"When Mac told me he was leaving, I cried and begged him to stay. He ignored my tears and pleas, waited until I had calmed down a bit, and then offered me his threadbare handkerchief to wipe my face. I can still feel the homespun, soft with age and wear." Wallace reached up and subconsciously touched his cheek, his fingers tracing the recalled trail of tears.

"He said something about how he didn't want to leave, but that was the way of it, and that we both had to accept it. Then he told me he had something for me. He hoisted me up to the sunny corner in the loft that he called his room and gave me a horse he had carved for me out of a deer antler.

"I remember how bare the room was; nothing in it save a pallet on the

190

floor and a small table with an icon on it, a small candle, burnt down to the nubbin, in front of it. I told him only stinkin' Papists burned candles in front of pictures. He said that he was a stinkin' Papist. I told him then I wanted to be a stinkin' Papist, too. So, he got some water and made the sign of the cross on my forehead, gave me this rosary, and a new name. He left the next week, and I never saw him again."

"What name did he give you?" I asked.

"Joseph. He said my name was now Wallace Joseph. I told him I already had three other names, but he said that Joseph was my Papist name." Wallace started talking softly again, "He said his name was Joseph, too," then looked over at Jody.

"By any chance, do you recall the groom's full name?" I asked.

Wallace looked back at me and shook his head. "I only knew him as Mac."

"Your father—Lord Julian, that is—knew his name. He was the one who arranged for Mac to work at your grandfather's estate as a groom. Mac saved your life the day your mother died. You were only a day old, had been stolen away, stashed in a corncrib, when he came upon you, blue and half-frozen. You probably didn't know about that either. Your mother gave you life, and Mac saved it. He stayed and watched you grow until Lord Julian came to marry your Aunt Irene. Mac baptized you with his first name before he left, to make sure you bore God's protection. His full name was...

"Joseph Alexander MacKay Pomeroy," Sarah, Jody, and Julian whispered softly in unison.

I broke the tension, quickly adding, "Where I come from, it's considered rude to use the word 'step,' as in stepfather. We just say father. We always considered and called stepfathers, godfathers, and biological fathers simply 'fathers.' Only lawyers used the clinical or legal prefixes with father. And that is why I said Lord Julian," I nodded at Julian, "was the father of his," then nodded to Jody, "Jody's, son."

I knew it was a lame explanation, but it was the best I could do on such short notice.

There was a collective sigh in the room. Mine was because I had been able to do some fast thinking to save myself from the wrath of Lord Julian. I hoped Wallace's sigh was of satisfaction at my explanation. I don't know what Jody, Sarah, or Julian's sighs were for, but at least no one was cursing, screaming, or getting red-faced with choler.

Wallace stood up, mute, but intense. I could see the bubbles brewing

191

behind his eyes. He looked down at his hands, then at Jody's, large, long-fingered,and with wide palms like his own. He walked over to his newly acknowledged godfather, stopping less than a foot away. He gazed into Jody's sky-blue eyes, a mirror image of his own. He put his left hand on Jody's shoulder and said, "Thanks for saving my life. I'm very happy to have found you again," he swallowed a hard gulp, and added, "father."

Jody didn't even try to stop himself from responding. He put his hand on Wallace's shoulder and, one blink later, the two of them were hugging.

Jody was overcome. To hear Wallace call him father was more than he could ever have wished. For so long, he had hoped his 'surprise' child would remember the man who had baptized him with his own name of Joseph. He could never share his last name, Pomeroy. That would entail Wallace giving up his title, land, and a fortune. But now, thanks to Evie, he was his son's acknowledged godfather. That was close enough. They could be in each other's lives forever, God willing.

"Thanks for giving me life, too," Wallace whispered in Jody's ear just before the two pulled away from each other.

Jody clasped the joy close to his heart. He could rejoice later, in private.

Wallace turned and addressed everyone, declaring, "You're right, Miss Evie; it does feel better to say I have two fathers. Thank you for letting the truth be known."

"You're very welcome, sir. I guess I let the cat out of the bag after I let the two men out of the bags." I giggled, then covered my mouth in embarrassment at my lame pun.

The men looked at me as if I were speaking Swahili. "It's just a saying from where I come from. It just means I revealed a secret. Oh, and I'm not a Miss, I'm married. I'm Mrs. Ian Kincaid."

"What? Ian got himself a wife?" Jody exclaimed, acting surprised. He didn't want Sarah or anyone else to know that he had intercepted Ian just moments before. "Why dinna anyone tell me so?"

"Well, it was a bit exciting around here," answered Sarah. "Ian came by this afternoon and asked me to look after his wife. He said she hadn't been feeling well lately. He went to find you. Just after Evie got to feeling better, I got a message that my help was urgently needed at the Dunmore's. It seems Mrs. Dunmore almost cut off her thumb. It took a lot of time to get the bleeding to stop, and then to stitch up the wound. I thought Dottie and Betty were going to stay here with Evie, but next thing I know, they're both following behind me. They said there was a ruckus at the house, that I should come back quickly, and bring some strong men with me. I couldn't just leave my patient, so I told Dottie to go to see if the Thorpes would come and help. When I got back, Evie was in here taking care of Wallace's bruised head, with Julian looking *very* angry. Evidently the men had been kidnapped, stuffed into gunnysacks, and brought here. Evie took her fancy little tool here and got them ungagged and unbagged, and shooed off the kidnappers in short order. Oh, and did I tell you that she and I are family?"

"Nae, ye dinna mention it. Pleased to meet ye, Mrs. Kincaid. Are ye feeling well now? Did Sarah have a chance to tend to ye yet? It sounds as if ye've been verra busy today."

"Uh, yeah, I mean yes, sir, I'll do, and no, sir; Sarah and I haven't had time to address my problems."

I know I'm bug-eyed and trembling as well as tongue-tied. Here he is, Himself, big as life—no, bigger! He really does fill a room when he's in it. He's tall, broad shouldered—big, all right—but the man has a presence about him that is twice his physical size. And when he asked about my health, he was genuinely concerned. And he called me Mrs. Kincaid. How wonderful!

Jody must have said something else to me. "I'm sorry. I missed what you were saying."

"How long have ye and Wee Ian been marrit?"

"Well, we didn't have a calendar, but it's been almost three moons, er, months. Did he find you? He did say his trip wouldn't take too long. I thought he'd be coming back with you."

"No, I'm sorry lass. But dinna fash. I'm sure his business willna take long. He'll be wantin' to return to his new wife *ere lang*."

Now it was Sarah's turn to take the floor. With a mixture of professional sternness and parental pride, she said, "Wallace, if you're up to it, would you escort your fathers outside? It's time for me to perform the long overdue examination of my good sister."

"I'm sure we could all do with a bit of fresh air," Jody said, his arms wide to usher the men to the door. "Let's see if we can do a bit of investigatin' around the barn. Maybe we can find out who was behind the kidnappin' of ye two."

Sarah shut the door after them. "Now what is this?" she asked as she held up my lantern.

"Oh, this is just too cool. See, it has a built-in dynamo so it creates its own electricity. It also has a radio, but since there aren't any radio waves yet, it's useless. But see," I said, and cranked the unit, "light!"

"Great. Now I have a light for my examination that doesn't flicker or stink and won't burn the house down. So, what seems to be the problem?" she asked as she guided me to the chaise.

"Well, look," I joked as I pulled my shirt taut across my belly, "as William Penn said to his very pregnant wife, 'Thou Swell.' However," I added more somberly, "I'm only two or three months pregnant. I think this is a bit bigger than normal. I don't know if I've ever been pregnant, but if I keep growing this fast, I'll explode!"

Sarah motioned for me to recline. "Lie back," she said gently, "and let me take a look."

I pulled up my shirts, gathering them under my breasts, as she tugged down the elastic waistband of my pants. She gently pushed on my belly, starting low, at my pubic bone, and worked her way up my firm womb until she found mushy gut, just below my belly button. It was as if she were measuring my womb by finger widths.

I had been doing my best to ignore the pregnancy. It was easy to do at first. When Little Bear performed his exploratory physical and announced that I was four months pregnant, it shocked me back into reality. I was terrified at the prospect of motherhood in this strange, primitive place. Women were having babies here, but I didn't even want to think of how hard it would be for me without disposable diapers and washing machines, stores nearby for baby food or formula, new clothes when the baby grew a size or three, immunizations, a home with a roof and a solid door... Shoot, I'm getting overwhelmed again.

"Have you felt the baby move yet?" Sarah asked, bringing me out of my trance of insecurity.

"I don't know if it was a baby moving, but it must have been. I felt something like butterfly wings fluttering in my lower belly. I didn't feel any arms or feet, though."

I sat up straight. She was my doctor and I had to tell her. This was important.

"Ian told me that when he found me—just before we were married— that I was, as he called it, on my courses. I was having a period, so I know I didn't come to him pregnant."

"Well, women have been known to continue menstruation for several months into pregnancy. It is possible you were already pregnant when you, um, married." Sarah was being gentle, but clinical. "However," she said, a look of hope shining in her bright amber eyes, "when did you feel the fluttering?"

"I first felt it a week ago. I still feel it now and again when I'm lying down and holding still. I don't think I was pregnant when we got married, though, because it hurt like the dickens the second time we made love. I thought it would hurt the first time if I was a virgin, but it was the second time. Is that possible?"

"Oh, very possible; the hymen could have been moved aside and not penetrated during intercourse. So, because you felt the baby moving for the first time last week—that's called the quickening by the way—and you were a virgin when you married, I'd say you were having twins. At least. Congratulations."

"Uh, did you say twins…*at least*?" I gasped. "This can't be!"

I was glad I was sitting down or I would have fallen down; I was feeling faint again.

"Well, I've never delivered triplets, but you do seem a bit further along in size than a woman carrying twins. Do multiple births run in your family?"

The new memories I had recalled earlier weren't personal. They were world history, generic modern day knowledge, and that strange insight into her family and friends' lives. I still knew nothing of myself, my life 'BI'— Before Ian. "I don't know. That's my other problem: amnesia."

**26 Double Amnesia?

"Is there such a thing as double amnesia?" I asked. "I mean, it seems that I already had amnesia when I first appeared here. I have no idea how I got here either, so please don't ask; it just frustrates me more.

"Sometime later, I don't know how long—an hour, a day, a week?— it's kinda fuzzy—I rescued a man I didn't know, that would be Ian, from a gang of thugs. I do remember that I rescued Rocky first because he helped me drag the bagged-up Ian into to a cave. That's where I tended to Ian's wounds and we hid out from the bad guys. He told me later that they had bound him and thrown him into the gunnysack, beat him with sticks, then forced him to walk over burning coals and broken glass. As a result, his feet were a mess and his hands not much better.

"Then, for some still unknown reason, I climbed up on top of the tall, rocky crag above our cave. I tripped and tumbled ass over teakettle to the ground. I cracked my head hard enough to lose consciousness for a day, maybe it was two, and when I awoke, Ian was tending to me...and I couldn't remember anything.

"I still have general knowledge, like how to speak, do math, a lot of what I learned in science and history, but it's not of this colonial time period. It's 21st century recall: save and back up files before shutting down the computer, and what's a good price for toilet paper. Do you want to know who's president in 2012?"

"Does it matter?" asked Sarah.

"No, not really, especially if we're going to stay here for the rest of our lives. Actually, so far, I like it here. I don't remember my personal past, so I don't miss anyone. I get random spurts of memory, like when I told Julian I was born in New Haven. But so far, that's all I know about me: I was born in America. True, I miss hot showers and bananas and music, but not the hectic pace, noises, and pollution in general."

I sighed in frustration. I needed to share my uncomfortable suspicions with her. "I think Ian knew I was pregnant. We never talked about it, but I'm sure he knew. It was pretty obvious, considering how close we were. But the reason he brought me here was to see if you had something in your little stash of herbs that would restore my memory."

Sarah bit her bottom lip and took a deep breath, bracing herself to give the bad news. "I'm afraid only time will take care of your memory.

There have been cases when it came back all at once, sparked by a word, a sight, or an incident. Other times…well, you might want to get used to your new life."

"When I awoke here earlier today, I suddenly had loads of memories flooding my brain. Before that moment, I didn't remember anything. But what I *did* recall, didn't make sense. I was bombarded with knowledge about events and people who had no personal relevance to me. How and why would I know about Mona and Wallace? I've never met them before. Do you think it's because I'm next to you?" I gave a big sigh and lay back into the chaise. "If that's the case, I don't want to get in a crowd. My head would explode!"

"When you confronted Julian and Wallace's erstwhile kidnappers, did you 'feel' anything with them?"

"Nope, I felt nothing but disgust when I was near them. Could it be because they weren't *fairies* like we are?" I asked, my mouth twitching to contain my smirk at the word.

"Fairies?"

"Isn't that what they call time travelers who just 'pop' into another time?"

"Aye, we're fairies," she agreed in a Scots accent with a shoulder shrug of acceptance. "Now, this other thing…" Sarah's lips pursed and her eyes narrowed to focus her deep thinking. "That's a very real possibility. If we ever encounter any other *fairies*," her mouth turned up in a full grin, "we'll check out your theory. But for right now, to take care of your *delicate condition*, all you need to do is eat right, drink lots of water, and exercise…which is easy enough to do in these times. Goats don't milk themselves and gardens don't plant, weed, and harvest themselves, either. I'll be glad to have the help *and* the company."

"Well," I added, "at least until Ian returns. I don't know where he wants to go next. I actually hope he wants us to stay here with you, though. It would be nice if that's his plan."

"Ian isn't the type of man who plans," explained Sarah. "He seems to attract situations, and then reacts."

"Oh, so is that why he left? He was reacting to the 'un-planned' part of me getting pregnant?" I was on the verge of tears. "Was looking for Jody just a ruse so he could dump me on you?"

Sarah reached out and held me close. "Evie, family men here don't look at pregnancy as a negative event. They celebrate it. Big families are an asset, and the men brag about how many children they have."

197

"Well," I sniffed as I pulled away and looked at her, "Ian told me he lost a couple of children, and I think he's afraid that this one will die, too. Or two will, but he doesn't know about the 'twins at least' part. No, my gut feeling is Ian wanted to get away from me because I was pregnant. He probably felt that if he just left me here, you and Jody would take care of me. After all, it's not as if I had any friends or family of my own around to watch out for me."

"You are family in more ways than one, and we'll take care of you. Don't give up on Ian yet, though. There may be more to his disappearance than we know about. In the meantime, we'll get some quilts for you and partition off this little area as your room." A big smile came across Sarah's face as she finished, "Then we can divvy up the chores."

**27 Depression and Gimpy Return

Sarah had arranged for two women, Dottie and Betty Rourke, to tend to the house and animals while she and Jody were out 'takin' care of business,' which was her code for working to help America gain independence. Sarah trusted the women to make sure the chickens and goats were fed and the woodpile kept full. They lived nearby and were glad help the cause in their own small way.

Business could take many forms and be for any length of time. A short trip generally meant Jody would be gone by himself for up to a day, maybe two, gathering information locally. But if he knew he would be gone for more than forty-eight hours, Sarah would be by his side. I knew he respected her insight on the situations involved with the conflict, but he also wanted her healing hands nearby if any bloodshed should occur.

At least that's what he said.

I knew she had a separate body from his—well, except for at intimate moments—but they shared the same soul. Neither could stand to be apart from the other—period. I wasn't jealous of their closeness but did marvel at it.

Jody had established a very dependable network of spies, but like any good crop, they needed cultivating. He would try to visit with each of them on a semi-regular schedule, asking if they had heard or seen anything suspicious. If they didn't have any special insights—or even if they did— he would ask specific questions. Invariably, what his operative had thought was nothing important, would be valuable information for Jody—at least, eventually.

Just his appearance was inspiring to the undecided who wondered if the conflict with Mother England was worth the fears and fighting it was causing. Many people here had lived through the Rising in Scotland and were afraid that if a young America lost, all hell would break loose, and the resulting restrictions and retaliations would make their lives even worse, with still more suppression, repercussions, and taxes.

"This is neither England nor Scotland. This is our home, America, and we have the right to enact our own laws, gather our own taxes fer our own needs. We shouldna be forced to have the British soldiers take our food, or anything else that strikes their fancy. Let the British Loyalists go back to their own land and kiss the King's arse. Leave us here to build and

199

govern *our* country."

Jody was passionate, but his words—although important and inspiring—were not as valuable as was the enthusiasm and optimism he brought to the people with his impromptu gatherings.

Julian and Wallace had finally agreed to stay missing from their unit. Wallace was in favor of fighting for the cause of America's freedom, but Julian wanted him to lie low; there was the matter of his lands and titles to consider. No matter how passionate Wallace's political feelings, Julian wanted him to be able to retain his vast land holdings and property. Declaring his advocacy for freedom from British rule was a bad fiscal move. If their former outfit had seen the two of them being kidnapped, the officers probably figured that they were being held hostage. They would reasonably assume that their families would either pay the ransom or not. If not, they would remain prisoners or be killed.

Julian surmised that he and Wallace could always surface later—after the conflict was over—and reclaim their estates, if indeed their properties were still intact at that time.

"Dinna worry about money, son," Jody told him. "It willna buy ye health, and no matter what anyone says, it willna buy ye happiness either. Yer safe here and now, and the Lord willin', we'll be able to keep food on the table fer all of us. Jest keep yerself alive—the money isna important."

When Julian first heard what Jody had said, he was furious. Falls Church—the huge plantation in Virginia he had helped establish for Wallace—was more than just a few dollars. But he realized that he would give it up at once if it meant that its loss would save Wallace's life. And so the two men joined Jody, Sarah, and me in our life of near poverty.

Ж Ж

Dottie and Betty came by, but not for a visit. They had all their belongings stacked and tied onto their brother Jess's wagon. The three of them were moving out.

Dottie explained, "Jess heard that there was some good trappin' out west. He's a good farmer, too, he is. I wager he could get corn to grow out of a rock! He can do the plantin' in the springtime and gather furs in the winter. We figure if we go far enough west, there willna be any more war, and no one will try and conscript him into the army. I'm sorry, Mrs. Pomeroy, I jest canna stand to be around all this fightin' any more. We already lost our ma and pa to the smallpox, and we're all we have. Ye have the two extra men—dinna fash, we willna tell anyone—and yer sister here to help ye. Please," she handed Sarah a twine-tied bundle, "would ye give this to Miss Evie? She can use it to make a proper dress fer herself and maybe a gown or two fer the bairns."

Dottie had given Sarah a large roll of fabric secured with bits of twine knotted together. It looked as if the sisters had been gathering rags with some wear left on them and had pieced the better portions together into a long length of cloth.

I had stayed inside the kitchen doorway, hardly visible in the shadow of the doorframe, while they were explaining their personal reasons for leaving. When I heard Dottie ask Sarah to give me the cloth, I came out to accept the gift in person.

"Thank you so much. You really didn't need to give me anything, but I sure do appreciate it."

I took the bundle of fabric and opened out the end of it. The women were very talented and did a beautiful job. They had used fine stitching and kept the colors similar, so it didn't look like a large dishcloth. "This will make a proper dress for me, and I'll be sure to let the babies know that their first gowns were made from a gift of love." I gave a little curtsy to each of the ladies in thanks.

"Is there anything you need before you leave?" Sarah asked with concern. "Did you pack a lunch? Evie, do we have any of those cookies left?"

I ran into the house and grabbed two fistfuls of the oatmeal and dried currant cookies I had baked earlier. The men hadn't come back from their wood gathering expedition, so we still had lots left. "Here, sweets for the sweets. Maybe this will help the trip go a little easier."

"Thank ye. We'll miss ye. And may God keep ye all safe in His bosom."

Ж Ж

Sarah had gone on another 'business' trip with Jody, and Julian and Wallace were off in the woods de-limbing trees for a secret project Jody had planned. I really didn't care what it was, and that was my problem.

I didn't care about anything.

It had been two weeks since Ian dropped me at the Pomeroy's doorstep. No one had seen or heard from him since. Jody had his friends, contacts, and spies—or whatever—looking for him. Any way you looked at it, I had been ditched, deserted, abandoned, and probably forgotten. There were at least fifty ways to say what had happened to me, but they all brought up the same negative feelings.

That first evening when I initially encountered Sarah, I was so happy.

I was going to have someone to talk to, and she would have someone to share chores with. That sounded wonderful to me. I would have a purpose. But now she was gone with Jody, and the few chores to be done were being taken care of by Wallace.

I had used the fabric Dottie and Betty had given me to make a skirt and a shawl for myself. That kept me busy for a few days. However, there wasn't any leftover for the babies' layette, and that frustrated me. Then I realized that I could use the shawl now—while it was cold—and just before the babies were born in late spring or early summer, I could cut it up and use it to make a couple of gowns and some diapers. At least my babies would be covered in something. I'd have to wait to do that, though. It was chilly and I needed the shawl to keep warm. However, if I could somehow manage to make another shawl, not only would I be able to get a head start on cutting and sewing the babies' layette, I'd have something to do, something to look forward to when I woke up in the morning.

I knew how to crochet, but I didn't have any yarn or even a crochet hook. I knew that somewhere, at some time, I learned how to spin yarn, but there wasn't any wool available or even a critter to get it from. I even thought about gathering a bunch of that weed fluff that was all around—stuck in the bushes and scrub—to see if I could get enough of it to spin. I realized how ridiculous that idea was. I couldn't make something out of nothing, no matter how clever I thought I was.

It was gloomy outside—gray, but not precipitating—but gloomier inside, so I decided to go for a walk. Actually, the depression was getting so bad, I was seriously thinking of taking a long walk out onto a partially frozen lake. At least that way there wouldn't be a messy corpse—actually no corpse at all until maybe summer. Nobody would care. Certainly not Ian; he'd never know because he'd never ask. Sarah and Jody were busy. They'd be sad, but life would go on for them. It always did. Wallace and Julian would make do. I really wasn't a part of their lives anyway. Besides, Julian always seemed to land on his feet, and Wallace was young, good looking, smart, and Jody's son. Anything and everything was possible for him.

And then there was me. I was unwed by conventional standards and pregnant, which put me on about the lowest social level there was in this era. My caste rating was just about the same as that of a prostitute. No, wait—probably lower since I never made any money out of what I did. I had nothing to offer society—no skills or talents—so how could I expect to support my children? It would be probably be better if they didn't make

202

it into this world and I just made an early exit.

All these thoughts were compounding as I picked up a short, fat stick on the way to the creek. I knew if I followed the poor excuse for a stream, I'd wind up at the lake. I'd never been there before but had heard about it. I'd make my decision about taking the long, wrong walk after I got there.

The club felt good in my gloved hand. It was almost the weight of a baseball bat. I picked up a rock, tossed it high in the air and—wham!—I hit at least a double. The handle was a bit rough, though, so I took out my Leatherman and used the sharp knife-edge to narrow and smooth out a grip. I hit a few more rocks then decided that I'd better whittle off the rest of the bark or I'd put out an eye with the shrapnel that came off with the rock's impact. "Good grief, girl. You're thinking about suicide, but worried about getting bark in your eye. Make up your mind."

Well, I guess I had already made up my mind. The self-preservation instinct I had to protect my eyes was the revelation I needed. I really wasn't in a life-taking state after all. Then again, I couldn't take my life without taking the lives of my babies. And—whether I had asked for them or not—they were alive, and I had no right to kill them. I shivered at the thought of it. "Nope, it's all gonna be all right," I said, picked up another rock, and batted it out into the creek.

I heard a crunching noise and froze. Another elk was my first thought. And then I heard it. "Are ye thirsty, lass?"

I turned to run but wasn't fast enough to escape the filthy hands that came out of the bushes and grabbed me without regard to which body part was being clutched. I ducked and squirmed but tripped just as I managed to twist out of the vile monster's grasp. I was knocked flat on my face, and before I could get up, three despicable heathens dog-piled on top of me.

"Keep hold of the bitch. She's a wily one, she is."

It was Gimpy, the one who had kidnapped me two months ago and taken great joy in spitting in my face. Only the intercession of the woman called Ma had saved me from his perverted attentions.

Gimpy's two raggedy and stinking male companions slithered off me, but kept me pinned, each with a firm grip on a forearm and an ankle. I was splayed out like a hide to be tanned and hurting. My right arm was twisted so far around that my shoulder was ready to pop out of its socket. I was now face up, though, and able to see my assailants.

"Yup, that's her all right," Gimpy boasted, as if he had just captured Big Foot.

I looked at the two men holding me down. It wasn't Abe or his erstwhile brother who had been involved in my first encounter with Gimpy, though. These two strangers were beyond help. I could see the wildness in their eyes and in their slathering mouths. A comb or soap hadn't touched their heads...well...probably ever. The clothing they wore were literally rags and hides that had been crudely sewn together. The word dreadlocks came to mind when I saw their wild hair pulled back from their faces with something—a piece of string, a thong, a dead snake—I didn't look that closely. Their beards were tangled and matted with leaf and twig bits, and slick and smooth under their mouths from food, drink, or I didn't want to know what that had fallen from their mouths.

Still, I looked from one to the other with what I hoped would be perceived as a plea for help. I didn't want to yell—at least not yet. The thought of a gag in my mouth turned my stomach. I hadn't thrown up yet in my pregnancy but had had a couple of close calls where mind won out over body when the reflux hit. I didn't think that I'd be able to control myself in this situation though.

"Those bubbies look even bigger now, they do." I tried to twist away as Gimpy reached down to grab a handful of breast. His associates grunted at me and tightened their hold which I took to mean 'hold still.' Gimpy reached down with both hands and yanked open my shirt, just like the first time. This time he was paying more attention.

"What?" he asked, wide-eyed and opened-mouthed, looking even more like an idiot.

'Where'd the buttons go?' was probably what he was thinking, but I certainly wasn't going to explain the concept of snap closures to him—now or ever!

His confused gawk left when he looked down and saw my pregnancy-enhanced breasts crammed into my sports bra. He grabbed and kneaded them. I felt the bile rise in my throat when he flicked the nipples to make them hard. Trapped. Beneath him. Helpless. I closed my eyes and did the only thing I could: concentrated on keeping the vomit down.

He only had one hand on me now. I forced one eye open to see what had happened. My bile rose further. His other hand was on the front of his pants, clutching and tugging on his own little pull toy. He caught me looking at him, leered at me, then climbed off and moved to my feet. He grasped the hem of my skirt and raised it up and down, making it pouf out like a parachute.

"Having fun?" I sassed. *Crap, me and my big mouth. What am I thinking!*

"Oh, the fun is jest about to start, lassie." He pulled the rope belt from his pants. "Here," he said, and with that, Gimpy threw the skirt over my head.

I felt him move around to the side of me. He took over the grasp of my wrists from his minions. They still had a firm grip on my ankles, though, and when I tried to bring my knees up to my chest, they roughly pushed them back down. I never stopped struggling, but Gimpy was strong and quick. He managed to wrap the rope around my wrists, pulling the coarse cording up between them, making a sloppy knot I hoped would be easy to untie.

"Pull those pantaloons down, boys. I want to go first. Ye can have 'er next; I dinna like sloppy leftovers."

I grimaced as they pulled down my pants but didn't resist anymore. I was glad—if you could call it that—that my face was hidden under my skirt. The blue patchwork fabric covered my humiliation and shame, and the tears that had squished out of my eyes from being shut so tightly. There were three of them and only one of me. I couldn't subdue them and had already failed at trying to run away. I wanted to tell them to hurry up and get it over with, but bit my lip to keep the words contained. I didn't let up on the biting either. The pain and taste of my own blood was distracting me from what was going on.

Or actually, what was not going on.

I relaxed my clench and paid attention to the noise the rapists-in-waiting were making. "No, I ain't gonna stick my pecker in that...that...thing! When they're biggen like that, they're likely to s'plode," said one of the other two, not Gimpy.

"Then jest hold her down and let me show ye how it's done. She won't explode, ye idjit!" Gimpy didn't sound too sure of himself but was trying to put on a show of bravery for the other two.

I heard him fumbling with his sexual member, but—evidently—it was showing the fear his voice had been trying to hide.

Now I remembered... When I was attacked before, he was turned on by my struggling. This time, when whatever it was deep down inside me knew it was futile, I had gone limp out of self-preservation...and I guess my limpness was contagious.

"All right, all right," Gimpy hollered, "maybe there is somethin' to that bloated belly curse. But this'll work."

All of a sudden, there was bright light. He had pulled my skirt back down. "Come here, sweetie," he cooed maliciously. "Are ye thirsty?"

And then he did it again. He spat in my face.

"Clyde, keep hold o' her legs. Clayton, you take her arms, here, above her head, like this," Gimpy had twisted my wrists when he tied them so I couldn't bend my arms. Now I didn't have the control for clawing out his eyes and blinding him—my first wish—or for escaping—second on my list.

"*Slurp*," Gimpy was making a loud sucking noise, "Oooh, here's another one," he said, and then spat in my face, the glob landing just beneath my right eye. "We want yer purdy lil' face to be nice and slick now, don't we," he mocked. Apparently, he was only aroused with gross perversion.

My jaws clenched tight. I tried not to move but turned away from his stinky club of flesh by reflex when he poked it under my nose. He rubbed it all over my face. Almost. I'm sure he knew I would have bitten off that foul piece of misshapen reproductive organ if it came near my mouth.

He spat in my face again and again. I sought the only protection I could find: turning inward. I pulled my essence deep inside my core, away from the unholy and revolting assault on my body. I was faintly aware of the rhythmic pressure on my face, but now I was deep within my womb, keeping my babies next to me, protecting them from the sickening storm outside, the heathen battering my soulless, paralyzed-but-breathing carcass.

The booming roar of a familiar voice brought me out of my protective Zen state.

"I said, get away from her! Now!"

I opened my eyes. It was Wallace, with an enraged look that would rival that of an avenging angel. Broad shouldered and towering, he had nothing for a weapon but a clenched fist and the drawknife he had been using earlier for debarking trees. I looked away from his commanding stature back up to the creature sitting on my chest, his limp dick, now spent, in his hand. He shoved it back into his pants with one hand as he pushed down on my chest with the other, slowly swinging his leg across me to stand up.

Gimpy began babbling in fear. "We wuz jest havin' some fun—ye ken how it is? Hey, ye wanna go first?"

Then he stopped. His attitude changed. Gimpy's slumped, cowering figure straightened up to stand as tall as physically possible, his chest puffed out, full of confidence. "Or ye can be the fun," he sneered.

I moved my focus from Wallace to where Gimpy was looking. Clayton had backtracked and was standing behind Wallace with my roughly hewn baseball bat. He swung it across the back of Wallace's knees, knocking my would-be savior face forward to the ground. The knife flew out of his hands as he reached out to try and break his fall. But the fiends were fast. One—I think it was Clyde—jumped on Wallace's back and grabbed his hair, pulling it back hard, as if he were reining in a strong horse. The other one ran in front to kick the knife further away, out of reach. At the same time, he grabbed Wallace's wrist, pulling and twisting it—out, away from his body. Wallace hit the ground chin first, his right arm pulled back like a wing. The weight of Clyde on his back made for a bone-cracking sound as he slammed the forest floor.

I scrambled, moving as fast as I could, to get up to attend to him, but my hands were still bound. I didn't know what I could do but had leapt up to help on instinct.

That was a mistake.

"Oh, no you don't, missy," Gimpy growled, just as I realized that Wallace was unconscious.

Twack!

Something hit me hard across the cheek, and then I, too, saw only black.

I awoke to the sound of celebrating. I did my best—which evidently was pretty good—at keeping the sound and rate of my breathing the same, hoping they wouldn't realize I was awake. I ventured a peek. All I could tell was that there weren't any legs or feet nearby. The laughs and cheers were coming from the area where Wallace had fallen.

"Yee haw, let me ride, let me ride. Come on, if you canna get that thing to work right, let me try. I'll get 'im slick fer ye."

It was Clyde. He had Wallace trussed over a fallen tree and Clayton was buggering him.

I rolled over and puked.

The boys were too busy whooping it up and hollering to hear my vomiting. Clyde had his fist wrapped around his stiff member, stretching and pulling it in anticipation of his turn.

"Yer sick, ye two. Dinna ye ken yer supposed to do it with a woman, and with 'er turned over to t'other side?" Gimpy hollered. I noticed his hands were in his pants—playing with himself—even as he ridiculed the other two for enjoying sex with a man.

"Aah aah aah aah oooh!" crowed Clayton. I guessed he had just finished, because he was pulling out of Wallace's backside. "Yer turn," he panted as he stumbled toward the other end of the fallen tree to sit down.

I was stunned at the sight of this hedonistic display. It took place in only moments but seemed like hours. I shook my head, trying to break the trance. I was probably in shock, but quickly coming back to reality. I managed to work the knot out of my rope handcuffs. It was a struggle to get up, but once on my feet, I found my strength.

"Get away from that man, you pigs!" I had only my voice to wield, but I had to do something. I couldn't just sit there and let him be defiled.

Defiled again...

"Oh, the lass is jealous, is she? What's the matter? Dinna I give ye enough attention? I still have plenty left fer ye," Gimpy said as he held open his arms and wiggled his hips, showing the obvious erection contained in his pants.

A horrible screeching yowl interrupted us. I recognized it as a cougar, as did the others. Wallace was still unconscious—gratefully. "A painter," the three of them said, almost in unison.

I didn't wait for any more banter. "Lady, lady," I called. "What's new pussycat, whoa, a, whoa, whoa," I practically screamed the song, terrified, but still trying to mimic the singing voice I had used when entering the cave I lived in last winter. I hoped that cat was Lady, my wounded cougar friend, who had stayed with me for those few days while she recuperated from near death.

"Yaa oww!" This time the screeching roar was closer, very close.

"Lady, help me," I screamed, trying not to break down into tears. "Lady, oof!"

Thump. Gimpy tackled me to the ground, knocking the wind out of me. He was fast for a lame, short man, but I had also been surprised. I was trying to turn over—attempting to get his filthy, vile body away from me—when I was knocked down again, this time by someone—or something—on top of Gimpy.

Lady had attacked the man who had attacked me. I turned halfway over and could see her. Her massive mouth encompassed the entire back of his head. I watched as Gimpy's eyes nearly popped out of his face when she crunched his skull.

I crawled out from under the two of them, scooting away as fast as my heels and hands could dig into the soft earth. Gimpy was still alive, but paralyzed—either by fear or from his skull being crushed. His mouth was the only thing moving, soundlessly opening and shutting like a fish out of water.

Lady looked at me, and then shook him quickly and hard, flipping him like a dog with a stuffed toy. I heard the distinctive 'pop snap,' the sound of his neck being broken.

His head in her mouth, Lady walked over to me and dropped it, and him—practically in my lap. I flashed on a house cat that would bring me dead mice as tokens of her love for me. I grimaced at the gesture—sweet yet sickening. "Thank you," I said to her as she backed away from the kill.

Clyde and Clayton were awestruck—paralyzed with shock—and had forgotten to run away. Clyde was still standing behind Wallace, his mangy pants down around his bare ankles. I hoped he hadn't yet made contact with him. Stunned and quivering, he was certainly not in any shape to do Wallace any shame now. I could also see that he had shat himself—streaks of brown goo marked the backs of his legs. Bug-eyed Clayton, panting in fear, was standing at the other end of Wallace, holding his unconscious head near the front of his pants, as if to assault him further in a different way.

In the split second it took for me to realize that those two were still touching Wallace, I was yelling at them all over again. "Get away from him or—I swear to God—I'll kill you!"

Well, actually, I can't remember what I said, but I remember well the heated emotions of hate and vengeance as they coursed through my body, racing ahead of each other to see which one would reap retribution first. I felt Olympian—as if I could shoot thunderbolts from my hands.

Clayton got a head start because Clyde was clutching and grabbing at his pants, trying to pull them up so he wouldn't trip over them.

Lady went leaping after the pair, and I let her. My concern was for Wallace. He was still unconscious, or at least I hoped so. I didn't know what I would do if they'd killed him. "Vengeance is mine, sayeth the Lord," I said as I untied his hands, trying to rid myself of the overwhelming hatred that had just flooded my spirit.

Wallace's cheek moved away from the log at my voice. "What did you say?" he asked in a coarse whisper.

"Vengeance is mine, sayeth the Lord," I repeated slowly, clearly, and with great conviction, the tears welling up in my eyes with joy that he was still alive.

"Hmph!" was his one-word, succinct reply. He set his head back down on the wood, took a deep breath, and stretched his arms out in front of him, as if he were a nude Superman flying through the air.

I quickly changed the subject. "Here, let's get you cleaned up and find your clothes—oh, here they are."

I turned away as Wallace painfully got off of the log, his unintentional gasps and groans stifled, but still audible. "Here, use this to knock off the bark and stuff," I said, holding out my shawl, my head turned, averting my eyes so I didn't see his nakedness. He took it, and I stepped away to give him some privacy.

"Just a minute," he said. "Come here."

I turned back and walked to him, my eyes focused high on his. He took the edge of the shawl and wiped my cheeks where the spurts of Gimpy's joy were still on my face.

"Close your eyes," he said. Just a couple seconds more, and he was back at cleaning my face, this time with water. "There's a puddle on the rock—don't worry, it's clean."

"Thanks, I'll just wait here for you," I said. I heard him, brushing tree litter from his body with the cloth. I blurted out, "Oh, Wallace, I am so sorry," trying not to cry.

"Sorry? What did you do? Here, would you wet this and wipe off my back?"

"Uh, okay." Wallace stood perfectly still as I wiped off his shoulders and middle back. "How far down should I go?"

"Get as much of the filth off as you can," he said resolutely as he bent over, presenting his backside to me.

And that is when we heard him.

"What in the hell is going on?" he roared.

It was Julian, red-faced and fuming. He glared at me—wiping Wallace's fanny—then looked down at the body on the ground. His scarlet countenance quickly paled as he took in Gimpy's contorted face and bulging eyeballs, obscene in its death scowl.

I handed Wallace the shawl to cover himself, but before either of us could speak, we heard two men screaming and the yowl of a cougar—my Lady.

Wallace grabbed my elbow and pulled me to him, clutching me close to his tense chest, while we waited for the terrifying noise to finish. I wasn't afraid. The feel of his skin on my face—cold and fuzzy on top and hard muscles, heated by anger and excitement, beneath—distracted and comforted me.

Julian was doing a pirouette—spinning around in confusion—trying to find the source of the commotion. Then the source came prancing up to greet me.

Lady looked from side to side, taking in the new addition to our little group. Seeing that I was at ease, she continued with her entrance. Julian looked pop-eyed at her as she walked past him with something in her mouth. She stopped in front of me and, very ceremoniously, deposited her present at my feet.

"Thank you, Lady. You'd better go home to your babies now," I said, completely composed—which very much unsettled both Julian and Wallace.

I had noticed her swelled udders or teats—or whatever they call them on a cat—as she walked—no, she *strutted*—away from us. She must have a home nearby with her babies, and the shouting and ruckus had disturbed her.

I didn't know she had been tracking me from the cave and watching over me these past few weeks. Well, at least that's how it felt when I looked over at the man she had killed in my defense, and the little present she had laid at my feet.

"What is it?" asked Julian, looking at the small pile of fresh meat at my feet.

"Vengeance," said Wallace, as he looked right at me.

A screech came from above us. An eagle was circling overhead. We all stepped back as it swooped down and grabbed the pile of male reproductive parts that had been at my feet. "Soon to be eagle poop." I added.

I looked up at Julian, took a deep breath, and said with finality, "I don't want to talk about it now."

Julian didn't reply with words, but he nodded, wide-eyed and mute. He probably didn't know what to say or ask right now, anyway.

Wallace kept me at his side as we walked back to the scene of his rape. He found his shirt and put it on mechanically, his eyes fixed on some distant, unseen object. I located his pants in a heap at the other end of the log and handed them to him. He put them on and walked to the spot where his boots had been tossed. Using a stick, he picked up the shawl we had wiped away each other's shame with. He walked over to Gimpy's corpse, and tossed it over the face, forever frozen in terror. "We'll get you another shawl, Evie."

I bobbed my head up and down. I swallowed hard and managed to say without letting the tears fall, "I want to go home."

Julian was shifting from one foot to the other, curious again. I knew

211

he wanted to know what had happened. He looked at Wallace, but before he could ask, Wallace said, "Like she said, Papa, let's not talk of it now. I want to go home, too."

**28 Wallace's Recovery

There was an uncomfortable silence, like a sooty fog, hanging over all of us for the long hour it took to walk home. I knew Julian wanted to ask about what had happened—there was a dead body and his son's nakedness involved, after all—but he respected our wishes not to talk about it, 'at least not now.' It wasn't as if someone was going to find a body killed by a 'painter' and come looking for us to blame.

Well, what Julian didn't realize was that 'that' was a real possibility. I didn't know if he had seen that the 'eagle chow' was actually the remains of a man's genitals. If the now dick-less Clyde—the one I was sure had been attacked and castrated by the cougar that appeared to be under my supernatural command—had survived and was able to talk, we had a problem. He was likely to want revenge.

Duh? Who wouldn't? If Clayton—his heinous partner in the rape of Wallace—had escaped the wrath of Lady, he would be another person who might come forth and make accusations. That is, if the two of them were brave enough to face Wallace or me again.

I doubted Clayton and Clyde had many social contacts beyond each other. From their dress, manner, and excitement in the ravishing of Wallace, I'd say they were butt buddies, at least. But I didn't care if they were backwoods lovers—they still didn't have to attack an innocent man like that. Those two didn't appear to have an ounce of ambition between them and—without a leader—would probably, hopefully, stay hidden in the hills.

The recently deceased scumbag I referred to as Gimpy didn't exactly have a societal personality either. I hadn't seen his old chums Ma and her boys around—I guess they had parted ways, which was a good thing. They had seemed decent enough people, although a bit short in the social graces. Yes, I doubt there was anyone in Gimpy's life who cared enough about him to even lift a sling shot to avenge him.

On the morbidly bright side, it was possible those two moldy maggots did not escape but had been attacked and killed by my feline protector. No, no—I shouldn't wish anyone dead, but their deaths were a real possibility. On the other hand, if either of these rapists had survived, it was possible they would seek revenge. And their revenge would not—probably could not—be against the attacking wild cat, but against her apparent diabolical controller—me.

I doubt I could legally be accused of any harm or foul in the death of Gimpy—whatever his real name was. But it was a marginal possibility I might be associated with the dismemberment of Clyde. I was willing to bet, though, that these wild mountain men wouldn't have the nerve or insight to have the local law authorities arrest me—not that there were any around. The 'CL' boys could, however, have some low-browed cavemen cousins who would believe their ridiculous story about a white witch and her familiar—an eight-foot long mountain lion. In that case, we might have a Paleolithic posse seeking revenge.

The three of us trudged along like two-legged machines—mobile, but without souls. I didn't know what was going on in their minds, but mine was full of doubts and fears of retribution. But as soon as I saw our humble little shack of a house, I started running to it as if it were my long lost mother.

I stopped long enough to pull up a bucket of water from the well. I hiked up my filthy skirt and cleared the porch steps, barely touching them. I burst into the house and was glad it was empty. I definitely didn't want to talk to Sarah or Jody about what had happened. I grabbed the hook from the front of the hearth and pulled out the large kettle containing the meager stew I had set on for supper this morning. I grabbed all of the bowls from the cabinet and started filling them, stopping only when I ran out of stew. I splashed some water into the empty pot, swirled it around, and divvied up the slurry among the bowls, thinning the stew into soup.

I poured the water from the ewer into the cast iron pot to capture the residual heat, swished it around, and poured it back into the ewer. I dumped the rest of the water from the bucket into the now semi-clean pot, set it back over the fire, and shoved three split logs into the coals, pushing them around them until it was blazing. I took off my skirt, snapped flannel shirt, and pants, and threw them into the big pot of rapidly warming water. I didn't have any soap handy, but I had to get the slimy filth removed from the only clothes I owned as soon as possible, even if only with boiling water. I grabbed a long stick of wood from the woodpile and used it to agitate the clothes. I worked furiously, wearing nothing but the tee shirt and white cotton panties I had arrived in this aulden world with.

Then I remembered the fancy bar of soap I had been saving for the babies. It was the only item I had for their layette. With my shawl gone, I didn't even have a piece of cloth big enough for a gown for one baby, much less two—at least two—babies.

Oh, boy—what now?

I didn't want the initial use of this sweet-fragranced bar to be for removing the remains of my sexual assault, but I had to use something. I was fuming with hate for those three men as I debated the need for cleanliness over the desire to maintain the purity of my babies' only worldly possession. I stood in front of the fire—the bar of soap a treasure in my mind—trying to decide what to do. Should I make this sacrifice or not? It was more than just soap to me.

"Lord, forgive me," I said softly, "but I sure hope those two degenerates…um, followers of Satan…didn't make it. Or at least that they learned a lesson and won't be back to bother Wallace or me again. I know vengeance is Yours, but thanks for sending one of Your creatures to help me—us—in our hour of need. Amen."

I hadn't yet decided whether to use the soap or not when Wallace walked in—stiff-limbed and staring, moving like a zombie—with two more buckets of water. He didn't look at me, scandalously clad only in my skivvies, but just stood motionless in front of the roaring fire. I knew he had heard my prayer, though. His eyes were glazed—the light of the fire reflecting the emptiness of his spirit.

I didn't know what to say, so said nothing. I stirred the pot again and set the stick down. I took a deep, calming breath and said, "Put down the water and give me your pants."

He didn't say anything, but set down the buckets and, one by one, took off his boots. He worked the buttons on the front of his trousers and let them drop, kicking them toward the fire with his bare feet. His long shirt fell almost to his knees, but I doubt he would have shown any modesty even if he had been naked as a newborn. He was in shock.

He had kicked his trousers so hard, they almost landed in the fire, but I grabbed my improvised laundry paddle and pulled them back. I wiggled the stick into the middle of the pile and twirled, pulling the pants onto the wood like spaghetti onto a fork. I lifted the mass and dropped it into the middle of the hot—but not yet boiling—water. I put down the wood, poured one of his buckets of water into the pot, and stirred.

"My Leatherman!" I exclaimed and used the laundry stick to fish in the pot for my fleece pants. I had forgotten to take the tool out of my pocket before starting the laundry.

Wallace's body burst from its stiff cast as he reached across me. He grabbed the pants as I lifted them up, searching the soaking mess with both hands for the pocket that held my multi-tool. He found it, picked it out

215

with his thumb and index finger, and let the pants drop back into the water. He tossed the scalding hot knife back and forth, an awkward, almost comical, juggling feat, as he turned around and stepped up to the table. Two more toss ups, and he decided that the blue quilted tea cozy was a good place to set it.

Wallace smoothed the folds out of the fabric carefully, the Leatherman now a treasure in a quilted frame. His face was still a mask of non-emotion as he said in a disembodied, far-away voice, "I think it will be fine if we put some oil on it."

I moved past him to the chaise and pulled my backpack out from underneath it. I opened it and found the treasured bar of sweet-smelling soap Sarah had given me. I took down a small pot and poured some of the fresh water into it, picked up and dried the Leatherman, opened out the sharp blade, and started shaving slivers of soap into the water. I put the pot into the embers and turned to Wallace. "Do you have another pair of socks?" I asked.

He glared at me, practically shouting in an angry whisper, "After all we went through, you ask me if I have another pair of socks?"

I didn't take the attitude personally—I knew it was misdirected hostility. "Well, yeah! How can you keep pulling me out of trouble if you catch pneumonia and become bedridden?" My reply was softly spoken, half-serious and half-irritating. I just wanted to goad him into showing *some* kind of emotion.

"Oh, Evie," he cried, and gathered me into his arms. He held me as if he had just recovered something he thought he had lost—a little boy who had just found the teddy bear he thought mama had thrown into the trash pit.

My maternal instincts were kicking in. I grabbed the tea cozy, dipped it into the porridge pot with the now warm soapy water, and started washing his face. He took the cloth from my hand, poured the stew-tainted ewer water into the basin, rinsed the cloth in it, and then dipped it back into the soapy water. He began by washing my face. We took turns cleaning each other's face, neck, and shoulders—rinsing with rabbit-stew-scented water.

At some point, I grabbed Sarah's tortoise shell comb and started combing the twig and leaf matter from his hair. When I was done, he held out his hand for the comb so he could tend to mine. I think he had some paternal instincts kicking in, too. It didn't feel sexual, or even like we were siblings.

Siblings. I flashed on that feeling, so I guessed I must have had one or more in a past life. I shuddered at the thought of me having a life other than this one.

"Are you cold?" he asked.

"Just a bit; let's get closer to the fire."

Wallace put one arm around me to guide me closer to the hearth. I inched nearer still, grabbed the potholder, and poured our bath soap/water mixture into our laundry. Normally I wouldn't dream of washing clothes in a food pot, but this impromptu laundering had been an emergency. I'd deal with scouring out the soapy residue later. Right now, a spiritual cleansing was more important than off-tasting soups and porridge.

"You know, I wasn't unconscious the whole time," Wallace said softly, as if admitting a fault. "I felt like a coward because I didn't do anything to protect you. But that bast... monster had a knife to your face. He threatened to carve you a couple of new eye sockets if I moved. He told the boys to throw me over the log and fu...er, use a small log to...to..."

Wallace couldn't finish, but I didn't want him to feel like he had to. "I get the idea," I said gently, cutting him off so he wouldn't keep fumbling for words.

"Then the two boys—or men, I guess—couldn't lift me, so the gimpy one who was holding you took his knife and started shaving your face. He said he'd start carving into it if I didn't put myself over the log and pull off my own pants."

I reached up and felt my face. The right cheek was completely soft and hairless as was half of the left side. There was also a small nick on my chin where he had missed and brought blood—or maybe he hadn't missed and brought blood on purpose.

"The boys refused to use a stick on me—they said they wanted me for themselves. They argued about it for a minute, and then the old man gave in and said to go ahead and do it their way, as long as they taught me a lesson. Then the two of them fought over who got to...to," Wallace's voice softened to a whisper, "do me first."

I reached out to give him a hug, but he put up his hand for me to wait—or leave him alone. I was taking it as a wait because I wasn't going to leave him alone.

"Then the one said he won because his manhood was bigger and he'd make it easier for the other one. He...he...started, and I couldn't help but squirm. That's when you got the cut on your chin. I thought he was going to slit your throat. At least, that's what he said he was going to do—the one with the knife. He said he could, 'Have his way with you, breathin' or nae.' I couldn't do anything to save you, but if I held still, at least he wouldn't kill you. So, I just pulled myself inside my, my, pulled my soul into my body. I guess that's what it would be. After that, I wasn't aware of what was going on outside of my body. But I could actually see and feel my heart pumping. It was as if I were part of the blood flow—going in and out of the heart chambers. I didn't hurt at all—didn't feel or hear anything until I heard your voice."

By the end of his story, I had gravitated into both his arms. Our bare legs were starting to get the hair singed from our nearness to the fire. We walked away from the heat as if we were one body.

"You know," he said, "I know there are homosexuals in this world—men who have sexual relations with other men—but I don't see how it's possible to be human and enjoy that kind of...of..."

I reached up and slapped Wallace hard across the face. "What was that?" he asked angrily.

I then put the same hand on the cheek I had just smacked, caressing the cheek softly, working my way around to tickle his ear.

"What happened to you was an act of violence—not love or even sex. You didn't ask for it, or even agree to it except under threat of my life. This same hand that can love and treasure you, could hurt you, destroy you. It's the same concept with any other part of the human anatomy. Rape is an act of hurting a person—showing domination, and inflicting humiliation. It *is* possible for two men or two women to love each other and make love with whatever parts of their bodies are accommodating. I believe there is nothing wrong with two people loving each other—no matter what their genders. I also believe that some people's sexual attractions are not the same as mine—and obviously yours—but that doesn't make it wrong. A man loving another man and not caring to be intimate with a woman is no different than a person being left-handed and automatically lifting his left hand in defense of something coming at his face."

I knew I had him identifying with me on this one—both he and Jody were left-handed. "God made us all different. Not even identical twins are just alike. And I think I know why God made us all different."

We were both mute, just standing there. "Well," he asked impatiently, "why did God make us different?"

"To teach us tolerance and acceptance," I replied self-assuredly. "I never read anywhere in the Bible that I was supposed to hate someone because he was different. It's just the opposite. Remember, Jesus taught us to 'Love thy neighbor as thyself.'"

"That has always been my favorite scripture, and one I've tried to live by. Today was too much of a trial, though. I don't think I can forgive them for quite a while, if ever. It's too much for me to believe I could ever love those two. And I can't say I'm sad that that big cat killed the man who hurt you."

Wallace's eyes lit up with recall. "And where *did* that cougar come from?" he asked, his own personality suddenly taking over and, hopefully, conquering the zombie persona forever.

"Oh, she and I have a history. Remember the story of Androcles and the Lion?" *Before he got a chance to answer, my head raced through history. I relaxed when I recalled that there was a good chance Wallace had heard Greek fables in his extensive education.*

"Do you mean the story about the slave who took the thorn out of the lion's paw?"

"That's the one. I'm the slave and Lady—that's what I called her when I found her with cut-up feet—is the lion. I helped her mend, I suppose. At least, I fed her for a couple of days—gave her water and, well—I guess we gave each other comfort in the cave when I was all alone. I suppose the moral of the story is—a kindness given is a kindness remembered. Or maybe a good deed is repaid by a good deed. And God takes care of His own, too. Thank You, Lord!"

"Aye, I guess you're right. Bashed, battered, and humiliated—at least our bodies are still whole and we are alive to see tomorrow. Oh Lord, Evie; I didn't even ask—are the babies okay?" Wallace turned me to him to look into my eyes for forgiveness for not inquiring sooner.

"I'm pretty sure they're fine—they have a Level One security system protecting them." I said, and wondered what that meant. "I mean, a woman's body is set up so the baby is totally protected by bones, tissue, and water. Did you know that they're floating in a sac of water so that any blows will be absorbed by the fluid."

"No," Wallace said, blushing at his own innocence, "I know about horses, but I'm not very familiar with the human reproductive system."

"Don't worry 'bout a thing. Anything you don't know, I can tell you. And if I don't know, we can find out about it together, okay?"

I blushed and bowed my head at my impertinence. To recant it wouldn't be right and would call more attention to it. He was probably just as embarrassed as I was at my remark. We remained mute—still standing face to face and very close to each other, so close I could feel his body heat next to mine. I guess the sibling attitude of my body was changing. My womb was tightening with anticipation of something I was pretty sure I wouldn't be receiving. I was also close enough that I could feel Wallace's mood indicator rising toward the 'happy to be with you' level.

The sound of footfalls on the porch steps shattered our little reverie. "Oh, crap," I muttered as I pulled away, suddenly aware of my near nakedness by current standards.

By the time Julian walked through the doorway, Wallace was tending to the wash kettle, and I was wrapping my sleeping quilt around my middle like a skirt. "What is going on in here—or do I want to know?" he asked suspiciously.

"Just helping Evie with the laundry," Wallace said with a totally detached innocence.

"And setting the table for dinner," I added.

Julian looked at the table set with five bowls filled to the brims with a watery stew. "Are we expecting company?" he asked.

"Uh, I thought maybe Jody and Sarah would be back. I guess with all the excitement, I was a little confused," I offered lamely.

Julian gave me the 'you're not fooling me, little lady' look, but I felt it best to ignore his unspoken scolding.

He turned his attention to Wallace, bent over the wash kettle, transferring the steaming clothes to the water bucket. His long, bright-white legs were exposed to the air from the bottom of his shirt to the ends of his bare toes. "And dare I ask what is going on here?"

"Nope," Wallace answered succinctly, picked up the bucket full of hot, sopping laundry, and walked out the door.

Julian's face reddened at being so curtly dismissed by his son. He was standing by the door, obviously deciding whether or not to go outside and have words with Wallace about his rudeness, when I came up and put my hand on his arm. "Please, let it go."

He turned to me and stared into my eyes, checking to see if I was hiding something. But I wasn't and he could tell.

He pulled his shoulders back and stood as if at attention, took a deep breath, and said, "I don't know what went on this afternoon, but I do know that it was—shall we say?—highly emotional. I did overhear some of what you said to my son just now, and I hope to God what I think happened, did not."

220

He didn't take his eyes off of mine as he spoke, searching for his answer in both my reaction and my words.

I didn't say a word, but my face couldn't lie.

"Oh, good God, no," he said.

"I don't know if he'll ever tell to you about it, and I really don't want him to," I said.

Julian gave me a scornful look. He apparently didn't like me making the decision on whether or not his son should talk to him about 'the incident.'

"He'll tell you if he needs to, but," I faltered, uncomfortable with the conversation, "well, if he does, that means he has to relive it, go through it emotionally all over again. I'd just as soon he didn't. We're both alive and both healing. Can't you just leave it at that?"

"I can," he said as a sigh. "When I was outside, I heard you explain your—attitude, shall we say—about men, women, people who are..." his voice softened, and then he was silent.

I grabbed his hand and shook my head indicating that he needn't say more. I'd do the same for the father as I had for the son. I didn't want people I cared about feeling uncomfortable with their words.

"Well, it's not just an attitude—it's the truth, right?" I moved my hand to his shoulder and looked into his eyes. It was my turn to be looking into the face's book of truth. He took another deep breath, started to say something with his proper English persona, then stopped. His face really did change between his Lord Julian Hart mode and his friend and father modes.

"Yes, you are right. I just wish others saw it as you do, Evie. It would make life so much easier," friend Julian said, "so much easier."

I heard the horses approaching at the same time as Julian. The mood was over; we were both back in protected mode—our emotional walls erected to keep others away from our inner, true selves.

Julian went outside to see who it was, and I shuffled over to the chaise to recuperate. All of a sudden, I was exhausted. I didn't want to deal with any new issues, so decided to play the 'pity the poor pregnant lady' card and lay back with my feet up. Julian was more than able to take care of any new situation that arose.

As it turned out, little needed to be seen to: Sarah and Jody were back. I heard them tell Julian that they both felt something was wrong. Sarah was afraid the babies and I were in danger, and Jody...well, he wouldn't elaborate on his uneasiness, but I'd bet my last dollar—oh, wait;

I didn't have one—that he knew Wallace was in peril. Julian made a strong show of composure, assuring Jody and Sarah that everything was under control. Well, that was true. He didn't lie. He just didn't tell them that all hell had broken loose earlier.

"What in the hell happened to yer pants, man?" Jody called out when he saw Wallace throwing the last of the laundry over the bush by the side of the house.

Wallace looked over at him and said, "There was an incident, but all's right now. Evie has dinner ready to serve. I think she was expecting you. Good evening to you, Mother Sarah," he said, and nodded to her in acknowledgment.

Sarah stared at him, her mouth hanging open at the sight of his naked legs. She realized she was slack-jawed, and closed her mouth, replacing it with a polite smile. "Good evening, Wallace. Is Evie all right?"

"She's just inside. You might want to ask her yourself. She didn't get a chance to make any bread, but there's some nice rabbit stew ready for us. Here, let me see to your horse," he offered, his hands out for the reins.

"I'll take care of the horses," scolded Jody, still mounted. "You'd better get inside before you catch cold." He started to say more, but I saw Julian's hand touch his leg. He didn't look down to see what Julian wanted. He knew. Julian was telling him to be still and leave it alone.

Sarah hustled into the house, frowning with concern, followed by a nonchalant Wallace. I supposed Julian went with Jody to see to the horses. Right—see to the horses and explain at least a little to Jody so he wouldn't pester Wallace for more information.

I was lying down—watching the older men through the open door—when I remembered I hadn't set out the spoons. Wallace looked at the table and saw what I had just been thinking, went to the sideboard, and drew out all five of the carved wooden spoons. He looked up at me as he set the table and smiled.

Gee, that polite and good-looking young man is really starting to get to me—and in a positive, thrilling way I hadn't expected.

"Now, what's going on, Evie?" Sarah asked in her clinical tone, interrupting my warm musings.

"Welcome home, nice to see you, too," I said dryly. She waved my words away with a flourish of her hand, as if she were shooing mosquitoes. "I'm okay, I guess," I said. "I just thought I'd better take your advice and rest my feet. I did a lot of walking today, and I guess I overdid it."

I looked up at Wallace and saw his eyes roll back into his head. I was glad to see a bit of mirth make its way back into his personality.

He had really run the gamut of emotions today—trying and failing to defend my honor, then made to watch my assault; raped by two men; humiliated, chastised, and then comforted by me. He had rebuked his father's concern and displayed his bare-legged indecency in front of his fathers and stepmother. And, since we were running through the range of emotions—and we did have a little personal arousal in there, too—we might as well add mirth to the mix.

Sarah bowed her head over my belly, feeling around the outside of my panties with the quilt pulled back, pushing the womb side to side, measuring with her fingers its size from pubic bone to the top of the womb—fundus she called it. I looked up and caught Wallace's attention. I stuck out my tongue and crossed my eyes. He snorted with a short laugh, then brought it down a notch to a big smile. Yup, we were in tune and on the same path: the path to healing and—if my sixth sense was right—to even more than that.

Ж Ж

"What?" Jody yelled. "How in the hell did this happen? Where were ye, and why did ye let Evie go runnin' around the woods? Ye ken there are horrid men about, scourin' the country, jest lookin' fer trouble, up to nae good."

"Do you really think I could tell Evie what to do?" Julian huffed in exasperation. "I thought she was inside, doing whatever it is women do inside in the early spring. I was outside with Wallace, stripping the limbs and bark off that timber like you asked. Next thing I know, he's gone. I thought he'd gone to the privy, but after half an hour, I went looking for him. He wasn't anywhere to be found, and Evie was gone, too. I finally located them two hours later—they'd gone down by the creek for God only knows what reason. I know Wallace knows not to go in that direction, but if you never said anything to Evie—I know I didn't—and she took off that way, Wallace would follow after her, safe or not."

"Ye said ye found the two of them with a dead man and some spare body parts. Do ye think they murdered the man?"

Julian took a deep breath, delaying his answer, trying to find a way to explain that his son—their son—had been raped by two men in the wilderness.

Jody tried to make the answer easier for Julian. "I'm sure if Wallace kilt a man, he deserved it. What did he tell ye?"

There was Julian's out. "He didn't tell me anything, except that he would tell me about it when he was ready. I agree with you that Wallace wouldn't kill a man except in self-defense, even if he deserved it. But Wallace didn't kill anyone. A cougar did."

"Yer not makin' any sense, Julian. If a painter kilt a man, and Wallace and Evie were there—even if they were someplace where they werena supposed to be—why the mystery?"

"I think I will respect Wallace's request that we leave him alone on this. And Evie, too. I believe he was protecting her and, well, she may not be his to protect, but she needs someone. You're her family, but you're gone so often, I think he feels the duty has fallen to him to watch over her. Actually, I think he wants the responsibility. He seems quite fond of her."

"I dinna ken whether to be glad or sad that someone else wants to watch over my family," Jody said as he kicked a stone across the ground in frustration. "Weel, if Ian isna gonna to take care of his wife and bairns, I guess the good Lord saw fit to bring someone else from my family to be their protector. I'll respect his right to tell me when he's ready, but I canna help but feel that ye ken more about this than yer telling' me, Julian."

"Jody, I feel like we are all family here, but anything I know has not been *told* to me by either Wallace or Evie. What I *can* tell you is that there were signs of violence. A man was killed by a cougar and there was a pile of bloody flesh that was taken away by an eagle before I had a chance to get a good look at it. The two of them are now back home—safe. Let's hope it stays that way."

**29 José: The New Man in the Neighborhood

Julian wasn't sure if Wallace had been awake that first night and heard the revelation that Sarah and I were from a future time and that we knew the British would lose this war. But he *was* sure he wasn't going to ask him if he *had* heard us.

Like most young men of title in England, Wallace had been eager to buy a commission into His Majesty's service. Since he was so prone to seasickness, he wouldn't even consider enlisting in the navy. Therefore, whether Julian liked it or not, Wallace followed in his footsteps and joined the army.

Julian knew military service was a rite of passage into the upper echelon of British society, but he was sick and tired of wars, death, and subterfuge. He had lived the life of a soldier and didn't want it for his stepson.

"A good education will be a valuable asset, son," he told him. "Learn and become prolific in all the languages you can. You have the talent for it; make use of it. His Majesty has soldiers and ambassadors in countries all over the world. Not everyone speaks English, you know. More opportunities will be available to you if you speak and understand the languages of the people involved in the negotiations and alliances that keep this world in a semblance of balance."

But Julian's real reason for extending Wallace's studies had been to keep him safe in England. The additional years in school would delay his entry into the army so—just possibly—he wouldn't be sent to that abyss of social graces: America. The conflict in the colonies involved active warfare, not just negotiations. He figured that if he could keep Wallace busy in school for an extra three years, the Americans would be subdued by the time his education was completed. Wallace could then buy his commission into an army that was not engaged in any active military conflicts and be safe.

And that was how it played out, except four years later, the war with America was being still being fought.

Wallace had purchased his commission last year. Julian had come out of retirement soon thereafter, calling in a few favors so he would be 'requested' as special liaison for His Majesty's army, assigned near his stepson in order to keep tabs on all the players. This conflict with America was like all others from the beginning of time: rife with spies and officers with dual allegiances. Julian didn't necessarily know whom to trust, but he did know many who should *not* be trusted.

However, their military assignments, and whom they knew, didn't make any difference anymore—they were away from their units and stuck in American patriot territory, bound by their word to stay put.

Julian wasn't completely convinced that I wasn't crazy but was unsure enough to accept that I was correct—the Americans would win the war. Julian, Jody, and sometimes Sarah and I, would discuss the current state of economics and politics with Wallace in the evenings. We hoped he would see the American point of view and decide to change allegiances on his own. Nobody wanted him to rejoin the fight on the British side.

Julian and Jody could have saved their proselytizing—they were just throwing pennies at a millionaire. Wallace had always been sympathetic to the colonists' causes. He had long ago found in his heart that he was an American. So, the British Lords agreed to remain 'missing, presumed dead' from their companies, keep a low profile, and stay with us.

None of us asked how Julian and Wallace happened to be apart from their unit. That was their business, and since its eventual outcome was their mysterious kidnapping, none of the Pomeroy household wanted to bring it up. It was an accepted mystery that had a happy ending—at least so far.

Because Wallace was an officer, he probably had been reported as killed or missing in action. Julian was an adviser and went from one outfit to another as requested; his whereabouts weren't as closely monitored. When one adviser couldn't be found, the commanders just went down their list to the next man available and filled the vacancy.

Troops on both sides were very disorganized and kept poor records— if any at all. It also helped ensure Julian and Wallace's safety and anonymity that the official roster of soldiers in Wallace's unit had conveniently been left in his pocket along with his new orders. His whereabouts in His Majesty's army were not on any current record. Julian Hart's name had also been on that list as an advisor. When I asked him where the list was, Julian said he had mistakenly used it to start a fire. "Oh, well," he remarked, in an uncharacteristically casual manner, "one soldier, more or less, really shouldn't make a difference to His Majesty."

冰 冰

226

The weather was getting warmer, and I wanted to get out of the cabin—probably an early case of spring fever. It was still too wet to dig in the garden, and I didn't want to go anywhere without an armed escort. I had seen scat on the way to the privy, and knew the bears were waking up. Yogi Bear may have loved his picnic baskets, but bears in the wild were omnivorous—they'd eat anything—or anyone.

Finding a companion and an excuse for a daytrip was easy. "Julian, do you think we can go into town and see if there's any fabric available. Sarah said I could take some of her sweet smelling soap to use for barter. We also need a few other things, like salt and soda. I'd go by myself, but I don't know the way." I batted my eyelashes and grinned at him. He knew my ruse, and I knew that he knew.

"We could do that. It's still early enough that we could leave and be back by sundown. Are you sure you want to go with me, though? Wouldn't Sarah or Wallace be better company?" he asked sincerely.

"Nah, you're great company. Besides, Sarah is riding up to the MacPhersons' to check on the old grandma, and Wallace is going to help Jody clear the area south of the cabin for a new garden."

Julian chuckled at the 'Nah' part and shook his head at my silliness.

He was definitely loosening up his cast-iron stays. He laughed and smiled and joked now. I doubted he was aware of how uptight he used to be. He had relaxed when he realized he could finally stop double thinking everything he was going to say.

However, we were still careful not to talk about Sarah, me, and our involvement with the future. If Wallace knew about it, he wasn't letting on. My gut feeling, though, was that he knew and was playing the 'don't ask, don't tell' card, just in case.

I had memorized the short list of supplies we needed. I was hoping we would be able to get at least half of the items. We had little in the way of money but did have some goods to barter. That didn't always make a difference. The war had left many commodities in short supply or completely non-existent. We were better off than most—we still had a few goats and chickens, and seed for the crops we would be putting in soon. We were rich in men, but made sure Wallace kept a low profile. Julian was older, smaller, and less likely to be drafted. Involuntary conscription into military service for either side of the conflict was still a frightening possibility for a strong young man.

Julian brought the buckboard wagon right up to the front steps. My legs weren't very long to begin with—just long enough to reach the ground—but now my belly was in the way of lifting my foot high enough to climb into the wagon unaided. Wallace was aware of my dilemma, so had built an easy access step on the passenger side for me. The rope and wood step was a convenient addition and swung out of the way when we were riding. When the babies came, maybe Ian could build a little swing for the babies using the same design.

Shoot, what am I thinking? He'll never come back. I shake my head, trying to rid myself of that uncomfortable feeling of abandonment that has snuck in. Again. As always, unwanted and unbidden. Pregnant and abandoned.

The ride took three hours. It would have only been two and a half, but I had to keep stopping for potty breaks. Julian was the perfect gentleman, helping me up and down from the wagon seat, and turning his back as I headed into the scrub to pee. I still couldn't figure out how I could pee more than I could drink. I was appreciative of the fact that he didn't complain about having to stop all the time. He knew I was self-conscious about it, and would never think to add to my discomfort.

We finally arrived in Gibsonville about noon. I went to the general store to see if I could find some gray or other neutral tone fabric to make jackets and trousers for Julian and Wallace. When Julian found out that I wanted the fabric so the two of them would have clothing that was not obviously modified British uniforms, he gave me a couple of coins to take care of the purchase.

I was able to buy a bolt of a light brown—kind of tan—heavy wool. It reminded me of the fabric used for Carhartt coveralls. Strange how that memory came: I saw the fabric, then the name label, and then the blocky style and design of those coats and coveralls just appeared in my head. I wondered if Levi Strauss had come along with his heavy cotton canvas jeans with the riveted seams yet. Nah—that was a California Gold Rush era design. Still, I'd remember to ask if brass rivets were available. Maybe a relative of Levi would see the pants I planned on making and would pass the information down the line to his grandson. I wouldn't be changing history. After all, I wasn't taking out a patent or anything.

I was able to get most of the items on my unscripted list without having to trade any of Sarah's sweet soaps. The one item I couldn't get was baking soda. When I asked for it, the man didn't know what I was talking about. I even told him that it might be in an orange box with a drawing of a strongman's arm and heavy hammer on it. Andrew, the storekeeper, must have thought I was crazy, but was very polite and told

228

me he didn't carry it at his store. He was definitely happy to get Julian's silver coin for the goods, though. He even threw in some cinnamon bark in the deal. It was a small gesture for him but meant so much to me.

The promise of cinnamon rolls or coffee cake for breakfast made me hungry, and now my stomach was making low, growling noises. I reached into my bag and took out one of my little sandwiches. I had figured out how to make mayonnaise from egg, oil, and vinegar. It went together well with Sarah's cheese and the sourdough bread I had baked earlier, and it also kept the sandwich from sticking to the roof of my mouth.

The shopkeeper had loaded the wagon for me, and I was ready to leave, but Julian was nowhere to be found. I wandered around the almost-a-town looking for him, rather than asking if anyone had seen him. He was still trying to keep a low profile, so I didn't want to draw any attention to the new resident in the area.

Attention had found him, though. There was a gathering of angry men about hundred yards away, and Julian was right in the middle of it, trying to quell the fracas—or at least keep the crowd from turning into a lynch mob. His arms were out and to the side, figuratively protecting a good-looking young man from the grasping arms reaching out from the angry, fist-shaking crowd. Well, maybe it was literally, but I knew Julian was unarmed.

He and his charge were standing in front of a colorful enclosed wagon. Two magnificent pale gray horses, their rear ends dappled black, were tied to the back of it with a coarse rope. The steeds weren't hitched to it, but looked as if they belonged with it. They were Andalusian horses, rare in this century in any country other than Spain. Four Angora goats, apparently a part of the menagerie, were tied together on a long lead, idly grazing the sparse grass, ignoring the to-do around them.

The carriage was basically brown—its natural wood color—with ornately carved trim. That alone was impressive, but it was also painted with stylized critters on the back and sides—dragons and butterflies, maybe. The outlandish green, blue, and yellow creatures were gathered around what appeared to be a big dish of apples.

However, the gypsy/hippie-looking rig wasn't the focus of the excitement. A short, ugly man was trying to work the crowd into frenzy. He was calling for the death of the petite, dark-haired young man—the apparent owner of the wagon and the exotic breeds of four-legged critters.

Julian was doing a good job of holding his ground. He wasn't very tall or physically intimidating—about the same size as the scared young man next to him—but he more than made up for it with his boldness. I guessed all the anger and frustration of being on virtual house arrest, having to hide out at the Pomeroys, was spewing forth—he was letting the crowd have it at top volume.

"Just because a man comes into town with strange-looking animals and an unusual wagon, does not mean he is evil. Let him be on his way. These are obviously his goods, and no one here has a right to them."

The short, ugly man who appeared to be the leader of the mob stomped the ground angrily as he approached Julian, shaking the coiled whip in his hand.

"How would you explain this then? It's a whip like the one that scourged our Lord. And look at his wagon: it's covered with images of demons feastin' on human hearts. This fiend has come to ravage our families and animals! He's even brought the Devil's own familiars with him. We who read the Good Book know the goat is the symbol of the Evil one. And these aren't *real* goats, the ones He made to give us milk and cheese: they're freaks! And those stallions! They're not *real* horses like we use for ridin' or pullin' a plow. They're the spawn of Satan himself! None of us is safe while this follower of Satan is around. He must be hanged by the neck until dead, and then drawn and quartered to make sure he doesn't come back in one piece to haunt us!"

The whole time he was ranting at Julian, the enraged townsman was making broad, crowd-inciting movements with his arms and body, pointing to different people in the crowd with the whip clenched in his fist, urging them to agree with him. He reminded me of a little Hitler without the mustache and armbands.

Julian held up his hands to try and quiet the horde so he could speak. They settled down enough to hear him. "What does the accused man have to say about all of this?" Julian asked the instigator, his voice an octave lower than normal, his face scowling at him.

Short Ugly spoke out boldly as he shoved his way through the crowd to claim center stage, not in the least bit intimidated by Julian. "The man speaks in the tongue of the Devil. He won't even talk to us in English! He is evil from the top of his black-haired head to the bottom of his snakeskin boots."

I looked down. Sure enough, the man had on snakeskin boots. Oh, boy. What we had here was a cowboy.

"May I ask him a question, please," I interrupted. I waddled forward and elbowed my very large pregnant form into the middle of the crowd.

Stunned, everyone stopped babbling to hear what the big-bellied woman had to say. *"¿Habla usted Español?"* I asked the frightened newcomer.

"Si, si, señora. ¿Es usted mi amiga?" he asked, a spark of hope showing in his dark brown eyes.

"Si, momentito, por favor," I replied, sharing with him a genuine smile of hope. I changed focus. "Julian, do you speak Spanish?"

Julian, flustered and angry, literally had his back up against the visitor, protecting him from the encroaching crowd. "I can read it, but speak very little. Do you think we can help him?"

"Oh, I'm sure of it," I replied loudly and with self-assurance, locking eyes with the short, ugly tyrant to make sure he heard me.

I leaned in and whispered to Julian, "I think I'm going to have to get creative, shall we say, on what I know. I know some of what's going on here. I think it's obvious to you and anyone else who hasn't been taken in, that Short Ugly wants at least those two beautiful horses. Will you support me if I jump into the middle of this, or do you want to try to handle it by yourself?"

Julian grinned. "Give it your best defense, dear. If they turn on us, I'll just claim it was your 'delicate' condition," he said and looked at my broad belly, "giving you delusions."

Everyone's eyes followed me as I waddled up to the front of the group. They were quietly curious, but I wasn't fooled. Docile sheep-type crowds could quickly change into a lynch mob under the right—or wrong—leader.

"Here's what we're going to do," I said, commanding their attention with both my booming voice and attitude. "I'm going to touch everyone here. If I tap you on the arm, you're to go sit down in the tavern by the window. If I tap you on the head, you can stand outside the tavern and watch the proceedings or go home—your choice. We're going to find out what's going on here Alaska-style."

I went through the crowd, tapping high and low. The slow, dim-witted looking people were 'touched in the head.' I was also gently head-thumping the ones who looked ready to turn violent. Those I tapped on the arm were going to be on the jury. The others were the audience.

"Everyone inside," I hollered. "Now, sir," I said to Short Ugly, "Please untie the accused so we can get this trial a-movin'!"

Short Ugly was rough as he grabbed the man's wrists, and nearly sliced his captive's thumb when he cut the rope. He pushed him through the tavern entryway, knocking him against the wall, and tried to kick his feet out from underneath him on the way in.

"Untie his legs, too," I ordered, hoping he heard my glaring omission of the word please. He grumbled but did as he was told.

All of the men and women gathered by the window or sat with hat in hand—if they had one—and waited for me to speak again. When everyone had settled down, I began. "All right, now what is your name," I asked Short Ugly.

"I'm Richard Short, owner of the property down by the creek. I found this man there, lettin' his animals eat my grass and drink my water. As soon as I saw his wagon, I knew he was from the Devil."

I put up my hand to stop his dissertation. "Okay, I mean, all right; just give us the facts. Save your guesses for later."

I turned to face the crowd of townsfolk, all of them staring at me, slack-jawed in anticipation, waiting for my directions. "All right, everyone, what we are going to do is have a trial."

I felt like a female Perry Mason addressing the jury, getting their full attention before I even started with my opening statement. "This is how we're going to do it. Mr. Short, you will tell us your side of the story, part of which you have already shared, and then I will ask you some questions. Then we will have others tell what they saw, and you and I will ask them questions—that is, if you have any. Does this sound fair to you?"

"Well, I s'pose so, but what does that do?" he asked, obviously confused.

"When we're done, we'll ask these twelve fine ladies and gentlemen who were selected as our jury by a touch to the arm, to confer amongst themselves. We'll let them figure out if this man deserves to die *just because* he has a colorful wagon and beautiful animals." I batted my eyelashes and smiled coyly, accentuating 'just because' to gain their sympathy. I was enjoying my role as Ms. Perry Mason, endearing myself to the men and women of the jury, even before the trial started.

"And don't forget, them demon animals was eatin' my grass and drinkin' my water, too," he bellowed.

"All right, shall we begin?" I asked rhetorically, totally ignoring the excitable man's outburst.

I wrung my hands and addressed my nemesis. "Mr. Short, have you ever driven any of your animals from your place to another site and had them drink by a creek not on your own property or eat the grass by the road?"

"Well, yes, ma'am, but that was a long time ago. I had to get my critters to the place I just bought. There was no other way to get them there," replied Mr. Short, nodding and looking around at his peers for validation.

"So, in the past, you have done the same thing that this man has done?" I asked, sweeping imaginary dirt off of my skirt.

"Yes, ma'am, but I was on my way to my own place," he insisted, taking his excitement level down a notch or two. "This is different."

"Now, you were talking about the Bible earlier. Don't you think the Lord, who has given us the water that flows and the grass that grows, don't you think He'd want us to share with other travelers?"

"Well, I guess so, but this man has devil animals, and he was goin' all over the countryside, cursin' people," he exclaimed, rising from his seat, all wound up again.

"Mr. Short, I would like to remind you that the Lord created both goats and horses. Many of us around here have these same animals, although maybe not with the same long hair or coloring. Therefore, I do not believe his animals are an issue here. Now, have you or anyone else received a curse from this man? And if so, what was it, and did anyone else hear it?"

"Well, he said somethin' that I didn't understand, but I think it was a curse. Will Severson heard him, didn't ya, Will?"

A tall blond man stood up. "Ja, I heard 'im say sumtim, den he starts vavin' his arms, jumpin up und down. I dunt know if twer a curse, bit it was sumtim else to see."

"Just a moment, men," I said. My Spanish-speaking defendant had figured out the gist of what was being said and was waving at me. At least he understood the last part, when Mr. Severson imitated him.

"Blah, blah, blah, *serpiente, malo, muerte,* blah, blah," was what I heard—but it was enough.

"Mr. Short, Mr. Severson: have you ever seen big snakes, like water moccasins, down by the creek?"

"Ja, I kilt one right after dis devil man started screamin'. If I hadn't, it vould ha' kilt Herr Short!"

"Do you think this man could possibly have been trying to tell Mr. Short that there was a snake and to be careful?"

"Ja, Ja. Ohhh, so dat's vat it vuz! Sorry, mein herr. And tank you fer lookin' out fer us," He bowed as he thanked the stranger. "Tank you verra much."

I drew a deep breath. "So here we have a man who doesn't speak our language, who stops to water his animals, and warns a man about a deadly snake—actually, in a way, saving his life—and you want to repay him by hanging him? Come on now, folks—is this the way to treat a new member of our community?"

I looked over at Julian and our new friend. Julian was waving a piece of paper at me. "Just a moment, please, people." I strutted over to Julian as only a very pregnant woman could, maintaining my 'I am in charge' attitude.

"This is a land grant," he whispered. "His property is between here and Jody's place. He's going to be our new neighbor. He isn't a transient—he was almost home when he stopped to water his animals."

"Wow," I said softly. I got back to my center-stage position. I paused to make sure the murmurs of the crowds, both inside and out, came to a complete stop. I wanted their complete attention before I addressed my impromptu jury.

"Fellow community members, it appears we have erred greatly. This man," I looked down at the deed to find his name, "José Rojas, is your new neighbor. His property is right next to Mr. Pomeroy's. I think we should all offer him an apology, ask his forgiveness, and welcome him into our community. Señor Rojas," I extended my hand to José as he rose at his name, *"Lo siento mucho."*

Everyone came up to José to shake his hand and offer apologies. It seemed I'd won over the crowd without even asking for a vote. Everyone except Mr. Short, that is. He remained standing near the door, scowling, his arms crossed tightly across his chest. He had just lost the two horses he had planned on getting through deceit. We'd have to watch out for him.

**30 José's Ranch

Julian walked out of the three-tabled tavern with me on one side, José on the other. I grinned at my driver and said in a low voice, "In my time and place, a person is often listed with his last name first. That means you would be referred to as Hart Julian."

"I'm familiar with the way of listing names. We often do the same now. What does that have to do with anything?"

"What is the nickname for Richard?"

"Well, there's Rick, Rich, Dick and…" Julian paused. "Yes, I get it— Short Dick. Evie, you are such an uncouth person at times," he scolded, paused, and then grinned as he finished, saying, "but always entertaining."

"Maybe there is something to names after all. He did seem to have a complex, didn't he?" I asked sheepishly.

"That he did," said Julian, smiling at our little shared joke.

The three of us arrived at José's brilliantly adorned wagon, its style reminiscent of a gypsy's mobile home. His horses and goats were all well fed and rested. They had eaten and drunk their fill, and were idling, swishing flies with ears and tails, enjoying a bit of early spring sunlight. I walked over to the mural on the side of the wagon. I pointed to the bowl that Richard Short had said was full of hearts. "*¿Cuales son estos?"* I asked, hoping I wasn't butchering the Spanish language too badly.

"*Estas son manzanas rojas, como mi appellido,"* he replied animatedly, pointing to the apples and then back to himself.

"*Claro*, of course," I replied. I turned to Julian, "You're not going to believe this, so maybe I won't tell you for a while. Anyhow, can we escort José to his new home? I have a few sandwiches left, so we can have a little 'welcome to Gibsonville' meal once we get there."

Julian looked over at our new neighbor as he spoke to me, a smile of appreciation on his face. "That sounds like the least we can do after the way Short Dick treated him today."

Julian wasn't as guarded as he used to be. I could tell he was checking out the new man. My gay-dar perceived that the youthful—but not too young—José was aware of, and enjoying, his perusal/inspection. The feeling appeared to be mutual. I caught him giving Julian the once over—twice—checking him out when he thought no one was looking.

"*Andalé, vamos a ir a su casa*, José," I called. He hopped up into his wagon, smiling broadly, and waited for us to get into ours. "I think we should lead, Julian. I suspect we know the way better than he does."

Julian took the reins, turned to José, and lifted his chin in salutation, "*Andalé, amigo, andalé.*"

We led the way with José's colorful wagon and menagerie bringing up the rear. We made it in an hour and a half, with only one potty stop for me, to where the deed indicated the property was located. At that point, José pulled up beside us, and waved for us to follow him.

We trailed behind him, the wagons barely able to negotiate the narrow path that followed the creek. We managed to make it to a small clearing just before it got impassable. José jumped down from his wagon, ran ahead of us, and pulled on what looked like a bush. It was actually brush attached to a swinging gate, plenty wide for a wagon to enter.

Then we saw it. Down the shaded road, not even a hundred yards away, someone had built a little paradise amidst the grove of tall, dense oaks—a Spanish-style home with stuccoed walls, arched doorways and windows, and a luxurious broad porch with pink-blossomed bushes spilling over the dark wood trim.

We followed his wagon down the broad lane and stopped in front of the sweet smelling veranda. José hopped off his wagon seat and ran over to help me down. "*Con su permiso,*" he said, his hand held out for mine.

"*Gracias,*" I replied, and let him help me to the ground. He scurried over to the door of the manse and pushed it open for us. Julian followed behind me with our little picnic basket.

The surprisingly cool room had a breathtaking centerpiece–a massive, dark wood table, its edges and legs ornately carved, its top accented with an embroidered, lacy table runner. Beside it, a matching china cabinet with floral etched-glass doors showcased brightly painted dishes—the red apple and floral design similar to the wagon's—and elegant cut-crystal glassware. Beautiful—could they be Persian?—rugs carpeted the floor. Dark, ornate picture frames held bright oil portraits of men and women with Andalusian horses, the apparent family pictures softening the brightness of the white walls.

I was stunned by possibly the most beautiful room I had ever seen—I knew it certainly was for the short span of my current memory. "Wow," was all I could say. It was stunning—a classy parlor and dining room that didn't need to be large to be impressive.

José opened a drawer in the china cabinet, grabbed a tea towel embroidered with the familial apples and apple blossoms design, and used it to dust off the table and a chair for me. He then did the same to the chair for Julian, smiling sweetly as he looked up. When he realized he was looking at him just a little too long, he got busy, did a bit more dusting, and took a pitcher from the hutch. He said, "*Momentito, por favor*," and headed out the door, wearing a smile that didn't stop at his face, but continued all the way down to the spring in his step.

"Julian, I think he likes you," I whispered across the table.

"Hmph" Julian replied.

"Oh, like that is it? You sound just like a Scot when you do that."

"Don't be ridiculous," he replied in his formal, British aristocratic tone.

"Uh-huh. Is that 'don't be ridiculous' about sounding like a Scot or about José liking you?" I couldn't help but smile from eyebrows to toes. "Someone's got a crush on you," I sang.

"Eev-vie," he said. His stern admonition—stretching out my name in an unnaturally low baritone range—was cut short by the reappearance of our new host.

José had filled the pitcher with water and brought it and a bottle of wine to the table. He set them down and took three glasses from the hutch.

"*¿Platas, tambien?*" I asked as I put the small package of sandwiches on the table.

"*Sí, sí,*" he replied and handed me three small dishes. I unwrapped the sandwiches and placed one on each plate, then set the table, making sure I was opposite them, the men's settings next to each other on one side.

José filled the glasses with the dark red wine, and we all sat down. He lifted his crystal chalice and toasted us, "*¡Salud! Gracias por todo lo que has hecho, mis amigos.*"

Julian and I replied, "*¡Salud!*" and sipped. Well, I sipped the dark, sweet brew, and Julian gulped it.

Julian raised his half-full cup again and said boldly, "*Prost!*"

I had no idea what that meant, but tipped my glass just the same, wetting my lips, enjoying the sweet nectar without swallowing more than a taste.

José refilled their chalices several times. They were drinking heartily, but I continued with my sipping. After the first glassful, I decided to substitute water for the wine. I took the initiative, hoping I wasn't insulting our host, and refilled my own glass from the water pitcher while they chatted. Women of this era drank while pregnant, but I knew its dangers.

I also knew I had to keep my calorie intake up. I didn't know what the protocol for social drinking and dining was in Britain or Spain, but I was hungry. I daintily picked up my sandwich and did my best not to wolf it down. I restrained myself by taking a small bite, putting it down, and looking around the room as I chewed.

I finished my little one course meal and watched the two men as they tried to communicate. It sounded as if the more Julian drank, the better his Spanish became. I also noticed that José would try to communicate a word or phrase to him, then put his hand on top of Julian's as he tried to get the message across. I'm not sure what he was trying to say, but when I saw Julian look down at José's hand and smile, I knew that his message was coming through loud and clear.

I waited until there was a pause in the bilingual conversation to ask, "Julian, do you think José would mind if we stayed here tonight? I think I've had a bit too much to drink and, well, I would really like to lie down if there's room."

I really hadn't had very much to drink, and certainly wasn't incapacitated, but I was tired. I also knew this initial connection, or bonding, would be hard to recapture on a future visit. They were on a roll, and I didn't want to stop or slow down the momentum.

Julian said something to our host, then put his hand on top of José's shoulder for to make sure he understood. He left it there just a tad too long, but José looked over at him and smiled. The two of them arose and came over to me. José put out his arm and asked me to accompany him. He led me to a very nice bedroom off the main room. It was complete with fluffy feather bed, ewer and basin, and a chamber pot. Julian looked over the room and then left quickly. He returned just as fast with the pitcher of water that José had brought in to the dining room table. He set it next to the bowl, swapping it for the empty ewer, and asked with a wine-induced glowing smile, "Is there anything else you require, ma'am?"

"I seem to have everything I need for the evening. Don't forget to take care of the animals."

"Oh, I can't believe we did that! José, *¡los caballos y cabras!*"

"*¡Aye, carumba!*" José rushed out to untie, feed, and water the horses and goats.

Yup, the two men had eyes for each other only. When a man forgets about his livestock, he is definitely smitten.

I reached out to Julian before he left. "I need a hug," I said, my bottom lip pooched out like a pouting three-year-old.

He gave me a big hug and long squeeze. "Do you really think I can't see through your 'I've had too much to drink' ruse? I don't know about you, Evie," he said as he rocked me back and forth like a child. "You have an old soul for such a young body."

He stopped rocking and set his hands on my shoulders, making sure I could stand by myself. "Good night and sleep well, you rascal," he said and kissed my forehead. I turned around, and he gave me a pat on the bottom. Oh, boy, he was sure wound up! Good wine and good company were working for him tonight. I was glad someone was going to get lucky.

I washed up as best I could with the cold water. Something wasn't right, but I couldn't quite put my finger on it. Then I got an idea.

I went into the main room and listened for the men. They were walking back from the barn, laughing, but still keeping a gentlemanly distance from each other.

I came out onto the porch. "Julian," I called out, "I think maybe José can help you tonight with your back." I looked right into Julian's eyes as I was talking and hoped he could see the 'just trust me on this' look I was giving him.

It must have worked because Julian replied, "Why don't you tell José what is needed, and see if he wants to be of assistance." He paused, then looked away from both José and me. I wished I could have seen the look on his face. I wanted to know if he was laughing, scared, mad, or disgusted. I couldn't see, but I was sure it was at least one of the four reactions.

I took a deep breath and started, *"La espalda de Julio es dolor.* Oh shoot, how do you say rub or massage?" I started making the movement of rubbing. "Julian, come here, please."

Julian came to me obediently, his bottom lip sucked in to try and keep his mask of detachment in place. I spun him around and used his back to demonstrate upper to lower back massage. *"Es mejor con aceite."*

José heard this and rushed into the house. Julian was confused, his mouth now hanging slack, his whole body wavering slightly from the wine and the uncertainty.

"Well, Julian, I'm off to bed—now that I've left you in good hands. And don't forget to take off your shirt…at least. I don't want you to get oil on your clothes."

"Oil?" he asked. "What's this about oil?"

"Oh, it just makes the massage more effective. It's also lots of fun to play slip and slide if you decide to get carried away—and I hope you do. I really like José, and I think he likes you, too."

239

José came out on the porch with a bottle of what I assumed was oil. Julian bent his head and brushed invisible lint off his jacket. I watched as his face did a perfect transition from an embarrassed blush to a glow of anticipation. He looked up and put his hand on my shoulder, pulled me to him and gave me a one-armed hug, and then placed a long, hard kiss on my forehead. "Goodnight, my dear Evie. Don't wait up for us. Sweet dreams."

I half walked, half waddled up the steps of the porch, pausing when I encountered José, "*Buenas noches*," I said with a polite and gracious smile to our host, "*Hasta mañana.*"

Back in my room for the night, I shut the door, finally able to release the huge grin I had been holding in check. I started to sing softly, "Matchmaker, matchmaker, make me a match." I rubbed my twice-kissed-in-one-hour-spot on my forehead. The world was spinning in the right direction today. I lay down on the fluffy feather bed and sighed deeply. The last thing I remembered was my head sinking into the pillow.

**31 A Partnership Evolves

I awoke the next morning content and happier with life than I had been in a month, maybe two. The dappled sunlight slipping through the leaves outside the honest-to-goodness glass window painted ever-changing patterns on the walls of my borrowed sleeping chamber, almost hypnotic in its movement. A rooster singing his 'get out of bed, sleepy head' song broke me out of my peaceful trance. I smoothed out the clothes I had slept in—still the only ones I had—ran my fingers through my hair, and drank about a half-gallon of water. Where there was a rooster, there were usually hens—and what hens produced. It was time to hunt eggs for breakfast!

I tiptoed through the main room so I wouldn't rouse anyone. I didn't see them, so they were still be in one—possibly, but unlikely, two—of the other rooms. I opened up the hutch and took out a big china bowl. It was a high dollar egg basket to be sure, but I didn't know my way around this place, and I didn't want to make a lot of noise looking for the right container.

I made my way down the porch steps toward the barn, the fancy bowl tucked under one arm. I grasped a fistful of my skirt with my other hand to facilitate my seek-and-find stance and began the hunt. Large brown-feathered chickens were pecking the ground right in front of the barn doors, gleaning bugs or seeds from the spilled straw. Hopefully, there was a coop where they had their nests. I didn't want to have to go traipsing through the brush to gather eggs. It was hard enough to reach down without having to try and see over my big belly at the same time. I already had to pick up low-lying objects by approaching them from the side.

I cracked open the barn door to investigate and—*voila!*—cute little boxes with hens setting on straw nests. It was time to reach under and rob a few components for our breakfast omelets.

As I walked through the door, I heard rustling noises. I froze. I didn't know what critter was moving around, and I didn't want it to find me first if it was un-penned, big, and ornery, like a bull. A moment later, I was able to discern the sounds. People—someone was making happy people noises. I grabbed half a dozen eggs and sneaked out as quickly as possible.

It seemed the men had stayed overnight in the barn. If they wanted to talk about it, I'd let them. But if they wanted me to believe that they had been in separate quarters—well, I wasn't going to embarrass the two of them. Of course, I'd have fun making Julian squirm and blush later, when we were alone.

As I walked into the kitchen, I noticed braids of onions, chilies, and garlic hanging from the rafters. I twisted off an onion for the omelet and walked in, making as much noise as I wanted. I found a crock of what appeared to be lard in the kitchen, a large bin of flour, and a small painted ceramic jar of what I hoped was salt. I dipped my finger in it, tasted the white grit, and found out that my guess was right.

Now it was time to stoke the stove for breakfast. I was going to make fresh tortillas and put together egg and onion burritos. I was just finishing up the last of the tortillas when a sheepish-looking José came in.

"*Buenas días, señora,*" he said, nodding to me. He went to the cupboard, pulled out a coffee pot, and took it outside to the well. When he came back in, he snatched half an eggshell from my little compost pile and dumped it and a tin cupful of ground coffee into the pot. He carefully moved around me and set it on the back of the stove. He smiled and said, "*¿Café?*"

"Yes, thank you. It should go well with the egg burritos." I knew I could make better conversation in my pidgin Spanish, but he might as well learn English with the immersion method. I wasn't going to use Spanish unless absolutely necessary. He'd catch on faster this way, for sure.

I turned around to see if I could find some cheese and walked right into Julian. He grabbed both my shoulders to steady me, and then looked me right in the eyes with a 'don't mess with me' glare. "Good morning, Evie. It looks as if you've become the lady of the house once again. Something smells good." He gave me a fatherly hug, then pulled away and asked, "May I help by setting the table?"

"That would be great. I think everything is in the hutch."

I went back to the small, dark pantry off of the kitchen and found neat rows of fresh red tomatoes! "I'll be just two more minutes. I think I found something else for us."

I gently squeezed a couple of tomatoes until I found one that was perfect, not too firm. I chopped it up, along with a small onion, added crushed cilantro, and a double pinch of salt. *Voilà*—two-minute salsa.

We had a nice, but boring, breakfast. It was good food all right, but the men were quiet—uncomfortably quiet. I saw them steal quick glances at each other under their long lashes. Why, oh why, did men always get the long eyelashes? Anyway, the mood was too glum for me. I wanted to steer this breakfast social to where I wanted it to go.

"Ahem. Hey, guys, I need a few questions answered before we leave. José, is there anyone around to help you with the ranch?" I was already using the English immersion program on him.

He gave me a blank stare and I gave in a little, "*¿Quien ayudas te?*" I was pretty weak in my grammar, but did know that "*quien*" was who, and "*ayuda*" was help.

Julian broke in. "José doesn't have anyone here to help him. His mother and brother lived here until they took ill. The one hired hand they had, Robert, was the one who sent the urgent message to Spain for José to come to America and help take care of the family and the ranch. Robert stayed here and did all he could. Two months ago, mama died. Brother passed two days later. All Robert knew was that they had chills, then very high fevers. He remained here by himself, taking care of everything as best he could. When he heard that a man with two magnificent gray horses had arrived in town, he came out to greet his deceased mistress's son. Robert introduced himself to José, received his wages, and then the trouble started. Robert had planned to come back to help José with the ranch and new animals, but when the threats, pushing, and shoving started, he panicked and left.

"The man we now know as Dick Short admired José's horses. He offered José a small amount of money for both of them. Of course, José said no. He may not have understood his words, but a couple coins rubbed together and a nod at the horses was plain enough. José's negative reply didn't go over very well. That is when Mr. Short decided to see how much he could take from the man who didn't speak English. He didn't want just the horses, though—he wanted everything the Rojas family had. Old 'Short Dick' intentionally started the panic about demons and Devil worship. If we hadn't come along and shown the townspeople how ridiculous the accusations were, it would be Mr. Richard Short sitting here eating eggs, and José would be...well, we came at a very opportune time to save his property and perhaps his life."

"Ho-kay, I think we need to get him some help. And of course, I have a plan." I turned away and made sure José couldn't see my face. I spoke softly to Julian alone, my cheeks nearly cramping from my huge grin, "And I know you like my plans, so here goes."

I turned back and spoke up to include José in the conversation, at least figuratively. "How about a partnership for you two? Julian, you have experience with horses and could make sure José isn't taken advantage of when buying supplies and such. And you know people, both here in this country and abroad, who would love to have one of his Andalusians, or even the use of one of his stallions as studs for their own horses. Oh, and I think the goats might actually be more valuable, pound-per-pound, than the horses. Did you notice that they're Angora goats?"

"I'll answer your last question first. No, I did not notice they were Angora goats, and would not know what to do with one if I did know what one was. On the other part, you little minx, yes, I do believe a partnership would be welcomed on both parts, but not because of what your little gutter mind is thinking. True, José needs help here, but any strong back could do that. As far as running a profitable horse stable, that would be where I think I could help most. I have some money, and I would be happy to invest it in more horses. I also believe that this location and occupation would be less conspicuous for me as far as the, ahem, other issue is concerned."

"Right," I drawled, "Hide in plain sight. A little homespun and a straw hat, and you'd blend right into the countryside." I smiled at José and nodded. "Do you think José would like the idea?"

"We talked about it last night and then again this morning," Julian said. I raised my eyebrows and glanced down at my plate. "Yes, you see," Julian picked up my chin and looked at me with an innocent smirk, "the more wine I drank, the better my Spanish became. And it turns out that José knows a bit of English, too. He's just afraid to speak it because of his accent. But I digress. Yes, a partnership is desirous," another smirk, this time from both him and me, "for both of us."

"Okay, but before we leave, I want to walk around the property with both of you. I want to see what you're getting yourself into, property-wise. But let's make sure I get back to our...er...the Pomeroy's place, and that there's someone there to stay with me, before you change your mailing address."

"You know, Evie, if you were anyone else, I'd call you out for some of your crude remarks. I would have challenged a man to a duel for even one of the innuendos you have made in the last 24 hours, but..."

I interrupted, "But you love me and I love you." I popped a quick kiss right on his lips and said, "Just give me a minute, and then I'll be ready to go with you on a tour of the premises."

I had been so absorbed with Julian that I didn't even notice that José had gathered up the dishes and was in the kitchen, cleaning up my mess. Wow, just what I need—two husbands: one to kiss and one to clean. Yeah, right...both gay. That would mean I'd have to take a lover or another

*husband just so I could get laid. Oh well, I'm happy with what I have now,
no matter how crazy it is. A good friend is better than a lousy husband,
any day.*

On our walk around the property, I explained in plain English the
value of Angora goats. Their coats were extremely soft and were evidently
rare since Julian didn't know about them. Goats would eat just about
anything, too, and their wool harvested twice a year.

José had a surprise for us, too. He had three young mares in the back
pasture. He explained in broken English that they had come to America
when they were young, so no one knew their value. Now that they were
grown, their compact yet sturdy form was definitely noticeable, their
manes and tails already long. "Did you know that their manes will grow
faster if you braid them?" I asked José.

He didn't understand, so I walked over and, after talking softly and
gaining the fairest mare's confidence, started braiding the hair just above
her withers in narrow one-inch plaits. I used a blade of new spring grass as
a ribbon for the end. I visualized them, Julian and José, out in the pasture,
braiding the manes of the horses, a very soothing thought.

"I want to go home, Julian," I blurted out. I was on the verge of tears.
There was no reason for it other than I suddenly wanted to curl up on my
poor little excuse for a bed. I could feel the start of a mood swing. The
hormones were bubbling to the surface, interrupting my composure, and
stifling my sanity on their way.

"All right, Evie, if that's what you want. Let's get some food and
water put aside first, and then we can be on our way," Julian said, a
puzzled look on his face.

I started to say something—to try and explain—then realized how
much concern he had for me. Julian didn't understand what was
happening, but he would do anything for me. Realizing that had the tear
glands working even harder. I blinked back the wetness, a brainstorm
replacing my anxiety. "Wait, wait, before we go, I want to do something.
We can do it in the *sala*…er…main room."

We walked up the porch steps together, one man at each elbow to
steady me. I saw Julian and José look at each other, wordless, yet with
complete understanding, just like an old married couple. Such a warm,
soothing sight—I was happy again. Good grief! Crying one minute, then
smiling and perky the next—what was left?

I pulled myself together. Recharged and ready, I had a task, a positive
mission to accomplish. "Okay guys, come here, we're going to have a little

traditional—at least where I'm from—rite, I'd guess that's what you'd call it." I reached out and held one of their hands in each of mine. "Okay, you guys want to form a partnership, right? You both understand?"

Julian and José looked at each other and then at me. Julian said, "Partners," and José copied him in his thick, sultry Spanish accent, "Partners."

"Okay, go stand together, side by side," I said, indicating the sunny spot by the front window. José moved over, stood up tall, and smiled. Julian walked over and stood three feet away, wearing a frown of uncertainty. "Get closer," I ordered.

Julian stepped nearer and looked at me with a slight sneer of defiance. "Closer—this is a partnership, and the whole idea is showing the symbolism of you two guarding each other's backs in all adversity, trials, blah, blah, blah."

"Is that how they do it in Alaska?" asked Julian. His frown had vanished. I could tell he was ceding all authority in this rite to me—he was smiling again.

"Huh?" I answered, totally baffled at his mention of Alaska.

"Yesterday at the 'incident,' you said, 'We're going to find out what is going on here—Alaska-style.' Is this little ceremony Alaska-style, too? And where is Alaska?"

"North, way up norrrth," I sang.

'North to Alaska' was sing-songing in my head. I shook my head to physically move the words away, along with any memories that might be sneaking in.

"Let's talk about it later, Julian. Remind me because I might forget."

Forget again, I thought.

Julian was six inches from José's elbow at this point. They looked so cute together. They were pretty much the same height and build, although José was at least ten years younger, maybe more. José was staring at me—oops! I had been gawking at the two of them for more than just a moment.

"Ahem, sorry about the wait, guys. I, uh, was just trying to remember the words," I lied. Well, it sounded like a good excuse to me. Now it was time to see if I could think fast on my feet again.

"Dear Lord, we are gathered here to ask Your blessing on this new partnership between Julian Wallace Hart and José Rojas."

"José Alejandro Rojas," José whispered to me.

"Julian Wallace Hart and José Alejandro Rojas," I corrected. José's chest puffed up at his name. I had intentionally left out Julian's title and

246

didn't know why I knew his middle name was Wallace. At least, I think I was right; he didn't correct me.

"Do you agree to help each other in your pursuit of health, happiness, and prosperity in taking care of this property and of all the creatures that reside here, your business needs and…" I paused, not wanting to sound too mushy, "Non-business needs, so long as you both agree," I paused again and looked down, "or live, whichever works out best?"

I looked at the men, waiting for an answer. They looked back, confused, seeking direction. "Say, I do," I whispered softly.

"I do," they said together.

"Lord, we ask You to give these men Your knowledge and understanding, compassion, and caring in all that they do. We ask Your blessing on them in sickness and health, poverty and wealth, trials and celebrations. In Jesus's name, Amen."

The two men looked at each other and then at me. I nodded my head, urging them to respond. They both replied, "Amen."

"Okay, a hearty handshake and a big bear hug, and you're partners in the eyes of all of us here, including Him," I said as I looked up to heaven.

José clutched Julian's hand in a big two-handed shake, exaggerating the up and down movement. Both of them were smiling as if they had just won the lottery. José paused for half a breath, then threw his arms wide and enveloped Julian in a big bear hug, actually lifting him off the floor. Julian's eyes were bug-eyed at the intense show of affection, and then he realized that he had nothing to hide, nor anyone to hide it from. His whole face relaxed and shone with its natural radiance, reflecting his unbridled joy.

"*¿Como oso?*" José asked me after he finally set Julian down.

"Yes, like a bear," I replied and walked over to wrap my arms around both of them, my belly squished between the two of theirs, my head touching both of their shoulders at the same time. "My bears," I added.

My beautiful, 'cuddly teddy bears,' I thought—but I certainly wouldn't tell them that.

I still wanted to go home, and Julian respected that. The men got the wagon set up while I waited, all aglow with the success of my matchmaking. Julian helped me into the wagon seat and José bid us a cordial, "Good-bye," taking care to enunciate both words of the simple phrase.

Ж Ж

Julian drove me back to the house. He'd make sure all was secure and that someone was home to watch out for me so he could he return to José and the ranch. It was quiet for a while, both of us in our own little worlds. He spoke first. "I don't know what I did to deserve you, lady. Sometimes you exasperate me so much I want to, to..."

"Throttle me?" I asked.

"I'm not sure what that means but, yes, probably. And other times I...well, if I weren't who I am—and I know I don't have to explain *that* to you—I'd ask you to marry me. But you are in my life and, for better or worse, as you say, I'm glad of it."

"Wow, an almost proposal—thank you!" I looked over and saw Julian was both embarrassed and ticked at the same time. "No, really, thank you. You have no idea how it feels to be pregnant and alone and well, to be literally dumped on the doorstep of other people—no matter how nice they are—by someone who you had felt so strongly for...ergh!"

"Well, it's his loss and our gain. We have a unique family here, Wallace with his two fathers and Sarah with a sister who really isn't a sister. Yes, I know the circumstances are most unusual, but we all love each other, and look out for each other. What more could anyone ask?"

"A last name for my babies?" I replied, my bottom lip blossoming into a full pout. I really wasn't looking for sympathy, but deep down I wondered: if I pouted well enough, would it cure me of my abandonment issues?

"Well, I'll tell you what," Julian said as he used the knuckle of his index finger to gently nudge my bottom lip back up to where it belonged, "if that big, strong, intelligent son of mine doesn't ask you to marry him soon, I...I..."

Julian was stammering, something I had never seen him do before. "You'll just have to have a *long* talk with the boy, that's all," I said in a jesting manner a la Jed Clampett.

"Yes, that's right, that's what I'll do, except I think he is waiting until...oh, I don't want to betray a confidence. You understand, don't you?"

"Yes, I understand." He hadn't said too much, but what he said, and how he said it, definitely brightened my morning. Shoot, brightened my whole month...at least!

I sat next to him, in a daze. I was worthy as a wife—at least to Julian and, apparently/hopefully, Wallace. And these men weren't self-serving, avenging skunks either. I sighed at the prospect of a new life; one where I didn't have to hide my thoughts or feelings for fear I'd get someone in trouble. I flashed on Little Bear and the gentle kiss he had given me on my hand. 'I hope he's safe,' went through my mind. I shook off the uncertainty. He'd be fine—at least until Ian caught up to and took care of the remaining seven foul judges...or however many were left of the original eight who had tortured him.

I snapped out of my jumbled emotional stew of bliss and fear when the wagon hit a bump. I reflexively clutched at the non-existent seat belt across my chest. Julian looked over at my odd gesture but didn't say anything.

"Oh, and I was going to tell you," I said as I re-adjusted my skirt under my thighs. "Remember when we were talking about names just after we first met José?"

"Yes, and you were going to tell me something about his name. What was that all about?"

"José said that *rojas* referred to the color of the apples, his family's emblem. Apples are *pommes* in French and *roy* means red in Gaelic. José means Joseph and so, you just had a civil ceremony joining you and Joseph Pommes Roy in a partnership for life, or as long as you both agree—but I don't doubt that it will be for life."

Julian paled at my explanation and I knew why.

I wasn't supposed to know that Julian had once had a major crush on Jody. That was some of the info I 'knew,' but didn't know why I knew. Shoot! I shouldn't have said anything, but it was too late now. Ah, what the hell...

I babbled on, acting as if I knew nothing of the crush. "Yup, you and another 'Red Jody'—partners for life. Weird, huh?"

"Yeah, weird, huh?" he replied, stunned.

Ж Ж

I did fine for the rest of the ride home—fine in the fact that I didn't cry or have any other signs of pregnancy-induced mood swings.

José had given me some of his long-keeper tomatoes and his extra tortilla griddle as gifts of appreciation. I think he was trying to say it was for performing the partnership service, but he probably would have given them to me anyway. He also let me have as much food as I cared to gather. I grabbed a couple of garlic bulbs and some dried chilies to bring back for seeding my little kitchen garden. I had found a few other plants that had gone to seed and gleaned seedpods from them for my mystery rows. I was pretty sure there were some greens in there and maybe a few carrots. Now if I just knew where I could get some cucumber and squash seeds and maybe some sprouting potatoes, I'd have everything I wanted. I'd start the tomato and chili seeds as soon as we got home.

I was very content. Now I had something to look forward to. The depression I had had that led to chaos, death, and disaster was gone. Now, if the guilt of my running away and being the cause of it all would just leave, too…

**32 But I Want to Go

February 23, 1781

"But I want to go, too! I can help you, you know I can."

I didn't like begging, but that's what I was doing. Sarah was going with the men to an area called Haw River. There were rumors that the Loyalists were gathering near there, and someone named Badminton Tarleton—or some goofy name like it—was coming to lead them into battle against the patriot militia. There had already been small skirmishes, but something big was in the wind. Our scouts had seen an 'officer-looking' man in a green coat leading a large group of foot soldiers. Scores of Loyalists, both young and old, followed behind him like little lambs. There were too many wound up tea-suckers—and with a leader—too close to home for me.

Sarah and I had been bickering about where I belonged all morning. "I know it's not safe for me, but it's not safe for anyone else either. I also know it's not a good idea for me to be here alone. If Julian or Wallace has to stay here to watch out for me, then Jody will be one good man short if there is fighting. So, how about if I go with you, do as I'm told, and keep out of harm's way?"

Sarah gave up the argument with a sigh. "I'll speak with Jody and see if I can persuade him to let you come with us. If there *is* fighting, there'll be injuries, and I could use your help. You aren't afraid of blood, are you?"

"Only my own, and I always do my best to grab the right end of a knife."

As if on cue, Jody appeared. "Would ye two come out here fer a moment," he said, and then turned around, not waiting for an answer, certain that we'd follow.

Sarah and I looked at each other, wide-eyed and stunned at the male haughtiness that had just made an appearance. "Hmph," I grunted.

"Hmph," Sarah echoed as we joined elbows in perfect accord, ready to meet with the man—on his turf and at his terms.

Jody was standing next to the horses, scowling like a man who had come to a decision he hadn't wanted to make. Julian and Wallace were a few yards away, fussing with their saddles, obviously trying to look busy. I knew they were trying to be unobtrusive, but they also wanted to be near enough to find out what was going on.

"I've come to the conclusion that Evie should come with us. I've arranged fer Todd Gillespie to come and take care of the animals. I canna risk leavin' her by herself, and I'll need Julian and Wallace by my side if fightin' should break out. She'll be safe with us…" He took a deep breath and stared into my eyes, either scolding me or challenging me—I'm not sure which—"as long as she does what she's told."

I unlocked his gaze then looked to Sarah. I shook my head back and forth, as if I were upset or undecided, then moved into her shoulder, giving her a big hug, burying my face into her hair to hide my grin. Finally composed, I pulled back, actually managing to keep a straight face.

I addressed Jody, my entire demeanor totally submissive, "If that's what you think is best, I'll do it. What should I bring?"

"Bring yer coat and yer wee bag. Ye always seem to have somethin' we need in there. And use the privy before we leave. We have to make good time, and I dinna care to take more rests than needed."

Sarah and I figured that I was four months pregnant. I felt great; I had a wonderful 'super woman' confidence and more energy now than during the last three months. And I was also able to hold my water longer.

Wallace was waiting for me with my coat and my backpack when I came back from the privy. "I'm glad you're coming. I agree with Jody that you'll be safer with us. Besides, I'd miss our conversations if you stayed behind."

Wallace offered his hand to help me onto my little nag of a horse. She was gentle and somewhat lazy, preferring to tag along behind the other horses. Well, I tried, but I just couldn't reach the stirrup—my belly was in the way. Baby belly didn't squish out of the way like fat belly. "Could you give me a leg up, Wallace? The stirrup seems too high for me all of a sudden."

"My pleasure, madam," he replied as he knelt down and cupped his hands for me to step into.

"Are ye gonna be all day gettin' into the saddle, lass?" barked Jody. "We need to make use of the daylight. It gets dark early, and we have a long way to go." He reined his horse around and started off, expecting us to follow in right behind him.

And so we did. With the quick pace Jody set, we weren't able to talk. We made one short stop for a toilet break and to grab our 'to go' food. I had started making tortillas after José gave me the griddle. I showed Sarah how I made sandwich wraps with the quick-to-make flat bread. Wraps were easier to eat one handed and packed well for travel. She had made a bundle of them the night before so we could eat on the road.

I watched with relief as the sun sank closer to the horizon. That meant we would soon stop for the night. My fanny was numb from riding all day. I wasn't accustomed to saddles, or even to sitting in one place for more than an hour or two. Wallace was aware of my discomfort and was standing next to my pony when I started to dismount. I had both legs over the saddle, ready to put my feet on the ground, when I realized that I couldn't feel them. Wallace must have anticipated it: he had a firm grip on my elbow. Because of him, I didn't fall down when my boots hit the dirt.

"Don't let go of me for a minute, okay?" I asked. "I need my legs to wake up before I can stand on my own."

"Here, let's move around a bit to get the feeling back in them." Wallace put his arm around my waist—well, where my waist was supposed to be—and walked with me to where Julian and Sarah were setting up camp. Jody had remained mounted and now was riding further down the road, operating as the forward scout, giving me an added sense of security.

Our camp was all set up and dinner was cooking when Jody returned. "It looks like Tarleton has been in the area with his cavalry and a small band of infantry. He's looking for that traitor Pyle so he can escort him and his men to General Cornwallis. I'd sure like to get in the middle of those two before they join forces."

"Are you talking about Dr. John Pyle?" Julian asked.

"Aye, that's him," replied Jody as he grabbed a couple of corn dodgers from the pan.

"Didn't he cause hard feelings with the locals in the War of the Regulation," asked Julian.

"Aye, he did, but he wasna at the Battle of Alamance. The word is, he's sent a request to Cornwallis, askin' for an armed escort fer him and the Loyalist troops he's been gatherin'. He wants protection fer his trip to the general's camp. He's a smart man, but a traitor. He kent the truth back at Hillsborough."

The men continued talking politics, but all I wanted to do was sleep. I excused myself and crawled into the pile of quilts that was my bed.

I slept hard, totally worn out from the ride. I didn't even wake up once to pee. Maybe utter fatigue was the answer to an overactive bladder.

We spent the next day waiting. Late in the afternoon, a colonel, along with a couple of his aides, came into our camp to speak with Jody. He had heard about Captain Jody Pomeroy and his part in the Battle at Moore's Creek Bridge, where Jody's creative thinking and fast acting saved patriots' lives. His brilliant plan to disable the Loyalist cannons in the middle of the night and sabotage the bridge by removing planks and greasing the support poles was legend. The colonel was hoping to be able to get some advice on this situation, too.

"Captain Pomeroy, I understand your friend here, Julian Hart, was with the British Army until just recently. Do you think he would help us get some information?" the colonel asked.

"I canna speak fer another man, sir. Why dinna ye ask him yerself?' He called Julian over. "Julian, this is Lt. Colonel Henry Lee. Colonel, this is Lord Julian Hart." Hands were shook and 'nice to meet yous' were exchanged. Then it was time for serious talk.

"Mr. Hart, I have been led to believe that you are now sympathetic with our cause for freedom and independence from England. Am I correct?"

I noticed the lack of title when the colonel addressed him. I knew that Julian did too, but he wasn't going to allow the man to get under his skin with the intentional slight. It sounded to me like there was some male posturing going on.

"Yes, sir. You are," Julian replied. His terse, curt answer was a red flag that I hoped the colonel had noticed. Whether or not he used Julian's title—and I wasn't even sure if Julian still *owned it* in his newly adopted country—the colonel still had better treat my friend Julian, the seasoned soldier, with respect.

Colonel Lee noticed the tension and responded to it appropriately. His tone became friendly, almost too friendly, a half step beyond courteous, but not quite to the level of sucking up. "We're glad to have you on our side. If you were still with the king's men, we'd have more of a fight on our hands."

That seemed to work. Julian, like any other man, liked to be flattered, and acknowledging his skills as a soldier was the right approach for the colonel to use. "Thank you, sir. Now, how can I be of assistance to you and your cause?" Apparently, Julian didn't like small talk when it came to business.

"I was hoping you might be able to flush out some of the Loyalist officers for us. I thought that if you could ride out along the Alamance Road and appear to be looking to join the Tories, maybe you could separate an officer or two from the group so we could get some information. So far, we've only been able to interrogate infantrymen. We need to speak with an officer so we can find out their plans and which direction they're headed."

"I can do that. I would like it if my son and Captain Pomeroy could follow behind me, though. I trust them to make sure the situation doesn't get out of control. Captain Pomeroy, Wallace, would you be willing to aid me in this endeavor?" he asked, looking at each of them in turn. I noticed that he had addressed Jody as Captain, too. He had switched gears to military mode.

"Aye, ye can count me in."

"And you can be sure that I will assist you in any way I can, Father."

I didn't know if the colonel knew that Wallace had been a British officer, too, but if he didn't, there wasn't any reason to bring it to his attention.

"Would tomorrow morning be soon enough?" asked Julian.

"I was hoping we could count on you," replied Col. Lee. "Yes, that would fine. We are located two miles east of here, on the banks of the Haw River, a mile south of the crossing. If you do capture an officer, please bring him to us right away. We understand Tarleton's dragoons and infantry are in the area to escort Dr. Pyle and his Loyalist troops to the Cornwallis camp, wherever that is this week. We want to intercept them before they gather into a major force."

"Consider it done," Julian said. "Now, if there is nothing else, sir, I'd like to confer with Captain Pomeroy and my son about our plans for tomorrow morning."

I liked the way Julian was dismissing the colonel. He was only an emigrant now—a dirt-digging, horse-breeding farmer—but this former British officer was still a commanding figure and able to put the full-of-fluff colonel in his place.

The men said their farewells, and life at our camp began to hum into pre-game mode; we had a tournament to win. Sarah and the men plotted and scheduled their plans for the morning startup. All they were lacking were the white board, markers, and the little x's, o's and arrows.

"If you don't need me for anything, I want to go to bed, er, sleep," I said. I was stumbling as I walked toward them. I think I had a bit of a hangover from the previous day's overexertion.

Sarah put her arm around my shoulder. "Go ahead and get some rest for you and the babies. If we need you for anything, I'll wake you."

"Okay, thanks. Goodnight, guys, I'll see you in the morning. Or maybe not, depending on when you go and when I wake up. Anyhow, I love you all," I grinned at Wallace, "good night, oh, I already said that, didn't I? I had better get some sleep."

I snuggled under the quilts that were my bed. I had forgotten to take off my boots but managed to kick them off without uncovering.

That was the last thing I remembered until I heard men's voices. Jody, Julian, and Wallace were getting ready to leave. "Wait," I shouted as I struggled to get up.

"What is it, lass," Jody asked, his brows crowded into a frown of concern.

"We need to pray before you leave. Here, I'll bless you all, including the horses. I'll be quick, unless you want to do it," I added as I realized how bossy I was being. Jody was the leader of our little clan—spiritual and otherwise—not me.

"No need to be quick with the Lord, but go aheid, get started," he said with a nod to proceed.

"Bless us all, Lord, and please keep us from harm. And bless this whole new nation, and guide us with Your knowledge. In Jesus's name, Amen. Okay, I love you guys, be safe."

"Aye, and thanks fer the blessing," Jody said, then turned back to his horse to double-check his gear.

Julian was a few steps away, but I caught up with him before he got in the saddle. I reached around him and gave him a big hug. "Thank you for doing this, Julian. I know you don't have to, but, well, thanks." I walked over to Wallace and squeezed his hand in farewell, blushing for no reason other than this was the first time our hands had touched. "You, too. Thanks."

Jody had given Sarah her good-bye hugs and kisses already, and was astride his big white horse, Aries, ready to leave. "Now, I dinna want to see ye or Sarah unless I call fer ye. If ye hear shots bein' fired, hide. If anyone finds ye, Evie, make sure yer big belly is showing. Yer less likely to be harmed if it's kent yer with child."

So the men took off, and Sarah and I stayed in camp. I didn't know what we were going to do with all the time we had, but I soon found out. "Would you like to see what I have in my medical kit?" Sarah asked. "You should be familiar with it if we see action."

I managed to sit down—with a grunt, two 'oofs,' and a hand from Sarah—next to her on a fallen log. She opened up what Jody called her wee bag. It had several bottles of alcohol that contained suture thread or catgut—I didn't ask which because I didn't want to know—and needles, as well as a bottle of alcohol, and bundles of rolled clean rags. There were also bags of herbs for brewing teas, a rolled-up cloth package of long tweezers, probes, knives—or scalpels—a saw, and lots of cotton wadding.

"I'm glad to see cotton's available," I remarked, "I wish we had a bolt or two of cotton cloth for clothes. This patchwork skirt won't last forever, and I'd like to get a head start on a layette or two for the babies."

"The cotton gin hasn't been invented yet. I've seen what the locals call calico, but it's imported from India and probably pricey. Linsey-woolsie shouldn't be too expensive. Maybe we can afford to buy some after harvest this fall." Sarah signed in resignation. "We'll find something for the babies, I'm sure," she said, placing her hand atop mine in consolation.

"So, what am I supposed to do here?" I asked, nodding to her bag, changing the subject and the whole atmosphere of our little *tête-à-tête* from one of financial disappointment to one of practicality.

"If there's hand-to-hand fighting, there are bound to be wounds that need cleaning and stitching. If there's shooting involved, then it's clean the wound and extract the musket balls. Broken bones happen frequently where there are horses to fall from or be knocked off of. Have you ever put in sutures?"

"No, but I don't think that should be too hard. Just show me which stitch to use. I can sew and should be able to handle it if the men don't scream too loud. But maybe that's what the cotton wadding's for," I said, smirking, trying to lighten the mood, "to stuff in my ears if the yelling gets too loud."

"Nice try at trying to get me to feel better," she said with a half grin, half grimace. "You and I both know this is serious. The worst part is, there isn't anything but willow bark tea and alcohol to dull the pain. If only we had antibiotics and morphine, so much pain, suffering, and death could be avoided." She took a deep breath and exhaled in frustration, obviously exasperated with the inadequacies of her medical supplies.

"Would it help if we gathered some ice and snow to help numb areas to be stitched and reduce the swelling of, well, whatever?" I asked, trying to offer positive options. Enumerating what we didn't have helped no one; finding substitutions for them would at least keep our minds off of our fears and frustrations.

"That sounds like a good idea. Let's see if we can pack some ice and snow in the cook pot. It should stay cold in there for a little while." She went to the side of the fire, grabbed the pot and a rag to insulate the handle. "We might as well get it now while it's still cold. The men won't be back for some time. We have at least a few hours, maybe even a few days. Either way, it will give us something to do."

**33 Pyle's Massacre

We heard his approach long before we could see him, the frantic sounds of desperation intruding on the still morning. The horse was snorting and breathing hard as it raced up Alamance Road, its hooves flinging clods of earthen road behind it as the rider broke through the ground clouds, parting the fog like a schooner through seawater.

The shaggy-haired youth reined in his steed, shimmering in sweat, to a fast stop. "Afternoon, ma'ams," he said breathlessly, trying to catch his wind. He quickly slipped off his horse. "Captain Pomeroy says fer ye to come quick and fer both of ye to bring yer bags. I'll get the horses ready while ye get 'em."

The young soldier—at least I assumed he was a soldier, even though he wasn't in uniform—was quick to grab the tack and our horses.

Sarah and I didn't waste any time making a quick trip around the campfire, gathering our bags and bedding. When we got back to the horses, we saw that he had saddled them in record time. He appeared to be waiting patiently on the outside, but his eyes betrayed his true need for urgency. "Here, let me help," he said, not trying to rush us, but eager to help us mount our humble steeds as quickly as possible.

He held the head of Sarah's little pony as she gracefully settled herself into the saddle. "Don't worry about the rest of yer things," he said as he handed Sarah her medical bag, "I'll send someone back to gather 'em up and fetch 'em back to our post. We have to hurry, though. It's a bloody mess out there, er, beggin' yer pardons, ma'ams."

"That's quite all right, soldier," Sarah said as she accepted the reins.

"What I mean to say is, yer healin' skills are needed right away, ma'am." The young soldier, red-faced in embarrassment, nodded up and down as he spoke, as if he were trying to ensure we understood his correction.

I felt helpless and frustrated, waiting for them to finish their conversation. While he was apologizing, I was trying to get onto my saddle by myself. No matter how hard I tried, I just couldn't get my leg up high enough to put my boot into the stirrup without losing my balance. The young man finally saw what was happening and rushed to my side.

"Sorry, ma'am, I didn't notice that ye were with child. Are ye sure ye can ride?"

"Oh, I can ride, all right, as long as I have help getting onto the horse." I graciously accepted his boost up, and then ungracefully landed hard, my fanny creating a loud *thump* as it smacked the leather saddle. I adjusted my coarse homespun skirts about me, trying to find some of the dignity I had lost in my awkward landing. "Ready, Sarah?" I asked.

"As I'll ever be; show us the way," she said to the soldier as he took the lead.

There was no more conversation after that. We rode at a fairly fast pace. I was sure we could have ridden faster, but the soldier's horse was already spent when he came in, and he was also being considerate of my delicate condition.

At one point, he looked over his shoulder to check on us. His face had gone blank: delayed shock. He was running on autopilot—instinct and familiarity with the area taking charge of the *corpus trepidus*.

Actually, the atmosphere of dread was heavy over all of us. I knew Sarah was going over medical procedures in her head, making an intellectual inventory of the tools in her bag; wondering if she had everything she needed. I didn't know why she worried so much. She would do the best she could with what she had when she got there. There was nothing to do now but pray. So that's what I did.

About twenty minutes out, we got to a rise. The soldier raised his hand to signal us to stop. "Ma'ams, I'd take ye further, but I dinna think this horse can make it. I dinna wanna kill her. We got all the Loyalists under control, so ye willna be in harm's way. The camp's jest down there, to the edge of the trees, almost to the river. Captain Pomeroy has a man on the lookout fer us. There should be a rider coming out to escort ye the rest of the way. Thank ye for comin', and God bless ye both."

"God bless us all," Sarah and I replied at the same time. We looked at each other and shrugged. "And God help us," she added as she looked toward the chaos that was the camp.

Just then, we saw a horse soldier—this time in uniform—racing toward us. We trotted up to meet him.

"I'm here to escort ye the rest of the way, ma'ams," he said as he turned his lathered horse around, eager for us to follow.

"Just a minute, please," I said to our new companion. He frowned but didn't argue.

Sarah and I turned around. "Thanks," we chorused and waved farewell to our shepherding young soldier. I was happy to see that he looked better than he had earlier, his mouth now turned up in an embarrassed smile at the appreciation he was receiving.

The new soldier led us to where we hoped we'd meet Jody and the others. They weren't there to greet us, but our first escort had been right: the area *was* a bloody mess.

I didn't want to imagine what had happened to cause so much spilled blood. It was obvious that there had been lots of hand-to-hand combat with sharp objects. The ground was uneven, churned up in areas where boots and hooves had dug in. The most ghastly aspect of the landscape, though, was the dark, tacky, maroon goo that covered the dormant winter meadow in large splotches, creating what looked like an immense half-eaten raspberry syrup-covered waffle. It was so gummy that it made squeaky, squishy noises as we walked across it. It was also slippery, as I found out when I took an extra-long stride across a little rivulet on my way to wherever it was we were going. I almost fell backside-first into it, but was saved the indignity by the soldier who was ushering me. "Watch yer step, ma'am," he warned as he caught my elbow. "It's a bit on the slick side, it is."

Sarah was walking ahead of me with her two young guides. Anyone could tell by her bearing that she was the woman in charge. Then, just over the rise, we saw it. Tarps had been strung up between the trees, and oh-so-many wounded bodies were lying beneath them, a field of fallen men in sunshine and shadows. Since the bodies were still moving, I assumed this was the hospital and not the morgue. "Come on," Sarah said. "We're needed."

I hadn't heard her, though. I was stunned and just stood there, unable to move, unaware of time or thoughts passing.

Sarah had to turn around to come back and get me. She grabbed my hand and pulled me along with her, not scolding or saying a word.

I was in shock at seeing so many moaning, broken, bloodied bodies—carpeting the ground as far as I could see. Earlier, when I thought about helping Sarah, I had imagined a few injured soldiers, not more men than I could count. I didn't have a long-term memory, but I was sure I had never experienced anything like this before.

I moved along behind her, doing whatever she told me to do. "Hold this, wash this, lift his head, move his feet, pull this skin together so I can stitch it..." I worked mechanically and obeyed all of her demands, but I had no initiative. At least, I didn't at first.

The atmosphere in our work area was truly thick, and I found it difficult to breathe. The air was moist from being trapped under the canvas ceiling. The smell of sweating, scared men vomiting and/or losing control of their bowels was more than my stomach could handle. The wounds, pain, and fears were indiscriminate. There were frightened soldiers of all ages here, waiting for relief—either from the doctor's hands or from death. It was becoming too much for me.

I had to get away—for a minute, at least—so asked Sarah if I could step out to get some fresh air. I didn't tell her I felt as if I were losing it, and that I needed to find a way to isolate my sanity from this mess, to find a place to tuck it away until we were done here.

Then I saw him. He was half-hidden behind the tree. He couldn't have been much more than eight years old. He was trying not to sob, but the tears were racing down his dirt-smeared cheeks, snot running past his lips and off his chin. Something clicked to 'on' in me.

"Here you go," I said as I wiped his tears, then his nose and chin, with a short strip of bandage. "Now, how can I help you?"

He pulled his hands away from his belly and I saw his problem. He had a slice across his abdomen. It wasn't too deep. It could probably do with a few stitches, though. I grabbed a clean cloth and put it over the wound. "Hold this here, and I'll be right back, all right?"

He bobbed his head up and down, "Yes, mum."

I weaved my way through the wounded men, some sitting, some prone, and approached Sarah. I quickly explained about the boy. She was palm deep into an older man's shoulder. Most of the wounds were saber and knife inflicted, but a few soldiers had managed to fire their muskets or pistols. Sarah was digging out a musket ball but could still talk to me. "Can it wait? I really need your help here with the more severe cases," she said, never taking her eyes off her patient.

"Yes, I suppose it can. Let me tell him to stay put, and I'll be right back to give you a hand."

I quickly made my way back to the boy. "I need to help some of these other men with bigger cuts than yours. Do you think you can make sure no one comes in here with a sword or a rifle meaning to harm us? I need a sentry, and there's no one but you to help me right now."

"Yes, mum, I'll watch fer ye." He pulled back his shoulders and reversed his frown, his eyes blinking back the last of his tears, feeling better for having a responsibility.

I returned to Sarah. "Looks like you're about done there. Have you had a chance to do triage yet?"

Sarah lifted her head from the bandaging. "Triage?—you can perform triage?"

"I'm feeling better now. Let me see what's out there. I'll move the men about so the worst cases are closest. Then I'll get right back here to help you."

I didn't know if I was skilled or even experienced in 'triage,' but the word just popped into my head and, well, I threw the ball up in the air, caught it, and now I was willing to run with it.

I grabbed a bundle of clean rags and headed outside to the impromptu north wing of our hospital. If the man could walk and talk, he was at the furthest end. Those capable of talk only were a little closer, and so on. I took care of profuse bleeding cases on the spot. I was surprised that these men didn't know how to apply direct pressure to a wound to keep it from bleeding. I also gave quick field instruction on tourniquets and when to back off on the pressure.

Most of the injuries had happened right where we were. We learned that our friend, Colonel Henry "Light Horse Harry" Lee, had come directly into contact with Colonel—a.k.a. Dr.—John Pyle's troops. Somehow, the Loyalists under Pyle thought that Lee was with Tarleton's troops, and that he and his men were on their way to join General Cornwallis. Just as they were greeting each other, face to face, one of Lee's men, who was new to the area and a little too eager, saw the red strips of cloth on Pyle's soldiers' uniforms, a sure sign of a Tory. When the patriot asked where his loyalties lay, the man said, "King George."

The patriot's response was a hearty clout with his saber. It was soon apparent to Pyle's men that Lee and his legion were not who they seemed to be. The Loyalists were spooked, confused that the soldiers in green uniforms—like the ones worn by their hero, Tarletan, and his men—would be fighting against their own colleagues.

The Americans started slashing their swords and firing their muskets at whoever wore the red strips of cloth—a sure sign of Tory allegiance—regardless of the jacket color. All hell broke loose as the mounted patriots, with a militia to back them up, soon routed the Loyalists, who were mostly afoot.

And now Sarah and I were dealing with the aftermath.

The Americans most definitely won this battle. At least I didn't see too many men whom I recognized as patriot militia. There were well over 200 men here who needed attending to, most of them Loyalists. Many of those who *could* talk, were cursing and complaining about the deception they had fallen for. I supposed it could have been worse.

I was glad Sarah and I weren't alone in our ministrations. I saw two others, men, who were doctoring the wounded. Still, there were more than enough wounded patients to overwhelm our small crew of medics.

I took care of triage, and then took a break to check on my young sentry. I decided not to stitch his wound. Instead, I improvised a little honey bandage to keep the shallow gash joined and sealed. I was just tying off his cloth bandage when I paused and turned around. The hairs on the back of my neck were sticking up as if someone had just blown across them. Did someone step on my grave? That was the old saying that came to mind when I turned in answer to that strange feeling.

And there he was.

"Ready for one more?" he asked soberly. "He can't walk, and I think someone should look at the back of his head—there's a lot of blood. Is Sarah nearby?"

It was Wallace. He wasn't wearing his jacket and was covered with blood from shoulders to knees.

"Uh, she's right over there. You'd better take him to her right away."

I finished my young friend Nathan's bandage, gave him a big hug, and then thanked him for being the lookout. "See if you can find your family. I'll bet they miss you. Make sure you eat something, and don't lift anything heavier than a dead chicken, okay?" I didn't know how to get it across to him not to lift over five pounds, but a chicken weight was close enough.

"Yes, mum. When I'm done, can I come back and be sentry again?" he asked, his big pale-green eyes imploring.

"I'd appreciate it if you would. Make sure your mother knows where you are, though, you hear?" I was firm, but ended my command with a smile. Kids—cute little buggers, and I was going to have two. At least.

Wallace! I suddenly remembered he had just come through. What was he doing here? He was supposed to be keeping a low profile.

And there he was—laying out the injured British soldier on the impromptu operating table in front of Sarah. I rushed over and quietly stood at his side. I wanted to reach out, turn him to me, and give him a big hug, but the timing wasn't right.

"I'm sorry, Wallace, he didn't make it. The wound on the back of his head wasn't too bad, but he also had a broken neck. He was probably alive when you picked him up, but it was just a matter of time. You knew him, didn't you?" she asked gently.

"Aye, er, yes, ma'am. But maybe it's just as well; he said he couldn't

264

feel his arms or legs. I'll take him out...oh, God, Sarah, where's the morgue?" Wallace's brow furrowed, as if he were about to cry. He looked around, unsure of his surroundings, now taking in big gulps of air, trying to keep from losing it.

"Here, let me go with you," I said. "We can stop on the way back and get you cleaned up a bit. Hopefully none of that blood is yours."

Dang, that was the wrong thing to say! What is the right thing to say, though, when a man has just lost a friend?

There was really nothing I could say, and an apology would have made my *faux pas* more obvious. I put my hand at his elbow, barely touching him lest I invade his personal mourning, and walked beside him in silence. I knew his fallen friend was heavy, but he still strode straight and tall. I glanced up and saw a single tear making a track through the dust and grime on his face.

I led him to the area that had been set aside as the morgue. I noticed Wallace said a little prayer, and then made the sign of the cross after he laid his friend's body down to rest. He saw me looking at him and said, "Jody told me what to say for the dead. It may not be much, but it's all I can do. And he's right; it does make me feel better." He sniffed and wiped his face with his sleeve, not showing any embarrassment at wiping away the tear.

We headed down to the creek. Wallace stumbled a bit but managed to grab a tree to steady himself. He took off his shirt and rinsed it in the water, then used it to wipe the blood off his chest and belly.

That was when he saw it.

He had a slice through the groin area of his pants and there was blood—his blood. He pulled apart the fabric and looked inside. He paled at the sight of it and plumped down hard on a big rock at the river's edge.

"Are you okay?" I asked.

He was stunned—silent—staring into nothingness, his eyes as empty as a Greek statue.

"Can you make it up there?" I asked, pointing to the small ridge we had just descended. "I don't want to check you while you're sitting on a rock." I started the ascent, then looked behind me and saw he was still seated, a stone mounted on stone.

"Come up here and lie down where there's more sun." I waddled down to him and held his arm, helping him back up to the flat area I had indicated. He obeyed at the touch of my hand but hadn't seemed to hear my voice. I didn't know if he was in shock, but I wasn't going to chance it.

"Here, lie down and put your feet up. Let me have that wet shirt." He obeyed my commands only because my hands were pushing or pulling him as I spoke. "Now, cover up with my shirt, and let me put my scarf around your neck." I took off my flannel shirt and scarf and bundled him up as best I could.

Now *Wallace* was the robot. I was sure he was in shock. His soul had left his body, but maybe that's what shock was. He was too big for me to move any further, and everyone else around here was in worse shape than he was.

I rushed back to the 'hospital' and grabbed a couple of blankets, a fistful of clean rags, and the little suture kit and bottle of alcohol Sarah had given me. I didn't say anything to anyone, and no one said anything to me. Fine: the light was fading fast, and I had to be quick about whatever it was I was going to have to do.

I looked down at his prostrate body and saw more than I should have seen through the slashed gap in his trousers. "I have to take these pants down and see the wound. Lift your bum and I'll try to get them off." Wallace's hips moved up a little, and then dropped down hard. "Here," I urged, "You're going to have to help me. I can't lift you, and I have…"

I glanced up and saw that Wallace was crying. He was sobbing without the noise. The chest heaves were there, though. He was utterly devastated. "Okay, then just hold still, see what I care. That just means I'll have to *cut* off your pants. I don't know where you're going to get another pair on such short notice, though…."

I looked up, hoping that I had smacked him into reality with my ridiculous remark. Nope. He was still crying, the tears now streaming down his cheeks. He was oblivious to what I was saying or doing. I sliced through his pants, trying to cut through the seam's stitching so they could be sewn back together.

Then I saw the actual wound: a slash across his groin and lower belly. I used a wet rag to wash away the dried blood. There was lots of it, but it was only from the surface capillaries being cut—it wasn't a deep gash. When I pulled the pants away further and exposed him all the way, I realized why he was so upset. Beneath his curly red pubic hair, all that was visible of his penis was a sliver of skin, sliced and ready to fall away. It looked as if his manhood had been cut off, and all that was left was a small, humiliating tab of flesh. I pulled at the skin and saw what the problem really was. He was so cold that everything else had just shrunk up; it was just foreskin that was hanging on by a scant eighth inch of skin.

266

Then I looked lower. He had no balls. Really, his testicles had disappeared, but there was no wound down there.

I realized what had happened, then snorted, and smiled.

That got his attention.

I looked up and saw he was staring at me, as emotionless as a mannequin. I giggled again, trying to elicit *some* response. Any noise, any emotion, was better than the silence of the soulless.

I turned away from him and stared into the sky, spotted with clouds, the only peaceful area around. Then I looked back at his less-than-magnificent male equipment. I snorted again and reached for my surgical scissors and alcohol. Another giggle sneaked out.

Come on, mister—speak to me. I need to hear you talk again.

He had finally had enough. "What's so damned funny? I lose my cock and you sit there, laughing?"

"No," I drawled, "But what *is* so funny is that I'm here in a war zone, performing a *bris* on you. Do you know what that is?"

"No," he replied curtly.

"It's the Jewish rite of circumcision. If I leave that flap of skin on, it will just get irritated, infected, or in the way. So, hold your breath and count backwards from twenty."

"20, 19, 18, 17," he rattled off rapidly.

"In Spanish," I said, "otherwise you'll go too fast. I want you distracted, okay?"

"Fine, then: *viente, diez y nueve, diez y…*"

One quick snip and that was that.

"All done." I covered up the wounded area with a clean rag bandage. "That wasn't too bad, was it?" I asked as I spread the blankets back over him.

"Fine, now I have a Jewish prick and no balls. How is that going to make me a good husband and father?" he said curtly, his previous blank stare replaced by a scowl.

"Oh, darlin', let me help you," I cooed. I reached under the covers and warmed my hands on his stomach—flat, six-pack tight, with lots of curly hairs on it. He flinched a little at my touch, but that was probably because he was trying not to be ticklish. I reached my now warmed right hand even lower, putting it over the area where his left testicle should have been. Then I reached up a few inches higher and found the depression. I gently pushed down, and plop, down it came. I reached across and performed the same manipulative procedure to the right side, releasing his testicles from his abdominal cavity.

"Did you know the Japanese Samurai soldiers used to practice sucking up their testicles so they wouldn't be cut off or injured in battle? Looks like your body didn't need instructions—it just came naturally."

Wallace flashed a chagrined smile, blushed red as an embarrassed teenager, and said, "Thanks."

"See, all better," I crowed. Then I took it down a notch, assuming the healthcare-giver persona again. "I think you were in shock, but your coloring's back now. Do you think you can sit up without falling over?"

He leaned to one side, brought his knees toward his chest, and sat up effortlessly. "Oh, I think I'll manage," he said, grinning.

There was an awkward moment. I wasn't sure what else to say since I had just been so close to his private parts, and acting way too flip and casual toward him, even for a 21st century woman.

He cleared his throat. "I do want you to know, though, I was scared pretty bad there. I think I would rather be dead than emasculated. Thanks for, um, bringing me around," he said, wiping his face with the sleeve of his shirt, trying to hide his embarrassment.

"Oh, I'm glad I could help. Then again, I'm relieved that it wasn't life threatening. I'd want you with or without, the, um, fringe benefits."

I blushed as soon as the words left my lips. "Did I just say that? I'm sorry. How brazen of me to suggest that we would, could…"

Wallace pulled me to him, cutting short my blathering with a passionate kiss that must have been a full minute long. I finally had to come up for air.

"Phew, the kisser's sure in good working order." I looked down and saw the tent pole bump in the middle of his blanket. "And it looks like everything else is going to be just fine."

**34 Healing

Wallace wrapped one of the blankets around his middle, and together we walked back to the hospital tents, rather, to the tarps suspended over the injured. There were wounded men all around us, but by the look on Wallace's face, he was inside the same cocoon of peace that I was.

I saw the pierced and battered men lying on the ground, leaning against the naked trees, but I chose to think of them as the once fallen who were now healing. Their warfare—for today, at least—was over. No one was going to ride through here again tonight and bring more chaos and destruction. "Let the healing begin," I said to no one in particular.

The patch-up crews were on duty. At least, most of them were. I had been absent too long and needed to get back to my job at the body restoration shop, otherwise known as surgery. Sarah had at least forty patients lined up to see her.

I found her just as I had left her, bent over a wounded man. I was sure this was a different one, but after a while, they all started to look the same. All the men had the same drab-colored clothing, covered with dirt and blood, lots of blood. The faces, whether young or old, fat or thin—and most of them were thin—all looked the same: haggard.

I walked to the other side of her patient and asked Sarah, "Do you know where there's a sewing needle and some thread? I had to cut through Wallace's pants to perform some first aid. They need repairing before he can go out into the field again. His quilted sarong really isn't suitable for riding or walking."

Sarah looked up at me with a glare between anger and frustration that could have cut through steel, if we had any. I knew she had been working non-stop since we arrived. Wallace was beside me, and it was obvious by the glow on our faces that we had been doing something other than working in the hospital effort. "Over there, in the pocket of my cloak, is a little sewing kit."

She bent back to her work. I could tell she was just about to say something else, but I cut her off as I grabbed the kit. "Sarah, I'll be quick about this, and then I'll be right back to help you. I'm sure Jody and the others want Wallace back in action right away, too. I took care of his wounds, so all that's needed now is his modesty returned."

I had the needle threaded by the end of the sentence. I reached up and rubbed my thumb and forefinger up and down the sides of my greasy nose, then slid them over the length of thread. I felt Wallace staring at me. I looked up and said, "The oil makes the thread go through the fabric easier and helps to keep it from knotting. Just a few more, there – done. These are basting stitches and only meant to hold the cloth together to keep you decent. They won't last long, though. When you get back this evening, find me, and I'll put in smaller stitches."

Wallace took the pants from me, the sparkle in his eyes and the dimples in his cheeks showing that he was holding back a full-blown grin of anticipation. He wanted to be with me as much as I wanted to be with him.

"Thank you for the doctoring, Miss Evie, and for the quick tailoring. Sarah, is there anything I can do to help you?"

Sarah was intent on her task, her head and shoulders hovering above her patient's thigh as her hands pierced and tugged a long series of stitches. The man might wind up walking with a limp, but she had probably saved his leg.

"Yes," she said, her clipped tone and pursed lips letting us know she was trying to hold her frustration in check, "stay alive and in one piece. And bring your fathers back the same way, please." She paused her suturing at the end of her request to find Wallace standing at her elbow. She looked up to face him. "Be careful out there," she said softly, her brow wrinkled with worry.

Wallace bent down and kissed her on the forehead, smoothing the stray hairs out of the way after the fact, trying to ease her fears with his touch. "You be careful, too. I don't think you realize how important you are to all of us. And I don't mean just your healing skills. You are a generous, selfless woman, and we, I, love you."

Sarah's face, at first stunned, was now glowing. "Thanks, I love you, too. Now, go out there and look after those fathers, would you?"

She was trying to put on her matronly nurse demeanor, but it wouldn't quite slide over her maternal radiance. She had suddenly realized that Wallace was not just her husband's son, or her friend Julian's, but hers as well. This six-foot-five-inch young man, whom she had cared about since she first met him, had just bonded with her for the first time. Now it was my turn to glow. My wonderful family was getting lovelier and closer, all the time.

Ж Ж

"Sarah, what can I do to help?" I asked, bringing both of us back to the reality of our barely civilized, extremely unhygienic, field hospital. I was standing next to her, blotting the oozing blood from the suture site on the young man's thigh.

"Check on who's coming in next. Take one of the healthier men with you to help get my next patient onto this table," she said, indicating the other rise of sawn timbers that was our second surgery platform. "And when you get back, I need a latrine break."

"Okay, but make sure you take a sandwich with you when you head out of here. I want you to eat something before you fall down. You can't sew up the wounded while you're lying flat on your back," I scolded.

"Yes, mother," she replied wryly, then was back to business. "There, all done. Where did you say the sandwiches were, Evie?"

I already had a cheese and onion wrap in my hand for her. "And take a minute to throw water on your face. I promise, it will make you feel better."

Sarah took a deep breath, "Do I really look that bad?" she asked as she pushed her hair away from her forehead with the back of her hand.

"No, you just look tired. The cold water facial is for your benefit, not for those who have to look at you. Now scoot, and drink lots of water with that sandwich. It's cheese, and you know what happens if you eat too much cheese," I said, making a face like I was in the privy, grunting.

"Yes, mother," she said again with a grin. She took a big bite of the tortilla-wrapped sandwich. "I'll sure be glad when we get a smoked ham. The cheese is good, but a ham and cheese sandwich will be, oh, so wonderful. I'll be right back; don't start without me."

Wallace's kiss on the forehead, along with a five-minute lunch and necessary break, gave Sarah a strong second wind. I was sending her patients like cars through an express lube shop. Having the patients in order of urgency and someone—me—to tell her about the wounds, their severity and location, really did speed up the process in the surgery. I was right at her elbow, anticipating her needs: when clothing needed cut away, wounds washed, or suture needles threaded. It was almost as if we were sending and receiving psychic messages. She would start to ask for something, and I would already have it in my hand, ready to put it in hers.

No matter how I tried to convince myself that we were doing well—there were few who had died after the initial conflict—it still bothered me to see these men wounded. I was glad young Nathan appeared to be the only child injured in the skirmish. Not all of the men were young. I was sure many of them had wives and children, parents, and maybe even

271

grandchildren, who depended on them for a livelihood. There was such a wide range of ages.

Almost all of these men were Loyalists and our foes, but Sarah and I were respectful to them. They were still Americans in the making, as far as I was concerned. They lived side by side with the patriots but were afraid to break away from the strong and domineering Mother England. Good manners and graciousness on our part might just help sway them over to the red, white, and blue side.

We were courteous when we asked each injured man—and they were all men—where he was wounded. Sarah would also inform her patient what she was going to do next and usually warn him that it was going to hurt. We really didn't have anything in the way of painkillers. We had the makings for willow bark tca, but didn't have the time to stop and brew it.

I saw my little friend Nathan standing guard outside the surgery area. He was staring at me, almost begging me with his eyes to come talk with him. When Sarah got to a point where I could break away, I did just that. "I need to be excused for a moment, Sarah; is now a good time?"

"You know it is," she replied as she followed my line of sight over to the little boy. "Go ahead, but don't take too long."

"I did like ye said, mum," Nathan said. "I told me mam where I was. She said to thank ye and to ask if there was anythin' ye be needin'?"

"As a matter of fact, there is something she can help us with. Does your mother ever brew willow bark tea?"

"Yes, mum; she makes it fer me sisters when they get the miseries. She always has lots of it put away. Did ye need some?"

"Yes, we do. Can you see if she'll brew as much as she can, and then bring it up here? On second thought, it might be easier if she just brought a big pot and the bark up here to brew. We have a few able-bodied men who can fetch the water for her. And ask her to bring a few cups if she has them."

"Aye, I'll do it right away," Nathan said. He straightened up, saluted me, and turned to leave.

"Whoa, whoa, whoa, wait just a minute, young man. I don't want you to carry anything heavier than a chicken, remember? You can carry the tea and a cup or two, but nothing else, you hear?"

"Oh, yes, mum; I'll get me sisters to help mam. I tole 'em about ye, but they wouldna believe me. Now they can come and see fer theirselfs."

"What wouldn't they believe, Nathan?"

"They dinna believe that a woman as big in the belly as ye could work with ailin' men. They said that it would hurt the bairn to be around so much blood, and that a respectable woman wouldna do it. Oh, I'm sorry. I dinna mean anythin' was wrong with ye helpin'. I think it's great! Can I go now, mum?"

"Yes, you can go now. Nothing heavier than a chicken, now, you hear. And that's a dead chicken, not a thrashing chicken that you're hauling off to the butcher block."

Nathan just waved as he ran off, happy to be helping in the cause.

**35 Crocs, Cabin Fever, and a Cell Phone

March 3, 1781

Other than with my immediate 'family,' I seldom felt as if I fit in with the people of this time, but I tried to at least *look* like I belonged. I wore a simple drawstring skirt as a courtesy to the people around me. Women in trousers were...well, they just 'weren't'—weren't accepted as ladies in this society. Based on my recent uncomfortable and nearly tragic personal encounters—the impressions by degenerate males like Gimpy, that a woman in pants was automatically wanton—I decided I should dress according to the prevailing fashion.

My simply gathered homespun garment provided the required 18th century modesty, but little warmth. I didn't have the benefit of a petticoat, so I kept my polar fleece sweatpants on underneath my blue rag-pieced skirt, the waistband of the gray pants shoved beneath my rapidly growing belly. I wore my green buffalo-checked flannel shirt over my white tee shirt in lieu of a feminine blouse, but usually had Sarah's cream-colored spare shawl across my shoulders to soften my appearance.

I wouldn't have worn the women's shoes of this era even if I could have afforded them. Their construction was weak—partly because of the materials used—but the design was lousy. Shoemakers of this era didn't differentiate between right and left shoes. The leather uppers got stiff if they got wet, unless you rubbed loads of bear grease into them, and then they stank. The pegs that attached the uppers to the soles fell out when it got too cold, or they'd simply shatter from wear.

I had something to keep my feet dry and warm though. The hiking boots I had been wearing for—well, ever since I could remember—were still in great shape. I had resorted to tucking the laces inside the boots, though, wearing them like slippers. My belly was too big for me to bend over to tie the bootlaces, and I didn't want to ask anyone to act as my foot servant. My feet were swollen by the end of the day anyhow, so it was just as well that I left them untied.

I would have been better off with my Crocs, but they were gone. Several weeks earlier, Sarah and I had gone to that little cluster of businesses we called 'town' for supplies. When we entered Gibson's sparsely stocked general store, a short and very obese man was talking with Andrew, the proprietor. He said he was looking for a comfortable pair of boots. He didn't have any money, but said he had barter goods in the wagon.

That was normal for these times. Bartering commodities—like bacon, tobacco, and grains—were often more valuable than silver for purchasing everyday supplies. His Majesty's money was not allowed out of England, so other forms of currency were improvised to transact business. Spanish silver coins—if one could find them—were often cut into eight pieces. These 'bits' as they were called, found their way into the backcountry. That's why in the 21st century, twenty-five cents was called—or will be called—'two bits': the value of two bits of a silver dollar.

I tried not to eat much, but an extra person—or two or three with Wallace and sometimes a visiting Julian at the table—depleted the pantry in a hurry. The men wanted to help, but didn't have anything in the way of money they could use without raising red flags. They were soldiers, or had been, and their script was worthless outside of His Majesty's service.

Our little clan didn't have much to trade, but we were going to try with what we had. Sarah was hoping to future barter—if there was such a term—two of the kids that were due next month. Two of her nannies were pregnant and, although it would have been nice to keep all of the kids for ourselves, right now we needed flour and salt more. Coffee and sugar would have been nice to have, too, but we would be fortunate just to get the essentials.

We waited for the storekeeper to finish with the heavyset man looking for shoes. I inspected the entire inventory of Andrew's puny fabric department—all three bolts of cloth—while Sarah bided her time checking out the small, dusty, colored-glass bottles and their contents on the back shelf.

It wasn't too long before the big man's temper began to flare. "What do you mean, you don't have any? I come all this way for some decent boots, and you don't even have *one* pair? How about what you're wearin'? Come here—let me see if they'll fit me."

It was desperation speaking; I could hear it in his voice. I looked down at the wide man's feet and saw that he had rags wrapped around them.

"Mr. Leuga, we've never kept shoes here fer sale, and those of us what have 'em, need to keep 'em. Lookit here—see, I had to put strips a' cloth around mine, jest to keep 'em together. They ain't worth much, but I'm gonna keep 'em, jest the same."

Andrew's shoes were in poor shape, and they wouldn't have fit his customer's feet even if he were willing to give them up...er...rather, sell them.

"Excuse me, sir," I said. "I might be able to help you. I don't have boots to spare, but I do have a pair of fancy Italian sandals that might work for you. You'd need to wear warm woolen socks with them at this time of year, though."

"Socks?"

He shook his head at the unfamiliar term, and then realized what I meant.

"Those ain't a problem, I got plenty of stockings. What I need is something to protect the bottoms of my feet and not bind me." He lifted his pant leg, "The boots I had rubbed the skin clear off. I got so mad that I threw 'em in the river!"

I gasped at the sight of his open wounds. He saw my reaction and liked the attention. He smirked and added, "You think those are bad? The ones under these bandages are even worse!"

Sarah had come over to see what the commotion was. Anyone who needed medical attention was going to get it if she were around. No one was left untreated on her shift—and she was always on shift. "Let me see, please."

I moved aside so Sarah could examine the man's feet. He leaned against the counter that held the store's ironmongery—shears, hinges, nails, and other odd-shaped metal pieces that I didn't recognize.

Sarah crouched on the ground, her skirts gathered close to her to in an attempt at keeping them off the dirt floor. She carefully untied the knots in the rags that bound his feet. I could see the ring of raw flesh above his thick ankle where a boot top would have been. He cleared his throat and said, "Sorry to be troublin' you, ma'am. We ain't even been introduced. My name is William Leuga. Do you think there's somethin' that can be done about them sores?"

She glanced up, gave a congenial smile and said, "Sarah Pomeroy; pleased to meet you," then looked back down, resuming her examination of his feet. "Yes, we can take care of them."

I didn't need to be a podiatrist to know what this man needed. First order of business would be to wash his feet. I could smell them from across the room, even though I had taken to breathing through my mouth at the first whiff.

"Andrew, do you have any goat's milk soap?" Andrew nodded. "Mr. Leuga, use this soap, not lye soap, with warm water to wash your feet at the end of every day. Dry them with a soft cloth and then put a balm on them. If you happen to have a clear vegetable oil, not animal fat, use that as the balm. I don't have any lanoline, but oil will do. Let the fresh air get to them as much as possible. After they're completely dry and the oil has soaked in—then, and only then—put on clean, dry, soft stockings. Don't wear shoes when you're sitting down and put your bare feet up at the end of the day. And don't walk any more than absolutely necessary until they're healed."

While Sarah gave her foot care instructions, I went outside and retrieved my backpack from under the seat of the wagon. I grabbed the bright green Crocs out of it, hid them under my jacket, and went back into the store. I popped in just as the hygiene lecture was finished.

"Mr. Leuga, hi, you can call me Evie. If you'll allow me, I'll see if these will fit." I grabbed the counter for support, squatted down beside him, and put one shoe next to his now exposed foot. His feet were probably EEE width, but that didn't make a difference. No one here used that sizing method. My Crocs were wide, soft, durable, and according to my quick side-by-side size comparison, would work just fine for the man. "I think we have a winner," I announced.

Sarah leaned over to look at the shoes and grinned. "Now don't be wearing those until your feet are washed, dried, and oiled up, okay? Andrew, do you have any oil for Mr. Leuga to buy?"

Bill cut in, "Oh, I have plenty of that in the wagon. Sunflower oil will work, won't it? I just built me a press and got lots of it."

I looked over at Sarah's suddenly glowing face. "Oh, yes, that would be perfect," she crooned.

Bill saw the look of desire in her eyes and heard it in her voice. He smiled like a dog with a stolen sirloin steak and said, "Now, I think it only fair that I square things up with you for the doctorin'. Would a skin of my fine sunflower oil be enough?"

"Oh, yes, yes," Sarah gushed, "thank you so very much."

"And Miss Evie, I think I owe you quite a bit for these Eye-talian shoes. I don't have much, but how about I give you a big bag of rice and another skin of that sunflower oil? I know you won't need that much oil, but Andrew here might just trade you for what you do need."

Andrew had been quietly following the proceedings and joined the conversation. "I could use the oil, and we have lots of goods here. Just let me know what you need." Andrew nodded in our direction, and then over to Big Bill. "Will there be anything else for you, sir?"

"No, no, all I needed was a pair of shoes, and I got them and a doctor's visit at the same time. And I already have some of that goat's milk soap. Ladies, it's been a pleasure meetin' both of you. If you're ever in need of help, don't hesitate to call on Big Bill Leuga." With that, he tipped his well-worn three-cornered hat, and waddled out the door, his pretty green 'Italian' sandals cradled under his arm.

Ж Ж

I guessed they called it cabin fever for a reason; I felt 'ick' all over, and it was hard to breathe. Claustrophobia could wield its evil little panic attacks in small houses, too. After living in the cave for so long, I thought I had grown stronger and braver, but that phobia still had a mosquito bite of control over me: irritating, but not debilitating. I could only tolerate staying inside for so long. Our four walls were not much more than an arm's reach away in any direction, and the air was thick with the smells of ashy smoke and simmering stew. But, then again, maybe it wasn't claustrophobia and I just wanted to be outside, to bask in fresh, moving air, to view and commit the springtime beauty of my new surroundings to memory.

The call of spring won, so off I went. I realized once outdoors, it was warm enough that I didn't need my coat. I took it off and left it on the porch; I didn't want to go back inside so soon. I inhaled deeply, feeling super-charged with my self-declared emancipation from the confines of man-made structures; the ability to come and go as I pleased a gift I had given myself.

I sauntered to the clearing west of the house toward that tree with my name on it—figuratively speaking—the threadbare quilt I planned to sit on draped around my neck like a patchwork boa, my empty fabric tote bag nestled under my armpit.

Bright green splashes of fresh grass dotted the ground beneath the south sides of trees and rocks everywhere, adding color to the otherwise dreary gray and amber hues of late winter. The warty willows, easily identified by the fuzzy silver catkins that covered them, were additional indicators that spring would soon be in full bloom. The thought of fragrant blossoms bursting forth—perfuming and pollen-dusting the air— immediately made my nose twitch in subconscious response. Hay fever. Hmm, at some point in my life, I must have had seasonal allergies.

"That's snot something I want to have here," I murmured, then chuckled at my own pun. My voice disturbed a magpie and he—or was it a she?—joined my silly cackling, brightening my mood even more.

Soon I was at my private little resort, just out of sight of the house. I laid out the quilt and leaned against my very own 'let it be' tree. When I relaxed and didn't think about my past, little memories would sneak in, like recalling the sneezes of hay fever. I wasn't searching for the whole story of my past, but I wouldn't mind a smidgen of instant recall, either...as long as it was pleasant.

I looked up at the sky and realized how quiet it really was. True, the little birds—I still didn't know which ones were called what—were making their happy little noises, but they were just that: happy noises. I didn't hear the plague of planes, trains, and automobiles zipping by, echoing the stress of their drivers and passengers while spewing toxic and noisome crud into the air, soil, and water. Here and now, the air was healthier. There weren't any plastic bags or containers littering the landscape, no oily sheen on puddles, no howling train whistles, or roaring roadways. True, stores weren't stocked with arctic grade outerwear or diesel-powered generators, but wool, candles, and a blazing fireplace were working fine for me.

Speaking of blazing fireplaces, I had discovered that a warm, wide hearth was an ideal place to settle back to design and produce needful items in the evenings. Throughout the ages, BT—Before Technology—families would gather in the main room, where it was warmest in the cold winter months, to visit and do handiwork. Quilting, spinning yarn, sewing or knitting clothing, or carving dinnerware, tools, and/or toys for the children—all these arts and skills will almost disappear in modern times with the introduction—and intrusion—of vacuum tubes, transistors, and computer processors.

Families of this era know one another, help each other, and generally try to get along. Technology is—will be—a poor replacement for the family structure it inadvertently sabotages. Two parents laboring outside the home just to get more, or bigger, 'stuff' doesn't work—rather won't work. A family working together for a common cause—food and housing—has worked for eons. Yup, these were just a few more aspects I really liked about living in this time. Of course, I didn't have a choice...

I pulled out the folding tote bag I had made last week: the ultimate ecology-friendly bag. "Only naturally harvested, renewable ingredients were used in the manufacture of this reusable conveyance, constructed and designed by one very human Evie—not even an electric sewing machine was employed," I said aloud in an infomercial monotone, chuckling at my own silliness, my laugh echoed by my magpie companion who was now foraging in a brush pile.

Today I'd use the bag to carry river cane and other greenwood for weaving into baskets. Well, eventually they'd be baskets for laundry or gathering, but their first use would be as bassinettes. Not quite as romantic as Nile River reed baskets, but they should work fine for my little early Americans.

Ж Ж

I returned home from my mood-lifting excursion with a growling in my empty belly, a toteful of greenwood over one shoulder, the folded quilt over the other. I stopped at the porch bench and set down my woodland harvest. I'd unload it later. First, I needed to get something to eat.

My jacket was still on the bench where I had left it. I picked it up to take it inside and froze. It felt as if the world around me had just throbbed—a powerful, invisible, soundless pulse.

My first thought was that there was a tremor in the Force—whatever that was. I called weakly into the house, trying not to show the fear that was rising, "Hello, anyone home?"

No response—no one was here. I sniffed around—Rocky had taught me well—but I didn't smell anything out of the ordinary.

It must have been those pregnancy hormones kicking up again. I didn't mind the fatigue or claustrophobia that came with being in a family way, but I didn't want to become paranoid. Oh, well. I'd eat a quick snack and then figure out something for dinner. That would keep my mind off this eerie feeling—I hoped.

Ж Ж

I was alone at the house today. Jody didn't like me being by myself, but his sources said all military activity had moved south. Everyone but me had somewhere special to be, and I insisted that I'd be fine. He gave in to my request for 'some time alone.' I knew he didn't understand my independence, but he accepted it. "Yer jest like yer sister," he said with a big smile, blinking both eyes as he tried to wink at the word 'sister.' He knew we weren't related by blood, but by the fact that we were both from a future time and 'thought' differently.

Sarah was at the Donaldson's for the delivery of what Mr. Donaldson hoped was his first son. They already had four daughters. He had told Mrs. Donaldson he'd have to get another wife if she couldn't figure out how to

280

make a boy. Jody was glad that he'd been there when he'd said that. The twinkle in the hardworking man's eye made it clear that he loved his daughters as much as any man could love a son. He always did like old Mac Donaldson.

In the past, Sarah had preferred to let the midwife take care of the deliveries, but the woman who had seen to the mothers-in-waiting, Mrs. Luebke, had moved west with her family. She and her husband had decided that they would rather take their chances with the Indians than with the volatile Loyalists and their erratic laws and taxes.

Hannah Althouse had accompanied Sarah today. The bright young woman knew how to prepare herbs and tonics and could take care of simple dressings for cuts and burns but had never assisted in—or even witnessed—a human birth before. Young Hannah was the likely candidate for the midwife position, but first she had to get some hands-on experience.

Wallace and Jody, protesting mildly, had left early this morning to visit Julian, José, and those fancy horses. Jody had wanted to see José's sturdy and compact Andalusian horses ever since he had found out that they were 'jest next door.' He had read about the Spanish 'royal' horses, but couldn't believe they could be that much different from any others. He wanted to see them for himself. Since they were so close, he could be there and back—visiting just long enough to see their compact form up close and observe their unusual gait—then he would return to watch over me.

José gave Jody a tour of his well-furnished house, the outbuildings, and the property. Jody could see that the ranch had lots of potential, but needed long hours and strong backs to return it to its former glory. For the past three years, only one man—Robert, the hired hand—had taken care of the buildings, the animals, and, at the end, José's infirm family. It had been a lot for just one person, but at least he left the house livable, the livestock healthy, and the property recoverable.

Julian and José's partnership had a good chance of becoming prosperous with José's rare, spectacular horses and Julian's good business sense. Julian had also managed to exchange some of his military script for a bit of silver, so they had funds for supplies until the mares started foaling and the ranch became productive.

Jody could see that Julian and José were more than just business partners, and that was fine with him. Everyone should have someone special in his life, and Julian deserved a someone as much as anyone else did. He didn't understand the male-to-male attraction but had lived withSarah and her modern thinking long enough to accept the concept that two members of the same sex could love each other. Now, seeing Julian with José—laughing, smiling, working side-by-side—it was easy to see them as a happily married couple, at least in spirit.

Wallace would stay with the men at the ranch for a while and lend his strong back, getting the heavy work done. It probably wouldn't be too long before he returned to Pomeroy's Place, to be with Jody and the women. Or rather, to wherever Evie was. Wallace loved his stepfather, the man who had reared him, but it was obvious to the men and to Sarah that he wanted to be with Evie. It didn't seem to matter to Wallace whether she and Ian were handfasted, married the Indian way, or not at all. All Wallace saw was what Jody saw, too; Evie was a wonderful woman who was alone, not because of something she had done, but because Ian had abandoned her.

Ж Ж

It was still early, but Jody was ready to leave. He apologized to José, telling him that he was sorry he couldn't stay and lend a hand, but he had to get back home to take care of some unfinished business.

As they walked to the barn, Jody confided in Julian that he had a knot in his stomach as if something was wrong. He had lived longer than he should have by heeding his wame, and he wasn't going to stop now. Julian understood and said that he, too, felt uncomfortable, that something wasn't right.

"God speed, dear friend," Julian said as he patted the neck of Jody's horse in farewell.

"Thank ye, and pray fer us all," Jody said, casually saluting Julian as he left.

Julian waved at the quickly disappearing horse and the tall redheaded rider. "Lord, keep them safe," he prayed with head bowed, "and all of us here too. Amen." Julian raised his head and went back to the pasture to work with the other two men he loved: his son and his partner. "And thank You for all You have given me. I appreciate it. Amen, again."

Julian spent the rest of the day with Wallace and José, mending fences and marking trees to be felled for more pasture. This was his home now, and the many chores were labors of love.

He was glad his son had stayed behind. Wallace told him that he actually liked doing hard physical labor—it helped him relax, he claimed. Julian knew that the necessity of laying low, staying out of sight of the soldiers from both sides, frustrated his son. Yes, working hard was good for both Wallace's sanity and self-esteem. And it didn't hurt that the ranch would be back in good working order in half the time with the strong young man's assistance.

He also knew that it wouldn't be too long and Wallace would be back with Jody and Evie. Or rather, he would be leaving to wherever Evie was. Julian really liked Sarah's sharp, yet sassy, 'little sister,' and was glad that Wallace did, too. She was such an intense and interesting young woman—it was hard to believe she was so young.

Ж Ж

Jody liked Evie, too. She was a brave young lass and, like Sarah, had adapted well to this time period. She could have been a whimpering, weak woman—bemoaning the absence of her husband and looking for sympathy with that big belly of hers—but she didn't. She helped Sarah with all the chores and pitched in with some of the men's tasks, just to lighten the load for the lot of them. She always worked as part of the family and didn't ask for any special privileges.

If his no-good nephew Ian wasn't coming back for his wife and their bairns, then he would be more than happy to have them stay as part of his family. Of course, that probably meant Wallace would be staying, too, and that was fine with him. He'd have to add on to the house, though. At least this time, he'd have Wallace to help him. He'd built enough structures, both by himself and with others, to know that he didn't want to construct anything by himself again.

As he rode closer to the house, Jody could see Evie sitting under 'her' tree with the little satchel she had put together with rags and wee scraps of cloth. The bag was overflowing with long pieces of vine and green shoots. He'd have to bring out the wash pot a day early, he thought. She'd need to soak her woodland bounty before she could weave it.

He stopped at the edge of the clearing and looked over his little homestead with a slightly biased eye. It wasn't as big as his last home on Pomeroy's Point, but land and buildings weren't everything. He only had the two buildings, but he also had at least one male and one female of each of the animals he wanted for his stock. He didn't need much more than hard work to improve his humble estate. Most importantly, he had a contented family.

And now he had his son in his life. Their hidden relationship, awkwardly revealed by Evie when she let it be known that Wallace was his godson, had been seen through by everyone present—they knew it was only part of the story. Later, Wallace had privately thanked him for giving him life. Jody hadn't sired him on purpose but was glad of it anyway…and relieved that his son understood, without explanation, why he hadn't been there for him while he was growing up.

Wallace couldn't have had a finer stepfather than Julian. The titled British officer was another blessing Jody hadn't asked for. Fair, dignified, just, and with a good heart—his former gaoler and political foe was the perfect surrogate father—well, except for the British part. Then again, Julian's citizenship and status had made it possible for Wallace to have more in the way of education and travel than *he* could ever have offered. Who would have thought that a friendship could evolve from spending six years together as prisoner and subjugator? Their status relationship was secondary to their respect for each other and their life situations, neither one lording over nor rebelling against the other.

After all these years, he and Wallace were together at last, sharing their chores, meals, and idle time, able to play an occasional friendly game of chess or a hand of cards, living as a family who cared for one another should. Yes, he had everything he needed, and should never pass up the opportunity to say thanks. He dismounted, knelt down on one knee, and said a short prayer of thanksgiving before continuing home.

Just as he was looking over his small cabin, visualizing its expansion potential, he noticed movement. He stepped aside to get an unobstructed view and saw it. There was a man on his porch. And he was rifling through Evie's coat!

"Lord, keep her safe," he prayed quickly as he flipped the horse's reins over a branch. He looked back to make sure Evie was still at 'her' tree, and then quietly sprinted through the woods to the back of the house.

The visitor never looked up as Jody neared. He was intent on the object in his hand, unaware that Jody had approached from his blind side, and was standing right behind him, just over an arm's reach away.

"Takin' to theivin' there, have ye nephew? Or do ye still consider yerself my kin?"

Ian dropped the item, spun around, and grabbed his dirk, all in one fast, smooth movement. "Jeez, Jody, I coulda killed ye! Dinna ye ken better than to sneak up on me?" Ian, extremely embarrassed, quickly tried to regain his brave Indian warrior persona, lowering his voice to a scold by the end of his speech that had started out as a squeak.

"What's yer answer, Ian?" Jody asked stonily, not allowing any emotion to show on his face or in his voice.

"No, I ain't theivin', and I guess yer the one to say aye or nae on the kin part, ye see..."

Jody didn't let him finish. "I ketch ye hot-handed with somethin' ye took outta Evie's coat, and ye say ye ain't theivin'? Why are ye riflin' through it then?"

"It's this," Ian said gruffly, still trying to be strong. He handed Jody the little black box that had been in the inside zippered pocket of Evie's jacket ever since he had returned it there months ago.

Jody took it and rubbed his thumb over its smooth surface. Then he held it up to the sunlight to get a better look at it. He hadn't pulled his dirk on his nephew and was glad of it now. He wanted to use both hands to hold and examine the strange piece.

Ian watched him silently, waiting for his uncle to speak first.

Jody knew his nephew wanted him to start the conversation, but that's not what he wanted. He'd wait and see what the irresponsible cur had to say about his absence. Jody continued his examination of the small, solid object with metal inserts, holding it further away from his face, squinting to see better.

That was Ian's opening. "Eyes nae so good anymore, eh, uncle?" he asked jovially. Maybe his little-boy-nephew attitude would work with Jody. Right now, all he wanted was to get away before someone else showed up. He hadn't planned on meeting anyone, especially his uncle. He had seen Evie out in the woods, sitting quietly; he knew she wouldn't be here soon. No telling where Sarah was. Hopefully he wouldn't meet up with her either. He had just wanted to get one more look at that box, and then he'd be gone forever.

That wee box: it haunted him when he tried to sleep. Even when awake, he heard the voice. "Hi, tell Danny you found her fone." The face—the woman looked just like Evie, but was so much older, and that voice—it had to be hers. He had to see that face and hear the voice just one more time...

"Weel, when ye get older, the eyeballs get firmer, Sarah tells me," Jody said, bringing Ian back to reality. "Oh, she's still my wife, and I keep her by my side as much as I can," Jody added snidely, looking down his nose at his nephew who had managed to make his way to the bottom step of the porch.

He returned to a civil tone and continued, "And, when they get all hard like that, they don't react to light like they did when younger. I doubt ye'll have to worry about it, though." He glared at Ian. "I dinna think ye'll live that long."

Ian unintentionally gulped, then realized the rip he had just revealed in his emotional shield and stood up straight. "I meant to return earlier and tell ye, Uncle Jody, that I canna come back as a husband to Evie. Ye see, right after I left her here, I got tangled up with some rather unsavory sorts and weel, they…er…um…weel…"

Ian slouched and shook his head in mock dejection. "I'm not a whole man anymore. I couldna serve a wife properly. Evie would be better off with another husband. She could jest say that she was a widow, and that would be almost right since I'm not a whole man anymore. I guess that would make her almost a widow. I jest dinna think she should be tied down to me like that."

Ian was sweating even though the air was cool. Jody had been a card player long enough that he could tell when someone was lying. And Ian was definitely telling a whopper.

Jody looked away from him and held the shiny part of the small box up toward the sun. As he turned it, he noticed a little orange flash appear, as if a wee fire had been lit. He glanced over at Ian, who looked as if he was trying to keep from soiling himself. He hadn't seen the orange light. "What did ye want with this?"

"Oh, nothin', I guess. I better be goin' now," Ian said as he sidled away, unwilling to look Jody in the eye. He started walking backwards, eyes still on the ground, moving faster as he spoke. "Tell Auntie Sarah 'hallo' and tell Evie I'm sorry it dinna work out."

Ian turned around and practically ran away, his brisk trot not quite a sprint, never looking back.

Jody started to yell out after him. He wanted to say, "Why dinna ye tell her yerself, ye coward?" but stopped before the first word was out. Even if Ian still had his balls—and he probably did—emotionally, he didn't. Evie was better off without him, like he said.

The little orange blinking spot on the box was now green and steady. He sat down hard on the bench, suddenly fatigued—physically and emotionally. He and Evie had a lot to talk about, and it wasn't going to be easy.

"My horse!" he exclaimed, suddenly alert and energized. He had completely forgotten about Aries and left him in the woods. He took a deep breath, looked at the wee box one more time, and then stuck it in his sporran. He slapped his knees and got up. "What's an uncle to do?" he said. "Jest keep puttin' one foot in front of the other, I suppose, jest one step at a time."

Ж Ж

Jody sneaked back to his horse and waited, making sure Evie returned to the house before he did. He watched as she walked up to the porch. She looked puzzled. Did she know what had just happened? Had she seen Ian? Well, the puzzlement didn't last long. She hollered to see if anyone was home, picked up her coat, and went inside. He did notice, though, that she had turned around and looked long and hard into the woods before she went inside. She must have sensed something—or someone.

He went into the barn, unsaddled his horse, and gave him hay and a fistful of oats. "Ye sure have it easy, Aries. No women, no balls, and yer food brought right to yer face. Then again, I'd rather work fer my food than be without my woman or my balls." Jody chuckled and walked to the house without even the slightest idea of what he was going to say to Evie.

He didn't have to worry about it, though; Evie started the conversation.

Ж Ж

"Oh, hi, Jody," I said when he walked in. Jody always made sure he made plenty of noise coming up the steps. I knew it was because he didn't want to scare me. "I'm glad you came back early. Either I'm going crazy or something weird is going on. You don't think I'm crazy, do you?"

"Nae, I dinna think yer crazy. With what ye and Sarah have been through—comin' here from a forward time—it's amazin' that yer sane at all. What's botherin' ye, lass?"

"Just a while ago, when I came back from gathering wood for the baskets, I could swear that someone had been here. I couldn't see or smell anyone, and nothing was out of order, but…well, I could almost *swear* that Ian was here, or had been. It was as if I felt his presence rather than saw or heard him. Do you know what I mean?"

"Aye, I ken what ye mean. Keep listenin' to that little voice inside of ye, lass. It seems to guide ye well. I came back earlier today and found Ian on the porch. He was riflin' through yer jacket. This is what he wanted." Jody reached into his sporran and brought it out, "This wee black box with the green spot on the side."

"A cell phone? I had a cell phone in my coat?"

"Weel, if that's what this is, then that's where it was. He seemed to want it terrible bad—bad enough to come here and chance bein' found. After he had it, he dinna seem to want to take it. What is a sell fone?" Jody asked as he offered it to me.

I looked at it suspiciously, but didn't take it. Instead, I went to the kitchen chair, sat down, and stared at the door with unseeing, vacant eyes, stunned. Jody didn't say anything to me, but respected my newly attained shocked status, and quietly let me gather my wits.

Jody was very curious about the shiny flat box. It reminded him of the little Bible he had had in prison. This was a bit smaller and seemed to be solid. One side had a shiny surface—like smoky glass. He held it up again and noticed that it was as reflective as a high-quality mirror. He set it into the clay candlestick holder, propped up against the unlit candle. The little speck of green on the side had turned red.

I took a deep breath and blinked rapidly as I came back to myself. I tried to lay my head down on the table—my belly was in the way, though. Actually, I wanted a deep, dark closet to crawl into, but I had to deal with this. I sat up—elbows planted on the table, my chin resting in my hands—and began my soulless dissertation.

"A cell phone is a communications device. It often has a GPS in it, that's global positioning system, which uses satellites to pinpoint its location. This smartphone version can take pictures, cruise the internet, do calculations, play music, and much, much more."

I looked over at Jody's wide-eyed and slack-jawed reaction to my explanation. "Oh, when I remember 21st century stuff, I forget that you don't know what I'm talking about. That probably sounded Greek to you, didn't it?"

"No," Jody began slowly, "I ken how to speak a bit of Greek, and that's no Greek. The only words I recognized were pictures and music. Are ye tellin' me that this wee box can make music and all those other things ye were talkin' about?"

"Yes, but I don't know if I want to turn it on. I'm afraid it'll be like Pandora's Box. I don't know if there are any evils in there, but I'll bet there *is* information about my past life in it. I don't want to know about who I was and where I came from—at least not yet. I like it here and now in 1781."

"Are ye sayin' that ye canna miss what ye dinna ken ye had?" Jody asked.

I paused. I started to speak, then stopped, started and then stopped again. Finally, I managed, "How do you say it, 'better the devil you know than the devil you don't'?"

"Aye, that's it, and true it is. What do ye want to do with this? Ye could use it as a mirror. It has a wee light on it. It would be easy to find in the dark."

"And why would I need a mirror in the dark?" I asked with a chuckle.

"Thanks, Jody, you always seem to make me feel better. Just put it in a safe place, and if I get curious about it, I'll come to you. We can look at it together."

"I'll put it back in here," he said and put it into his sporran. "It's unlikely anyone will take it without me kennin' about it if it's in here. Now, since it's jest the two of us, how about an early dinner? I'll chase down some eggs if ye wouldna mind fixin' some of those egg burritos. José sent along some more of those long keepin' tomatoes fer ye."

"Sounds like a good plan. I'll get right on it."

I began to gather together the flour, lard, salt, and a bowl for the tortillas, and Jody went outside on an egg hunt.

And that was all there was to it. I had a possible link to my past life in Jody's sporran. I didn't want to access it now—and might not ever want to know what I was all about BI—Before Ian.

I wasn't even sure if it was my cell phone, but I did feel a certain familiarity with it. I knew that the little green light Jody mentioned meant that someone had recently put the phone in the sun so the solar panels had charged the battery. If it had been in my coat for all those months, the battery was surely dead when Ian grabbed it earlier today. And if Ian had returned just for the phone, it had to be because he had seen it before. He had probably seen it when the battery was charged, too. That would be within the first few weeks we were together, if the phone was fully charged when I first 'got' here.

I wondered if Ian had seen something on the phone that made him dump me on Sarah and Jody. Well, to hell with him and wondering! I was here now, with people I had chosen as my family. If Ian couldn't stand to be with me, at least his Cousin Wallace, Uncle Jody, and Aunt Sarah wanted me.

"Pbbbt on you, Ian Kincaid," I said, then paused. "Did I just say that out loud? Uh, oh—I'm talking to myself again." I grinned from ear to ear. "I am not talking to myself," I declared loudly, "I am talking to my babies. Babies, you have a mother and lots of other kin on hand, and one day you'll also have a father to hold you and love you and help your sometimes frazzled mommy. Now, let's get something to eat. We're hungry."

**36 Twins

March 3, 1781

The gloominess of the overcast late afternoon made finding eggs a challenge for Jody. The chickens were out 'free ranging,' as Evie called it, darting about, exploring the dark places underneath bushes and stacked firewood, scratching and pecking for the protein portion of their daily fare, and possibly a stray seed or two that hadn't already been devoured. Unrestricted by their little boxes, they laid their eggs whenever and wherever the urge hit them. It took him a while, but Jody found eight eggs—nine, if he included the one he had accidentally stepped on. That was more than enough for just the two of them.

He was almost to the house when he heard it: a horse was approaching, and it sounded winded. Someone had been riding hard, but was smart and was letting the animal cool down before coming to the barn. As it got closer, he recognized the sound of the horse's gait: it was Sarah's pony. He set the egg basket down on the porch and ran up the path to greet her.

"Ho, there, Jessie," he called out as he grabbed the small horse's halter. "Sarah, what are ye doin' home now? I thought ye had a bairn to bring into the world. And why are ye ridin' so late in the day? Ye ken it isna always safe."

"Hello, Jody; nice to see you, too," Sarah replied coldly.

"Sorry, ye gave me a fright," Jody said. "Are ye ailin'?" Sarah shook her head in reply and accepted his help in dismounting. "Then why did ye come back so soon and so close to mirk?"

Sarah snuggled into his arms and shrugged her shoulders, letting him know wordlessly that she didn't know why. Jody gave her a quick kiss, took the horse's reins, and the three of them walked together to the barn.

Once inside, Jody quickly unsaddled the horse. He grabbed the brush from the peg near the door and started brushing the pony dry. Jessie wasn't lathered, but she *was* quite sweaty.

Sarah reached into the wooden box that held the oats and scooped out a cupful for her horse. Jessie deserved it. She wasn't a powerful pony and making two long trips in the same day was more than she was used to. A journey into town once a month was the usual extent of her travels, with maybe a couple of doctor's visits in between. She was an older horse, but still obedient and strong. Sarah decided to reward her with a second cupful of grain for her efforts.

"Now dinna be givin' her a sair wame with too many oats," Jody scolded. He reached up and murmured in Gaelic to the nag. "Yes, yer a good mare and I thank ye, but dinna be lettin' well-meanin' women knot up yer wame."

He turned his attention back to Sarah, who had overheard his admonishment and was returning the second helping of oats back to the lidded box. "What happened out there today? Are Mrs. Donaldson and her bairn awright? And where's Hannah? Did she stay with her?"

"Mrs. Donaldson is fine. I think she miscalculated her due date by a month. She's plenty big all right, but not ready for delivery. I'm not positive, but I'm pretty sure I heard two heartbeats when I checked her. I left Hannah with her, just in case. She'll be a big help as a babysitter, cook, and housekeeper. Those four little Donaldson girls sure have a lot of energy. If Mrs. Donaldson is having twins, she should be on bed rest for the next few weeks. I don't think Mac can handle his chores, the cooking, cleaning, and all those little girls without an extra hand. Hannah was more than willing. Girls would rather do anyone else's chores but their own. That, I think, will never change. Mona was the same way."

"Then why did ye come home tonight? Ye could have waited fer the morn and not afeart me."

"Oh, that isn't why I came back early. I know it sounds crazy, but I felt like Ian was here. I wanted to get back here and give him a piece of my mind. Now that I'm here, though, I wonder why I acted so impulsively. He's not here, is he?"

"Nooo," answered Jody slowly, "but he was."

"I knew it!" Sarah exclaimed, and then chewed her bottom lip, trying to figure out what her errant nephew could be up to. She huffed, angry and disappointed in him. "What happened? Did he see Evie, and did she see him?"

"Nae, they dinna see each other. He dinna want to see me either, but I came up behind him—and he dinna get a chance to run and hide, the coward. He dinna even ask about the bairns, or bairn. I dinna think he kens there's more than one. He lied to me, sayin' that he'd been castrated, that Evie should go on with her life and get marrit to someone else."

"The bastard," Sarah huffed. Jody's eyebrows went up at hearing her coarse comment. "Sorry, no disrespect meant to your sister."

"Aye, the word may be wrong, but I feel the same. By the way, he did say to say 'hallo' to you."

Sarah's mouth twitched for a moment. She didn't know whether to grin, frown, or say something profound. Instead, she issued an "Hmph" and let it drop.

"I agree with that," Jody said. "Come on in. We're havin' egg burritos for supper, a la Evie. By the way, she dinna ask about Ian, and I dinna offer up what he said. She's in a good mood now, and I dinna want to spoil it."

Sarah led the way into the house, with Jody and the basket of eggs following.

Ж Ж

"Sarah!" I shouted as soon as I saw her. After giving her a big, heartfelt hug, I grabbed the eggs and started on the scrambled egg part of the burritos. Jody grabbed the wooden plates and set the table. Sarah noticed the fresh tomato and onion I had set on the cutting board, and began preparing fresh salsa.

"Are you sure you wouldn't rather sit down and take a load off?" I asked and nodded to the chaise. "You must have ridden all day today, or at least I'll bet it feels like it."

"That's for sure. By the way, it looks like Mrs. Donaldson is going to be the first to have twins in the neighborhood. It turns out she isn't due for a month or so. I left Hannah with her to watch the girls and take care of the house so she could get some rest. You are putting your feet up several times a day, aren't you?" she asked, using her head-nurse tone.

"Yes, ma'am, I am! Hey, I have some news—unless Jody already told you."

I felt perky and knew it showed in my words and voice. Sarah looked at Jody, but he just shrugged his shoulder. Okay, I guess there's something else going on, but I really don't care to know about it right now.

I continued as if I hadn't seen any of their unspoken conversation. "Ian came back. And get this; he didn't come back for me..." I hesitated and added sarcastically, "big surprise," then bounced back into pert and sassy mode. "He came back for my old cell phone!"

"Cell phone," asked Sarah, "as in cellular phone?" I nodded my head vigorously. "Where did you have a cellular phone hidden? I never saw you take one out of your bag."

"It was in one of my coat pockets. I didn't even know I had one. Jody, show it to her."

Jody pulled it out of his sporran and handed it to her, pinched between thumb and forefinger, his pinky out as if he were removing a dead shrew.

"Well, I'll be. They sure got small, didn't they? Too bad there aren't any signals, you could... Oh, sorry," she apologized when she saw that my excitement had turned rancid.

"Sarah, cell phones do more than just make phone calls. Like I was telling Jody, you can type notes to people—they call it texting—and they'll get the message immediately. You can also record and play music, take pictures and look at them right away, even make movies with that little thing in your hand. It has a bunch of different types of calculators and language translators in it, and a radio—which wouldn't work here and now, of course, since there aren't any radio signals. Neither would the phone..." I stopped when I saw how stunned Sarah was.

"It's real scary how fast technology is moving—or rather, will move. It's all so quick and disposable in my time, my former time. Sarah, I don't want to go back!" I walked over to her and held her hand to my chest. "Good grief, I don't even know how I got here, so how *could* I go back? And, as I was telling Jody, I don't want to know about the old me—who I was—before all 'this' happened." I gestured to the small living quarters that I now called home. "I'm fine just as I am," I said, and hoped they could see how proud I was of how well I had adapted, how content I was.

"Hey!" I let go of Sarah's hand and looked down at the phone.

I was flabbergasted at the sight of it.

"When did this happen?" I asked Jody, trying not to show too much apprehension. "When did the light go from green to red?" The green battery-charged light was now red for recording in process.

"I first noticed it when I tried to give it to ye as ye were sittin' at the table. Why? Is there somethin' wrong?" He snatched it from Sarah as if it was a bomb, and she might get hurt.

"No, not wrong," I said as I stared at the red light flashing near his thumb. I pushed the button next to it, and it returned to its steady green glow. "I think we just made a movie."

It was total silence and stares for a full minute. Sarah spoke first, "Jody, put that thing away, please. We won't need it for anything." Jody obeyed, wordlessly putting it back into his sporran.

"Thanks," I said as I leaned into Sarah for a big face-in-her-shoulder hug. I wasn't even near crying, but I was burying all my fragmented, disassociated emotions into her collarbone. It felt as if I had been full of static electricity, and had now discharged all my tingly sensations into her body. I pulled away and smiled. My emotions didn't hurt anymore. "Thanks, I needed that," I said to her. I straightened up, smiled again, and asked, "Is anybody hungry?"

Ж Ж

Life went on. A week had passed, and Wallace still hadn't returned from helping Julian and José at the ranch. I assisted in the delivery of a couple of kids—goat kids, that is—but other than that, nothing exciting had happened. Sarah was frustrated at not having anyone to mend or deliver, and she was getting on my nerves.

"Sarah, why don't we go and check on Mrs. Donaldson? If nothing else, I'm sure she and Hannah will appreciate the adult company."

Sarah looked at me, opened her mouth as if to protest, then stopped, closed her mouth, and put her hands on her hips. "You're right, you're absolutely right. Even if Mrs. Donaldson was a month off of her estimated due date, twins are frequently born early. Two weeks early would mean that they could be here at any time. Are you sure you're up to traveling?"

"It's been weeks since Pyle's Massacre, and if it's just two women traveling, I'm sure we'll be safe. Pretty soon I won't be able to travel, and I'd like to talk to Mrs. Donaldson about babies and, well, stuff."

"Jody, do you mind if we leave by ourselves?" Sarah asked.

Jody shook his head as he looked at the two of us, one at a time. "Do ye think I could stop either of ye if ye got it into yer heids to do anythin'?"

"Thanks, you're a dear," I said and gave him a one-armed hug. I grabbed my backpack and said to Sarah, "I'm ready."

Sarah opened the door and looked out. "Well, it's early enough, and the weather looks like it's going to cooperate. Put together some food for the road while Jody and I get the horses ready so we can leave right away. No use in waiting for tomorrow."

I looked at Sarah with mock sincerity. "Don't you know that tomorrow never comes?" I gave her a big grin and added. "Okay, okay, I'm going," my hands up to protect myself, as if she had smacked me for my corny remark.

"Well, at least with ye around, Sarah will never be lackin' fer entertainment," Jody said and blinked. His attempt at a wink was a failure, but the broad, familial smile that came with it was a comforting coup.

Ж Ж

It was a practically perfect day for a one-hour ride with my favorite sister. The aroma of birch tree buds breaking open, lovelier than any Paris perfume, and the translucent tinge of green along the naked, gray tree limbs, were welcomed promises that spring was indeed on its way. Although it was chilly, it was sunny, the air still. The brightness gave the illusion of warmth. Of course, I also had a built in heater with my pregnancy. My additional body mass made me feel hot, even when others around me were shivering.

We could see them from afar. Three bright-faced little girls and Hannah, holding a fourth one, greeted us at the gate to the Donaldson's homestead.

"How did you know it was time?" Hannah asked. "Mr. Donaldson left for town this morning and, not an hour later, Mrs. Donaldson's water broke. Oh, how rude of me…here, let me help you down."

Hannah offered her free hand to assist Sarah, who was perfectly able to dismount by herself. She still had the youngest Donaldson daughter on her hip when she came over to help me. "Oh, dear," she said when she saw how big I had become.

"Don't worry. Sarah, would you help me down before you go inside?" It was obvious that Hannah wouldn't be able to hold the baby and help move my bulk at the same time.

"Here you go." Sarah, feet planted firmly, stood in front of me, and grasped me about my ribcage. I braced my hands on her shoulders and was able to touch down safely, her strong hands and body stance absolutely necessary for my dismount. "Take it easy," she warned, holding me close as we walked side-by-side to the front steps. She knew I had 'horse legs' and wouldn't be sure-footed for a few minutes, at least.

Sarah led me to a chair in the kitchen, made sure I was okay, and then transformed into midwife mode. "Hannah, put some water on to boil. Oh, I see you've already done that. Good. Now, did you get some clean rags put aside?" She turned to her patient and saw the pile of clean cloths neatly folded by the side of the bed. "Good job. How are you doing, Mrs. Donaldson?"

"The pains, they're comin' right close together now, they're…oh, my," she blurted, then groaned and held her breath.

I rushed to her side. "Breathe, breathe," I said. Her eyes squeezed shut in pain, popped open and stared at me in disbelief at my command. "Take a breath in, blow it out, in, come on now," I instructed.

She obeyed, but only because she was shocked that I was the one telling her what to do. She had already birthed four children and knew what she was doing. Sarah was the midwife, and Hannah was the trainee. I was just the very pregnant young woman who had come along with the midwife.

Sarah looked at me, her face pinched into a frown of disbelief, and asked, "What are you doing?"

I sidled up to her and whispered, "I don't know, but it seems to work. I guess it's one of those things I 'know' without knowing how I know. Let's go with it as long as I'm comfortable with what I'm doing, okay?"

"Okay, but let me know *discreetly*," she stressed, "if you stop 'knowing' what you're doing, okay?"

"Okay," I said. I pulled a chair over to the side of Mrs. Donaldson's bed. "I'm going to help you with the babies, okay?"

Mrs. Donaldson nodded and said, "Okay," very meekly.

I could tell she didn't have much—if any—confidence in me, but that would come later...or never.

"First thing I want you to do," I said, "is relax."

That was easier said than done. The woman was as stiff as an oak board. "Okay, I want you to lie on your left side like you're trying to go to sleep. Don't worry; I'll let you know when it's time to start the breathing. First you have to take a slow deep breath in, and then let it out...slowly."

Mrs. Donaldson looked at Sarah, then Hannah, with a 'help me' expression on her face, and then back at me with a weak, insecure smile. I had my hand on her belly and felt a contraction start. "Take a slow breath in now and go limp. Breathe, breathe."

She was following my instructions but inhaling and exhaling too quickly. "Slow down, slow easy breath in, then slow blow out. Again." The contraction stopped. "Now take a deep breath in and blow it all out."

She followed my instructions well this time. Her eyes lit up with surprise. "Lawdy! That weren't bad at all." She smiled at me, then looked at Sarah as if she wanted her to believe this miracle, too, and repeated, "Really, not bad at all."

"Now, I want you to do the breathing when I tell you to. If you start too late, or try to talk during one of the contractions, it'll hurt again. This will work for most of the contractions, and there's no magic way to stop all the pains, but the breathing...um...patterns...will help. Oh, get ready, here comes another one!"

And so the Lamaze method of labor management was introduced into 18th century North Carolina. The twins were born a relatively short two hours later. There was just a little manipulation needed to bring the second child's—the second son's—head into alignment for a proper presentation and delivery. The boys were both small, but very strong.

We had just cleaned up the second boy, and the first one was nursing, when Mac came bursting into the house. "What...where'd ...Oh my, they're here?" he asked.

Mac was accustomed to his little girls coming out to greet him when he came back from town. When they hadn't come outside, he was concerned. They were all in the house, safe and being held in check by Hannah, as best she could. The youngest girl was squalling because of all the excitement, and the older ones were shoving each other aside, trying to get a better view of their new brothers.

"Papa, Papa," called Miranda, the eldest, "we got brothers; two of 'em, and they got huge balls 'tween their legs."

"Aye, just like their..." Mac started to brag, but realized just in time that this was the wrong audience. "Just like they're supposed to," he said. "Boys are different, you know."

He picked up the two youngest girls as the older two crowded next to him. He walked over to Mrs. Donaldson—I never did find out her first name—and said, "Well done, well done." He gave her a kiss on the top of the head. "Only two more to go, and then we can have an even number."

"Not for a while, Mac, not for a long, long while," she said with a grin.

The girls were almost too excited to eat, but I told them they had to finish their supper so they would grow big and strong, so they could help Mama and Papa take care of their baby brothers. They all finished in a hurry—except for baby Rebecca who decided it was more fun to wear her oatmeal than eat it.

A quick but thorough hand and face washing after their privy visit, and the girls were ready for bed. The excitement was almost too much for them, so I decided it was time to see if I could recite a bedtime story. I gathered all the girls together in their great bed and sat in the chair next to them. I knew that if I lay down with them, I'd never be able to get back up without a lot of help. I settled myself in the hard kitchen chair and just started to babble.

"One fish, two fish, red fish, blue fish." The littlest girls just looked at me as I rattled on.

"We don't know that story," scolded Miranda.

"Well, maybe you can learn it," I said. "Black fish, blue fish, old fish, new fish, this one has a little star, this one has a little car." I took a deep breath and paused. "I mean this one has a little scar, he got hurt, but he's all better now." *This wasn't going to be as easy as I thought.*

Two of the girls were soon residing in dreamland and Miranda's eyelids were flickering, battling sleep. "One fish, two fish, red fish, blue fish," I repeated, softer and slower, two more times. It worked—all the girls were asleep, and I was still awake.

Mac was sitting next to his wife, holding one of his sons, positively beaming with pride as he studied the boy's face, gently stroking the wispy hair on his soft spot. "Have you decided on names yet?" I asked.

He looked up and presented his son to the world. "George Washington Donaldson and his brother," he pointed with the son he held to the one his wife was nursing, "Nathanael Greene Donaldson. May they be as strong and wise as their namesakes. May God bless America and my family."

"God bless us all," I said, then shrank back a bit. I realized I was being disrespectful by adding to the man of the house's blessing.

"You're right, Evie, God bless us all."

Ж Ж

The next morning, I peeked over Mrs. Donaldson's shoulder as she was changing little George's diaper. It was easy to tell the difference because the boys weren't identical twins. Little George was fair-haired and Nathanael was dark-haired like his mother. "Is that normal?" I asked.

Sarah came over to join us. "What, you mean the big balls?" she asked bluntly.

"Um, yes," I said meekly.

"Perfectly normal; they grow into them, although sometimes it takes a long time," she laughed.

I didn't know if she was serious or not. She saw the look on my face, and Mrs. Donaldson didn't look too sure herself.

"No, really, they're fine. Just keep them clean down there and wash and boil the clouts—don't just let them dry out and reuse them. And if the room is warm, let their little bottoms air out for a bit without anything on them. Keep the boys warm, dry, and well fed, and they'll grow up just fine. What am I saying? You did a great job with your daughters."

"Thank you," Mrs. Donaldson said. "And thank you, Evie, for the help with the birthin'. It was the easiest for me ever, even though there were twice as many to get out. I'll have to remember that next time," she said as she looked over at her husband, who was holding and admiring little Nathanael, "...if there is a next time."

I knew Mac had heard her, but he was ignoring her comment.

"You're such a fine young lad, and one day you're going to be a wonderful big brother, too. That is, a big brother to a little brother or two." He turned and winked at his wife. "Fine work, Mrs. Donaldson, fine work."

"What's today?" I asked. "Sarah, you'll have to record the births in your book and in the family's Bible.

"It's March 13th, not quite the Ides of March," she answered.

"Oh, crap," I said softly.

Sarah looked at me, but I was stunned and didn't see her. She reached out, lifted my chin, and asked—obviously not for the first time, but the first time I heard her— "What's. Wrong?"

I looked at the joy of the new family, at the bright sunny day outside the window, and then back at Sarah. "We have to go. Now," I said emphatically. "Hannah, can you stay here a little while longer? I have to take Sarah somewhere. Right. Now."

I knew I sounded cryptic but hoped that everyone—except Sarah—would chalk it up to my pregnancy.

"Yes, ma'am, no worries. I wasn't going back home for a week more anyhow. Are you sure you're okay?" Hannah asked with concern, a deep worry line marking her otherwise flawless young forehead.

Sarah answered for me. "She's had a lot of excitement. I think I had better get her back home to her own bed right away. She'll be fine."

Mac gave wee George to Hannah and went out to saddle our horses, while Sarah gathered up our bags and my coat.

"Are you sure you'll be all right with her?" Mac asked Sarah when we got to the barn. "She looks a bit off," he said softly.

"We'll be fine. You take good care of that family of yours, okay? If you need anything, just send Hannah. I want you to stay here with them, do you understand?"

"Yes, ma'am," he replied.

I waddled up to my horse and let Mac help me up; Sarah was all ready to go. "God speed," he said and smacked the horses' rumps, sending us on our way.

We rode as fast as Sarah dared with me and my big belly. When we were out of sight of the Donaldson's homestead, she pulled up in front of me and signaled me to a stop. "What's going on?" she asked.

"The Ides of March wasn't just a bad day for Caesar," I said. "It was the day of the big battle at Guilford Courthouse. We didn't, or won't, win this one."

"Oh, crap," she said.

"I remembered it when you told me today's date. Mac named one of the boys after Nathanael Greene. He was, or rather is, a great general. He's going to turn the tide of the war with this battle. We won't win it—but neither do the British, really. From this battle on, we're in charge and, well, you know we'll be victorious in the end. I wish I could do something to help us win this one, but I don't know what I—we—could possibly do. I do think we'd better tell Jody about it, though."

"That, my dear, is the only thing I'm sure we should do. Come on, if you can't keep up the pace, don't worry. I need to ride as fast as little Jessie can go. Even at that, I still won't be too far ahead of you. It's not that far until we're home, and I need to talk to Jody right away."

**37 Wallace and Me

March 17, 1781

Jody, Sarah, and Julian survived the bloody Battle of Guilford Courthouse without injuries. The two Pomeroys rode in late on the 17th, tired and filthy, but intact. Sarah looked as if she had just entered her own little bliss café when I told her that I had a hot dinner of rice and gravy—her favorite meal—ready for them. Jody, although visibly relieved when Wallace volunteered to take care of the horses for him, still looked as if he were carrying all the woes of the war on his back.

Julian had gone home directly to José. His body hadn't been wounded, but Jody said that he saw the conflict in his eyes when warring with men who had been his allies up until a few months ago.

"Don't worry," I said, "I'm sure José will make him feel better. I mean…"

I stopped talking rather than stutter. I didn't want it to sound as if I were insinuating that any potential intimacy between the two men would take care of everything. Now I had to try and recover two people's dignity—his and mine…

"What I mean is, when he goes back to José and the ranch, he'll realize that he was fighting for the right to own and control what belongs to them. No one will be able to take their property or goods, nor tax them without due process, when we win this war."

There were shrugs and nods of agreement all around the table at my comment, but no words. I knew that voicing my belief made me feel better, and I hoped it had helped them, too.

The simple dinner for four remained quiet and somber. I knew I needed a creative plan and extra effort to return us to our comfortable home and hearth mode. It was *my* turn to fight for what was mine: my family.

"If it's okay with you two, Wallace and I are going to do a little camping out tonight. I haven't slept under the stars for months now. It's clear and not too cold, and I think it might be fun."

Wallace looked sideways at me, but didn't say a word. I hadn't cleared it with him—I was making this up as I went along—but he was used to my spontaneity, and didn't protest.

Jody lifted his head slightly and squinted at me, giving me a scornful 'Now what are ye up to?' leer. I didn't let it bother me. He needed to get back to normal, and I was here to help get that done.

I kept on with my scheme. "I put on some hot water. You two can clean up and have a little privacy tonight." I looked at the very tattered and dirty Jody and added, "Besides, I don't want to be around to hear you hollerin' when Sarah scrubs all that pitch out of your hair. You almost look like a brunette!"

My little joke didn't even get a chuckle from Jody, Sarah only groaned, and Wallace decided it was best to stay quiet and neutral.

I walked up to Jody and said, "Brunette, as in 'there's so much crud in your hair, the red doesn't shine through anymore.'"

"Aye," Jody said glumly. He got the joke, but didn't think it was very funny.

"Jay, Kay, El, Em" I replied sarcastically, my chin stuck out in defiance.

"Eh?" he asked.

"Bee, Cee, Dee, Eee!" I said with self-assurance and a smile.

"What are ye talkin' about?" he groused. His mood was moving from dejection to irritation, which is what I wanted, sort of. I hated depression in me or anyone else and would rather have him mad at me than moping.

"It's a game I just made up," I explained.

"Oh," he said, his lips pursed, obviously thinking about my little wordplay rather than his disappointment at not being able to win the Revolutionary War single-handedly.

His eyes lit up suddenly and he grinned. "Pee, queue, arrrrh, ess! Now I get it." He shook his head and said, "Yer right, life is too short—fer some of us, that is—to worry about the past and what we could or couldna accomplish, aye?"

"Jay, Kay, El, Em," I answered, beaming with pride at the success of my mood-elevation exercise.

Ж Ж

The game of chess he and Wallace were playing was meant to be a distraction, but instead, it brought back vivid memories for Jody. The battle at Guilford Courthouse last week was short-lived, but intense. General Nathaneal Greene must be a great chess player, Jody surmised as he studied the board; he was definitely a great strategist.

He looked at his thinned out row of pawns, recalling the first line of soldiers in that battle. Those inexperienced men—most of them farmers recently called up for an eighteen-month tour of duty—were raw, inexperienced, and terrified. The tremendous loss of life wasn't his or Greene's fault. There were always casualties in war, but the British firing on their own men, just to take out some of the patriots, was both irrational and irresponsible. He made his move—castled his knight—and reflected on the waste of life, glad that he, Sarah, and Julian had returned unscathed.

War and fighting, and thinking about them, always brought out the family man in Jody. "Lord, please keep them safe—Mona, Gregg, Benji, and Becky," he prayed, as he always did when he thought of them, asking for protection for his daughter, her husband, and their children who had returned to the 20th century. He had the rest of his family here with him now, in this time, and they were his to protect.

And now it looked as if his son had someone he wanted to keep safe and care for, too. Jody hadn't told Evie or Wallace about Ian 'releasing' Evie from their marriage, saying it was because he wasn't a 'whole man' anymore. Maybe now was the time…

"Wallace, there's somethin' I need to tell ye and Evie. It might be best done together, but, if ye want to ken first, I'll tell ye by yerself."

Wallace sat up straight on the stool and raised his chin, accepting the responsibility of taking care of the woman he loved and any decisions that concerned both of them. "Go ahead then," he said his hands on his knees, braced for whatever his father was going to tell him.

"Ian came here nearly a month ago. He, um, stopped to check on somethin' Evie had in her coat. He left without it, but told me to tell her that some bad men had injured him intentionally—that he wasna a whole man anymore, that she should go on with her life, find someone else, and remarry. I never told her what he said because, weel, there never seemed to be a good time fer it. And she dinna seem too interested in him, or anythin' havin' to do with him, either. She's been happy lately, and I thought if I brought it up, weel, I dinna want to upset her, her bein' in a family way and all."

"I'll see to it. And you're right, now is not a good time. She's a strong woman, no matter *when* she's from, but she needn't be burdened with this now. I'll tell her when the time is right. Thanks for letting me know."

Ж Ж

Every day held new adventures for me. At least it was novel for the first few weeks. I must have read about early American laundry methods but reading about them was much easier than trying to move a big wooden paddle around in a pot filled with boiling water and sopping wet clothes. It was more than strenuous; it was nearly impossible. The chore seemed like punishment, but it was necessary in order to have clean clothes. At first, I couldn't see why the water had to be boiling, and then I found out that lye-based soap wouldn't come out of the fabric without it. I didn't want itchy soap crud next to my skin, nor want anyone else to be uncomfortable because I was a poor laundress.

I didn't have the upper body strength to move the heavy mass at anything but the slowest agitation speed. Even the simplest daily tasks were extra labor intensive for me because my big belly was always in the way. I really couldn't do the job well but didn't want to ask for help.

As I was making a valiant attempt at lifting out a sodden mess of steaming clothes, I felt a warm body reach around my right side. "Allow me, please," said Wallace as he took the long wooden paddle from my hands. "Where would you like them?"

Wallace's sudden appearance at my side had startled me and left me breathless. "Uh, over there," I gasped and pointed to the slatted wooden table that today was being used as the first stage of the spin cycle. I figured that hand wringing—the second stage of the spin cycle—would be easier if I let gravity claim the first few pounds of water from the clothes, the excess water dripping between the boards to the ground.

I composed myself quickly—I didn't want him to know that he had spooked me—and walked over to the porch to retrieve my bag. I had talked Sarah into letting me set up a clothesline but had forgotten to bring out the rope.

"Can you help me? I need a sturdy place to tie this. I want to set up a clothesline." I gave him one end of the blue and white striped nylon rope. "Drying our clothes on bushes isn't too bad, but I don't like wearing the dried leaves and stems that are left behind. Here, can you tie your end around the top of the porch beam? That should be high enough."

Wallace turned the cord over in his hand, checking out the tight weave of the precise braid, and the stark white and brilliant blue hues. He was intrigued, but didn't say anything, instead just reached up and quickly tied a simple but sturdy knot.

"Okay," I said and looked around, trying to figure out where the other end should go.

I was standing on the porch and he was at ground level, so now I was as tall as he was. I had the sudden urge to grab him and give him a big hug. There wasn't a real reason—it wasn't lust or passion. I guess it's just because I needed one. I took a deep breath, hoped it didn't sound like the wishful sigh that it was, and continued with supervising the project.

"Now, where should we attach the other end? It has to be low enough so I can throw the clothes over it to dry, but tall enough that they won't drag on the ground. Do you think you can tie it off over there?" I asked, pointing to the mulberry tree.

"I could, but I don't think that's the right kind of tree. The fruit will fall when it's ripe and stain the clothes. And birds that come to eat the berries will leave little 'presents' on the clothes, too." He chuckled when he saw me smile. "How about back here? There's plenty of sun, and it won't catch riders in the throat as they come up to the house."

"Hence the phrase 'getting clothes-lined'—good choice," I said. "Clothesline pathway, coming through."

After a few minutes of our joint effort moving a few fallen branches and pulling some tall, dead weeds, we had the ground beneath our solar dryer cleared and the bright rope secured.

"I like working with you, Wallace. How come you aren't married, if you don't mind me asking?"

"I guess I wanted to make sure I didn't get 'clothes-lined' by the wrong sort of woman." He laughed, and then continued on a serious note. "Actually, as a soldier, I didn't think it fair to marry and then take off." There was an awkward micro-moment when neither of us spoke. Wallace quickly realized what he had said and apologized, "Oh, I just said the wrong thing, didn't I?"

"Well, where I come from, the phrase is, 'truth hurts, doesn't it.' But you're right. It wouldn't be right to marry, take off, and then maybe get killed, leaving a young widow and maybe a child or two." I looked at him quizzically and asked, "What is this, saying the wrong thing day?"

We both laughed at the awkward remarks, relaxed in each other's company. Wallace asked, "Will you let me help you on laundry days? I know you can handle it by yourself, but I can use it as an excuse to spend more time with ye. Listen to me now, I said 'ye' instead of you. It seems like Father...er, Jody, is rubbing off on me."

"What it sounds like to me is that you're starting to relax. Have you always had to live up to someone else's expectations?"

"I can't remember when I *wasn't* told how to sit, talk, or eat. I drew the line at being told how to think, though. I would say, 'If you didn't want me to think, then why did you bother sending me to so many schools?' That would stop the arguing right away."

Wallace and I hung the clothes on the line. We tossed the few items that wouldn't fit, over the bushes. After we were done, we walked back to the porch to sit. He held my elbow to make sure I kept my balance—or at least that was the pretense. The truth was that we both liked touching each other. It wasn't a romance thing, at least not for me. It was a 'gesture of comfort'—or so I kept telling myself.

"I never did thank you for telling me about my fathers. You know I knew, didn't you? That Jody is—had to be—my natural father. What did you call it, biological father?"

"Yes, biological father is the cold, but accurate phrase. How did you know?"

"I always knew someone else was my father. I didn't look like the paintings of Lord Cavendish or anyone else in his family portraits. I used to study them, trying to see some similarity, but there was nothing. I never saw my mother but was told that my hair was like hers. Growing up, I was often called 'bastard' behind my back—and a few times to my face. I wouldn't tell Papa, Julian that it, what was going on, but I think he was aware of it. He made sure I knew how to keep my temper in check, but also that I knew how to fight properly. He would show me off at little exhibitions just to keep my peers aware of my skills. When I grew to over six feet tall, that in itself was a deterrent. It didn't take much for me to avoid verbal conflicts and fisticuffs—I'd just stare down my nose at anyone foolish enough to challenge me. The antagonist would usually find an excuse to leave the area in a hurry. Funny, though, you wouldn't think so many men had sick mothers they suddenly had to tend to as soon as trouble started, would you?"

We both laughed at his joke. I stood up and rubbed my lower back. It hurt for me to sit down for too long. Wallace took my hand. We walked down the steps, my hand resting in the crook of his elbow, as if that was where it belonged. We headed away from the house, the laundry, and the responsibilities.

"No, really, it wasn't too bad after a while," he continued. "Then I came to America. One look at Ramona and I knew it was more than coincidence that we looked so much alike—especially when I saw Jody again. I had seen him several times as a youth, but back then, I didn't know—or care—what I looked like. Now as an adult, here in his world, I have been mistaken for him several times. Someone would see me from afar, come up to greet me, and then realize that I was younger, and didn't have that flaming red hair. They would say something about me being a younger twin, or ask, 'Does Jody know he has a son?' Others would just stare, turn and walk away, but always taking a second or third look back at me. Now that you've related the 'godfather' story, and given me an excuse to call him Father, it makes it easier for me. And for the rest of us, I'm sure. Sarah and Julian know, don't they?"

"Like you said, one look at you and Jody, and anyone would know. I'm sure you'll hear the whole story one of these days, and I'd kind of like to be there when it comes out. I'm not involved in this, but, well, you know that I *know* things, but don't know *why* I know them? For once, I'd like to hear the story outside of my head, not from the inside, if you catch my drift?"

"Yes, I think I catch your drift." Wallace paused. "I've never heard that phrase before. I like ye for so many reasons, and one is that every day I learn something new. You're so bright and fresh and, well, fun. Fun is something that wasn't part of my curriculum when I was growing up. I'll make sure it isn't left out when I have children."

"Wallace," I felt the heat of a blush rise up my cheeks as I spoke, "do you want children?" I looked down and began digging a stone out of the ground with the toe of my boot. I was embarrassed, but wanted to—had to—know.

"Oh, yes, definitely. As a matter of fact," he took my right hand in his left, put the other one on the spot where my waist was supposed to be, then started dancing with me—to music that was only in his mind, "I would like to see if I can get a head start on having a family. If only I could find a worthy woman who is already with child who will have me... Do ye know of one?"

"I do believe the lye fumes have gone to your head, Wallace. But before you come to your senses, yes, I do know of one. See, she figures that because of the tradition of handfasting, when her babies are about three-months-old, it will have been one year and a day since her handfast marriage. At that time, she'll be unmarried again—unless that rascal, coward of a man comes back before then. And even if he does return, she would have to agree to remarry him, this time in front of a priest or parson. And I'm *sure* she wouldn't say yes to that! So, it appears she will be a single woman soon. Oh, you do realize I am speaking about me, don't you?" I rolled my eyes at the end of my dissertation to avoid looking into his, embarrassed at my own boldness.

"Really?" he said, shoulders back, jaw dropped and mouth opened, in mock surprise. He relaxed and smiled in contentment, his eyes now locked on mine. "That's the best news I've heard all day." He swung me around quickly, and said, "As a matter of fact, it ranks right up there with being acknowledged by my father! I'm so happy, I don't know if I can hold it in."

After his own introduction, Wallace began his serenade. I didn't know that he had heard me singing while I worked in the garden, but he was now belting out my favorite song, "Oh, what a beautiful morning," in his rich, baritone voice. He started dancing with me again, deftly picking me up, swinging me over the small rocks and roots as they appeared in our makeshift ballroom floor.

At the end of his melodic refrain and our clumsy, but spirited dance, he carefully brushed back my hair and placed a soft, warm kiss on the middle of my forehead.

"Oh, boy," I muttered. On the outside, the buss wasn't any more than a father would give a daughter, but I was overwhelmed—twitterpated—by my own intense reaction to such an innocent kiss.

"I'm sorry," he said. He quickly brought his hands down to his sides, and stepped back, away from me. "That was rude, improper, disrespectful…"

I moved forward two steps, grasped his hands in mine, and said, "Yeah, well, maybe you thought so. I *liked* it! After your little…um…surgery, I thought you'd never let me kiss you again."

"Me, *let you*, kiss me? I thought it was you who *let me* kiss you."

Wallace was both flustered and blushing—and I was hot and bothered in a different way. I think he was confused about how to behave with me. There was his proper British upbringing—how to treat a lady, 18th century-style—and my very liberal, and obviously innate, 21st century attitudes.

I knew I was a flirt. I didn't try to be—I just was. 'The look' given to me by others reminded me to hide it every time it popped out. I didn't behave that way on purpose, and I seldom apologized for my forwardness—to do so would only draw more attention to it. I just hoped to be given the benefit of the doubt, that my words or actions had been misconstrued or misinterpreted and weren't simply bad manners or rudeness on my part.

"Would you kiss me again, a little lower this time?" I asked, trying to be demure and bold at the same time. "I'm not really married any more. Sarah said that Ian 'released me' from our wedding vows. Ian didn't tell me himself, but I know she wouldn't lie to me, especially about something like that."

Wallace brought my hands up to his mouth and gently brushed his lips across each knuckle. "Aye, Jody told me, too. I wouldn't have kissed you, even here," he kissed my forehead again, "if I thought you were married to another."

I saw the desire in his smile, and tipped my head back, shut my eyes, and waited for the kiss I knew was imminent. I was *very* ready.

"Therefore..." he began slowly.

I opened my eyes again, frustrated at the substitution of words for passion. I didn't protest verbally, but let my intense frown speak for me.

Wallace laughed unexpectedly, his serious preamble dissipated by his chuckles. "You look so cute when you do that—is that the phrase?"

"Yes, but no. That's the phrase, but I don't feel too cute. What were you going to say?"

"So, in your *other* time, would it be acceptable for a divorced woman to kiss another man? I mean, could she kiss her fiancé?"

My grin came back, broader and wider than ever. "Uh, huh," I cooed as I bit my bottom lip coyly, hoping his words were done. "Fiancé?" I squeaked as I realized what he had just asked.

"I wouldn't have it any other way." He bent forward and placed a soft, reserved kiss on my lips. He started to pull back—for propriety's sake, I'm sure—but I wasn't feeling very proper.

My hands slipped away from his, and reached around his neck, holding him in place to make sure he didn't try to speak again. The rest of the world had disappeared for me. I was only aware of his mouth on mine—warm, soft, and tasting of maple syrup.

His bashful kisses quickly became firmer and more insistent. My world of newfound passion expanded as I became aware of my womb, now contracted and hard, having tightened with the excitement. Wallace pulled me closer, undeterred by my swollen belly. He let me take the lead as our cravings and ardor increased. I opened my mouth slightly, and his followed. I gradually let my tongue slip into his, and he both relaxed and tensed. His lips softened, but I could feel a part of him firm against my belly. I snuggled closer still, rubbing against him in a way that I'm sure made him feel very good physically, but probably made his 18th century ethics quiver...or evaporate completely.

Well, the kissing, rubbing, and physical quivering continued. We were both reacting physiologically...and procreative-ly...if there even was such a term. I hungered for him, and tried to climb into or onto him—or maybe both—I don't know which. I grabbed his head and pulled it down to my chest, burying his face in my bosom, caressing the back of his head, and then pulled him up again for more intense kissing. I didn't want to stop whatever it was we were doing, because the effort of it was the joy.

We finally broke apart, both of us panting. We leaned back against my 'let it be' tree, side by side. I was unable to open my eyes, too satiated to move any voluntary muscles. I finally managed to sneak a quick peek at Wallace. His face was radiant, his eyelids shut, heavy with the same contentment I felt. I looked down at the front of him. He had a wet spot on the front of his bulging pants. I started giggling. "Well, I got mine, and it looks like you got yours, too. You are a true gentleman, dear—you let the lady finish first."

"Um…well…I was a bit overwhelmed, I guess. It's going to be hard to keep away from you for the next few months. Oh, I'm sorry. I didn't do this right. Evie," he asked as he got down on one knee, "would you be my wife?"

"I would be delighted," I answered and took his hand, offering to help him up.

He dusted off the dirt and leaf matter from his knee and asked, "Do you want to announce the engagement right away, or should we keep it quiet for a while, just for your honor's sake, and wait until the handfasting has expired…and when is that?"

"One year and one day from when Ian and I took the vows…about Halloween, Sanhaim, I think. But then again, I have amnesia and I'm not too sure about the dates." I lifted my eyebrows up and down as if hiding something. "How about we say that it'll be six weeks after the babies are born. Then," I grinned and looked him right in the eyes, "I'll be able to resume, or rather start, relations—if you know what I mean."

Wallace smirked, and blushed all the way down to his elbows, but didn't reply to the inference. He wasn't experienced, but if the rest of our marriage came as easy as the kissing…

"Well," I said to spare him further embarrassment, "I don't think we need to say anything unless someone makes a comment. I think even a blind man could see something's going on by the way we're both glowing right now. I seriously doubt it will fade in the next hour, day, week, or decade. I feel like I just can't get enough of you."

I reached up for a simple, closed-lipped, sweet kiss, and a comfort hug. I didn't think my womb could take any more of the tightening that came with his full-bodied smooches and caresses…at least for a while. "Do you think we've been missed?"

"Oh, I doubt it," Wallace answered with a sigh. "We should be getting back, though. Jody wants to head out on another scouting mission…er…hunting trip, and I need to find out if he's taking Julian or me. If he sees me too soon, though, I think he'll take *me* just to keep me away from you. Oh, and I want to stop by the well before we leave. I should spill some water down the front of me. I don't need to be showing off the results of our little dance in the woods."

"You are so clever. Come on, I'll help."

We held hands, swinging our arms like playful five-year-olds, as we walked back to the house. I grabbed a small pail, dipped it in the rain barrel, and said, "Oops," as I threw water at his crotch. "I'm sorry," I feigned, "I slipped. I think you'd better dry off or put on your other pants. Someone might see you and think you had an accident."

"Well, a happy 'accident' it was. I'll get the goats milked. The pants should be partially dry by then. Did you need anything else, ma'am? I am at your disposal," he mocked and gave a deep bow.

"Thank you, sir, but I have been served well already. I'll try to have dinner in an hour. Hopefully, everyone will be back by then. I'm surprised, but very glad, that they're not here yet."

****38 Rumor Had It...

The sun was getting low, and I knew I needed to get something started for dinner. We still had some ham left, and there were a few wintered-over cabbages in the garden. It wouldn't take much time or effort to whip together some of my sourdough corn bread, now Jody's favorite food. I could get the ham bits and cabbage cooking while the bread was baking. "Fast food, colonial-style," I said, "coming up."

I had just placed the Dutch oven, filled with the cornbread batter, into the fire when I heard the commotion. I walked outside and saw the horses in front of the barn. Jody and Wallace were taking off the saddles, and Sarah was coming toward me with her bag, wearing a ten-pound frown. Julian was dusting himself off, following right behind her, his head-down posture unable to hide his scowl, nearly identical to hers.

I joined Julian and Sarah in their somber walk back to the house. They both looked worried—so worried that I didn't even want to ask what was going on. I was sure I'd hear about it soon enough.

I acted the hostess, offering them both a drink. Sarah asked if I could make a crème liqueur for her. Julian wanted his whisky straight.

"Julian," she said, "I think you might want to try the Evie special. It will be easier on your stomach, and the effects are the same."

"All right then—make that two Evie specials, if you would, please?"

His face didn't look right to me. His expression was a mix-up of mad and sad, with a big dollop of frustration thrown in to add an extra wrinkle. Something was definitely wrong.

I put their drinks together in a hurry. I wasn't stingy with the whisky, either. "Do you think I should make one for Jody and Wallace, too?" I asked brightly as I handed them their drinks. I wasn't going to let their attitudes bring me down. I was still on my kissing and hugging high.

"Jody will want his whisky straight and, Julian, do you think Wallace will need a drink?"

"I don't know, Sarah, I really don't know. Oh, Lord, help us all."

"Okay, do I need to fix a drink for me? You two are starting to scare me."

"Go ahead and make two more drinks, Evie; one for you and one for

Wallace—just in case he wants one. If he doesn't drink his, I certainly will. Lord Almighty in a bucket! Why?"

I looked out the door. Wallace and Jody were talking. I could tell by their body language that it wasn't casual chitchat, nor was the subject comfortable. Wallace was facing the house. Even as far away as he was, his displeasure was evident. Jody was obviously giving him bad news.

Rather than join Sarah and Julian's 'frayed nerves and worry party,' I ignored them, and busied myself in the kitchen. I set the other two crème liqueurs on the table next to an empty glass and the bottle of whisky. I decided I'd pass on the one for me; Sarah could have it if she wanted. I'd never seen Wallace drink, so the second one would probably go to Julian. He still looked tense to me, and he had admitted that he liked the new concoction.

Somewhere in the back of my mind, I remembered something about when you don't know what else to do, eat. I knew I was getting hungry, and I was going to have supper no matter what was going on: I had babies to feed. I also knew that empty stomachs wouldn't make disclosure any easier. Jody and Wallace would be in when they were ready, but maybe the aroma of a hot meal wafting from the house would help soften the blow of revealing whatever was going on.

I rinsed and chopped the cabbage and threw it into the pot that already had the ham and water in it. The wooden plates were set out, along with a crock of butter, a jar of honey, and the spoons. When I smelled the cornbread, dinner would be ready. My part of the job was done.

I took a big gulp of goat's milk. Its comforting warmth filled my mouth, slipped down my throat, and tingled all the way down into my tummy, as if my cells were grabbing nutrition from it all along the way. I hadn't realized that it had been so long since I had eaten until the milk coated the lining of my empty stomach. Ahh, another wonderful sensation.

I wrapped my hands around the cup of milk. I was staring at, but not seeing, the earthenware mug, as I relived my earlier excitement with Wallace in the woods. I didn't want to look at Sarah or Julian. I could hear them pacing, performing their uncoordinated two-step shuffle in the small room. They were obviously too uncomfortable about whatever it was to sit still. Apparently, they were staying inside so Jody and Wallace could have some privacy.

I refused to worry about anything. Worry never solved a problem, took lots of energy, and half the time, the worry wasn't needed. Life's events seemed to have a way of sorting themselves out. Plan for—and be aware of—but don't worry about 'stuff.'

My olfactory baking alarm went off. I grabbed the hook, pulled out the Dutch oven, pushed off the lid, and saw the cornbread was perfect. The pot of cabbage and ham bits came out of the fire next. "Dinner in five minutes or less," I announced to Sarah and Julian. "If you don't eat with me, I'll dine alone. I'm hungry!"

I was trying to be light, but levity wasn't working in this household. Well, I wasn't going to let them drag me down, too. Hmph!

I took the ewer outside and filled it from the well. Jody and Wallace looked across the yard at me. There was no emotion on either of their faces.

"Do you realize that you both look like clocks without hands? Your faces are positively blank. Put a smile on 'em and come eat dinner. We have cornbread and honey butter, and ham bits and greens. I'd rather not dine alone, but will if nobody's gonna come join me." I didn't wait for an answer, just turned around and walked back to the house.

I poured water into my plastic water bottle, dished ham-flavored greens into my bowl, and set aside a small piece of the cornbread. I wanted more, but knew my stomach was squished to about half its normal size. I had to eat half as much, but twice as often.

I prayed loudly and boldly over my dinner to ensure everyone heard me, "Lord, thank You for this food, and please bless us all. And whatever is bothering everyone, well, Lord, I know You can handle it, so please do. In Jesus's name, Amen."

I started spreading butter on my bread, then paused. "Food's been blessed, come and get it while it's hot." I really didn't care if anybody joined me or not. It tasted great and was beginning to fill the empty spots the goat's milk had missed earlier.

"Do you like that, my little lion cubs?" I asked of my belly. "Greens will help you grow big and strong and smart." Then I added loudly, for the benefit of Sarah and Julian, "Smart enough to eat when there's food in front of you."

I hadn't noticed, but Jody and Wallace had come in. I was sure they heard the last part.

"Dinna let it be said that I passed on eatin' good food prepared by a fine lady," Jody announced as he sat down next to me.

Wallace sat down on the other side. "Dinner smells delicious. Wasn't this cabbage out in the garden just an hour or so ago?" he asked, smiling as if nothing had happened.

"It was. And if you care to have an aperitif, I made one for you, and there's one extra…just in case anyone wants it. Jody, I assume you still like your whisky naked?"

"If by naked, ye mean without the honey and cream, that's still true. *Slante*," he toasted.

"Health and happiness to us all," I said.

Julian and Sarah appeared at the table and joined the toast, "Health and happiness to us all," they chimed in.

"Now about this dinner, madam, you have set such a wonderful table with such meager resources; I salute you in your efforts. I am sure it tastes as good as it smells."

Julian had changed his outlook, as had Sarah. Whatever it was, it wasn't bothering them now. Jody and Wallace seemed to have had a change of heart, too.

"See," I said to myself, "worry not; want not." I was glad to have my family happy again, even if it was just when they were with me.

**39 The Rumor

Julian, Jody, and Sarah had just come back from town where the story was spreading like the itch of poison ivy. Jody would have to tell at least one of the two young lovers what he had heard, and he wasn't looking forward to the task.

"Watch where yer goin' there," Jody warned Sarah. "It appears the two of them have been busy, stringin' a rope across the yard fer Evie to hang her washin' on."

There was no way that the clothesline restricted access to the barn. Jody had just wanted to announce their arrival as subtly as possible. He needed to speak with Wallace and hoped that he would come out to greet him.

And so he did. Sarah and Julian very conveniently went into the house as Wallace came into the barn, alone.

"Rumor has it that Ian was seen," he said brusquely as he unsaddled his horse, glad that he had a chore to help dissipate the anger and frustration he felt. "A family came into town last week fer supplies. They were all excited, tellin' everyone about their adventure. It seems a white man dressed as an Indian had saved their child from drownin'. The young couple hadna even noticed that their three-year-old lass had wandered away. Then a strange-lookin' man came up quietly to the edge of their camp, carryin' their daughter. She was soaked to the bone, shakin'. He put her down and quickly disappeared into the woods. The lass told her parents that an angel with stars on his face reached into the water and saved her when she fell into the creek."

Jody paused to see his son's reaction to the story. There was none—he was emotionless—at least on the outside. This must be what Sarah sees me do, he thought.

He continued with the tale, wanting to get the unpleasant task over and done with quickly. "This happened in the late winter when the ice was thinnin', they said. That means that Ian—it had to be him—was as close as 10 miles from here less than two months ago. That's twice he's been in the area and never stopped in to check on his wif...," Jody stumbled, and then recovered, "to check on Evie."

Jody shifted his shoulders uncomfortably. "Julian and Sarah heard the rumor, too," he said softly. "They dinna want to tell Evie about it, and I'm nae too eager to let her know either, but I felt ye should ken, at least."

Wallace had remained stone-faced during the entire revelation. Jody needed to know, though, and asked, "Do ye think Evie should be told?"

Wallace said icily, "Let sleeping dogs lie." He stood tall, stuck out his chest, looked Jody in the eyes, and vowed, "I'll mind Evie from now on," then walked to the house, his claim to Evie now declared to his father, her brother-in-law.

Jody was terribly upset, of course, that twice his nephew hadn't stopped in to check on his pregnant wife, damn him. Even if he had 'released' her from marriage, she still carried his child, his children. Why would he be so cruel as to not even inquire about her welfare, their welfare? Jody wanted to set out right away, find him, and thrash him for being so heartless and irresponsible. But he knew that Ian couldn't be found if he didn't want to be. Ian knew the Indian ways and could live off the land indefinitely. At least he had come out of hiding to save a life. Ian also knew that his uncle wouldn't let any harm come to his kin: Evie was safe.

Ж Ж

A few days later, Wallace had asked to speak with Jody in private. He said it was personal, and that he couldn't talk to his other father—Julian—about it. The two of them went out to the barn, the oppressive silence choking Jody. He glanced at Wallace; he didn't look too comfortable either. He tried not to imagine what Wallace wanted to talk about that he couldn't speak of with Julian, his stepfather, the man who had reared him.

Wallace got right to the point. He asked Jody if he knew what it was like to yearn for a woman he couldn't have. Was there a way to ease the pain of it? He said he felt like he was literally being torn into small, jagged bits for wanting this woman.

Of course, Jody knew who he was talking about—there could be no other. He also knew what it was like to want a woman so badly that life didn't seem worth living without her. Phew! The lad comes to him as a son to a father for the first time—and what counseling does he seek?

Well, being a parent wasn't supposed to be easy. He told Wallace the truth. Yes, he knew what it was like to burn. He hadn't had Sarah with him for twenty years and had missed her horribly the whole time. He never stopped wanting her, thinking about her; he felt incomplete without her.

Now that he had her back in his life, he would risk everything to keep her, and had. If Wallace felt this way about his woman, he shouldn't hold back.

"Evie's worth it, from what I see of her," he said, eyeing Wallace knowingly. He sat down on the stool next to the very pregnant nanny goat, and shifted his position. "I dinna imagine it could be any other woman, ye ken. Life can be difficult—but it's always interesting—with a woman from another time."

Wallace nodded. He hadn't told anyone that he had overheard Evie explain to Julian that she and Sarah were from another time. He accepted it the same as he accepted gravity—just because he couldn't explain it, didn't mean it wasn't so.

Jody looked deep into Wallace's eyes, waiting for an answer, making sure that Wallace knew what he was talking about.

He hadn't tried to fool his father about what he knew or didn't know about Evie, but now Jody was asking for acknowledgment. He gave it, nodding again that he knew about her: go ahead with the rest.

Jody settled back and continued his counseling. "They dinna think the same way women do now. They're very independent, ye ken. But a fine woman, no matter what she looks like or what time she's from, is worth takin' and cherishin' as a wife."

Neither one of them brought up Ian or where he fit in the picture. Ian was a cad—the whole family knew it—and there wasn't a valid reason on earth for it. Wallace had already said he'd take care of Evie, and now had indirectly acknowledged he wanted to do so as her husband.

"So, ye want to wait until after the bairns are born to be marrit?" Jody asked, keeping his eyes on the nanny. He didn't want to make Wallace uncomfortable. That had to be the reason Wallace was 'burning,' but he didn't want to address *that* subject, now or ever.

"Aye. Whether Ian really 'un-married' her or not, she will truly be free from the handfasting when the babies are six-weeks-old." A red blush rose in Wallace's face. *And at six weeks, they could have relations.*

***40 Time of Confinement

Sarah was frustrated—again—unconsciously huffing and snorting as she paced; first inside the house, then out, trying to find challenging tasks to keep herself occupied. There wasn't much to do these days, and she was used to being busy. Besides the omnipresent housework, there was always sorting, drying, and grinding herbs; and taking care of people's health needs, either at 'the little table' in the kitchen, or calling on them in their homes.

It wasn't like that anymore. The house calls were nil, and no one was coming to visit. Many families in the area had left because of the fighting—or fear of it.

Sarah's anxious energy had already placed her ahead of schedule on performing the mundane, but necessary, chore of creating home-manufactured goods. Her woodland harvested and garden-grown pharmaceuticals were processed and stored, and our cupboards were filled to capacity with soap, candles, and dried foods. We had at least a two-month supply of our everyday consumables and no place to store more.

I insisted on helping with the household chores, despite my very advanced stage of pregnancy with 'at least two' babies in my belly. I did the prep chef work—washing, peeling, and dicing vegetables—and all the mending. I even took the initiative of modifying the men's britches, adding double knee patches before they wore out so they'd last longer between repairs. Wallace volunteered to take care of washing and hanging out the laundry, in addition to his daily tasks of seeing to the animals—feeding, milking, and cleaning out their stalls—and making sure the wood box stayed full. Because of my super-man's boundless energy and ambition, Sarah only had to cook the meals and tend to the garden.

The spring rains had come on time. The peas and potatoes were up, and she had put in the beans, squash, and corn last week. It was still too wet to hoe, but the sun was coming out every afternoon, drying off the leaves and making the air smell fresh and promising. Unfortunately, the stench and noise of cannon and small arms fire still came in occasionally, reminding us that all was not well in America right now.

Jody had taken Julian with him several days before on a 'hunting trip,' a reconnaissance mission to the south. Jody joked that he and Julian were going to get fresh meat for the table, but we all knew they were making sure our area wasn't in the path of militia movements of either side. With both Julian and Jody out riding, one could pose as captured and the other captor if needed, depending on who they ran into. They would still do their best to stay undetected, of course. It would be bad for all of us if either one of them were taken away as prisoner.

Jody would have taken Wallace but didn't want to leave Sarah and me alone. He knew Sarah could take care of her own needs, but she had to see to me, also. I still had a couple months to go until I was due to deliver, and the multiple-births aspect of my size was not only obvious, it was restrictive, the simplest of tasks now onerous. I would have been angry at Jody's insinuation that it took two adults to look after me, but I think he knew that Wallace wanted to be with me, and would be thinking, or worrying, about me the whole time and not paying attention to 'hunting' or scouting.

These were uncertain times with desperate and dangerous deserters from both sides roaming the countryside. Wallace was a skilled and well-trained warrior and was tall and powerfully built. He could easily take on several men at a time if Sarah and I were in danger. He would certainly be better at intimidating any potential attackers than the older and diminutive Julian. Jody was also more comfortable with Wallace safely ensconced at our little homestead rather than visible: he was prime material for conscription into whoever-found-him's service.

Ж Ж Ж

Both men had made it back from their trip without incident—Julian to his ranch with his partner, José, and Jody to us. Now it was Sarah's turn to travel. She had heard that the women in Miller's Flat had herbs, dyes, and assorted kitchen items they wanted to trade with other ladies in the area. I guessed it was sort of an annual colonial swap meet.

Women came from far away to do their own trading. Most of them brought their children along. The men and older sons either were at war or were staying near their homestead to keep it safe from marauders. Make no mistake about it, though—these women were well armed. They may not have had muskets or pistols, but they had their butchering knives and clubs. They had also spread the rumor that their menfolk were hiding in the woods, just waiting for someone to make the mistake of attacking their women and children. A good rumor was as good as an armed escort in these suspicious times.

Sarah only had to go a short distance to reach the MacPherson family farm. Ten women and children were traveling in their group. They were excited to have Sarah accompanying them, and Sarah was glad to spend time with them, too. Eleven-year-old Elizabeth was passionate about herbs and medicines; she practically tied herself to Sarah's elbow whenever they were in the same neighborhood, asking questions about tinctures, teas, and poultices—volunteering to help with any task, even the distasteful ones.

The womenfolk's trip to do their trading would have them back home in a week or so, depending on the weather and how much visiting they did. The mothers and children were happy to be away from their regular surroundings, their daily chores and routines. They had more than just homegrown and handmade goods to swap with each other—they also had recipes, patterns, and stories to share. No one was in a hurry to get back, so they didn't rush the experience, enjoying their vacation and the nearly perfect weather before weeding, reaping, and preserving took up all of their time.

Before she left, Sarah had put me on house arrest—bed rest, that is—and insisted that I use the ceramic indoor accommodations for all of the 'minor business,' and save the trips to the privy for the more malodorous bodily functions. I wasn't happy with the restriction, but knew it was in my best interest. Of course, it was better than it could have been. I had help, didn't have to eat my own cooking, and wasn't responsible for the usual, and always arduous, daily tasks.

Both Jody and Wallace remained behind to keep the Pomeroy place functioning, but it was Wallace who stayed close, taking care of me as the concerned and doting fiancé that he was. He had his chores to do, too, but he always found a reason to be near me.

He brought in the firewood and refilled the water vessels with a smile and a bright attitude that seemed to shout, 'Look what I got to do for you today!' Some of his small projects, like sharpening tools or mending harnesses, wound up being performed at the porch bench, a close and comfortable conversation-length away from me.

I was glad that he was coming to me. It was getting more and more difficult for me to move. I was huge—as bulky and awkward as a 200-pound chicken with three legs. Actually, I didn't have a scale, but it felt as if I were gaining a pound a day, and at least an inch or two of girth. It was an engineering wonder that my belly still stuck straight out—no sagging—and had stretched to such a humongous size without splitting or becoming marked.

The worst part about being so big was that it had become necessary to ask for help getting up from the pot. I could get onto it just fine but couldn't manage to get back up again. It was both humbling and humiliating, but Wallace was right there to attend to my needs, always polite and considerate.

Wallace felt sorry enough for me and my challenging situation that he did something about it. He took several planks from an old broken door and designed and constructed a commode chair with sturdy arms on it, just for me. He made sure it was well-sanded, too. I was most appreciative of the attention he paid to the finely polished surfaces. Splinters in the fanny would have been both uncomfortable and impossible for me to remove. It took him less than two days to cut out and finish the chair. He probably could have completed it sooner, but I had to keep calling him in from the barn to assist me with my necessary breaks.

He was such a gentleman about the interruptions, too. "May I be of assistance, madam?" he would ask.

I would have been mad at him, but he always said it with a deep tone of exaggerated diplomacy, sparkled with a grin. I couldn't help but return his smiles and say, "How kind of you, sir?" or "Oh, my knight in shining armor, here to rescue me again." He truly was a treasure.

Ж Ж Ж

Sarah came back from her trading vacation with lots of new seeds, herbs, and ideas. I was glad to have her home again, but not nearly as happy as Jody was. She really did complete him, and the other way around, too. Julian was with José at their ranch, and I had my Wallace. There was peace in the land; there hadn't been any battles, skirmishes, or even Tories in our area in ages. Our little clan had settled back to where it was meant to be. The rhythm of life and its comfort had returned.

As content and boring as life was, now that warm weather had arrived, there were no empty hours in our days. Sarah and the men had those never-ending summertime chores to do. I was willing to assist, but there wasn't much for me to do but take care of the babies within me.

I was no longer frustrated with my 'strongly suggested' bed rest limitation—I knew I was doing what was best for the babies. Sarah didn't need to tell me that an early delivery, and the lower birth weights that were sure to accompany it, would lessen the babies' chances for survival. So, rather than carp about my restrictive lifestyle, I ate my greens, drank lots of milk, napped, and grinned. I knew I wouldn't get much sleep after they were born, so reveled in the rest while I could.

When day was done and meals were finished, I began my job. I had taken on the role of entertainer, sharing stories and poems with my enthusiastic audience.

"'To talk of many things: Of shoes and ships and sealing wax, of cabbages and kings—and why the sea is boiling hot—And whether pigs have wings.'

"That was written by—or will be written by—Lewis Carroll in *Through the Looking-Glass,*" I said. "I sympathize with Alice, and I'll tell you more about her later, but I have to get the story straight in my head first. Hey, I wonder if that's how I got here. Nah; couldn't be, there weren't any mirrors around when I woke up."

Books and stories were not the hot topics, though. Sarah was interested in modern surgical techniques. I explained Lasik and laparoscopic surgeries, deep brain stimulation, and anything else I could remember. Modern drugs were a bit of a joke, I opined. I told her how many of the new medicines had side effects worse than the original problems they were meant to treat. She agreed with me that many 20th century ailments were unknown here in the 18th century. Parkinson's disease, with the whole body shaking, was unknown in this time. I told her that one theory was that it was caused by pollution from the Industrial Revolution.

Of course, the term industrial brought up the subject of new innovations in engineering, machinery, and tools. We spoke of bulldozers, airplanes, helicopters, oil pipelines and tankers, underground and underwater highways for cars powered by everything from fossil fuels to the sun. We never ran out of topics to discuss.

Wallace accepted as fact that the Americans were going to win the Revolutionary War. He was positively fascinated with Benjamin Franklin and Thomas Jefferson. He knew of them as contemporaries who were innovative in both civics and scientific inventions. He confided in me that he would like to meet them. Heck, I wanted to meet those two men myself!

"Post offices and a standardized system for delivering mail—zip codes?—how clever."

"Lightning is composed of electricity which man can also make with water or coal or oil? You can save it, contain it, and distribute it with wire, and use it to provide light as bright as day? And you turn it on and off with the push of a button?"

"How can sound and pictures travel through the air without being seen?"

"Writing without pen or paper on a computer? Explain computers again, please?"

I was happy to speak about the good things in the 21st century, and didn't elaborate on the problems of crime, broken families, drugs, and corruption. They had those same problems now, but not on the same magnitude as we had—or will have. Was the trade-off worth it? The more time I spent in this era, the more I felt that this was the right pace for life. What did we gain by traveling faster? We got a polluted planet and stressed out human beings to name two big consequences.

Both times had problems with alcohol. Booze has always been a part of human culture, its abuse an ever-present challenge. And there have always been deaths from wars and passion, but the suicide bombings that were almost a side note in modern daily newspapers were unknown before we became 'civilized.' Large-scale kidnappings and killings as a result of the oil and drug cartel wars—those were totally modern-day casualties. Eating disorders, heart disease, cancer, Alzheimer's, rampant diabetes, AIDS, and all those broken families due to drug addiction were horrible additions to the human race caused in part, I believed, by modernization and all the chemicals, corruption, and conveniences that came with it.

On the other hand, we didn't have slavery in modern America. Homosexuality would be accepted, grudgingly by some, but still recognized as a normal aspect of human life in the United States, and in many other parts of the world, too.

Why can't people just accept each other as what we are?—souls with a mammalian shell. We shouldn't have to live in fear. We're at the top of the food chain, but have to be wary of others who share our top rung. I figure it must be part of God's big plan to see how we cope with the situations in our own era. Then again, after all the pains, joys, and sorrows people go through while on earth, heaven seems a wonderful place to go when our physical bodies wear out.

The sun streaming through the window—and the fact that there was nothing else for me to do but philosophize more—brought me to the conclusion that now was a great time for a nap. I really was expending a lot of energy just growing babies.

I was always hungry, but my stomach was so crammed up into my chest, I could barely eat a cupful of food at a time. What I really wanted was a banana. I knew that was an impossible fruit to have, but I could dream, couldn't I? I grabbed a chunk of sourdough bread, rolled it up into a banana shape, and spread a little of Sarah's delicious peanut butter and honey mixture on it. It wasn't quite the same but was still good and would probably hold me through my nap.

I dreamt of deserts and snakes. I wasn't afraid of these snakes: they had no rattlers. I walked closer to the one sitting on a rock because he looked like he was talking to me. As I got to within a foot of him, he leaned his head back and blew on the whistle he had been holding with his tail. The ground beneath me suddenly opened up, and I dropped into a pit filled with water, so deep that I couldn't feel the bottom. I panicked, my arms flailing about, reaching and grasping the empty air.

My thrashing and moaning woke me with a start.

"Are ye okay, lass?" a male voice asked.

My heart was thumping in my throat, choking me—it was Ian!

"Ian!?" I yelped, shrugging away from the hand on my shoulder.

"No, I'm sorry, lass; it's only me, Jody. Sarah took Wallace outside fer a bit to help her bring in the surprises we brought back fer ye. I said I'd keep an eye on ye. Can I get ye anythin'?"

"How about a husband who won't ditch me?" I said under my breath, ill at ease with the phantom voice of Ian still echoing in my head. "Oh, I'm sorry," I said aloud, shaking my head to try and Etch A Sketch erase it. "I think it's just those raging hormones of pregnancy."

"Ach, I dinna ken anythin' about ragin' whore moans, but I do ken that a woman gits a bit out of sorts when she's carryin' a bairn, especially toward the end of her time. How far gone are ye now?"

"A little over eight months. I don't think I can get much bigger without bursting. Look," I said, and pulled down the waistband of my skirt, "I don't know if I'll ever get my belly button back again. I do want to carry the babies for as long as I can, though. They're much easier to take care of and feed while they're on the inside. I still have to find more cloth for diapers…er…clouts, too. Did you find anyone who had cloth for trade? Right now I'd swap one of my gold nuggets for a bolt of good cotton."

"Weel, ye can keep yer nugget. I happened to meet a man who was stopped on the road. He had too much packed onto his wagon, along with another problem. I asked if he needed help with his lame mule. He said he'd appreciate it. I dug a stone out of the mule's foot, trimmed her hooves as best I could with my dirk, then she was right as could be. He asked what I would be wantin' fer payment. I saw he had quite the load of dry goods. I thought this hank of pretty green cotton cloth would be right nice for a proper dress fer ye, and maybe some garments for the wee bairns."

"Oh, thank you!" I gushed. "I'd hug you if I could." I made a valiant try at getting near enough to him to reach around his neck, but my belly was in the way. Instead, he bent over and hugged me about the shoulders.

"Ye willna always be this big. I'll let ye owe me the hug. Julian has somethin' fer ye, too."

Julian walked in, holding a dead pheasant by the legs.

"Ooh, pretty feathers," I said. "Are they good to eat?"

Julian smiled and said, "Well, I don't know if the feathers are good to eat, but the meat is mighty tasty. I'll ask Wallace to pluck it. Sarah can manage to cook it, I'm sure."

"I'm starting to feel worthless," I said. "Isn't there something I can do?"

"You can eat well, stay healthy, and promise to tell us about Alice and the looking glass after supper," said Wallace as he walked in, hiding something behind his back. "And you might try showing me how to work these while the food is cooking."

Wallace held out his hands. He had carved two crochet hooks for me. I had told him what they looked like, and that they were made in different sizes. He presented me with one, very small—just the right size for baby booties—and the other one, larger, perfect for a shawl or blanket.

"And you can get started with these." Sarah handed me a small basket loaded with hanks of yarn in a wide range of colors. "When Jody told the man with the wagon what the cloth was for, he offered this for you with his blessings for a safe and healthy delivery for you and the babies."

"Oh, they're such beautiful colors," I said, then started crying unexpectedly. I sobbed and sniffed, then excused myself as I wiped my nose with my sleeve. "Raging hormones again, I guess."

"Sarah, when ye git a moment, would ye care to explain about ragin' whore moans to us menfolk so we can understand." Jody grinned at me, then Sarah, as he said it. He was doing his best to make me feel at ease. I was on an emotional roller coaster, for sure. "Yer doin' jest fine, lass, jest fine," he soothed.

Ж Ж Ж

Sarah put the freshly plucked and butter-basted pheasant into the clay pot, wiped her hands, and grabbed the bolt of fabric. "You'll need new clothes to wear after the babies are born. That skirt isn't going to last much longer," she said and poked her finger into a patch that had come loose, tickling my sweatpants-covered leg. "Those pants you wear are sure durable. What did you say they were made of?"

"Polar fleece; it's a manmade fabric that stays warm—even when wet—stretches, wears like iron, but feels oh, so soft. It also washes well.

326

I'm glad these had a drawstring waistband. Even though I have them slung beneath my belly now, I'll be able to wear them again as regular pants after I deliver. They're much warmer than a petticoat could ever be."

"Now can ye explain to me what a polar is?" Jody asked. "My sister had some Merino sheep that produced some verra soft wool, but yer fleece is maybe softer still, and its verra warm, ye say?"

"I guess you weren't around when I was explaining man-made fabrics, Jody. They actually make all sorts of cloth out of petroleum...that is, oil...products. I think they've already discovered oil in Pennsylvania, but the technology to make this is a couple hundred years away. I don't know how, but somehow they spin the oil real fine, and then weave it so the fabric has air pockets that can trap the body's heat. It's good for really cold weather, like they have at the North Pole, so they call it 'polar' fleece. I don't think we'll be able to get any more of this, though." I sighed at the loss; it would be so warm and comfortable next to a baby's skin.

I quickly snapped out of my funk, more for Jody's sake than my own. I didn't like making others uncomfortable, and here I was acting like a ninny at the loss of a chunk of fabric. "I'm sure I can help Sarah construct a dress and a shift," I said, "or maybe another skirt and a blouse. I'll see if I can put together something convenient to wear when nursing babies so I won't offend the folks around here—that is, if we ever see anyone else again. Sarah, we'd better get started on my new trousseau soon. I doubt I'll have time to sew if I'm taking care of twins."

She pulled out a length of the new cloth, hummed, and folded, as she designed my new apparel in her head, assessing me through one squinted eye to imagine me as a normal-sized woman.

Julian spoke up, "I'm sure the people will return soon. This is good farmland, and there's still time to get in some crops. They'll need food for the winter. From what Jody and I have heard the last few days, most of the fighting is to the south. I doubt there's anything here of strategic military value for the British."

"I guess some days it's good to be poor and isolated," I said. "Sarah, how long until that fowl becomes feast? Do we have time to start cutting out the skirt? Shoot, maybe we should make the babies' gowns first."

"Oh, I'd say we have an hour or so until dinner. Are you feeling up to the task? You look a little peaked."

"I'm okay. I've just had a horrible backache all day. I guess the pain is showing on my face. There's no way I can get comfortable anymore. Now, if we just had a big, warm swimming pool, I could float in it, and get the load off my legs and back." I got up to walk around the room, hoping to work out some of the stiffness in my joints.

"Oh, no! Oh, no, no, no! Sarah, I think I just started to make my own swimming pool. I think my water broke. I didn't feel any gushing, but it's dribbling down my legs. Oh, sorry, guys—that's a bit graphic… But, hey, we're going to have babies! Yahoo!"

Sarah put down the bolt of fabric and walked over to the chaise where I had been sitting. Gross—she stuck her finger in the wet spot and sniffed it. "Sar-rah!" I shouted.

"Oh, don't worry, I was just checking. I think you're right; your water broke. That wet spot isn't urine. You men may want to make up some beds in the barn. It's likely to get noisy in here before we're done."

"Aye, I remember the skellockin' my sister Elly let out when she was birthin' her bairns. I guess we'd better find a bottle of whisky, too. It willna help the women, but it might quieten some of the noise comin' from the house." Jody gathered up the spare blankets and grabbed the rest of the loaf of bread from my afternoon snack, gathering goodies for his self-imposed banishment to the barn.

"Uh, hello, guys?" I said and waved my hand, lightheartedly looking for attention. "I'd really appreciate it if you stayed around, at least until it *does* get noisy. I don't plan on yelling, and I'd really like your company."

Jody snorted. "Weel, a woman never does plan on yowlin', but when the time comes, the rarin' isna from the menfolk nor the midwife."

He sighed and shook his head in resignation at the sight of my frown, changed emotional gears from sassy to sweet, and nodded, "But we'll stay in here with ye a bit, if it makes ye more comfortable."

"Thank you; I'd really like the distraction. From what I've heard—or read, or whatever—about labor, the first several hours are uncomfortable, but tolerable. It's the last hour that's rough. So, I'll save my breath and make sure to give you fair warning when I plan on getting loud. Lord knows, I wouldn't want you to suffer from sore ears," I said dramatically, the back of my hand on my forehead to complete my theatrics.

I sat back down but was too antsy to stay still. I got up again, and then realized how small the room really was, even more so with everyone inside. "Julian, why don't you and Jody stay in here and play chess. And Wallace, would you take me for a short walk *al fresco*? Maybe it'll make the time go by faster. I think it speeds up the delivery, too. Is that okay, Sarah?"

"You can walk just until you're tired, but make sure you hold on to

Wallace the whole time. No more than half an hour, and then I want you back in here so I can check you. Before you go, though," Sarah ripped off a 3-yard-length from my newly gifted bolt of fabric, "make yourself a sarong. I don't want you wearing those pants anymore."

I went behind the privacy screen, dropped my drawers, wrapped the Calcutta 'calico' cotton fabric—green, interspersed with rusty-nail red and high-noon blue flowers—around my middle, and secured it by tucking it under my very heavy breasts. I emerged with a big smile, "Dorothy Lamour never looked so great."

"I'll agree with that," said Sarah, "and Bob Hope and Bing Crosby never were as prone to trouble and excitement as Jody, Julian, and Wallace are."

"I don't know who Bob Hope and Bert Crosby are," said Jody, "but I dinna think ye need to look farther than to the end of yer own nose to see someone who is as attractive to trouble and excitement as ye are."

We all laughed, then settled into our zones—Sarah to the kitchen fire, Julian and Jody to the chessboard, and Wallace and I to the door. I turned back before we went out and said, "I don't know what's going to happen in the next twenty-four hours, everyone, but I want you to know that you are the best family anyone could ever ask for. I love you all, and thank you for all you've done for me."

I hurried out the door, pulling on Wallace's arm to get us away before my tears started to flow. I stopped at the bottom of the steps, sniffed, wiped my face, and turned toward him. "I'm a little scared; well, maybe a lot scared. I know childbirth is a dangerous time for a woman in any era..." Insecurity was overwhelming me, but I had to get this out. I took in three quick gulps of air, trying to avert a full breakdown. "So would you be the godfather to at least one of the babies if something happens to me?"

Wallace straightened up in shock. He was stunned, but regained his composure just as quickly as he had dropped it. "Evie, I would be most honored to be the godfather of any or all the children. I hope you know, though, that I don't ever want to leave you, or the babies. If only we could be married right now..."

He grimaced, a fleeting squint of anger—probably at Ian—shadowed his face, and then disappeared. "I know the importance of fathers, and godfathers, in a child's life. It would take more than this war, or any war, to tear me away from my new family. You honor me with your request, but I *know* you'll come through this delivery fine. You're the strongest, bravest, and sweetest woman I've ever met...or ever heard of." He bent down and kissed me gently on the mouth. My lips were an easy target, too—I tilted my head up to accept his kiss before he bent down to give it.

My arm went back into the crook of his elbow and we walked, both of us at peace, crisscrossing the yard like a giant word-search puzzle. There was just enough of a breeze to keep the mosquitoes at bay. I didn't talk much—I was breathless from being so big—and was also out of shape. In the last three weeks, I had seldom walked more than thirty steps at a time. Our pace was slow, but comfortable, my earlier worries about dying in childbirth forgotten. I knew the Lord had it all under control, right down to providing me with a moral support coach, Wallace.

We must have been outside for forty-five minutes when Sarah came looking for us. "I told you no more than half an hour. Come back inside and let me check you."

When we came in, Julian and Jody were still playing chess. I never liked the game—too much tension for me—but I could tell something was going to happen soon. Julian was holding his drink to his lips to hide his excitement. I think Jody was getting ready to fall into a trap. If Jody was aware of Julian holding his breath, he didn't show it.

"Damn, Julian, ye got me again," said Jody, as he knocked over his own king. "Should we try cards next? I might be able to best ye at that."

"Evie, come over here. I've set up a little labor and delivery area for you." Sarah had moved the privacy screen and chaise so they were near the fireplace, and arranged the two tables on the other side of it. The fire would provide better light than candles for a while, and the screened-in aspect would create a warm and toasty area to greet the newborns. The two little greenstick baskets I had crafted months ago were nearby, getting pre-warmed. The baby nests were padded with well-worn, but clean rags, too small to be used as anything other than batting. Wee blue and red quilts rested atop each, pieced from the linings and softer parts of Wallace and Julian's former military jackets.

Sarah had the kitchen table loaded with a basin and ewer of water, a stack of clean rags, and my crank-operated dynamo lantern. Her little medical kit and a bottle of medicinal alcohol were set out on the side table adjoining it. She had torn more fabric lengths from the bolt of green print cloth, rinsed out the residual inks and dyes, and had them hanging out to dry on her simple little twig and twine drying rack. These were apparently the first batch of diapers—or clouts as she called them. I'd have to wrap the babies in swaddling cloths for the first few days until we could make some gowns for them, but that had been working for newborns since mothers started using homespun instead of animal furs.

"Men, I don't want you over here unless I call you," Sarah said, using her loud 'I'm-the-person-in-charge' tone, then lowered her voice, speaking only to me. "Evie, scoot your bottom down here and bring up your knees. I need to see if you're dilated."

Sarah grabbed the lantern, wound it up a few times, and switched it on. She held it between my knees and peered up to inspect my privates.

"Are you having any pains yet?" she asked, her head bent in concentration.

"I have a horrible backache. It feels like cramps, only much worse. It comes and goes, but it's tolerable. I'm still having those contractions in front, too, but they're much stronger than they've been in the last month."

Sarah put her hand on my belly. "When you have your next contraction, I'm going to put my finger inside your cervix and see if it's dilated and effaced."

"Sure, go for it," I said to her then raised my voice. "Hey, Jody, is this when I'm supposed to start yelling?"

"Ye can yell whenever ye want, but when ye do, we're headin' fer the barn, and takin' the whisky with us." Sarah and the men all laughed at Jody's remark—and it wasn't a nervous laugh either, I was glad to note.

"I'll make you a deal then—you can't drink whisky until I scream. Then you can keep drinking until the babies are here, okay?"

"I think we can make that sacrifice, don't you, men?" Julian said. "All right, we'll just sit here playing cards without the benefit of drink while you do your job. But hurry, will you?"

Julian's time spent with this family and with José had loosened up his staid British demeanor. He was evolving into a laid-back, happy American, a wonderful transformation that I was happy to be partly responsible for.

"Jody, you can knit some booties for the babies now that we have yarn," I called out from behind the screen. "Ouch! Sarah, what are you doing? And no, that is not yelling, guys!"

"I had to wait for a contraction before I could check for dilation. You're doing fine, but I don't want you out walking more than twenty minutes at a time." She pulled my sarong back down, and stood up. "Men, can I get an escort for the lady in waiting."

"My turn," said Julian. "I could use some fresh air."

***41 Delivery

June 21, 1781

Julian was almost smiling as we left the other members of our 'unrelated-by-blood-but-as-close-as-possible-without-wearing-the-same-clothes' family. It wasn't a full grin of glee, nor the stifled smirk at a silly joke that he sported. No, I glanced over and realized what it was. He was staring at the sky, one side of his full bottom lip pulled back into the near-perfect smile a person wears when contented with life. I flashed on the first time I had ever seen him: an angry, bound and gagged British officer, kidnapped and contained in a dirty gunnysack. Who would have thought we'd be here, like this, less than six months later?

We walked together, arm in arm, in a comfortable silence. Well, he was walking, and I was waddling. "I'll be glad when this is over," I said. "At least I won't be the size of an elephant and can tie my shoes again."

"Have you ever seen an elephant?" Julian asked, wide-eyed at the possibility. "I've read about them but have never met anyone who has actually seen one."

"Oh, yes, we had them in zoos; everything from exotic insects to elephants, and even killer whales were held in huge artificial tanks...er...ponds. Visitors could see animals from all over the world—polar bears, camels, anacondas, ostriches. I don't remember what town I was in, or how old I was, but I'm positive I've seen elephants, and all of those other animals. They impressed me on a deep emotional level, I guess. Most big towns had some sort of zoo. I think you call them zoological gardens. The groundskeepers had to grow special plants to feed some of the animals: bamboo for pandas from China, and eucalyptus for koala bears from Australia."

"I've seen the zoological gardens in Paris, but they didn't have the animals you named when I was there. I've never heard of most of them. And, is Australia the same as *Terra Australis,* the land Captain James Cook explored recently?"

I stumbled, and Julian caught me before I completely lost my balance. Ever the gentleman, he didn't make me feel like the klutz I knew I had become.

"Perhaps we can talk about this later, when you're feeling better," he said. "You seem to being getting a bit breathless. I believe we should return you to your bed."

"Thanks, I think you're right." I realized that I was practically panting and let him guide me toward the house.

"Oh, no—hold on a sec." A major contraction was having its way with me. It took all of my concentration to keep from yelping—and there was no way I could walk through it. Two more of those paralyzing pauses hit me before we got inside. My labor had increased to a more intense level, so it was desert tortoise pace back to the house for us.

"Sarah, I think the lady is in need of your attention," Julian announced as we walked through the door. He turned to me and said with mock formality, "Madam, I thank you for accompanying me on a stroll. Our conversation was, as always, most engaging. I look forward to hearing more about those strange and unusual animals you have seen."

"All right, sweet sister, it's time to check you again," Sarah said, her hand reaching out for mine.

"Ooh, wait," I gasped and hunched over, immediately breathing in and out with a slow, even pattern. It wasn't helping much. This contraction was almost unbearable, but I wasn't going to scream, no matter how much it hurt. I started huffing and puffing next, but it kept getting worse. I resorted to panting to avoid pure panic. The pain abated and finally ended. I exhaled in relief, then scurried like a fat basset hound with a soup bone to my labor bed before the next one hit.

"Oh, it's like that, is it?" Sarah asked. "You're progressing rather quickly. Have you timed your contractions?"

"If you mean how long between the start of one to the start of another, they're about three minutes apart. I don't know how long the contractions themselves are. I do know that I can't talk or walk through them, though."

Sarah helped me settle in as I arranged my makeshift sarong around me, loosening the fabric so I could cover or expose myself, depending on who was looking in on me: her or one of the men. I inched myself upright with my elbows—I had lost all abdominal strength two months ago—and pulled my knees up in anticipation of the next examination.

I sucked in a deep breath and attempted to ignore the world around me, hoping I could create oblivion, to block all thoughts and sensations, especially the pain that was imminent with her poking around. Meditating on nothingness failed. Over and over, like a needle stuck in a groove on an old vinyl record, I kept wondering how and why I was here?

How and why was I here?

How and why was I here?

What a heck of a time to get philosophical, woman, I thought. Considering that I couldn't do much except breathe and think, I guessed it was as good a time as any to reflect on the question of the centuries that I had been ignoring for nearly eight months: how and why was I here?

I tried not to care about Ian. We hadn't been together very long before he left me. I had been here in this time longer without him than with him. I had Sarah and the men to keep me company, and I knew they were all fond of me. I loved Wallace dearly, and he was going to be my husband and the father to these babies soon, but dang it, I wanted the biological father here, too!

After I punched him in the face—and oh, how I wanted to do that—I might be big-hearted enough to let him share in the joy of the birth of my babies. I couldn't find myself generous enough to consider them his babies, or even our babies. And if he were here, he could darned well bear some of the pain, too. I wanted to grab his bony hand during a contraction and squeeze it until it turned blue.

He knew I was pregnant when he dumped me on his aunt and uncle. I wasn't paying attention to what was happening with my body, but he had seen all the symptoms before. He didn't tell me much about his first wife, but I knew she hadn't been able to carry his children to term. That had to be why he left—he couldn't stand the thought of losing another child. But this was me and my body; he couldn't have known how I would have handled a pregnancy.

"Pfffftt—Men."

"Are you okay?" asked Sarah.

"Oh, just thinking about men," I said casually. I changed my attitude, lowered my voice, and asked, "Do you think Ian abandoned me because he thought that this wasn't his child? Hmph—that couldn't be—he knew better. Maybe because I was pregnant, he figured that another one of his children was going to die, and he left because he couldn't stand to be around when, not if, it happened?"

Sarah and I had discussed Ian leaving quite a while back, but for some stupid reason, I couldn't stop thinking about him. I hadn't thought about him this much in the last three months.

"Uh, I don't know, that's possible...no probable...no, hell, how would I know? He's just being a jerk." Sarah frowned at me, exasperated. I watched as the wide eyes of realization overtook her scowl, "Oh, now I understand what you meant when you said, *men*."

We both knew that our men could hear us, but neither one of us cared. I made a gesture, elbow bent and fist to mouth with neck tipped back—like I was drinking whisky—and grinned broadly. I knew they wanted to drink, but they had given their word that they wouldn't if I didn't holler. I had only had the urge to scream once, and had stifled that one, along with the groans that had tried to escape. Their pain wasn't nearly as bad as mine was, but my misery loved their company.

I heard the chairs scoot across the floor; the men were going outside. If the ladies' conversation was heading toward male bashing, they didn't want to be around, and I didn't blame them. I smelled the brusqueness of Julian's cigar. He was smoking a bit prematurely; cigar smoking was supposed to come after the baby was born.

Sarah put her hand on my belly. I could see the strong, leathery, but delicate hand rise up with the contraction before I could feel it. I started my slow, steady breathing right away. If I started the routine too late, I felt more than uncomfortable—I felt helpless.

I experienced a flash memory. My uncontrolled labor pains reminded me of falling down that hill eight—or was it nine?—months ago. When that event occurred, I had nothing to grab onto, no way to steady myself, and had known an intense pain was imminent because I hadn't paid attention to what I was doing. Strange, this was the first clear memory of that day. I was certain more pain was coming with this situation, too, but I was going to use all the help offered me from my new family.

Sarah moved the light toward the foot of the chaise and pushed up my sarong. She looked right at me, then closed her eyes in concentration as she slipped her hand inside of me.

"Oh, poop," I grunted. The pain of her invasive examination was much worse than the cramping of a normal contraction. I giggled at my non-cursing expletive, and then tried to get back into my pain-reducing breathing regimen. I panted, huffed, and puffed. After what seemed like forever, I was finally back to the normal, tolerable discomfort level of a bloated multi-birth, late-stage pregnancy, and able to speak again.

"Phew! That was a big one. Having you poke around there doesn't help, either."

"That's true, but I have to see how you're coming along. I would say you're at seven centimeters and totally effaced. One of the babies is down in the birth canal, so it won't be too long. Hmmm, something smells good. Jesus! The dinner!"

Sarah rushed to the fireplace, grabbed a kitchen cloth to use as a

335

potholder, and pulled out the clay pot with the pheasant in it. She started to put it down on the kitchen table, but there was no room: it was loaded with her medicine box and supplies for the delivery. She turned to the small table, but it had the basin and ewer on it. She mumbled and snorted, her hands burning through the thin damp cloth that held the searing clay pot, looking for an empty spot to set it down. She two-stepped about the small area, did a quick pirouette, and clumsily dropped it four inches onto the hearth.

"Aaaagggghhhh!" Sarah hadn't said one discernible word as she danced her hot-pot shuffle, but made up for it with her one syllable shriek once it was out of her hands.

Jody ran in from outside, knocking Wallace out of the way in the process, his eyes only for his wife. "What happened? Jesus, Sarah, talk to me," he demanded, his voice breaking with fear.

Sarah was now sitting on her haunches, rocking back and forth, glassy-eyed, her hands cradled at her chest, breathing hard with an occasional mumbled curse word escaping as she tried to recover from her grasp of the vessel that was hot as hell in a forest fire.

"She burned her hands on the clay pot. Sarah, put your hands over the basin, and Jody, pour some cold water over them," I said. Suddenly, I was the medic in charge. "Sarah, keep them wet. Cold water is the best thing for a burn. Jody, if that water isn't cold, get some more. The colder the better and leave them in there for at least ten minutes. Uh, oh...here's another one..."

Another contraction hit, and I was huffing and puffing, almost from the start. I blanked out everyone's presence to concentrate on inhaling and exhaling. As soon as it was over, I called to Wallace. "I need your help. I want you to put your hand on my belly. When you feel it start to get hard with a contraction, I want you to squeeze my hand. In the meantime, I am going to try and sleep."

"Uh, all right. Can you do that?"

"If I'm asleep, it means I'm totally relaxed, and that eases the pains. So I'm going to sleep between the contractions. When you squeeze my hand to let me know one's coming, I'll wake up enough to do the breathing. Hopefully I can stay on top of them but won't have to be fully awake to do it. I don't know how I know about this, but I believe it's the best way to go. Sleeping's an easy way to make the time go faster, too."

"Would you like a drink of water first?" he asked.

"Thanks, I could use one." With the mention of water, I realized that my voice was hoarse, and my mouth dry, from all the deep breathing. I took a small sip. I didn't want to have to use the chamber pot again. As it was, I was wet from the amniotic fluid constantly dribbling out. I couldn't seem to keep a cloth between my legs to staunch the flow and didn't want to ask one of the men to help diaper me. Childbirthing was inconvenient in so many ways.

I didn't know how badly Sarah's hands were burned—it would probably be a while before she would be able to use them—but I wasn't worried. I had an overwhelming sense of calm that must have been supernatural. Whatever it was, I embraced it. I knew everything was going to be fine.

I was asleep before I knew it and had no idea how long it had been when I awoke in a surreal fog. Wallace was next to me, faithfully squeezing my hand so I—we—could handle the contractions together. Then, all of a sudden, I was wide-awake. Life was crystal clear. It was as if bright lights had been brought into the room. It was I who was radiant, though. I knew it was time; the adrenaline had kicked in.

Julian, Jody, and Sarah were sound asleep, sitting up. Julian was in the straight-back chair, his head nearly resting on his right shoulder in what looked to be an incredibly uncomfortable angle for his neck. Jody had his arm wrapped around Sarah, enveloping her protectively as they leaned as one against the cool side of the hearth. She wore the unmistakable frown of pain on her face. Her hands, still wrapped in damp cloths, rested in her lap.

Wallace was half-asleep, but still doing his part in the laboring process. His left hand was on my belly, and when my womb contracted, his right hand would squeeze mine. I shifted my body, and he awoke all the way. "Is there something I can get for you?" he asked, suddenly bright-eyed. His adrenaline had kicked in, too.

Just then, another contraction came. It caught both of us off guard. I was floundering in desperation. I started to hyperventilate, sucking in air rapidly to keep from screaming. Two hours past forever, or so it seemed, the pain was finally over.

"Wallace, I want you to grab one foot in each hand." He wrapped his large hands around them. "Use your thumb to press in under my soles, yes, right there. Now back off, but when the next contraction comes, press there."

For some reason, I knew about the pressure points on feet for childbirth pains. I wondered, was I a nurse? I was knowledgeable about many medical procedures and pharmaceuticals, but I had told Sarah that what I knew was common knowledge in my time.

I felt Wallace squeeze my hand, and then reach for my feet, pressing his thumbs to the sweet spots. Another contraction hit; they were practically on top of each other now. When the last one was over, a big smile lit up my face. "Sarah, it's showtime!" I called out in a lilting tone.

Sarah tried to stand, then halted, letting Jody get up first so he could help her. She grimaced as she walked uncertainly toward me, her hands held close to her chest. "Evie, I'm sorry, but I think I'm going to have to let the men take over for me. Would that be okay?"

I started to answer, but Wallace squeezed my hand, and came around to my feet to press those magical points that took away nearly half of the labor pang. I put up one finger to Sarah as in, "wait a minute." After the contraction was over, I gave my final cleansing breath and said, "You know that there's no modesty in a maternity ward. Jody has assisted in many a birth with horses and other critters—the mechanics are all about the same so... Uh, oh; here comes another one."

Wallace had squeezed my hand as I was speaking. He seemed to be more in tune with my body than I was. As soon as the contraction was over, I said, "Sarah, can I use the chamber pot? I feel like I have to go number two."

"Number two?" asked Jody as he leaned over Sarah's shoulder to see what was going on.

"Never mind, Jody. Evie, your body wants to push the baby out. That's what you're feeling. Scoot up and get ready. Jody, you'll have to wash your hands and check inside her to see if she's fully dilated. She's supposed to be at ten centimeters, that's four inches. If she pushes too soon, well, let's just say we don't want that to happen. Here, Julian, step over here and hold the light. Wallace, keep doing what you're doing. And everybody pray."

Jody looked down at his hands. "I dinna ken if I can do this, Sarah. My hands are verra big and dinna move as they should. The lass is a lot smaller than a mare, too. Are ye sure it wouldna be better fer Julian to check her and have me hold the lamp? He has the small hands."

"Now wait a minute. I didn't sign on to be a midwife. I know nothing about such things," Julian argued.

"Papa, wash your hands, and come over here. No one said you signed on for this, but it's what family does for one another. Maybe if someone had helped my mother, she'd still be alive today. My hands are too big, too, or I'd be offering. Hold on, Evie. I know this is distracting. I'm sure Papa is just being bashful." Wallace was multitasking: performing foot rubs, comforting me, and chastising Julian, all at the same time.

"Oh, all right," said Julian. His body shivered from head to foot in an involuntary shudder. "Please, excuse my reluctance. I really am unsure about all of this."

I looked up and saw that Jody was holding onto Sarah's arm, literally holding her back. Evidently, she had wanted to say something about Julian's unwillingness, but Wallace had stood up for me, and now nothing else needed to be said.

The contractions were practically on top of each other. "Julian," I squeaked, "I'd really appreciate a hand, yours if you please. Just pretend I'm a mare...ohhh...shit!"

Julian stuck his hands over the basin, and Jody splashed them with the alcohol wash. "I really wish you had started screaming earlier. It would be easier if I had a fair amount of whisky in me before doing this....task." His little preamble about his chore started stern but ended with a smile. "Do I need some oil, Sarah? I'd hate to hurt the lady."

"I'm past hurting," I snarled, "Just reach up in there, and make sure it's safe to push, oh no, not again..."

I stopped talking and held my breath. Julian stuck his hands out again, and Jody poured oil over them. "This should help grease the way so the bairn can slip through easier. Now, ye just put yer oiled finger around the..."

"Evie, keep breathing," ordered Sarah. "When you hold your breath, you're pushing. Julian, is she up to ten centimeters?"

"Uh, I think so, but there's a head down there. Jody, bring the light."

Jody held the lantern and leaned over to see. Sarah and Julian bent over at the same time, and all three clunked heads. Assorted exclamations and curses ensued, but quickly evaporated as the two men let Sarah in to see. "She's ready, Julian. Keep oiling and stretching. Rips are hard to mend, and I can't perform an episiotomy with these hands."

"She's a mare, Julian, a small, prize mare, just a little while longer." Julian mumbled his own little mantra to himself, but it was audible to everyone because of the very close quarters.

I sat up and started pushing. Wallace had my back and was supporting my shoulders, Jody was helping me hold onto my knees, and Sarah was standing over Julian's shoulder, poised like an umpire behind a catcher at a baseball game. I couldn't see Wallace or Julian, but Jody was beaming.

This wasn't his child coming into the world, but he or she was his kin. Sarah had the detached emotion of a bricklayer. She was 100% clinical, but she had to be. She was performing obstetrics via verbal instructions to an untrained—and very uptight—man.

I pushed again, and Julian hollered, "Sarah, is the face supposed to be pointed down?"

"Yes, now ease the shoulders out one at a time."

Sarah talked Julian through pulling my first child into the world. I could hear the baby screaming, which meant he was hale and had good lungs. "It's a boy," she announced.

Jody took the baby and started cleaning him up, wiping off the vernix. "Hey, everybody, I think he's gonna have red hair like his great-uncle. I've wiped off the blood and white stuff, but the copper fuzz is stayin'. Ye did good lass, he's wee, but a hearty one."

I leaned back for a rest. "That's uncle or grandfather, Jody," I corrected, "and there's another cub in the lion's den, still waiting to get out," I puffed. "It ain't over yet."

A dozen more contractions and at least three dozen more pushes, and I still hadn't produced another baby. I collapsed back into Wallace's arms, too worn out from pushing to sit upright by myself, much less to open my eyes. "Can you see his head yet, Julian?" I gasped.

Julian grimaced as he took on the distasteful part of his midwife task: he bent down and looked up between my legs for the baby's head. "No, no head, but I think he's shaking his fist at me. Sarah, is this normal?" he asked.

Sarah bent down to look. Sure enough, a little hand was grasping at the air. She took a deep breath before speaking. She was more than just concerned about this new development. "Evie, lie back and relax every muscle in your body. Do *not* push. We have to get this baby's hand back in, and then see if we can move him around so his head will come out first."

I didn't hear anything else she said after that.

I went totally limp and let my essence slip into a delicate bubble of solitude. Any stress or movement would shatter it—and the little person inside my womb who depended on me. No sound, pain, thought, or emotion was allowed. All I was aware of was my slow, even, shallow breathing.

Sarah directed Julian's movements. If he had any protests about his duties, he didn't voice them now. His eyes, shut tight, concentrated on the

340

shapes of the baby's body parts that he was feeling inside the womb. The baby's hand that had pushed through the cervical opening, was safely back inside. Julian followed the hand up the arm to the shoulder. From there he maneuvered the small infant's body, so the head was down toward the cervix. He felt the umbilical cord wrapped around the babe's neck.

"Hold on, everyone," he said, but was really directing his message to Sarah. She had been instructing him, but he hadn't been listening; he was concentrating on what he was doing. He stuck a finger under the cord and pulled it over the infant's head. He knew about cord strangulation, and it wasn't going to happen when he was at the helm!

Julian pulled out his hand, grabbed a cloth, wiped himself off, and said, "The baby's in position." Then, in a very good imitation of Jody, intoned, "We're ready when ye are, 'Darrrlin'."

Everyone looked at Evie. She was totally immobile, and her face was blank. She would have looked dead except for the slight rise and fall of her belly and bosom. Wallace lifted her arm—it was totally slack. Sarah's eyes were like saucers. Jody hollered at her, "Sarah, do somethin'. What's wrong with her?"

"Hell, if I know," she said, totally stunned.

Wallace took matters into his own hands, or rather fingers. He pinched Evie's inside upper arm and put his face right into hers. "Wake up," he yelled.

The combination of the two intercessions made me bolt upright. I didn't know if I had hypnotized myself or was half-dead, but either way, I was back. "Ouch, that hurt," I said. "What's going on?"

"Ye jest scarrit the piss out of us, that's all," said Jody. "Are ye ready? Ye got another bairn in there who wants to come out."

Right then, a contraction hit. I didn't know if I had been having them while I was 'out' or not, but this one definitely got my attention. Wallace was at my back and Jody at my knees as soon as I gasped at the onset of pain. Sarah and Julian stayed at their positions at the foot of the chaise. "I think we have another red head," declared Julian.

It only took two pushes to get my second son into the world. My first son had widened the path to the outside for him, I suppose. I lay back and relaxed as Julian took care of the placenta. Jody had handed Wallace the first baby and was cleaning up number two. "Yer right, Julian, we have another red heided boy. This one is a bit smaller than the first, but they're both bonnie-sized fer havin' shared the same womb."

"There's only one placenta. Sarah, does that mean they're identical twins?" asked Julian.

"Yes, most definitely. Congratulations, Evie. Did you know that Ian's mother had twins? They were fraternal, though. There's a big difference. You had one egg fertilized, and it split into two embryos. These two guys will look alike, but I assure you, they'll be two different persons."

"It's a good thing I have two boobs then. Is either one of them ready to nurse?" I asked.

Jody walked over with number two. "It looks like this one is hungry. The first one has already fallen asleep."

I was adjusting my smock down so I could nurse, when a horrible feeling came over me. I held up my hand, "Not yet," I groaned. I rolled over onto my side, extremely nauseous. "Wallace, pan," I yelped.

Wallace reached for the basin with one hand and passed off the firstborn to Julian with the other. He got to me just in time. I gagged and spit up slimy green bile. "Oh, this is not good," I moaned, and reached up to wipe my mouth with the back of my hand.

Wallace grabbed a fresh cloth and performed the clean-up for me. "Here, rinse," he said, a cup of water in his hand.

I obeyed, then asked, "Help me stand up, would you, please?"

Wallace put his arm around my much narrower middle and helped me take a few steps.

"Are you sure you should be doing that?" asked Julian.

"She probably has gas," said Sarah. "Walking will help relieve the pressure."

Sarah, Jody, and Julian gathered around the baby boys as we walked. Number two had calmed down without being fed, and was nuzzled into Jody's shoulder, his lips pursed, content to just make little sucking motions.

Wallace brought me back to the chaise. A sudden contraction hit without warning, and I bent over, helpless, clutching my middle.

"Chamber pot!" I yelped. I yanked off my birth fluid-soaked sarong and squatted over the pot. I didn't mind if Wallace or anyone else was watching me. I knew how crass I was behaving, taking a dump in the middle of a room full of people, but at this point, I didn't care.

"Oh," I groaned as another contraction hit. I called out hoarsely, "Wallace!" I felt the pressure, and started to stand up, my legs bowed apart. "Catch," I squeaked.

Wallace held his huge hands out just in time to catch my baby girl, the cord still attached to the placenta inside of me.

We were joined by a baby and her umbilicus.

"Good timing," I panted. "Uh, oh, here comes the rest." I squatted back down, and the placenta dropped into the pot.

Wallace looked up at me with a smile like a new summer day. This little girl was his by imminent domain. "Papa, we need a little help over here," he called.

Julian turned around and saw what had just happened. "Again?" he asked as he rushed over to attend to me.

He had tied off the cord and was just about to cut it. "Would you like to do this, son?"

"Aye, Papa, I thank ye for the honor," said Wallace with a Scottish flourish and accepted the dirk. The thick accent he was using sounded natural. I never realized how much he sounded like Jody before. The similarity wasn't lost on Julian or Sarah either. They were both wide-eyed at the sound of his reply.

"Uh, can I get something to cover up with, please," I asked to break the stunned silence. I was standing in the middle of our multipurpose family room without anything on but a shirt. It covered my private parts, but I had become used to this era and its moral standard that a woman's legs were not to be bared except in the bedroom, and maybe not even then.

"Here," said Sarah, "use this." She motioned for Jody to grab the cloth that had never been used as my lap sheet for delivery. "And give her these, too," and gave him a couple of cloths for me.

They all turned their heads as I cleaned and dressed myself. "Thanks," I said and stuffed the cloths between my legs. I made myself another sarong with the sheet, went to my chamber pot chair, and sat down. "Now, will someone bring me one of my babies to hold? I still haven't seen any of them up close."

The men performed a little ceremony as they presented me with each of the babies, making sure I knew which was son number one and which was my second born. I looked at the boys closely. "Can you tell the difference between them? I can," I bragged. "Go ahead and swap them around. You can't confuse me."

Jody and Julian both took this as a personal challenge. They turned their backs to me, and moved the cloth bundles back and forth between each other. Jody held his bundle out to me. "Now dinna be goin' by the swaddlin'; we may or may not have changed them around."

"This is number one and, if that one has a penis, he has to be number two. I'm glad there aren't three boys. They'd be harder to differentiate."

"How did you do that?" asked Julian. He knew I was correct, but wanted to know how I had managed their shell game.

"Easy; look closely. Number one has a cowlick on his left forehead. Number two's is on the right side. I think we had better not let them know about their little 'tell.' I'm sure they'll try to pull the old switcheroo on us more than once as they get older. I want to stay one up on them as long as I can."

Wallace still had my little girl bundled close to his chest. I had better start thinking of her as 'our' little girl. She was squalling and putting her fist into her mouth. "I think she's hungry," he said as he offered her to me.

I discreetly bared my breast and she latched on with a powerful grip. "Umph," I squeaked. "She may be the smallest, and the last one out, but she sure has a mouth on her."

Julian and Jody looked at each other. "Don't say it, Jody," warned Julian.

"Oh, there's no harm in tellin' her that the wee lass takes after her in that respect."

"Ha, ha," I mocked. "If she has a big mouth that gets her into trouble, at least she'll probably to be smart enough to know how to use it to get herself back out."

***42 Naming

"I guess I had better name these children pretty soon. I don't want to be calling them boy number one, boy number two, and girl, you know." I breathed a deep sigh. "Ian Kincaid, you blew it, dude," I said to the ceiling with a bit too much hostility for the occasion.

Sarah was sitting at the table, turning her hands over, looking at the blisters that were rising on the palms of her hands. She was listening to me, but didn't say anything. I could tell she was thinking about it, though. I changed focus and saw that Jody was standing behind her now. I wasn't sure if he had heard me grousing or not; then he spoke and removed all doubt.

"I dinna ken what 'blue it' means, and I dinna think that Ian is deid," he tipped his head to the ceiling like I had, as if I had meant that Ian was in heaven, "so if ye mean he made a great error in judgment, I agree. I canna understand why he would leave ye like he did. But to his credit, he did leave ye with his family. Sarah and I care fer ye and are more than happy to have ye and yer beautiful bairns stay with us as long as ye'd like. But I happen to ken a fine young lad jest achin'," Jody was stroking his chin, trying to control the words spilling out of his mouth, "well, let's jest say ye have a proper man now. He's willin'—nae, wantin'—to take care of ye and the bairns. I dinna think a number eight cannon could blast him away from ye. Now, that bein' said, have ye found proper names fer the wee uns?"

"Well, since I always referred to my belly as the lion's den, I'd like to give them names having to do with lions. I thought of Judah for number one, and maybe Leo, or names like it, for number two."

"Ye do seem to ken yer Bible, and a bit of Latin, too. Where did ye go to school? Oh, I'm sorry, ye still dinna remember, do ye? Aye, Judah is a fine strong name. Did ye ever hear of Leonardo da Vinci? He was a very fine man with many talents."

"Oh, yes, Leonardo da Vinci is still famous and talked about in the twenty-first century. I could talk for hours about him and his inventions. Oh, and did you know it was rumored that he was a time traveler by the name of Leonard Vincent who was really from the 20th century?"

Just at that moment, Wallace and Julian walked in. "I hope we're not interrupting," said Julian.

345

"No, not at all," I said. "Actually, I'd like everyone's input on this. We were just talking about names for the babies. I like Judah and Leonardo as first names for my boy cubs. They shared the den with their little sister, but I don't have any ideas for her name."

"How about Danielle, as in Daniel in the lion's den?" asked Wallace. "Danielle is the French feminine form of Daniel."

"I like that! Now all we have to do is figure out the other names." My mood dropped like a rock into an empty bucket. "Do I have to assign their last name now, or will it be Kincaid by default?"

I looked up and saw two empty male faces, a young man with slightly reddened ears, and a blushed Sarah. She spoke up, "Right now, it's up to you. The only recording of the names would be in the family Bible." She grinned and said in a teasing manner, "Do you happen to have one of *those* in that little bag of yours?"

"As a matter of fact, I do. There's a pocket-sized Bible tucked into one of the inside pockets. I didn't remember that I'd seen it there until you said something. It seems a bit ironic, though, don't you think? I'm recording a maxi birth in a mini Bible. I hope there's enough room for all their names."

"Write very small," said Sarah, "and leave room for a last name later. No one will see the names until you want them to. Does anyone know what day it is? I haven't been paying attention?"

"It's June 21, summer solstice," said Wallace. "They were born in the zodiac sign of Gemini, the Twins." He walked over to the littlest of the babies, Danielle, and stroked her pinkish bronze-colored hair. "Twins with a bonus baby. She sure is beautiful. Danielle, *ma belle.*"

Wallace's ears had lost their pink tinge of embarrassment, but now he was glowing in a different way: with pride. He was clearly infatuated with Danielle, his little girl.

"You know, I think this is going to work out just fine. The babies may not have a father," I blushed and looked down, and softly said, "yet," then took a deep breath and continued aloud, "But the Lord has provided me with three fine gentlemen to be godfathers. Wallace, will you be Danielle's godfather?" I asked.

Wallace paused before he answered, sharing a smile so wide, I could see his molars. "I would be most honored," he said. He bent down to peer into her little face again. "My little girl," his smile bloomed again, and I swore she grinned back at him. "She smiled at me," he said. "She knows who I am!"

"I don't doubt that a bit," I said. "And Sarah, don't even think about suggesting that it was just gas. She's a lady and knows a gentleman when she sees one."

"Oh, I believe you," she said. She looked over Wallace's arm. "She's quite content, I'd say, even if she is a bit of a flirt already."

"Watch what you say about my daughter now, Sarah. She's jest verra polite, that's all," said Wallace.

"Aye, and she'll probably have more than her hands full with two brothers her own age," I said, using the same accent that Wallace had unknowingly used. "Jody, would you honor us with being the godfather for Leonardo, and Julian, would you be Judah's?"

Jody and Julian looked at each other with mirrored smiles. "Sharin' the fatherly duties again, are we Julian?"

"Aye, and glad of it," mocked Julian in a good-natured imitation of Jody's voice. "Now just make sure you get the right one, Jody."

"Leonardo with the left cowlick, that's easy enough to remember. The boys are mirror images of each other. I'll wager one is cack-handed, most likely this one since he's mine," said Jody. "Not that there is anythin' wrong with bein' right-handed. I'm sure both will be bonnie fighters, either way."

"Let's not talk about fighters or fighting, please," I said. "How about if we claim that they'll both become bright artists, inventors, or leaders like Leonardo da Vinci and Judah?"

"We can claim that, too, for Danielle," said Wallace. "You see, there are two women who I have grown close to in the last six months who have shown me that a woman can do just about anything a man can do and," he used Danielle to point to her brothers being held by their godfathers, "a few things that men cannot."

"Aye, Lord, we ask Yer blessin's on these three young bairns; please protect them and their parents in health and happiness; give all of them Yer wisdom and guide them in Yer ways; and please Lord God, grant us all peace. Amen."

"Well said, and thank you, Jody. Now, if it's all the same to you, I think I'll grab a nap while the babies are asleep." And with that pronouncement, I threw a blanket over the chaise, lay on my side, and fell into a deep sleep.

***43 Life was nice and boring

Life was nice and boring. Fighting in the area had headed south. That meant Julian would be able to take a long leave—or maybe even retire—from his intelligence gathering and return to the ranch and his life with José. I knew they were in love, but I also knew they had each led a bachelor's lifestyle before their partnership.

"The separation is good for us," Julian confided in me.

"Yes, and the hellos and good-byes are nice too," I said, blushing. Once again, I had spoken before thinking with the 18th century side of my brain.

He gave a half-smile, shrugged one shoulder, and held up the spindle he had been carving for the babies' playpen. He had avoided a verbal reply, but as always, was being honest with his body language.

He set the wooden piece on top of the others in the recycled quilt tote I had crafted. "There you go," he said, referring to the pile of at least four dozen bark-stripped and smoothed two-foot-long saplings. "You should have enough of these now."

After a long silence, he said, "I'll be leaving in the morning," He turned the knife over a few times then set it down. "Remember how we met?" he asked.

I put baby Leo down on the bed with his siblings, grabbed a kitchen chair, and sat down in front of him. I took a deep breath, blew it out, and said, "Boy, howdy."

I looked over at him, and saw his pursed lips and furrowed eyebrows that meant, 'Huh?'

"Very much so," I said. "And you stood on your word and stayed. I'm kind of glad we never found out what happened. I'd hate for you to leave me, us." I tucked my chin down and lowered my eyelids. I didn't want to see his reaction, nor did I want him to see the sadness in mine.

"Oh, Evie," he said, and grabbed my hand. "I don't think I could ever 'leave' you. You are a part of my life, my son's life, and have given so much to all of us. Sarah, Jody, Wallace, José, me, and now the babies—we're all family because of you. Not even a war can break us apart."

I looked up to see his face and saw that Jody was standing behind him now. It was unsettling, still, that the big man was so quiet, and could just pop in without being heard or sensed. Then again, I'm sure that ability had saved his life, or at least spared him a thrashing, more than once.

Jody hadn't said a word, but Julian saw me look up, and turned around to see his friend, looming tall behind him. Jody realized that he was towering over us, so pulled up a kitchen chair and sat down. "There's somethin' I've been meanin' to share with the two of ye, but weel, I never seemed to remember it at the right time. It may never be the right time, so I'll jest spit it out. I dinna mean it, but 'I' might be the reason ye and Wally were kidnapped."

I don't know if Julian's eyes had popped open as big as mine because I didn't have a mirror. But mine sure felt huge, and I knew his were. Jody looked from Julian to me and back again. "I dinna do it on purpose! I jest mentioned I was lookin' out fer two friends. I gave yer descriptions to the men at the blacksmith's shop and I, weel, I happened to mention that I'd give anythin' to see that the two of ye stayed safe and werena hurt in the conflict. I dinna mean fer anyone to go out and steal ye!"

The tension was as thick as four-day-old pea soup. It was too much for me, so I started giggling. I kept it up until I was in full-blown belly laugh mode, snorting and gasping for air. The two of them just stared at me until Julian finally asked, "What's so damned funny?"

It had started out as a nervous giggle, but had grown into a big, hooting, roaring laugh because all I could think about was, 'how am I going to explain this laughing?' I settled down and said a quick prayer for inspiration as I caught my breath.

And then it came to me.

"It was divine intervention," I said with confidence. "What Jody had said as an innocent remark was misinterpreted by three simple men who, well, you remember them. They weren't capable of an intelligent plan, and never even asked about a reward. But you and Wallace are alive and well because of it. Right?"

Julian sucked in his cheeks as he recalled the kidnappers. I could see that he was now confused about the incident—the lack of hostility in the men who had stuffed him and his stepson into the sacks, and the strange fact that the odd trio had simply disappeared after I had come in and released their hostages, never to be seen or heard from again.

Julian looked over at Jody and asked, "And you never gave them anything for 'saving' us?"

"I dinna ever ken who did it!" Jody said, his eyes wide and backbone straight, indignant at the suggestion. "If ye recall, I wasna even around. It was Evie here who rescued ye, and I dinna even ken who she was at the time." He changed his focus to me, and Julian's eyes followed his. "If there was any divine intervention, I'd say it was Evie here who was the angel."

"Who…whoa…what? Me? ME! I'm about as mortal as they come!"

"Weel, I dinna ken if ye were brought here by divine intervention or nae, but ye did fall from the sky, so to say, and ye did jest happen to have a lot of bairns all at once without any problems…"

"Maybe I didn't have any problems, but the pains were real—whether I was yelling or not. And remember, I did bleed, and it's milk that comes out of these boobs, not manna," I said and pulled the neckline of my blouse down an inch, sticking my chest out in a bold, defiant gesture.

I heard a woman gasp and looked up. Sarah and Wallace were in the doorway. I didn't know how long they had been there, but probably long enough to get the gist of the conversation. I didn't know if I *should* have been embarrassed about my final words, but I wasn't. Either way, I wasn't going to apologize to anyone.

I heard a baby mew but waited to see if he'd go back to sleep. It was Judah starting to rouse; he'd slept through the last feeding. Julian got up to get him. Jody started to say something to him—he was probably going to admonish him to let the baby cry a bit more before picking him up—but Julian continued. He rewrapped him in his little blanket, chatting to him the whole time, and then brought him over, cuddling him close one more time before handing him to me.

"You're a blessing, Evie. There isn't a 'nothing more than, nothing less than' when speaking of a blessing. And I thank the Lord that you are in my life."

I took my now wide-awake, screaming little boy from him. Julian patted my head as I started to feed my son.

"Thanks, I love you too, Julian," I said as the baby latched on. A tear rolled down my cheek, and it wasn't from the powerful suckling. I was that happy with my family.

***44 The Fifth Fourth

July 4, 1781

Today was a day of celebration for many of us, and just another summer day for the Tories and Loyalists. Independence Day number five was an affirmation and show of unity for all of us who had kept the faith and persevered, and who were still striving to win the conflict with England. Tonight, all up and down the eastern seaboard and in all thirteen colonies, American patriots would observe the fifth anniversary of the signing of the Declaration of Independence with parties, drinking, banners, and bragging. There would be cannons blasting, guns saluting, and rockets painting the night sky with festive fire, acknowledging our gratefulness to God, our soldiers, and the Continental Congress for working together toward our deliverance from English tyranny.

We were still at war, but I knew beyond a hiccup of a doubt that we would win this. My faith was contagious to others, too. Jody was aware of the outcome before I showed up because of Sarah and her knowledge of English and American 'history,' but he was absolutely passionate about our new form of government, as if he had discovered it himself.

I felt privileged to be able to observe his finesse in promoting the push for our new country's independence. He was easily wound up and preached whenever he saw an opportunity. He knew how to use his size, bearing, and voice to great advantage. He would start low, just a comment or an aside, to someone in town. "Better a free mouse than a slaved cat," he was fond of saying.

The crowd would grow as people curious about the tall red-haired man would stop, watch him gesticulate with those long arms and broad hands, and listen to his booming voice hawk the merits of self-rule. The crescendo moved into an awesome finale, a passionate speech, sweeping all within earshot of him into a roaring fever of patriotism and hope. Then, to make sure they understood the concept, he would give his short comprehensive summary of what we were fighting for.

"We will make this a great country. We will have the right to say how we govern ourselves; we will elect our own people to *enact* the laws, *interpret* the laws, and *enforce* the laws. This will be the greatest nation on earth: one nation, under God, indivisible, with liberty and justice for all!"

His powerful speeches and the boldness of Angus and other printers to publish booklets and broadsheets to spread the word even further enabled the masses to understand how great our potential was. There were other great speakers around, and I'm sure glad they were all Americans. The Loyalists evidently didn't feel as if they had to support or prove their side of the conflict. I guess the fine art of political debate would have to wait a few generations until broader venues were available.

Not all of the well-spoken American patriots made it, or will make it, through this war, though. "I regret that I have but one life to give for my country," were powerful words spoken by a very young twenty-one-year-old, Nathan Hale, just before he was executed by the British in 1776. These words helped inspire the fight for a new nation. Jody's words may not be remembered 230 years into the future, but he didn't—oh, my God, I hope he doesn't—die a martyr.

Maybe the pen *is* mightier than the sword. If Hale's affirmation and the words of others had never been written down and shared within this fledgling nation, would we have been as brave and fearless? Young America was certainly underpowered as far as weapons, money, and a navy were concerned. Yes, the American spirit, shared in voice and spread in ink, was definitely what won—will win—the war for independence.

I couldn't—wouldn't—live in fear for my life or the lives of my family. Our future Constitution and Bill of Rights would be to protect us from fear. But today, right here, right now, lingering Loyalist factions were still pressing their interests, both personal and respective to the Crown, into our lives.

Word came through the usual local news network—paranoid gossip with a smattering of fact thrown in—that a motley crew of disgruntled Loyalists was roaming the area, collecting taxes without regard to who the property owners were or their delinquency status. As far as we knew, the 'maybe they were, maybe they weren't British soldiers' had no valid basis for the tax they were collecting. These bandits were working solely by intimidation. If the landowner couldn't pay hard cash, they would take anything of value they could put their hands on. If the landowner refused, bloodshed ensued. There was a term for this course of action in my time: extortion.

We had heard the rumors and were cautious, and never left our little homestead unattended. Today Wallace was the sentinel, staying home with me and the babies.

Jody and Sarah had gone into the little big town of Gibsonville for the latest news, salt, and a few other staples. Sarah had insisted on bringing the wagon, hoping that they would be able to bring home some of those flat stones that were down by the creek. I guessed what she wanted were what I called flagstones.

"I want a solid floor, Jody, and one without splinters, one that I can cover with rugs in the winter and have cool to my feet in the summer. Nothing can stay clean with this hard-packed earth as a floor. Pretty soon the babies will be crawling, and we don't want them scooting around on this, do we?"

She had a good argument, and he knew it. Julian said that José had more rugs than they could use at their house. Evidently his mother, Señora Rojas, had been quite the collector. José, although he probably would have given them to us just to be rid of them, was glad that he could offer them as gifts for the babies. He had only seen the wee'uns once, when he had come to bring Julian back to the ranch the week after they were born and had fallen in love with them at first sight.

"Tres, um, three? At the same time?" he asked.

José had taken to heart my suggestion and was speaking English as much as possible. He looked at the petite crew, sleeping in one heap on the middle of Sarah and Jody's bed. I had only made two little baskets for use as bassinets when I was pregnant—not knowing I would need three—but they slept better when snuggled up together and fussed when separated. I guessed they had lived in close quarters for eight months and weren't quite ready to be apart.

Julian had just about completed their new bed. "Wally, can you finish this for me? I thought I'd be done by now, but I didn't plan on, ahem, doing other things," he carped, then grinned. Julian had been roped into doing all of the cooking. Sarah's hands were still tender, and I was always busy tending to the input or output of the babies.

"I'll be glad to cook, Julian," I teased. "You just come over here and whip out your boob and feed these little guys." He glared at me and went back to cracking eggs for our dinner omelet. His eggs were always good, too. Why did men always make the best omelets? Maybe it was because that was the only dish they ever cooked. Practice makes perfect and all that, you know.

So, Julian was back with José, and Sarah and Jody were out harvesting river rock flooring, possibly until tomorrow. Wallace and I had time to ourselves. Well, sort of—we still had the babies to tend to. I took out the little Bible. "Is it okay if I get a head start on finishing the birth records? I…well, I want to give them their last names now, if it's okay with you. You see, in my time, a baby can be given any last name, not just the mother's or father's surname. You might think I'm a bit twisted, but I think it would be kind of cute if they had your last name before I did."

"I would be honored to give them my name," he said proudly. He sighed then added, almost apologetically, "The way the country is now; it's only the name of Urquhart I can give them. I think I have forfeited my title and the Falls Church estate as a result of changing allegiances. It looks as if we will all be wearing homespun for a long time."

I looked up to see if I could read anything in his face after his last soft-spoken remark. I could. The love he was radiating was undeniable. He saw the insecure look in my eyes and said, "A small price to pay for a bit of heaven on earth, I say. Even without the babies, you alone are worth it."

"Wow, um, thank you." I put down the mini Bible and reached up, clasping my arms around his neck, to give him a smooch worthy of Burt Lancaster and Deborah Kerr in 'From Here to Eternity.' I composed myself after the kiss but couldn't manage—and really didn't want—to get rid of my huge grin of satisfaction. "I'd better be careful; if I don't stop smiling so big, my face will freeze like this forever."

"That would be fine by me. I like seeing you happy. Now let me see that Bible."

A card fell out as I handed it to him: a business card. I hadn't seen it when I put the babies' birth date in the book; it must have been stuck between the pages. He picked it up and glanced at it, then stared at it, as if he couldn't believe what he was seeing. "Where did you get this?" he asked coolly.

"I don't know. It's new to me, which really isn't saying much. Here, let me see."

He let me take it but didn't move his hand to offer it to me. He was shocked—at it or something on it.

"It's just a business card—see," I said and waved it in the air, showing off how harmless it was. "I guess it was in my backpack and…oh, my," I looked at the card, "isn't your uncle Lord Melbourne?"

"Yes, and that's the family's coat of arms. But my uncle's name isn't James. I've never seen a card like this. The paper is so smooth and shiny, the letters are raised, and the printing is so, so perfect. What do all these numbers mean?"

"Those are phone numbers. Remember when I told you about telephones? Phone numbers are how we kept everyone indexed, sorted, and how we accessed them, I mean… Well, there are also faxes, which need numbers, too, and emails, which use letters and/or numbers. And gosh, look at that—he even has his own website."

I set the card down. This wasn't working, and it wasn't because I had overloaded him with my rambling about numbers and modern technology. This 21st century business card was from someone with his family name, actually his kin by the use of the coat of arms and title. And I must have had it in my possession since…well, at least since a minute before I arrived here from the 21st century.

I lifted my suddenly insecure fiancé's chin and fixed my eyes on his half-closed ones. "Wallace, I think this is from one of your relatives, or rather your relative's descendants. But I swear I don't know how I got this. I don't have any feelings for or about this card, or this 'James Melbourne' person, at all!"

I hadn't started out to be emotional or excited about a silly old slip of thick paper. Good grief, it was just a business card. I received cards like this all the time in my previous life. I think. But this was 'when' I was, here and now. It should be no big deal after seeing the smartphone a few weeks ago, but this had something to do with Wallace and Julian's heritage. Or whatever the opposite of heritage was: *descentage*?

Wallace's head was bowed and still. I looked at the card again, then gave it back to him. He rubbed his thumb over the embossed lettering. "Oh, well," he remarked nonchalantly, then lifted his head to gaze at me with a weak smile, "another mystery."

"Like bumblebees," I said with a one-shoulder shrug of agreement.

He raised one eyebrow and looked down his nose, asking me wordlessly, "Explain, please."

"Aerodynamically, bumblebees aren't supposed to be able to fly, but they do. You know, fat little bodies and itty-bitty wings? An eagle soaring, that's easy to see, but those chunky little buggers popping from flower to flower, mathematically and scientifically shouldn't be able to fly. A mystery, but real; something we accept and don't try to explain."

"Okay, a bumblebee," he said and shoved the card back into the Bible.

"Maybe we can do the names a little later," I mumbled, suddenly feeling insecure.

He looked over at me and saw that my big happy smile had managed to totally disappear and was now approaching a frown. "We have the first and last names. Why don't we figure out a few middle names before we enter them in the Bible? After all, we aren't going anywhere."

"Okay," I chirped, popping right out of my funk, "fine by me."

And it was. Now what were some good middle names, and how many should I give each child? Those were happy posers for me to consider and didn't even begin to drag me down into curiosity about my unknown past.

Ж Ж Ж

Wallace went to the barn to continue with his woodworking. He was finishing the babies' playpen/crib that Julian had started. I was hoping to get a few minutes to myself before a baby woke up. I grabbed a clean cloth and filled a small pot with fresh water. I sat on the porch and untied my shirt. I felt icky, covered with baby spit-up and sweat. I wet the cloth and wiped from my forehead down to my neck. I rinsed the cloth and washed the top of my breasts then rinsed again. Ah, now the best part. I lifted one of my heavy breasts and washed away the perspiration and spilled milk. The babies all nursed well, as in vigorously, but they all seemed to fall asleep with a mouthful of milk. It dribbled out their lips, and down and underneath my breasts. It wasn't always possible to clean up after each feeding. There was always another one waiting to be fed or changed.

My little sponge bath was just the pick me up I needed. I felt almost as clean as if I'd taken a whole bath. Maybe I'd be able to do that later on tonight.

It was still early, but looked like it was going to be another miserably hot day. There wasn't a white spot in the sky, which was good. I didn't mind the heat, but I hated the humidity that came with the clouds and haze. I decided to be brazen and leave my shirt open so I could thoroughly dry out. I knew I'd be able to hear anyone coming before they could see me, so I put my legs up and kicked back on the porch bench, ready to catch some rays and vitamin D.

I looked up at the north end of the porch through squinted eyes and visualized a swing. I'd have to show Wallace how they were made where I came from—or would that be when I came from? It would be nice to have one wide enough for two adults to share. And it shouldn't take much more effort to hang three little swings from the porch beam.

I was fantasizing about swinging and fresh air when someone threw a cloth over my chest. I looked down and saw it was a diaper off of the clothesline.

"Cover up, quick," a husky voice ordered.

I did, hurriedly tying together my blouse underneath the cloth—at the same time, looking for my modesty policeman. I didn't see him but did see

356

a rider coming in at a fast pace, kicking up a twisty, tan dust cloud, followed by a wagon with three men.

I searched again for the cloth-tosser but didn't see anyone. I called for Wallace, but he didn't answer. Something fishy was going on, and I was starting to get scared.

The rider, a scruffy-looking British soldier, jerked back hard on the reins when he saw me, and came to a gravel-crunching stop. He had kicked his horse hard and repeatedly to get her to the house so quickly. Fresh blood was oozing from the gouges in the long-legged black mare's flanks. I looked over and saw that, although the man was dressed in a tattered and filthy British officer's uniform, he was wearing Spanish spurs—mean, ugly, sharp ones that would give the SPCA and PETA fits.

I walked to the edge of the porch to greet the stranger. "Can I help you, sir," I said in my bravest voice. My knees felt watery, but gratefully, they still held me up. I reached out and held onto the porch post in order to give myself more stability. My courageous demeanor would mean nothing if I passed out from fright right in front of him.

"I'm the new tax collector and I see that," he pulled out a little booklet that looked like one of those cheap dirty novels that made the circuit, "this household has not paid any taxes this year."

I leaned in closer to see if I could see the name of his little novella. He quickly pulled it close to his chest and shoved it back into his jacket pocket.

He was lying, and I wasn't the least bit subtle with my distrustful leer, letting him know that I knew he did not have a tax-roll book in his jacket.

"I think you're mistaken, sir," I said with a newfound confidence, "we are current on our taxes. Someone must have given you the wrong book." Then I glared at him, daring him to challenge me.

That was probably a bad move. He was not a nice man by the looks of his horse's bleeding flesh. I quickly backpedaled, "I'm sure it wasn't your mistake though, sir." I batted my eyelashes, hoping to cover my tough northern girl persona with a charming young southern belle flirtation. "Good help is so hard to find nowadays," I added demurely.

I should have continued with the engaging debutante role and asked if he would like a drink of water, but I really wanted him gone. Just as I was wondering what to do next, my decision was made for me. The creepy soldier jumped up onto the porch and literally got in my face.

"What's a sweet young thing like you doing out here all alone? Did your menfolk go out and get themselves killed by the mean old British soldiers?"

His breath reeked of rum and rotten teeth. I took two steps back to get away from him, but he advanced three.

"If you're lonely, I can be real friendly," he cooed.

His hands reached for my hair, but my reflexes were fast, and he didn't get a chance to touch me. Instead, it was I who reached out. I instinctively slapped him across his stubble-whiskered cheek before I could think.

"Oh, you shouldn't have done that, little lady. I don't take to violence. At least *I* don't like being hit. I do like to inflict a little pain every now and then, though. I find it—rather, arousing…"

He dragged the last word out in a most perverse manner. I had ducked and drawn away from him with the slap, but he was closing in on me, making sure I didn't have an escape route. He was between me and the steps now. I could hear his heavy breathing and smell his rummy breath. He reached down and grabbed the front of his pants. "Give the taxman his due, little lady, and maybe he won't take too much from your little bitty home. The wagon is fairly full already, but what I'd really like…"

"Mama, Mama," the little boy said as he popped up between the extortionist and me. "I'm back. Did ye miss me?"

I reached down and clutched the unknown dark-haired boy to me and hugged him hard. "Oh, I did miss you," I said sincerely, keeping hold of this little person who had just stopped an assault. He was about ten years old and wiry—hard, skinny, and definitely clever.

"Father says that he'll be right back. He and uncle and cousin and all the men from the…the…the store will be here any minute. He says he loves ye and misses ye."

The little boy stammered on where the menfolk were, and I hoped the taxman—or whoever he was—had missed his little sign of lying.

"Thank you, dear," I said as I brushed his wayward hair out of his eyes.

I gasped, glad that my back was toward the soldier. I suddenly realized who this boy must be, and I was sure the look of shock showed on my face. He had to be Ian's son! His features, that hair that wouldn't go where it was supposed to, and those soft brown eyes—if he wasn't Ian's son, I was a rhinoceros.

My momentary trance was broken by the sound of a baby crying. It was little Danielle. If I didn't get to her soon, she'd have her brothers awake and screaming with her. "I need to take care of my daughter," I said as I excused myself, not waiting to see if he had any objections. No one was going to keep me from my babies.

The little boy followed me inside. He literally stood guard at the door as I sat on a kitchen chair and bared a breast to both quiet and feed her.

"Get out of here," growled the little boy. "This house is for family only."

There wasn't any sign of fear in his voice, and I realized why. I think he knew I was feeding his sister; she *was* his family.

My back was turned away from the opened door—I wanted at least a modicum of privacy in nursing—and I didn't see it coming.

"Move out of the way, boy. I wanna see what we have here." I heard the shuffle of bodies in contention and turned around just in time to see Little Ian fly through the air. The taxman had lifted him bodily and tossed him into the corner like a dirty shirt.

I stood up and backed away from the man as he neared me with a lusty smirk. "Ooh, a little one, but she's *too* little right now. Give her a couple of years, and she'll be just right."

"Keep away, you bastard," I hissed, controlling the urge to scream—I didn't want to startle the baby. I saw movement out of the corner of my eye. Little Ian had come to his wits and was inching our way.

"Now lookie there; she is a fresh one, isn't she? I'll bet you and your husband—if there even is a husband—haven't had relations since she was born."

He reached up to brush my breasts with his huge, filthy hand, but I feigned right and dodged him. Now I was on the other side of him, and could easily run outside. But I couldn't leave him in the house with my other two babies. One of them was sure to awaken soon.

He glared at me, angry at my clever escape. It was a stare-down, and I won. Sort of. His eyes changed focus and peered down, leering at the opening of my blouse. Then he looked up to my gold nugget necklace, and another kind of lust appeared.

"Aarrgghh!" I caught sight of the tanned buckskinned-clad boy just as he tackled the taxman behind the legs, effectively knocking the much bigger man flat on his back...and evidently the wind out of his lungs. The man's mouth was moving, but his chest was still. He couldn't draw a breath

"Hmph," I snorted. I didn't care if he ever breathed again.

Little Ian stood above his prey, a dirk in his hand, his foot ready to stomp on the man's windpipe if he should try to rise. "Shall I cut him?" he asked.

"Yes," I answered angrily in emotional reflex. "Cut him? Oh, no," I said as I suddenly realized what he meant.

"Too late," he said.

I was afraid that he had meant kill him, but he hadn't. Nevertheless, he really had cut him. The taxman had a 'Y' cut into his cheek. He still couldn't breathe, though, and was beginning to turn blue. Little Ian stepped back and kicked him hard under the ribcage. The man gasped, and his color started to return with the intake of air.

I heard a noise in the doorway, saw that it was Wallace, and was relieved.

And then it was terror time all over again.

I noticed the look in Wallace's eyes and the knife at his neck—he was being held hostage. Three men were standing behind him, grinning like cats at an overstocked fishpond. The taxman's reinforcements had arrived.

Judah and Leo chose that moment to wake up and call for their lunch. I let them scream. I knew an infant's cry was irritating to a human male's eardrum. The high pitch actually caused men physical pain...or so I recalled reading or hearing...somewhere. If I could irritate the intruders in an unobtrusive manner, maybe they wouldn't be able to think clearly. Then Wallace, the boy, and I could find a way out of this mess.

The boy! If Ian's son was here—and how in the hell did he have a son that he didn't, or wouldn't, tell me about?—then Ian was around here somewhere. That made me feel better—I had an invisible ally.

Surely Ian would want his prey out in the open where he could see them. Now I felt like I was part of a rescue team, and my partner was out there somewhere, just waiting for me to flush out his quarry.

"How about if we go outside where it isn't so noisy," I suggested as I put Danielle down into the nest of quilts on the bed. I picked up Leo—he was protesting the loudest—turned my back on the men, and let the baby start nursing. There was no reason for him to be deprived of lunch. And right now, I needed him as much as he needed me.

Leo and I followed the gruesome foursome outside. I hoped Wallace, the boy, the babies, and I had someone—my modesty policeman maybe?—to help us.

The taxman was a bit loopy from his assault, but managed to grasp onto one of his cronies, and made it to the porch bench. Little Ian—or should that be Wee Ian?—had picked up little Judah, and brought him outside to be with me. He was cooing and cuddling the baby; actually

360

doing a great job of distracting the little two-week-old—oh my, Judah was his little brother!

I took a deep breath to compose myself. Too much had just happened, and I couldn't handle it, even with the aid of my little dark-haired champion. "Lord, help us," I prayed softly to the man upstairs.

"Who you talkin' to," asked the skinny man who still had a knife to Wallace's neck.

"God," I answered with self-assurance. I suddenly felt braver because I knew He would help us. "You know, the man who gave us 'thou shalt not kill' and 'thou shalt not steal' and about eight other good 'thou shalt nots' to live by."

"Hmph," was the monosyllabic reply from the man who looked like he had a single digit IQ.

Okay, maybe I could work this in my favor. The taxman was evidently the head honcho in this little extortion ring. Right now, he was pretty much out of commission. His three apes were apparently trying to keep up the intimidation and theft gambit, and weren't quite sure about what to do next.

"Would you believe that you have a knife to the neck of General William Howe's son?" I asked. "You do know who General Howe is, don't you?"

Skinny looked at the other two, and they all shrugged their shoulders.

Gee, maybe these guys were too dumb to fool. "General Howe is a big time British general, and his brother is 'Admiral' Richard Howe. You know him, of course. *Everybody* knows him," I said dramatically.

Skinny started bobbing his head, then the others did, too. "Yeah, we know 'em; *everybody* knows him," the bald one said enthusiastically. He was lying and I knew it.

Of course, I wasn't lying. I hadn't said that Wallace was the general's son. I had said 'Would you believe?' and they did.

"Now," I continued with great sincerity, "if the Howe family found out that you hurt one of their own kin... My, my, there would be, pardon the vulgarity, hell to pay."

The boys were getting nervous now. "But we can't leave without takin' somethin'," the bald one—evidently the new leader—said.

"Now, how are you going to get your—captain, is he?—home with all of this 'stuff' in the back of your wagon?"

I walked over to the wagon and lifted one edge of the canvas tarp covering it. I couldn't see what was in the little barrels, but I *could* smell it.

They had gunpowder. Kegs and kegs of gunpowder. I wasn't a betting person, but still I'd bet those long boxes under the seat had rifles or muskets in them.

"I'll tell you what, why don't you just unload this wagon here, and then your captain can ride in the b…"

"Shut up, bitch," boomed an angry voice from the porch. Taxman had regained his senses and was reclaiming control. "I'm going to take you for everything you've got. Including that little boy of yours, the bastard," he said as he reached up to feel the wound on his cheek.

I needed to think of what to do next, so I stalled. Leo had finished nursing, so I moved him off the breast and covered myself in one smooth move. As I walked back up the porch steps to be near Danielle, I put him over my shoulder to burp him. Five seconds passed, and I still hadn't had a brainstorm.

Taxman had moved from the bench to the porch post, and was trying to stand up straight by himself, testing his balance without using his cronies as crutches. They were mumbling amongst themselves, but I couldn't hear what they were saying.

I was scared, staring off into space, not knowing what to do next, when I felt the tugging at my elbow, a small hand trying to get my attention.

"Here, Mama, I'll take him," Wee Ian said as he handed me Judah who, although not screaming, was making faces and shaking his fists in frustration. I swapped out babies and saw the boy's eyes shift to the barn.

"Thank you, dear," I said. "You're such a good big brother." I got Judah started on lunch, then turned to face Taxman. He was able to stand alone now, only touching the porch post for security.

I cleared my throat to get the captain's attention. He looked down at me with disgust, but I didn't mind. I'd rather have him look at me like that than with his earlier ogles and leers. "Sir, I don't think you have the situation under control like you think you do."

My confidence level was Rocky Mountain high, and I was letting it shine. I tossed my hair back and stuck out my chin. "You see, right now you are being targeted by a very angry man. He doesn't take too kindly to his kin being threatened. So, I suggest that you let his cousin go…*right now!*" I dipped my head down to accentuate my guttural threat, and glared into his eyes, an angry bull daring the toreador to approach.

Skinny let his knife fall away from Wallace's neck, but Taxman interceded. "Not so quick there, mate," he said. Skinny brought the knife

362

up again, straightened his back, and froze, as if he were at attention.

"There's still the matter of the taxes, you see," Taxman said as he worked his way toward me.

I sidled around him, keeping eye contact. He had changed his demeanor back to letch mode. With it came that ugly, lustful sneer. His eyes moved from my one covered breast, ignoring the baby actively nursing, to the other side, and then back up my throat to the gold nugget necklace.

"Oh, and I *know* that you're lying about a marksman in the barn," he said. "My men looked in there, and all they found was this wee little patriot," then he poked Wallace in the ribs with his silver-barreled pistol.

I looked toward the barn. I multitasked, holding the suckling baby with my right arm, lifting my left hand straight up to the porch beam to point to a spot two feet above my head. "Right here, Ian," I yelled.

Zing! Twack.

An arrow hit the spot I had pointed to. I looked over at our extortionist and grinned. "Now, let's talk terms, shall we?"

The captain glared at me, obviously thinking of his options. He didn't want to back down to anyone—especially a woman—in front of his men, and didn't want to leave empty-handed, either. He would have to let Wallace go, or get himself shot; that was obvious. And I was far enough away now that he couldn't grab me. I wasn't going to let him have two hostages.

Wee Ian had disappeared during all of this, and had put Leo on the bed with his sister. He was back now—his knife in hand and a squint in his eye—just daring the captain to make a move.

The tension was smothering. Taxman turned toward Wee Ian and spat on the ground, aiming for the boy's feet. The boy jumped out of the way and stabbed him in the thigh at the same time.

"Do ye really want me to cut ye some more? Jest keep it up, and we willna have to waste an arrow. I'll bleed ye right here and now." Wee Ian snarled with grim satisfaction. "Willna bother me none."

"Goddamn bastard," Taxman swore as he clutched his fresh leg wound. I could tell it was a deep cut, but because of where it was, the blood was only dribbling, not gushing. I was sure he hurt plenty, but the injury couldn't be as painful as the humiliation of being attacked by a child in front of his minions.

I glanced toward the barn and realized that Ian, my first husband, the man who just two weeks earlier I had been wishing was by my side to share in the pain and joy—in that order—of the birth of my children, was less than a hundred feet away. The man who had abandoned me, the one who I had longed for once upon a time, was just across the yard. Flashbacks of the beaten and burned man I had rescued, the weakened man who with his first flush of strength made love to me after promising to never leave me, the man whose seed had spawned my three babies…

Focus, woman, focus! He's just a tool in the woods, a weapon to help resolve this conflict.

I stopped staring and started glaring. Taxman was still grumbling about his leg and tying a handkerchief around his thigh, eyes down on his first aid ministrations. I glanced over and saw that Skinny still had the knife to Wallace's throat. Wallace's eyes were on me, but were vacant. He wasn't letting anyone know—including me—what he was thinking.

"Wee Ian, take the baby back to the bed, please. And don't stab anyone unless I say so, okay?" I covered myself up, put my finger in between my son's mouth and my nipple to break the bond, and then offered the bundle of baby to his big brother.

Wee Ian sheathed his knife and walked over to me, but kept his eye on Taxman, his stare somewhere between mocking and sheer hatred. "Asshole," he said, as he looked the bigger man in the eye.

I had to stifle my laugh—it was such an appropriate name for the brigand. Wee Ian took the baby from me and walked backwards into the house, throwing a quick glance in my direction, making sure I was still safe. I nodded that I was okay, and then he passed through the doorway, disappearing into the shadows.

As soon as the two boys were safely inside, I squared my shoulders and growled, "Take that effin' knife away from his throat." Skinny dropped his knife—from either shock or obedience—and Wallace stepped away, to stand at my side.

Taxman looked up, one eyebrow raised in satisfaction. He had finished bandaging his leg and figured out his next strategy: humiliation. His acne-scarred face screwed up into a complete sneer as he asked Wallace, "Do you always let the woman do the talking?"

"She seems to be doing all right. If she needs help, she'll ask." Wallace nodded to me to dismiss himself, then moved past the Taxman, intentionally bumping into the man's wounded leg on his way into the house.

"Good job, lad," he said to Wee Ian as he walked inside to check on the boy and the babies. Wallace knew he wasn't leaving me alone—the master archer was still watching over me—and, as he said, I'd ask for help if I needed it.

"Okay, Captain Asshole, is it?" I asked, not really wanting an answer.

He glared at me. He had no intention of replying and I knew it. I'm sure he didn't want me to know who he was. I was definitely the type who had no qualms about spreading the name of the crooked British officer who illegally collected taxes. And I'd also let everyone know that the dirtbag had been overtaken and marked by a boy not even old enough to have a whisker.

"So you want to collect some 'taxes' from us, even though we're current?" I asked sarcastically.

His reply was to stare at me, to try to intimidate me with his clenched jaws and barely audible growl.

It wasn't working. I grinned in response, just to make sure he knew it.

"Well, what I want is for you to be gone, and never to return again." I paused for effect—and for the muscle strength to return to my shaky legs. I shook my head at him with disgust, "And since you are wearing a British uniform, you should be under some sort of code of ethics."

A snarl escaped his raised lip at my remark, but I ignored it and continued. "So, I'll let you go with a bargain. You see, if you take anything from us, it would be considered stealing since your 'tax record' is, shall we say, out of date. If I *voluntarily* give you the taxes for the next ten years in advance, you'll never come back. Sound like a deal?"

Wallace was standing in the doorway now, pale at my words, but quiet out of respect for my negotiating. Captain Asshole, the taxman, nodded.

I continued, letting a slight grin of superiority escape. "But you have something I want, and if I am to pay with this," I fingered my gold nugget necklace, and his eyes widened, "I want a full measure of compensation."

"Yes, ma'am," he said. His threw his shoulders back and straightened his spine. His whole attitude had changed with the promise of the nugget necklace without a fight. He was now respectful and at full attention. He was looking at my upper body again, but not even glancing at my bosom—his eyes were fixed on the gold.

"So, I'll take that wagon, all of its contents, and your horse. You can have the necklace, but I want your word as an officer and a subject of the Crown that you will never tax or bother this property, or its residents, ever again…or suggest to or order anyone else to do the same."

"Yes, ma'am," he said, his tongue literally licking his lips in anticipation of getting the gold, his eyes still fixed on the necklace.

"Oh, and one other thing I'll be wanting. You can consider this compensation for the harassment and duress you have inflicted on members of this household."

His face froze—the transaction wasn't going as smoothly as he had hoped.

"I want those spurs," I said. "You can ride the wagon horse back to whatever privy-hole you came out of, but you have to do it without spurs. Deal?"

"Yes, ma'am," he said and stuck out his hand.

I didn't know if the hand was to seal the transaction or to claim the necklace, but I didn't want to touch it either way. "Wallace," I said as I looked over to the doorway. My betrothed walked up to me and waited while I took the necklace off my neck with a jerk. It was a tricky clasp, and I hoped I had broken it. I put it in Wallace's hand and looked toward the captain.

Wallace held the necklace in his left hand and stuck out his right. The captain was gazing at the gold, and then realized that Wallace was waiting for him to shake his hand. Wallace took the hand offered him and squeezed hard, barely shaking it at all, until the man winced and squeaked from the pain. He let Asshole's hand go at the squeal, then dropped the necklace into the waiting, throbbing palm.

Skinny and Baldy were standing by, fidgeting, not knowing what to do. The captain saw Wallace walking over to the wagon and extended a bit of unexpected courtesy. "Curly, help him with the gear. I'm riding the bay out. I got the tax payment. We'll be leaving the wagon here. We can make good time getting back to New Bern now," he said with a voice of authority.

The bald man—ironically, he must be Curly—walked up to the horse and started removing the harness and reins, throwing them onto the wagon seat. He grabbed a little bag from the back, and was going to take it with him, when I hollered, "The wagon, and all that's in it, stays here. All you get is the horse," I said.

I was taking a liberty here. It was probably just their rations, but I didn't care. I made a point of catching the captain's eye, and then looked to the barn, a subtle reminder that my marksman was still watching them.

The Taxman saw my gesture and ordered his men, "Leave it there." I think he started to say, 'Do as she says,' but bit off the words, his pride stopping him. He looked over to me and asked, "I do get my saddle, don't

I?"

"Sure," I said, and turned to sit down on the porch bench. I was getting weak all over now and wanted to conserve enough energy to at least keep my voice strong.

"Put my saddle on the bay," he told the third man. I noticed he had a limp, but still managed to get the job done.

It took a long five minutes, but they were finally ready to leave. "Good day, ma'am," the captain said as he sat tall on the swaybacked wagon horse.

"Not so fast," I said, "You're forgetting something." I looked down at his boot.

"Pardon me," he said sarcastically, and bent down to remove one, then the other, of his spurs. "You'll need these," he said as he waved the shiny metal and leather devices. "The horse may look fine," he grinned like he knew how the deck of cards was marked, "but she won't break a run; she won't get past a trot." He tossed the spurs to the ground in front of me and said, "Let's get the hell out of here, boys," and was gone with a gallop, his three stooges obediently following behind him.

Wallace reached down to get the spurs. "It was just gold," I said, "and it never had any sentimental value for me. I don't even know where it came from."

"You know I don't care about material goods—were you harmed? I couldn't tell what was going on from the barn," he said.

I wasn't sure if it was embarrassment or an apology, but he definitely felt inadequate about not protecting me.

"Not a scratch on me or the babies, but Wee Ian," I asked my little protector, "are you okay?"

The young man was standing in the doorway, watching the bandits as they disappeared into a trail of dust. "Aye, I'm fine, but why do ye call me Wee Ian?"

"Well, because you look like your father and his name is Ian. Actually, when he was young, he was called Wee Ian because his father's name was Ian, too."

All of a sudden, I remembered that Ian was in the barn or in the woods or somewhere where he had a good shot at the house and its enemies. I looked up and saw that Wallace was already walking toward the barn. I patted the boy's hand, put it down, and followed after Wallace. Wee Ian ran after me, reached out, and retook my hand, escorting me as if the two of us walked hand in hand every day.

Wee Ian and I caught up, the three of us undoubtedly a very intimidating triad. Wallace called out coolly, "Cousin, you can come out now."

Ian jumped down from the rafter of the barn, but neither Wallace nor I got a chance to speak. Wee Ian strutted up to him purposefully and stopped three feet in front of him, his hand on the dirk in its sheath. Wallace and I looked at each other, then back to the confrontation.

"She says yer my father; is that right?" the young man demanded. After what he had just been through, it was easier to think of him as a young man rather than as a prepubescent boy who was not much more than four feet tall.

Ian closed his eyes and brought his hand up in front of his brow. He squeezed his forehead with long, knobby fingers, thinking about his answer. He dropped his hand to his chin and brought his forehead down in a gesture of shame. His hand remained at his chin momentarily. He sighed, lifted his head, and then dropped his hand to his side—limp—no fight or resistance left in the sentinel.

"Aye, I suppose I am yer father," he said. "At least that's what yer grandmother said, and I was marrit to yer mother when...weel, I dinna ken ye were even born until three moons ago!"

"When were ye gonna tell me?" the boy demanded, his fists on his hips, making Ian look the child who had just been caught shaving the cat.

Wallace walked up to Wee Ian and put his hand on his shoulder. "It's a funny thing about this family. Some of the men are a bit slow to admit that they're a father. It happened to me, too. But at least we did find out. I'm sure it's just that Ian didn't want you to care less about your other father. You mother, uh, remarried, right?"

Wee Ian had been glaring at Ian during Wallace's little chat but let his shoulders slump at the last remark. "Aye, she did, and I have two wee sisters. They're with her now. But my other father, their father, is deid. That's why I went with Star Walker." Wee Ian stopped and squinted at Ian. "So, what am I supposed to call ye now?" he asked.

Ian chewed on his lower lip a couple of times, then said, "Ye can call me Da, if ye like. I mean, I'd like it if ye did."

I could see Ian's eyes getting moist, as if he wanted to cry. All of a sudden, I had bucket loads of compassion for him. His father was probably dead, and now he was waiting to find out if this 'surprise' son—the boy he had known of for only three months—could, or would, acknowledge him. And I had named this bright and brave young man Wee Ian after him.

368

Wee Ian thought about it for a moment. "Okay—Da," he said in a stilted manner, as if this was the first time the name had crossed his lips. He looked up from Wallace to me, and then said to his father, "I think they want to talk to ye, too."

Wallace nodded at the boy, and then fixed his eyes on Ian. He said, "Thank you," and turned away to escort me back to the house.

And that was that.

Apparently, Wallace felt that he didn't need to say anything else.

We were half way to the house when we heard Ian yell after us. "The bairns: there were two of 'em. Did ye have twins?"

Wallace stopped. He looked at me, his back still turned away from the man who he had only recently found out was his cousin. "I can't do this to him," he told me. He took a deep breath and turned halfway around.

"No, we did not have twins," he said.

I could hear the smile in his tone and was concerned. Was he being cruel? I looked at him and saw that he was not being mean, but was teasing.

"But there were two! Do they belong to someone else? Evie, I saw ye feedin' 'em..."

Ian, the tough mountain man who had lived for years as an Indian, was distraught—his voice squeaking with his plea, anxious to find out about the babies.

I was still mad at him for leaving me, but I would get over it. I had Wallace and was happy, happier, the happiest that I could ever be because of him. There really wasn't a reason to punish Ian for the rest of his life, or for even the next five minutes.

I grinned at him and shook my head. "Oh, you saw two of them, all right, but they're not twins, not really. You saw two of them, but there's one more. Wallace and I had triplets! Come on in and see."

I grabbed Wee Ian with one hand and kept hold of Wallace with the other. Ian ran to catch up with us, but stayed six feet away, off to the side of us. I guessed any closer than that would have made him uncomfortable.

The babies were still asleep in the clutter of quilts. They hadn't suffered through the day's ordeal, and I was grateful for that. Actually, the only wounded one, besides Wee Ian's possible bruising from being tossed across the room, was Captain Asshole. And nobody cared about him.

Ian stayed outside, just beyond the porch steps. I remembered how it felt to have a roof over my head after being in the open for so long. He probably didn't have claustrophobia, but I didn't want him to feel uneasy either. I picked up Leonardo and brought him out to the porch.

"Here's Leonardo, he was the first one born," I said.

Ian took slow deliberate steps up to the bench and sat down. He held his breath as I handed him the bundle of sleeping baby boy. "He's got red hair!" he exclaimed in a soft whisper.

"They all do," I replied, "just like their Grandpa Jody."

His eyebrows crowded together in a frown as he realized that I hadn't said great-uncle Jody. Then he looked up at Wallace. Wallace cocked his head and shrugged his shoulder as in, 'Yeah, I found out your Uncle Jody is my father,' and then brought Judah to him for inspection.

Ian now had a baby tucked into the crook of each elbow. He looked from one to the other. "These two look jest alike! How do ye tell them apart?"

Wallace pointed to the cowlicks on their foreheads, mirrored images of each other, and said, "They'll be a handful, but I think they're worth it."

I came up with the last swaddled infant. "It's easy to tell this one apart from the others," I said as I pulled back the clout, "She's a girl. Our little bonus baby was a big surprise. I thought I was finished, and then boom! There she was."

Ian handed off the boys to Wallace, and I gave him Danielle. "Weel, thank ye fer lettin' me see 'em. I woulda understood if ye dinna ever want to see me again, here or anywhere else." Ian's head was bowed down, his long finger stroking Danielle's fine pink hair, ashamed of his previous actions, but fascinated with the baby girl, the first living daughter he had ever seen.

Wallace said to his cousin, "Thank you for them," he nodded to each of the babies, "and for Evie. She and I will be married in front of a preacher next month. I just thought you should hear it from me." Wallace said it sincerely, without a trace of malice, and by the blinking of Ian's eyes as he looked at him, he could tell.

"Aye, thank ye fer tellin' me. I wish ye both well," Ian said sincerely, almost embarrassed at his admission. He swallowed, closed his eyes in deep thought, then opened them again, looking at Wallace as if to ask a favor. "So does this mean I can come see 'em every once in a while, since they're my cousin's children?" he asked.

Wallace looked at me to see if I had any objection to having Ian back in my life, even if only on a very limited basis. I shrugged my shoulders. It was okay with me. Now that I had seen Ian in the flesh, my flesh was neither craving him nor hating him. That was a relief, and a reaction I hadn't expected.

"There's one more thing," Wallace said, "If it's all right with you, Evie. We were talking of middle names earlier today. Wow, it was only today, wasn't it? Anyway, if it's all right with you," he nodded to me, "could we use Kincaid as a middle name for the boys? I mean, he was their protector, and the protector of their parents, too."

"Sounds like a good idea to me, a very good way to say thank you forever. As long as it isn't Danielle's middle name," I said, giving Wallace an exaggerated scowl wrapped around a grin.

"How about Wren?" asked Wee Ian. "She has a pretty cry, like a wren, not a crow."

Wallace and I looked at each other. "Well, it's better than Magpie," he said. "Okay, then her name's Danielle Wren Urquhart, unless we find another name to throw in with those three."

I looked over at Ian and smiled. "Oh, and since we're saying our thank you's—thank you for being the sperm donor, Ian."

"Sperm donor? What's a sperm donor?" asked Wee Ian.

Wallace and I couldn't help but laugh. "Welcome to fatherhood, Ian. You get to explain that one to him, not me," said Wallace.

Ж Ж Ж

I was famished, so decided to bring out the leftover noodles I had set aside for a pasta salad. All I needed were a few more items to stretch the meal. "Ian," I called.

"Yes, ma'am," came the quick response from both of the Ians. They looked at each other and grinned.

"Okay, Ians, would one or both of you go into the garden and bring me three ripe tomatoes? I saw some turning red a couple of days ago, and they should be ready."

"Red already?" and "What's a tomato?" were the questions from both of the Ians at the same time.

"Come on, and I'll show ye," said Ian the elder as he led the way to the garden.

"And ye can tell me what a sperm donor is while we're out here," said the younger Ian as he hurried to catch up.

Ж Ж Ж

Wallace and I, and the babies of course, were alone and not under duress for the first time in hours, or so it seemed. I took a deep breath and strolled up to him, ready for a big hug and a long kiss. He was ready, too. The soft kiss sealed the contentment that we both deserved. I sighed as he

371

pulled away, the dreamy look warm on my face.

"I have to ask you," Wallace said softly, trying to hide his embarrassment. "I've never heard that word before. What does effin' mean?"

"Um," I stalled and glanced around the room, avoiding his gaze. The blush that had begun on his face was spreading and was now rising to a full bloom on mine. "I really, really wanted to say another word, but just said the first letter instead. It's nasty and crude—and I did almost say it—but I wasn't going to let anyone make me mad enough to use *that* word."

"Oh, I think I know which one you mean," Wallace said and swallowed a smirk. He reached up and pushed a stray hair behind my ear. "What about Ian? I thought you wanted to—how did you say it—'punch him out'?"

"Nah, that would take an intense emotion and, believe it or not, I don't have any strong feelings for him either way. I mean, I don't hate him, and I don't love him. I'm grateful for the babies, and very glad that he at least had the courtesy to leave me with Sarah and Jody. He didn't just drop me under a spreading chestnut tree or something. No, I think I'm worthy and well, he just blew it!"

"Blue it?" asked the confused young man standing in the doorway. "And he left ye? And those bairns are my brothers and sister? And, and ye dinna hate him fer leavin' ye?"

Wee Ian looked at me, then at Wallace, still very closely linked. I stepped away. "Come here and see the babies again," I said.

He followed and sat on the edge of the bed next to me. 'Lord, give me the right words,' I prayed silently. Okay, start small and work up to the big stuff.

"Blew it means he made a big mistake. Have you ever seen anything swell up really big, then bigger still, and then 'kaboom!'—it blows up? Well, if that occurred in the past, it 'blew' is what happened."

Wee Ian was listening intently to my explanation. "I saw a raccoon once that had been deid for a long time. Its belly was swelled up real big, and when I poked it with a stick, the belly popped, and there were stinky innards all over the place. Is that what ye mean when ye say 'blew it'?"

"Exactly. And if you 'blew it,' it's like a dead raccoon's exploded bloated belly. It's kind of hard to, no, it's impossible to put it back together again like it was, right?"

Wee Ian nodded that he understood, so I continued. "Well, your Da 'blew it' with me, but it's okay. It all turned out fine. As a matter of fact, if

Ian hadn't left me, he never would have found you or your mother and grandmother. And then you would never have met me or your, um, kin," I said and pointed to the babies.

"So, are these my brothers and sister or my cousins?" he asked.

"Yes," I answered. I paused, wanting to end it there, but the brokenhearted frown made me feel guilty for my short, succinct response. I amended my answer, "Both, but that might be confusing to other people, so let's just say they're your kin. Wallace is your kin, too, and he's their father now, and Ian, well, he kind of gave up the right to be their father, but he's a cousin and kin, too. It's nobody's business how we're kin. Kin is a good enough explanation for anybody, all right?"

"Okay. Does this mean yer my kin, too?"

"Oh," I paused to think about it for the first time. "Aye, I am." I grinned. "Now, where are those tomatoes?" I said, effectively ending the thread of the awkward, but revealing conversation.

I cut up the tomatoes and tossed them together with some salt, onions, garlic, dried blueberries, and herbs. I threw in a healthy dash of vinegar and oil, stirred, and added them to the leftover egg noodles. It was red, white, and blue pasta salad for our Fourth of July lunch, with forgiveness for dessert. It was turning out to be a spectacular day.

Ж Ж Ж

After lunch, we passed around the babies for closer examination and appreciation by their new family. Wee Ian couldn't keep his hands off of his newfound kin. He seemed to know all about babies. He held them correctly, could get the burps out without spit-up, and made funny faces that amused me as much as them.

It naturally progressed that we began to share stories. Wallace bragged about my stoic composure during delivery.

"Ye mean she dinna yell or even curse?" asked Ian, eyes wide and jaw slack.

Wallace beamed as he recalled that day. "She made us all proud," he said. "She's a very brave and strong young woman. But you probably noticed that this afternoon," he added with a gimlet eye to Ian, waiting for, but not necessarily expecting, an answer. Ian gave a brief, embarrassed nod, and Wallace continued.

"Danielle, Wren," he corrected as he nodded to Wee Ian, "surprised us with her appearance after her twin brothers' births."

I interrupted at this point, "Yeah, I hollered for the chamber pot because I had thought I had to, well, you know, but realized it was another

373

baby coming out. Wallace got to me just as I yelled 'catch!' She plopped right out, into his hands." I was smiling all over again, remembering that moment when he and I were joined by a little girl and an umbilicus. I glanced over and saw that Wallace was radiant all over again, too. Could it have only been two weeks ago? It seemed like at least a year had passed.

I looked over at Ian. He was fingering the cloth of little Wren's clout, pensive, and probably feeling guilty that he hadn't been there for her birth. Personally, I really didn't want him to feel bad. I wasn't mean, and it *was* in the past. And socially, well, I was still the hostess, and in charge of the good will and comfort of my guests.

"So, what's been going on in your life," I asked. I wasn't just being polite; I was truly curious.

Ian's eyes fixed on a distant point in the sky above the barn. He stared off into nothingness as he began an obviously planned dissertation about how after he had left me with Sarah, some unsavory sorts caught up with him. I was only half listening. I was mad that he was lying to me, to all of us. I couldn't help but glare at him and would have shot rubber bands or thrown marshmallows at him instead if I had had them.

"I was injured and so dinna think I should come back..." He looked up as he continued—probably ready to add in the old sympathy lie about getting castrated—but stopped cold at the sight of me.

My jaws clenched, I shook my head slowly, as if to say, 'Don't go there, dude,' so he didn't. He knew I didn't approve of his personal vendetta with the gang that had captured and tortured him and his dog, Rocky. He was a cad for his single-minded vengeance, but he could at least be respectful and not speak of taboo subjects—and certainly not lie— while a guest in my, rather his uncle's, home.

I swallowed the bile that was rising with my rage. "How about if you tell us how you found Wee Ian," I suggested. I didn't want to hear fabrications, and hopefully there was nothing in this recent event that needed to be distorted or embellished.

He had gone back to check on Robin—his first wife—he said. He wasn't returning to the village to reclaim her—he was only going for a short visit to see her. He had heard she had remarried and had a child, and went back to make sure it was true. He thought he had ruined her by giving her two dead babies. The grief at the loss of their bairns was terrible, but the guilt of her not being able to have more children with another man was even worse.

He found Robin in a Cherokee village three days journey from here.

She was very polite, showed him her new home, and verified that she now had three children, but she was also distant. There was nothing left of the relationship between the two of them. As he was leaving the village, a young boy approached him. He said he was Robin's son. They talked for a short time. The lad knew all about him; he had heard about Sky Walker from his grandmother, his mother's mother. The boy said his grandmother told him that he had Star Walker's—Ian's—spirit.

"It was too much to hope for—that this sharp and fast young lad," he said as he looked over at Wee Ian with pride, "was my son, so I dinna ask. I left the village and returned to my...er...um, business, and tried to forget about him."

Ian looked away as he continued with his recent history. "I had been *hunting*," he glanced over at me to see my reaction to his new word for vengeance, "fer two months when I heard that Robin's husband had been kilt by a bear. It was a brave way to die, but still hard on a woman with three wee 'uns.

"By the time I had made it back to her home, she had found another husband. The man was fond of the two daughters, but dinna want another man's son in the house. The boy was sent to live with his grandmother, even though she was verra old and in poor health. I went to visit the grandmother," he paused to take a drink of the whisky I had brought out for the reunion. I recalled that this was the woman who had made Ian leave Robin, her daughter, after the death of their second child.

Ian settled back on the porch step and continued. "She was blind, but recognized me as soon as I came to her side.

"'I was wrong to send ye away, Star Walker,' she said. 'I canna change what has happened, but I would ask yer forgiveness and a favor. Take the boy with ye. Teach him the ways of the Indian, and the White Man, too. Teach him yer language. He's a fast learner. He will need to ken the White Man's world, but should ken what is right, too. The world as I kent it will soon be gone. He still needs to be taught more of our ways, the true ways, and our stories. Of how to hunt and fish, he already knows much, but there are things only a father can teach."

"I dinna talk while the old woman spoke. I let her finish. She closed her eyes, and I found the courage to ask: is he my son? I looked at her and saw her smile. She was happier than I had ever seen her. But she wasna breathin'. She died givin' me a young lad to watch over. I could only hope that he was mine."

Ian leaned forward, and then looked over at me. "And it wasna until today when ye called him Wee Ian that I kent fer sure that he was mine. But I had no right to claim him after what I had done to ye and the bairns; the leavin' and all…"

Now I was uncomfortable, and didn't feel like I should be, so I changed the subject. "Why were you here today?" I asked. Ian hadn't expected that, nor did anyone else on the porch, although it was a valid question.

"I was followin' those three men," was all he said, then rose to stand, looking as if he were going to excuse himself.

"Those are some of the…the…*them*, aren't they?" I accused.

He looked guilty but didn't answer.

I was persistent, though. "And you're going back after them, aren't you?" I asked, not really wanting to hear the answer that I knew was coming.

"Aye, the last three," he said almost apologetically. "Come on, let's go, lad," he said to Wee Ian.

The boy looked up at him, and then over at me nursing one of his brothers, and then back to his father. "We can stay here longer, maybe a day or two. I nicked a mark in the horse's hoof, and then put camphor on it. If we canna smell 'em, we can see 'em. It has my mark on it."

"Your mark?" I asked.

"Aye, the lizard's tongue," he said simply.

"The lizard's tongue?" Then it dawned on me. "You didn't carve a 'Y' into the Captain's cheek, did you? It was a lizard's tongue?"

"Aye, that's my mark," he said proudly.

"Well, I thought it was a 'Y' for yellow, as in cowardly." I popped right back into mommy mode and dared to ask, "Ian, if you want to go on your 'hunt,' that's your business. But it's okay with me, and I'm sure it's okay with everyone else in this household, if Wee Ian stays here until you've completed your *business*." I couldn't help but add with a black splash of nastiness, "Because you know how I feel about that *business*…"

"He comes with me," Ian said with a coldness that was flat scary. He had his 'possessed by an alien hate force' face on. He was back in vengeance mode.

I couldn't stand the thought of Wee Ian becoming like his father, callus and jaded about taking another human's life. I wanted him to retain at least some of his innocence and humanity. "Well, he's our kin, too, and I think we have a right to want to keep him safe," I argued.

"Safe?" Ian yelled. His face was red, and he was breathing so hard, he was almost snorting.

Well, at least he wasn't cold and emotionless…

"Ye call what went on here today, safe? If I hadna come by, ye would be dead…or worse!"

"And who's to say that you didn't drive them here on purpose, huh?" It was a totally irrational question, but I didn't care. My maternal hormones were raging again; I had a child to protect. I felt Wallace's hand on my shoulder, his gentle pressure urging me to back down.

"I'm sure he didn't send anyone here, Evie. At least, not on purpose," he added with a stern look at his cousin. "Wee Ian is kin, and he is more than welcome to wait here for you to finish your blood feud. I understand that he is your responsibility, but he *is* still only a lad."

"I'll go with Da," Wee Ian said solemnly, his chin out, hands behind his back like a patriarch watching over his family. He stepped next to his father and said, "Someone has to watch out for him, so he doesn't 'blew it' again." He looked right at me as he used the colloquialism incorrectly, but accurately.

I couldn't help it. I rushed over and grabbed Wee Ian with Judah still at my breast. I squeezed the two of them to me, not wanting to let the elder boy leave to watch his father kill people in retaliation for deeds done months ago.

I looked up to Wallace for help, knowing there was nothing he could do. But he tried. He looked right at Ian and said, "Vengeance is mine, sayeth the Lord."

"Not this time, cousin, not this time," Ian said right back at him, and then headed down the porch steps toward the woods.

Wee Ian went over to his little sister and kissed her on the head. "Good-bye, Wren. Watch out fer yer brothers, hear?" Then he ran outside, and caught up to his father who looked down, made sure the boy was with him, and with a definite relief shown in his bearing, continued down the path the horse and the men had taken.

Ж Ж Ж

"You don't think I'm a coward, do you?" Wallace asked.

His question took me completely off guard. "No; why would you ask, or even think, that?" I replied, truly baffled.

"Because I don't fight, didn't fight, when the taxman came, and when the…those…um..."

I didn't want him to fumble, so I just popped in, "the incident in the woods?"

He nodded sheepishly.

"Well, if I remember correctly, you came armed with nothing but a draw knife, ready to fight three men for me. I have no doubt that if they hadn't had a blade to my face, you would have—shall we say—taken out every one of them. You risked your life to protect me; you suffered a hideous indignation worse than bodily death rather than allow me to be hurt. I'm just glad I was able to get you back." I walked up to him and put my hand on his face, and looked deep into his heart by way of his eyes. He saw I was speaking the truth, and smiled weakly.

"And as far as Captain Asshole, I was the one dealing with the situation first, and you let me continue until it was resolved. I think the greatest thing you did for me today was to let him know that you had complete faith in me and my abilities. And you were right; I would have asked for help if I needed it. Well, I did ask for help, but I asked Him," I said as I looked up. "And He is the One who gave you to me—and I always thank Him for that. You're always there when I need you. Besides, any man with a hand can make a fist and throw a punch. Not many know when and how to deal with situations so that a punch or an arrow or a gun isn't needed. That is where you excel."

Another weak smile appeared, but I could tell he still wasn't mollified. "Okay, what do you want to tell me?" I asked.

"I almost killed someone once, actually four someones. Papa had been very diligent in teaching me the many ways to fight—properly, of course. I could fence, use a broadsword—which isn't an easy task, by the way—shoot a pistol, and he even had a man from the Orient show me some unusual ways to use my body to disarm and even kill a man. But Papa was also insistent that I knew that being able to tactfully avoid physical or armed confrontation—while at the same time having all parties satisfied with the arrangement—was much more valuable than fighting. Diplomacy is the civilized man's warfare, he'd say. I did listen to him, but I was young, and didn't really understand what he meant.

"I was sixteen years old and full of myself. I was tall and proud of it. My classmates weren't even up to my shoulders. The girls had just started to notice me and were fluttering around me like pigeons after breadcrumbs. The other boys didn't like that at all. They knew that they couldn't beat me. I was too big. Fighting would get us all expelled from school, too, and our fathers wouldn't care for that..." he looked at me and grinned.

"So, they lay an ambush for me when school was out for the holidays.

It was Christmas Eve, and I wanted to get Papa one of those brandy-soaked cakes; you know, the kind you light on fire just before eating it? Well, I heard there was a shop in town that still had some of them left. I left Uncle Tony's house early in the afternoon—we often spent the holidays with him—and hoped that the shop was still open. Somehow, they found out where I was going, because when I got there, four of my classmates were waiting for me.

"I ignored them as I went in. They didn't like that. They started calling me names, but I was determined not to let them bother me. 'Boot-licker,' 'bollocks-breath' and 'shite-pile'—they were just frustrated teenagers, trying to sound big, saying all the nasty sounding words they could think of. But when I heard the name 'bastard,' I froze. Evie, I could take just about any name but that one. I'd heard it since I was old enough to—no, even before I knew what it meant. When I came to London to attend school, I thought that stigma would stay at Richwood Hall, but it didn't. In retrospect, they probably didn't know about any of the rumors. It was probably just a dirty name to them. But I let them get me angry. Then someone threw a snowball with a rock in it. It caught me in the head, right here," he said, and parted the hair in front of his left ear to show me the scar.

"Between the pain in my head, and the rage at hearing that name again, I lost it. I was livid and, well, it was as if I was somewhere above my body, watching this frenzied madman beat four of his peers until they stopped moving. I stopped swinging and kicking because…well, maybe it was because I was tired of not getting any reaction when a punch or kick landed. I regained my senses—slowly at first—and then saw the pile of muddy, bloody bodies I had created, all because I had let my mouthy classmates make me mad.

"Evie, it was just me, unarmed, and I almost killed those boys. I didn't know what to do, so I ran. I forgot all about the plum pudding cake. When I got home, I asked to be excused for my disheveled appearance, saying that I had fallen down and hit my head," Wallace pointed to the same scarred spot near his ear, "and I was sorry that the dessert had been spoiled. Papa never called me out over it. I was sure he suspected something was amiss, though. You see, I never was a good liar.

"Well, the four boys recovered and never called me names again. Actually, they never talked to me at all, and would walk to the other side of the courtyard rather than come near me. They spread the story that they had been waylaid on Christmas Eve by a gang of ten highwaymen, were beaten and robbed, but were still able to inflict grave bodily injuries on their assailants."

Wallace grinned weakly at the memory of his attackers' fabrication. "But I received my punishment with the guilt I had to carry. It would have been easier if I had been whipped for it, but Papa didn't believe in the belt. I never hit anyone in anger again. I knew I couldn't control my rage once I started. But if you hadn't been under Gimpy's knife, I would have, oh…" Wallace's words stopped as he sucked in a deep breath to compose himself, jaws clenched in recollection.

I put my arms around his neck and brought myself as close to his body as our clothes would allow. "Let's hope we never get in a situation like that again, all right?" I gave him a quick, sisterly kiss. "You've received the fighting blood from the Pomeroys, and the tutelage and temperance from Julian. Now, I think you've managed to overcome the reaction to fight with knowledge of when it is appropriate, and the smarts to know how to avoid it all together. I think you're quite well-balanced."

I purposely tilted off center to force him to catch me and bring me back to center, still in his arms. "Well-balanced and practically perfect in every way," I said in a dead-on imitation of Mary Poppins. Then I planted a long, very un-sisterly kiss on, in, and around his mouth. "Perfect."

***45 Wedding Day Blues

August 3, 1781

I'm getting married.

Again.

I wasn't sure if my marriage to Ian was actually legal since we hadn't had any witnesses. Jody assured me, though, that since Ian and I had performed the traditional rite of handfast, we were indeed wed, but the marriage was only valid for a year and a day. Ian's surprise visit last month sped things up a couple of months or so—I didn't want to do the math because I really didn't like reflecting on the past. But it didn't make any difference because he essentially 'released' me from the handfasting, and wished Wallace and me well in our upcoming marriage. I was no longer obligated to wait for the entire 366 days to pass before having a proper wedding. I didn't care if this was my first or fourth wedding; it was going to be my last. I had met Mr. Right and he was mine.

The babies were six weeks old now, and Sarah said I should be able to resume—or in the case of marrying Wallace—commence 'relations.' Resume, commence, either way, I was more than ready for my wedding night—I was eager.

Sarah hadn't examined me since the babies were two weeks old, and I wasn't looking forward to another one of what I called 'those physical indignations.' She wanted to give me the customary six-week postpartum checkup to make sure I had completely healed.

"Thanks for the offer, but honestly, Sarah, my modesty has returned. A pregnant woman doesn't seem to be shy that way, and when she's in labor, well; she'll let anybody check her bottom end if it means getting the baby out faster."

"All right, but would you at least let me feel your belly? I want to make sure you haven't developed any abnormal masses. Your uterus expanding big enough to carry three babies could cause problems with clots…and you wouldn't necessarily feel any pain or discomfort."

Sarah had asked my permission in a clinical, sisterly, and pleading manner. The last two aspects of her request, and the furrowed forehead of extreme concern, persuaded me to let her poke and thump my tummy.

I sat down on my chaise and pulled off my winter shawl, tacky with sweat, which had stuck to my bare skin. The air moving across my damp neck and shoulders immediately produced an evaporative cooling effect. I sighed at the brief, blissful moment of feeling cool, if only on a few inches of skin.

I had decided to spend the day covered with my shawl, in self-imposed misery, because I didn't want to appear semi-decent or offensive to our guests. I refused to wear a corset and didn't want my unbound body shape offending anyone. Uncorseted women were called 'loose' women, and although they meant it literally, its connotation was the same now as it would be in the future. I knew Sarah and the men didn't mind that I wouldn't wear stays, but we had company coming soon, and I wanted to be courteous.

I kicked off my slippers, lay back, and tried to relax. Another sigh escaped as I felt that same wonderful cooling on my bared feet. Lying down in the middle of the day felt great. Why should I stress over whether I needed the exam or not? I decided to give in to it and enjoy the rare, and guilt-free, moments of idleness.

Sarah helped me hike up the skirt of my new green calico gown. She chuckled when she saw them. "You still like those white cotton briefs, I see."

I growled at her like a dog at a stranger. She grabbed a handful of skirt, playfully threw it over my face, and then got down to business. She pulled my panties down to just above my pubic bone and started kneading my flesh with two fingers, as if she were looking for lumps of flour in bread dough. I peeked over my skirting as she worked over my much smaller, but still mushy, belly.

"I don't see how you swelled up as big as," she looked around for a comparison, "well, as big as this house, and still didn't get any stretch marks. I only had one child at a time, and my belly looked like a road map."

"Good genes, I suppose," I said as I worked the rest of the skirt out of my face with my chin. "It certainly wasn't because I used fancy designer creams or lotions." I unbuttoned the top two buttons of my blouse and looked down at my huge breasts. "Looks like I'm going to have candy-striped boobs, though. These red lines will fade to silver ones, right?"

Loud footfalls, boots stomping up the porch steps, interrupted our conversation. I yanked up my underwear and the two of us tugged at my clothing to get me presentable. I buttoned up as I sat up, sucking in deep breaths of composure, then relaxed—it was Wallace.

It had become a standard, unspoken protocol that when one of the men approached the house, he was to walk heavy as he came up the porch steps to the door. If I was nursing—and it seemed as if I always had at least one baby feeding—I would have a chance to cover up. It might have been different if it was winter, but this was July. Our small, un-air-conditioned southern home had only one small window. It was hot enough inside to bake bread by late morning—or at least it felt that way to me. The skin-to-skin contact necessary to feed the babies was hot and sticky for me *and* for them. As a result, the red blush of prickly heat spread from their cheeks to my breasts. When alone, or only in the company of people under ten pounds, I tried cooling down by baring as much of my upper body as I could.

It was impossible to keep our home environment comfortable. Still, I did my best, stealing random moments of bareness for me, keeping the babies in their sleeveless little green calico gowns and skimpy clouts rather than swaddled. The babies were small and didn't fill their diapers with much output. For right now, I'd rather suffer a wet spot in my lap than deal with diaper rashes on their behinds. I still wasn't brave enough to hold and feed them bare-bottomed though.

Wallace and Julian had constructed and set up what I called a playpen. The men laughed at the name but agreed that it was an apt description. Right now, since they were still small and didn't move much more than a fist or a foot, the child container was perched atop sawhorses. With this arrangement, I didn't have to bend down to floor level to pick up the babies, and the airflow was better for cooling them. I had to admit, I was a little jealous of their life of leisure. When they were hungry, they got their hot dinner brought right to them on the second or third screech or cry.

"Ye canna be feedin' them at the first wail. Ye need to let them work up an appetite," Jody said. "At least that's what my sister Elly told me. Otherwise, ye'll be feedin' them all day and all night. Ye need yer rest and time to yerself too, ye ken."

Jody was careful about speaking of his family. I knew Jody's sister, Elly, was Ian's mother. I didn't know if he had written to her to let her know that she was a grandmother again, and that Ian had fathered three babies at the same time—and with the same woman.

I snorted at the very idea. Fathered; I guess I should say he sired three children because he sure didn't take to fathering. Oh, well, his loss, Wallace's and my gain. I stamped my foot and twisted the sole of my handmade slipper into the ground. Sarah looked over at me like 'am I supposed to know what you're doing there?'

I repeated the stamp and squish into the ground movement. "Bad thought, struck down and buried," I said.

She tipped her head back, sucking in a sigh of understanding, and nodded. Yes, she knew what I was talking about. It was cool to have someone around who was like me. It was also nice that I didn't have to over-explain my idiosyncrasies.

Wallace—my betrothed and the man I loved—was a great father. His fathers, Julian and Jody, were both delighted with their grandchildren. Julian had never been a grandfather, had never even been a father to a baby before, so infants were new to him. Jody had been close to his nieces and nephews in Scotland, and then lived right next door to his daughter Mona's children. Those first grandchildren were a cherished part of his daily life until they time traveled with their parents, back to the late 20th century for medical support. Jody loved babies and spent as much time as he could spare with his new wee kinfolk.

The men were all tuned into their own godchild's cry, too. Jody, who was essentially tone deaf, could differentiate Leonardo's cry from the other two's, but couldn't tell the difference between Judah's and Wren's squalls. Julian would know if his godson was the one fussing. He'd be on edge, trying not to interfere, but would give me 'the look' if I didn't attend to his godson, Judah, right away. He even asked if I needed help on occasion. I knew he didn't want to change diapers, and he certainly wasn't equipped to feed the baby, but he was definitely little Judah's advocate and quite good at settling him down for sleep after a feeding.

Wallace was still partial to Wren, but was on hand to help with all of the children. He was more attentive and helpful than most men of this time. I take that back, he was probably more helpful than most men of *any* time. He told me that he hadn't had any brothers or sisters and had always wanted them. He was lonely as a child, with only adults and animals for company. He knew early on that he wanted a big family, but hadn't been in a hurry because he wanted to make sure he had a good wife. "I didn't know I would find the perfect woman and get a big family all at the same time. God sure has been good to me," he said as he rubbed little Wren's back. He kissed her on top of her pink fuzzy head. "He's been verra good to me."

Ж Ж Ж

Jody and Julian had stayed outside at the corral fence when Wallace went into the house to check on Evie and the babies. The morning was hot, and a break sounded good. The two of them were leaning on the fence, not doing anything but waiting for a bit of breeze to blow across their sweat-soaked bodies.

Julian was deep in thought, going over and over it in his mind. Why had he not talked to Wallace sooner? He had planned on telling him the basics of human reproduction and how it was accomplished when he was entering puberty, but that window of opportunity had long since passed. He should have taken Wallace to see Mrs. Abbott when he caught him with his classmate's book, *London's Women of Pleasure*. Surely one of the girls in her employ could have delicately and tastefully shown an innocent yet inquisitive lad of sixteen the basic mechanics of heterosexual sex. He, or someone, would have to tell Wally today, before the wedding, how it was between a man and a woman. After the ceremony, there might not be a chance to speak with him in private before his wedding night, as it were.

"If this fence gets any harder to hold down, we'll have to call Wallace to help us," Jody joked.

Julian pushed together a small pile of stones next to the base of the fence post. He was smiling at Jody's joke, but didn't say anything. Jody looked over and said, "Are my jokes that bad, or is there somethin' botherin' ye?"

"I want to ask you a favor," Julian said with a large intake of air, finishing with a gust that could have blown out a candle at twenty paces. Yes, Jody could tell Wallace how it was between a man and a woman much better than he could, that was for sure. He took another deep breath, paused, blew it out, breathed in deeply, and then said, "I'd appreciate it if you would talk with Wallace about his wedding night and what to do." He paused, kicking the pebbles hard across the yard, trying to gather courage. "I know the ladies liked him, but I really don't think he's—how should I say—experienced? I've not been married in a long time, and you're still married, and well…"

Julian was fumbling for words, getting red faced with frustration and embarrassment. He looked at the ground for inspiration and couldn't find it. He took another deep breath as if to say something, but no words came out. Not only did he not know the right words to use, he didn't know how to put even the *wrongs* ones together into a coherent request. He was also starting to get light-headed from all the deep breathing. Then he felt the heavy hand on his shoulder.

"I'd be glad to help with this, shall we say, responsibility?" Jody gave an expression that was half grin and half grimace. He was proud of the fatherly task he had been asked to undertake, but was also scared, unsure of what he was going to say.

"Ye ken, the men who told me about what to do and what to expect on my wedding night werena exactly right. My father dinna get the chance to give me the talk. He died before he could see me with a wife, or even a girlfriend. I dinna ken exactly what to say to the lad, but I do ken a few things *not* to say," he said, laughing.

The blush of tension was gone from Julian's face, and the start of a smile was on Jody's. "I'm verra glad that Evie has been marrit before. She'll ken what to do, but I dinna want him goin' to his marriage bed without an idea of how it should be done. I," Jody faltered, then regained his composure, chin out and spine straight, ready to shoulder the responsibility. "I had better have that talk with him now, before I lose my nerve. You can stay here and hold the fence down, or move some fresh straw into the stalls. We willna be havin' too many people over this afternoon, but there's no need to have a foul smellin' barn fer their horses. Besides, if some of them take to drinkin' too much, they can jest sleep it off on the clean beddin'."

Jody reached over and grabbed the wooden pitchfork, propped against the fence. "Use it well, my friend. Ye have the easy task." Jody wiped the sweat off of his upper lip with the back of his hand. "Aye, ye have the easy task," he mumbled as he walked away.

Ж Ж Ж

Jody stomped his feet as he climbed the steps, trying, but not succeeding, to crush his childish insecurity about discussing sex.

I could tell the difference between Jody and Julian's footfalls, but not between his and Wallace's. Since Wallace had just come in, it had to be Jody. "Come on in, Jody, I'm decent," I hollered.

"Of course, yer decent. Who said ye werena decent?" Jody asked, truly confused. Then it dawned on him what I had meant. "Oh, all right. Weel, ahem, I came to ask Wallace to come help me outside fer jest a bit. I need a hand movin' a couple of fence rails, and Julian is busy with a...another chore." He smiled at the mental image of Julian holding down the fence as his other chore.

"I'll be right there," Wallace said. "I just came in to see how my little family was doing." He turned from looking at Wren to me. "Do you need anything before I go?" his hand still stroking little Wren's forehead.

"Yes," I replied, "please send in a cool, gentle breeze, but not too gentle. I want to be able to feel it, but I don't want to get knocked down

386

either."

"I'll do my best," he said, smiling, then turned to Jody. "Ready?" he asked.

Jody took a deep breath, held it, and then blew it out in a huff. "Ready as I'll ever be, I guess."

Wallace and I stared at him, both of us wondering how much trouble setting fence rails could be. He repeated it again, softly this time, and without the hurricane blast. "Ready as I'll ever be."

Ж Ж Ж

Julian saw the two tall men coming out of the house, picked up the pitchfork, hailed them with it, and then walked around the back to the haystack, relieved that Jody doing the deed, not him.

Jody walked up to the same spot where he and Julian had been standing. A slight smile appeared—now it was Wallace's turn to help him hold down the fence.

"Where are we going to put in the rails? This one looks fine." Wallace saw the slightly contorted scowl on his father's face. "Are you all trigh? You look like you're choking on a bone or…"

Jody snorted and said, "No, we dinna need to be changin' out perfectly fine fence rails, and I'm not chokin' on anythin' but words. Ye see, yer other father wanted me to have a talk with ye about yer, um, yer…"

"Wedding night?" Wallace suggested, an open, inquiring look on his face.

Oh my God, Jody thought; he doesn't have any idea of what's going to happen! He looked at Wallace again and saw that he had the most innocent, pleading look on his face. He had a 'please tell me, father, I need to know: will it hurt, will she bite me, am I going to explode' expression of a scared three-year-old.

Wallace burst out laughing. "I got you, didn't I?" he said. He kept laughing as his father's face changed from shock, to anger at being made fun of, to laughing right along with him.

"Aye, ye got me," Jody conceded. His laughter turned into light seriousness. "Now, yer father said that he never had the talk with ye. He wanted to make sure ye dinna have some wrong ideas about…weel, ye ken, the weddin' night. And, weel, it will be more than jest one night if ye have a good wife, and I'm sure Evie will make ye a good wife."

"I'm sure she will. And for the rest of it, I was reared around horses and other animals. It can't be that much different, can it?" Wallace asked with total sincerity.

Jody rolled his eyes, leaned back against the fence with a small thud, and said, "Yes, it can and *is* that much different." He looked into his son's eyes, trying to gauge if he was teasing again. "Ye really dinna ken, do ye?"

"Well, no, I've never 'been' with a woman, although I have kissed a few. Things 'happened' when Evie and I, well, we got carried away kissing, but we had our clothes on the whole time. I know what a woman looks like without clothes, sort of, but I never touched one all over. What I did touch felt mighty good, though," Wallace said with alacrity, indicating that he was definitely looking forward to being married.

Wallace came out of his reverie and asked bluntly, "So what's different with what happens between a man and a woman, and between two other mammals?"

"Weel, first off, ye do it face to face, mostly. Ye can do it jest about any way the, um, parts will fit together, but fer the first time, I suggest face to face." Jody was flustered, but didn't want to leave Wallace ignorant on his first encounter. "And use yer elbows. Ye dinna need to be squeezin' the air out of yer new bride, after all. And if she makes a verra ugly face and little squeakin' noises, that's a good thing. Make sure she makes the faces and squeaks before ye, er—before ye finish…"

Jody looked over at Wallace to see if he understood. At first, there was a blank stare of uncertainty. Then, all of a sudden, his eyes widened— he knew.

"I've seen that look!" Wallace said. "One time when Evie and I were…kissing, she made this horrid face, and then she went limp, almost collapsed. And she was grinning…" His focus drifted off with the memory of their encounter in the garden. "She said she got hers first, and then I got mine. Well, I know what I got, but now it makes sense. Women get that, too?"

"Aye, they do, if yer doin' it right."

Father and son became silent, looking away from each other into the woods, neither of them ready to return to the awkward discussion. Then they both spoke at the same time. "If ye have any questions," Jody began, just as Wallace said, "If I have any questions…"

They both laughed and stared at each other's shoulders, still too embarrassed because of the topic of their conversation to look each other in the face. Then Jody put his hand on his son's shoulder, looked him in the eye, and said, "Dinna worry; jest love her, respect her and protect her, and ye'll have a wonderful marriage. It worked fer me, and I'm sure it'll work fer ye."

Wallace said, "Thank you, father, thank you very much," and started to walk past him to the haystack, intending to help Julian with the straw redistribution task.

Jody's face flashed recall, and he raised his hand to stop his son from leaving. "I have somethin' fer ye. I ken ye canna get yer hands on yer money to buy yer wife a proper ring, but ye'll be wantin' to give yer bride a token of yer marriage. So here, Sarah gave me a bit of ribbon to use as a necklace fer it."

Wallace opened his hand and Jody put a length of black silk ribbon with an ancient silver coin attached to it. "I think that's Athena," he said as he pointed to the face on the coin, "and I'm sure this is Pegasus on the back." He turned over the coin to reveal the struck impression of a flying horse. "See, someone punched a couple of holes here, so the ribbon went right through to make a lovely necklace."

Wallace looked carefully at the coin, and then up to Jody with a raised eyebrow, asking 'where did you get this?' without words.

"It's a long story, but whether it's worth lots of money or nae, there isna anyone here in this land who could change this coin into anythin' but a pretty piece of jewelry. Jest dinna let one of the bairns put it in his mouth when he gets older. It's a bit messy gettin' it back," he said with a smile of remembrance.

Ж Ж Ж

I decided that a salad would be good for lunch. It was too hot to cook inside, and I had just been given two fish as a wedding present by our neighbor Hannah's younger brother, Jedediah. The fish could be wrapped in mud and set in the fire outside to slow-bake. It wouldn't be tuna salad, but flaked trout mixed with mayonnaise on greens sounded yummy. Jedediah said he wanted to give me a present because I was so pretty, but I think he just wanted an excuse to come see the babies.

"You had them all at once?" he asked.

"Well, not exactly. It was kind of like a cat having kittens. They came out one right after the other," I said.

"Did it hurt?" He looked over the edge of the playpen at the babies who were getting their air bath in the late morning shade. "Hannah says the ladies always scream somethin' terrible when the babes are comin'. She puts wadding in her ears, it gets so bad."

Just then, Jody hopped up the steps to the porch. "Weel, some women screech and holler so bad, ye'd think they were dyin', but Miss Evie here, she was quiet as a...as a fish in the water."

"Really?" asked Jedediah. "Do you mean that it doesn't hurt when you have three at a time?"

"Oh, it hurts, all right," I said. "I just found out that it hurt *more* when I yelled."

"Oh, oh, oh, I almost forgot. Da would give me a whippin' for sure if I didn't tell you. Mr. Pomeroy, Da said that there was some soldiers muckin' around the mill yesterday afternoon. He didn't know who they was, but he figured they was up to no good, and that I should tell you right away. Except that I forgot about the right away part. I wanted to bring Miss Evie and the babies something, so I stopped and caught these fish. It's okay, isn't it? That I didn't come here right away, I mean." Poor Jedediah looked as if he could feel the spanking on his bottom while he was talking about it.

Jody said, "Ach, its fine. You had better go on home and tell yer da that ye told me, and that I'll look onto it. And ye dinna have to tell him about the fish, aye?"

"Yes, sir, thank you, sir," he said as he walked backwards away from the house toward the trail. "Thank you very much," he said again, and then turned around and began his race home, sprinting like a short distance runner in an heroic attempt to make up the time lost with the fishing expedition.

Jody looked at me, shrugged, and explained, "No use the boy gettin' whipped fer doin' a good deed fer ye. I canna go back in time and start checkin' on the soldiers sooner. I dinna think the lad will be makin' the same mistake again—with or without the strap. I'll leave with Julian now to see to it. You stay here and let the others ken what's goin on."

I watched dejectedly as Jody strode purposefully toward the barn. He stopped suddenly and turned around sharply. I could tell by his face that he had just remembered something. He came back to where I was, wearing a grin like the fox that had just found the key to the chicken coop. He patted his sporran, and then opened it. "Jest fer the ceremony, here, take the somethin' borrowed. That is, of course, unless ye want to consider it somethin' new. I'll be sure to take it back after the weddin' so it wilna be hauntin' ye. I heard someone is comin' by later with the somethin' blue, and I ken ye have a somethin' old comin' yer way soon. Dinna fash," he consoled, "We'll be back before ye can miss us."

"But..." I started to say something, but thought better of it. I'd heard that phrase 'be back before ye can miss me' one too many times. "God bless," I said instead, hoping that Jody hadn't heard the fear in my voice.

He was halfway to the barn when he called back to me, "Oh, and tell Wallace that we'll be back fer the weddin'. We wouldna want to miss that."

I pulled apart the rag-wrapped parcel he had given me. Jody had 'gifted' me the smartphone he had been holding onto for the last couple months. Now I would have it as a something borrowed, or ironically, something new, 'jest for the ceremony.' Funny man. It was new as in 'this cell phone is so new that it hasn't even been thought of yet, much less created.'

I stashed it in my pocket. I really didn't want it. I didn't like to be reminded of the life I used to have but knew nothing about. At least I didn't have to clean it, feed it, or worry about it giving me fleas. "Nice pocket," I said softly, "you just stay here in this nice pocket, wee black box, and don't give me any reason to toss you down the privy."

***46 Clyde Returns

Wallace and Evie's wedding day

All the major chores had been completed in time for the big celebration. Wallace was behind the house, musing while he busied himself with the never-ending project. The steady tug, tug of clearing out the weeds in Evie's vegetable garden was soothing. He really didn't mind the task; it was actually therapeutic. Yanking and pulling out the bad stuff, and seeing immediate results for his effort—if only life was that straightforward.

However, no matter how much time he spent on gardening, the weeds always found their way back. Wedding and weeding. Evie would be sure to have a joke or a pun about how he was burning hours on one, waiting for the other. "Wally weeding while waiting for the wedding?" he recited to his audience, the magpies in the tree, eating the last of the mulberries. "I'll have to try that one out on her and see what she thinks. Even if it is a groaner, she'll smile for me. Helen of Troy may have had the face that launched a thousand ships, but Evie has the face that lights up this whole colony."

He hoped that there were enough weeds to keep him busy until the wedding. He had been waiting for this day for months. Well, not so much the wedding day, as the wedding night. The warm glow he felt was more than just the weather, exercise, and thinking about his first day and night of being married. He realized that after this evening, he and Evie would be together forever—a well-matched and contented husband and wife like Sarah and his father, Jody.

The summer's heat had really kicked the garden into high production mode. Those tiny seeds Evie had salvaged from the tomatoes and dried peppers from José's ranch really took off after she planted them outside. She had sowed the seeds early, when the garden was still frozen in places. She insisted on keeping her little dirt-filled rag pots in the house so her tomato and pepper plants could get an early start. He had extended the windowsill for her so she could set the seedlings in the sun. "Besides, the soil has to be warm for the seeds to germinate. When it stops freezing at night, I'll plant them in the garden. I'll bet we have tomatoes by the Fourth of July." And she was right; they had tomatoes by the Fourth of July and dozens, scores, more every day.

He had brought along one of the large woven baskets she had made when pregnant to collect today's harvest. That seemed so long ago. Back then, he had been dubious about eating a tomato, but she assured him they were not poisonous, and actually had lots of vitamins and antioxidants in them. He had been a bit embarrassed because he didn't know what those were. "Oh, they're just fancy words that mean they're good for you. You won't get scurvy if you eat one of these every day."

Wallace was contentedly picking the red fruit—what he had been told once upon a time were love apples—when he looked up and saw Jody and Julian quickly and quietly saddling their horses. It was obvious by the sharpness of their movements that they were in a hurry. Something must be wrong for them to be leaving so soon before the wedding.

Wallace sprinted toward them, hurdling over the rail fence like a two-legged jumper horse. Jody saw him approaching and pulled Aries around so they could speak before he left, motioning for Julian to proceed.

Julian nodded in acknowledgement, then turned back to look at Evie. She was on the porch, arms crossed in front of her chest, helpless and frustrated that she couldn't assist her friends and family. The frown on her face was almost enough to pull the brightness from the sunshine. Julian waved his arm to her with a wide good-bye. She grimaced in reply; his false smile hadn't fooled either one of them. He kicked his horse's flanks and swiftly took off to investigate the commotion, hoping that whatever was wrong was easy to repair.

Wallace grabbed the halter of Jody's skittish horse and didn't even get a chance to ask 'why?' when Jody volunteered the answer. "Wee Jedediah jest said his father was concerned about a fuss at the mill. He asked if we would make sure that there was nothin' amiss. Julian and I will look into it and be back in plenty of time fer yer weddin'."

"Don't worry about us; we'll be fine. And I hope you know that we wouldn't think of starting the ceremony without the two of you."

"Aye, we'll be quick about it then," Jody said, and turned the horse around.

"Godspeed," Wallace said, slapping Aries on the flank, hoping it would make a difference in the horse's swiftness and getting the situation resolved.

Wallace stood with his knuckles on his hips, helplessly watching the backs of his two fathers disappear into the trees. It could be nothing, or it could be a major confrontation that they were riding into. Nowadays, nothing was safe or simple.

Of course, they wouldn't—couldn't—have the wedding without the two fathers. After all, someone would have to give Evie away, and it looked like that was going to be the responsibility—no, make that the privilege—of her father-in-law, Jody. Papa was also part of the wedding party. Even though he was legally Wallace's stepfather, Julian was offered, and had accepted, the honor of being his best man.

Ж Ж Ж

I was trying to suppress an intense negative emotion as I stood on the porch and watched Wallace walk back. He didn't look too happy about the men taking off, either. I didn't want to be mad at Jody and Julian for leaving because I knew it was what they had to do; it was a matter of duty. What I had was a case of intense frustration—there was so much going on with this war, and I couldn't help, or do a darned thing about it.

I was sure the two fathers didn't want to leave, but they were soldiers. To them, answering the call to duty was as natural and essential as, well, eating. The gut feeling of frustration that I had was good in a way, though. I didn't have any anxiety or worries that they weren't coming back. At least Sarah and Wallace were still here. If I got to feeling too bad, I could always whine at them.

I wiped my brow with the back of my hand and tried to compose myself. We had guests coming soon—mostly women and children. They probably wouldn't like it either, but would understand about the delay. Young Hannah, who was now acting as au pair to the four young Donaldson girls and the twin baby boys, was coming along with Mrs. Donaldson. The amiable teenager had decided it was safer to stay with the Donaldson family than to follow Sarah around, learning the doctoring trade, at least for the time being. Sarah had agreed it would be best for her to continue her medical training when 'things settled down'—meaning when the war was over.

Wallace hadn't come back to the house but had returned to the barn and was finishing the clean hay exchange. I could really use a hug but didn't want to call him back just for that. My frustration was beginning to segue into moping: I hated the idea that I had become so selfish, clingy, and needy.

Darn it! The wedding ceremony wasn't set up to be a huge or lavish affair, but it was still supposed to be our day! Ergh! Not now, woman... I shook my head and tried to find a positive outlook. Nope, I couldn't find one.

I had fed the boys before the hullabaloo, and now *I* was hungry. I didn't feel like making a sandwich, so settled for polishing off a few tomatoes waiting to be sliced for our celebration meal. I heard one of the babies start to fuss and, sure enough, little Wren was winding up her little pink fists, getting ready for her lioness roar of 'feed me now!'

I scooped her up into my arms, hopped up the steps, and in three long strides was inside the house, settled back on my chaise, having managed to unbutton my dress and bare a breast as I did so.

As soon as she smelled skin, she latched on. It was a phenomenon that never failed to occur; as soon as a baby started to suckle, I would get thirsty. I tried to make sure that I either had a cup of water or milk within reach when I sat down to feed a baby. I had been drinking lots of water today, but water didn't give me the calories I needed to make breakfast, lunch, dinner, and snacks for my three little redheads. I got up and grabbed the pitcher with my free arm. Not bothering with a cup, I slugged down nearly a quart of still-warm goat's milk without stopping for a breath. I wiped off my milk mustache with my quilt and wished that I had a big bowl of fruit salad loaded with bananas for dessert. Even an apple would do. Maybe Sarah knew of a good substitute. I was craving fruit big time, and the endless supply of tomatoes wasn't cutting it.

I laid Wren down on the bed and reached up as high as I could. My fingertips weren't even close to touching the tall ceiling, but I tried to, just the same. I didn't want to get round-shouldered as so many women did, from hunching over babies and chores all day and night. I raised my other arm high, dropped it, then repeated the exercise on the other side. Yoda—at least, I think that's what this was called—was part of my daily routine now.

My workout session was interrupted by light footsteps coming up the porch. It wasn't the normal stomping the men used to announce their arrival. My blouse was still unbuttoned. I had been airing out as I worked out; damp nipples soon developed into cracked and bleeding nipples. I quickly threw my shawl over my shoulders and stood up straight, ready to look any stranger in the eye.

It wasn't a stranger, though; it was Wallace. "I didn't walk heavy coming up the steps because I didn't want to wake the babies if they were asleep. I figured you'd know it was me. Sorry if I frightened you."

I hadn't realized how staid I must have looked, straight-backed, wearing a shawl in this insufferable heat, the milk pitcher in my hand, readied as a weapon. I put down the pitcher, turned around, and buttoned up under the shawl. I looked over my shoulder at my betrothed, gave him a mischievous grin, spun around, and with a grandiose flourish, flung the shawl onto the chair. "Better?" I asked.

His head literally flipped back at my almost obscene gesture. I guessed if it had been anyone other than a husband—or a soon to be one— that gesture would have been outright nasty for this time, even though I was flashing a fully-covered bosom.

His mouth worked around a smirk, trying to clean it up to a smile. He hadn't responded to my question but knew he didn't have to.

"I have something to give you," he said, his eyes shining, dimples stretching. "It's not as pretty as your *ravishing* neck and shoulders," Wallace paused as he took in my shocked expression, "or any of the rest of you."

I couldn't believe that he had just made me blush, especially since I had just been playing the vixen, but he had.

"Oh, you are beautiful, all over: nose, elbows, toes... I'm sorry if I haven't told you enough." He gave me a quick kiss on the end of my nose. "Nothing can come close, but I thought this might suit you since you had to give up your pretty gold nugget necklace to…well, we don't need to talk about that now, do we?"

"No, we don't," I agreed sheepishly. "But you really think I'm beautiful? Beautiful all over?"

"I always have and always will. Here," Wallace got down on one knee and put out his closed hand. He slowly opened out his fingers, and the ribbon expanded like one of those Fourth of July black carbon snakes after it had been lit. My mind raced through thoughts of Independence Day, fighting, gunpowder, and then slammed shut. Nope, not today. I hoped. I didn't want to think about any kind of war or explosions, *especially* today.

"Are you all right?" Wallace asked.

I guessed my eyes had glazed over, fearing armed confrontations. "Aye," I brightened up, and replied in a Scottish accent, "its jest the lack of sleep. I'll bide fine in a wee bit." I changed back to the appropriate voice for the occasion. "What do you have there?"

"It's something for you until I can get you a proper ring. I'd like you to have a gold setting with lots of big diamonds around another, bigger diamond, or maybe you'd prefer a ruby or sapphire in the center. But for now, would you accept this as a token of my love? I'd like you to wear it for our wedding ceremony."

I looked down at the ribbon that was pulling away from the coin in an unplanned, but stunning, animated formal presentation. Wallace had threaded the shiny disc onto a black ribbon, which offset the silver of the pendent beautifully. I picked up the coin and walked through the doorway to see it better in the bright sunlight. "Oh, my," I said, unable to contain the low groan of dread. I lost my legs and sat down quickly on the porch bench.

I looked up and saw the shocked expression on Wallace's face. "Oh, my," I repeated, but with an inflection of adoration rather than recognition. "This is beautiful, so beautiful that it took my breath away."

I doubted that I had fooled Wallace, but he probably would rather believe a lie than to ask me more about it. I recognized the coin, sort of, but didn't remember from where. I sucked down the enigma and asked, "Would you put it on me? I'm afraid I can't tie a good bow or knot behind my neck, and I don't want to lose this—ever."

Wallace took the black and silver treasure from my hand. I twisted my hair into a rope and pulled it up into a knot. We did a tiny tango, turning around each other until we were positioned so my neck was presented to his slightly trembling, but warm hands. "It's beautiful, Wallace. And I don't care if I ever get a gold ring. I have the biggest treasure right here," I said as I turned around and put my arms around his neck. "I'm serious, you know. I can't lose you."

I buried my face into his chest. I wasn't brave enough to look up at him. My tears were brimming, being held back by the rise of my bottom eyelashes. I sucked in a breath of bravery and pulled away to look up into his face. His eyes were every bit as full of tears as mine. I jumped up to kiss him just as he leaned down to kiss me, and we bumped noses.

"Ouch," we both squawked at the same time. I reached up and wiped away the tears in his eyes that had spilled over, and he did the same for me. "Love hurts," I giggled.

"Hold still," he said. I grinned and let him lift my chin, my eyes shut in anticipation of a long, warm kiss.

But nothing happened. I opened one eye. He was bent over to kiss me, but was looking away, his eyes focused on something in the distance. I turned my head and saw a cloud of dust heading up the road to our place.

"Now you hold still," I said. I put my hands on his shoulders and tip-toed up to get my kiss. It wasn't much of a kiss, though, because he was preoccupied with the thought of company. "It'll be a while before they get here," I reminded him softly.

He turned me away from the distracting view of the road, literally sweeping me off my feet, and gave me a kiss commensurate with the giving of an engagement token. "Much better," I said and smiled. He gave me a quick reassuring hug, and then turned both of us around to face the incoming company.

Wallace took a couple of steps forward to see better, his eyes squinting, searching the distance. I came up beside him and looked. I knew who it was. "That's the Donaldsons," I said. "I recognize the horses. Besides, who else would have that many little people on board?"

I hurried back into the kitchen and got the ewer to refill with fresh water. The gang was sure to be thirsty after the long ride. I also grabbed the plate of oatmeal cookies I had made for the reception. On second thought, "Not a good idea," I said. "We don't want the girls amped on sugar." I reached into the little cooler I had devised and pulled out the veggie tray that had been soaking in chilly water. The radish roses had filled out and the carrot sticks had curled. The cucumbers were just slices, but I told Sarah I was going to call them cucumber coins. The girls would get a kick out of having their own money.

I got the fresh water and cups gathered together while Wallace waited for the wagon, ready to grab the harnesses and bring the horses to the barn. The wagon hadn't even got to him when the girls started trying to climb out.

"Whoa there, young ladies. Wait until the wagon comes to a complete stop before trying to get out. We don't want anyone to get hurt. Now," he said when he had a hold of the horse's halter, "if you can wait just a wee moment, I'll give you a hand. Let me help the women first."

"Miss Evie!" Miranda squealed, a fistful of blue ribbons in her hand. "Look what I got for you!" She had leaned out so far that she was starting to fall. Wallace saw what was happening and lifted her out the rest of the way.

"Might as well let them out first," said Mrs. Donaldson. "It takes a bit longer to unload us," she observed matter-of-factly. "Miranda, watch out for your sisters, hear?"

"Yes, mum," she replied. She looked toward me and waved, but turned back to her mother, still in the wagon, ready to assume her sisterly duties.

Wallace had all the girls out in three quick lifts and set downs. The Donaldson daughters all held hands as they came running towards me and the house, a chain of calico and curls. "Come on, sisters, I'll bet Miss Evie has more stories to tell us," encouraged Miranda.

Wallace helped Hannah and Mrs. Donaldson out of the wagon, the two women passing the twin boys between them with an ease and familiarity that seemed to be as second nature as scratching an itch.

Within minutes, our little house had added four little girls, two baby boys, and two women, all talking or squawking. I counted Hannah as a woman although she was only about fourteen years old. My babies were used to being around household noises, family talking, or me singing; we didn't pussyfoot around them either. I wanted them to be able to sleep through everyday sounds. However, the addition of eight more voices, and a new octave range, into their lives woke up every one of them at the same time. I had to admit the cacophony was tremendous.

I looked up and saw Wallace through the open door; it was too hot for closed doors today. He was craning his neck, trying to get a peek at me, I think. I picked up the loudest of my babies, little Wren—she had fallen asleep while eating earlier—and fumbled with my buttons to bring out the buffet. As soon as she latched on, I took my free hand and waved at my very, very soon to be husband. He waved back and headed to the barn to take care of the horses.

What a wonderful noise I was breathing in. The prattle was like oxygen, feeding my heart and nourishing my spirit. The women were talking on top of each other, admonishing the fidgeting girls, telling their baby boys to hush, while straining to look at my two yowling redheaded sons in green calico diapers. I flashed back to my life before I got here, my trek through the wilderness with Ian and Little Bear. I remembered wanting to be in the presence of another woman and estrogen. Well, I was more than in its presence; I was in an ocean of it now.

I was also surrounded by the smell of babies and what babies do. Only it wasn't my babies.

"I told you it was too soon to be givin' the babies porritch. It jest makes their messes stink," Mrs. Donaldson said to Hannah. "I know you were jest trying to help me, but we'll be fine. See, I got lots of milk now."

The front of Mrs. Donaldson's dress was soaked. "Here, give me one of those we'uns," she told her and pointed to little Judah. "I want to see the difference the three months makes on the sucking."

Judah was squalling and hungry but didn't recognize the source of the milk. His head twisted and turned away from the proffered nipple. "Here," I said as I tossed her my shawl, "throw this over your shoulder, and see if that helps."

She did as I asked and sure enough, Judah shut up and started suckling, his little fist clutching the edge of the shawl. "How about that?" she said. "Ooh, now that feels right nice compared to those little fiends of mine." Hannah handed her little George who was making his wants known, too. Mrs. Donaldson leaned back in the kitchen chair, a babe at each breast, and sighed. I think she was actually enjoying the gentle suckling of my baby boy.

"Here, let me have Leo," I said to Hannah. "We might as well get all of mine fed at once. Hopefully Jody and Julian will be back soon, the babies can take their naps, and we can get on with the wedding. Oh shi... oh dear, where's the preacher?" I asked as I arranged my two babies, so they weren't kicking each other.

"Oh, Pastor Lawrence said he'd be right along. He was going to stop and pick up Mr. Rojas. He wanted to see those horses and goats he's been hearing so much about. By the way, where is Sarah, er, Mrs. Pomeroy?" asked Hannah.

"Well, speaking of goats, she's out in the shed, trying to help little Sharona bring forth her twin kids. Or maybe she's having three. That seems to be the magic," I quickly corrected myself to these superstitious women, "I mean, the special number around here."

The little girls were giggling and dancing around the table, inspecting the colorful vegetable tray I had laid out, hands dutifully held behind their backs. "Did you know I made those radish roses and cucumber coins just for you? Go wash up, and then you can have two of each one." I said.

"Can we buy Da a new gun with the coins?" Miranda asked in complete sincerity. "He's always saying how he could sure use a better one."

"No, these are just pretend coins and roses." All the girls' faces fell with disappointment. I added brightly, "But you can eat them. They taste mighty good." I sighed, exasperated that I couldn't help their father, or anyone else, and said gently, "I'm sure your Da will get a new gun when the time is right."

Lord, when is the right time for hoping or praying for a new, or better, gun? Well, I guess now is the right time with our new country on the brink of becoming either firmly established or totally suppressed. "Lord, give us Your strength and wisdom and the tools needed to ensure the success of the independence of this new country, our home, America. In Jesus's name, Amen."

I looked around and noticed it was suddenly very quiet. I must have been praying out loud. Both the little girls and the big girls were staring at me. "Amen," Hannah and Mrs. Donaldson said solemnly.

"Amen," added all the younger ones, including little Rebecca's, "may men."

Mrs. Donaldson handed little George Washington Donaldson to Hannah, who put him to her shoulder for burping. Then she picked up my little Judah, wiped off the milk dribbling out of his slack mouth, and put him to her shoulder. She gently rubbed his back and said softly, "My husband went to the mill yesterday. He heard that there were soldiers out there, tryin' to take it over, meanin' to keep all of the flour and wheat that was in there still. I guess they're serious about tryin' to starve us out. Anyway, he was supposed to be back by last night, but he never came home. I didn't want the girls to worry so, well, Hannah and I decided we should go ahead and come here for your special day. Maybe that would take their minds off the conflict and their da bein' gone for so long. Do you think we did the right thing?"

"I'm sure that's what Mac would have wanted you to do. Who knows, maybe Jody and Julian will be coming back with him this afternoon. That's where they went, too: to see about a disturbance at the mill. If any two men can help, it would be those two," I told her with exaggerated confidence. "Here, let's see if we can fit all the babies into the playpen. Your boys aren't rolling over yet, are they?"

Changing the subject seemed to help everyone. It was a Kodak moment without a camera: five babies in a homemade playpen. "America, the next generation," I said with pride. 'God willing,' I beseeched silently.

Before the ladies could say anything about my remark, we heard a "Ho, the house," from a man coming up in a wagon. It sounded like José and the new preacher had made it to the festivities. Now all we needed was the rest of the men.

I wanted to go outside to greet the new arrivals, but didn't want to be rude and leave Mrs. Donaldson and Hannah with four little girls and all those babies. Then I thought, 'good grief; they do it all day and night, every day and night, so why should today be any different?' My three were asleep and contained. The girls were proper little duchesses from what I had seen. I didn't think they'd do anything bad on purpose, but I didn't want them pulling the playpen down off the sawhorses for a better look at the five sleeping babies either. I didn't need to worry, though. The girls were well distracted playing with their gourmet cut vegetable *hors d'oeuvres*.

I went outside, eager to meet the preacher who was new in the area. I saw that Wallace had already made it to the wagon, and Sarah was on her way, wiping her hands on her apron. She was radiant, with only a smear of blood on the apron, so I guessed all the kids came out okay. I caught up with her on the way to the wagon and our guests.

"How many?" I asked.

"Three, of course; all healthy, and Sharona's doing fine, too." Sarah's face suddenly fell, and I followed her gaze.

There were four men standing next to the wagon parked under the big mulberry tree, their backs to us. I recognized José's fine form right away. Ever the king of courtesy, his hands were already on the horse's halter, ready to assist Wallace. There were two other men, though, not just one in the person of the new preacher who we were expecting. Sarah and I strolled up to the wagon.

The second man turned around. "Good day. I'm Jacob Lawrence the Third," said the dark-skinned man as he extended his hand, "the new preacher."

Everyone was stunned but me. "Hello, glad to meet you," I said as I reached out and shook his hand. "You know, you might get a bit of resistance around here. There's quite the Catholic influence at this house. But, since there isn't a priest anywhere, and I'm the one getting married and not of the Catholic persuasion, I'm glad you could make it. Would you care to come in for refreshments?"

"Yes, yes," added Sarah, "please do come in out of the sun. It's unbearably hot today. But, then again, it seems like it is every day." Sarah started to walk ahead of the new preacher to lead the way to the house, then stopped and turned around. "Master Simon?"

I turned to follow her stare. The sight of a good-looking man—most definitely of African descent—dressed as a white-collared preacher was enough to make anyone in this area stare. It had also been enough to take our attention away from the third man standing by the wagon.

"Simon?" I asked incredulously, wondering why and how I knew that that was his name.

Sarah realized that she had just stopped the new pastor from coming in out of the sun. She looked as bewildered as I felt at the introduction of this new—or was that old?—character of Master Simon into our sheltered life here in the backwoods of North Carolina. "Just a moment, please, Pastor Lawrence. I...I..."

I saw her dilemma. We were both curious about Simon—for different

402

reasons, I'm sure—but wanted to be gracious to our new guest, too. However, we couldn't just lead him into a very small house that was currently overcapacity with little girls, babies, and worried women. In this era, a black man—even a free black man—normally wouldn't interact with white women and children, except as a servant. Sarah and I were both aware of this and stared at each other with the 'what now?' look on our faces.

I knew that slavery was a part of Colonial life, but it hadn't impacted this area. The dirt farmers and tradesmen were too poor to own a slave. By the suffix of Pastor Lawrence's name, I'd say his father or grandfather was a shrewd man who knew, or at least hoped, that being 'the Third' and being a man of the cloth would help protect his heir in this racist region and era. So far, so good.

Then I knew what to do. "Miranda!" I hollered. "Bring me the water and three cups, please." Shouting across the yard was rude, but I knew that little girl was like my magic wand. She would do anything for me, whether it be serving water to our guests or digging privy holes in a rainstorm.

I walked over to our three recent arrivals. "Sorry for the shouting," I said. I looked at Sarah. She looked like a landed fish; she was in some sort of mouth-opening-and-closing shock, and I was beginning to feel a bit overwhelmed, too. "Our house is so small, and right now there are two ladies and nine children in there, five of them under five months old. We haven't had a chance to set up the tables and refreshments yet. It's..."

I didn't get a chance to finish with my excuses. Wallace's hand was on my shoulder, gently telling me with his touch that it was okay. "Sure is hot today, and here she comes," he said as Miranda came up to him with the tray. I noticed that she had eyes for no one but the two of us, and that was a good thing.

"I put some of the Continental coins and other treats on the tray for you. Mum said we couldn't eat them all 'cause there was more company coming."

Wallace took the tray from her and set it on the corner of the wagon. Just then, Miranda spotted the three men. She saw José first, and gave him a big grin that bordered on flirting. Then her eyes went to the other two men. She didn't say a word, just stared at the man with cocoa-colored skin. I walked over to her and tapped her on the shoulder.

"Thank you for your help. You'd better go back to the house now, all right? I'll be in later."

I had thought about introducing her, but remembered that 'children should be seen and not heard' was the attitude of this time. I never subscribed to that theory, but today, I was glad of it.

The horses and wagon were in the shade, so that's where we stayed to enjoy our little tea party. I served the cups of water then offered the plate of vegetables to our guests. Pastor Lawrence accepted a couple of curled carrot sticks from the plate, commenting on how elegantly I had prepared a simple root vegetable. José said 'thank you' and took a couple of the radish roses.

I was glad that José had not refused to eat the food after a black man had touched the tray. Evidently, segregation was not the way of life in Spain. Simon was mum, just looked constipated and agitated, and ate nothing.

Sarah was beginning to come out of her trance and had accepted a 'Continental coin' cucumber from me. She hadn't stopped staring though. She was just about to say something—profound, I'm sure—when we heard it.

There was a horse coming up to the house at full speed. Wallace walked away from our soirée and stood in the middle of the road, ready to intercept the rider.

The lathered horse came in with a raggedy young man clutching its mane. The spindly roan didn't have a saddle on it, and if it had ever had even a blanket, it was long gone. The man dropped off his ride as soon as it came to a stop. He almost fell down, either from being no-saddle sore or fatigued, but either way, he had lost his legs. Wallace gave him a hand up.

The raggedy man looked up at Wallace and gasped, "It's you!"

Wallace recognized the man immediately and quickly stepped away, rubbing his hand on his pants, as if it was soiled.

It was Clyde, one of the men who had raped Wallace six months before. We had both been attacked, although Wallace much more brutally. We thought that my feral friend, Lady the puma, had devoured or at least killed Clyde. She had killed my attacker, Gimpy, and castrated and possibly killed Clayton, the other rapist. All we ever found of him were the remains of his genitalia.

If looks could kill, Clyde would be dead, but instead, he was on his knees, pleading. "You have a right to punish me, and I'll let you do it later, but please, first, help me! My brother and sister are holed up at the mill with your kin. There's three Redcoats there holdin' 'em with guns. The Captain said as soon as the rest of his men get there tonight, they're gonna line everyone up and shoot 'em all, make an essample of 'em. I knowed

404

the way around the back, so I snuck out to get help. Your kin tole me to get you to come and rescue 'em. The Lobsterbacks didn't see me sneaking out, but I wasn't who they wanted anyhow. They wanted the big man with red hair—your father, I reckon—and anyone that joined up with him. We can sneak back in and blindside 'em if we hurry. There's only the three of 'em right now. Please, help me."

Clyde was prostrate on the ground now, his hands cupped as in prayer on top of Wallace's boots. Wallace took a step back and said, "Get up." He paused and added, "We'll need fresh horses," then turned and headed for the barn.

"I'm coming, too," shouted Sarah as she ran after him.

Wallace stopped and turned on his heel. I saw him take a deep breath, the look of fire ablaze in his eyes. I was sure he was going to tell her to stay put. He blew out his breath in a huff and said, "Then get your bag and let's get on with it."

Wallace took long strides to the barn, grabbed the jackass's reins, and threw them over the hitching post for Clyde. He wasn't going to give him one of our horses to ride, and didn't even want the man inside our barn.

I didn't blame him on that one. I looked over and saw Clyde bent over the trough, using both hands to bring water to his face to drink. He felt uncomfortable, and as uncharitable as it was, I was glad. I didn't want to talk to him, nor did anyone else. I shuddered at the thought of him.

I ran after Wallace, my heart ready to tell him that he couldn't go—it was our wedding day—and caught up to him as he swung the saddle over the horse. He just missed my head with a stirrup as I popped up on the other side of him.

"I'm sorry, Evie. What kind of man would I be if I let my fathers be murdered? I have to go."

"I know," I said, as I held the horse's halter for him. Tears were streaming down my face, but I didn't want him to see them. I had left my shawl in the house, so had to settle for wiping my tears on the shoulder of my blouse.

I felt a hand come under my chin and lift it. "Here, blow," said Wallace as he offered me his beige embroidered silk handkerchief. I blew, then quickly tried to wipe away my sadness with the edge of the cloth, only managing to get the wetness removed.

"We may have to delay the wedding a day or two, but I will marry you, I promise," he said. Then he lifted me off the ground and gave me a hard, quick—almost painful, but passionate—kiss. He set me down just as

405

fast as he had lifted me and snorted, his face taut with anger. He turned away and mounted Thor, Jody's latest acquisition, a still not completely broken Arabian mix. "Sarah will have to catch up. Kiss the babies for me, aye?"

"Okay, and I'll save another one for you," I said and pushed his silk handkerchief back into his pocket.

Sarah came running up with her bag in hand. "I hope I have everything," she said frantically as I helped her get her horse ready.

"You always have the best-packed medical bag in the colonies— maybe even the world—and you know it." She shrugged at my remark, her lips tight with frustration. She handed me the bag, then put her foot in the stirrup to climb up. "Let's just hope and pray that you don't need it," I added as I handed it back to her.

It hit me again; I couldn't contain the emotional eruption. I grabbed her leg and clutched tightly, "Bring him home, please, please! I don't want to be a widow before I'm a bride." A huge wail came out of me, then two big hiccups. I sucked it back down and tried to put on my brave-little-soldier mask. "Go, go," I said as I pulled on the horse's rein and led her out of the barn. I slapped Jessie's behind so Sarah had a chance to catch up to Wallace, almost out of sight, and Clyde, just ahead of her, hanging on for dear life on the bare back of that sturdy but ornery jackass, Prince Charles.

***47 Rescue at the mill

I watched the three of them take off, my hopes and dreams for a happy wedding day riding grimly astride Thor's saddle. The unlikely trio was on their way to resolve a disquietingly odd scenario. Wallace, the former victim, was blindly answering his attacker's request, heading into a hostage situation in order to help members of this horrid man's family. Well, Wallace did have a personal interest in the liberation effort, too, so I guessed it wasn't that odd. His fathers were also being held against their will. At least it was a rescue mission and not cold-blooded vengeance. I snorted. "Forever Pollyanna, eh—always looking for the good in a situation—at least it's not vengeance…"

I tried to compose myself and wiped my face on my damp sleeve, only to realize that it was too wet to be of use, so I leaned over and employed my apron. I straightened up, pushed the hair out of my face, and sucked it up, gazing one last time at the vanishing trio. I was standing resolute in my newly recovered respectability when I noticed it. It had flown out of his pocket—the embroidered handkerchief used to wipe away my tears just moments earlier. To hell with respectability and dignity: I ran after that cloth as if it was a lost part of his body. To me, it was, in a way. It was the last object we had shared that I could touch.

I bent over and picked up the now dear and precious memento: my fiancé's crumbled and dusty silk snot rag. I stayed crouched on the ground and shifted side to side on my flat feet, clutching the cloth to me as if it was a pouch of gold coins. I reached in front of me and grabbed a golf-ball-sized stone. I rubbed it hard with my thumb a few strokes, pressing my anger and aggravation into it. I stood up and hurled the rage rock down the road where the three mismatched rescuers had disappeared. "You'd better come back in one big piece!" I shouted at my long gone fiancé.

I turned around and headed home, angrily kicking stones in front of me. I knew no one had heard my scream. I was still a long distance from the house, and the riders were too far away to hear me, but it felt good to both vent and be bossy.

"Damn…damn…damn…" puffed an angry young voice from the direction where I had just thrown my attitude adjustment rock. For a moment, I thought I was hearing myself curse, but the sounds were coming from behind me.

I turned around quickly and saw a totally naked young girl half-running, half-falling down, on this same trail that Sarah, Wallace, and Slug Mold had just traveled. She must have recently emerged from the brush on the side of the road. I stared at her for a long moment, and then realized that the falling down aspect of her movement was going to win out over the running part. I raced up to her, my skirts pulled high so I could move faster, and caught her just as she stumbled one last time.

What do you say to a naked young lady? In this case, nothing. I could see that she needed water before any questions could be answered. Her lips were swollen and cracked, and it looked as if her tongue was too big for her mouth. "Come here," I said as I bent over and helped her wrap her arms around my neck. "Lift your legs around me and I'll carry you back to the house. We'll get you something to drink and some clothes."

I heard mumbling and crying in my hair. She was wrapped around me like a blonde spider monkey puppet and sobbing, "Damn, damn, damn, damn," over and over again.

The barely lucid young lady—by her budding body parts, I'd say she was about 11—was so lightweight and leggy that it had been no burden to carry her like a toddler. It was a natural progression for me to treat her as one, too.

I stopped at the barn, got her some water to drink, and then gave her a rag I had dipped in the horse trough. Her overheated body was covered in a red flush. "Wipe yourself down with this, and stay put," I said.

I ran over to the clothesline and grabbed a length of the green calico fabric I had prewashed and hung out to dry. It seemed like that bolt of cloth never ended, which was a good thing. I could hear our guests on the porch enjoying themselves. The little girls were teaching Pastor Lawrence some of the songs and stories I had taught them. "One fish, two fish," the girls were chanting. I stayed mum, covert in my laundry retrieval. I didn't want to draw any attention to this new situation.

I rushed back to the barn and saw that Master Simon was looking inside, possibly for me. All of a sudden, his head snapped back, as if he had just been hit on the chin. I couldn't see anyone else, but I realized what had happened: he must have spotted the girl and seen that she wasn't wearing any clothes. A true gentleman, he quickly averted his eyes from the little Lady Godiva, and was now walking my way.

Rather than wait for his questions, I took the proactive approach. "I haven't a clue as to what's going on, but I'll find out once she gets decent. Stick around, though," I said as I turned and walked backwards away from him. I shook my finger at him and continued my admonishment, "I want to talk to you, too."

I still wanted to know about Sarah, him, and me, and what we all had to do with each other. Something was niggling at the back of my mind, and it wasn't the current situation, or rather situations, at hand.

I tore three thin strips off the end of the cloth. The girl had cleaned the road dust off herself as best she could. Her frightened blue eyes peered out from behind a wayward tress of long, blond hair. Her face was pink, puffy, and lopsided, and it wasn't that way solely from crying: it looked as if she had been hit recently. The skin was crimson on the left side, although it didn't showing any sign of bruising yet.

"Here, hold your arms out like this," I said. I took a hasty measurement, folded the long length of cloth in half then once again sideways. I used the sheep shears to cut out a piece of the double folded corner. I opened out the makeshift dress and threw it over her head. I grabbed two of the short strips, tied them together, and made a belt for the ensemble. The third strip I used as a headband to pull her hair out of her face. The poor girl was shaking as I clothed her, her arms now held close across her belly. She was stunned, possibly in shock, sobbing silently, gulping air, and trying to steady herself.

Simon very gingerly walked over to us. He held the vegetable tray that had been passed around earlier. It had been resupplied with little pinwheel sandwiches and tomato wedges. He held it out to the little girl and waited for her to take one. She looked up at him, wary of his motives. It appeared she wanted to make sure he wasn't going to grab her when she reached for the food. Seeing her distrustful, frightened look, he put the tray down on a barrel top and moved away. She took two cautious steps to the food, then reached out and grabbed the whole plate, clutching it to her chest, cramming the little sandwiches into her mouth as fast as she could.

"Whoa there, little lady," I said and pulled the plate away. I didn't want her to choke. "Don't forget to chew before swallowing, all right?"

She nodded her head twice, then went to the trough and cupped up water with her hands, quickly and efficiently swallowing her big mouthful of food. "It was a trap!" she exclaimed. She started crying again, but managed to spit out her words between gulps of air. "I hollered at them as they were riding by, but they didn't hear me," her head dropped low in shame, "or see me."

"Who didn't see you, and what do you mean it was a trap?" I asked, hardly able to contain myself. I wanted to pick her up and shake out the answers but resisted the urge.

"You see, they let my brother Clyde escape so he could come and git the other big one. The first ones was just wantin' the flour and to talk to the big red-haired man, but the captain, he wanted trouble, I could see that. He said he wanted to bring in the Big Red and the son, too, and then arrest 'em both…and anybody else that had been listenin' to 'em."

"So how did you get out?" I asked. If they had let one person escape, maybe this was a trap, too.

The young girl put her head down in embarrassment. She didn't want to talk, but I wanted—needed—to know. I realized I had to get her confidence first. Evidently, feeding and clothing her weren't enough. "What's your name?" I asked.

"Jenny. And don't go makin' jokes about me bein' a female jackass either," she said defensively.

"Okay, Jenny." I paused to savor the name, hoping to earn her trust through flattery. "That's a fine name. Did you know that's the name of Big Red's mother, too? I certainly wouldn't think of teasing you about your name with his mother having the same one. He loves her very much."

"Oh," she paused to think about it. "Really? Okay, I guess I can tell you, seein' as you know him and his kin and all. The Redcoats stopped by the mill yesterday and decided they was gonna take all the flour for theyselves. But the man they called Mac was there, and the miller and Clyde and me and my t'other brother, Clayton, and a couple t'others, too. Well, Mac said they couldn't just be takin' what weren't theirs. I guess he and t'others had been readin' that paper about liberty and stuff. So the Redcoats, they say they're gonna shoot 'em all, but I don't think they really wanted to do it. So they just tied 'em up and took all the flour and started loadin' it into a wagon. One of the men that was there at the mill—Mac's friend, I think—he rannned off, and so two of the soldiers took off and chased him, but I don't think they ever caught him.

"Then this afternoon, the Big Red and the one they called the Turncoat—he's a little man, but kinda pretty—they showed up. Clyde took 'em aside and told 'em he knew a way they could all sneak out if one of 'em could addle the soldiers. So Big Red, he just starts talkin' to the Redcoats. And the soldiers, they was about to let everybody go and just keep the flour and the wagon, when another Redcoat come in. He said he was a captain, and he was in charge now. He was mean and ugly, and said they was still gonna keep the flour and the—the sons of liberty, I think he called us—they would have to pay the tax, or they would all get dee ported!

"Well, the first soldiers just wanted the flour, so they took it, and most all of them went off. That only left the two soldiers there with the captain to watch 'em all. Clyde was all set to slip out—he didn't want to get dee ported either—but Big Red asked him if when he left, would he follow this here road," Jenny pointed to the road she had just come down, "and tell his son to come back with help. But he said to make sure he brought back the kegs or cakes or somethin' like that. But I'm not sure Clyde got that part. He's not too bright and can't remember two things at once. But I *know'd* he got out and come down the right road 'cause I just saw him headin' back to the mill. But he musta forgot about t'other part, 'cause he didn't have no cakes with 'em. And, and…"

Little Jenny started crying again and couldn't talk, and I was losing patience. "And what?" I asked sternly.

"After he left, the big ugly captain told one of t'other soldiers to stay outside and watch to make sure Clyde got away. And to let him know when he got back with the, the son, and then they would line 'em up and shoot both the Big Red and his son. And he wasn't just talkin' like t'others, he really meant it!"

I fell back hard against the center post of the barn and slid down in what felt like a controlled faint with consciousness, if there even was such a thing. "Oh, shit," I said.

"Yeah, oh shit is right!" Jenny agreed. "So, I wanted to hurry up and catch Clyde and tell him it was a trap, but I couldn't just run out, me still bein' a prisoner and all. But you see, the ugly captain, he took to starin' at me, wantin' to set real close to me. He came up to me and started runnin' his hand down the side of my face, and then down to my neck and, and… Well, the Big Red told him to take his filthy hands off-a me, but the captain, he just laughed, then kicked him real hard. I thought he hurt him real bad, but he didn't because then there was some scufflin' and next thing ya know, the Big Red has his knee in the captain's throat. But then t'other soldier came by and kicked Big Red in the head, and he rolled over and didn't wake up."

I was even more stunned, wide-eyed with wonder and worry.

Jenny paused to look over at me. "He wasn't dead, though, I checked—you see, they hadn't tied me up." Jenny was concerned about me and made sure I knew that Jody was going to be okay. "But I bet he has a big headache when he wakes up. But then the captain, he starts rubbin' his hands on me again, and then I get an idea."

Jenny's voice changed. She continued but was obviously embarrassed about what she was saying. "I watched a woman do a dance once, and it made the men just stare, and they couldn't even move, except their hands was on their...you know, stuff, and then she took all their money, so I figured that maybe I could do somethin' like that. So I tell t'other soldier why don't he put down his gun, and I'll do a dance for the both of 'em. But I told him that they can't touch me. The captain, he don't like that much, and he smacks me upside the head for bein' sassy. But t'other soldier, he's got the rifle, and he says he wants to watch, so fer him to keep his paws off-a me.

"So, I start dancin' around a little, and my brother Clayton, he starts to holler and tells me don't do it. But then the captain punches him real hard, and then he don't talk no more. I don't think he got killed, though, 'cause he kept groanin'. So, I start doin' the dance, and the miller and Mac just cover their eyes and start prayin', but I tell 'em I'm gonna be all right.

"Then the captain says I have to take off my clothes. So, I take off my dress, and he says I have to take off my shift, too. I can see he's gettin' all worked up, so I tell him he has to take off his clothes, too, if I'm gonna take off mine. Well, he starts to do that, and that's when the other soldier had to hit Mac and the miller to get 'em, get 'em, quiet.

"So, the soldier takes off all his clothes first, and I think he wants to do the nasty with me, but the captain says he has to wait. I didn't want to take off my shift, but the captain smacks me, and says that if I don't, well then, he's gonna do it for me, and cut me, too! So, I take off my shift...and he pulls down his pants and, and..."

Jenny paused. I looked up at her, throat tight with terror. It felt like an iron fist was squeezing my heart.

"And I ran like hell!" she bragged. "They had their pants down, and there was only two of them. One of 'em had to stay with the prisoners. I heard 'em yellin' and arguin' as I was runnin' away, about who was gonna do the chasin' and who was gonna do the stayin'. I was flyin' down that road, hopin' to catch up with Clyde on the way back from fetchin' the Big Red's son, but then, then, I got a bit bashful 'cause I didn't have on no clothes, and I hid in the bushes when I heard the horses comin'. I thought they might be more soldiers again 'cause there was more than just two. By the time I got back out on the road and saw it was them with a lady, they was already gone. They was ridin' real fast! I didn't know what to do, and then somebody almost hit me with a rock, and then I saw you. I wasn't afraid of you 'cause you was a woman, and really, I was just too tired and too sad to care about anythin'."

With her last revelation, I realized the need to take quick action. "Okay, so what we have is five men tied up and kicked around. Hey, where was Julian, the pretty Turncoat, during all of this?" I was afraid that something had happened to him that she hadn't revealed.

"Oh, him? The first Redcoats, they stuffed him into a flour sack and said they was gonna beat him with a stick. But they shoved him out back and forgot all about him when they left. It's a good thing, too, I think, or he would be back with those Lobsterbacks, and I don't think they like Turncoats too much."

"Thank you, Lord," I said softly and got up from the barn's dirt floor. I brushed off my skirts, now ready to get back into boss lady mode. "So, right now Julian is safe because they don't even know he's around. That leaves Clayton, Jody, Mac, the miller, and his friend—that's five—and Clyde, Wallace, and Sarah—three more—are on the way." I enumerated the captives, or soon to be captives, on my fingers. "Eight. Ho, boy. But you say that there're only three soldiers?"

"Well, no; that's the bad part," she said. I tipped my head and looked her in the eye, urging her to continue. "I saw six more coming in from t'other way when I was runnin' to catch up with Clyde. That makes ten."

"No, three and six makes nine, but that's still a lot of men for you and me to overpower if Wallace, Sarah, and Clyde get captured."

I paused for a moment, waiting for inspiration. "Cakes; what did you say about Jody and cakes?"

"I don't know if he said cakes or kegs," Jenny said. "Why would he be wantin' food or whisky at a time like this?"

"Oh, oh, oh! Yes!" I burst into grin. "He said kegs! We have lots of kegs: kegs of gunpowder. Simon, we need you to drive us up to the mill in the wagon. Before we actually get there, though, I'm going to do a little sabotage. I may not have C4, but I do have gunpowder, fuses, and a plan. I'm going to do a bit of distraction and diversion while you, little Missy, sneak back in and cut loose the hostages. Those Redcoats won't even know what hit them."

It was first things first, though: I needed to take care of my little family. Right now, that meant I needed to have a talk with Mrs. Donaldson. I walked up to the house and saw that José, Pastor Lawrence, and pretty much everybody who could walk except for Mrs. Donaldson, were outside playing catch with a rag ball. I waved to them, then ventured in through the open front door, my emotions as tangled as an eagle's nest.

"I need to ask a big favor," I said to my bosom buddy, my heart rising to my throat, nearly choking off my words before I could say them. Mrs. Donaldson looked at me as if I was sick, but I held up my hand for her to let me finish. "I have to run a little errand, and I'm not sure how long I'll be. Could you and Hannah take care of my babies? I mean, you'd have to feed them if I didn't get back in time, but...but..."

My words were failing, fumbling out because I was now looking at all three of my babies, sound asleep in their little playpen next to the larger George and Nathanael Donaldson. I sucked it up and continued, "They shouldn't be too much trouble. I just have to take this little girl back to her family. I'm not sure how long I'll be, and she doesn't feel comfortable going with a man, so if the babies need feeding, do you think that you..."

Mrs. Donaldson interrupted me with a compassionate hand on my shoulder. "Of course, my dear; we already know about the shawl trick now, don't we? My boys can have some porritch if they get hungry. It might make their messes stink, but they're gonna have to start eatin' it sooner or later anyhow. You just go on and take care of that little girl. Oh, here she comes now."

I turned around and saw Jenny in the doorway. She glanced sideways then turned her complete attention to the pen full of babies. "Are they all yours?" she asked, her mouth hanging open.

"No, no, only the three little ones; the two bigger ones are hers. Mrs. Donaldson," I nodded the introduction.

"Wow. Are they comin' with us?" Jenny asked, her eyes as big as teacups.

"Oh, no; they'll stay here with me. Are you ready to get back to your family?" asked Mrs. Donaldson.

Jenny looked over at me for an answer, and I dipped my head slightly in acknowledgment. "Yes, ma'am, I'm ready," she replied. She turned to me and asked, "Can we leave now, uh, ma'am?"

I realized that I had never told Jenny my name. I grimaced slightly and tried to recover with the words, "Yes, let's go. Thank you, Mrs. Donaldson."

The two of us scurried out of the house, then almost ran to the barn. "My name is Evie," I said when we got inside. I grabbed two of the long boxes containing the rifles and ammunition from under the loft, set them on the tailgate of the wagon, and pushed them under the seat. I showed Jenny where the kegs of gunpowder were. "Here, these need to go into the back of the wagon."

414

These kegs were the goods received from my gold nugget necklace trade with Captain Asshole, the taxman. I was pretty sure he knew his lamebrained accomplices had gunpowder in their wagon of stolen goods, but he had let the valuable commodity go in trade. Gold lust will do that to a person. Besides, he probably figured he'd just get more of it down the road. However, I was pretty sure he didn't know that what he had was state of the art—for 1781—ammo propellant. Jody had marveled at the texture of this new powder; it was very consistent and didn't clump. I grunted as I lifted one of the kegs onto the wagon tailgate.

"Simon, would you help her load these?"

Simon had been busy while we were in the house. The team was ready—it never had been unhitched—but he had watered the horses and given them hay. Now, the man with the scholar's soft hands was hefting kegs of gunpowder to the little girl in the wagon. Jenny was strong for her petite size, and was managing quite well, maneuvering the kegs by rolling them on their rims to the front of the wagon. "Don't bump those into each other or anything else," I warned. "And would you ride here in back and make sure they don't move?" I didn't know how explosive the kegs were, but I didn't want to find out until I was ready.

I ran into the corner of the barn and dug out the spool of fuse cord and the lighter from my secret cache. I had left the two items together for rushed times such as this. I patted my pockets and made sure I still had my Leatherman and the smartphone. I grabbed the shovel and carefully placed it next to the six kegs of gunpowder. "I think a six-pack should be enough to get this party rolling. Come on, Simon; let's go."

I climbed into the wagon. "Here, you drive," I said as I handed the reins to him, "I still haven't got the hang of these two-horse powered vehicles."

A cosmic pulse of *déjà vu* throbbed as soon as the words were out of my mouth. It felt as if Simon and I had been out driving around the countryside together once before.

It was too noisy for conversation while riding in the wagon on a rocky road, but I couldn't help staring at him. He must have felt my eyes on him, though, because he turned to look at me. "Later," he said simply, returned his focus forward, and flicked the reins, urging the horses to speed up.

We rode in an uncomfortable silence for half an hour. Simon never said a word nor looked in my direction again. Jenny rode quietly, too, scanning the roadside, absorbed in her own thoughts. I made good use of the time cutting fuse cord, and praying—for inspiration, and for the safety

415

of our friends and families.

"Here, here!" Jenny called out suddenly, pointing to a little pullout on the side of the road. "We can't ride up past here or they'll see us." She turned around and looked at the armament, scowling. "Master Simon told me these would explode. How do you make them do that?"

It was a valid question. I guessed Simon—she called him Master Simon, so I supposed he had introduced himself earlier—must have given her a brief lesson on explosives. "Leave that part to me. Now, help me bring those around here."

Just a few yards away was a slightly sloping glen that would be perfect for my pyrotechnics display. If I could get the explosions to shoot up past twenty feet high, they would be in the line of sight of anyone near the mill. Sight, sound, and maybe smell: a perfect distraction so we could rescue the hostages.

The three of us worked in a well-coordinated effort and had the wagon unloaded, the kegs set in more or less a large circle, within minutes.

I turned my attention to Simon. "Give me about fifteen minutes to do my thing, and then very slowly drive up to the mill. You can claim the horse has a sore foot or whatever. I just want them to be watching you as you make your approach. When you get there, ask them if they have your flour ready. Make up some story about how your brother brought in two bushels of wheat or something, and that you want the flour. Just talk, okay? And talk real slow and act stupid."

The indignant look on his face was priceless. I still didn't know who this Master Simon fellow was, but he was definitely a 'master' of something and didn't look the simpleton at all. Maybe this would be harder than I thought.

"Here, unbutton your shirt and re-do it wrong, you know, so you have one button too many left over. And put your hat on crooked." I reached up to shove his hat askew and he pulled back, as if I was trying to wipe a smudge off his face with a spitty finger. That gave me an idea. I reached down and grabbed a juicy weed, pulled it between my thumb and forefinger, then picked up a pinch of dirt. "There," I said, and used my dirty digits to paint the side of his nose and one cheek. "That looks much better."

Jenny was doing the 'me too, me too' dance, eager and more than ready to do anything to help. "Jenny, your job is to sneak around the building and get in the back door. There's probably a guard there, so you'll have to wait until the coast is clear."

I saw her tilt her head in confusion, so I reworded my instructions. "Don't go in until it's safe, and you know you won't get caught. Here, use my knife to cut off the men's bindings. Make sure you tell Jody, that's the Big Red, and his son that I have a *well-stocked wagon* out front. They'll know what that means. Now, this is how it opens up."

I opened up the Leatherman and turned it back on itself to reveal the hidden blades. I debated on whether to show her how to use the wire-cutter feature. That might be too complicated for her. I used my thumbnail to pry the blade up so she could see where it was. "When you're ready, pull it out all the way. It'll lock in place."

I looked up at her face to make sure she understood. She understood, all right. She was about to receive a magnificent piece of equipment and probably thought it was magic. "It's Italian," I explained casually with a shrug of my shoulder.

"Oh, right," she said, nodding politely, but obviously unsure of what I meant. I put the multi-tool in her hand, and she straightened up with pride; she was going to help fight the British. "I can do this, I know I can. But how will I know when it's safe to get out of there?"

"Oh, I'll give a big signal. You just listen for a really loud noise, one like you've never heard before. When you hear it, run like hell. The men will be able to take care of themselves.

"Master Simon," I said as I put my hand on his back. I had true admiration for this man who was putting himself in harm's way for people I didn't even know if he knew. He looked at me with an open face, waiting for his orders, "as soon as you hear the noise, I would suggest you find a good place to hide."

It wasn't showtime yet, and we wouldn't be able to have a dress—or any other kind of—rehearsal for our performance. It was definitely time to set the stage and wire the props, though.

We had spaced the kegs about twenty yards apart. I found a soft spot for each one and quickly dug a hole, buried the keg, inserted the fuse, and covered it. If I couldn't bury it completely, I piled rocks or wood on top of it. I wasn't trying to disguise them—the kegs weren't going to be intact long enough for someone to find them. I needed the added mass for compression, though, so the explosions would be big, loud, and hopefully, distracting.

I heard voices down the road. One was Master Simon, talking slowly and stupidly. Well, at least slowly. I couldn't distinguish his words but could hear the soldier talking to him getting angry. "Spit it out, man," he hollered.

I didn't want to eavesdrop, especially when I realized that I recognized the voice. "It's just some soldier," I mumbled. "It could be someone else."

Yeah, right, I knew better, but worked at securing my last bomb, focusing on the task before me rather than speculating as to who was at the mill. That's all I needed—another confrontation with Captain Asshole.

I had precut all of the fuses on the wagon-ride in, each cord a little shorter than the one before it. This way, after they were inserted into the power kegs, I could light all of them at the same time, but they'd blow up sequentially. I was hoping for at least a two-minute delay between explosions.

"Thank you, Lord, for the lighter," I said softly as I finished lighting the last fuse. "You've given me the ideas, Lord, now if You would just help me execute them, I'd appreciate it. The ideas—not the people," I added to make sure He understood, "In Jesus's name, Amen."

I ran to my next assault position. I was hoping to do a little shock and awe. At least, those were the words that came to mind as I raced to my next site. I didn't know where that phrase came from, but it sounded like a good description for the misdirection I was trying to accomplish.

Sound is an amazing property. If done correctly, it can both reflect and be directed—just like light with a mirror. My plan was to do just this. Hopefully, I had all the factors figured correctly.

I stood behind my shield, a mammoth, odd-shaped boulder with a flat face. It was located at the edge of the clearing, about 100 yards away from the mill. The exterior wall of the building facing me had a tall, flat, uninterrupted surface. When the time came, this would be my sound mirror.

I could see and hear Simon pleading with a soldier. He was getting pretty good at playing dumb. I had had my doubts about his acting ability when we first got started. Now it sounded as if he was immersing himself in the role. "But I have to bring home the flour or my wife will beat me. Please, sir," he whined convincingly.

I dared to peek out and verify that this was indeed the evil Captain Asshole beleaguering our Master Simon. It wasn't. I must have imagined his voice. I knew fear played tricks with the mind, and I guessed mine had just been *abra cadabra'd*.

All of a sudden, we heard a big 'poof,' then the noise of rocks and pebbles raining down from the sky. It sounded like I didn't get that first charge packed tightly enough. Four of the Redcoats came out of the mill and looked down the road at the source of the commotion. They could see a big cloud of dust settling, but no people or animals.

I looked back toward the mill again and saw Jenny's blond hair move through the trees, but not the rest of her. Her little green calico smock was good camouflage. I probably should have covered her whole head. Fortunately, though, the soldiers were all focused on the unusual dusty apparition down the road. They hadn't seen the fair-haired waif running to the back of the building.

"Bang!" The second explosion made a much louder noise. Now two more soldiers came out to see what was going on. That meant that if Jenny really did see six new arrivals, and there were only three of them when she left, there were only two soldiers remaining inside.

I looked at Simon to see how he was reacting to the show. I was glad to see that he was still in character. He had pulled his hat off and was shading his eyes with it, peering off into the area of concern. Just then, a third blast went off, not quite as loud as the second, but much better than the first.

Evidently three explosions were enough to get the soldiers to take action. I heard orders shouted like 'find out what's going on out there' and 'hurry up' and 'take corporal so and so with you.' Two men mounted up and rode out toward my little Gunpowder Park. It was at this point that the officer came outside.

Captain Asshole.

"Where are the men going?" he barked. "Who said they could leave?" He was angry and wanted answers right away.

"I sent the detail out to check on the source of the explosions, Captain. I'm Sergeant Josef Betz, and these are my men to command," was the quick and concise reply, spoken in a broad German accent by the stocky blonde non-com.

"They may be your men, but I am the superior officer here. You will do as *I* say! Now, I want the men sent out in twos. Take two and head that way, and two back behind, and two up there," he ordered and pointed right to where I was standing.

"Oh, shit," I mumbled and hoped another bomb would go off.

"Right. Now!" Captain Asshole screamed into the sergeant's face.

Sergeant Betz stood his ground, looked the captain right in the eyes, and sneered. "You are not my commanding officer, and my men will do as I tell them. Do you understand *me*?"

I got the feeling that Sergeant Betz believed that the captain was simply an asshole and not a captain of anything. I giggled at the exchange, and boy, was I sorry. No one had been talking, nor were bombs exploding, at that moment. It was dead calm except for the sound of my sniggering. I was sure I had been heard.

I pulled back to the other side of the rock, scurried into the wooded area, and hid behind a low-branched tree. I wanted to climb up and disappear into its lofty branches, but realized that once I was up there, I wouldn't be able to move laterally. I decided it would be better to stay low and mobile.

The captain strode right up to where I *had* been, then another bomb went off. That made four. I looked to the mill and saw Jenny run into the woods, followed by Jody, Wallace, and some of the other men. I needed to move, too, but my escape was cut off by the captain's advance.

Kerboom! Another one of my bombs exploded, and it was the biggest and loudest yet. I really felt the ground shake with that one. I looked back at the captain and saw him spin around, checking behind himself nervously. He acted as if he was being chased, but I think it was only his paranoia catching up with him.

The captain hadn't found me or anyone else, so retraced his steps, going back the same way he had come in. I threaded my way through the trees, making a big loop, and returned to my original location as he headed back toward the mill, his head jerking from right to left, looking for his transparent enemies.

Sergeant Betz and his four men had positioned themselves in front of the mill entrance, an apparent unwelcoming committee for the unpopular captain. It didn't seem to faze him, though; Captain Asshole strode right up to the sergeant. I couldn't see his face, but he was obviously angry by his gait. The sergeant's other men remained stone-faced and at attention. I think they believed that they were still guarding their prisoners: the rabble-rouser Jody Pomeroy and his cohorts. It was too bad—no, it was a good thing—that they hadn't gone inside and found out that all of their prisoners had escaped.

Oh, crap. Sergeant Betz was ignoring the captain's angry approach, turning away from a possible confrontation. He was leaving his men and heading back to the entrance of the mill. Shoot, why was he so smart?

I held my breath and squeezed my eyes shut as he walked through the front door, as if my not seeing what was going on would help. After a long minute and no yelling, I cautiously opened one eye to see the fuming

420

sergeant exit the front door and march toward the captain. Both of my eyes popped open when I saw how mad he was. Sergeant Betz was moving sharply, as if his thigh muscles were made of thunderbolts. I was sure glad he wasn't coming at me!

The sergeant screamed in the captain's face, "You left the prisoners unguarded, and now they've escaped, you fool!"

The captain didn't back down an inch. He snorted and said, "Don't call me a fool, you kraut-eating son of Satan. I was left with only one man, and he just left for a minute to take a piss. I can't do everything by myself!" Apparently, the captain didn't care for people of German descent nor was he fond of being yelled at.

"He only left for a minute? And you didn't ask for a replacement or to be relieved? Don't you have any sense of protocol? I doubt you're even an officer. You are such an asshole!" The sergeant's face was ripe tomato red and looked like it was going to explode.

The sergeant was right, and the captain knew it. He wasn't going to admit it, though, especially since there were other soldiers watching the altercation. So the captain did about the only thing he could do under the circumstances. "Do *not* call me an asshole," he said low and threateningly.

The sergeant pulled himself as tall as his vertically-challenged body could, and glared back. What the man lacked in height, he more than made up for with intensity. "Ass. Hole," he said coldly and clearly, belittling his adversary in front of the other soldiers with the drawn out, emphatic word.

I was really getting into watching their little pissing contest, but before it could get any more intense, a soldier rode in at full speed. He stopped short, right in front of the two adversaries, his horse's hooves kicking up a thick cloud of dust that blocked my view. When the dirt settled, I saw that there was another rider right behind him, his hand atop the green bundle across his lap.

Jenny had been captured.

The first rider gave his report to the sergeant. "Just up the road, it looks like someone rigged six kegs of gunpowder to explode. There's still one left back there. I wasn't sure if it was going to blow up or not, so thought it best to leave it there." The soldier saw the look of scorn on the sergeant's face and added, "Best to leave it there until you told me what you wanted done with it, Sergeant."

"We'll leave it there then," the sergeant agreed. "Did you see any sign of who might have done it?"

"No one was there, sir. But there were lots of footprints there at the site, and a wagon had stopped there recently. There were three sets of footprints including those of a barefoot small person. Apparently they unloaded the gunpowder from a wagon," he said, glancing over at Master Simon and the wagon as he finished his report. The sergeant also looked at the wagon and driver, but before he could say or do anything, a ruckus started.

"Let me go, you rotten Lobsterback!" The green package slung over the front of the other soldier's saddle suddenly burst into screaming, kicking, and writhing.

"Let me have her," ordered Captain Asshole as he strode over to the mounted soldier who was struggling to keep the little dynamo contained. "She's mine," he growled.

The sturdy sergeant stepped between the captain and the squirming young girl. "She is not yours. Here, put her down," he ordered the soldier, who was more than ready to be rid of her. He let loose of her wrists, and Jenny immediately fell to the ground, landing hard on her bottom. The sergeant stepped up to her and congenially offered his hand to help her to her feet.

"Thank you," she said courteously as she rearranged her makeshift dress, shifting it around to re-cover her partially exposed body. She looked over at the captain, sneered, and covertly stuck her tongue out at him. She then turned around to face the sergeant, sporting a sweet smile to match her now polite and ladylike behavior.

"You little bitch!" the captain screamed and grabbed for her.

The sergeant picked her up by the armpits and swung her away, out of the captain's reach. "Men, restrain the captain," he ordered. He set her down and turned back to address the officer held in check. "I think you have forgotten what your mission is," he paused then added, "Sir."

Two of the foot soldiers approached to apprehend him, but he ducked and spun around, grabbing Jenny by the hair as he did so. He yanked her hair so hard, he pulled her off her feet, tugging her into his grasp like a trout on a fly line. He held her close and high, so her feet couldn't touch the ground, his inner elbow clamped around her neck. He clutched her so tightly that her face began to turn scarlet. Her little hands clawed at his sleeve, futilely trying to penetrate the thick cloth to get to his skin. She was kicking with the fury of a newly branded mule, but to no effect. She was barefoot, and although she may have inflicted some minor bruising to his shins, the captain was oblivious of anything but keeping her away from the good sergeant and his men.

"Let her go," the sergeant said calmly. "We have a job to do, and she will only be in the way."

Captain Asshole felt her body go slack—she was as limp as a rag doll. He lessened his chokehold to let her get a breath. He didn't want to kill her. Yet. He knew she was either unconscious or pretending to be.

Jenny took a couple of shallow breaths, and then I saw her body tense.

Evidently, the captain felt the change because he resumed his iron-armed hold on her...but not before she had moved her head enough that she could sink her teeth into his bare hand. She wasn't loosening her bite, either. He released his chokehold, and was now batting at her head, using one hand to try to knock her off the other. That didn't work, so he literally swung her away from his body, pivoting in a tight circle, causing her body to fly away from him as if she were on a carnival ride. Even the centrifugal force of her own body weight wasn't enough to cause the little viper to let go, though. Captain Asshole stopped the flinging, reached down, and grabbed the knife out of his boot. "Bite this!" he yelled as he brought the blade to a spot just under her left ear, piercing her skin.

I saw the flow of blood from where I was but didn't know what I could do. I had no idea if Jody and his crew had had a chance to get to the rifles in the wagon yet. This wasn't the distraction that I had planned.

Distraction! That was it! Now was the time!

I squatted down in front of my broad-faced rock pillar and pulled out the smartphone. It was fully charged. I had made sure of it by covertly placing it in the sunlight on the ride in. I pressed the little treble cleft button and the screen lit up. I found the little American flag emblem and tapped on it once. I slid the volume bar all the way to the right, tapped the icon of the fuzzy-haired hippie twice, and set the phone on its little rock stand.

The blare of 'The Star Spangled Banner' *ala* Woodstock was deafening to me, and I was off to the side of the speakers with rock amplifiers, not getting the complete effect of the full-tilt volume like those in front of me.

My plan worked. Everyone in the mill arena was covering his ears and looking at the wall that seemed to be the source of the alien noise, the sound of an electric guitar being put through its paces by the master musician and former US Airborne paratrooper, Jimi Hendrix. Even the captain had loosed his grip on Jenny and dropped his knife away from her neck, at least for a second.

Jenny hadn't been distracted, though. She had been expecting a sound like she had never heard before and had taken advantage of the captain's diversion—she was now running, hauling butt away from the area at top speed.

I looked up and saw Clyde running in to intercept his little sister. Talk about mixed emotions. I was glad she had a protector, but the sight of him still made my stomach churn. It was a gut reaction I had to shut down. I was not willing nor wanting to deal with those feelings now or ever. I scanned the area and saw Jody and Wallace running for the soldiers' horses. My men each had a rifle, and it looked as if they were planning on cutting off the captain's retreat.

Master Simon had wasted no time in leaving. He was already heading back down the road we had come in on. I didn't see anyone else I knew, though, and that worried me. Then again, if I didn't see them, nobody else did either.

But it was too good to be true. One lone soldier was leading Mac and Julian in at gunpoint. Or I guessed that would be at musket muzzle. Either way, they were captured and definitely in harm's way. I didn't recognize the soldier, and then realized that this must be the one who was inside with Captain Asshole and had disappeared to take a leak while on watch. One of Sergeant Betz's men came up beside him to share the captors' duty, so now they each had a prisoner.

At this point, I decided to turn off the noise and listen to the proceedings. Everyone stopped at the sudden sound of silence and looked around, but no one commented. I couldn't help but wonder if they all thought that they had been hallucinating.

Sergeant Betz straightened his shoulders and walked up to the prisoners. "Who are you?" he asked of Mac first.

"Mac Donaldson, sir. I was just here to pick up some flour, when this man," he turned his head back to indicate the first restraining soldier, "and this, this thing in a uniform," he nodded at the captain, "detained me and my neighbors without cause."

Sergeant Betz let a minor smile sneak across his face at the description of Captain Asshole. The prisoner had enough smarts not to call the captain a derogatory name in front of his vanquisher. "And who are you?" he asked Julian.

"My name is Julian Hart, and I am visiting friends and family in the area. I, too, have been detained without cause." Julian's hands were still tied, and it looked as if they had been bound for a long time. They were swollen and deep purple, and if someone didn't remove the bindings soon, it looked as if his hands would fall off.

The sergeant saw his hands, too. "Cut him loose," he commanded the errant soldier. The soldier just looked at him as if he had heard a noise but wasn't sure what it was. I didn't think he wanted to take orders from him.

That didn't sit well with Sergeant Betz. He huffed and strode over to Julian, unsheathed his own knife, and cut the bands off of Julian's hands himself. He looked Julian in the eye—to make sure he was okay, I think—and then flashed recognition. I noticed he recovered quickly, and if Julian had seen it, he didn't react to it. The sergeant looked at Mac's hands and saw that he wasn't bound. He continued with his interrogation.

"By what right are you detaining these men, soldier?" he asked.

The still-nameless soldier looked to the captain for direction. The captain, his child-bitten and bloodied hand held close to his chest, strode over, eyes afire as if he was going to enjoy this confrontation. "This man, *sergeant*," he spat out the title with intense disgust, "is a deserter from His Majesty's Service. He is to be brought in and tried for treason." His smug smile was more tactless than scary.

I had the distinct impression that he was bluffing. Julian certainly didn't look threatened by the accusation. He turned to face the captain with an incredulous look on his face. "What?" was all he said, but with complete innocence. Julian was making his accuser squirm and fidget with his complete lack of distress and fear. Even though his face didn't show it, I was sure Julian was enjoying his captor's backfired ploy. Now I was positive that the captain was bluffing.

The sergeant saw the accusation as a sham, too, and came to the rescue. "I don't think that good manners and proper speech are an indication of either enlistment with or desertion from His Majesty's Service. Are you a deserter, sir?" the sergeant asked Julian with a gleam in his eye.

"No, sir, I am not," replied Julian.

Julian wasn't lying. I remembered him saying that he had just chosen his own retirement time, not deserted. He was answering like the honest and respectable gentleman he was.

"And are you a deserter?" he asked Mac, not even trying to hide the capricious grin on his face.

"No, sir, I am not," replied Mac, using the same words and intonation as Julian had. I could just hear him *not* saying the words 'I wouldn't be a part of your stinkin' army, no way, no how!' but the insinuation of the sentiment was flashing like a neon sign in his eyes.

The sergeant looked as if he was getting ready to dismiss the two prisoners when Captain Asshole spoke up, very dryly. "Then you wouldn't be interested in the reward for catching their friend, the Big Red, then?"

Sergeant Betz glared at him, almost daring him to try and pull a fast one on him, but the captain remained stoic.

None of us in our little community had ever heard of a reward for Jody. He was sometimes a nuisance, but the few British soldiers who were left in the area had pretty much turned a blind eye when Jody took to his patriotic preaching. The British were employing the divide-and-conquer tactic, fighting two distinct campaigns. Most of the battles were being fought either further south or far north of us. That left North Carolina as an area of little interest. The local civil disobedience was so minor that it was easier to ignore it than to respond to it.

The sergeant looked to Julian for his reaction to the reward rumor. I was beginning to believe that these two had a history. Julian's eyes made the slightest twitch indicating the falsehood of the captain's accusation.

The sergeant had seen and believed the answer in Julian's eyes and decided to run with it. Now it was time for him to spin his own web of deception. He walked in a circle around the prisoners and the two soldiers, as if he were pondering his next chess move. "Oh, *that* reward," he deadpanned. "Yes, I did hear that they were paying for the capture of seditious traitors. However, they stopped having any interest in them quite a while back. They are more interested now in catching that scoundrel wearing a British officer's uniform who has been traveling through the area, illegally collecting taxes, and then keeping them for himself. Come to think of it, you fit his description. What unit did you say you were attached to, *sir*?"

Captain Asshole squirmed, chewed his bottom lip, preparing his answer, but before he could reply, Wallace walked out of the woods. All eyes were on the tall, striking young man entering the field of fallacies and fabrications. He stopped ten feet away from the thief who had not only misrepresented himself as a British captain and tax collector, but who had also held him at knifepoint in front of his fiancée.

"Have you turned over the taxes that you extorted from us," Wallace asked as he sauntered in closer, his eyes squinted in an intimidating scowl, until he was two feet away, "or have you decided to keep them for yourself?" Quick as a rattlesnake, Wallace reached out and jerked the gold nugget necklace from around the captain's neck that had been hidden, tucked under his stock, but had fallen out and become visible during his skirmish with Jenny the biter.

The captain lunged forward to take back the necklace, but Wallace took a step to the side, and the thief stumbled forward, landing right in the middle of Jody's chest. "Ach, taxman, are ye?" Jody asked. "Here," he said, and launched an uppercut, landing his fist squarely on the bottom of the captain's chin, knocking him to the ground, senseless. "That's fer hittin' the lass."

Jenny ran up to the prone, momentarily incapacitated molester, and kicked him hard in the head. "Yeah, and this is for hitting Big Red."

"Here, here," the sergeant said, arms spread out defensively, trying to bring order to the mini melee and keep more blows from being struck. "Miss, don't kick a man when he's down, *verstehst?* It is very unladylike. Besides, I think he's had enough."

Sergeant Betz called over four of his men, and then turned his attention to Wallace and Jody. "Is this the man who has been taking goods from the local residents under the guise of a tax for His Majesty?"

Before Wallace could give an affirmative answer, Captain Asshole, flat on his back, sprawled out like a snow angel on a dirt canvas, screamed, "He's lying." He rolled over and scrambled to bring his knees beneath him, so he could stand and face his accuser with some trace of dignity.

But it was too late for that. A quick scan of the gathering crowd showed that all the soldiers were disgusted with him. It was time for a plan B. Captain Asshole looked over and saw that his quick-thinking cohort had come from the back of the group and grabbed little Jenny and was twisting her arm up behind her back.

"Well, I think I'll leave you all to finish this party by yourselves," the captain said as he picked up his black silk-trimmed tricorn hat from the ground, knocking the dust from it onto his britches. He walked tall, full of self-assurance, toward the little beauty, and the beast who had her contorted into submission.

Well, sort of submission. He was controlling her like a marionette by her left arm, but he couldn't control her mouth. "Let go of me, you rotten pig fornicator! I'll have my brothers cut out your liver and eat it for supper, you no-good privy dweller!"

Captain Asshole walked up to her and, without even pausing, swatted her across the face, and continued his trek to the horses. "Let's go, Ronald," he said, "and for God's sake, keep that little bitch quiet!" Then he stopped, waited a moment as if he were making a decision, and turned to face all the soldiers who were standing with the sergeant.

"Any man here who is tired of not getting paid by His Majesty, you're welcome to come with us. There's a lot to be had out there in the way of taxes. Just grab your horse and follow along."

I noticed two of the sergeant's men looking at each other, eyebrows raised, silently deciding to take the offer. I didn't know times were tough for the British, too. I thought the Americans were the only ones starving. They both shouldered their muskets and walked toward their horses.

"Ain't someone gonna do somethin'?" a voice shouted from the back of the mill. It looked like a two-headed monster rushing into the commotion. It was Clyde, and he was holding up Clayton—or they were holding each other up. Panicked, they were running up to the sergeant like two men in a three-legged race.

"Halt!" the sergeant called to the deserters and the kidnapping thieves who were hauling away Jenny. The erstwhile soldiers ignored his command. They kept walking, not even turning around, confident that they carried the 'get out of trouble free' ticket.

"Take aim, men," the sergeant ordered his remaining squad. They fixed their rifles on the captain and his crew, and waited for their next command.

Captain Asshole stopped and turned to face the militia. Ronald stopped too, his fist held high, still wrapped around Jenny's wrist, controlling her by her dislocated arm. She was in pain, had to be by the way she was almost turned upside down by her captor. Her jaws were clenched in hatred, and tears streaked through the dirt on her face, but there was no sobbing. Her eyes—squinted tight and thin—glared at Private Ronald. She was a time bomb ready to explode.

I was still watching the proceedings from the patch of woods across the way. Wallace, Jody, and Julian were gone—or at least weren't visible. All I could see was the standoff between the sergeant and his loyal men, and the cowards, ready to mount their steeds to unimpeded freedom and larceny. Captain Asshole grabbed Jenny from Ronald. "Go ahead; I'll catch up with you in a minute. This won't take long."

The captain had grabbed Jenny's uninjured arm. He was holding it up and back high behind her, her other arm now hanging limp and useless at her side. "If you want to see her again—alive that is—you'll let us go and not follow." His grinning, greasy face reflected the bloated pride he had in his blank check. He was going to have his freedom and be able to do whatever he wanted with the little girl.

Bang! Bang! Bang! I changed my focus from her to the shots being fired. Evidently the sergeant didn't take too kindly to his men deserting. His remaining soldiers were shooting at the deserters as they tried to get to their horses. I turned back and saw the captain running to join them, dragging the uncooperative and cursing Jenny behind him. He stopped, though, when he heard a voice call out.

Wallace's voice boomed, "Runnin' away like a sissy, are ye?"

I noticed that he had assumed the Highland accent, and then realized why. He was in warrior mode.

I didn't want to think it was vengeance, but it could have been. I preferred to think that it was the fighting Pomeroy blood rising in response to the stimulus of the battle. His fathers and an innocent—weren't they all at that age?—little girl had just been attacked. That would be enough to call up those hormones—or whatever they were. If it had only been pride calling, and he was still angry about being humiliated when the taxman had come to call... Well, I just couldn't believe that's what it was. I knew he was more of a man than that.

Wallace and the captain were the center of everyone's attention now. But what were they going to do? Fight hand to hand? Neither one was armed, as far I could see. The captain's boot knife was still lying on the ground where he had dropped it earlier, when Jimi Hendrix had come to Jenny's rescue. I scanned the trees and saw the flash of a rifle barrel, then another one. It appeared that Julian and Jody had Wallace's back. I'd have to remember later to tell them to put soot on their sights and barrels so they didn't reflect light.

"Did your wife let you go out all by yourself? Or is she back there," the captain asked, cocking his head to where I was, "making sure you don't do anything to embarrass her? Oh, she's a pretty one, all right, but a little old for my tastes."

He had to be bluffing about knowing where I was. I doubted that he knew I had left our house, much less that I was anywhere near here.

Wallace was grim, and hopefully he wasn't letting the taunts get under his skin. "Let the lass go," he said, his voice low, slow, and commanding. Then he suddenly growled, "Now!" startling everyone.

All but the captain. He was too sure of himself to heed the order from the young, apparently non-military male. "Oh, you want a little of this, do you?" he taunted as he pulled on Jenny's arm, causing her to let out an unintentional squeak. "I don't think so. She's mine, and she's coming with me. And if you try to get her, I'll let you have her, all right. You can have

429

her a little bit at a time." He sneered as he tilted his leg sideways to show off the knife in his other boot. "She won't need all her fingers or toes for what I want her for. Which end do you want me to start on?"

It was now time…time for the second, and hopefully the last, act of this drama. I had no way of knowing whether this would be a victory or a tragedy, but I couldn't stand by and let him take her. A finger slide, a couple of taps, a fast forward, and then the sky was singing, "And I'm proud to be an American, where at least I know I'm free," voiced by 21st century singer Lee Greenwood.

This time there were words, very loud, clear, passionate, and meaningful words, and not just strange noises, coming from the side of the mill. Jenny took advantage of the captain's momentary shock and slackened arm, and did a pirouette to face her captor. She pulled back, and with every pound of her body and ton of her anger, head-butted him right in the crotch. He reflexively let go of her hand and grabbed his jewels while she ducked and ran like a rabbit from a fox.

At first, she headed toward the sergeant and his men. Then she saw her brothers pointing towards an opening in the woods. She veered left and took off in that direction, her green calico smock twisted and flying loose, like the tail of a kite.

The words 'God bless the U S AAAay' were now blaring, but the captain was oblivious to everything and everyone around him. He was determined that he would have the little spitfire, Jenny. He gingerly regained his posture and, with eyes focused on his target, began half-limping, half-running toward the fleeing girl. He was obsessed with her, and not even the presence of muskets, men, and loud music distracted him. Jenny tripped on the front of her frock and stumbled, slowing her pace in order to find her feet. "Stop right there," he yelled at her.

Yeah, right, as if she would even consider listening to what he told her to do. I reached over and turned off the music, which was now distracting me in a negative way, and put the smartphone/media player contraption back into my pocket.

I saw the whole scene opening in front of me. The captain was zeroing in on her, like a hawk on a field mouse. She was back on her feet and shifting her weight, side-to-side, trying to decide which was the best escape route. Jody was coming in with nothing but his dirk from the left, and Clyde was running interception from the right. Jenny didn't see Clyde, so ran towards Jody.

Captain Asshole stopped, coolly and vindictively, pulled his silver pistol from his belt, held it over his forearm. Aimed. And fired.

Jody clutched Jenny to his chest. They dropped to the ground just as Clyde lunged out in front of them. All three bodies hit the earth at once.

One shot had been fired, but none of us knew who—if anyone—had been hit. Jody sat up, checked to make sure they were safe, and then unfolded his arms carefully. He looked down to see if Jenny had been hurt. She gazed up at her protector, marveling at his size and closeness, and then turned and saw her brother.

She hadn't seen Clyde leap in front of the shot—she had been enveloped in Jody's arms at the time—but she saw him now, flat on his back, lying still, eyes to heaven.

Blood was gushing out of her brother's neck. She rushed to him, put her hands on the bloody hole, and screamed, "No, no, no! Stop bleeding, you gotta stop!"

His whole bearing changed the moment he saw his little sister above him, working fervently to stop the inevitable. Clyde's pain and anxiety were replaced by pure love.

"No, you can't die, no!" she kept screaming. But it was already too late. The blood had stopped spurting, but only because his heart had stopped beating. Jody came to her side and gently turned her, so she wasn't looking into her dead brother's face. He bent down and shut the eyelids that had been staring out in peace, the slight smile frozen on his face.

The captain hadn't moved, but Jody made sure that Jenny stayed behind him, out of the monster's reach. He looked beyond the captain and saw the sergeant approaching with his men.

Sergeant Betz walked up to the scene and glared at the erstwhile captain, who was checking his pistol, looking at the sight, then down the muzzle, frowning, as if there were gremlins inside.

"Who *are* you?" the sergeant asked, holding his potential captive with his gaze.

"I am Captain Atholl MacLeod of His Majesty's Secret Service," he replied. "Now, if you will let me pass, I have work to do," and took steps to leave.

"His Majesty's Secret Service? There is no such division," the sergeant said, and stepped in front of the captain, blocking his retreat. "You know, you really should learn how to lie better if you plan on continuing this ruse. No, on second thought, I don't think you need to expend the effort. You're heading to the gallows. Right. Now." The

431

sergeant turned at the waist, called, "Men," and motioned for his soldiers to apprehend the shooter.

Suddenly, a horrific wail came from the lifeless form of Clyde. It wasn't Clyde, though; it was Clayton. While all the posturing of the captain, the sergeant, and his men had been transpiring, Clayton had come out to mourn his brother, and had been crying softly over his body. But now he was back in the world of the living, and aware of what was going on. His little sister had been assaulted, kidnapped, and nearly raped by their brother's murderer. His rage was at critical mass, and I could see that a nuclear explosion was imminent.

"Aarrggh!" Clayton's cry of vengeance was worthy of any Highlander. But his wisdom of attacking an armed man with nothing but his bare hands was classically stupid Clayton. He pushed Jody and Jenny clear, and charged the captain, tackling his brother's murderer to the ground. He glanced back to make sure that his sister was okay, then pinned the captain's shoulders down and bit off a chunk of his ear. Or maybe he bit off the whole thing if what I saw was the entire appendage being spit out. Either way, Clayton was going back for more.

But Jenny didn't want to be out of the way. She wanted payback, too, and didn't want a champion—she wanted to do it herself. She picked herself up off the ground, and was ready to jump into the fray, when Wallace ordered, "You! Stay!"

She looked up, saw the fire in his eyes, and that long arm pointing at her to remain where she was, and—I was both stunned and happy to see—she stayed put.

Clayton and the captain rolled around on the ground—kicking, scratching, and generally fighting clumsily, but fervently. The captain fumbled for his knife while Clayton, ugh, tried to bite off the man's nose.

Wallace loomed over the wrestling duo, and I thought for sure he was going to break them apart, but he just stayed off to the side, letting the two men beat on each other. He remained neutral, only observing the row— except for the one time he kicked the knife out of the captain's hand.

After ten minutes, it was becoming obvious that both of the combatants were tiring. "Break it up," Wallace said, "he's had enough."

"Yeah, he's beat, and you're next," the captain hissed breathlessly. "Coward."

"I was talking about you, asshole," Wallace replied coolly, looking down at the bloody and beaten pseudo-captain lying on the ground, his child-bitten left hand cradling the spot on the side of his head that used to

432

sport an ear. Wallace glanced up and saw the sergeant observing his four men bringing in the three rogue soldiers. "Sergeant, here's another one for you," he called.

I turned around and saw Sarah rushing toward the wounded, gathering her skirts with one hand, carrying her little black medical bag in the other. It seemed silly to follow her, but I felt as if I needed to protect her, even though there were now half a dozen men fully capable of doing that. I patted my pockets, made sure I had everything I came with, and followed behind her.

Sarah nodded to Wallace and Jody, letting them know that she could handle this. "Sergeant, I'm a healer, and I would like to tend to the, er," she cleared her throat as she tried to assign a name to the phony captain, "the, er, *man's* wounds. I wouldn't want them to get infected."

"Infected? You mean red and full of pus, fevered? I don't see how that will make any difference. He'll probably be hanged in a couple days anyway." The sergeant saw Sarah getting ready to protest, so acquiesced. "Go ahead and see to him if it makes you feel better. Personally, I think he got off easy. You should have let him finish chewing off body parts," he said as he looked over at Wallace. Wallace shrugged his shoulder and escorted Sarah to the captain, still lying on his side.

I hung back; I really didn't want to get too close to that ugly sack of cells with opposable thumbs. Just looking at him literally made my skin crawl. I never knew what that phrase meant until I saw him clutching at Jenny. Ugh, there it goes again. Memo to self: do not think of Captain Asshole ever again, or the sensation of centipede legs marching over limbs and belly will ensue.

Sarah quickly set to her task, focusing on the captain's wounds, totally ignoring Wallace, the sergeant, and the rest of the contingent of good and bad Redcoats. "I want to clean and bandage that hand and ear before you leave. There's no telling if they'll find someone else to take care of it," she said to her patient.

Jenny. I looked up and saw her holding, clutching, Clayton to her chest. She was trying to smooth out his wild hair and was crying. I didn't know whether it was from sorrow about Clyde's death or relief that this incident was over. I wanted to make sure she was okay, but I definitely didn't want to intrude on their private moment. I knew that the brothers were close—ugh, too close—but didn't know much about her. From the fuss she was making about his appearance and comfort, I'd say she was the parent in the relationship.

433

"I need some water," Sarah said.

"I'll get some for you," I offered.

"There's an empty bucket on the porch," the sergeant told me.

On my way over, I saw that Jody had joined Jenny and Clayton. They were all kneeling beside Clyde's body, and it looked as if Jody was saying a prayer. Wallace was not going near them, and I could understand why on more than one level. He left to go stand with Mac Donaldson and the other man. I passed them on the way to the well. "Are you all right?" I asked.

"Jest a little bruised dignity is all," said Mac. "This is my brother-in-law, Todd Gillespie," he said. We both nodded and smiled.

"Nice to meet you, Todd. Mac, the girls will sure be happy to see you. Everybody is at our place. They came for the wedding. Oh shoot, I have to get water for Sarah. Bye!"

I literally ran to get the water, hoping the tears wouldn't have a chance to catch up with me. "Yeah, wonderful *effin'* wedding day," I grumbled as I filled the pail with water.

I had to get back to Sarah soon, but since it was only to 'help' that creep, I didn't feel as if I should hurry. Besides, I couldn't run with the bucket full of water, so I walked slowly, taking the opportunity to calm down and think about what had just happened.

I still had a groom-to-be, and it could have turned out worse. I looked around at the minimal mess that had ensued. No one in my family had been injured, the phony taxman captain had been apprehended, and Jenny had been saved from the paws of that sadistic pervert. I guessed as dramatic as everything was today, I really hadn't sustained any losses. Maybe we could get home in time for a nighttime wedding. A preacher and plenty of witnesses were already on hand, waiting for us to come back. Yes, it had turned out okay, but I was still pissed off at having to go through all this drama just because of one rotten, greedy asshole!

Oh, Lord. Jenny. I have been so absorbed with how this has impacted me and my wedding day that I haven't even thought about her. She just lost her brother. She still has one more, and I'm sure they'll be fine, but still, darn it, no one needed to die today!

I returned to Sarah with the bucket full of water and a gut full of rage. If she had heard me coming up, she didn't acknowledge it. Her back was to me. She was seated on the ground next to the captain and had already bandaged his hand. By the lack of color in his face, she had used her alcohol blend as the disinfectant. He started to turn his head away so she could assess the damage to where his ear used to be, but paused long enough to snort with disdain as he glanced up at me.

My anger flared up again—actually exploded—and I lost control. "Here, let me help," I growled, and impulsively threw half a bucket of water at the captain's head.

The captain bolted upright and grabbed Sarah, all in the same efficient movement, as if he had already had it planned out.

"Oh, shit," I said. I started to set the bucket down, but stopped midway when I saw them. The sergeant was coming in, his musket raised, ready to fire. Wallace was racing past him, warrior scowl set, dirk blade shining—it was much scarier than the black powder contraption the sergeant had. I glanced to where Jody had been, and saw that he and Clayton were sprinting towards us, too. My spiteful, extemporaneous water toss had just started extreme drama act number three. When would I learn to think before acting!

"I'm sorry, I'm sorry," I said frantically, but I could see it didn't make a difference to the captain. He was purple-faced and furious!

But Sarah was cool, inexplicably mellow for the situation she was in, and then I noticed why—she had a scalpel in her hand. Unfortunately, she didn't know that Captain Asshole had his hand on the pistol in his belt.

I gulped in a quart of courage and changed my attitude right away. "Where did you get that?" I asked and nodded to the pistol, both as a diversion and to let Sarah know that she was under-armed. I could also see Jody approaching in my peripheral vision and wanted him to be able to get closer.

"Oh, our little sauerkraut-sucking sergeant isn't as bright as he thinks. I'll bet he keeps his pistol loaded, right?" he asked, turning around to glare at the sergeant.

Sergeant Betz looked down at his belt and saw that his pistol was missing. The color left his face. He didn't have to say that the pistol was loaded. It showed. "Uh, I'm sorry, miss, ma'am…"

"Ah, don't worry about it, Sarge. I was just waiting for the good missus to finish the bandaging before I took off. Too bad the other one wasn't closer, though. I would have had fun with her, even if she is a bit old," he said, looking straight at me.

I was terrified for the first time today. I had run out of gunpowder and gimmicks and didn't know what to do. I felt deflated, like an empty sack, without substance. Whether this scenario would have played out the same way without my water toss or not, I still felt guilty. Then I remembered the phrase, 'When it doubt, call out.'

Call out to the Man.

And so I did. My heart prayed fervently, but a mumbled, "Help us, Lord," was all I could get out past my lips.

"Oh, so you're one of those religious sorts, are you? I hear they're the lustiest ones. Being repressed all day makes the activities at night much more fun—right, big boy?" he asked Wallace.

Wallace glowered as he slowly walked towards him, ready to put him in his place. Sarah shouted, "Get back," and he froze.

"Oh, so I see you always mind the womenfolk. You have *got* to be the biggest sissy I have ever seen."

Wallace's face turned scarlet, but he breathed slowly and deeply, and rearranged the rage within him. Two breaths later, he was totally cool and composed. He grinned as he bragged, "At least I have women in my life who are worthy of listening to."

The captain didn't say a word, but jerked Sarah closer to him and growled, reminding us that he was the one with the hostage.

Wallace's tone and expression quickly changed to that of someone I didn't know: a teasing, cocky, barroom jackass. "What, you don't have a woman? Even your own mother wants nothing to do with you? You have to pay the whores twice the rate, and still they balk. You can't even get one to dance with you? You rob and pillage for months on end, yet can never get enough money for one to sleep with you?"

Now it was time for the captain to turn red. His mouth opened and shut, trying to find words to contradict the accusations, but "Shut up!" was all he managed to say. He shifted his weight, pulling Sarah up with him, clumsily getting to his feet. "Where's your God now, little missy?" he snarled at me.

"Look! Ducks!" Wallace yelled and pointed to a totally empty area in the sky.

It was a totally irrational call, but the ploy worked. The captain dropped his guard, looked up, and Wallace dived in. He wrapped his body around Sarah and rolled away from the kidnapper, depositing her on the ground next to me and the dumbfounded sergeant.

Wallace stood up, casually brushed off his trousers with one hand, and brandished a shiny pistol with the other, turning it so the sunlight caught its barrel, but keeping it pointed at the captain's chest.

The captain looked down and saw that he was missing his weapon. Wallace grinned at him, "Look familiar?" he asked as he turned it over in his hand. He had not only rescued Sarah, he had grabbed the pistol out of the man's hand in the process.

"Not bad, not bad," the captain replied with a nod of agreement. "But you always should have a backup," he purred, then swiftly drew a pistol from the back of his waistband and fired it right at Sarah.

I saw the intent of his movement and lunged out in front of her, my arms spread wide in the classic gesture of maternal protection.

The musket ball caught me in the left shoulder. I felt an explosion of fiery pain near my heart, and then my whole world was bright white light with no definition.

Ж Ж Ж

Wallace reached for Evie, and Jody went for his wife. "Get him!" Sarah shouted, pointing at Captain Asshole. She didn't believe in killing people, but Sarah didn't want to let her good-sister's shooter—oh, God don't let him be her assassin—go free. Jody scanned Sarah, made sure she was unhurt, and then joined Wallace in the pursuit of the assailant.

Captain Asshole didn't have a chance of escaping. His four strides were Wallace's two, and he was overtaken even before he had a chance to consider his destination. Wallace stopped right in front of him, blocking his escape. A second later, the sergeant joined them. The captain emitted a nervous laugh when he saw he was both outnumbered and out-weaponed.

"Here, I think this is yours," Wallace said and handed the sergeant his pistol, never taking his eyes from his prisoner.

Captain Asshole studied his options. The pistol he had shot the healer with was spent; the sergeant had his own weapon back now and was already heading back to his men. The big, red headed man was with the healer, tending to the sassy woman he had shot, and the big sissy in front of him appeared to have dropped his dirk in the chase. No one could hurt him now; he was almost home free. He snorted and looked up at Wallace. "I don't see how you could stand her. She was such a mouthy bitch..."

Wallace swept his boot out in front of him and took the feet right out from underneath the foul-mouthed fiend. The captain landed with a thud, flat on his back. Wallace stood above him, his foot held firmly on the culprit's larynx. "You know, I could fix that rude language of yours. One crunch," he pushed a quick pulse to the voice box, "and you'd never be able to talk, or even whisper, any of your curses or insults again. Or just a bit more pressure," he applied substantially more pressure and held it there, "and your throat would swell shut. You'd die a slow and painful death. Asphyxiation is quite unpleasant, I hear."

Wallace took his foot off the captain's throat, and then offered him his hand. The captain looked at it suspiciously but took it. Wallace pulled him up to his feet, and then quickly twisted his hand up behind his back, turning the captain's arm around so severely that he bent forward, and was nearly standing on his head.

"You know, my fiancée was a very smart woman, and she said that what goes around, comes around." Wallace yanked up so hard on the man's splay-fingered hand that the captain squealed like a piglet and pissed his pants.

"Have mercy! Doesn't your God say you should have mercy?" cried the teary, snot-faced, one-eared monster of a man.

"Aye, He does," sighed Wallace, his shoulders slumped in resignation. "Sergeant, would you please tie up this man and get rid of him?"

As soon as Wallace loosened his grip, the captain snapped back into attack mode. He had hidden one of Sarah's scalpels in his boot. He grabbed the razor-sharp implement and slashed at Wallace's face, aiming for his eyes.

Wallace stepped back from the assault, untouched. "Mercy's done, Asshole!" he growled, then shouted, "*Manu Forti!*" He brought up both fists and quickly spread them out, breaking his assailant's forward attack. One quick uppercut and the scalpel flew into the air, landing far beyond either one's reach. Jenny ran over, picked it up, and held on to it.

Wallace could have knocked out the phony captain in two punches, but drew out the punishment, savoring each well-calculated, painful blow, ignoring the bruising of his own fists.

One two, one two. Wallace was bashing the captain's face beyond recognition with bare-knuckle boxing combinations. The soldiers and most of the men from the mill gathered around the combatants and were urging Wallace to 'hit 'im again.'

But one man watched quietly, waiting for an opportunity to make his way into the arena. Ronald—the captain's right-hand man—had been detained by the soldiers earlier, but had managed to slip away from his guards when the confusion began. He had procured a rifle, but the weapon was empty, and he couldn't find any ammunition to reload it. He decided he'd avenge his captain's beatings with what he had, though: the gun's bayonet. The big, tall, quiet one who was now pummeling his boss wasn't going to die quickly or quietly. Gut stuck was a horrible way to die, and that was how he would take him out.

The watcher had a watcher. Clayton had been following Ronald's movements all afternoon with the intention of killing him as soon as he was away from the soldiers. This man had slapped, twisted, and dragged about his little sister just moments ago, and would have raped her earlier today if it hadn't been for her quick thinking and still quicker feet.

Rape. He had never thought of rape as a personal thing. It was just sex, a form of pleasure—or so he believed. It was true that he and his brother got carried away with Wallace months ago and, although it was fun at the time, they both realized after the incident that it probably hadn't been a good idea. When he saw the way the captain and Ronald had looked at, pawed at, and lusted after his little sister, unwanted sexual attention took on a completely different meaning. It wasn't fun for her, and if it wasn't good for both people, then it wasn't good. Period. All of a sudden, he had intense remorse for the attack on Wallace, this man who today had defended his little sister.

Clayton watched as Ronald began to move amongst the crowd, making his way toward Jenny. He flashed anger, hatred, and revenge—all at the same time. Clayton hadn't come unarmed this time. He had taken a long knife from the wall of the mill. He worked his way around the circle of men to get near Ronald. Maybe he could stab him when no one was looking.

"Hit 'im again, hit 'im again, harder, harder," the crowd chanted. Clayton took his eyes off Ronald momentarily to watch Wallace the punisher wail on his brother's murderer. He grinned. He was glad that the big man was relentless with his pounding on the man who had caused his family so much sorrow. He glanced back just as Ronald lunged forward into the brawl, his bayonet drawn, targeted on Wallace.

Clayton instinctively jumped in front of Wallace, the intended victim, his sister's protector and avenger. He defended him, retaliating by thrusting his own purloined long knife deep into the would-be assailant's belly.

In a bizarre twist of fate, the same man who had raped him months earlier saved Wallace from a potentially mortal assault. But the protection had come at the ultimate price for the defender.

"Arrgh!" Wallace didn't stop the pummeling when he heard two men scream in combat behind him. The sounds of bellies being punctured could have been birds flying overhead. He was focused on his task—the punishment of the man who had killed his fiancée—and nothing else mattered.

Two bodies fell onto Wallace just as he threw his last punch. He didn't let it distract him, but merely moved aside to let them fall, never taking his eyes off of Captain Asshole. He grimaced; he had lost control of his temper, and it would be a long time—if ever—before the captain's face looked like it had even an hour earlier. He took a deep breath of regret, then realized it was a moot point. The man was due to be hanged for murder, insurrection, and illegally taking taxes in the name of the King—and then, in ultimate stupidity, keeping the loot.

Lost in his own reflections of remorse for losing control, Wallace suddenly realized that there was a commotion around him, and it didn't concern him or the beaten prisoner. He kicked over the unconscious captain, so he didn't have to look at his mashed and bloody face, and saw the two bodies at his feet. Ronald had a long knife in his stomach, and Clayton—he winced at the thought of him—had a bayonet in his.

Then he heard it: Jenny screaming. The other soldiers were trying to calm her. The sergeant had pulled her away from Clayton, but she was fighting to get back to his side.

"Let her go to him," Wallace said calmly, but with authority. The sergeant looked up and obeyed. He recognized an officer, whether he was in uniform or not. "Now, have someone go and get Sarah, Mrs. Pomeroy, the healer."

Wallace went to Jenny and knelt beside her, knowing that Sarah would be with them soon. It was doubtful that anything could be done for either of the men. He knew about abdominal wounds, and survival was just about impossible. It was supposed to be the most painful way to die and wasn't quick either. Clyde had had it easier, he thought. Then he looked at Jenny, the real victim in all of this. She was a mess, crying and clutching at Clayton's head.

"Here," Wallace said as he lifted Clayton's shoulders, "you can hold him if you'd like."

"Yes, please," she sniffed, and scooted under her dying brother. "You're gonna be fine—I'm here now—all right?" she consoled, as if she were a mother, talking to a toddler with a skinned knee.

"Oh, God," Wallace groaned, and collapsed next to the little girl. "Mother, no mother," he mumbled in shock. Evie was dead. He had three little children to rear, and no one to feed them. His eyes rolled back in his head, and the sobbing began—this time, his own. He felt a heavy hand drop on his arm and looked over to follow it to its owner. It was Clayton.

"Please forgive me; me and Clyde for, you know. I am so sorry, and I know Clyde was, too, but I am the sorriest, for sure."

Clayton grimaced in pain, then coughed, and yelled out in agony. Jenny was stroking his forehead, pushing the hair out of his eyes, trying to comfort the man. The yelling stopped, but he was still alive. The hand came back to Wallace's arm, beseeching this time. "Can you forgive me, please?"

Wallace sniffed back his tears for Evie and wiped his nose on the back of his shirtsleeve. He looked at his attacker and saw the sincerity and need in his eyes. He started nodding his head slowly, and then moved up to a real assent. "Yes, I forgive you, you and your brother," he said.

Wallace didn't have anything left to give. He rolled over onto his side to face Clayton, his whole world empty except for the dying man and his sister holding him. "If I don't forgive you, how can I expect the Lord to forgive me for the wrongs I've done? That's what it says in the Bible, you know."

Wallace was now the preacher and counselor to the rapist and murderer lying next to him. He reached out and held onto the dying man's hand. He sighed. Now that he had forgiven him and reached out in compassion, his world didn't seem as dreadful as it had moments before.

Then he felt another hand on his. It was Jenny. "Would you say a prayer for him?" she asked, her big blue eyes red-rimmed and pleading.

Wallace looked over and saw the grayness of Clayton's skin. He didn't have long, if he was even still alive. Then he heard another groan, and knew the man was still a resident of this realm. He started to say the Gaelic prayer that Jody had taught him but realized that it wouldn't help either of them. "Our Father, who art in heaven, hallowed be Thy name...."

Ж Ж Ж

The sergeant ushered Sarah to the carnage. "What happened here?" she asked. Three bodies lay on the bloodied ground. Wallace was grim, reciting the Lord's Prayer to a young girl with one of the dying—Clyde's brother—in her lap.

Wallace looked up, tears rolling down his cheeks. "Was she in pain before she...she died?"

"Yes, I mean no, I mean," she took a steadying breath and started all over again. "She's in pain now, but she's not dead. She's..."

Wallace didn't wait to hear the rest of the story. He sprinted to the site where he had last seen his fiancée. He had seen her fall—a musket ball shot into her chest—then saw Sarah bent over her, shaking her head. He was sure she had been killed. But there she was now. Jody was sitting next to her, his hand holding a cloth over the bloody hole in her chest. The

441

wound was on her left side, and it looked as if it had gone straight into her heart.

Jody looked up and said, "She's not deid, but Sarah said she canna fix it. It needs a proper surgeon and tools she doesna have. Weel, she's a proper surgeon, but she doesna have any anestheez, that is, special pain medicine; or lots of other things she needs to get the ball out and sew the vein back together. Wallace, if only we could get her back to her own time some way, she could be healed. She said she dinna know how she got here, so how could she go back, even if she wanted to?"

"I think I can help with that," said a strange, yet familiar, voice behind Wallace. He turned and saw Master Simon walk past him to kneel beside Evie. "We need to take a ride to get you to help. Do you think you can make it?" he asked.

I forced one eye open and saw who it was. "I want to get married first." My eye fell shut—it was too much work to keep it open—and I resumed my slow, gentle breathing regimen. It had worked for labor, and Lamaze breathing was the only respite available for the fiery pain in my chest.

"Ye heard the lady, she wants to get married. Do we have any takers?" asked Jody with a lilt of hope and happiness that was contagious to all who heard it.

"I'd be honored," said Wallace brightly, keeping up the optimism Jody had initiated. "Um, Master Simon, do you have any credentials that would work for performing a marriage ceremony? I mean, you seem to be dressed for it," he said, nodding to Master Simon's black frock coat.

"Er, why, yes, but please, can we make it quick? We have to get to our, um, destination before dawn, and we have a ways to go. Oh, and it would be best if you or your father here would ride in the back of the wagon, just in case… Well, the ride may get bumpy, and I want her to be as comfortable as possible."

"Get on with it," I said, my voice low and eyes still closed. "I hurt like hell."

"Ahem," Simon cleared his throat and motioned for Wallace to scoot next to Evie. "This is the quickest rite that I am accredited to perform. It's a sweet little ceremony they perform in the islands just off the coast of Norway. They do it quickly because of the weather…"

"Hurry. Up." I said.

"Oh, yes, sorry." Master Simon grabbed Wallace's left hand and my right, put them together, and said, "Love, honor, and protect each other, no matter what happens, all right?"

There was silence, and then Wallace realized that Master Simon was waiting for an answer. "All right," Wallace and I said at the same time.

"You're man and wife, and I pity the poor fool who tries to separate you two. The marriage is good with or without, but you may want to wait for the reception and er, wedding night. Now, give your bride a kiss, and let's get going. The wagon is ready, and if you two will help load Miss Evie…oh, my. What *is* her name now?"

"Mrs. Wallace Pomeroy-Hart," Wallace said as he looked towards the still seated Jody. Julian was standing behind him, his hand on his good friend's shoulder. Wallace's two fathers had made it to the wedding ceremony.

Wallace bent down and gave me, the new Mrs. Pomeroy-Hart, a gentle kiss on my lips. He brushed his hand across my forehead. "I'll do better later, I promise," he whispered. I answered with a smile.

"Okay, fathers, let's load my lovely wife into the wagon for a trip to the hospital. Which one of you wants to join us for the ride?"

"Load first, please," Master Simon said. "And make sure she doesn't lose her necklace. She'll need that."

The Pomeroy Hart men looked at each other, confused at the comment, then gathered around, nodding to direct one another to lifting points. Wallace grabbed my shoulders while Julian steadied my head and Jody took my feet.

"Don't let her use her neck muscles," Sarah said. She rushed over to the wagon and climbed in the back, ready to position me in the impromptu ambulance.

I could tell by the feel that she had used a bag of rice to keep my head still, and it was as comfortable as could be under the circumstances, but the quilt had wadded up underneath my hips. "Move, blanket, butt," I said.

"Here, help me," Sarah said to Wallace. "Lift her hiney, and I'll get it straightened out."

Wallace did as instructed, then looked at Sarah and asked, "Hiney?"

She shrugged her shoulders and grinned. "It's a word I learned from your wife."

"Oh," he said, dropping the subject, but glowing with pride. He had a wife.

Ж Ж Ж

Sarah didn't know what was going on, but assumed, rightfully so, that Master Simon had arranged for a way to take Evie back to her own time for life saving surgery. Jody walked up to her with Julian at his side and said, "We tossed a coin and he lost—I get to go with the newlyweds. Sarah, take care of Julian, and dinna let him get into too much trouble, aye?"

Julian said, "He's making light of this because he's so concerned. Wallace, you take care of everyone, and don't let him get into too much trouble. Evie, I know you can hear us. Be strong, and hurry back home before I get a chance to miss you. Oops, too late—I miss you already, and you haven't even left yet."

I smiled in reply. When I first met Julian, he could barely laugh at a joke, much less make one. Knowing that he would be here when I got back was like cuddling a warm sheet right out of the dryer—or should that be right off the summer clothesline? Either way, he was a warm and fuzzy memory for me to cling to.

Master Simon took command. "We're leaving now. Mister Pomeroy, would you take the honor of driving? Wallace, you need to stay back here with us. Try to keep her from being jostled. Here, drink this," he said as he held a vial to my mouth. "Just a sip, now. It will ease the pain and help you relax. We don't want your muscles to tense and," he paused, obviously making a decision, "here; take another sip, just to make sure."

And that was the last I remembered of my journey, traveling in the back of an 18th century horse-drawn wagon to a 21st century hospital room in Greensboro, North Carolina.

***48 Voice sweet as chocolate brownies

I must have been in a deep sleep, because people don't wake up from being dead. And I was awake. Or almost awake.

I didn't know where—or when—I was, but I knew that I wasn't alone. I couldn't make out the words, but her tone was soothing, her voice as sweet and rich as double fudge chocolate brownies. "Mmm, brownies," I cooed.

"Brownies?" she asked. "Do you want a brownie?"

"That would be nice," I answered in a soft, dreamy whisper, "with lots of walnuts; no, pecans would be better. A nice tall glass of milk, too…" I rolled over to embrace my lusty wish and stiffened up with pain. "Oww!"

"Don't move," the velvet-voiced lady said in an authoritative tone, "you'll tear out your stitches. You have to stay on your back." Her hands were chilly, but gentle, as she lifted my upper body, and rearranged the pillows behind me.

"What happened, where am I?" I asked, now completely awake. I couldn't see. I reached up with my right hand and felt a bandage. It covered both my eyes. I patted the gauze and found that it seemed to be wound all the way around my head. I lifted my left hand to check, and froze with the piercing pain. "Ow, ow, ow! What in the hell is going on?"

"You were in an accident, I would guess. Let me see your chart. Hmm. This says your name is Jane Doe and that you had a musket ball removed from your left shoulder. It just missed your heart, but it looks like you're going to be good as new. Renaissance Fair accident, it says." The woman paused then added, "They didn't have muskets in the Renaissance. Jane Doe?"

"That isn't my name, it's, uh, oh, shoot. What is my name?" I asked. "Crap!"

"Well, I doubt it's crap. Let's see, it doesn't say anything here about why your eyes are bandaged. Let me check this out."

The nurse unwrapped the gauze strip around my eyes. "I can't see any signs of trauma; there's no blood or seepage." She got all the wrapping off, and then gently pulled off the eye pads one at a time. "Nothing obvious,

445

and there aren't any notes in your chart about ocular trauma. Open your eyes, please."

I did.

Oh, boy…

I knew her.

"Leah?" I asked.

"Mom?" she answered as a question.

"I think so. What's going on? I don't remember anything," I said. "I mean, really, I don't know why I'm here. Nothing."

I really didn't remember anything, but I knew that this was Leah—I was absolutely sure of that—and I had the gut feeling that I was her mother.

"You disappeared ten months ago. No body was found; not a trace of you. You look good now except for the hole in your shoulder. You've lost a lot of weight and your wrinkles are, well, they're gone. You dyed your hair, too—no more silver highlights, as you called them. You look good," she repeated, "almost too good."

I was scared beyond words. I slunk back into the pillows and started to hyperventilate, casting my eyes down at my slim midsection. "Thanks," I said softly in response to the complement. I pressed my lips together and just lay there, stunned, concentrating on my breathing so I wouldn't have to think about this uneasy situation. There was a hole in my memory, and all I could remember was that I had had amnesia before. I didn't know what to say, so I said nothing.

"Well, aren't you going to tell me what happened?" she asked, not even trying to disguise the edge of disgust in her voice.

Just then, the door opened. I looked up and saw a face and body familiar to me, but I couldn't place where this short, odd-looking man fit in my life. He didn't scare me, but I didn't get warm, fuzzy feelings about him either. "How's my patient doing this morning?" he asked cheerily.

"I'm sorry, sir. I don't recognize you. Are you her doctor?" Leah asked in a sharp, indignant tone. I didn't know if she was irritated with him or me, but I suspected both.

"I'm Dr. Em and Ms. Doe is my patient. I've come to see if she is well enough to travel. I would like to get her back to the clinic as soon as possible."

"Dr. Em? I've never heard of a Dr. *Em* at this hospital." Leah picked up the chart and looked it over again. She glanced up at me, then over at the doctor, and then back down at the chart.

446

"Okay. Dr. Em, first off, this patient isn't a Jane Doe. I think I know who she is." Leah's voice was commanding, as if ready to reveal who murdered whom and with what in a game of Clue. She didn't volunteer any names, though. It was obvious to me that she was testing the man.

"Yes, yes, my dear," he replied in a condescending tone. "We use aliases at the clinic to protect our patient's privacy." Dr. Em looked at me again and realized that he could see my whole face. "Why are the bandages removed from her eyes?" he asked harshly, his knuckles flying to his hips, his body language shouting indignation.

"It's my job to check dressings, sir," Leah answered with self-assurance. "There wasn't anything in the chart about her eyes or why they were bandaged. I wanted to make sure the dressings were clean and that an infection hadn't set in." The confidence in Leah's voice was ebbing. "There didn't seem to be anything wrong with her eyes, so I didn't re-bandage them." Her last words were spoken softly and with just a hint of guilt.

"And are you her doctor? Are you an ophthalmologist? Did it say in her chart to check the bandages? Miss, what is your name? I should report you to the nursing supervisor. This is very inappropriate."

"Sorry, sir, I just thought…" Leah stammered.

"You aren't supposed to think, you're supposed to follow orders, understand?" Dr. Em stuck his chin out, almost hostile toward the young nurse who had taken the initiative. He was short, but definitely had a superiority complex.

I stopped listening to the doctor and nurse and their debate on protocol, designated duties, whatever. Young nurse? She looked to be older than me. How could I be her mother?

"Wake up, wake up!" It was the doctor, practically shouting in my stunned face. "Come on, get dressed. We're leaving right now!"

I looked around and Leah was gone. Dr. Em shoved a robe at me and grabbed my good right shoulder, pulling me up into a sitting position. He carefully picked up my left arm—which hurt like hell—and put it into the sleeve. He positioned the plush pink terrycloth robe around my back and helped me put my right arm into the other sleeve.

"My necklace! I won't go anywhere without the necklace Wallace gave me!" I cried.

"Oh, yes, yes. We'll need that. Oh, here it is, in the bureau." Dr. Em pulled the Greek coin necklace laced on black ribbon from the little nightstand drawer. He gently pushed aside my hair, causing a shiver to run

447

up my spine. He quickly tied the ribbon, then let my hair fall back on my neck. "Here, take this," he said and shoved a small bluish bottle to my lips. "It will help ease the pain."

I let him pour some of the liquid into my mouth...but I didn't swallow. As soon as his back was turned, I spit the bitter brew into the pile of gauze that Leah had pulled off. Fortunately the liquid was clear, so it wasn't obvious that I hadn't swallowed it. My mouth was kind of tingling, though.

"Dr. Em, the head nurse would like to speak with you." Leah was back again, accompanied by a very fat woman in lavender kitty cat-printed scrubs that were at least two sizes too small for her.

"Yes, Dr. Em, Nurse Madigan says she thinks your patient is here under duress. I am going to have to ask you to come with me while we check out your credentials. You're not on our list of doctors authorized to practice at this hospital."

Miss Kitty Nurse was being polite and formal, but she was twice his size. If Dr. Toadface didn't cooperate, she could haul his butt out of here to wherever, if she wanted.

"Nurse, uh," the doctor looked down at her name tag, "Gata, yes, Nurse Gata, my patient is here on a discretionary pass. We do not use our client's names when we come to a public medical facility. We use pseudonyms to protect their privacy. Of course, my patient is not Jane Doe, but her real name is none of your business. Now, if you will kindly move aside, I am ready to transfer my patient to another location."

"Oh, no you don't, mister," Leah said, her cheeks flushed with anger. "I doubt you are even a doctor, and I have reason to suspect that this woman is a victim of kidnapping."

I felt as if I had a front row seat at a mid-morning hospital-themed soap opera: second-rate actors—an obstinate nurse, a clueless supervisor, and the classically-clad doctor—all trying to out-emote each other. My head turned side-to-side as I watched the dimwitted drama unfold. My mouth wasn't tingling anymore, but I probably had been affected by the funny-looking doctor's special medicine. I was feeling very relaxed, definitely more laid back than possible without chemical intervention.

"Out of my way, Ms. Madigan," Dr. Em said as he tried to elbow his way past her.

But Leah wouldn't budge. "I know this woman, and she knows me. She called me by name, and I want her to stay here until this is resolved. Nurse Gata, would you call security, please?"

The matronly supervisor left in a worried waddle, hands in the air as if she was praying to heaven for divine intervention—or she was giving up.

Dr. Em looked both angry and scared at the prospect of more people coming. "Of course, she knows your name; it's right on your name tag," he said and stepped forward to leave. Leah moved away from the door and let him pass.

He hadn't taken me, so she had won.

Or so she thought.

In two blinks of my still befuddled eyes, he was back—he had only left the room to get a wheelchair. He rolled it past Leah and over to the side of my bed, pushing aside the rollaway tray that held my discarded gauze bandages.

I looked up at him and wondered what the drug he had given me was supposed to do. Since I was mellow and not hurting anymore, it was probably both a painkiller and an anti-anxiety medication. But, given that I hadn't swallowed the full dose, maybe it was also intended to make me docile and submissive. I decided to play along, at least until I found a better option.

Leah and her boss didn't seem to be working well together on this. Nurse Kitty was big, but was as meek as a melon. Leah was going to have to be both the brains and the brawn in this confrontation.

Evidently Leah had come to the same conclusion. I looked over at her with awe, wonder, and maternal pride. Awe at how she was taking charge, even though it might mean losing her job by challenging a doctor. Wonder at what her plan was to keep me here, and maternal pride—that I couldn't explain. It was the same innate emotion that I felt when I held my babies.

Dr. Em had been ushering my oblivious body into the wheelchair as I recalled my babies. I was suddenly aware of how full and hard my breasts were. I hadn't fed them in I don't know long, but I would suspect at least eight hours. I could feel the coolness on my gown where my very large and painfully firm breasts had leaked milk. I looked down and saw the wetness. Leah followed my gaze and her eyes widened.

"Not so fast there, mister," she said. "She called me by my family name, not the name on my tag. We're related, and I'll be damned if I'll let you take her away from me—again."

Dr. Em had been ready for resistance. She was two steps away when he lifted his hand and flung the fluid into her face. She gasped, and sunk to her knees. Her head plopped forward and she fell, unable to stop herself, landing on his chest with a thud, her arms limp at her side, unconscious.

He backed away from her and gently, but with mild disgust, laid her on the hospital floor, her face turned to the side. She was alive, breathing shallowly, her eyes glassy and staring into nothingness, but would recover soon. He pulled the privacy curtain around the bed to block the view of her body. Her foot was sticking out, so he knelt down and dragged the leg to the side, essentially bending her body into an "L" shape so she wouldn't be visible to anyone who walked into the room.

I didn't know what to do, so I continued to play the drugged patient. Dr. Em maneuvered me in the wheelchair—stunned, scared, and silent— around her prone body and escorted me out the door.

I wish I knew how I'm supposed to be reacting. Crap! Nurse Gata is coming towards us. Dr. Em sees her, too, and quickly moves us into an alcove. How appropriate; we're in the chapel. "Please help us, Lord," I pray softly: I don't want anyone but God to hear me. I immediately feel a lessening of the tension in the air, and it's not from the drugging. I know I'm going to be okay now.

After a very long thirty seconds, we emerged from our hideout, Dr. Em pushing me in the wheelchair. I felt carefree, as if I was a baby in a stroller, and we were going for a picnic in the park. I started humming for some reason—probably a side effect of the potion. We passed a cart loaded with flowers, balloons, and a fruit basket. I reached out with my good right arm, grabbed a bunch of bananas, and clutched it close to my belly like the golden treasure I felt it was. I started singing, "One banana, two banana, three banana, four…"

"Hush," the doctor said. So I did. Sort of. I couldn't help but keep humming. Between the prayer and the anti-anxiety medicine, I was *very* content.

We made it to the emergency room entrance with hardly a head turned. I say hardly because we did receive a smile from a little boy holding a bouquet of balloons. The balloons were all blue and said, "It's a boy!" He was holding his father's—I guess—hand and waving at us as we passed. I felt moistness in two zones at his smile. I was leaking milk again, and tears were dribbling down my cheeks.

I missed my family, my home in the wilderness, the wildness of the late 18th century. I didn't know who Dr. Em was, but I was sure that he was my ticket back home. I felt sorry and confused about leaving Leah, but my lactating hormones were in charge right now. I needed my babies, and I'm sure they needed me, too.

"Get out, come on, you can do it. Hurry, hurry up." Dr. Em was urging me out of the wheelchair and into the vehicle. I had been oblivious to everything around me while grieving for my babies. I did as I was told, clutching my bunch of bananas as if they were my children, while I waited for the doctor to get in on the other side.

I looked up and saw the seatbelt hanging next to the window of the car door. "Sorry; no way, José," I said. "Ain't gonna put that on with my shoulder torn up and my chest ready to explode."

There was a commotion moving our way. Nurse Kitty was in the lead, speed walking, leading a crowd of uniformed people—male nurse-types in scrubs and a couple of rent-a-cops, or maybe they were real law enforcement officers. Anyhow, they were heading right towards us, looking at the man who had just climbed in next to me. And they didn't look happy.

"Good Lord," Doctor Em exclaimed. "Where's the steering wheel? Oh no, this is America, isn't it? They put the damned operator's station on the wrong side of the conveyance!"

Dr. Em had put me in on the driver's side of the car and was trying to make a getaway by sitting in the passenger's seat. "Drive woman, drive, NOW!"

The mob was getting closer, and I realized that I had just been given the upper hand. "I will," I said, "if you tell me what's going on." I stared at him with narrowed eyes, the medicine's effect was either wearing off or being overridden by adrenaline. "Tell me everything that's going on, or we stay here."

"All right, all right, just go!" he said, his hands flying up in panicked surrender.

The key was already in the ignition. I started the car, dropped it into drive, and floored it.

It was just like buttering toast; it all came back to me. "Where are we going?" I asked as I sped to the end of the parking lot. He could tell me all I wanted—needed—to know later. If the hospital posse caught up with us first, they'd haul him away, and then I would never find out what this last year had been all about.

"Head that way," he said, pointing east. "But go quickly, we don't have much time. They'll be blocking the roads if we don't get out of town soon."

I looked in the rear view mirror and saw that we were in an SUV with an infant car seat and booster seat in the back. There was also a flower arrangement with 'Congratulations' and little blue football and baseball decorations poked in amongst the daisies and carnations. We had just stolen the car that belonged to that smiling little boy's family. Well, they would just have to score another ride home. Something told me that this was my only chance to get away from the hospital authorities and get to wherever it was that I was supposed to go.

"How far?" I asked. I was traveling nine miles an hour above the speed limit. I didn't want to get stopped for a traffic ticket but wanted to get to our destination before the cops figured a way to keep us—me—from going home.

"It's only about 20 miles from here to the exit. After that, it's only six miles on gravel road, and then a mile and a half of walking." Dr. Em was looking around anxiously, rubbing his thumb back and forth over the side of the first joint of his index finger in a nervous manner.

"Chill out, Doc. We'll be fine. I can feel it in my bones, can't you?" I was trying to get him to relax. I wanted to hear the story of me from him, and didn't want him distracted when he told it. "Didn't you ever hear that negative energy attracts bad karma?"

"What? Negative energy, bad karma, yes, yes. You are right. How is your shoulder? I'm a bit surprised that you can still talk, much less operate one of these foul-smelling machines."

"My shoulder is fine when I'm not thinking about it. I didn't swallow that elixir you shoved in my face, and it's a good thing, too, or I wouldn't be able to drive. And this may be a foul-smelling conveyance, but it sure is comfortable and fast. At our current rate of speed, we should be at the turn off in just over 15 minutes. Six miles on a gravel road at 30 miles per hour is about twelve minutes and then, depending on the terrain, a thirty-minute walk. That means you have almost a full hour to tell me why I'm *here*, and why I was *there*."

Dr. Em squirmed in his seat. "Maybe I should have one of these on," he said as he played with the nylon seat belt at his right.

"A seat belt won't protect you from me if you don't start talking. We had an agreement, remember?" I was hoping that this man, this apparent time traveler, had the sense of honesty and integrity that made the men— the gentlemen of earlier eras—so appealing to me.

"Yes, yes, I do owe you that, I suppose. Well, you saved my life, and now I have saved yours. That's it," he said.

A satisfied smug stretched across his face. He didn't know how to smile correctly, though. It looked like his cheeks were going to split—his determined effort to look happy was apparently causing him pain. He gave up on his attempt at a smile, crossed his arms across his chest, and scrunched down in the seat, looking as if he was preparing to take a nap.

"Sorry, Doc, that version's too short to pass as a full and complete explanation. Let's start from the beginning. Who am I?"

"You're Dani Madigan. Next question?"

"You know, you're making this very difficult for me. You said you'd tell me the whole story. Do you want me to pull over here, to the side of this freeway full of fast-moving cars, and wait for roadside assistance from one of our ever-so-vigilant traffic safety officers?"

Dr. Em lost the slouch and scooted back up in his seat, his straight-backed body language practically shouting, 'No, thanks; I'll behave myself.'

"Who are you? I can't believe that Dr. Em is your real name."

"I'm Master Simon and I travel."

"Travel?" I asked. "Here and there, or now and then?"

Master Simon cleared his throat and said, "Yes," with a definite finality. He wasn't going to elaborate.

His answer was good enough for me. I wanted to get down to what concerned me and mine. "Okay, so what did Leah mean when she said she didn't want you to take me away 'again'?"

I figure I had better get as much out of him now as I can. The troopers—or highway patrol, or whatever they are—could still catch up with us even if I don't feint a breakdown. At least we're in a red SUV, and no matter who makes them—Toyota, Chrysler, Ford, Mercedes, Honda, or whoever—they all look alike. That should make tracking us a bit harder. And since this isn't a rental car or an emergency vehicle, there probably isn't a LoJack installed on it either.

I wasn't getting an answer out of Master Simon, so I let my foot off the gas, tapped on the brake, and slowed down. I turned towards him, gave him the evil eye, flipped on the blinker, and headed onto the shoulder of the freeway.

"All right, all right, get back on the road." He huffed in frustration. "Hmph! And hurry."

I turned off the signal and sped back up to my nine miles over the speed limit. He remained mum, so I growled at him, like a dog guarding a purloined steak.

"Sorry, I was just trying to figure out where to start. Let's see, I was going to meet a friend not far from here when you first met me. I had been assaulted and robbed, and you came to my rescue. You helped me retrieve my stolen map, figured out how to read it, and then took me to the park where you were supposed to leave me, and go home. I caught up with my friend there. All was going according to our plan. We were at the nearest high gate to Greensboro and ready to make the jump, but you had followed us. We did our best to, shall we say, sneak past you, but that plan failed. You stepped out over the point when my friend and I weren't watching you. You leapt out—chasing an illusion, I believe—and my friend and I grabbed you. We all fell, but you didn't know how to land. You fractured your skull and broke your back. It didn't look like you were going to survive. I felt a bit guilty; I supposed it was because you had hurt yourself trying to help me. It's not that I needed the help—I knew what I was doing. But I digress. You had major injuries and were 230 years from home and medical attention. So, I gave you some of my FOY water. I was trying to dribble a few drops into your mouth, but you latched onto the bottle and sucked it dry. It was the last of my supply, too. I had to return to Florida to get more so I could get out of this fiasco."

"Uh, okay. But before you go any further, what is FOY water, and what does it do?" I looked down at the steering wheel. There had to be a cruise control button somewhere. I didn't want to trust my reflexes to keep a constant speed with the story that Simon was telling me.

"Fountain of Youth; a couple drops of the water can keep you young or seek out broken body parts to mend. Actually, it replaces the damaged cells in the body, so if you have, say, liver failure, it will repair that. In some cases, it has even shrunk fat cells, and I see that it did that for you, too. I've used it for thous...er... many years with no ill effects. You drank so much, though, that it actually reversed your aging. I hear it also acted as a fertility enhancer in your case. Triplets, I understand."

"Hmm. So I *am* Leah's mother. What was I doing in North Carolina? All of the bits and pieces of memories I have are of Alaska and the desert."

I was only slightly bothered by my lack of personal history, but still very curious about why I was so far from Alaska. I was also glad that the cruise control was now engaged.

"I don't know about you personally. If you remember that you are from both Alaska and the desert, then it is most likely true. Since you met your daughter—I assume she is your daughter—at the hospital, I would surmise that you were there to visit her."

"Brilliant deduction, Dr. Watson. So, I have a daughter who is older than me?"

"No, you are still older in chronological years, but you have had a rewind of your cellular biology. I'd say you are about 18 years old physically. Are all your questions answered, madam?" he asked, looking at me for confirmation.

I turned to him, gave a half-grin, half-grimace, and said, "It'll do for now. Which exit do we take?"

Ж Ж Ж

About five miles and five minutes later, I had thought of more questions. "So, how did I get hurt? A musket ball wound, Leah said."

"You were in the line of fire, but you should fully recover. My potions can only do so much. Musket balls need to be removed before the healing can begin."

"Why did you bring me back? Couldn't Sarah fix me?" I paused, waiting for the response that didn't come. "She is okay, isn't she?"

"Yes, yes; at least she was when we left. She was afraid to operate so close to your heart. I was willing to bring you back to this time, but your—how do you say, 'menfolk?'— insisted I stay with you at the hospital, and then return you to them. They were *very* insistent," Simon was shuddering at the memory, "that you make it back."

"If you mean Jody, I see what you mean. He can be rather intimidating." I smiled, visualizing Jody lording over the short, squat Master Simon.

"Oh, not just him—it was the both of them. They told me I could bring you here to be mended and then returned to them, or they would pull me apart into so many pieces, that I'd never be whole again, no matter how many stitches were used. I'll get you back to the portal site, but I'd rather not face them another time. Besides, my work there is complete, and I have other places to go. You seemed to manage fine there by yourself before. This time, Sarah, your husband, and father-in-law will be waiting for you."

"My husband and father-in-law? That's right! I remember. You did a little Norwegian wedding ceremony just before the wagon ride. I'm married!" I suddenly felt warm and squishy all over as I realized that I had a husband and was now on my way back to him. A real husband and father for my babies…

My reverie popped shut. "Hey," I said, "Why did you leave me by myself before? I didn't even have any water, much less food or shelter. I could've been eaten by wild animals the first night!"

"Ah, but you weren't, were you?" he said. "You are stronger and smarter than you know."

"Well, you're taking a lot for granted. Oh, my God. Leah! She'll think I've deserted her again. Hey, she said she didn't want you to take me from her *again*. Did she know you were with me the first time I disappeared?"

"No, at least nothing for certain. When we were in the hospital room, I could feel her inside my head. She caught me off guard; I didn't know she was psychic. She couldn't tell much about you, though, because she was so angry with you for being gone. She has your strength and wits. She'll be fine. She's a survivor. Here, take this exit, then turn left at the stop sign."

I followed his directions without any emotion. I didn't know what I wanted to do. I knew I had to go back to my other family, but I also hurt—physically ached all over—when I realized that I was deserting my firstborn. Again. And this time, it was intentional. I had the choice of staying here—or going back.

Master Simon looked over at me and put his hand on my good shoulder, "She's an adult and can take care of herself. You have a new husband and three babies who *need* you. And Sarah could use your help, too. There's a new country that requires support for both its soldiers and citizens. Come on, let's get you back home."

***49 Back home again with bananas

"Now, I'm not going with you this time; you'll have to go by yourself. You probably don't remember how we made the trip yesterday because you were unconscious. I 'carried' you with me. This isn't the same method of transition we used on your first trip either, so don't worry about your landing. Actually, there isn't any kind of drop here—it's a horizontal pass through. There's a very strong magnetic distortion at this site—marked by those trees—but the coin should help defray the pulses and any potentially harmful static they cause. Take a deep breath before going through, and don't hold your own hands. You don't want to complete a circle with either your hands or feet touching. That could be, well, just don't do it."

"I feel sick," I said. "I think I'm going to throw up."

"No, no; it's just the magnetic field. If you couldn't feel it, you wouldn't be able to go home this way. If we went back to the monadnock—the hanging rock—you'd have too far to walk to get home to your family. Besides, they aren't expecting you to return there. You'd be all alone again. Please, just concentrate on your breathing and..." he looked down at the bundle I held close to my middle, "are you going to take that fruit with you?"

"You bet I am. I've wanted bananas for almost a year. I don't want to eat one of them now and lose it, though," I lifted my yellow potassium-rich booty as if they were trophy-sized trout, "so these guys are coming with me."

"That's fine. Just hold your coin and focus on your family. Do you see them in your head?"

I nodded in acknowledgement, sniffing back my fears and uncertainties.

"Now open your eyes and proceed through there." Master Simon pointed to a gap between two old trees. I walked forward and heard his voice, "Be safe, and I'm sorry I inconvenienced you..."

Ж Ж Ж

I awoke to someone patting my hand and someone else stroking my hair. "Get away! I need air," I shouted, thrashing my head side to side.

My movement woke me up all the way. "Sarah? Sarah?" I called frantically. I tipped my head back, looked up, and saw it was her. "Oh, sorry. *Déjà vu* all over again. Remember, Sarah?"

"Yes, yes, I remember. But do you remember me, and all of this?"

"Yes, I do," I said with confidence, and smiled at my handsome, hand-holding husband. The pride quickly drained away and frustration took its place. "Damn! I forgot to ask Dr. Em—I mean, Master Simon—how come I couldn't remember anything when I woke up the first time I was here."

"It doesn't matter, does it? You remember us and we remember you, right, Sally?" Wallace asked, grinning.

I snorted at his little joke, then winced in pain. I didn't dare laugh—I still hurt—but kept my smile.

Sarah grinned` and changed the subject, rubbing the edge of my hospital gown between her fingers. "They didn't give you much in the way of a trousseau," she said. "Although they did provide you with a nice traveling cloak," and nodded to the plush pink cotton terrycloth robe, folded beside me.

"Yeah," I said and peeked down the front of the standard issue cotton print smock. I was wearing one frontwards, the other tied on backwards. "But they took my underwear. I guess I'll have to go commando like everyone else."

I got blank stares from both Sarah and Wallace. "No briefs, I mean, small clothes. Never mind, it's just a phrase," I said, and shook my head. If I didn't elaborate on it, I wouldn't get embarrassed.

I put a cautious hand on my tender left shoulder. It wasn't too bad, so I decided to find my limits. I started wiggling, trying to scoot up into a seated position. Wallace saw what I was trying to do, and was right there with me, helping me upright. Sarah moved over to my other side and just kind of hovered, wanting to help, but unneeded. I caught my breath—it was harder to do than I thought—then continued with my challenge. Wallace gently guided me the rest of the way up until I was in a standing position.

I felt all warm and mushy, and I doubt it was from the exercise. My senses were waking up, too. The physical proximity of my husband, his voice, his smell... I looked over at Sarah. "Can you give us a moment, please?"

"Sure, sure; I need to go check on... Well, I'm sure something needs checking on," she said and left in a hurry, her cheeks pink with embarrassment and joy.

I turned into Wallace's firm body and looked up. "I need a hug," I pouted, my bottom lip stuck out in mock drama, and then added, "but be gentle with me. I still have an owie."

His eyebrows crowded together in confusion. It must have been the word 'owie,' but he figured it out. "How about this?" he asked and squatted down so he could hug me at my own, lower altitude. I appreciated his assumption of the awkward posture, so I didn't have to reach up. We were almost in an embrace when he stopped and asked, "What's this?"

I was still clutching the awkward bundle of bananas to my middle, and it was now poking both of us.

"Those are for later. Would you put them over there?"

"Anything for you, Mrs. Pomeroy-Hart."

Wallace put the bananas next to my new, pink robe, and then turned back to me. "Now, where were we?" he asked, the glint in his eye letting me know that he knew exactly where we had been.

I didn't say a word; just smiled and did my Groucho Marx double eyebrow pop, adding a 'come hither' purr.

And he did.

The kissing was as good as it could be, considering his awkward position, and my recently assigned status of injured reserved. He was starting to wobble, losing his balance, and reached out to steady himself on the ground. "I think we'd better continue this later," he said. "I think there are others who want to see you."

As if it was his cue, Jody showed up, Sarah at his elbow.

"Hey, Jody. See, I didn't forget to come back. And Sarah, look here: bananas!" I was so excited that I could hardly contain myself.

And then realization hit. I was probably not the only one who had been injured in the confrontation. "Oh, these can wait. Was anyone else hurt?" I asked.

"Yes, but let's not talk about it now. We need to get you back home," Sarah said. "Do you think you can handle the wagon ride back?"

I took Wallace's hand and let him help me into the back of the wagon before I answered. I think I was still in shock at all that had happened.

"Yes, I'm sure I'll be okay. But if it's all the same to you, I think I'll go back to sleep. Traveling 231 years twice in twenty-four hours kind of wore me out." I started to roll onto my left side, was rudely reminded on my recent surgery, and quickly decided to stay flat on my back. I wiggled my head to get my neck comfortable, heard the grains of rice in the burlap bag pillow shift, and then floated back into oblivion and the absence of pain.

I awoke to the familiar smells of home: herbs, eggs, and babies. I heard the eggs sizzling and felt someone touching my gown. It was Sarah. "Do you think you could try to feed Leo? We need to get your milk supply going again."

I scooted up on the chaise and gladly took my little boy to my breast. It was frustrating for both of us, though. Both my breasts were hard as brick cheeses from not nursing for so long, and my nipple was too firm for him to latch onto. Sarah handed me a teacup. "Try this," she said.

I must have done it when Leah was a baby. Expressing milk over the edge of a teacup came naturally. I pumped enough off of one breast to allow him to drain the rest. He didn't act as if he was very hungry, though.

"Just before you woke up, Mrs. Donaldson went home to be with the rest of her family. Hannah took all the girls and the twin boys home yesterday so they could be with their father. By the way, he didn't suffer from his ordeal at the mill, and the British soldiers didn't arrest any of the locals. Mrs. Donaldson stayed here to wet nurse your three. She told me you still had plenty of milk, but you need to feed the ones who aren't too hungry first. That way you'll still have some left for the others."

And she was right. I wound up feeding all three of my babies in that first hour of semi-lucidity. I was in my own mini-world, only aware of them and our need for each other. And my world was at peace. No muskets or mean men to ruin my day...or my body.

I looked around and saw that the adult members of my family had divided the childcare duties while I was gone. Sarah changed the diapers, Jody did the burping, and Wallace got them settled back to sleep, rubbing their backs to soothe them into a deep slumber.

Julian had returned to his job as the chef. The four of them had lunched in between cooking and nursery duties, but had made sure that there was a hefty portion of omelet left for me. A big mug of buttermilk completed my welcome home dinner. The simple fare was divine and literally restored both my body and soul.

My mind was clearing rapidly. "I'm back," I declared to everyone in the room, "I mean here, too," and pointed to my head. "And, in case any of you were wondering, there was nothing, nobody, here I was running away from. It's just the opposite. There were so many of you here who I cared about, that I was running *to* you!"

"Well, ye did have the bairns to come back to," Jody said. "It's not as if ye had any there."

He saw my face drop. "Lass, did ye have bairns there, back there in yer own time?"

"Well, yes and no," I answered as I looked at Wallace.

He wasn't guarding his feelings at all. He looked afraid, as if he was going to lose me again.

"I have a daughter," I said softly, and took his hand. I brought it up to my cheek and held his fingers so they traced the side of my face from the outside edge of my eye, down my cheek to my neck and collarbone. "Would you love me if I were old?" I asked, making certain I saw his reaction. I was sure he and everyone else thought I was still dopey from my ordeal, and that was fine—actually better.

He smiled and said, "Don't worry; I'll love you forever. We'll grow old together, God willing. Wrinkles won't make any difference to me. Age is just a number. Look at my father," he said as he looked towards Jody. Sarah's hands immediately went up to touch the crow's feet beside her eyes. "Jody doesn't care that Sarah is older than he is, right?"

Sarah saw that he was asking her the question. "Well, biologically I'm older, but chronologically he has me beat by about 200 years," she said with a tinge of sarcasm.

"See," he said, "it never made any difference to them."

"Yeah, well, this is different. You see, I met my daughter when I went back. Actually, she was one of the nurses who took care of me..."

Wallace's eyes widened. He looked over at Jody, Julian, and Sarah and saw that they, too, were as bug-eyed as grasshoppers. He started moving his head from one side to the other, gradually working up to a full-blown head shaking. "But how?"

"Not but how but will. Will you—would you—love me if I were old enough to be your grandmother?"

"I knew it!" exclaimed Julian. "Oh, sorry, it's not my place to speak."

"Go ahead; it looks like everyone else is tongue-tied," I said, and stumbled back to the chaise.

My chaise. I ran my fingers across the little bit of the original fine fabric that was still intact on the side of the chair. "What did you say?" I asked when I realized that Julian had been speaking to me.

"I always knew you had an old soul in that young, nubile body. Well, Wallace, I think you have the perfect woman here. Smart and wise beyond the, shall we say, obvious years of her body. How could you possibly have a problem with that?" Julian was grinning; so proud that he had perceived the real me before I had.

461

"I'll give you an A-plus in detective work, Julian. I just wish I had found out about it earlier," I said, unable to hide the grumble of regret.

"Why?" asked Wallace. "I mean, yes, I must admit that I'm a little shocked and yes, I definitely want to hear more about my stepdaughter—oops, sorry about using that four letter word 'step'—but what difference would any of that knowledge make, or have made? I still would have fallen in love with you, and I hope that you would still have loved me. Now what? You think that since you know you're so much older than me that maybe Julian would be a better husband for you?"

I laughed and giggled, and then started coughing from swallowing spit the wrong way. Wallace came over and patted me gingerly on the back to help me stop coughing. I looked over at Julian and saw his frowning, contorted face. "Would that be so bad?" he asked. "I'm not that old," he added indignantly.

I looked over and saw Jody and Sarah rolling their eyes. Both had their hands to their mouths, stifling grins or chuckles, or maybe even belly laughs.

"Julian," I said as I walked over to his side, the coughing fit over, "I love you; I've told you that, but," I leaned in and gave him a kiss on the cheek, "you're not my type." I walked over to Wallace's side and snuggled next to him, still too apprehensive because of the topic of discussion to give him a kiss or a hug. "You're just a little too straight-laced for me," I said as I looked back at him.

I turned to look up at Wallace. "I like a man who doesn't have to button up all his buttons." I put my finger under Wallace's chin. His top button was undone. He looked down to see what I was doing. I flipped my finger up, popping him on the nose as I did so. "Gotcha," I said.

"You sure do." He gathered me up in his arms, lifted me by the waist, and gave me a very long welcome home kiss. When we finally broke apart, he set me back on the chaise. "Now tell me about my other daughter," he said, beaming with joy.

His smile was genuine. It was as if I had just announced that he had won a new critter, and he wanted to know all the details. He pulled over the four-legged stool from in front of the hearth, eager to hear stories of his newly discovered daughter.

But I wasn't ready. I still had to find out what had happened at the battle at the mill. I couldn't have been the only one who was injured. There had been muskets, guns, and all sorts of commotions, and I couldn't remember much of anything. "First, tell me who else got hurt."

Wallace rose up from the stool, sat next to me on the chaise, and took my right hand. "I'm afraid that both Clayton and Clyde didn't make it. You were right that there had to be a reason why both of them lived after the...the attack."

Wallace's lips were tight, and it looked as if he were choking. "God, I hated them so much, and I felt like...like Ian had the right idea with vengeance, but I listened to you. Clyde was already dead, but Clayton apologized to me for both of them. I didn't want to accept the apology, but I remembered that part in the Bible that said if I didn't forgive, then how could I ever expect to be forgiven. I don't think I will ever, could ever, do anything that horrid, but, well, they needed to be forgiven, and so I gave it to them—forgiveness."

Wallace looked at me to see how I was reacting to his story. He rubbed my hand, "It actually felt good to forgive them. It wasn't just for them, though. After I forgave them, I found out that it helped me, too."

I gave a weak smile and scooted closer to him, not wanting to stop his recollection of the previous day's events. "Just before the fighting was over, Clayton stepped in front of a bayonet that was meant for me. And earlier, Clyde had jumped in front of an officer who was aiming his pistol at Jody. That bullet hit Clyde in the throat. He died immediately. Clayton didn't fare so well. He had been stabbed in the stomach, and held on for nearly an hour. I was by his side at the end. He just kept saying how sorry he was..." Wallace was choked up, the tears slipping down the sides of his red cheeks. "If I had gone out and killed them after they...they...did what they did to me, then they wouldn't have been there to save Father and me. And then where would you and Sarah be?"

A big frown covered me all the way to the ground. I looked over at Sarah and saw she had a similar reaction. I'm sure she was thinking the same thing I was: if our men were gone, would we go back to our former times?

"But that's not what happened, is it?" I asked, not really expecting an answer. "We're all doing fine here in 1781 and ready to take care of the families we have here and now, right?"

"Right!" came the resounding replies, the mood of everyone in the room immediately lifted.

Well, almost everyone.

I looked over and saw Jenny in the corner. I hadn't even noticed that she had come into the house. She had picked up, and was now holding and cuddling, my baby girl. I was going to have to remember to ask everyone to call her by her middle name, Wren. I didn't know if I was ready to let it be known that I had found out that in my 'other time' I was a Danielle. I had actually grown fond of her new name, and Wren seemed to fit her better anyway.

Neither Wallace nor I realized that Jenny had been in the room when we had spoken of her brothers. I still had a hard time believing that those two degenerates, Clyde and Clayton, were related to her. And now those two were dead. Since she was still here, I had to assume she didn't have any other family.

"Wallace," I called softly. "Do you think we could handle one more?" and nodded to Jenny.

"Absolutely!" he whispered with delight. I tilted my head in her direction again, squinted my eyes, and frowned, giving him the look that said, 'Well, ask her!'

Wallace gently moved away from me and walked over to the girls. "Jenny, would you like Wren to be your little sister?" he asked.

She looked up at him, surprised at his size as much as by the question, I think. I don't know if she had ever been physically that close to him while he was standing. She looked back down at the little red-headed girl in her arms, and then back up to face him. "Could the other two be my brothers then?"

"I wouldn't have it any other way. They're a matched set, you know. They all have the same birthday, parents, and everything."

Jenny's face worked a few emotional twists: a frown, a deep thought, a grin, and then a huge smile. "Does that mean you'd be my father and Evie'd be my mother?"

Wallace nodded, "Yes, that's what that means. Would that be okay with you?"

"A mother, a real mother! And a father, too!" Jenny was beside herself with joy, squealing with excitement. She was still holding onto her new baby sister, and the yelling was upsetting the little one; she started bellowing, too. "You're my new sister, you're my new sister," she sing-songed. "And I'm the big sister to all three of you. Hah!" she said with pride.

"Well grandpas and grandma, it looks like there's another one in the family. Can't say that she was any less pain to get," I said and rubbed my left shoulder, "but the pregnancy was sure a lot shorter."

Ж Ж Ж

It was evening. The adults were gathered around the kitchen table,

464

sharing stories. Life was starting to settle back into our old routine—with a welcomed modification. Earlier, Sarah had set up a sleeping pallet for Jenny on the floor next to the playpen. The new big sister didn't want to be far away from her new siblings. One of the babies started to fuss. I looked to see who it was, but Jenny lifted her head, saw where the movement was, and placed her hand through the rails and onto Judah's back, rubbing it softly until he went back to sleep.

Jenny had the most contented look on her face. I didn't know if there was a word for it, but what I saw was peaceful satisfaction. Just wait until they're in their terrible twos, I thought. Yes, and now there would be one more person to help me keep them out of trouble. Then I felt that 'peaceful satisfaction' smile come onto my face, and welcomed its presence.

Ж Ж Ж

The next morning started before the sun came up. It was the beginning of my first full day back home. First Wren started squawking. She didn't know how to crow, but was still able to wake me with her none-too-subtle wail. There was no hesitation on my part to rise to the call of duty as chuck wagon. I had learned early on to get the first baby 'busted in the mouth' right away, so the other two didn't waken.

But it was the second loud noise that woke everyone else in the household: my screaming. I hadn't planned on yelling. Then again, pain doesn't always give you that option. When I heard Wren, I immediately sat straight up. I was aware after the fact that I was stiff, but still hadn't had any trouble sitting up. But when I reached for Wren with my left arm, all traces of civilized behavior disappeared, and I was a screaming, shoulder-shot banshee.

I had been asleep—totally pain-free—and then risen, half asleep, to a ten plus on the pain scale. It was no wonder that I found it impossible to contain the hysterics. Of course, all of the babies were panicked by mama's screeching, and before I could even think to shut up, three men and two women, one very small, were at my side trying to find out the cause of the uproar. Each one of the men grabbed his godchild, and Jenny grabbed Wallace's leg, trying to make sure her baby sister was okay. Sarah was tending to my shoulder—or trying to. I was thrashing my head back and forth, trying to shake the pain away.

"Whisky," Jody called. "Get whisky down her throat."

"Coming right up; and I'll brew some willow bark tea," said Sarah. "She can use that as a chaser for the whisky."

"Aarrgh! This is worse than labor!" I screamed. I was losing it, and I

465

didn't care.

At least I didn't care for about two whole seconds. One look at the fear on Jenny's face and the concern on Wallace's was enough to shock me back from hysteria to just plain pain and frustration.

I stumbled over to the chaise, panting, clutching my arm. I hadn't screamed with labor pains because I used the Lamaze breathing method. Who was to say that it wouldn't work in this situation? I sat back, and huffed and puffed, eyes focused on the pink bundle on the cold hearth. Slow deep breathing in to the count of five, blow it out to five, and start again.

After a minute or two, I regained my composure. "Sorry 'bout that. It was the pain, you know. God, I wish I had something for it. Here, would you help me with Wren?" I asked Wallace.

He didn't say anything, but brought her to me, her tiny fists clenched as tight as her eyes, little tears making their way down her cheeks. I wiped away her tears and felt them reappear on my cheeks, my feelings of inadequacy manifesting themselves in saline drops. Wallace untied the 21st century hospital gown I had arrived in so I could bare my breast. "You'll be fine; you just have to give it some time. I'm here to help you now." He placed a delicate kiss on top of my head, then walked outside to check on our other children.

Jody and Julian had taken the boys outside and were employing the walk-and-talk infant sedation technique. It must have worked; I didn't hear anything but footsteps and grandpa whispers, the soft sounds of adult men talking to their progeny. I felt Jenny's hand move the hair out of my face. I looked up and saw the fear in her eyes hadn't disappeared.

"I am so sorry. I can't believe I did that. I'm sure I'll be better soon," I apologized.

She leaned forward and her lips brushed my cheek. "Mama. I can call you that, can't I?"

I nodded and smiled. Hearing her say that felt like a warm, moist kiss that covered my whole body all at once. I didn't have to wait a year to hear it from one of the babies; this one could—and did—want to call me by that wonderful name. I felt goose bumps all over and welcomed them.

"When you get better, can you fix my hair? I never had a hairbrush. I have to use my fingers to comb my hair. She," Jenny nodded to Sarah who was pouring a cup of whisky for me, "said that you had a comb and some sweet smelling soap that you would, uh, probably, maybe, could share with me? I tried to keep clean, all over clean, but we didn't have no soap.

You see, I saw that people treated you nicer if you were clean. I tried to tell that to my brothers, but they wouldn't listen. Do you think maybe you could put braids in my hair when...when your arms work better?"

"I would love to do that. But we don't have to wait. You can ask your Grannie. Maybe she can do it today. That is if she has the time," I said and looked at Sarah. She was standing by, waiting for me to finish my little talk with Jenny before handing me the drink. I saw that she had made me a crème liqueur.

"Ah, just what the doctor ordered," I said as I pushed my nose into the cup and inhaled deeply. I took a cautious sip, and then another. The warmth worked its way down my throat, then radiated equilaterally down my shoulders to the inside of my elbows. I set the cup down and let Jenny take Wren. She got a big, very unladylike burp out of her, and then set her back into the playpen.

"Grannie, Grannie, Grrrannie," Jenny was trying out the name of her new grandmother, letting the sounds play on her lips and tongue. I looked at her and couldn't help but think, 'Well, this one will be easy to entertain.' Then I noticed it again, the object of my earlier meditation.

"What's that pink package over there?" It didn't look like it was 18th century vintage, and I couldn't place where I had seen it before.

"That's the robe you had on when you, shall we say, walked back home?" answered Sarah, nodding to Jenny. She picked it up and handed it to Wallace, who had just given me Leo to feed. I settled back on the chaise, happy to be able to cuddle my little rascal again.

"Wallace, do you want to help her with this?" Sarah asked. "It's the only thing she has to wear other than those dreadful hospital gowns. Which, by the way," she said, turning to me, "are going to be reconstructed into useful garments for the babies. There isn't enough fabric in them to make anything decent for you. I think there might still be enough on that bolt of green calico for another dress. We, rather I, can get started on it today unless," she grinned, "someone else shows up with a musket ball in her shoulder."

Even though the fabric was relatively heavy, it would have to suffice for a day of so, even in this August heat. Wallace opened out the robe for me. It was soft and I recognized it as terrycloth cotton. "Look, there's something in the pocket, or rather pockets."

Wallace set the robe down on the table and started pulling items out of the pockets. "What are these?" he asked as he held up little white plastic bottles with color printed labels on them.

467

"Oh, my Lord!" I exclaimed. "I don't believe it. Are they all the same, or do they have different names on them?"

"Let's see—here, I'll set them out on the table. Amoxicillin? That sounds Greek. Percocet, Oxycodone, here's a couple of tubes of something: triple antibiotic and Bacatracin?"

Wallace was doing a pretty decent job of pronouncing the names of the medications, but I couldn't help giggle. I worked my way up into joyous laughter and exclaimed, "Sarah, wake up woman! Give me a glass of water and one of those Oxycodones. And we might want to get me started on the antibiotic, just in case. Sarah, Sarah?"

Sarah was in a state of shock, wide-eyed, pawing at the bottles as if they were the priceless commodities that they really were. She looked up at me with the question in her eyes, 'How?'

"I think Master Simon wanted to make sure I recovered completely. But I think there's more than enough here to treat me. Congratulations, Sarah, it's twins: antibiotics and pain killers."

"No," corrected Sarah, "it's triplets: antibiotics, pain killers, and a mystery bottle." She held up a little blue bottle, obviously not 21st century vintage. "Do you know what this is?"

"Uh, oh; my bad," I confessed. "I took it out of Master Simon's pocket, just in case. Well, I was kind of out of my mind and… Oh, shit. He's going to be pissed!"

"Who's gonna be pissed?" asked Jody as he walked in the door. I looked up and saw the full complement of the extended Pomeroy family.

"Oh, just the wagon driver, but don't worry about it. I doubt Master Simon will be coming back, at least anytime soon." I wasn't ready to explain Fountain of Youth water to anyone, except maybe my healer, and that would be done on a one-on-one basis. "Sarah, let's find a safe place for that bottle. It's more precious than gold or diamonds. And even I have a hard time believing what it is, so let's leave this one as a mystery, shall we?"

Everyone in the room looked at each other. Nods and shrugs of agreement bounced back and forth until everyone was satisfied. Everyone, that is, but Jenny. "Are these a mystery, too?" she asked as she held up the bunch of bananas.

"Nope. These are part of a balanced breakfast. Is anyone else hungry?" I asked, and shoved the bunch under my free arm, using the hand cradling Leo to pull free one of the yellow fruits, waving it in the air, showing it off like it was a juicy drumstick. "Let's have a taste of South

468

America, shall we?"

August 3, 2013
Moses H. Cone Hospital
Greensboro, North Carolina

The chaos settled down at the hospital after a couple of hours. No one knew of—or could find any history of—a Dr. Em. Leah did find that Dr. Swenson had performed the emergency surgery to remove the musket ball lodged near Jane Doe's heart but didn't know anything about the mysterious young woman other than, yes, she was lactating. Dr. Johnson, the anesthesiologist, confirmed that. He said she kept mumbling, "My babies, I have to get back to my babies," until he had her fully sedated.

"Wow, twins. At least," Leah mumbled as she walked back to the room where her much younger mother had been just hours before. Nurse Gata was there with an orderly who was changing the linens and preparing the room for the next patient.

"Nurse Madigan," the supervisor said formerly. "I need to speak with you in my office, please."

"Oh, crap," mumbled Leah. She'd probably lose her job, or at least get written up, for this debacle. "Yes, ma'am, I'll be right there," she said. She looked around the room one more time and shook her head. 'If I didn't have witnesses, I wouldn't believe it myself,' she thought.

Nurse Gata was waiting for her in her office. "I want to thank you for your help this morning. Your observations about the man were correct. I was told that the police found the stolen car, but the kidnapper and the patient have not yet been found. Now, that being said, didn't you say that the Jane Doe was a relative of yours?"

"I did, ma'am," Leah replied without emotion. She wasn't going to explain how she was related to the missing patient—to her supervisor or anyone else. No one would believe her anyhow. Nurse Gata had said something else. "Excuse me?"

"Here are the belongings that came in with the patient. Since we don't have anyone else to claim these, would you like to take care of them? There's not much for clothing—just her old colonial costume—but she did have a smartphone in her pocket. It's a rather nice one, and since she was family, maybe you can get it back to whoever should have it."

"Yes, ma'am; thank you, ma'am; I'll do that, ma'am," she said mechanically, realizing after the fact that she sounded like an idiot with all of those 'ma'ams' echoing out of her still stunned, empty head.

Ж Ж Ж

Leah's shift was over, and she was more than ready to be back to that little white-walled apartment she called home. She carried the little beige plastic tub that held the personal effects of the young woman who had been her charge for less than an hour this morning. She was certain that the woman was her mother, but she had no proof, and there was no one whom she could trust to tell her suspicions to. But it was a moot point. The patient was gone, and with her, any evidence she might have had that could connect her with her mother's disappearance.

Was she or wasn't she? Who would believe that the young, mysterious Jane Doe was her sixty-year-old mother? She could hardly believe it herself. She really didn't know for sure whether *she* believed it. Her mind was going in circles. She didn't even remember the ride home. She had been driving solely on response to the stimuli of traffic lights and conditions.

Leah unlocked her front door and went straight to the kitchen cabinet. She grabbed the new bottle of McCallum whisky and the old Flintstones cut-glass cup. It was her favorite cup for drinking. It was the last one left of the set her mother had given her as a house-warming gift for the playhouse she had built for her when she was six. She poured out a healthy splash of the high-dollar-but-worth-it single malt whisky. "*Slante!* Here's to you, Mom, wherever or whenever you are."

Leah pulled the green calico Colonial-style dress out of the plastic bin. She held it up, sniffed it, realized what she was doing, and sniffed it again without reservations. No one was around to make fun of her for the odd behavior. "Yup, smells like Mom all right." She fingered the neckline and noticed the fine hand stitching on the buttonholes. "Bone buttons, hmm, those could be dated. Yeah, but you can buy antique buttons, and it's still possible to make a dress without a sewing machine. What else is there? Ho Kay; talkin' to yerself are ye? Jest like yer mudder. Well, mudder, what did ye leave me besides this sweaty dress."

Leah poured another couple fingers of whisky into the cup before investigating the scant contents of the tub. She took a small sip, enjoying the feel of the cool liquid on her upper lip, before she relaxed her lower jaw and let the sharp yet smooth fluid burn down her throat until it settled warmly in her empty stomach. She set the cup down on the table and nearly knocked it over when she couldn't pull her fingers out of the handle.

She picked up the dress and held it up as if it were a mannequin and danced around the small kitchen-living-and-dining room combination. "Some enchanted evening, you may meet a stranger," she sang. "Yeah right; they don't come much stranger than Dr. Em, do they? Hey, what's this?" she asked of nobody but herself since she was her only company tonight.

"Ooh, a nice, crusty snot rag." She suddenly realized what a treasure it might be. "DNA! Looks like Abby and the forensics lab will get a challenge with this one!"

She ambled over to the chair and plopped down hard. The whisky had definitely relaxed her uptight muscles and was clarifying her muddy-water mind. She put her elbows on the table and dropped her forehead into her hands. She wanted to cry, but the tears wouldn't come. She pulled her head back and sat up with a renewed confidence.

"Well, I didn't cry the first time you disappeared, and I'm not going to cry this time either. You were alive a few hours ago, and I know you're still alive. I can't cry for the living now, can I?"

She looked over at the plastic tote on the table, and there it was: the green-eyed pixie box. The smartphone was identical to the one her mother had when she came to visit ten months ago, the twin of the solar powered prototype she carried in her pocket now. Could this be the same one?

Leah picked it up and closed her eyes tightly. She rubbed her thumb next to the micro USB port and found it: the telltale roughness of an engraving. She got up and hurried to the bathroom, nearly tripping over her feet, which seemed to have grown a size with each swallow of her drink. She grabbed the talcum powder and walked back to the table, slower this time, and with one hand on the wall to steady herself. She tipped out a small amount of powder onto the table, dipped her index finger into it, and rubbed some of it into the irregular surface next to the port.

And there they were. The initials DUM were visible, small and now bright white. Danielle Ursula Madigan.

She wiped the excess powder onto the leg of her scrubs and relaxed into the chair, relieved that she wasn't going crazy. She looked back and saw the steady green light was on. The smartphone was charged and hopefully still functional. "Well, what little treasures do you hold, my wee black box?" she asked, holding the phone by the edges. "Talk to me."

END

Preview of AYE, I AM A FAIRY follows.

Aye, I am a Fairy

Preface

August 12, 1781

"Dang, I wish there was a way I could call Leah; tell her I was sorry I had to leave, that I loved her so much, but that she had three infant siblings in the 18th century who I had to go back and take care of, that she was an adult now and could manage just fine and, that…that…" I was exasperated and couldn't finish my explanation, but I knew Sarah understood.

"I know what you're going through, and I think there might be a way to let her know. I mean, it's how I keep my sanity with having my daughter in the 20th century." Sarah reached into the cupboard and pulled out a sheet of paper, a small wooden box with an inlaid top, and a goose feather.

"What? Write to her?" I asked, stunned at her suggestion.

Sarah nodded silently, lips pulled taut in a painful grimace. She set the items on the kitchen table and picked up the paring knife. She scored the end of the feather, creating a reservoir in the end of the quill, and then offered it to me. "I write her about our life, the day to day things mostly, then put the dated letters in the box and let them accumulate. Eventually, I'll send them overseas to Barden Hall with a note for Jody's family to hold them, unopened, until the year 1980." Sarah opened the box, took out the small inkwell, and set it next to the paper and quill.

"If, I mean, I'm *sure* Ramona and Gregg will have contacted Sam Eastman, my best friend and former professor, by then. He was the only one I trusted to tell that I was going back, coming back here to this time. I'm certain he already figured out that's what happened to Mona when she disappeared; that she followed me to the 18th century. And now she has returned to his time, back to the 20th century, with a husband and two children."

Sarah sighed, shrugged her shoulders, and then relaxed into a smile. "Call me romantic," she said as she played with the nib on the quill, running her finger over the fresh cut to make sure it was smooth. "In 1980, I went back to Barden Hall in Scotland—that's the estate where Jody was born. I worked up the nerve to talk to the current owners. Of course, they didn't know who I was, and I wasn't going to tell them that I was the wife of the man who owned their place 200 years earlier!"

473

Sarah regained her composure quickly. "I just said I was intrigued by the location, and had heard a bit of its history when I was in town. They told me times were tough and that they were going to have to sell the property. I could hear the heartbreak in their voices. I decided right then and there to do what I could to help Jody's family, even if they were about seven generations removed from him. I bought the estate and let them stay on as caretakers. I didn't know what the future held, but didn't want the ancestral land and buildings to go to just anyone. I thought Mona might want to live there after she got out of school and was ready to settle down. Sam had the deed and was to give it to her when she graduated or got married or whenever. I left it up to him to determine when she would be receptive to the idea of living in Scotland. I told him just to make sure he gave the current occupants at least six months' notice before they had to move out. And well, I didn't even know if they wanted to stay as caretakers after they got the money from the sale."

"So, you're saying I should write a letter, or letters, now, and put them in your little box there, and then your daughter can give it, them, to Leah?" I asked.

"Well, that could work, but you might want to establish another destination—sort of an alternate backup site—for your letters, in case mine don't make it. You know what they say about putting all your eggs in one basket…" she joked.

I frowned as I realized what she had said. "Twentieth century, you said. But I came from the 21st century, 2012. Well, at least the first time. I just came back from 2013 last week. You're writing to, what, 1980?"

"It doesn't matter which decade it is. And it probably won't make a difference to them whether or not they even get these." She sighed and stroked the top of the inlaid wooden box. "I mean, it's not as if they know we're writing them. I'm doing it for Jody and me. He writes, too. It helps us feel connected with them. I *hope* they get the letters, but I doubt that they'll make a dramatic difference in their lives." She shrugged. "I can't take photographs, so they're getting written snapshots of our lives instead."

"So you think I could write a letter now, today, and ask for someone to get in touch with my daughter two hundred and thirty years from now? That then—in our future, their present—they could let her know why I had to leave and that I'm okay?" I was starting to feel better already.

"Well, continuity is the key; it has to be successfully passed down through the generations. You can write a letter and I'll put it in with mine, and maybe the 21st century Barden Hall group will forward it to her or, or…"

If only I knew whom I could send a letter to…even a card…a business card…

My eyes opened wide with a clear, distinct memory—bright, shining, and sparkled with hope. The business card Wallace had found in my backpack two months ago, just after the babies were born, was from a James Melbourne. I suddenly knew who he was! New memories were tumbling over each other. I met young, good-looking, James Melbourne the same day I first met Master Simon. It was in a café in Greensboro. I figured out a map, an ancient map… I shook my head. That wasn't important. What I needed to know was if James was from the same Melbourne family as those who were now living in London. Wallace's Uncle Tony, Julian's brother, was a Melbourne. And he was possibly— probably, hopefully—James Melbourne's ancestor. Well, I knew they shared the same coat of arms, and maybe, if they shared the same residence—hmm…

"Sarah," I said, bringing myself out of my own reverie. "I know of someone now whose family will still be around in the 21st century." I inhaled deeply and elaborated. "You said it would be best to have two sources of delivery, right? So I'll leave my originals with yours, and then send copies to, hmm. I need to talk to Wallace. Excuse me; I'll be write back. Get it? W.R.I.T.E. Oh, never mind."

Wallace was bringing out Aries for his daily ride. The high-strung stallion didn't like being cooped up and was easier to handle if ridden daily. I ran outside, my arms flailing in the air, signaling for Wallace to stop before he rode out. "Whoa, whoa, wait," I blurted out breathlessly.

"Is there something wrong?" he asked, pulling back the reins, ready to dismount.

"No, no. I just have to ask you a quick question. What are the chances your Uncle Tony would ever sell his place in England?"

"Which one?" he replied. I'm sure my shocked look wasn't what he expected. His sly grin at my reaction wasn't the least bit rude, but still made me feel silly.

"Well, I'm certain the last place he'd ever sell or relinquish would be his home in London. Country estates can come and go, but that house is as much a part of him as his right hand. He could go on without it, but he wouldn't like it." He scowled in concern and repositioned himself in the saddle, ready again for his boot soles to touch soil. "Are you sure you're all right? Should I put off the ride?"

"Oh, no, please don't. It's just that I think I found a way to tell Leah what happened—or will happen—so maybe she won't feel too bad that I left. I'll explain when you get back. Have a nice ride, okay?" I said and blew him a kiss.

Wallace reached out and gently retrieved the imaginary buss in the palm of his hand as if it were a butterfly, brought it to his lips, kissed it, and blew it back to me. "Share this with the children. We won't be too long." He reined the horse back toward the road and was off like his boots were on fire and his trousers were catching.

I skipped back to the house, unable to hold back my elation at finding a solution to my documentary-sharing continuity. Sarah and her treasure box of letters had sparked a memory for me. It was if I had seen it as a preview of a movie in the theater—an interesting clip, but not enough words or images to tell the whole story.

It had to be last year, maybe even the day before I woke up here in the past, that I met a descendent of Wallace's Uncle Tony: Lord James Melbourne. I'm sure he'd help me out if I wrote to him and asked him to contact Leah and pass on my information. I grinned as I recalled our little meeting with the curious map owner and, unbeknownst to us, time traveler, Master Simon. James knew right away that there was more to the map than Simon was telling us. Well, I'd explain that to him, too, in the letter.

"Mommy, Mommy; both boys want you real bad," Jenny hollered, almost running into me, unaware that I was moving so quickly in her direction. "And Leo has a poopy clout. Do you want me to change it while you feed Judah?"

I held onto Jenny's shoulders, steadying the two of us after our minor collision. "That would be wonderful. I don't know what I did to get such a great helper, but if I couldn't feel you under my hands right now, I'd swear you were an angel. Come on; I'll race you to the house."

I bent forward, dropped my hands to the ground, and crouched into a starting position. "Ready, set...hey! You were supposed to wait until I said go," I carped as I picked up my skirt to chase after my ten-year-old adopted daughter. It was a great day.

*1 Blasted alarm clock

Monday, August 5, 2013, Greensboro

*Good morning, good morning, good morninnnnngggg guhh guhh!
Nothing to do…*

Slam, thump, "Ouch! Son-of-a-bitchin' thing!" Leah finally got the alarm shut off on the fourth smack. She must have moved it when she got into bed last night. Or was that this morning?

"Ugh," she groaned as she turned over. She grabbed the gray stuffed hippopotamus, and plopped it over her throbbing head, effectively shutting out the world with the loftiness of the velour and polyester water-horse pillow.

*In the town, where I was born, lived a ma'a'aan…*thump. "Hah! Gotcha on the first try!" Leah exclaimed with pride then fell back and moaned, "Oh, no," the pain of her class one hangover trumping her momentary elation at winning the whack-the-alarm-clock contest. She rolled over and looked. It was 5:15. If she had to work today, she only had 15 minutes to get dressed and slug down a cup of coffee before it was time to head out the door. If she had the day off, she could roll over and sleep until noon if she wanted. It would be easy enough to check. She made sure she entered her work schedule into her smartphone every week as soon as it was posted.

"Okay, where did I leave you this time?" Leah was forever misplacing her phone. She was so notorious that she even customized a message for the opening screen page that said, "Tell Leah you found her phone. You can contact her at work at Moses H. Cone Hospital…." So far, every one of the three people who had found it, had returned it. "Mom was worse than me," she said softly, "she lost and found hers five times."

Then she saw them: the two identical solar powered smartphones. "Oh, crap." Traces of talcum powder were still visible on one. She had dusted it the night before, looking for the engraved initials to verify what she already knew: it was her mother's.

Her mother disappeared from Greensboro ten months ago, apparently falling off the earth without a trace. Yesterday, she reappeared at the hospital's emergency room with a musket ball in her shoulder, looking forty years younger, fifty pounds thinner, and with all the signs of being a nursing mother. Before they had a chance for explanations, Leah was knocked out by the phony attending doctor. He then kidnapped her mom and shuffled her out the door in a wheelchair. He forced her to drive away—drugged and still recovering—in a stolen car, leading the hospital personnel and police on a chaotic chase to a vacant lot at the edge of town. The police found the car within minutes, but its occupants seemed to have disappeared into thin air.

Leah, still stunned at her mother's sudden appearance then re-disappearance, had told her supervisor that she was related to the kidnapped woman. Nurse Gata, not wanting to be burdened with paperwork or inquiries, gave Leah the left-behind personal belongings bag. It's only contents: the colonial-style dress her mother had been wearing when she came into the emergency room and the prototype smartphone.

"I guess it wasn't a dream after all," she said as she softly touched the phone with the white disclosed initials DUM: Danielle Ursula Madigan.

Leah picked up her own phone, the one without the powder, and scanned her calendar. Cool, she had today off. She stumbled into the kitchen, opened the refrigerator door, and saw the carton of orange juice. "I don't think so," she groaned, "What I need is the hair of the dog that bit me." She shoved the juice aside. "Ooh, there's an idea," she said and grabbed the carton of vanilla-flavored soymilk coffee creamer. She took her dirty coffee cup out of the sink, gave it a fast rinse, shook off the water, and then poured a healthy slug of the sweetened coffee creamer in it.

"Ah, my little friend," she cooed to the bottle of McCallum whisky on the counter, and tipped a shot into the mug. She swished the cup, dipped her finger in it, and swirled the mix. She lifted the cup to her lips and sniffed. "Smells pretty good, but I bet it'd be better warmed."

She put the cup in the microwave, nuked it half a minute, then pulled it out and did the swish, finger dip, and swirl routine again to make sure the hot and cold spots were blended. "Ah, that's too good," she said as she sipped down half the concoction with her first taste. "That should take the edge off the hangover."

"Ding dong." Leah took her cup of homemade crème liqueur to the table and sat down in front of the two phones. The notification tone wasn't from hers; she had disabled the audio email and text message alerts long ago. She picked up her mother's phone and slid her finger across the face

478

of it. The little animated letter was dancing all over the screen. Her mother's email address was still valid, although there hadn't been any real activity on it for the last six months. The Alchemy spam blocker had virtually blocked all of the junk mail; this one must be legitimate. Leah took another sip of her liquid courage and double-clicked the letter.

'Remember meeting me in that little café in Greensboro last Halloween? Did that strange little man—Simon was it?—ever figure out his map? Hopefully you were able to finish your Revolutionary War sightsee and had a safe journey home to Alaska. I will be returning to North Carolina August 5th. After I take care of some business, I would like to visit your state. Is your offer for a three-hour tour still open? Please let me know so I can schedule flights on this end. Regards, James Melbourne'

"What the fu..." Leah looked at the properties of the email. The origination was a UK internet provider, and the name was 'Lord' James Melbourne, MP. Last Halloween—that was the last time she had heard from her mother. Maybe this man could shed some light on what happened.

Leah quickly typed in her reply. *'Please contact me as soon as possible. This is in regards to my mother, Dani Madigan. Thank you, Leah Madigan.'*

She hit send, then wondered if she should have included her phone number. "Nope, I doubt I'd be coherent over the phone. If he's going to be here today, maybe we can meet face to face." Leah touched her hair and realized she was a mess. She'd better clean up if she was going to meet the man, a British Lord no less, who might have a clue about what happened to her mother last year. She wouldn't tell him about yesterday unless... No, don't anticipate, she admonished herself. Just take a shower and go from there. One small step at a time: baby steps, lady, baby steps.

Thanks, in no particular order:

Thank you, Elaine Boyle, editor, historian, and cultural counselor, for your invaluable advice and insight on life in North Carolina and for being the grammar queen.

Thank you, Diana Gabaldon, for your words of encouragement to write, and for creating the *Outlander* series, the inspiration for the time travel saga *Lost* that is used in my stories.

Thank you, Amazon, for all the tools you provide free of charge to help authors and artists bring their works to others.

Thank you, Marty Haviland, for being a great guy who really does let me take charge and follow through in tough situations, and who trusts my judgment (and is gentle and discreet when I need a bit of redirection or correction). Oh, and being a wonderful husband, too!

Thank you, Kim Killion, and Hot Damn Designs, for the wonderful cover.

Thank you, Edye Rogers, for the picture on the cover. You didn't know when you took the selfie that you were wearing your 'other sister,' Evie's, coat!

Thank you, Leatherman Tool Company, for having such great multi-tools, that they're mentioned by brand name in my books. Everyone in my family has at least one of the tools, as do most of my 21st century characters.

Thanks, Crocs, for producing the most comfortable footwear, and in enough styles, that I can wear them all year round here in Alaska.

Thanks, Dr. Seuss, for your books that are so memorable, even two centuries and a tough case of amnesia can't stifle your rhyming words and rhythms.

Thank you, Lee Greenwood, for the powerful words and music of 'God Bless the USA.' I still think it's the perfect national anthem, and it brings tears to my eyes every time I hear it. It was also a great tune to stymie the British back in the Revolutionary War…at least in my story.

Thank you, Jimi Hendrix, master musician and former US Paratrooper, for your skilled guitar playing. You left us a great gift with your music. Rest in peace.

Other books in The Fairies Saga series

Ha'penny Jenny, Book Two. Learn more about newly adopted Jenny, her past, and her talent (or curse) of being able to see the future.

Aye, I am a Fairy, Book Three. Leah, Evie's daughter in the 21st century, has a new friend. And he's not who she thinks he is.

Dances Naked, Book Four. 21st century British Lord Marty Melbourne is found by the Cherokees in 1781.

Chasing Christmas, Book Five. Only love could be sweeter than freedom for the Cherokee slave.

The Great Big Fairy, Book Six. Back and forth between the 21st century and 1781 for our favorite 6'7" time traveler.

Little Bear and the Ladies, Book Seven. More about the trapper Little Bear and a few of the ladies from Dances Naked.

Little Drummer Boy, Book Eight. Can young Scout help find the way during one of the biggest snowstorms of the 18th century?

Never Too Young, Book Nine. Will a clever thief ruin Scout's chance for happiness with Jenny?

Time in a Little Blue Bottle, Book Ten. Could a young woman and teenage pickpocket beat Elvis and Mark Twain to the Fountain of Youth?

Kidnapped! Book Eleven. Could Benji rescue his sister from the MacLeods? And what about those letters?

Big Mac. A tall, curly-haired redhead has come into Benji's life. Was he really who he said he was?

"Sub-series" *Benji – The Early Years* includes *Luke the Unexpected* and *Pool Boy Wanted: No Experience Preferred*

*Check out www.danihaviland.com for information about the latest releases, series, box sets, and excerpts. While there, join **Time Travelers Anonymous** for freebies and sneak peeks at new books.*

*Follow us on **Facebook: Dani Haviland & Friends Readers Group**, www.bookbub.com **@Dani_Haviland***
www.amazon.com Type Dani Haviland in search bar, then click on name (under a book) and select 'Follow' button under the author image.
*Follow on **Twitter**: @dani_haviland and @gr8authors*

Cast of Characters

Abe ~ 18th century backwoodsman

Big Bill Leuga ~ friendly acquaintance, 18th century

Captain Atholl MacLeod ~ evil, phony Redcoat officer, 18th century

Clayton ~ degenerate 18th century man

Clyde ~ Clayton's degenerate brother, 18th century

Curly ~ rogue British soldier

Evie ~ 20th-century born older woman, transported back to 18th century, has amnesia, now in young body due to an overdose of Fountain of Youth Water.

Frankie ~ 21st century waitress

Gibson ~ store owner, 18th century

Gimpy ~ bad guy with a limp, 18th century

Hannah Althouse ~ helpful teenager, 18th century

Ian Kincaid ~ 18th century backwoodsman, aka Starwalker

James Melbourne ~ young British Lord, 21st century

Jenny ~ preadolescent girl, 18th century

Jody Pomeroy ~ 18th century patriarch, Wallace's father

José ~ Spanish emigrant, 18th century

Julian Hart ~ British Lord, 18th century

Lady ~ cougar (the feline type), semi-tame

Leah ~ 21st century daughter of Evie

Leonardo da Vinci Sr. ~ time traveler, 18th and 21st centuries

Little Bear ~ white trader, dresses like Indian, 18th century

Ma ~ 18th century backwoods woman

Mac Donaldson ~ 18th century farmer, father, patriot

Master Simon ~ strange man, time traveler 18th & 21st centuries

Mrs. Donaldson ~ 18th century homemaker

Richard Short ~ local troublemaker, 18th century

Sarah Pomeroy ~ Jody's wife, 20th century-born time traveler, healer, living in 18th century

Skinny ~ rogue British soldier, 18th century

'The Fireman' ~ bad guy, 18th century

Wallace ~ 18th century British soldier, Julian's stepson

Wee Ian ~ also known as Scout, about 11 yrs old, 18th century

www.ingramcontent.com/pod-product-compliance
Lightning Source LLC
Chambersburg PA
CBHW051429260626
47162CB00001B/14